Get a Lif

This is a complete work o ,
businesses, places, events ei-
ther the products of the author's imagination or used in an
entirely fictitious manner.

◆ ◆ ◆

Any resemblance to actual persons, living or dead, or actual
events is purely coincidental. Those people and places that
do exist are used in an entirely fictitious manner and I have
nothing but love and respect for them all.

Thank you to my darling man for not moaning about me having my head buried in my laptop for the whole of 2020.

Huge thanks to beautiful Vicky for your ongoing support and encouragement.

CHAPTER 1

"**G**et some knickers in a bag we're going travelling."

"What? Since when? You never mentioned this before!"

"Wasn't planned but I just rented the house out for six months, so you better get packing."

This was a typical day with my bonkers Old Man. I'd recently been living back with him since yet another relationship had crashed and burned...His, not mine...I'd given up on finding Mr. Right a long time ago. I found Mr. Perfect in 1985 at the tender age of eighteen but sadly Madame Karma had other ideas and saw fit to obliterate him in a motorcycle accident before our teenage dreams and plans really got chance to take shape...I must have done something really bad in a former life....

Hi, I'm Dil, short for Delilah Tallulah Tinkerbell Rainbow Blue; hippy parents have a lot to answer for! I'm currently a four foot ten, seven stone, purple dreadlocked, possibly menopausal, motorcycle mechanic. I've been most of those things for many years, the menopausal bit has just made a very unwelcome appearance. I am also a major adrenaline junkie, parent sitter, animal lover and social phobic with a nomadic lifestyle that a Tuareg would envy. Like the Tuareg I have got a thing for astronomy although my beliefs would probably be a bit too 'new age' for them.

I started my gap year in 1981 and haven't finished yet! Don't get me wrong I'm not a lazy scrounger and never have been, I've worked all over the world and never claimed an unearned penny for anything in my life. Come to think of it there's been quite a few well-earned ones I'm still to claim too. I'm just a seeker and, in the words of the song 'I still haven't found what I'm looking for'.

'You can't take the Kwak anywhere 'til I've changed that chain and sprocket. Its nearly dragging on the floor, you don't deserve that bike you heathen!" I yell.

"She's good for another trip around the clock ... she likes to be treated rough! Anyways we're only going 90 odd miles so what's the problem?"

"90 miles? How's that going to be travelling exactly? You goin' senile, old man?"

"Nope, we're going Isle of Man. I forgot to tell you I own some land down Jurby. Thought we could go build a house or something."

"When? Where? How and why did you buy land on The Rock?"

"Can't remember when, I just told you where, with money I got from a very nice accumulator bet on a lot of bike races, I predicted 1st, 2nd and 3rd in every race!" He proclaims proudly. "And I bought it 'cos the old lady and I thought you'd eventually like to be close to Jimbob then we found out you'd had him chopped up and fed to the birds!"

"He had a sky burial! He was Buddhist, he wanted to be chopped up and fed to the birds!"

"So you keep saying, seems an odd way to go; please don't do it to me. I want to be cooked and thrown down Route 66 with the old gal."

"Okay Pops, I promise to get you cooked now can we get back to the house building thing?"

"Yep, get packed and we'll go and see what's there." He turns and saunters off which means conversation over. He's almost deaf, probably due to so many years with his head right next to noisy exhaust pipes, so unless he's looking at me, he ain't listening to me. There's no point in arguing and why would I? I love the Isle of Man; I love my Dad and I love a challenge! I better go and pack my knickers.

All my worldly goods are loaded on my most treasured possession, my Ducati aka The Duchess, not the most practical tourer l admit but nevertheless she has taken me all around the globe without a hitch. I pack light; l learned long ago that material possessions just slow you down and are constantly reminding you of what might have been. Luggage consists of two small throw overs, my tent and sleeping bag roped on the pillion seat and a half full rucksack including that chain and sprocket. Dad's faithful old Kawasaki sits on the drive, 109000 miles on the clock and still kicking!

Dad locks the door and throws the key in a nearby plant pot "Ready Dilly girl? You need juice?"

"Nope, I'm good, filled up yesterday 'cos I was going to head over to Germany for a few days. What's with the centenary lid? I thought that only came out on special occasions."

"I'm off on a new adventure with my girl, that's special enough. Let's go, head down, arse up 'til you see the Liver Birds!"

I'm starting to think there is more to this trip than he is letting on. We've done this same journey once, twice or even more times almost every year for as long as I can remember and its never warranted his favourite crash helmet. That helmet has sat in a display cabinet since the day I bought it him. Either he's going daft or he's up to something.

The journey to Liverpool is as uneventful as always, the eternal roadworks on the M6 are still in place and the M62 is empty. l follow Dad through the run-down depression that is Liverpool and smile when l see the Liver Building. The Steam Packet company are as laid back as ever, plenty of food to buy and plenty of seats to choose from. We sit in our usual spot close to the coffee shop and acquire loads of sugar sachets and little milk pots 'cos we both forgot to pack any. Looking out of the windows, we watch the mainland disappear and the Island appear. We arrive at Douglas as it's getting dark and as we ride off the Manannan I take a deep breath of Manx air, my whole body relaxes, and l feel like l am home. l follow the old man down quiet, hedge lined lanes to our destination which I can't see much of. You don't realise how much light pollution there is until you come here, and nighttime means pitch dark with just the moon and stars to guide you. We pitch the tents on what appears to be a clear area close to some old buildings, crawl in and settle for the night. I sleep like a baby.

Next morning, not for the first time in my life, I find myself sleeping under canvas for the foreseeable future on an incredibly overgrown plot of land with probably no facilities, but the salty, fresh spring air and most amazing view makes up for everything. I am a typical cancerian, a moon child, a child of the sea, I am at peace near any water, sit me by a puddle, I'm happy. Everywhere I look I can see the ever-moving sea, rolling green fields, bluebell strewn hills and Snaefell, the mountain watching over us. Manannan Mac Lir was one hell of an architect.

Enough of the romantic stuff, on the practical side, we have a sea full of fish and a camping stove to cook them, appear to have a beautiful solid, and still salvageable, stone carcass of the cottage that once stood here and a huge, long and wide, stone barn with half a thatched roof and a rotten door. We also have some dazzling spring sunshine and the promise that it will continue for at least five days. I normally take no notice of weather forecasts, wherever l am in the world, preferring to simply look outside and see what's going on but Manx forecasts are amazingly accurate; if they say it will rain in Douglas at 3.36 pm you can guarantee that it will do just that and if you look out to sea in the direction they state, in fact you can actually see the rain arriving.

I corner my old man whilst he's supposedly inspecting the barn but is really mooching for anything old and mechanical that he can fix. "What's the plan, old man?"

He's standing under the thatch which appears to be home to half the wildlife in Jurby. "Dunno, shall we just reroof the other half of the barn? Plenty room in here."

"Have you got any actual plans? Surely we need planning permission to do anything?"

"Yep, I've got permission to build a three-bed bungalow and a treble garage and workshops...thought we might stay a while and sort some of the seriously neglected bikes on this island. We'll get extra work for TT with independent racers and the numpties that come over to spectate on bikes that haven't been out of the garage since last TT and conk out as soon as they give them some beans up the mountain. Southern 100 guys may need bits on older stuff, Manx will bring independents and spectators on older, temperamental bikes and maybe some off-road stuff when the trials are on. You could set up some tours and ride outs when the loonies arrive for TT or even over to Ireland for the races. You've still got your license to instruct as well."

"You said 6 months...that sounds like a much more long-term plan and a surprisingly well thought out one for you. It also appears to involve contact with lots of people and you know that's not my favorite sport. Cards on the table time, old man...what's going on?"

"Dilly Girl, I'm an old man and I ain't gonna be here forever so I wanna see you settled and sorted before the grim reaper comes callin'. We've done enough wandering and Jimbob, Marley and your Mama ain't never coming back no matter how long we mourn."

"Wow, that's deep! What if I'm not done with wandering and mourning?"

"Tough shit girly, I've made my mind up and I'm sure as heck gonna be dying sooner or later so humour me and stay a while."

And so, a very vague kind of decision is sort of made, this is as close as we both like to get to commitment... we're possibly going to be building a bungalow, probably going to build a business ... and maybe start rebuilding our lives.

CHAPTER 2

I'm happy in my daydream, roaming aimlessly on a people less, pebble beach with gulls wailing overhead and the sea crashing onto the rocks. Seals are basking on the waterline and bobbing around just in view. I've come to catch something tasty for tea. Tasty Mackerel are abundant and if the seals are about there must be fish around too.

I'm coming around to the idea of setting down a few roots here. I've always been drawn to the Island and spent many happy times here with my parents and then several blissful years with Jimbob. Dad raced here before I was a baby, Mama raced here when I was a baby, I raced here in my teens, twenties and thirties alongside my crazy little brother and Jimbob. Our whole life has always included this tiny rock in the middle of the Irish Sea.

We all knew it would claim one of us eventually, payback for the risks and reckless thoughtlessness for our safety. Ultimately, it took two... Jimbob and my spirited little bro, Marley Indigo Ocean Blue (hippy parents!!!). I feel them both when I'm here and so many other friends and acquaintances we've lost along the way to the great but cruel and insatiable gods of speed.

I'm very careful not to make new friends now as it hurts too much when they go. I'm lost in my own bittersweet reverie when I am grabbed from behind in a huge bear hug and lifted several feet off the ground.

"Dave! Where's yow bin? We missed ya. Ow am ya?" Says the bear.

The bear is one of my very, very few real friends, Billy. He's a huge 6 foot six, hairy Black Country escapee who's lived here on the Island for a long time. Think Hagrid with a Tipton accent. Strangely, he calls everyone 'Dave' including his wife and three kids. Too much Fools and Horses and League of Gentlemen when he was younger.

"Hi hun, how you all doing?" I lean into the bear hug and instantly feel protected and safe. Despite my phobia of people and relationships I do have half a dozen real friends who I would walk through fire for, Billy and his brothers are top of that list. "How did you know we're here?"

"Ha, ha, Dave. You're on The Rock, our old 'un heard your bikes coming off the boat last night. He'd know the sound of your Dad's old Kwak anywhere and the whole island could hear The Duchess. Our kid says he'll be down the pub after work."

"I didn't hear your bike, how'd you get here?"

"I'm working, I'm in the truck. Pack your shit up I've bought some crap for you. Come and help me unload."

We walk back up the beach and chat like we haven't been apart even though it's been two years since we last saw each other...true friends don't notice time. I've skyped a few times but always end up chatting to his missus and kids 'cos he's always in the shed or running errands for someone.

'Middle Dave pilfered your old YBR. He spent the winter sorting it out, finally took and passed his test a month ago and he's put over three thousand miles on the clock already. Surprised he ain't dizzy the amount of times he's been over the mountain!"

Middle Dave is his second child, Nathan, who I also love dearly, and I cannot think of anyone better to take on my poor, abandoned YBR that has sat in Billy's shed over here for several years. I used to teach bike lessons and it has had a lot of misuse and abuse over the years. One of my trainees, a very odd and distracted man who I am convinced was registered blind, rode it right into the sea off Peel harbour the morning of his test having totally forgotten how to turn and follow a perfectly good road, we had fun winching that out and all credit to Yamaha it started and ran as soon as it hit the tarmac and drained! Mr. Magoo didn't pass his test though, thank goodness. He failed for neglecting to stop at several junctions and doing a spectacular stoppie, with the back wheel a foot off the ground, when asked to do an emergency stop.

We get back and there's a huge R P Plant Hire lorry in the middle of the road. At home this would be causing absolute chaos, over here no one notices because there is enough space for everyone.

"Wow! Where are you delivering to? That's most of Ricky's yard on the back!"

"I'm bringing it here, Ricky said you're gonna need it. I've got a thunder box, two generators, strimmers, a cement mixer, space heater, field kitchen, scaffolding and whatever else the lads loaded s'morning. Where do you want it? Get the kettle on and hurry up I've gotta take little Dave to the dentist at 3."

I drop the fish in a cool corner of the barn and put the kettle on; marvelling at this idyllic island full of beautiful, generous people with huge hearts.

We unload everything and put it all in the barn or against the buildings. At home we'd be locking and securing it all and waking at any tiny sounds, panicking in case someone is trying to steal it. Here, life is more relaxed, and everyone knows everyone and everything so you'd have to be really brave or really stupid to take something that doesn't belong to you.

We drink coffee and put the world to rights, discuss the pros and cons of the new Triumphs and Billy takes off to get Little Dave, aka Sarah, his youngest daughter, to the dentist.

Dad still isn't back and didn't say where he was heading after his shopping chores, but I assume he's catching up with everyone. I grab some PPE and a strimmer from our recent delivery and start clearing the ground. The cottage carcass is a large, low rectangle and would have been an old, thatched building originally belonging to a fisherman or a farmer I imagine. I clear around it and venture inside too. The walls are remarkably sound and the earth floor inside is level and dry. There is still some evidence of the thatching and there's a huge chimney breast at one end which I can stand inside and see right up, apart from a slightly wonky top and lots of nesting materials it looks intact. There's a smaller chimney at the other end, a big solid oak dresser that's stood the test of time, a sturdy old oak table, a couple of wooden chairs and a beautiful old Belfast sink. I turn the tap, not holding out much hope but to my amazement the water runs clear and cold. I thank every star I can think of and a few gods and angels too. That reminds me I must get down to the Fairy Bridge and say 'Laa mie' to the fairy folk before they start making mischief here. There are some internal walls still standing and there's room inside for plenty of different ways to set it out into a cosy cottage.

The window frames have rotted to nothing, but the glass is sitting unbroken on the ground in a neat pile. The huge wooden front door is rotting from top to bottom but still hanging. I carry on clearing and find stone outhouse around the back with a toilet and another beautiful Belfast sink. I'm not so lucky here, chain from a very ancient high-level flush comes off in my hand and smacks me on the head and the tap in the sink will not turn unless I find a pair of mole grips. I'll add it to my 'to do' list. This might actually be an easier job than I first anticipated...don't say that too loud Dil, you know what'll happen.

I head across to properly check out the barn. Suddenly, I see an orange flash shoot out of the doorway with one of the mackerel in its jaws. I'm just thinking 'wow, that's a huge fox...hang on there are no foxes over here?!' when my Dad runs up from the road looking hot and flustered...

"Have you seen Jeff? I've only bloody lost it! We we're getting on so well and having a lovely walk and chat, getting to know each other like, then it sniffed the air and took off like a pony in the national." He collapsed in a wheezing heap on the grass and started giggling his head off.

I love him dearly and to see him laughing is enough to set me off smiling and then joining in with the giggle. I know him so well and it takes me seconds to work out that the hairy, orange, fish thief is bound to be 'Jeff'.

"Enough giggling you old reprobate! Does Jeff have four legs and a shaggy orange coat?" I ask wheezing for breath.

"Oh! You've already met? What have you done with her?" Dad looks around suspiciously as if I've kidnapped his new friend.

"Her? Jeff is a girl? We haven't formally met she just popped by to steal your dinner. Last seen heading for the beach."

"Oh bugger! Are you sure it was my dinner and not yours? And yes, I think it's a girl, but she looks like your uncle Jeff and the MSPCA said they hadn't had chance to name her yet. She's a bit wild they reckon." Dad tells me as he's wandering off towards the beach.

"She likes mackerel maybe you should take another one to tempt her back?" l yell after him heading to the barn to grab a fishy enticement.

Down on the beach lying on a flat rock in the sunshine, Jeff is happily munching on her stolen treat and eyes us with very little concern and no remorse whatsoever.

"Did the MSPCA give you any more details about Jeff? Like does it bite? How old is it? WHAT exactly is it?"

Up close Jeff is huge and definitely very orange actually quite similar to my Dad's youngest brother, a big hairy ginger hippy. Jeff, the dog, has a long but wide head and from the demise of the fish l would say very capable teeth and jaws. Its ears are furry and pointed but they point two different directions with the right one pointing to the sky and the left one at 90 degrees from its head and appearing to have half of it missing. Paws are like dinner plates and Jeff looks like it still has some growing to do although it's quite skinny legs are already ridiculously long and lanky. Hair is wiry and abundant, tail abnormally long and skinny, eyebrows that Dennis Healey would admire and the most beautiful huge, blue-grey soulful eyes.

"He or she is a bit of an interesting mixture apparently mummy was a Dogue de Bordeaux and daddy was an Elkhound. She seemed friendly enough and was more than happy to come out for a stroll." Replies Dad smiling at Jeff and sitting down on the closest rock.

"Have you walked from Foxdale? Isn't that about seven miles? Where's your bike? Have you got to take Jeff back?" Dad has never been big on planning ahead; Mama was the one that had always kept us all organised.

"Yes, why not? It's a beautiful day and Jeff likes walking. Yes again, it's 7.6 miles according to this tracker thingy." He waves his Fitbit at me...a gift from his last lady friend who wanted to keep tabs on him. "Bike's at Foxdale 'cos Jeff couldn't balance on the tank and we can walk back later to get it can't we? Any more questions?"

"Nope, it's all clear now...we can eat in the pub on the way back seeing as your dinner is in the dog." I laugh.

Jeff is looking at us both with her head on one side as if weighing us up. She's completely devoured the fish including head, tail and fins...no evidence remains. She sits up slowly with a huge sigh and ambles over to Dad. She puts her nose right up into his face, lets out a huge fishy burp, smiles at him and licks the top of his head.

"See, we're getting on fine." Dad and Jeff sigh contentedly in unison and Dad reaches over to tickle her ears. She leans against his hand and closes her eyes; trancelike she leans further and further until she nearly falls over.

"How exactly did you happen to meet Jeff?" I ask as Dad had mentioned no plans that involved dogs or walks or even Foxdale when he left this morning to go to Shoprite for some supplies.

"l was fancying a proper breakfast and you know theirs are ace. I offered to wash up for a discount and Nina said if I adopted a dog, she'd feed me for a week."

"Adopted? That does not sound quite as simple as a walk." I look at Dad and he is now cheerfully making Jeff a wig with a big chunk of seaweed. She is sitting still and enjoying the attention and looking fabulous with long, green ringlets.

"Does Nina know we're living in a tent?" I ask carefully, not wanting to ruin his fun.

"Nina knows everything, we're on the Island aren't we? Everyone knows we're living in a field and no-one is worried about it at all. Jeff and l had a chat about it on the way down and she really likes the idea." Typical Dad, he hates being asked to use his common sense or listening to reason.

We head back and Jeff follows without hesitation, possibly because I still have a rather warm mackerel in my hand. I find a washing up bowl and fill it with cold water into which she submerges her whole face and comes up a minute later, picks up the empty bowl and throws it at me. I refill it and she repeats her actions.

"What time do they close at MSPCA? You'll need your bike even if Jeff doesn't need to go back." I ask a few hours later when I've finally finished clearing all the weeds and grass from the barn while Jeff lay in the shade snoring peacefully with Dad doing the same next to her. Their walk had obviously taken its toll.

"Half four l think. Is it time to go? I'm starving!"

I have completely lost track of time so I reach inside my rucksack to check the time on my phone. "It's already half 7 you daft old bugger. You've been asleep all afternoon! We'll go get your bike in the morning...Lets go and introduce Jeff to pub." l laugh.

"Best idea you've had since we got here! I think they'll get along nicely together." Dad smiles at Jeff who is stretching like a cat, front down and bum in the air and yawning so widely her jaw nearly disconnects. "You gonna get washed first? You look like a navvy! What the heck have you been doing?"

After a quick scrub in the Belfast sink and a change of clothes we're off to the pub with Jeff leading the way. She appears keen to meet 'pub' and is dancing along looking very fetching in a rainbow bandana Dad has found for her. Its cooled down a little but the sun is still shining. There are plenty of people already settled in the beer garden drinking, eating, laughing, and relaxing. Kids are running around chasing each other and a scruffy little missile launches itself at me as soon as I near the gate.

"Granddad Dylly! Auntie Dilly!" The missile is Sarah, Billy's youngest. "I got my tooths cleaned today, look!" She opens her mouth as wide as she can whilst diving into my open arms. Kids are supposed to be wary at her age but Sarah loves and remembers everything and everyone and is never shy or reserved. She clings to my neck for a second and I feel her wipe her snotty nose on my dreads then she spots Jeff. "Thing!" She states and flies out of my arms and flings herself at the poor dog. To her credit Jeff doesn't even flinch. She patiently endures a big hug and kiss including another surreptitious nose wipe; she shakes paws, wags her tail and licks Sarah's head.

"What the heck is eating my child?" Sal, Billy's wife has appeared from inside the pub and grabs my Dad for a big squeeze. "It's been too long you old git, where've you been? "She gives me a hug and stands, hands on hips, watching Jeff and Sarah taking turns to lick each other. "I'm not sure which one to tell off." She laughs, "She's probably dirtier than whatever it is she's licking! What is she licking, exactly?"

"Jeff." Dad says assuming this is all the answer Sal needs and Sal, in turn, seems happy enough with this knowledge not to remove her child from the situation. "Want a pint of Okells? I've been working like a dog all day!" He adds.

Dad saunters towards the pub, he is a slight, rangy man with a mass of long white hair and beard, neither of which have seen a comb or scissors in over 40 years. He is wearing faded Levis which are probably older than me and a Metallica t shirt my brother bought him in the 90's. I get my build and fashion sense from him but he is still over 6 feet tall even at 78. My height comes from my Mama who insisted she was 5 foot but was really 4 foot eleven and a half!

He opens the pub door and is instantly swept off his feet in a Billy bear hug.

"Dave!" Exclaims Billy, expressing more love and affection in one word than I could put into a whole song. He puts Dad down without any further conversation and heads towards me and Sal. "Where's Dave?" He enquires.

"In the sandpit licking her new mate." Sal informs him.

"That's my girl." Billy laughs, looking over towards the sandpit "What the fuck is that? "

"Jeff." Sal and l reply in unison.

"Okay then." Billy replies and returns to his pint.

"If l hadn't given birth to her I'd swear she was Dil and Jimbobs." Confesses Sal to no-one in particular shaking her head whilst looking lovingly at her youngest child. Sal is the most elegant, smart and spotless woman l have ever met. She is tall and has the poise of a dancer. She is never seen without full make up and not a hair out of place. Nathan, her middle son, is the spit of her; he's handsome, immaculaate and always pristine. He's currently working for a bank on the Island; yet he also has his dad's knack of reviving anything mechanical and is often found in the shed in spotless overalls breathing life into lost causes. Max, the eldest is her daddy's daughter, like me. She is always covered in oil and grease, swearing like a trooper and taking apart anything with wheels. She is currently studying Advanced Motorcycle Engineering at Bologna in Italy. Sarah was a late arrival surprising everyone and horrifying Max who convinced herself that her parents had not had any intimate contact after 2001 when Nathan was conceived.

As the spring sun sets we are treated to an amazing display of Mama Nature at her best. A bright golden orb appears to sit at the end of the sea fanning out into a blaze of yellow and orange and red, the wispy clouds turning violet and silver blue. Dad and Sarah come closer to join us. Jeff, however, despite having a huge bowl of clean water, tours from table to table helping herself to any unattended beer. She then staggers back to us, looks lopsidedly at Billy, burps and farts simultaneously very loudly and flops down on the grass beside Dad with a contented sigh.

"Fair play, whatever you are! I'm impressed. You're gonna fit right in. Welcome to the family." Laughs Billy offering her the rest of his pint.

Ricky arrives as we are all tucking into cheesy chips and gravy - the unofficial Manx national dish.

"Yo bros, Shortarse, snot monster and hairy orange thing!" He plonks down on the grass next to me kissing

me on the forehead and raising his pint in salute to Dad. He pinches a handful of my chips. Ricky loves his food. He's as wide as he is tall, much of it is muscle as he spends his days lumping heavy plant and machinery around and wrestling farmyard animals during evenings and weekends. He owns and runs the Island's main plant hire business and lives in a cottage on his parents' sheep and dairy farm so he can help them out.

They upped sticks from Tipton when the boys were young but none have lost the accent. He's Billy's youngest brother, they are as close as brothers will ever be but they are opposite in so many ways; Billy loves family life and Island life, he married Sal, his childhood sweetheart, the first person he met on his first day at school over here, as soon as he could. He dotes on her, his kids, his brothers, his parents and pretty much everyone he knows and will run around after all of them without complaint.

Ricky is a total commitment phobe and has disappointed a long line of heartbroken ladies, both on the Island and around the globe, who have fallen for his easygoing charm and thought they'd be the one to settle him. He also has a wanderlust and has joined me on quite a few rides in Spain, Italy, New Zealand and Australia and I can always count on him to step up when I want to do go off doing crazy stuff like off-piste skiing, cave diving, bungee jumping and hurling myself off buildings and out of perfectly good airplanes. Chaz, the eldest is married to his career and I rarely see him now but we all know he would be here in a heartbeat if any of us were in trouble.

With Sarah curled up and fast asleep in my arms, we spend a beautiful evening relaxing, catching up, chatting, reminiscing, remembering adventures we've had together and separately, friends and family, those still kicking and those who have left us, races won and lost, favourite bikes, bikes from hell and bikes consigned to the scrap yard in the sky. I get them up to date on where I've spent the last couple of years; Indonesia; Bali, Java, New Guinea and Sumatra.

I catch sight of Dad, he's smiling and chilled, he enjoys the company but being so hard of hearing he tends to retreat from noisy conversation as he can't keep up with it. If they weren't such close friends I'd be right there on the sidelines with him. He's lying back on the grass with Jeff flopped with her huge head on his chest, her nose tucked under his beard. Dad is watching the sky, pointing out birds, stars, cloud patterns and who knows what else; Jeff is totally focused, looking adoringly into his eyes and listening to his every word.

With a deep sadness it suddenly occurs to me that he really has become what I have called him my whole adult life, an 'old man' and I'll be lucky to spend another ten or fifteen years with him. I vow to make a real effort to put down roots and make a go of this wild dream of his. This will not be easy, ghosts on this island always overwhelm me after a few weeks here and I usually run away as soon as I sense their presence.

CHAPTER 3

I am awoken rather violently by a washing up bowl being dropped on my head.

"Morning, Jeff." She licks my forehead and collects the bowl for a second assault. I rise to another beautiful morning with the sound of the waves lazily wandering up the pebbled beach and the gulls screaming a greeting to the day. I check my phone...its five to four in the morning! "Okay, Jeff we need to have a little chat about what constitutes breakfast time." She looks at me with her head on one side, ears almost mirroring the clock. She sighs deeply and picks up the bowl again in order to reiterate her point. "We'll have to go catch breakfast baby 'cos your dopey Dad forgot to do the only job he was supposed to do yesterday." I grab the rod and we head of to the beach leaving the old man snoring softly in his tent.

The beach is again devoid of people but far from deserted; black headed gulls, fulmars, gannets, chough and Manx shearwaters vie for sea and airspace as they dive and swoop and bob all busy getting breakfast. The seals are also up and about whooping and barking and heading in and out of the sea. It's high tide and there's plenty of rich pickings.

I negotiate with Jeff on the benefits of not eating the bait and finally cast the line. This is my idea of heaven, barefoot in my knickers and vest on a beach surrounded by sea and nature my only company being a slightly unhinged and probably hungover dog who is presently eating seaweed.

I'm lost in my daydream and then reality begins to muscle in...How long will the build take? Can we really build a house? How long will the weather last? Will we get enough work to pay the bills? Can l stay put for longer than a month? What will I do without Dad? What ......the hell is Jeff doing now?

I can hear woofing and whining and a wild-eyed dog comes running over to me with a very large and very affronted crab attached to her top lip. She plonks herself in front of me with her ears and fur standing on end, a look of absolute horror on her face and appears to be going cross eyed with her big furry eyebrows knitting into one. I can't help but laugh which makes her even more insistent, kicking me with her big front paw. Not without some effort I carefully remove the seriously unhappy crustacean and set it back on the shoreline, it shakes itself, helps itself to a chunk of bait and wanders off. I inspect Jeff for damage. She seems fine and is happy for me to look in her mouth, turn up her big, baggy lip and check her eyes are still intact. When I'm done she shakes herself from head to tail, licks my head and saunters off taking a mackerel I've just caught with her. l shake my head and laugh.

"Thanks both. Nice to be appreciated!"

I catch a few more fish and we head back to camp. I tiptoe past a still sleeping Dad and head into the barn to set up the field kitchen so that we can eat properly from now on.

After a quick set up and check and a rearranging of the barn so that I don't set fire to anything l have a workable kitchen area. The field kitchen is superb with a stove, oven, fryer, grill, sink and work surface all in shining stainless steel. The guys have even sent three full gas bottles to see us through and a folding picnic bench and a blue and white checkered oilcloth cover. I set it up amidst the reasonably organised chaos and with a tear in my eye I vow to repay them whenever and however l can. I put the kettle on and grab a jar of instant coffee out of my rucksack and promise myself that later in the week I'll make a trip to Ramsey to get some of Conor's really fab proper coffee. Coffee is my one vice. I rarely drink excess alcohol, can't stand the taste of many spirits, have never smoked and see not much point whatever in drugs but cannot go a day without strong, black coffee.

"Can l smell coffee? What's for breakfast? I'm starving!" Dad wanders into the barn absently scratching at his beard. He looks around and smiles "Looks proper homely, you been up all night?"

"Jeff requested breakfast at four. We've been fishing, crabbing and tidying ever since." l laugh handing him a mug of hot, sweet coffee in one hand and a plate of hot, fresh mackerel in the other and reaching up to kiss his cheek.

"Is it my birthday?" He enquires with a cheeky grin as he sits down at our newly set up table. "Got any plans for today?"

"We better go get your bike and some supplies. We can't live on mackerel forever and Jeff might appreciate some real dog food. Right on cue Jeff saunters in, washing bowl hanging out of her mouth. She is a little more polite this time, gently offering it to Dad with her head on one side and an expectant look on her silly face. Dad passes it to me and l fill it with cold, fresh water and hand it back with some chopped up fish on a makeshift plate. Jeff appraises the offerings, sighs happily and submerges her head in the water for several seconds before resurfacing and devouring the fish in one inhale and burping loudly in appreciation. We watch on in amazement, she appears to be a canine hoover.

"Wow, l think she may be a reincarnation of your brother." Smiles Dad as he hands her the last bit of his own breakfast.

I clean up and we're just discussing the logistics of fetching the bike and groceries with a large animal in tow as we hear a reversing beep and a huge horsebox backs into the lane.

Nina and a complete stranger jump out and wave a greeting then disappear around the back of the van. We head towards them and Nina bustles quickly over, she seems keen to keep us away from the vehicle.

"Hi both!" She booms, "Beautiful day again! You're all settled, I see." She announces confidently with barely a glance at our camp. She was a headmistress for many, many years before retiring and taking the helm of the MSPCA in Foxdale which she runs with the same control and authority as she ran her 'Ofsted Outstanding' rated school.

"Thought you might need your iron horse so I've bought it back." On cue the bike appears down the ramp with a rather hot and bothered looking youth struggling to push it backwards down a ramp and control its trajectory. This is a skill that takes time to master, trust me I've done it enough times with a less than perfect outcome. He also seems a little distracted by whatever else is in the horsebox.

Jeff is clearly familiar with the young man and launches herself at him from a nearby bush. To his total credit the lad manages to carefully lean the bike up the fence and catch Jeff in his arms. She licks his face from chin to the top of his head and he hugs her tightly and laughs before losing his balance and falling back into the bush she appeared from and being completely smothered by the hairy, dribbling hound.

Laughing, we extract them both from the undergrowth and we get to formally meet Joseph aka Joey. He's introduced as Nina's great nephew.

"Staying with me a while...Got himself into a bit of trouble on the mainland. My cousin knew I'd set him straight." Nina purses her lips and shakes her head. I'm not sure if she's unhappy about her visitor or overjoyed to have a new project.

"Our latest edition clearly approves." I laugh, as Jeff is alternately standing looking at Joey with adoring eyes then dancing around him, sniffing his pockets and then repeating her actions over again.

"Likes mints, don't she?" Joey states but doesn't offer her, or anyone else, one. He is clearly happier with animals than conversation. He has a broad scouse accent and a flop of unruly fringe hides his eyes. He looks about 14 or 15, like he should still be at school.

"Come on Joseph, we've lots to do!" Orders Nina. "Get the rest unloaded." Dad and I look at each other questioningly. Dad shrugs like he has no idea what's about to happen. "Old Lady Fairley has been taken into Noble's for a few days so I need someone to look after Giles and Isobel. You have your paddocks empty and I knew you wouldn't mind." As Dad and I absorb this information Joey reappears from the horsebox leading two adorable donkeys.

"Do we have a paddock?" I enquire. Dad looks confused.

"You have three, my dear." Nina replies as if talking to a rather unintelligent child, pointing to the fields around our camp. "That one, that one and this one." While l stand with my mouth agape taking in this new information Joey has found and opened a rickety, but secure gate and deposited the donkeys inside with half a dozen bales of hay and a sack of carrots. He walks back to us with a large trough.

"Water?" Dad points him to the cottage. He struggles back past us a few minutes later with the trough full and puts it down. Jeff immediately immerses her whole head in it.

"Come on Joseph! Time to go!" Turning to us Nina issues more instructions as she jumps into the driving seat. "Don't feed them rubbish and watch Giles he's a biter!"

Joey rushes from the field, tickles Jeff's ears and looks over at our camp

"Sick." He whispers shyly as he climbs into the truck and they are gone.

"Anything you forgot to tell me, Old Man?" I enquire with a raised eyebrow.

"Nope, knew nothing about any of that, don't look at me." He shrugs and saunters off to meet our new guests.

So now we are five!

CHAPTER 4

D ad is duly dispatched to Shoprite with a long list, an empty rucksack and very strict instructions not to return with any more livestock if at all possible.

Jeff and l get down to some proper work. She rearranging her makeshift bed which she has made from Dad's old army surplus coat which goes everywhere with him, one of my hoodies she's taken out of my tent, some material she must have found on the site somewhere and the washing up bowl which she has firmly claimed; me grabbing the strimmer to tentatively reclaim a bit more of the land that may, or may not, belong to us.

I clear away thick, spiky greenery, gorse and broom, from the paddock fence so that we can see and feed the donkeys without serious injury or having to walk down the lane to the gate. They watch on suspiciously from a safe distance.

At the back of the barn I clear away enough nettles to make soup and wine for a year, keeping a more regimented clump in order to do both. Under them l find a very welcome patch of wild garlic, my favourite smell and taste of spring, some forget me nots, the remains of a quite extensive herb garden all planted in old chimney pots and some rough raised beds made from old railway sleepers, a pile of garden canes, some rolls of chicken wire, an old hen house and a kennel. Whoever lived here seems to have been quite self-sufficient. It certainly hasn't been empty for twenty years. I must quiz the old man a bit more when he returns.

While Jeff snoozes in her newly made bed and the donkeys explore their temporary home, I spend a few more happy hours clearing, mooching and making pleasant discoveries before l hear the dulcet tone of the Kawasaki approaching. Dad rides up looking like he's moving home. The bike is loaded with bags and boxes, sacks and buckets and bowls.

"Got everything on yer list and a few extras just in case." Dad climbs out of the heap and gently hands me a small paper bag that had been sitting on his tank.

"Oh no! It's not a hamster is it?" l tease carefully opening the bag. It's my perfect gift....Coffee Mann Racer Blend ground coffee and a huge slice of bread pudding. "I just remembered why l love you." I smile kissing his cheek.

"Twice in a day? It really must be my birthday! Get the kettle on girly it's been a mission."

I grab a few more bags and head for the barn. Sometime later, l totter back out balancing my tray (piece of wood) loaded with mugs of decent coffee, buttered French bread smothered with pate and the pudding cut into two equal chunks each sitting on a piece of the ripped open bag they arrived in. Hardly afternoon tea at the Ritz!

Jeff has already started without us and is crunching loudly on a bone that was possibly the whole leg of a cow or a postman that wasn't quick enough. Whichever it is, she is really enjoying it.

"Fit for a king!" Dad announces as l put the tray down and join him on the grass. We eat in comfortable silence and savour the tastes, slowly and appreciatively.

"How was your day, dear?" I ask Dad jokingly.

"Brilliant but stressful." He laughs. "I went to Nina's place to buy dog food and ask what donkeys eat. I got sold a great big sack of dog stuff and was told we are not to feed the donkeys as Joey will come every day to sort them as he needs 'a sense of responsibility'" He mimics Nina's cut glass accent. "Poor lad, we need to rescue him. I roped the sack on the bike along with the bone, a bowl and a load of poo bags. Then l went to Shoprite and Pat Parker copped me and talked my head off for an hour. We're going there for Sunday dinner by the way, then I'd just balanced all the shopping perfectly and Paddy Mac spotted me and came over to shoot the breeze for an hour or so, then I took off to Ramsey to Conrods for your coffee. It was a mare to park and l didn't think the bike would stand up if l got off so l just phoned in and Emma ran out with it and stood chatting for a bit." Dad looks around the plot. "I see you've been almost as busy. Find anything salvageable?"

"Loads of great stuff. I think we need to get a builder to look at the cottage and barn to tell us if they can be saved and if not, what options we do have. Not sure where the money's coming from though I've only got a couple of thousand left in the bank."

"Ah, I think you have a little more than that." Says Dad. "The Old Gal was careful with her money and had us all very well insured after we lost Jim-bob. There was money for Marley and for her. She left it all to you and me but you took off as soon as we'd scattered her ashes and I was fine money-wise so l didn't get around to reading the will until a couple of weeks ago when a solicitor phoned. Not sure what it's worth now it's been invested for a while in some high interest thingy but it was about £850,000 five years ago apparently. You know your Mama, she worked hard all her life and was an excellent accountant."

I'm stunned. I sit opening and closing my mouth like a goldfish. Money has never featured big in my life. If I've needed money I've got a job, saved up, bought whatever I needed and then moved on. I've never had money to spare and definitely never had more than ten thousand pounds at any time in my life that was when l was saving for my beloved Duchess. Dad and Mama always asked if I needed money and I always declined. Mama used to say 'I'm saving it all up for you' but I never thought she was serious. This will take a while to process.

"Oh, okay then...I think I need more coffee."

CHAPTER 5

I sleep fitfully, having money appears to affect my slumber far more than having none. Outside the tent, Jeff lets out a low rumble and takes off down the lane. I emerge from the tent in my usual attire of knickers and a vest, dreads like a bird's nest. I hear an audible gasp. "Eh Laa, don't look, it's proper scary that!" I look over to see Joey with one hand over Isobel's eyes and one hand over his own. I duck back in the tent giggling and grab a pair of dungarees.

"Want a coffee, Joey?" I shout once l am suitably attired.

"Nah, coffee's for old folk, ya got any Coke?" He replies.

"Nah, Coke's for kids." l shoot back.

He takes this in for a second, with his head on one side like Jeff, then he smiles, a real cheeky grin, and laughs. "You're alright for a woolly you are. Gor any tea? Three sugars." I head for the barn and make coffee, tea and bacon sarnies for three. Only two sugars as Nina will have my guts for garters if his teeth fall out! When I exit the barn, I find Joey sitting on my bike, leaning forward on the tank and making revving noises as if pretending to race. He jumps off in a panic and looks extremely guilty.

"On me Ma's life I weren't gonna nick it!"

"Honey, I'm chilled you'll get nowhere with it on this Island, everywhere leads back to where you left. Relax, come and eat your sandwich and drink your cuppa." Hoping I've found a way in I try a conversation. "Like bikes do you?"

"Fuckin' love 'em!" He woofs down his food. "Me Da used to bring me 'ere for the racin' when 'e wasn't inside. Named me after Joey D...." He shakes his head as if he feels like it's just been invaded and jumps up with his half-eaten sandwich. "Gorra go, Neenaw'll be screwin'!" With that he dives on his pushbike and hares off waving his butty at the donkeys as he goes. "See yas tommorra!"

Dad unzips his tent. He's been listening to the chat. "You'll have cracked him by the end of the week. Ain't lost your touch, Dilly girl. Where's my grub?" He's referring to his breakfast and my ability to work with withdrawn and damaged kids. Mama and Dad emergency fostered hundreds of them while me and Marley were growing up and long after we'd left home. They were always so broken that l became a pretty good counselor over the years. I seem to have a knack of getting people to talk about stuff they don't want to. A healer l met in India told me I'm an empath and explained that I absorb people's feelings, hence l get sensory overload in big groups. Sounds like mumbo jumbo but who knows?

I give Jeff her breakfast and a fresh bucket of water, check the donkeys have everything they need and head in to wash up the cups and plates. I hear Dad yell a greeting to someone and wander out to have a nose.

It's Paddy Mac, a southern Irish expat. Word has it he came over for the racing in 1973 and forgot to go home. Rumour has it he left a very unpleasant and demanding fiancée at the altar and can't go home. Either way, he's now married to a wonderful Manx lady and has seven strapping boys and a very successful building business, McDonnagh & Sons. Dad and I have known him and his family a long while as two of his sons are road racers.

"Dilly Girl! There's nothing to you! Get up our house and get fed!" Paddy exclaims as he engulfs me in a huge hug. "Your Pa tells me you want a bit of work done. Do you want to rebuild and rethatch or bulldoze the lot and start again? It shouldn't be that bad it's only been empty about five years. Old lady Keogh was batty as a fruitcake but she survived here until well into her nineties. Your Da was a kind soul for buying the place and letting her stay on when her lease was done, so he was."

I'm not quite ready for this and haven't thought about it at all so l put the coffee on, drag the table out into the sunshine and the three of us discuss our options while Jeff snores gently in the shade and the donkeys look on from their field. Paddy produces dozens of plans and catalogues and samples and colour sheets and plonks them on the table. It appears that him and Dad had quite a specific 'shoot the breeze' yesterday. We chat and debate and good naturedly argue for hours over materials and finishes and prices. Suddenly Dad's stomach rumbles loudly.

"Oh Lord! Lunchtime!" Exclaims Paddy slapping his forehead with his hand and hustles off to his van. He returns with a huge cool box and sits it on top of everything already on the table. "Meave sent lunch." He announces. l play mother and start unpacking. It's a real feast! The sandwiches are like doorstops, homemade fresh bread packed with real butter, tasty roast beef and salad, there's quiche, cans of lager and a bottle of lemonade, huge slabs of homemade fruitcake, fresh fruit, chunks of cheese and a huge bone and two carrots.

"Nina was around yesterday." Paddy replies to my raised eyebrows and nods his head towards Jeff. I hand over the bone and deliver the carrots to the pointy eared onlookers who are more than willing recipients. Giles leans over the fence to grab a chunk of me as well as soon as l turn my back but I'm too quick for him. After our very enjoyable and seriously appreciated lunch we return to negotiations until the sun goes down.

"Okay right!" Paddy says standing up and stretching his arms above his head to loosen the kinks. "Okay, l better be getting off Meave'll have supper on the table. We're sorted on the barn becoming your workshop then? I'll be back tomorrow and see what we can do with the cottage." Bikes have always taken priority over beds.

Dad and I chat long into the night over coffee and the remains of Meave's cake. It turns out we do own the three paddocks one of which contains the remains of a stable block, the cottage and the barn, the land surrounding it down to some quite distant hedgerows, the driveway and part of the beach.

Dad's excited about having a proper workshop with space again and collecting some of the treasures he currently has scattered around both over here and back on the mainland. They've all sat in garages for a long while so I'm sure we'll have plenty to work on even if no customers turn up. Dad starts off the yawning then neither of us can stop. We clean our teeth, visit the thunder box, check on the donkeys, kiss Jeff goodnight and crawl into our tents, tired and happy. It's been a long but fruitful day.

CHAPTER 6

This morning's wakeup call is Paddy Mac and a truck full of Paddy juniors and a trailer carrying a JCB. Jeff, who's made her way into my tent during the night, opens one eye and theatrically puts her big hairy paws over her ears and goes back to sleep. I laugh and do the same. When I finally emerge from my pit I find a building site in full swing with Dad as labourer and Joey as tea boy. He hands me a perfectly made coffee in my favourite cup before l even reach the barn.

"Eh laa, what time d'ya call this?" He gives me that cheeky grin and wanders off with Jeff in tow. Dad gives me a thumbs up and a wink and nods his head towards Joey.

I savour my coffee then head off to find Paddy Mac. He's busy putting up some scaffolding at the back of the cottage

"Afternoon Dilly Girl, grab a trowel. We need to get all the loose stuff out so the boys can repoint it." He calls down gesturing towards a tool bag against the wall. I laugh and grab a trowel...it's actually about half 9 in the morning but it was a real lie in for me, that dog is a really bad influence.

I spend a few hours lost in a trance, thinking about everything and nothing, mindlessly scratching out loose mortar from between the huge stone blocks that make up the cottage walls. I become aware of a more hesitant scratching and look up to find Joey has joined me at a safe distance and is watching what l am doing and carefully copying. I nod in appreciation and we work in companionable silence for the rest of the morning until Paddy Mac declares its lunchtime and produces three huge cool boxes.

Young Macs descend upon it from all over the plot and much good-natured teasing and banter passes between everyone whilst I sit back and observe. Joey is cautious and constantly weighing up his situation but takes the teasing in good spirit and politely accepts all the food he is offered. He briefly looks over to me when one of the lads passes him a can of lager as if seeking permission, I nod and raise my own can in salute. Cold lager just really hits the spot on a warm day and he's more than earned it.

The talk inevitably gets around to bikes and racing past, present and future and Joey really comes into his own. He knows all the greats who were done or gone long before he must have been born. He competently debates with the boys whether Guy Martin would have won the year he turned his bike into a fireball and laments Conor's unplanned trip off the side of the Verandah in the same race, we universally agree it would have been Conor's race. He says he wished he'd been around to see the great Foggy v Hislop battle in 1992 and then in complete innocence states.

"I wish I'd met some woman called Delilah Blue as well, she raced 'ere at the same time and me Da proper fancied 'er, whenever 'e went inside me Ma told everyone 'e'd run off with Delilah Blue." The lads, to their credit, say nothing. Paddy Mac looks at his watch and declares it's 2 o'clock and time to get on with work.

Joey jumps up "Fuckin' 'ell! Neenaw'll be screwin'!"

"Neenaw?" Queries Paddy Mac.

"I 'ave to check in with Neenaw, who's gorra phone quick?"

"Leave her to me." Dad says reaching for his mobile. "I'll call her now and tell her we can't do without you this afternoon. Joey visibly relaxes and runs off after the lads, grabbing his trowel on the way.

"What's he mean, Neenaw?" Paddy Mac looks to Dad "He's not in trouble with a policeman over here surely? He's a good boy, so he is."

"Neenaw is Nina...she's got him under house arrest." Dad laughs making the call. "He calls her Neenaw 'cos he says she's a 'fed'."

Paddy Mac laughs "He might have something there. The boys still call her 'neighborhood watch'."

We work long past clocking off time and Paddy Jr. and Joey head off in the van to the chippy to get us all supper while we tidy up and clear away for the night. The place looks totally different already; mortar stripped from the front wall of the cottage, the inside completely cleared out, the woodwork from joists, doors and windows now on a bonfire around the back, scaffolding right up to roof height on both barn and cottage, a large trench dug around both and even the paddocks are mowed and the garden cleared.

Supper arrives and we all congregate on the grass. "Okay then." Says Paddy Mac. "Where are we at?" The boys take it in turns to reel off the jobs they've done and materials they need for tomorrow. They are a real slick outfit; l had no idea they were so good. Turns out plumbing to toilet and sink out the back are sorted and working and the outhouse has been reroofed and has a working light and a fuse board ready for the rest of the wiring. Everything has been measured for the wiring and a list is given. The chippies give a list of wood they want - roof joists, frames, floorboards and batons. The roofers have decided to tile the barn and thatch the cottage and give Paddy Mac their list too. "Anything we've forgotten?" Asks Paddy Mac after writing everything down in a well-used notebook.

"'Ow about somethin' to fill them dirty great gaps me and 'er 'ave made in that there wall?" Joey chimes in waving a chip towards the cottage.

"Don't worry son there's a bit of concrete coming tomorrow. We'll make a builder of you yet so we will." Paddy Mac laughs and ruffles his hair.

"Nah man, it's sick work but I'm gonna be a racer." Joey says earnestly. "I better go sort the donkeys 'fore l geroff." He heads off towards the field.

Paddy Jr. laughs "He's just been telling be about his plans in the van. He's coming down to Jurby to watch us test the next TT winner on Saturday. We've got the track booked for the whole afternoon. Bring The Duchess down we'll see if you've still got what it takes."

"I might just do that." l tease.

"Seriously, we could do with your expert eye we've got a new Beemer and we're struggling with our pre circuit testing. We've only got a few weeks to set her right before the North West"

"Sorted 'em. I better get off." Shouts Joey from the darkness of the lane.

"Don't be soft, lad it's black as pitch! Throw your bike on the back of the truck, we'll drop you off on the way."

"Dilly Girl, come and look!" Dad yells from the back of the cottage after everyone has gone and we're getting ready for bed. I grab the torch and run around the back expecting to see something nature related that has caught his eye, a robin's nest in the roof or something equally brilliant. l stand amazed, looking at something very man made but even better than a nest. As well as the roof, the light, the loo and the sink with working taps we have a water heater and shower. Absolute bliss!

CHAPTER 7

Paddy Mac and the boys are back bright and early next morning with Joey right behind them, literally - he's hanging on to the back of the truck and being pulled along. He sees to Isobel and Giles whilst they unload endless materials and I make countless mugs of coffee and tea and bacon sarnies and feed Jeff. She is in her element; with so many people eating so much bacon she barely touches her own breakfast and wanders around everyone in turn trying out her 'cute' face to get scraps. She scores every time then comes back and hoovers up a huge bowl of water. She retrieves the remains of her postman's leg from under a nearby bush and settles down for a good chew.

The guys all get off and do their thing while I fire up the cement mixer and start repointing the wall. At some stage of the morning a cement lorry arrives and the trenches that were dug around the buildings yesterday are filled and everything has to be dragged out of the barn and cottage to lay level concrete floors.

The lads are on the cottage roof and they're rebuilding the chimneys and lining them. They are also putting joists across both the barn and the cottage and repointing like ninjas. They work in complete harmony and seem to communicate by telepathy. No one gets in anyone's way and they occasionally break into song when something catches their attention on the radio. It's when they break out into 'Open Arms' by Journey that it all becomes a little overwhelming for me and l sneak off down to the beach with Jeff for a few moments to pull myself together. Menopausal hormones are hard to handle.

I sit down on the pebbles and watch the waves wandering in and out aimlessly and the birds bobbing and diving. I can hear the hammering and general hubbub on the site but l am far enough away to calm my thoughts and relax. Don't let em in Dil, you know it'll end in tears says a voice in my head. Jeff is off mooching and exploring, digging potholes in the pebbles with her huge paws and throwing seaweed in the air with her nose and making me smile. Clearly not scarred from her recent encounter with the unhappy crustacean.

The wind is blowing my hair in my face and as l go to brush it away l realise I'm already crying. This dream that is now becoming a reality was always mine, mine and Jimbob's. We always talked of living here on the Island permanently, setting up a business, fostering and maybe having a family of our own, dogs, horses, more bikes than we had room for, a huge garage with a mezzanine floor, a bunk house for Marley and friends to sleep over and a granny flat for Mama and Dad.....Oh lord, l remember we had gone on so much about this whenever we were all over here, dragging Mama and Dad around to look at places and drawing up scribbles and sketches of our dreams.

I'd blocked it all out, locked it away in the recesses of my damaged mind...too painful to remember. We'd found a farm house over at Scaard; lots of work to do but it would have been perfect, no way we could afford it but we were both frantically working all hours to get a deposit together and hoping no one else put in an offer.... l hear the pebbles crunching and quickly wipe away the tears and snot on my sleeve.

"Big Mac's broke out the scran." Announces Joey plonking himself down next to me, dropping a doorstep sandwich roughly wrapped in a paper napkin and a bottle of Coke in my lap. He says nothing, sits eating his own food, quietly looking out to sea. "Okay?" He asks eventually.

"I'm fine. I just needed a time out. Thanks for lunch."

"Try the Coke all the cool kids love it, it's bad for ya, full o' caffeine Neenaw says." He grins at his own joke then suddenly looks spooked and shivers. "I'm off, too many ghosts, fuckin' 'ell even me Da's down 'ere." He whispers and briskly marches back up the beach.

"Enough of this self-indulgent crap Delilah! Can't change the past. Get your arse up, sort your hormones out and get on with the future." I tell myself sternly, taking a swig of the Coke... it's pretty disgusting and all the gassy bubbles go up my nose and make me cough and splutter. "Face it Dil, you never was a cool kid and its far too late now." I laugh and walk back into the mayhem.

CHAPTER 8

Two days on and Saturday morning dawns with no break in the beautiful sunshine. The cottage floor is dry and we have windows and a front and back door. The lads have started the thatching which should take two or three weeks so hopefully the weather will be kind. The barn is already roofed and the field kitchen and table returned to their original spot inside. The electrics are well under way with brightly coloured wires snaking around the walls and sockets appearing everywhere.

I grab a sander and go to work on the dresser and table, l really want to keep them if l can, they seem to belong here. The table is fabulous; solid and scarred; what stories it could tell...burn marks, gouges, dents and scratched legs-maybe from a long-lost cat. I strip back the layers of dirt from the top to reveal a gorgeous grain. I yell Dad for a hand to turn it over so that l can remove the legs and get started on the bottom. He comes to help out and we turn the table upside down on the grass, then he disappears into the barn and comes back with tools and stuff to join me.

He removes the table legs and sits down to work 'old school' with sandpaper wrapped around a block of wood.

"You going to see how the boys are getting on later?" He asks. "You should go. It'll do you good."

"I'm good already. Sunshine, sea and you. What more could I want?" l tease.

"A bit of fun? Apart from our first night at the pub you haven't been further than the beach. The work's going well and we'll be fine even if the weather breaks. We can sleep in the barn if we have a hurricane and I'm pretty sure none are forecast. Relax and spend some time with the living." I shrug in reply, l can't deny anything, he's telling the truth.

We continue to work on the table, side by side but each lost in our own thoughts. Lunchtime is signaled by Dad's belly rumbling loudly. I head off to the barn to find something to eat. Stocks are getting a bit low. I make myself promise l will go to get the next shop, the old man is right l am becoming a bit of a hermit.

I butter crusty bread, hard boil some eggs, boil some rice, clean the fish l caught this morning and throw together a kedgeree.

When l deliver the food to Dad he's lying back on the grass, hands behind his head, eyes closed and a big smile on his face. Jeff is in what has become her usual position, flat out on her side with her head on Dad's chest and her nose in his beard.

"Hear that?" He asks not opening his eyes. "SC Project pipe. A great choice."

I cock my head to one side and hear the distinct high revving wail of a four stroke. It never fails to amaze me that the old man genuinely appears to be quite hard of hearing but he can still hear, and identify, anything on two wheels from miles away. The sound calls to me. I laugh.

"Eat up and we'll go up and have a look."

We settle Jeff with her postman's leg and her bucket of water inside the barn with the bottom half of the door closed just in case she goes wandering. I put some boots on and grab my lid. The Duchess hasn't moved a wheel since we arrived and she creaks, groans and spits in protest when I wake her. Jurby track is only two minutes away, an easy walk but I need to ride. Dad fires up the Kwak which doesn't complain in any way. He kicks it into first, looks down and then does a thumbs up at me when he notices I've done his chain and sprocket. He takes off down the lane and I follow, waving to the donkeys on the way.

The circuit is situated on an old airfield which still has the fabulous wartime airport control tower and communications block. It is surrounded by an industrial estate, the prison, the original and the newly built motor museum, a gorgeous little cafe called The Guardsman and a separate carting track. We pull into the paddock area, park up next to Paddy Jr's van and trailer and walk to the side of the track just as a white, red and blue BMW flashes by.

We watch and listen as Paddy Jr does a few more laps then walk over to meet him as he comes off track. The tyres are blistered and everything is tinging and pinging from the heat expansion. He jumps off removing his helmet, still full of adrenalin and with a huge grin on his face, talking fast and loud.

"She's a handful through the start finish chicane and the hairpin was a bit hairy but really not too out of shape anywhere else"

"Apart from the nut loose behind the handlebars?" Dad laughs.

Joey comes cycling up like the devil is chasing him, slams his brakes on and does a very impressive stoppie. "What've I missed? Neenaw 'ad me cleanin' out all the kennels 'fore she'd let me out. I smell like the fuckin' 'ozzie." He snorts in disgust, putting his head down and sniffing his t-shirt. He is giving off a strong whiff of Jeyes Fluid.

"Chill man, we're only just getting started." Juan, Paddy's brother laughs clapping him on the shoulder. "The big boys haven't had a go yet."

Paddy punches him playfully. "Get the stopwatch then let's see who's got the biggest balls. Five laps each - 1 minute 20 or less on your first run or you're out, who wants to go first?" Juan starts zipping up his leathers and grabs his helmet. He nods towards the van.

"Yours are all in there. We picked them up from Ricky's place last night."

"The ones from Ricky's?" I shake my head and laugh. "I've put on a stone at least since I last wore those. I've got no chance of zipping up!" I go off to the van to see what's in there while Juan goes off for his laps and Dad takes control of timing.

I pull my racing leathers out. Wow! Memories flood into my head; sitting on the start line waiting to go, flat out up Bray Hill, flying over the mountain, the relief of reaching the finish straight for the final time, the exhilaration of being part of such a unique event. Jimbob not coming in on lap 3, Marley not getting to the Gooseneck where I was waiting with a pit board....

"Get you kit on Dil! you're next." Yells Paddy Jr.

I shake the ghosts out and grab my long-abandoned custom-made Manx leathers; custom made for a six stone me...this will be fun! I strip off my jeans in the back of the van and manage to get all of the necessary arms and legs in the right holes with a bit of wriggling and a lot of giggling. Now for the interesting bit. I jump out of the van and lie flat on the tarmac in a desperate attempt to get the zip up.

The old man is having hysterics and trying hard to concentrate on his stopwatch at the same time. Paddy Jr. is hanging on to the fence trying to catch his breath from laughing so much. Joey is looking at us all in turn as if we are completely crazy. I get the zip up over my belly but have apparently developed boobs at some stage in the last five years and they do not want to conform! I stretch my arms to the sky and arch my back to stretch the well-worn leather and with a big deep breath in, a big grunt and a tug on the zip everything is finally contained. I just need to get up, do my boots up and get on the bike. I roll around on my back like a turtle until Paddy can stop laughing long enough to set me upright. The boots still fit like a dream and the leathers are starting to give enough for me to bend down and do them up.

Juan comes in all hyped and grinning from his laps. "She's a handful alright...how'd l do?"

"1.20, 1.19, 1.19, 1.27 because you went grass tracking and 1.19 again for the last one." Dad informs him. "You're consistent. I'll give you that."

"That bloody flip flop always lets me know when I'm getting cocky." Juan shakes his head and climbs off the BMW, patting the tank in admiration. "All yours Dil, let's see if you've still got it."

l climb on and rearrange my leathers, gloves, check my helmet is tight and my seating position is comfortable. It's been a while since l rode around Jurby and last time was just parade laps at the festival. I know the circuit well and it's easy enough but can catch you out especially around the Bus Stop. I approach the start line with some trepidation and a lot of adrenaline coursing through my veins.

I love the thrill of riding fast. You have to empty your head of everything; complete concentration on the next bend or change of direction. The bike is raring to go. I pull in the clutch, knock her into first gear and press the start button to activate the launch control, I smoothly relax my left hand and take off down the straight, left at Hodge, right into Runway, a quick right left right left around Kneens and steady into the Bus Stop. I can already feel how stable and forgiving the bike is. It's light and agile and has so much more power than I need around here. Left at Snuffles and I give her a push down the straight to Castle then rein her back in for Ballamenagh and Tyrers Curve then speed up down Knights and back over the start/finish line...Keeping my head down and my mind focussed I go for a fast lap. It feels good. It always amazes me how quickly I can get 'in the zone'.

I have not felt the desire to race for a while but as soon as I got onto the circuit today I felt something stirring. Having the track to yourself is bliss, you don't have to think about who is in front or behind you can just concentrate on the bike and the tarmac and 'go for it'. Lap four is a bit hairy when I cannot find the back brake for a second... a combination of a bit of a design fault and my size two feet! I lose a few seconds but that makes me even more determined on my final lap. I give it everything my rusty brain and body can and try to keep it smooth, controlled and consistent. I fly over the finish line and embark on a slower lap to bring her back around to the start line.

"Thanks for that, Delilah! You always let me know I'm shite at this game." Laughs Juan. "I'll stick to being pit crew! "

I'm buzzing as I take off my lid, grinning like a child at a birthday party.

"The bike is awesome! So forgiving, The Duchess would have kicked my ass more than once just then." I cock my head on one side and look at Dad. "Come on then Old Man, how was it?"

"Not bad for a has been. 1.19, 1.18, 1.17.6, 1.21 and a 1.17.4 on your last one. Is it my turn?"

"'Ang on Laa! Wind back...did you just call 'er Delilah?" Joey is standing with his hands on his hips looking confused and bemused.

"Sorry kid." Dad laughs. "You never were formally introduced... Meet Dil aka Delilah Tallulah Tinkerbell Rainbow Blue." Dad has a goofy, proud grin on his face but tries to hide it. "Get off Dilly let me show him how the old boys go!"

"I'm livin' my Da's dream! This is random and yous lot are fuckin' tapped!" Announces Joey shaking his head, trying to take another bit of information into his already mixed up head. "Wait 'til l tell me Ma I've run off with Delilah Blue!"

Dad takes off on the BM flatly refusing to use the launch control and puts in five respectable laps all under 1.20. He knows this circuit inside out. Like me he is all pumped up and hyper when he comes in. There is no feeling quite like it.

Paddy jr. goes off next and he is a joy to watch, he's really focussed and trying to be smooth and fluid with every change of direction and gear. He makes it look effortless and judging from the expletives being uttered by Joey, with the stopwatch, he is making good time. All his laps are all under 1.19 and he beats my best by two tenths of a second.

We continue to play around for the rest of the afternoon; focusing on different areas each lap...brakes, suspension, handling in different situations and finally launch control. Overall the bike is already a superb package straight out of the crate but a few tweaks will make it the perfect tool for the job.

We're just about to call it a day and Joey is sitting on the bike pretending to race... he's in a world of his own, lying on the tank saying the names of every point on the TT course in the correct order and leaning the right way for each one.

"PlayStation." He grins when he realises we are all watching him. Juan goes off to mooch in the back of the truck and returns with a pillion seat pad, rear pegs and a spanner.

"Get off Joe, let's feed your need for speed and blow away the stink of Jeyes Fluid, there's a one piece in the van that'll fit you." He sits for a second, eyes wide, with his mouth open then he moves like greased lightning and is in and out of the van in seconds. Juan takes his boots off and Joey puts them on. I hand him my gloves and helmet and we check everything is safe and tight on him.

"One word to Nina and she'll have you on the boat back home." Warns Dad with a giggle as he drops and locks the visor. Paddy Jr. takes him on a steady first lap to check he can sit still and won't panic and cause any issues but he's still and planted and l see him tapping to go faster. Being a pillion is so different from riding. You need to have complete trust in the rider and be able to move with them; you have no control.

Joey has often seemed guarded and unsure, always checking around to see what everyone is up to, always moving and animated, jumpy... but now he's lost in the moment, still and relaxed and l note with interest that his foot is twitching on the pillion pegs as if he is in control of the gear changes and occasionally rear braking when the bike is getting a little unsettled.

"Are you seeing what I'm seeing, Dilly girl?" The Old Man asks.

"He is a bloody natural! We need to get him riding." Juan exclaims.

Paddy Jr. pulls in and Joey jumps off.

"That was fuckin' boss!" He's full of adrenaline and dancing around like a loon, trying to undo his helmet but failing miserably. We all laugh as we know the feeling even if we express it a little more eloquently.

"Welcome to the world of the tapped." I laugh. "Stand still and let me get your hat off!" He dances around some more muttering endless expletives before getting it together enough for me to retrieve my helmet.

"You've clearly been on a bike before." Paddy Jr. states. "You're a better pillion than all my brothers, especially him." Pointing at Juan.

"Ain't ever been on anything but me pushbike...Ain't even sat on a bike 'til I saw Dil's at the camp an' couldn't resist. All me Da's cash went on smak and me Ma never 'ad any cash to start with! Cheers man, that was awesome!" We look at each other in amazement but say nothing. He turns away from us all appearing embarrassed, he's on a high and just let his guard down, shared a little more about himself than he intended to.

We pack everything away into the van including my snug fitting leathers, Secure the bike on the trailer and head off to The Guardsman for a debrief and a snack. We grab a table outside and sit down for a chat. I suggest an adjustment to the back brake and the others agree that it's not quite right. We talk about changing the brakes but all agree just a change of pads should be fine. We debate changing suspension internals and again decide to leave it for the North West 200 and panic practice week if we need to. We talk about trying different tyres but this is an easy fix and we can play about with several types as Paddy Jr is currently dating the young lady who runs the local tyre and exhaust fitters in Douglas and has easy access to supplies. She has already sorted that SC Projects exhaust system.

Joey paces around the table, shoving his food in like he's starving. He's still full of adrenaline and away in his own thoughts with a big grin on his face between bites.

We sit chatting until long after the food is finished and don't even notice it's starting to get dark until Joey jumps up and slaps himself on the forehead. "Eh Laa, I forgot to feed the donkeys!" He yells as he rides off on his bike towards our place. "I'll do it now then I best get back to Neenaw's. Today was epic." And with that he's gone ignoring our shouts to hang on for a lift.

"He does take his responsibilities seriously, doesn't he?" Dad laughs as Joey disappears into the darkness as if he's been shot from a cannon. We say our goodbyes and the lads promise to pick Joey up on the way home if they see him.

I'm tired and happy, muscles l haven't used for a while will be aching in the morning but the short ride back in the cool night air with my visor up reminds me again why I love this place and its people so very much.

CHAPTER 9

S unday dawns with the most amazing sunrise which l watch from the beach. My body and mind are totally relaxed and l take the opportunity to indulge in a bit of yoga. I can feel the dull aches in my shoulders and forearms and thighs, pleasant reminders of a wonderful yesterday. I stretch and pose and balance whilst Jeff looks on bemused. She stays away from me for the most part but tries to shake paws when l get into the warrior pose and then nips me on the bum when l bend to salute the sun.

Dad has joined me at some stage and as l look across is currently trying to do a downward facing dog pose with a large orange beast climbing on his back. He laughs and collapses on the floor rolling and playing with Jeff, he looks so much younger and full of life and l wonder why I've been worrying about his age. The peace and tranquility of this island seems to have taken the years off already.

"What's the plan for today?" I ask after we've been sitting in pleasant silence for a while watching the day arrive in a spectacular burst of colour.

"Dinner at the farm at three. I'm gonna get that mezzanine up in the barn and make some calls to the mainland to get my tools sent over. Why don't you go see Billy or Rick or take Joey down to Murray's?" He tentatively suggests.

"And who's going to keep an eye on you if I go out to play?" I tease.

"Jeff. She's very resourceful and may be a distant relative of Lassie." Dad replies earnestly, tickling a besotted Jeff under her chin. "She will come and find you if anything happens or she may just phone the required authorities if she thinks it's more appropriate."

I laugh and stand up, holding out my hands to pull Dad up.

"Come on you crazy Old Man. Let's go and have some breakfast." We walk up the beach arm in arm with Jeff running circles around us.

We're well into our third coffee when Joey arrives to see to Isobel and Giles. He is riding his push bike bow legged with a huge sack of food hanging over his crossbar He grins and waves to us as he jumps over the fence heading towards the donkeys with the sack now balancing on his head. The Island's magic is working on him too. He looks less anxious and drawn, he's tanned and more relaxed and is singing 'Funky Moped' loudly to the donkeys. How does he even know that song?!

Jeff appears with her washing bowl as Joey comes over with the bucket to fill the trough. "Come on Laa, I'll sort ya." He says as he passes us and Jeff willingly follows with her bowl.

"Want a cuppa, Joe?" Dad asks.

"Yeah, I'll put the kettle on while the buckets and bowls are fillin'. Got no official orders for today apart from 'donkeys at 7.30am and lunch at 1.30 prompt'" He mimics Nina's cut glass accent perfectly. "What does that word even mean?"

Jeff returns and shakes her shaggy wet head all over us and Joey appears with a mug of tea. "What's for scran, Dil? I'm starvin' Neenaw gives me bird food for breakfast"

I zip into the barn and rustle up three slightly improvised full English breakfasts with the last of our supplies. I really must go shopping later or tomorrow. We sit and eat and I watch in wonder as both Dad and Joey shovel in mouthfuls as if they haven't eaten for a week and good naturedly fight over the last piece of fried bread, eventually breaking it in half and sharing. Dad shrugs as he catches me watching. "This sea air gives us working men an appetite."

"Want a 'and with that floor?" Joey asks pointing his fork at the barn.

"No, son, have a day off. Go and show Dil where the cool kids go on this Rock."

"As if I'd know, Laa." Joey snorts. "Me Da couldn't do without the smak and me Ma wouldn't let 'im take me if 'e had any so we'd come for the day and just walk up to the paddock. 'E'd be rattlin' by teatime so we'd 'ave to get back. Never bin out o' Douglas 'til Neenaw picked me up off the boat." I can see he's not bitter, it's all he's known and he still counts it as some of the best times of his short life. "I got to stay one year when 'e scored on the boat over and went AWOL."

"Where'd you sleep?" Dad asks careful not to sound too shocked.

"Slept in the park. It was great. Got loads o' scran off the race teams in the paddocks and a big, hairy bloke who was checkin' the bogs every mornin' and night kept bringing me drinks and stuff. Me Ma 'ad a meltdown when me Da went back without me and the feds came lookin' for me on day three. I watched every race and practice l could, was lovin' it." He smiles like it's a happy memory and then shakes his head regretfully. "That was the last time she let me come over and he went proper off the rails after that, scrappin' and robbin' all the time. He got banged up again just after-wards and they found 'im od'd on spice, lemo and meth in 'is pad before trial. Soft Lad! Dead as a fuckin' doornail at 32. What a waste!" He lets out a huge sigh and it seems as if a huge weight has been lifted off his shoul-ders, talking to someone who doesn't know or judge you is always great therapy. "Enough o' this shite! What we doin' before dinner? D'ya want the garden sortin' or l can rub down that cupboard thing?"

"See if my lid rattles around too much on your head." Dad says reaching down for his helmet. "If it's safe enough Dil might take you a run over the mountain as payback for all the stuff you've already helped with." Joey's whole face lights up, his grin is electric and there's no way l can refuse. Cunning old man!

We kit him out in Dad's centenary helmet with a crochet beanie hat underneath to keep it snug, my spare pink gloves and my Power Puff Girls buff. He's already wearing a battered leather jacket, jeans and huge boots. "I'll take it steady." I promise Dad, laughing at his worried scan of Joey from head to foot. He always insisted on decent riding gear when we were kids and never let us ride in jeans. I do it too often now and he still hates it even though mine are now all padded and lined with Kevlar. "No chance of a twenty-minute lap in that outfit."

Joey looks himself up and down. "Eh La! Let's get on 'fore I scare the donkeys."

I pull on my jeans and jacket, grab my lid and lace my boots and coax The Duchess into life. She growls and spits and roars. Joey jumps on.

"Enjoy! Don't forget he's gotta be back for half one." Yells Dad as he pats the tank. "Ride safe. love you."

Despite having a back seat and pegs, I rarely carry a pillion so l go super steady for us both to get used to it. We head down to the Fairy Bridge to take an offering to the little folk and I tell Joey about the tradition of always greeting the little guys in order to have good luck and a safe ride. He laughs at me then starts mooching through his pockets to find a token to leave. He finds a pretty shell. "Will this do? I found it on your beach. I was saving it for y ....me Ma."

"Keep it for your mom if you want." l say giving him a pound coin to place in the wall.

"These fairies have got a right racket goin!" He exclaims when he sees all the coins in the wall. I've never 'ad that much ackers in me life."

We ride a little further on and into Murray's Museum. It's a gold mine of old bikes and memorabilia and Joey is mesmerized. He's running from bike to bike, from floor to floor and then gets even more excited when he finds the donkeys that live out the back. I've seen the place a hundred times but find something different every time l go, it's a great place to spend a rainy afternoon and they happen often during TT and Manx GP. Seeing it through Joey's eyes is a real pleasure. His excitement is genuine and he's desperate to take in everything, shouting me over and over to look at something he's found.

I remember being the same when l was about eight or nine when the museum was in its old home at The Bungalow up on the mountain. The ever present, Peter Murray is beaming with pride.

"Delilah, come and have a coffee and a chat and leave him to it." He calls waving a mug and biscuit tin at me after he's spent an enjoyable hour relaying tales of Joey Dunlop and other legendary riders with our Joey hanging on his every word then asking question after question, hungry for knowledge.

We sit and chat outside while Joey continues in search of 'more input'. He finally emerges to see where we've gone.

"It's boss 'ere!" He announces, throwing himself down on the floor next to me and pinching my biscuit.

I punch him playfully in the arm.

"Have you had enough now? Where do you wanna go next?" I tease, knowing he's keen to go over the mountain. He looks at me for a moment as if he's scared to ask for more.

"Can we do a lap? It's okay if you've 'ad enough o' me now, l get it." He says smiling.

"Joe, you're a real pleasure to be with, honey. We'll do steady lap then l better get you back so you're not late for lunch...times running away." He says a thousand thank yous to Peter and offers to help him out if ever he needs anything.

I head towards Douglas so that I can give him the full start to finish lap. There's a bit of traffic about and l just go slowly. As soon as we ride towards the start line he realises where he is and he gets excited. l can hear him muttering away to himself, saying the names of places he can see and pointing at the park to show me where he'd slept. I go off up Bray Hill at a sensible speed.

It always feels strange when it's a normal day and traffic and people are using the roads and pavements. We pootle around and l point out a few things to him and he yells questions back over and over. We reach Ramsey and l am tempted to stop at Conrod's for some coffee but manage to resist. I lean the bike right over to go around the hairpin and Joey sits as still as ever. Traffic is clear and we head up and over the mountain going a little quicker than Dad would approve of.

There are no speed limits on the mountain which is very liberating. I stop at the Bungalow for Joey to meet his namesake. He looks in absolute awe at the statue of Joey Dunlop sitting astride his SP1 and approaches with reverence.

"Climb on the back. I'll take your picture." I say getting my phone out of my pocket.

"Ahh ehh! I can't touch it!" He looks from the statue to me. "Can l?"

"Course you can if you're careful. Dad has at least a dozen pictures of me sitting there."

He climbs on talking to Joey all the time, apologising for his actions. I take a photo which by no means captures the full beauty of the moment but he is smiling if not totally relaxed. He dives off the second I've taken the picture and apologises to Joey some more, wiping his sleeve over where he was sitting as if he'd left a mark.

"Come on Sunbeam! We better get back." I say noticing the time on my phone. We have a superb run up the mountain mile and all the way down to Windy Corner and around past the Creg ny Baa. The Duchess is loving it and behaving impeccably. I slow down when I get to Hillberry and we hit a bit more traffic going back into Douglas. I cross the finish line with Joey waving his arms around like we just won the Senior Race.

I head straight back to our place. If it's too late for Joey to push bike back to Nina's I can drop him there and fetch him in the morning.

Dad is waiting for us at the top of the drive with his phone in his hand looking worried.

"I've got some bad news for Joey." He says. "Nina has fallen down the steps at church and broken her hip. She's in Noble's. " Joey goes white. All the colour drains out of him.

"Is she gonna die?" He asks. I put my arms around him and he stiffens for a second then relaxes into me and starts to sob.

"No, Joe she's made of tough stuff and a broken hip will mend but she will be out of action for a while. We'll head to the hospital now and you can see for yourself."

"She'll send me 'ome! I can't go 'ome!" He sobs "They'll 'urt me. They'll 'urt me Ma."

"Who will? " Dad asks. "No one is gonna hurt you, son."

"They will! That's why I'm here. Me Da owed a lot of money to nasty people. They came round after the funeral sayin' I could work for 'em to pay it off. Me Ma rang Auntie Carole who stuck me on the boat. They think we've run off. Ma is out the way, in Manchester. We'll 'ave to go back to the flat. They'll come lookin' for me as soon as I get there. I ain't sellin' drugs for no-one even if it does get me Ma out the shite." He takes a deep breath and tries to pull himself together, he looks so young and totally defeated. "How do I get to the 'ozzie? I gotta ask Neenaw if I can stay. If I can't I need to get me stuff and do one 'cos I'm not goin' back."

I look at Dad and I can see his heart is breaking. He's seen and dealt with so many of these vulnerable kids but it never gets easier.

"You haven't got to go anywhere. You can stay here. She's classed as a responsible adult." He laughs pointing at me. "Not as comfy as Nina's but not so far to go to sort the donkeys and we kind of miss you when you're not here." Joey looks at Dad in disbelief and then at me for confirmation.

"We'll have to go and buy you a sleeping bag which ain't gonna be easy on a Sunday afternoon on this island." I say in mock horror, "But nothing else is a problem. Come on let's head for Noble's to let Nina know you're safe and sorted then to the farm for dinner. I bet Ricky'll lend us his camping gear so you can have your own space. Oh bugger! You're wearing Dad's helmet!" I suddenly realise.

"Don't worry. Keep it on. I'll get Billy and Sal to pick me up in the car. Tell Nina to rest and not worry. Don't be late for dinner! Ride Safe."

Nina is bossing the doctor about when we arrive. He smiles at us with relief and seizes his chance to escape. "If I need a new hip they need to get on with it!" She aims loudly at his retreating back. "I've got things to do, people who depend on me. Ah Joseph! What am I going to do about you? I need to ring your m....."

Joey looks genuinely relieved to see she is far from death's door but doesn't let her get started. He holds up his hand as if stopping traffic to cut her off.

"Chill Auntie Nina, got everythin' under control." He announces confidently. "I'm stayin' with Dil and Dylan so I can keep 'elpin' with the donkeys an' the buildin'. I'll go to the kennels every day and check they're doin' everythin' proper. If anyone needs 'elp with an animal I can go an' sort it. I'll go by the house an' bring ya post an' whatever ya need. Trust me, I got it all covered." He's clearly done a lot of thinking on the way over here. I realise all the muttering I could hear from the pillion seat must have been a rehearsal.

Nina is stunned into silence; either because he dared to silence her or because he called her Auntie or possibly because that's the most she's ever heard him say or maybe it's the fact that she actually needs to let him take on all and more of the responsibilities that she claimed he needed. She glares at him as if she is going to start a lecture then just seems to deflate and suddenly looks exhausted.

"Oh Joseph you are such a good boy! I can't expect you to do all that. Is Dylan happy about you being there? Are the donkeys well? I need to check up on Lady Fairley.... "

"Enough mitherin'!" Joey chides. "I'm goin' to 'andle it all 'til ya sorted, end of discussion. Write me a list an' I'll come and get it in the mornin'. Get some shut eye. We're off for some scran now, even that's sorted." I realise Joey has had to step up and sort the grown-ups on more than this occasion and I wonder if it was his Dad, his Mum or both?

Nina can either see she's beaten or really is in too much pain to argue. She agrees to Joey's proposal and hands over the keys to her house and the kennels. She insists that a full list of instructions will be written and waiting by 9.30am when visiting is allowed and takes mine and Dad's mobile numbers. She kindly suggests we all stay at her's but Joey is looking forward to camping out and tells her no. Eventually, she is appeased and informed enough to let us leave with a firm promise to be back in the morning.

"That wasn't as much stress as l thought." Grins Joey as he puts his crochet hat and helmet back on. "This dinner better be big 'cos I'm starvin'." I smile at his ability to take everything that comes at him and kick The Duchess into first.

We arrive at the farm at ten to three and are met by four huge dogs including Jeff who's looking very happy about her new friends. Next attack comes from Sarah Snot Face who dives on me and then after a brief appraisal, Joey. He laughs and hugs her even though he's no idea who she is.

"Dave!" Shouts Billy from the farmhouse door. He waves over and spots Joey. "Fuck me it's little Dave from the paddock! You still livin' down in the park?" Joey takes a second to realise Billy is 'the big hairy bloke' who'd looked after him when his Dad got off. He holds out his hand to shake Billy's but is mashed and lifted off the ground in a Billy bear hug. Next assault comes from Pat and Will they hug and kiss and hug some more and welcome Joey with open arms. He's not quite sure what to make of it all and clearly isn't used to such displays of affection but accepts all the cuddles with good grace and then retreats to sit by Dad on the big, comfy sofa. Sal hands me a mug of coffee and tells Sarah to go and fetch her Uncle Ricky from the cottage next door.

Ricky arrives with Nathan in tow and we all sit down to a proper Sunday feast; roast beef cut from a joint big enough to feed fifty, Yorkshire pudding, mash and roasties, cabbage, carrots, green beans, cauliflower cheese, horseradish sauce, onion sauce and a bucket of gravy. It's all heavenly and we all eat way past being full up. Pudding then arrives - rhubarb crumble, apple pie, pineapple upside cake, brownies, a fruit salad, ice cream, custard and thick, sweet fresh cream.

"Help yourselves!" Pat invites.

I choose cake and ice cream. Dad and Joey try to get a bit of everything in one dish but have to go back for more as they've chosen big bits. Pat watches indulgently, smiling and encouraging everyone to eat more and more until we're all fit to explode. Sarah lets out a huge fart and giggles.

"Full to farting, Gramma!" She announces and we all collapse in a fit of laughter.

Sal and I start collecting plates, glasses, dishes and cutlery when we summon up the energy and head into the kitchen to wash up. Pat joins us and we chat pleasant nonsense while we clear away. Joey sticks his head in the door and asks if he can help but Pat chases him off with her tea towel.

"Alright if l go outside for a bit?" He asks shyly.

"Of course it is!" Pat exclaims. "No-one stands on ceremony here and I've a feeling you're going to become a regular visitor and a very welcome one. Go and have a nose around. Take the dogs with you if you want some company."

Nathan comes up behind him.

"I was just coming to see if you want to come and mess around on the crossers. Me and Ricky were having a play before dinner."

Joey looks apprehensive and excited at the same time. He looks over to see what I've got to say about it.

"I ain't bin on one before." He's quick to admit.

"Go on. You'll love it but take my helmet. Dad'll cry if you scratch his." I prompt.

"No need, he's got his own." Nathan smiles and hands Joey a helmet. "You can keep that one if you want it. It's not new but it's not very old, I treated myself to a new one when I passed my test and don't worry about being a first timer we'll take it steady. Dad and Ricky taught me and I ended up in Noble's with a broken wrist didn't I Mom? So I know how not to teach you." Joey is speechless. He takes the helmet and follows Nath out the back door.

Two minutes later we hear the motocross bikes start up and Nathan shouting clear directions and loads of praise and encouragement. I shed a few quiet tears of thankfulness and am engulfed in a big hug from Pat and Sal and told to 'stop being a soppy tart!'

I pull myself together and we finish tidying, make a huge pot of tea and a big pot of coffee and Pat loads up plates with homemade cakes and biscuits and we go and join the guys who are all glued to the TV watching a recording of last year's North West 200. They've clearly all seen it a dozen times before as they are commentating on what's coming next, urging each other to look out for specific corners or specific racers or a bit on a bike that looks out of place. This is us. We cannot help ourselves and within seconds I'm joining in.

After an hour of analysis, banter and lots of coffee and cake Billy looks up.

"Where's Dave?"

"He's outside trying not to break Joey." Sal replies. "You ought to go and check if they're okay and take this hairy orange thing with you because it smells worse than our youngest!" Jeff is flat out on the rug under Sal's feet and, like Sarah, doesn't have any qualms about sharing her bodily functions with us.

Billy, Ricky and I troop outside with Jeff and Sarah in tow. The field at the back of the farmhouse has been a motocross track since Billy and Ricky were kids. Will has always encouraged them to ride and still rides himself. The track has become pretty technical as the years have passed and the kids have grown. Sarah grabs her helmet off the floor, jumps on her own little KTM and flies off to chase the boys. Like her Grandad, Dad, Uncles, brother and sister, she's been riding since she could walk and is fearless. Sal loves her road bike but isn't as keen to get knee deep in mud.

My suspicions about Joey being a natural rider are confirmed as he comes flying past us in pursuit of Nathan and takes a huge jump in his stride, landing correctly. He corners without losing too much speed and gives Sarah plenty of room as he passes her on the straight. She catches him on the next bend and he lets her through safely and with good grace, shaking his head in amazement.

Nath spots us and rides over.

"He's really good! I showed him the gears and clutch and he's followed me round getting quicker and quicker. He listens and asks and wants to know stuff. He's a pleasure to teach. I'm going to get him on the YBR soon so he can get his license. Oh! If that's alright Auntie Dil?" He adds remembering the YBR is mine.

"It's fine! The YBR is all yours, sweetheart. You've sorted it out and you can keep it. When you want something bigger you can use it as a trade in. If you're lucky someone will give you 50p for it." I tease, then realise something important. "Hang on! Is he old enough to ride on the road?" The minimum age over here is 16 for a learner bike.

"He will be in a fortnight." Nathan informs me with a wink.

Joey pulls up all hyped and talking loud and fast. "Eh Laa! I'm buzzin'. Wish I'd had teachers like 'im when I'd bothered to go to school. 'E explains proper like. Thought l was doin' good but l just got showed by a munchkin." He laughs pointing at Sarah.

"Don't take it to heart!" Ricky laughs. "She's seen me off a few times. She's a demon on a bike. Have you lot had enough 'cos l think Nan's sorting tea?"

I can't resist a quick blast around with Billy while Joey watches us from the sidelines. We hare around jumping high and turning fast, kicking up dirt and dust, vying for the best lines and bumping and pushing each other good naturedly. It feels so good but I'm hot and knackered after half a dozen laps. I pull up next to Joey and take my helmet off. "Man, I am so unfit!"

"You're old an' shouldn't be doin' daft shite like that!" He teases.

"It's a good job I'm old and unfit else you'd get your bum kicked." I laugh pointing over to where Billy has just disappeared. "Ride over to the barn and put the bikes away, it's teatime."

Back at camp tired, full and happy we put up the tent Ricky has kindly lent Joey and Dad shows Sal and Billy around.

"Never 'ad me own pad." Joey grins as we get the bed and sleeping bag in. "It's proper nice in there."

"I wanna camp!" Sarah announces. "I'm staying here tonight with Auntie Dilly."

"You're not, little miss stinky pants!" Sal laughs. "You're going home for a bath and bed. You've got school in the morning!"

We say fond farewells and they take off home. Joey goes off to feed the donkeys, Dad goes off for a shower and Jeff and I head for the beach to watch the sun set.

CHAPTER 10

Monday morning madness arrives with a truck full of McDonnaghs. I dispatch Dad to the butchers for sausage, bacon, eggs and bread so that l can sort breakfast and I settle down to write a list of what else I need to get later. I sit in the sunshine with organised chaos all around me; pointing being finished, thatching carrying on, new doors being hung on the barn, the mezzanine floor finished off, wiring snaking from barn to cottage, internal walls being erected to separate the bedrooms off and Joey busy tidying the garden. He smiles and waves when he sees me. He must have slept okay, him and the Old Man were snoring their heads off when l got back last night.

This morning I can hear him chatting happily with Paddy Jr as he's digging over the raised beds. He's recounting his biking adventures from the weekend and questioning Paddy Jr. relentlessly about the North west 200 and the TT. Again, I marvel at his ability to take everything life has thrown at him and just accept it and move on, l resolve to be more 'Joey' from now on and stop dwelling on the past.

The list goes from food and essentials to stuff for Joey's birthday, what do you get a sixteen-year-old? Next l list furniture for the cottage, we will need beds and bedding and a settee and a couple of chests of drawers, l want to buy veggies for planting and chickens or ducks for the henhouse which l need to reclaim from the undergrowth and then my mind takes a turn to bikes and tools we can get over here, stuff from the mainland we need to send for and by the time l hear the Kwak bringing in the breakfast I'm well into writing a business plan....careful Dil you might be starting to grow roots.

I drop the list and jump up to go and put the kettle on and make food for everyone. By mid-morning everyone is fed and watered and Dad has taken Joey off to get his instructions from Nina, run her errands and check the house. I head into the garden to mooch about for a few hours. Before l start getting dirty I text Nathan to see what he knows about Joey's birthday. I get a text back in less than a minute.

'gr8 kid bdy 9ma thnks u thnk es 16 dnt wna go bk cos es 2 yung yey prtyXx'

I text him back;

'Please translate! I don't speak teenager. Are you saying his birthday is 9th May and he hasn't told us because he assumed we thought he was old enough to be riding bikes and looking after himself? Are you organising a party or asking for one? Xx'

'Sorry Auntie Dil, I forgot you are anal about punctuation and grammar. AND OLD! Yes, you are correct about his birthday and reason for not mentioning it although I got the feeling that he's not had any epic birthdays ever. I am happy to help you organise a party. I will sort some music and invite some of my friends so that not everyone there is ancient. Ha Ha Luv ya xxxx'

'Thank you, you cheeky little shithead. 9th is a Saturday so shall we go for his birthday night? Let me know what l need to sort. Love you too xx'

Okay, I've got six days and he's going to be running plenty of errands for Nina so no worries. I let Paddy and the lads know what I'm planning and they're all up for a party.

"We're off to North West on Monday so that'll give us a day to recover." Juan quips. "Shall we take him with us for a birthday present?"

I get back to gardening but Joe has already dug over all of the raised beds and they are ready for planting. I give the herbs in the chimney pots a bit of attention and then head to the overgrown corner where the hen house and kennel are. Both are a little rickety and the mesh around the hen enclosure is more holes than fence. I strip it all away and wrap it safely so that Jeff doesn't get tangled in it. A skip has appeared at some point and l throw it in there along with a few other rusty bits and pieces that l unearth while clearing.

I lift the roof off the henhouse and find perches and shelves still intact. I grab the dustpan and brush and sweep it all then scrub it inside and out. Then get some offcuts of wood, nails and the end of a roll of tarpaulin to recover the roof. Paddy brings me a pot of paint and a brush over.

"I've just finished painting your doors. Do you want your henhouse the same colour?" He checks out my workmanship. "You're doing a good job! I'll send one of the boys over to replace that corner post and help you put the fence back up."

I finish the painting and fetch the chicken wire l found during my first tidy up. With help from one of the lads I get it all enclosed and it looks really sweet.

"All we need now is some chickens!" Dad says coming over and putting his arm around my shoulder. "It just so happens that there is an assortment of feathery inmates at Nina's place. Shall I bring some home tomorrow?"

"Better let the paint dry first." I laugh then look around to check Joey isn't nearby. "Where's Joey? We're having a party for him on Saturday. Nathan is going to find some cool kids and sort the music; the Macs are all up for it and said they'll bring some food and drink and I'll do a barbecue if you can cut a barrel in half for me. Where shall we have it?"

"We could go down in the field at the bottom or on the beach. He might like a beach barbecue. He's talking to his mom on my phone just now. He hasn't spoken to her since he came over because he says he can't find a payphone and didn't want to ask Nina. "

"Hasn't he got a mobile?" I'm shocked to realise l now assume everyone has a mobile phone. It's not that long ago that we'd never even heard of them.

"Nope, never had one apparently. Mom couldn't afford it and he said he'd got no-one to call anyway. Don't think his short life has been very luxurious, I reckon he's been a lonely kid with a lot of grown up responsibilities. I just had to convince him he needs to ring to tell her where he is because Nina can't do it. He even asked how many minutes he can stay on for. I think a party will mean a lot to him. Hopefully, he'll leave his mum's number in my phone and maybe we can get her over."

"Old Man, you're a clever bugger!" l stand on tiptoe and kiss him on the cheek. "I do love you so much. Thank you for bringing me back."

Joey comes sauntering across to us and hands Dad his phone back his face is a mixture of emotions like he's trying to process his conversation.

"Me Ma just 'ad the shock of her life, 'ad a right turn she did, thought l was callin' cos l was in trouble. Told me off then asked me fifty questions an' didn't give me time to answer and then cried. Women are weird! Can l ring her again next month? I won't stay on long."

"Son, you can ring her whenever you want. I get millions of free minutes and I don't know enough people to ever use them all. Dil uses even less than me so you can use her phone as well." I nod in agreement.

"Cheers but she'll do me nut in." He changes the subject. "Nice chicken 'ouse. Want me to sort the dog'ouse now?" He takes the broom and disappears into the old kennel and Jeff follows him. "Watch ya feet laa, don't tread on anythin' spiky."

Dad and l head off to see how the Macs are doing. The doors are hung and painted on the barn and the cottage door is a beautiful rich blue and the door furniture is on. We have a chunky brass doorknob and a cast iron bell on a bracket, with a little shaped motorbike on top, hanging next to the door. It makes me smile.

"Meave picked that when we went to get the hinges and knobs." Paddy Mac explains. "She said you must have it."

"It's perfect Paddy, it's all perfect." I sob, wiping tears and snot on my sleeve. "Thank you so much for everything."

Paddy reddens in embarrassment. "You haven't even looked inside yet!"

We go into the cottage and can't believe how much has changed. The walls and the fireplaces are pointed and whitewashed and there is even kindling in the hearth and logs stacked. There are lights hanging and switches and sockets on the walls. The room is open plan with one end empty and the other end has the table in the centre and the dresser, which has been rubbed down and waxed, against the wall. A sink unit has been built under the Belfast sink and a space for a huge cooker and fridge is evident. Beyond the kitchen a stud wall and short passageway has been erected with two opposite doors into small but adequate rooms which also have lights, sockets and radiators.

"You've a back burner in the fireplace." Paddy proudly announces. "You've room for a double bed in both rooms but not much else." He ushers us towards the back door which previously led to the garden. "Come and see the piece de resistance." It now leads into a cosy, whitewashed, passageway which still has a door into the garden but also leads to the toilet and shower room. "No having to go outside for a pee!" He laughs. "There's space and plumbing for a washer and dryer here too. Roof's not finished but it is watertight if you want to move in. The boys just need to put another layer on. I've never known them work so fast. They should be done before they go off to Ireland."

"Let us have the bill so we can make sure they're paid before they go." I say though floods of happy tears. "Don't forget to include all the extras you've done like mowing the paddocks and sorting the dresser and chopping the logs and feeding us and....." I want him to know I've noticed and appreciate all of the lovely kind touches they have added.

"Enough! It's been a pleasure and we've eaten a hundred weight in breakfasts." Paddy says giving me a big hug and shaking Dad's hand. "I'm off to another job tomorrow but some of the boys will be here to finish the electrics in the barn. I'll send the bill with them. Call me if you find anything you don't like." With that they all pile into the truck and disappear.

Jeff and Joey appear from around the back, both looking tired and dusty and matching the front door in several places.

"Doghouse is done! Jeff 'elped with the paintin'." Jeff gives a proud wag of her blue tail as if to back up his statement. "We gor any scran? I'm starvin'."

"Go and get showered and we'll go and eat down the pub. I'm gonna check out the workshop." Dad says and Joey saunters off to his tent for a towel.

I follow Dad into the barn and its quite dark with the doors on. He flicks the light switch and it's amazing; huge bright work lights beam down on a smooth floor. A work bench runs along one wall and Dad's toolboxes are sitting in a row at the end. His two big bike jacks and a selection of paddock stands and other useful bits and pieces are neatly in place.

"I rang Charlie with a list last week and they came over yesterday. Paddy picked them up from the boat." Dad informs me. There is a small office in one corner and a basic kitchen area with a sink and space for a fridge and kettle and a toilet and shower. The mezzanine is huge and industrial with lots of head height and a raised platform to put a mattress onto. It's also enclosed on all sides for privacy but has a window looking down into the workshop and another in the roof.

"Wow! It's better than I ever imagined, Dad. I can't believe this has all happened so quickly." I'm sobbing again and shaking my head in wonder trying to take in everything. "I wish Jimbob and Mama and Marley were here too."

"I'm done. Just gorra sort the donkeys. Fed Jeff." Joey yells as he passes the doorway. I pull myself together and go and get showered even treating my hair to a thorough scrub.

We walk to the pub with miss blue tail leading the way and order nearly everything on the menu between us.

CHAPTER 11

I wake to another flawless day and head off to the beach for some meditation and yoga. I've been there for a good hour before Joey comes wandering down.

"Are ya doin' some new age 'ippie shite?" He asks with a grin.

"More like middle aged hippie shite." I laugh looking at him upside down as I am standing on my head. "It helps you focus and calms your mind and makes you super strong and flexible which means you can ride a bike like a demon." I wink.

"Can ya teach me some?" He asks suddenly interested. "Can't stand on me nut! Can't even do a 'andstand but if I'm gonna be the best road racer that ever lived I better start learnin'." He's always so willing and so optimistic.

I turn myself up the right way and begin to show him some basics. He's such a keen learner and so eager to please that we progress well. Dad and Jeff join us and Dad shows off to Joey that he can still stand on his head, shows him the shoulder pressing pose, the peacock and the firefly. All are pretty advanced moves and need a lot of core body strength.

"That's epic! I wanna be that boss when I'm you're age." Joey announces.

"That's nothing. I can teach you the Karnapidasana, knee to ear, pose. You kinda stick your head up your bum!" Dad tells him.

"Err, no thanks! Show me that warrior one again, I can do that an' it 'urts so it must be doin' somat." We practice and lark about for another hour or so and then Dad and Joey go off to do their Nina duties. I consent to the bringing home of whatever fowl wants a bike ride and wave them off.

I start to make a big stone circle on the beach so that we can safely have a fire and maybe a roast for Joey's party. Jeff discovers her calling and brings me endless driftwood and big, smooth pebbles from far and wide. By the time we're done there is a six-foot round pit surrounded by a foot-high wall full of firewood and dried seaweed.

We head back to the cottage and the boys are on the roof. Jeff barks a 'hello' to them and then plonks down on her bed for an afternoon nap after consuming a bucket full of cold water. I offer them a drink too then head inside the cottage to continue planning what I need to buy. My phone rings and I jump a mile it's such a rare occurrence. It's Sal.

"There's an auction at Sarah's school tonight. I've just seen them taking some nice settees and wardrobes in. Do you want me to pick you up later? It starts at half 7. I'll bring the van in case we see a bargain. I'm going into Tesco in Douglas afterwards too if you need a big shop, our cupboards are bare." Sal is a sucker for a bargain and loves to shop whatever it's for.

"Perfect timing, I'm just writing a 'need' list. I'll do a shopping list too. I'll ring Euronics in a minute and see if they'll bring me a fridge."

"I'll pick you up at seven so we can earmark the good stuff. See you later. Love you."

I can't believe how well and how quickly everything is falling into place. Madame Karma appears to have finally found some time for the Old Man and me and l am truly grateful for it. It's scary how I have very quickly adjusted from scraping by to spending money far too easily. I need to sort permits and paperwork out so that we can start working from here and put a bit back in.

In the meantime, I ring the electrical guys and spend a bit more. Within an hour l have a fabulous double cooker, a washing machine, dryer and a fridge freezer. The delivery men wire in the cooker, plumb in the washer and dryer and even plug in the fridge. Service over here is second to none and salesmen are very persuasive. They hand me all of the paperwork along with boxes containing two kettles, a very sexy coffee maker, a fancy toaster, a microwave and a complimentary set of saucepans. I realise that at the grand age of 52 I have just taken delivery of my very first white goods, none of which are actually white but a lovely brushed stainless steel.

I waste no time testing them out. I put the coffee on to brew, filling the kitchen with a fabulous aroma and grab all the left-over veggies and spices from the barn and the meat Pat sent us home with yesterday and make a huge pot of thick, spicy, stew. Once its cooking I move all the kitchen stuff out of the barn and clean and neatly stack all the plant Ricky had lent us, move the few utensils we own into the kitchen and make a list of other bits we need. I seem to have become a prolific list maker and have to admit to finding it very therapeutic.

"Fuckin' 'ell! 'Ave ya robbed Curry's?" Joey exclaims as he comes into the cottage to find me in amongst the boxes. "Somat smells nice, I'm starvin'. Come an' meet the ladies."

Dad is down by the hen house chatting away to our latest editions. "Chickens on a Kawasaki, two up is quite eventful." Dad informs me and Joey grins in agreement. Both are covered in poop and feathers.

"Good job we've got a washing machine." I reply.

"We haven't." Dad says looking at me like I'm going bonkers.

"We 'ave." Joey tells him. "Dil's ramraided the leccie shop while we've bin off workin'. What we gonna call these chucks?"

I look in the enclosure at three very indignant looking brown hens and two ruffled white bantams. All are busy scratching the ground, exploring and rearranging the straw. The guys have already put in food and water for them.

"If I name them I'll get them mixed up, I can't tell them apart!" I laugh.

Joey looks at me like I'm a complete idiot.

"Some are brown and some are white." He points out. "Look at the 'en's 'eads. That one 'as a black patch by 'er eye, that one is miles bigger than the others an' this one is a lighter colour. Bantams are different an' all...that one's fat! "

I apologise to the birds for not being more observant and suggest some names. "How about Tikka, Masala and Balti?"

The Old Man joins in "Or Rogan, Josh and Korma, the little ones can be Chapatti and Naan?"

Joey shakes his head and laughs. "Yous two a' tapped! What about Jemima, Matilda and Ethel? The bantams can be Nellie and Ellie."

"Whatever you say is fine but you'll have to make me a sign for them so that I can remember who's who." Dad chuckles. "I'm going for a shower." Before he disappears I let him know my plans for the evening and tell them both to write a list of what they want from Tesco and help themselves to dinner.

"Socks!" Dad tells me. "Someone keeps nicking my socks." I laugh and look down at my feet.

"Don't want nothin' ta." Joey tells me.

"What about socks?" I ask. "Or any food? You must fancy something food wise. What foods have you missed over here?"

"Nothin' at all! Ya shouldn't 'ave to keep buyin' me stuff. l need to get a job an' pay me way. I never et so much in me life! Food 'ere is boss. Donkeys are gonna need some carrots soon though and l dunno what chickens eat l just bought the stuff that was in the cage with 'em."

"Chickens are a lot like you. They eat anything you give them." I laugh and realise he's not had money since he arrived. "And as for paying your way, you haven't stopped doing so since you arrived. We're really happy to have you here, feed you and buy your socks to pay for all the work you're doing. If you want a weekly wage we could make an official chores list and agree an amount."

"Fuckin' 'ell Dil! I'm real sorry! I din't mean I want ya dosh. Ya can't do more for me. You're better at lookin' after me than me Ma's ever bin. I meant get a job so I can pay board an' stuff. Then maybe I can stay 'ere even when Neenaw is better." He looks genuinely worried that he has upset me.

"Joey, sweetheart, you can stay here as long as you like and do whatever you want job wise or maybe college if you fancy it. You won't go hungry and although l am spending money like water at the moment it's only because I've never had any until recently and it's quite a novelty and I've found out I like buying stuff especially for people I love." I hold my arms out to him and he gives me a big hug.

"In that case can I have some socks and boxies?" He asks with a cheeky grin, "And some Coke but Tesco cheapie stuff is good, 'onest. If l 'ave a shower can I come with ya? Never bin to a' auction an' I can carry the shoppin'."

Sal arrives on time. Nathan waves from the back seat of Billy's crew cab pick-up which has plenty of ropes and straps rattling around in the back. A spruced-up Joey has bolted down two bowls of stew and is ready and waiting, he's really happy to see Nath.

"You bought the muscle too?" Sal comments as we both climb in. The boys are soon chatting away like old friends in the back and Sal and I catch up on our day. We get to the school and park up. The hall is packed with locals and auction lots and the lads go off to look at the garden tools and bikes. Sal and l head for the furniture.

She stops and chats to a few neighbours and gets a bit of gossip about where some of the stuff is from. "We shouldn't have too much competition." She whispers. "Most are just here for a nose at the stuff they've brought here from Lady Fairley's place and the big old manor up at Greeba."

"Why are they emptying stuff out of Lady Fairley's? We've got her donkeys which weren't supposed to be permanent residents."

"Her daughter is having a big clear-out to get the place ready to sell. She's come over from The South of France and is deciding whether to take her mother back over there or put her in a home here. Apparently she's as nutty as a fruit cake. The donkeys had been living in the house with her. They might be at your place a while longer. What's the going rate for a donkey? We could have bought them to the auction." Sal laughs. "Wow! This is you Dil." She is sitting on a huge, sturdy 1920s Chesterfield sofa in well worn, deep red leather. It is stunning. It comes complete with a matching wing back armchair. I flick through my program and put a big asterisk by the lot number.

We also pick out a lovely red velvet big squidgy settee as a backup and another leather armchair. I asterisk three different sets of dining chairs and some fire irons. Then we look at the bed frames. I decide l want a single and a double so I can have an irresistible French oak dressing table with drawers and the Old Man will have a big enough bed. We asterisk half a dozen lovely wooden headboards and bedframes because it's something I don't want to go away without. There's a big oak pantry there which is gorgeous and would match the dresser and table, I don't think it'll fit in the kitchen but l asterisk it anyway in case it's too cheap to miss. Sal is a bad influence. She spots a blanket box, an art deco mirror and a big box of Denby crockery. She reminds me I need some cutlery and glassware too.

The boys come back and say they're going to auction the garden stuff outside at the same time as the inside auction. I give them a limit of £300 and trust them to get all the best stuff. Joey looks panicked but Nathan tells him they can handle it and they shoot off outside to do some sums.

In typical Manx style they don't get started until way later than planned as the auctioneer is chatting to his mates and forgets he's supposed to be working. There are about sixty lots and once he gets started he rattles through like his tea is getting cold. There are only one or two bids on most things and neighbours know not to bid against each other else competition gets fierce and they end up paying loads more than they wanted to just because they don't want to lose.

I win the crockery for £6.20 and the mirror for a tenner. I get a full set of cutlery in a wooden box for £ 3. I can't believe the prices. I miss out on the fire irons and the first double bed but win the single one that l liked the best and the dressing table. I have a bit of a battle to get the lovely chesterfield and chair but refuse to give in and eventually win. No one bids on the big red squishy sofa and l feel sorry for it and buy it for £20. I get six kitchen chairs for the same price.

"We're going to have to ring Ricky and get him to bring the lorry." Sal laughs digging in her handbag for her phone. She texts Rick and warns him to be on standby just in case.

I win the pantry and the next double bed and a couple of antique rugs we hadn't even noticed before. The blanket box is the last lot and most people have gone off to the pub so I get it for £25. I go and pay my bill and we start to collect all our bargains. The older school kids have been acting as porters and have kindly put everything in one place near to the exit. A very snooty school commissioner tells us they can help load the van for a fee as we need to be 'off site' in one hour.

"No thanks, we bought our own loaders." Sal tells her as the boys come running over. Joey gives me an invoice to pay.

"We ain't spent it all. We got a big petrol mower an' Nath checked it works, an 'edge trimmer an' a big load of shovels an' stuff, some pokers and stuff for the fire an' some old metal TT signs, they were mega cheap, thought Dylan'd like 'em in his workshop." I look at the bill and they've spent less than two hundred quid.

"Let's see if we can get everything on the pickup and remember to leave room for the shopping. We're going to look like the Beverly Hillbillies."

We cart everything outside and Sal parks as close as she can. We're just about to load up and Billy and Ricky arrive in the lorry with Sarah.

"Bloody hell, Shortarse! Have you bought everything they had?" Ricky asks dropping his arm around my shoulder. "You really are planning to stick around this time. Mam's sent you a load of bed stuff. It's in the cab. You lot piss off to Tesco before they shut and we'll take all this over to Dil's. You do know half of it ain't gonna fit in the cottage don't ya?" He laughs and kisses me on the head. "Bring some beer, we're gonna need it."

We pile back in the pick-up with Sarah between the boys and head to the supermarket. Sal and I show the kids up by standing on our trolleys and racing down the empty aisles. Nathan gets his own trolley and says he'll take Sarah and Joey off to find the good stuff.

"You've got twenty-five minutes to spend fifty quid each because I love you all but I don't want to spend all night here." I laugh and Sarah doesn't wait to hear any more she's off to the toys dragging Joey with her. Nathan follows them. "Show Joey where the clothes are please, Nath." I yell after them.

Sal and I do 'ninja' shopping; flying around at high speed throwing every-thing in the trolleys food, fruit and veg, spices and more herbs to plant, sweets and ingredients to bake and make cakes, cleaning stuff, loo roll, kitchen essentials, shampoo and shower gels, beer for the boys, some bed pillows and duvets, towels and cushions, candles, party stuff, frozen stuff to fill the freezer, proper Coke for Joe, socks and boxers and a couple of T-shirts and some shorts for Dad.

"They're selling bargain electrical stuff over there." Sal points out, so we get a telly and a laptop too. We can watch the North West highlights next week and I can actually see what I'm Googling rather than squinting at my phone all the while. We meet up with the kids in the clothes aisle.

"I've got two reading books, a colouring book and a writing book and some posh pens and some slime and a 'Jeff'. Can I get a telly too?" Sarah asks waving a huge, hairy, cuddly, orange dog at us.

"No, baby." Nathan explains patiently as her bottom lip starts to quiver. "You've got 50p left. You can get some sweets." Sarah quickly decides sweets is much better than a telly and heads off to the sweet aisle. "I've got that game l was saving up for, thank you." Nathan lets me know as he follows Sarah.

Joey is standing in front of the socks looking lost. "Eh laa how do I know what size me socks are?"

"Tell you what, I'll get your socks and skidders you go and choose a couple of T-shirts. They've got TT ones over there. Get medium if you want it to fit and extra large if you want it super baggy." He grins and shyly kisses my head before running over to the T shirts. I pick a few pairs of both thick and thin plain socks and a pack of seven pairs of boxers for him and grab him a pair of trunks, some shorts and then decide to get some dressing gowns and sliders for all of us. I get me a pack of knickers, some white T shirts and a swimsuit and head for the tills.

Sal joins me in the queue and the cashier looks mortified. We laugh as Nathan brings up the rear. Then takes pity on her and heads to the next assistant. I pay for mine then run over to pay for his. We load everything in the back of the pickup and secure what we need to. Joey is already wearing his new top and I remove the label as he gets into the back seat.

Back home everything is unloaded and stashed away or dumped on the kitchen table for sorting later. The guys are sitting on the newly installed chesterfield which looks like it's always been there. The rug is in front of the fire. Dad looks comfy in the armchair and a set of fire irons are dropped on the hearth.

"Yer beds are up and yer girlie drawers fitted in. We've stuck everything else in the barn. Where's the beer?"

"In the freezer for five minutes." Sal says. "Get that telly off the van and set up and we'll make some food."

As the sun starts to set we all head down to the beach with our bottles and huge plates of food. We sit by the unlit fire pit and chat and drink and eat and then paddle along the shoreline splashing and laughing until way past everyone's bedtime.

CHAPTER 12

I crawl out of my tent to a cooler, windy, cloudy morning and can hear the waves crashing onto the rocks. I grab my hoodie and head for the beach to retrieve all my new crockery and the bottles we left safely piled in the pit.

The waves are really calling to me so I forget the cleaning up and l go down to stand at the waters' edge watching the clouds move and change in shades of steel blue, silver and grey. I can taste the salt on my lips and feel the spray on my face and eyelashes as it smashes against the jutting stones and covers me in a fine sea mist. It makes me feel so alive; barefoot, I jump from one stone to another like a child, searching in the rockpools that have formed and picking up shells and pretty pebbles.

I land on a large flat rock and sit down to meditate for a while. After a few minutes of quiet contemplation I realise I don't want to meditate, I don't need to get away from reality. I want to stay in the here and now and think about what's happened recently and what's happening around me right now. I recall the fun we had last night; the auction, shopping and the time together on the beach. I think about my trip out with Joey and the wonder in his eyes at Murray's Museum and Joey D's memorial and our afternoon at Jurby. How good it felt to be on a track again. I remember my first encounter with Jeff. My trepidation and doubt when we woke on the first morning after we arrived, feeling so overwhelmed by all the building work and builders on site. I realise too how much more active and interested Dad is in everything now. Since we lost Mama he'd been lost too, like me, he'd barely picked up his tools in the last few years but now he's constantly tinkering in the workshop or around the land. He absolutely loves running errands with Joey and showing him how to do things, they really enjoy each other's company. He didn't disappear either when we were all on the beach last night, he stayed with us chatting and laughing right up until we all said goodnight.

I think of the sullen, suspicious, monosyllabic, undernourished Joey we were introduced to and see him last night filled out and sun tanned, laughing and splashing in the sea, spinning Sarah around and kicking a ball about with Dad and Nathan.

This Island is truly a blessing for us all. I miss Jimbob and Mama and Marley so much every day but before we came here it was always like a physical agonising pain, something I needed to get away from. I was always running as if to suspend reality. Although I'm still so sad that they're not here, l find myself thinking 'Mama would have loved this' or 'Marley would have done that' now it's a nice melancholy feeling rather than an unbearable hurt. I sense them here with us but in a good way if you know what I mean? Jimbob I'm not ready to deal with yet. Living our dream without him seems somehow disloyal and cruel... Enough Dil! That can go back in the box for another day.....

I look up and Jeff is heading towards me with her washing bowl so it must be breakfast time and the boys probably aren't up yet. I stand up to go and meet her and laugh at my wet bum where I've been sitting in a puddle. I retrieve the crocks and the recycling and head into the cottage to find dog food.

The Macs are on the roof and I wave hello and ask if they've got the bill.

"Tomorrow." They tell me.

As soon as the sausage and bacon start cooking the boys appear and sit down at the table which is still piled with shopping. I ring to sort an internet connection whilst I remember.

"There's goodies in that heap for both of you." I tell them. "See if you can work out what's what and find somewhere to put them." They both dive in the bags like it's Christmas and Joey finds my purple tie dye swimsuit and holds it up against himself.

"Must be yours, Dylan. It ain't my colour." Joey teases. They argue good naturedly over the socks and then find the trunks and shorts and argue whose are the best. They find my t shirts and Dad puts one on to model...it's a crop top on him and they both fall about in hysterics. Joey rips his boots straight off and puts his sliders on. "Eh laa that's boss I've only 'ad me Da's boots on for the last year!"

"I couldn't get you trainers because I don't know your size." I shrug.

"Neither do I." Joey admits. "Them boots a fuckin' massive! These are all boss, Dil, Ta very much." He dashes off to put them in his tent.

"Cheers, Dilly girl." Dad says folding me into his arms and kissing my head. "For the clothes and for looking after him and for making me feel like we have a home again and for my chair. Dish up I'll throw these in my room." He walks off and I wipe away more happy tears.

"Who says it's your chair?" I tease when they both come back for breakfast.

"It's a proper man's chair and I'm a proper man so it must be mine." He laughs. "I might make myself a pipe. It's definitely a pipe smoker's chair. That settee is big enough for six, don't be greedy." We all continue to tease and torment until the food is eaten. Joey washes up his plate and goes off to feed the donkeys and chickens.

"I spoke to his mother last night. I think she's a bit of a madam, was more interested in the size of our place and who was coming to the party than how Joey was. Asked if l could send her money for the ferry ticket and if Nina would mind if she stayed at her place." Dad looks concerned. "I might have done the wrong thing in inviting her."

"Don't worry. It'll be nice for Joey and I'm going to sort our mattresses today so she can stay in one of the tents and we can put her back on the boat Sunday afternoon if she's a pain."

The rest of the week goes by in a flash. We are connected to the 'interweb', as Dad calls it and the mattresses arrive. While Joey is busy at the MSPCA, we manoeuvre one up onto the mezzanine platform along with the squidgy settee, floor rug and the blanket box. I make up the bed with a well-worn and super soft, cotton duvet covered in motorbikes which must have belonged to Billy or Ricky, that Pat had sent. Dad screws some of the TT signs onto the walls and makes a couple of shelves from drift-wood. When we're done we stand back admiring our work and go back downstairs to make up our own beds and wait, not very patiently, for Joe's return.

We introduce Joey to his new bedroom hoping he will like it and his reaction makes us feel so good. He is way beyond 'over the moon'. After his initial stunned silence he goes to shake Dad's hand but Dad hugs him and then he can't stop hugging both of us and muttering strings of expletives. He picks me up and dances around the room with me like I'm a rag doll then puts me down and checks I'm okay. He moves around and around the space, initially trying to avoid walking on the rug then taking his boots off and sinking his toes into it. Then he reverently sits on the bed, feeling the duvet between his fingers after he's checked they're clean, then sits on the sofa stroking the arm. Looking in the box which contains a spare set of bedding his few bits of fresh laundry I've just done in my new whizzy washing machine, he sticks his head right inside and takes a huge sniff and swears some more. Finally, he stands admiring the signs and Dad's handmade shelves.

"We thought you might be missing your own room and you can't sleep in a tent forever. You can put whatever you want in here, make it however you like."

"Never 'ad me own room to miss. Never 'ad me own bed, always slept on the settee. Me Ma 'ad the bedroom. The whole flat ain't this big." He replies matter of factly with his back to us, still reading all the signs.

Dad and I look at each other and squeeze hands but say nothing. Neither of us want to spoil his happiness by crying. As we finally head down for some food Dad turns back halfway down the stairs.

"Pass us that rag, Joe." He gestures to one of his old bandanas hanging by the doorway. Joey pulls it down to reveal a beautifully hand painted little driftwood plaque which says, 'Joey's Place'. He does a double take, touches it and stands staring then sits down heavily on the top step, drops his head in his hands, and sobs. I run up and hold him, sobbing too.

"They better be happy tears after all this work." I tease.

"You twos a just fuckin' unreal." He informs us which we take to mean he's happy enough and go and put the coffee on, leaving him to his own thoughts.

We're on our second coffee when he appears with a huge bunch of wildflowers he's picked for me from all around the place and the first two fresh eggs from our very own chickens for Dad.

"Can l sleep in there tonight?" He asks.

"Course you can, soft lad!" Dad ruffles his hair and hands him a cup of tea and a huge piece of cake.

With a lot of rearranging, swearing and much laughter and a complete reenactment of an episode from the Chuckle Brothers we manage to get the larder into the cottage and as close to the kitchen as damn it. I scrub it clean and fill it with the last of the shopping and we finally have a clear dining table and a fully working home.

The herb chimney garden is right outside the back door and I add my most recent purchases to the empty pots. Joey waters them all. Then we go and tidy up the inside of the tents and pack away Ricky's so that he can pick it up with all the plant later but I tell him to leave mine and the old man's up on the pretense of 'drying them out'.

Plans for the party are going well. Pat, Meave, Sal and I have made and stored a load of food ready to bring out on Saturday. Dad rings around and invites a few people we know and Nathan invites loads of work and old college and school mates who are closer to his and Joey's age and tells me his mate will DJ and some friends in a band will come and play. I bake a huge chocolate sponge cake, Joey 's favourite, which I'm going to decorate but Dad and Joey accidentally eat most of it while I'm out getting new coffee stocks, banners, balloons and some candles at Ramsey.

On Friday I bake another one and hide it from the gannets. Joey is completely oblivious to any plans and is carrying on as normal apart from permanently having his head in a bike theory test book that Nathan has lent him whenever he's not doing chores. He eats an evening meal with us and stays with us in the cottage or on the beach every night until about half ten then he retires to his own room after doing his impression of The Waltons; shouting goodnight to us and to Jeff and the donkeys and the chickens and the bantams one by one by name.

As soon as he's gone off to bed The Old Man and I hang Happy 16th Birthday banners, blow up and hang dozens of blue and silver balloons, place loads of garden torches ready for lighting tomorrow. We wrap the gifts we've bought; a pair of trainers, some new jeans, a TT hoodie, some bike boots and bike gloves and a proper bike jacket and loads of little bits like bike books, racer autobiographies, a docking station for his phone and a funky 3D lamp for his room and some little nut and bolt bike ornaments Dad has made. We've got him a mobile too and we set the ring tone to Happy Birthday Sweet Sixteen, we think he'll probably not even notice it's a song about a girl and if he does he'll just think we're taking the pee about his hair. We turn it up as loud as it will go and pop it back into the box and wrap it up. Dad sneaks it outside his door before we go off to bed.

I'm so excited for the morning to come and the weatherman says it's going to be a scorcher. I think I'll never sleep but as soon as I climb into my cosy little bed and turn out my light I am zonked until Dad knocks my door at half eight next morning. He sits down on my bed and we ring Joey's new number. It's so loud we can hear it from the cottage. It goes to answer phone so we sing a quick 'Happy Birthday Dear Joey' then redial again. Joey comes running in wearing just his boxers and socks and dives onto the bed with me and Dad. "I dunno what to press to fuckin' ansa it!" He laughs. We stop it and give him a crash course in how to use it and then it rings again. It's a text;

"Hapy 16 Birfdy frm Sarah Delilah Parker age 4"

And again;

"Happy 16th Joey Have a fab day! Loads of Love from Billy & Sal xx"

And again and again;

"1st bk lssn 1/2 3. Hppy Bdy Bro Nath"

"Happy 16th Birthday Joseph. Enjoy your day. Love and thanks from Auntie Nina x

"Merry Christmas Dave"

"Happy 16th Scally. Av a good un. Rick"

"Happy Birthday Joey lad from Meave, Paddy and the boys xxx"

By nine o'clock he's received at least a dozen texts and is reading and rereading them in amazement. None are from his Mom even though Dad has given her the number and I'm glad Joey is unaware of this.

"Do you want that ringtone changed now?" I laugh after it goes off yet again.

"No, it's boss! I'm leaving it on 'til it drives ya nuts." He grins.

"It'll ruin your street cred." I tease.

"Never had any to start with." He shrugs.

Dad gets up to go and put the coffee on.

"There's a couple more presents here on the table." He calls to Joey.

"More? Where from?"

"Dunno, think the tooth fairy left them. Or maybe the chickens, the donkeys and Jeff? Go and see." I tease.

He leans over and kisses my cheek. "Thanks Dil." And he's off. I quickly pull on my dungarees and follow. He sees the pile of presents and his jaw drops.

"I never 'ad this many pressies in me life." He informs us and carefully reads all the tags and finds they are indeed from Jeff, the chickens, the bantams and the donkeys but the tooth fairy has forgotten him again. He laughs and keeps all of the labels.

By the time I've made breakfast he's completely dressed in his new gear and would be looking very smart apart from the fact he's wearing one bike boot and one trainer and eating toast with his gloves on.

After a leisurely meal Dad and Jeff disappear into the barn whispering and conspiring together.

"What they up to?" Joey asks.

"Search me!" I reply with a giggle. "He's at that funny age now, we have to accept his marbles are going and make allowances."

Jeff comes running back in to Joey with her bowl. He stands up straight away to fill it for her and finds an envelope inside. It contains his provisional license, L plates and some keys.

"Forgot I need a license. How come I signed it?" He looks confused. "What's these keys for?"

On cue Dad starts up Marley's old DT125R that arrived from the mainland when him and Joey were running errands and I'd hidden under some covers in the barn. Dad's been tinkering with it and getting it roadworthy again whenever Joey was busy elsewhere.

"You signed it the other day. It's the thing I shoved at you when you were in the middle of cleaning out the chickens. You signed without even asking what it was for." I laugh. "You better go see what that noise is.

"Happy 16th, Joey!" Dad says handing over the bike. "If Nathan's coming at half three to give you a lesson you're probably going to need a bike."

Joey is speechless yet again. He jumps on the bike, swears a lot, realises he has odd shoes on, swears even more, jumps off and runs inside to get his other bike boot and then into the barn to get his helmet. "Fuckin' 'ell! God! Shit! Fuck! I really fuckin' love yous two." He yells as he goes. He runs back and dives on the bike. Dad talks him through the controls and reminds him of the gears and off he goes to the end of the lane and back seemingly oblivious to the fact that several helium filled balloons are tied to it. Dad grabs his helmet and keys and they go off for a pootle round the quiet lanes to get Joey bike confident and give me chance to ice the cake, cook the last few bits of food and get the party sorted.

I fall over a hastily discarded trainer in the doorway. I pick it up and take it and all Joey's other presents up to his room and leave them on his sofa.

I go to get showered and dressed properly and tidy away all the wrapping paper from the kitchen table then put everything that needs cooking in the ovens and am about to start the cake when Billy and Ricky arrive to take away all of the plant. When I go out they're unloading a second portaloo and several huge packs of beer and cider.

"You're gonna need it for tonight. Dave's invited half the Island." Billy informs me. "You better get the fire going for this piggy else we're gonna be eating at midnight." He hands me a huge piece of pork already threaded onto a long metal skewer so that I can roast it on the beach fire.

They load up all of the other stuff and I tell Ricky to send me a bill for the hire of it all. He respectfully tells me to 'Fuck off!' kisses me on the head and they're gone until later.

I decorate the cake with sixteen sparkler candles and a wonky iced happy birthday message and put it in the larder to stay cool and safe. I prepare the pork, putting salt in the scored skin to make yummy crackling and head to the beach to get the fire started. I throw a load of barbecue charcoal in the pit with all the dry wood and seaweed and it lights easily. Dad has already stuck in two Y shaped metal poles to rest the skewer in so as soon as its white hot I put the meat on. I nip back every half hour to turn it a bit and throw on some bigger logs. By the afternoon it's smelling fabulous. Dad's cut my barrel in half too so l can barbecue. I fill that and get it ready but don't light it yet. I get the other half, put it in the shade and half fill it with cold water ready to put some ice and the cans and bottles in when everyone arrives.

Dad and Nathan time it perfectly to meet at the end of the lane at half three so that Dad comes in and Joey goes off with Nath and still knows nothing about the party. Nathan's going to try to keep him away until at least half five but I have a feeling getting him back will be much harder than keeping him out.

Dad puts both of our bikes in the barn out of harm's way and takes over the tending of the fire while Jeff and I drag up big flat-topped rocks for people to sit on. A lad arrives and informs us he's Luke the DJ and starts setting up on the beach, carefully running cables to the cottage and covering them over with stones so that no one trips over them.

"What music do you like?" He asks when he's all plugged in.

Dad thinks he's clever and tells him "Bad Company" expecting him to say he hasn't got any but he messes with a computer and seconds later 'Feel Like Making Love' is blaring very loudly across the beach followed by 'Seagull' and 'Shooting Star.' Luke informs us he can access pretty much anything and that he's going to set up a few playlists ready for later. I tell him a few bands everyone l know likes, give him some drinks and sandwiches and leave him to do whatever.

Then a van rolls up with several hairy youngsters inside.

"Hi, you must be Dil, right? We're the band, where do you want us?" I tell them to look around and choose the best spot. They seem to know Luke and are quickly all working together to organise themselves. Sal and Meave arrive next with a mountain of food that they and Pat have prepared. They set it out on the kitchen table or stow it in the fridge then take off to get dolled up. I do the same; shower and let my dreads down to hang right past my bum, put on a clean white t shirt, my favorite and only patchwork dungaree dress, my purple DMs and some make up.

Joey and Nathan arrive back around six and Joey jumps off his bike and grabs me in a big hug, spinning me around.

"It's perfect, best birthday I've ever 'ad." He says and then looks me up and down, looks around and finally notices the banners and balloons. Nathan is starting to welcome a few mates who are beginning to arrive and Joey finally twigs "Why ya spruced up? Are we 'avin a party?"

"Just a little one." I tell him. "You better go and get your coppin' off kecks on."

"I'm stickin' with the bike." He laughs. "Only bit of advice me Da ever give me was stay away from girls. Shame 'e never followed it. I'll go an' get washed though, smell like a docker." And off he runs, taking his bike into the barn with him.

He's back out in a few minutes with wet hair and wearing his new shorts, a birthday t-shirt and trainers. He grins over at me and runs to meet Nathan and his mates. Everyone keeps arriving and in true Manx style they bring drink, food and their own chairs.

A few of Dad's old pals from over here have come to see the place and he is proudly showing them around. The kids are on the beach dancing and chatting. Me, Sal, Ricky and Billy are chilling by the cottage so we can grab food and drink if anything gets short. A taxi arrives and a skinny, dirty, bottle blonde who looks like she's dressed for a night club; plastered in make-up, wearing a gold strapless mini and four-inch heels gets out. Billy starts singing "Who let the dogs out?" Then yells to Nathan. "Dave! If this is a mate of yours don't ever bring it home. Your mother will kill yow." Nath looks up and shrugs to say he doesn't know her.

Sarah who is sitting on her Dad's lap asks very innocently. "Daddy why is that lady wearing 'fuck me shoes' outside the house?" Billy holds his palms up and gives her a big shrug, desperately trying to keep a straight face.

"I dunno Dave, why don't you go and ask your Mam?"

Joey, who fortunately was out of earshot the whole time, comes running over.

"Fuckin' 'ell! 'ow come me Ma's ere?" I notice he doesn't sound particularly excited about it. He rushes over with arms out to hug her but she stops him short.

"Pay the taxi Joe." She orders. He gets some of the birthday money Ricky and Paddy Mac gave him earlier out of his pocket and sorts the taxi for her. He then brings her over to introduce her to us. "This is me Ma, Sienna." She looks us all up and down as if working out who is most useful to her, decides none of us, ignores us all completely and says to Joey.

"Ain't ya got any mates ya own age? I need a drink an' some scran an all, I'm starvin'. Where's the auld fella what owns this gaff? It's probably worth a few quid even if it is in the arsehole of nowhere. Is 'e single?"

Pat has been watching from the door of the cottage. "Thank goodness his appetite is the only thing he inherited from his mother!" She exclaims. "We only gave him fifty pounds in a card and he's kissed me and said thank you twenty times already and shook Will's hand off. I didn't even hear her say thanks for the invite. Spiteful woman hasn't even wished him a happy birthday."

We all watch in wonder as she drapes herself all over Nathan and his mates, then tries to chat up Luke the DJ, then each of the band in turn, bumming cigarettes off anyone who smokes and totally ignoring Joey, who, to his eternal credit, is removing her as soon as she gets over friendly. He is clearly used to being her minder. Dad goes down to meet her and she starts fawning over him. Ricky digs Billy in the ribs.

"Me thinks Joey's mommy is a brass. Only our Dil could invite a hooker to a kid's party." They both dissolve into a fit of giggles.

"Oh my God!" I start nervously giggling too. "There's the Old Man and me thinking she's some poor struggling young widow and single mom whose had a hard life trying to bring up a child on her own and dealing with a heroin addicted husband. I am so bloody stupid!"

"I could have told you she didn't give a fuck when I told the coppers 'e was alone in the park the first day I saw him. The authorities asked everyone to look after 'im, said 'e was well known to Liverpool Social Services an' better off staying 'ere. He'd bin 'ere three days an' she hadn't reported 'im missing. Our Dave told me the Dad went home on the evenin' ferry the first night. Said when the Liverpool police went round they were both so wrecked they didn't open the flat door until day three." Billy tells me.

"Oh shit! She's a junkie too? Why didn't you tell me? Poor Joey, what have we done?" I shake my head in despair.

"I didn't know yow was planning a mother and son reunion. I better go and check she ain't dealin' to the kids." He laughs and heads off to the beach. "Although she don't seem like the sharing' type."

"If she offers my Son anything I'll rip her head off!" Growls Sal following him.

"Our Sal." Pat laughs proudly. "That's how a proper mom should be."

I leave them to deal with the lovely Sienna and grab Joey for a chat. He's looking seriously flustered.

"Oh my God, Dil! I'm real sorry l should 'ave told the truth an' not made out like she was a good ma. I'm really sorry. After all you've done for me...."

"You have nothing to apologise for, Joey. We're the ones who invited her. We should have asked you if you wanted her to come and even asked if you wanted a party instead of trying to completely take over your life. We've been so busy trying so hard to make everything perfect we've forgotten you might have a very different idea of perfect. I'm the one who's sorry, really sorry, I'll back off and stop trying to be your Mum."

He puts his arms around me and holds me tight.

"Promise ya won't ever stop. You're brilliant at it and 'ave bin more of a ma to me than she ever 'as. It's not all 'er fault, she was a care kid and she 'ad me when she was fourteen. I've tried to make 'er change but she won't. She's a walkin' disaster. She thinks the world owes 'er. At least me Da tried to spend time with me. Kept tellin' me it wasn't my job to look after 'er. I thought it was all normal 'til I come over 'ere; you an' Dylan, Billy an' Sal with Nath an' Sarah, Even Will an' Pat an' Meave an' Paddy Mac 'ave all shown me 'ow parents an' kids should be. I'm sixteen now so I'm old enough to make me own way. I've decided to stay 'ere, if that's okay, and not worry about 'er anymore. She's already told me I ain't worth any benefits to her now so I can't go back unless I agree to start dealin' for 'er mates an' sign on so she can get regular money. I told her no way I'm sellin' drugs an' I told 'er no chance when she asked about stayin' 'ere. She even 'ad the nerve to say she couldn't afford to buy me a present 'cause she'd 'ad to pay to come over 'ere but l know you an' Dylan must 'ave paid or she wouldn't be 'ere at all."

"We did." I sigh. "Shall we put her on the next boat back?" I ask.

"Yeah please. That really would be a perfect end to the best birthday ever!"

"Go back and have fun with your mates and enjoy what's left of your day." I tell him. "Do you want to say goodbye to her?"

"Naa, I just wan' 'er gone for good."

I have a quiet word with Billy and Ricky and ask them to name their price to escort her to the van and drop her off at Douglas ferry terminal in plenty of time for the next boat back. They laugh at me take great pleasure in playing the heroes. I follow behind them on the way to the van listening to her offering a price for a threesome. Ricky politely thanks her for her very kind offer and tells her she is not his type and he wouldn't touch her with a barge pole and also that he has no desire whatsoever to see his brother 'on the job'. Billy asks if she has a death wish and suggests fetching Sal to help with negotiations. She immediately turns on crocodile tears when she sees me.

"It could only 'appen to me." She wails. "I spent my life pretending me fella 'ad gone off with you and now me kid really 'as!" I advise her to go back to Liverpool and have a really good think about why that might have happened and not to try to return. I make it very clear that this is Joey's choice and Joey will contact her when he's ready. I suggest she might want to seek professional help to sort herself out and make him as proud of her as she should be of him. I also can't resist telling her Karma is a bitch. Ricky and Billy take her off to the terminal and ask a mate who works on the docks to make sure she gets on the next ferry.

They return to a huge round of applause and a standing ovation led by Joey and, as the sun goes down the party gets going properly. The DJ plays a string of appropriate records to celebrate Sienna's departure including 'Good Riddance' from Green Day, which lightens the mood even more. The band is excellent and everyone is soon up and dancing.

Jeff is still bringing wood for the fire, drinking everyone's beer and clearing leftovers from any unguarded plates. She likes parties. Sarah is dancing with Joey, teaching him the moves to 'Baby Shark'. In true Joey style he's already moved on from the drama and is giving Sarah his full attention, desperately trying to remember which shark comes next and what arm movement that entails.

I stand down by the water's edge and look up at the stars; naming and thanking every one of them for bringing us here and bringing us Joey. Dad comes down to join me and we walk, arm in arm, along the shoreline. I can hear the party in the distance and I swear I can hear Mama's laughter and Marley's out of tune singing.

"That was a close one but crisis averted and lessons learned." Dad says kissing my head. "Come and have a dance with your Old Man."

The tempo drops and the youngsters make room for the oldies to get up for a slow dance near the fire. I put my head on Dad's chest and with his arms wrapped around me I lose myself in the music and want this day to last forever.

CHAPTER 13

"Y ou better open all these cards and presents so as everyone can get to the table, sleepy head." Dad laughs when Joey finally wanders in a little bleary eyed. He grins sheepishly and collects them all up and plonks them on the sofa and starts working his way through them. Taking his time to read every card properly and asking who's who if he doesn't recognise a name. Judging from the expletives his muttering he's got some nice stuff and a few quid too. Sarah and Jeff help him with the unwrapping and Sarah tells him off whenever he swears. Suddenly, he stops dead with an open card in his hands.

"Ya fuckin' kiddin'!" Sarah chastises him and he apologises instantly. "Really, Juan?" He turns to look at Juan and Paddy Jr. he's holding a North West 200 wristband.

"Yes mate, we're happy to take you, if you want to come. You can help out in the pits. All you need is your tent. You'll have to talk nice to Dyl and Dil to see about them doing your chores for the week."

"I'm fine with it." Dad and I reply in unison. He doesn't need to ask.

Billy, Sal, Sarah and Nathan stayed over because Sarah wanted to camp and none of them were fit to drive. Jeff is none the worse for the excesses of the night before and willingly takes up present opening duties. Ricky is here to fetch the portaloos and Paddy Jr. and Juan are here to finish off the roof.

We all have a full English followed by birthday cake for breakfast. We had totally forgotten to light the candles last night so we sing happy birthday once more and Joey blows them out.

Sal and I get to clearing up the beach with Sarah and Jeff helping, Ricky goes off to work, Juan and Paddy Jr. get up on the roof. Dad, Nathan and Joey go off to do Joey's maiden ride over the mountain. After much coaxing, Billy joins them on The Duchess to keep them all in check. Complaining that she's a bitch to ride and he's sure she will try to kill him.

We play hide and seek with all of the bottles, cups, cutlery and plates that appear to be hidden in every nook and crevice within a two-mile radius. Sarah thinks it's a brilliant game. We stack it on the table and return for more until we're sure we have everything and then start the mammoth washing up task.

"Remind me to just order pizza next time." I groan. I wash, Sal dries and Sarah puts away; we have a perfect production line and it's soon sorted.

"Can we go swimming now?" Sarah asks. "I bought my cossie."

"Yeah, great idea! I'll go and get mine on." We grab a blanket and some big towels and Sarah and I go running into the sea. It's freezing and takes our breath away but we get aclimatised and are soon swimming and larking around. Sal sits on the beach on a blanket reading a book and taking photos of Sarah with her phone.

The lads come back all hyped up and hot and bothered relaying tales of heroics from their ride. Billy strips down to his boxers and dives in the water, Nathan strips off his bike trousers and jumps in in his shorts and Dad and Joey go off to find drinks and snacks and their own shorts and trunks, returning five minutes later to drop a load of food and drink on the blanket and join us for a swim. Dad, Nathan and I race each other right out towards the horizon. Sarah is a really strong little swimmer but is having too much fun using her Dad as a diving board. Joey stays in the shallows.

When we return to the beach Sarah is patiently teaching him how to swim, he is listening carefully and doing everything she tells him. We sit in the sun to dry off; grazing and drinking and chatting and dozing. By the time it starts to cool down Sarah announces that Joey can now swim. He demonstrates with a half breaststroke half doggy paddle for about 20 metres and we all applaud loudly. He comes out of the sea holding hands with Sarah and they both take a bow.

"Wow! It's half seven already. What time are Juan and Jr. picking you up?" I ask. The air turns blue and Joey flies off up the beach, with a towel flapping from his shoulders like Superman, to pack a bag. We saunter up after him and wave bye to Billy, Sal and a very worn out Sarah. Nathan goes into the barn to help Joey get sorted. They appear after a short while and Nathan drops his sleeping bag and tent by the front door and tells him to have a great time and send photos then heads off home too. Someone has bought Joey a rucksack for his birthday and it's now packed and ready to go including his phone and plenty of birthday money. Juan and Paddy Jr. pull up with the bike trailer fully loaded.

"I've written ya a list of stuff to do. I know ya like lists." Joey grins handing me a screwed-up bit of paper. "Don't give Isobel treats she's getting proper fat. I'm really gonna miss me bike! See ya in a few days." He gives Dad and me a quick hug and jumps in the van, yawning his head off.

"Have fun. Enjoy yourselves. Ride safe!" We wave until they are out of sight.

"He'll be fast asleep as soon as they get on the boat." Dad laughs. "Sarah wore him out this afternoon but he was determined not to let her down. I'm going to miss him."

"You're going to be too busy doing his chores." I tease. "We better start by putting the chucks to bed and feeding the donkeys."

We head over to the to the field with carrots, apples and parsnips already chopped small enough for them to eat safely. I distract Giles whilst Dad jumps in and fills their trough from a bucket. He's already jumping back over the fence when Giles realises he's been fooled and makes a lunge, narrowly missing removing a chunk of left buttock.

"Ungrateful bugger!" Dad giggles. "You can run the gauntlet tomorrow. Joe's right, Isobel is looking a bit portly. Oh dear!"

We both realise what's going on at the same time.

"He's obviously been much more friendly with Isobel. I'll call the vet in the morning. Looks like we may have a pregnant donkey." I smile.

The chickens are much less eventful and we laugh when we see Joey has drawn a very childlike drawing of the chickens and the bantams with each difference highlighted in a cartoon fashion and the names next to each one. Despite their slightly unflattering portraits, they all look relaxed and settled and have presented us with two lovely eggs. We feed them and shut them up safely for the night.

"Come on Old Man. Coffee, cake, shower and bed!"

"Sounds like a plan, Dilly girl. I must say, I'm loving my new bed. I've not slept so well in ages."

We head inside with Jeff in tow and put on the coffee machine. Dad cuts the cake whilst I clear the last of Joey's birthday detritus from the chesterfield and stand up his cards on the fireplace. I find his list and check to see what we have to look forward to in the morning;

1. feeb chuks
2. Feeb bonkees
3. Neenaw ½ 10 evry mornin
4. Go MPSAC. Chek everfink ok finb duchis yull lyk im
5. Look afta me bike
7 Mek choklat cake for wen I get dak (plees)
8. Tayp tely racin
fanks for
1. best birfdy eva
2. best present eva
8. best room eva
4. sortin Sienna
3. putin up wif me
an a milyon otha fings
Luv ya bof iyl fone
Joey xxx

I wipe my eyes, show it to Dad, drink my coffee, eat a huge piece of cake and head for the shower. Jeff has taken to sleeping on Dad's bed and all three of us are tucked up and fast asleep before ten o'clock.

CHAPTER 14

My phone wakes me at half eight. It's Joey, full of so much excitement, he tells me all about the lumpy Irish sea ferry crossing, the beautiful Irish coast and countryside, the noisy campsite, the even noisier pits, all the famous racers he's already seen, the insanely narrow roads, the plans for the day and what his jobs will be all week. It's so good to hear it relayed with all the newness and wonder of seeing it for the first time. I get up and put the phone on super loud speaker on the table so that Dad can hear too. He smiles and hands me a coffee. We listen happily whilst Joey doesn't take a breath for at least twenty minutes.

"Gorra go, Juan needs me. Ring ya tonight." And he's gone.

"Good job we got him a contract with unlimited calls." Dad laughs. "Are you coming to see Nina with me this morning? It'll be nice to have company."

"Are you scared to go alone?" I tease.

"Yep, I always hide behind Joe." He grins.

He feeds Jeff, the chickens and the donkeys while I transfer money to pay Paddy Mac's very reasonable bill and ring a local vet for Isobel. He says he will pop over on his way home and check her for us. We have a bowl of cereal and another coffee then head off to face Nina.

"Good morning! Where's Joseph? Is he still sleeping off the excesses of his party?" Nina is sitting up in bed and looking much more comfortable than last time I saw her. "They're taking me into theatre this afternoon now all the swelling and bruising have gone down. I should be good as new by teatime. I'm so annoyed that I missed Joseph's party. I hear you saw his awful mother off. The darling boy sent me a thank you message for my thank you message as soon as he got his phone. I am so sorry; I do wish I'd warned you about his mother. He was over here because Liverpool Social Services had contacted Carole saying they would have to take him into care because of his age and they knew he would run away if they tried so they asked if she could find an alternative solution. One doesn't usually share family problems as too much gossiping goes on."

"I think you might need to rest a little while longer than tea time and you don't need to apologise." I smile not even asking how she knows about our encounter with Sienna; that's the Island for you, if something happens everyone knows. We tell her all about the rest of Joey's eventful birthday and his current trip and assure her we will do whatever chores she has until Joe's back. She's really grateful and hands us a list of jobs for the day.

"Please go to Mr. Jeavons' farm down at Scaard. He rang to say his cat has had half a dozen kittens and he's going to drown them if we don't go and get them. Be careful with him he'll probably greet you with a loaded shotgun if he doesn't know you. I'll try to contact him and tell him you'll be coming."

Apart from Mr. Jeavons the list is easily doable. Get the post and a few toiletries from Nina's to take to her in the morning, take any money from MSPCA to the bank before five and check to see if they need any help in the cafe at lunchtime. We say bye to Nina and wish her well with the operation.

"Okay, kittens first, then MSPCA, then Nina's" I say jumping on The Duchess.

"Sounds like a plan. You go first, I don't want my old Kwak shot up!"

We get down to Scaard and I realise it's the farm next door to the one Jim-bob and I had set our hearts on. I look over and can see its still unoccupied and in a far worse state than it was when we'd chosen it. It's possible it's been empty ever since we first found it. I'm unsure if I'm happy or sad about this fact but don't have time to think about it further as an old boy and a very scary looking dog come hareing up the track on a big old farm quad. The old boy eyes us both up suspiciously while the dog bares his teeth and rumbles a warning.

"Who are you? What do you want?" He demands, looking like he'll be unhappy with whatever reply he receives.

"Hello Mr. Jeavons, Nina sent us from the MSPCA to get your kittens." I tell him from a safe distance.

He shushes the dog, smiles a big toothless smile and turns into a completely different person.

"Oh, you must be the Dils? Nina said you were on the way. Wasn't expecting the bikes, that's a fine-looking Ducati you have there, missy. Come on down to the house." He u turns the quad and shoots off back the way he came. We follow.

The kittens are in the barn all safe and snuggled in a box with some straw. "The mom's disappeared. I didn't know what to do with 'em. Asked Nina if I should drown them because I think they're too young to survive on their own and she went bonkers. Good job she's in Noble's else I'd be in real trouble." He chuckles.

Dad has his eye on something else in the barn, a wheel peeping from under a sheet. "Is that a Manx Norton?"

"Sure is, I raced a bit in my youth but she hasn't run for a good few years now. Bloody mice have eaten the wiring loom. Just keep her for nostalgia." He uncovers the bike and Dad is smitten. We all chat bikes and investigate possible causes for the Norton's original demise. We explain that we've moved onto the Island and are going to set up a bike mechanics and restoration business and Mr. Jeavons offers his beloved Norton as our first customer. "If I can just hear her running again I'll die a happy man."

We agree to collect the bike as soon as possible and settle the kittens and their bed into my rucksack and head for Foxdale.

We hand the kittens over to Milly, one of Nina's many dedicated volunteers and she takes them off to get them checked by the vet. I scrub my hands, don a very fetching hairnet and serve in the very busy cafe for an hour while Dad walks a lovely family through the adoption of a beautiful little terrier mix called Ted and helps an older couple pick out the best-looking cat. Once the cafe is closed I help with the washing up and cleaning and then we count up all of the takings ready for banking. It's been a good day and there is quite a bit of cash. "Don't call me horrible." Milly says, "But everyone has heard Nina is in the hospital and are coming in while she's away because she scares them when she's here or sends them off with a pony when they came for a rabbit because she's so persuasive."

I laugh and promise not to tell her. We're sitting at one of the cafe tables putting the money into coin bags when this massive bruiser of a true, tailless, Manx cat comes strolling over. He's ginger and white, the size of medium dog and appears to only have one eye which is almost in the middle of his face. He heads straight for me, jumps on the table in front of me and head butts me so hard I nearly fall off my seat.

"Oh my goodness!" Milly exclaims. "He's been here six months and never shown the slightest interest in anyone before. Won't let anybody near him. He only just tolerates Joey. He's bitten me a dozen times already the little bugger. It's a shame really, he's missing his partner in crime, that hairy reprobate your dad took home. They used to roam around here terrorising the visitors. Nina thought all her Christmases had come at once the day she saw your Dad's bike pull up but Duchess took flight before she could talk him into a job lot. Duchess, get down you mad cat." She waves to get him off the table and he snarls at her like a dog. She backs off and leaves him to his own devices.

So this is who Joey wanted me to meet. I put my open hand out slowly for him to sniff but he's just standing staring into my eyes. He carefully snags one of my dreadlocks with a huge paw and has a little chew, not talking his eye off me then comes up really close and sniffs my face and my hair and then my t shirt. He sighs loudly, jumps off the table and marches off.

Dad arrives with his jacket on. "Everything is fed, watered, cleaned and locked up are you both ready to go? Was that Duchess?" He enquires. "You are highly honoured. He totally ignores me whatever I try. You must smell more like Jeff than I do" He giggles.

We lock up the front barrier, say bye to Milly, grab Nina's few bits and check the house and head to the bank in Ramsey, nip into Conrod's for a crafty coffee and bread pudding and then home to a very welcoming Jeff who smells my hair and gives me a funny look then throws her washing bowl at me.

We've been in five minutes and Joey calls to check we've done our chores and tell us how his day has gone so far. He's still awestruck by everything going on over there and we sit at the table listening and drinking in his enthusiasm for half an hour. Then he's gone again to help with setting up for practice.

We hear a Land Rover pull up and I go out to meet a very tired and disheveled looking vet who smells a little ripe to be honest. He explains that he's been doing his farm rounds which involves a very long day of cantankerous farmers with cantankerous animals and lots of being kicked and bitten and sworn at. He visibly pales even more when I explain that the donkeys belong to Lady Fairley. I call Dad so that we can keep Giles away from the poor man as they have obviously met before.

By allowing him to chase us around the field we manage to distract Giles long enough for the vet to examine Isobel and he is extremely grateful. He confirms that she is quite heavily pregnant but otherwise in very good health. He says most donkeys will give birth without any issues but just to keep an eye on her and call if we notice any changes or are worried at all. I ask for the bill and he says there's no charge, he was passing by on the way home anyway. On the mainland we'd be paying a hundred pound call out before they even turn up. We thank him and head off to sort the chucks.

With jobs all done we get showered, have a sandwich for tea and settle down to watch the North West practice coverage on the TV. The familiar drone of the bikes lulls us both into a gentle sleep within ten minutes, me and Jeff flat out on the sofa and Dad snoring gently in his armchair. Good job I'm recording it all for when Joey gets back.

CHAPTER 15

O nce the North West racing gets underway the Island wakes up to the fact that it's got to get ready for the annual madness of the TT. Ricky and Billy are always ridiculously busy from dawn 'til dusk as they provide all the barriers, the tiered seating, the compressors, the portaloos, the flooring and lighting and anything else anyone needs. Nathan and Sal muck in and they've already talked Joey into working with them as soon as he gets back, he's agreed on the condition that he doesn't miss any racing so he'll have to be up early and working late but I'm sure he'll be more than happy to be involved and will earn himself a good wage. Everyone rents out something for TT; spare bedrooms if they are sociable, holiday cottages if they are business minded, own homes if they want to escape from the madness and need the rental money to book a flight, camping space in a garden or field if they want an impromptu festival, garage space and even cupboards under the stairs. The Manx people know TT is an opportunity to have fun and make money.

There are a couple of free municipal campsites which are usually full of Manx families who have given up their own homes for the fortnight and earned at least two month's mortgage payments. Many rent to the same folks every year for decades and become close friends. All the places of worship set up tea rooms and cafes and make welcome funds for restoration of beautiful buildings. These are by far the best places to eat as the food is all local and the cakes are all handmade and everything is served by lovely little old ladies of the parish who delight in feeding you and can tell endless fascinating stories about the area and local characters. The government allows all this to happen without hassle or threat of extra taxation. They understand how important the event is to the local economy.

Straw bales and barriers are placed around the course to ensure the safety of the riders insofar as they can and to keep spectators from harm. Make no mistake this is dangerous racing on a dangerous circuit. There are brick walls, stone walls, iron railings, bumpy roads, blind bends, curbs, encroaching trees, greasy patches, whole spectrums of weather and livestock and birds to contend with. You have to be a real professional or a total nutcase to race here.

"Okay Old Man, what's the plan?" I ask over breakfast. "Chickens, donkeys and dog are sorted already. We need to pop to Douglas and sort work permits and some bits of paperwork and do our Nina duties but that shouldn't take all that long today and the extra volunteers are at MSPCA to look after the cafe so we just need to check for banking and lock up later on."

"How about we get the bottom paddock TT ready and advertise online for some campers? It's far enough away from us and we can sort the gate so they can get straight on there from the lane, I know we're a long way from penniless but it'll get some money in and be fun." Dad suggests. "If this weather holds out it'll be a bumper year and people will struggle to book somewhere to stay. If Ricky can spare a toilet and shower block we'll be able to sort everything else."

"You are becoming scarily forward thinking." I laugh. "Are you sure you don't want to just enjoy this TT and then take campers for Southern 100 in July or Manx GP in August? It'll be less full on."

"Nah, let's just go for it. Shall we?"

The phone rings and Joey takes us on our morning North West adventure. He shares every tiny detail and remembers timings and what happened to whom on which lap. He tells us how he's doing in the pits, what he's learned, how quickly he can now do a wheel change and what he's eaten. "Anything 'appenin there?"

Dad winks at me and puts on his best stern voice. "It's come to our attention that a young lady you've been spending a lot of time with is having a baby."

The line is quiet for a second while he processes this information. "Fuckin' 'ell you daft twat! Isobel's up the duff ain't she?" He giggles.

We tell him about the visit from the vet and our plans for TT and he's really excited. I tell him about my encounter with Duchess the cat and he is happy that we've met. We all chat for an hour or so and then wish each other a safe day and all promise to be careful and have fun.

"Ring ya later, love ya both!"

We take ourselves and Jeff for a long, relaxing walk along the beach, following the coastline to Smeale and back and we don't see a soul. We settle Jeff and head to Noble's to check on Nina. She's had her operation and is looking extremely sprightly. She's dressed and sitting in the armchair by her bed.

"Everything went smoothly. I'm having some physiotherapy in a little while and hopefully I'll be home before the weekend." She announces cheerfully. "Carole is coming over to stay and help me out now she's finally managed to get rid of Sienna. The cheeky Little Madam phoned her and asked for the train fare back to Manchester after you put her on the ferry. Carole told her to go home to her own flat and learn to look after herself. Joseph can come back to mine whenever he wishes but I have a feeling he's settled well with you two. He told me all about his new room. He's a good boy and very thoughtful. He rang last night to see how I was."

We promise to take in some clothes for her in the morning and tell her about Isobel. She offers to pay the veterinary fees immediately but doesn't mention any plans to return Isobel and Giles to Lady Fairley or her daughter.

We head into the work permits centre and hand over our forms and £ 60 each and within a few days we should be legal and able to start work on Mr. Jeavons' bike. We also pick up some college and apprenticeship information in case Joey fancies getting some qualifications when they all start back up in September. Rick has already sorted him a work permit but if he chooses college we can always support him with the reading and writing bits.

We pop into the Town Hall next and chat with a very patient and friendly man who talks us through how we register as residents, everything else we need to do to run a business on the Island and comply to Manx laws and even how to get the cottage listed on the postal route. I tell him we've been getting all of our post and parcels without any problems, even when we were living in the tents. He's not surprised but advises we do it anyway just in case. We thank him for all his help and he tells us they have recently installed a new TT exhibition at the Museum that we should check out if we have time. Our TT field prep can wait, we can't resist a look and ride straight there to spend a really pleasant afternoon immersed in ancient and modern Manx history and wildlife. We realise the time is getting away and we dash to Foxdale just in time to help feed and bed down all the furry inmates.

Duchess the cat is nowhere to be seen. Milly tells me he likes to wander around at night so she always leaves his door open. Mr. Jeavons' kittens are happily settled with a surrogate mum who is fussing over them all. The turnover of animals is brisk here and they'll all soon find good homes. I've always been an animal lover and have volunteered in some god-awful sanctuaries around the world and seen the pain, neglect and suffering that humans can inflict upon animals. It's nothing like that here, animals come in if something major happens like an owner's death or inability to cope, a new baby arriving or a child developing an allergy, an injured animal being found or an animal having unexpected babies. All are settled, sorted and rehomed quickly once Nina has vetted the owners thoroughly. The smell of Jeyes fluid is the only hint at institutionalisation.

We finish off and go to grab our helmets and bags ready to leave. I go to pick up my backpack and can barely lift it.

"Has everyone paid you in pennies today?" I laugh, assuming it's the banking that's weighing me down.

Milly looks confused and waves her bag at me. "Banking is all in here, I've got some of my own to take so I was going to save you a trip."

I gently lift the flap on my pack and as we watch a huge ginger paw reaches out and slowly closes it back up. I try again and he pulls it back closed.

"Looks like we've got another lodger. I hope he's a good pillion." I smile and Dad gently lifts the pack onto my back. "He's going to have to have a name change though. How did he end up with such an inappropriate moniker?"

Milly shrugs. "Nina went to check on a farmstead up near Cronk y Voddy because neighbours reported the cows hadn't gone in for milking. She found the old boy had turned up his toes in his armchair and Duchess was sitting on his chest trying to breathe life back into him. Cows went to next-door farm; old boy went to heaven and cat came here. Nina said it needed a pretty name to attract some new owners and we assumed it was female until we caught him being very unladylike with another resident. The name had stuck by then."

"How about Cyclops?" Dad grins and an audible groan emits from my backpack.

"Let's just stick with Dutch. It suits him much better." I suggest and get what I take to be a tap of approval from behind.

Milly hands Dad a couple of tins of cat food. "Looks like he's definitely decided who he wants to live with. At least have his tea on us!" She laughs.

We arrive home safely and Jeff runs to greet us with the enthusiasm of a dog that hasn't eaten for a few hours. I put the pack carefully down onto the grass outside and Jeff immediately investigates. Dutch sticks out a paw and has a feel around, he touches Jeff's nose, then his head and then leaps out of the bag like he's been fired from a cannon. He hugs Jeff, literally wrapping his front paws around her neck and rubbing his face against hers. I grab my phone to record the beautiful moment and send it to Joey.

"Well someone has clearly missed you, Jeff. That's definitely what I would call 'letting the cat out of the bag'. Shall we all go and find you both some tea?" Dad waves the cat food and goes to find a can opener closely followed by our, still intertwined, star crossed lovers. I go and check on the rest of the menagerie. The chucks have laid us three lovely eggs and Isobel is looking even fatter than she did this morning. Giles is getting even more protective and leans right over the fence to try to get a piece of me as well as his food. I jump back and shake my head in wonder at the growing bunch of weird and wonderful damaged, misfit creatures that have been drawn to this little haven, me and Dad and Joey included.

CHAPTER 16

I manage to wake early enough to enjoy what promises to be another spectacular sunrise. I make coffee to go, pull on my hoodie and head outside with my cup. The odd couple come piling out of Dad's room amid much ouching, swearing and groaning as they trample him on the way. They walk with me down to the beach but then go off to do their own thing, Jeff proudly giving Dutch a guided tour of our little cove, while I take up residence on my flat rock by the sea, savour my coffee, watch the day arrive and then indulge in some yoga. It's pure bliss.

The North West 200 comes to a close today and Joey will be back by tomorrow night. The regular calls have conveyed his epic falling for motorcycle racing. He is smitten and more determined than ever that he is going to become a road racer. As much as I want to dissuade him I would never do so because I know I have no rights to stand in the way of his dreams and I know only too well that racing is an addiction, a virus, it gets into your head, your blood and your heart and it takes over your life. You just have to let it run its course.

I haven't told Joey anything about Jimbob and although he knows his DT belonged to Marley he's tactfully avoided asking me about him. Maybe Dad or Nathan have told him some tales of Blue's deep, dark history.

Dutch and Jeff wander back to me and get involved in a few yoga poses. Jeff is extremely good at downward facing dog. Then Dutch headbutts me quite forcefully in the back of my knees to remind me they haven't had breakfast yet. We go back off to the cottage sort their meals and get the coffee on. Turns out Dutch prefers dog food and Jeff is very partial to cat food. Go figure. They share breakfast, literally, and then they both settle down on Dad's recently vacated bed, for a snooze. Dad comes in from feeding donkeys and letting the chickens out. He's carrying two eggs.

"No baby donkeys yet but she seems to be producing milk so I think it'll be happening soon. Shall we have boiled eggs for breakfast?"

"Yep as long as we have enough to make Joey's chocolate cake later." I look in the egg box and we have plenty so l boil us the two biggest ones and cut some soldiers. This was one of the ways I deduced that Joey had suffered a terrible childhood; he laughed when I made him a boiled egg for the first time and gave him soldiers. He'd never seen them before. What kind of mother must Sienna have been to never give her child eggy soldiers? Marley and I had them for Saturday breakfast forever and sometimes Sunday tea too.

We are joined for breakfast by Joey, Juan and Paddy Jr. via the phone. It's a big race day and you can hear the anxiety mixed with the excitement.

Paddy Jr. is currently riding well and the bike hasn't missed a beat so they are in with a shout which puts far more pressure on everyone but they sound like they're all keeping it together, just about. We talk through tactics for every obstacle and corner, wish them all the luck in the world and send loads of love and tell them to 'ride safe!'

"Right then! I've rung Ricky about a shower and loo block and he can spare one but it's only four loos, four basins and two showers apparently that means that legally we can have about a hundred and twenty tents! Personally, I was thinking of something a bit easier to manage, maybe ten or fifteen? Shall we go down with the mower and strimmer and see what's there first?" I ask Dad. "We're close by too if baby donkey chooses to make an appearance. I've been Googling and they usually arrive at night but better safe than sorry, eh?"

We stagger down the lane with a huge assortment of tools and machinery, not thinking twice about leaving the front door wide open for Jeff and Dutch to come and go as they please. The entrance to the paddock is hidden behind a tangle of greenery so I strim us a pathway in and Dad gets to work with his cordless drill and screwdriver in order to make the rickety old wooden gate swing freely and safely on its hinges. I help him with some lifting and holding and then once we're in I fire up the mower the boys bought at the auction. Dad has worked his magic on it and it's running like a dream. I walk behind it for miles, up and down and up and down what seems to be a never-ending field until I run out of petrol.

"We appear to own rather a lot of land, Old Man." I smile as I look over towards the cottage, across another overgrown field I can see the newly mown donkey field with Isobel and Giles happily grazing and beyond that our gorgeous new thatch which is a real work of art.

"Petrol can is there." Laughs Dad pointing to the pile of tools and stuff by the gatepost. "You haven't got time to admire the view!"

I refill the mower and keep going until I get to the end. Dad has strimmed all the edges, earmarked the flattest place for the toilet block and bike parking and started to make a fire pit, in the least combustible place, from some stones left over from an old, long collapsed wall. I park up the mower and help him. We work harmoniously together, me passing stones and him placing them.

Suddenly, we hear a loud groan and a whimper from the donkey field and Giles starts braying loudly as if shouting for help. Jeff comes flying up the lane to fetch us. We run down and find Isobel lying down and Giles having a panic attack, braying madly and swaying from side to side. We're about to run the gauntlet to keep him from accidently hurting Isobel and are fully prepared to be kicked and bitten when Dutch arrives and to our amazement he saunters past us, jumps onto Giles' back, puts his head close to his ear as if he is whispering and begins to stroke Giles' neck very gently with his paw whilst purring softly as if to soothe him. Giles visibly relaxes and we all watch in awe from a safe distance as Isobel delivers a big, healthy, leggy, boy. Dad videos it all to share with Joey.

Everything goes so smoothly and Isobel is an absolute star. She's not fazed by Jeff lying close by to give her emotional support or us gawping from a safe distance, Giles' fussing or anything else going on around her. He dives out feet first and once he fully arrives I check he's breathing okay and his airways aren't blocked and then leave them alone. She quickly begins to bond with her foal, drying, nudging and licking him as soon as she's got her breath back and within an hour or so of his arrival he is wobbling to his feet and feeding, gaining all the vital strength and anti-bodies he needs from his mother's milk.

We give them some space but Dutch, the donkey whisperer, stays in the field to keep Giles in check. We keep a close eye on Isobel to ensure she delivers the placenta and I ring the vet to update him on our new arrival and book a checkup for all of them tomorrow. Before calling the vet, I text Joey a picture of mummy and baby and caption it 'Wonky Donkey! It's a boy!' He immediately sends back a string of hearts and kisses emojis.

Dad and I take a very late afternoon tea break. We toast the new arrival with a can of Guinness each and both devour doorstep cheese, tomato and onion sandwiches and a family bag of crisps before heading back down the lane to finish work on the fireplace. We get done and stand back to see what space we have. It's huge and we could easily fit fifty or sixty tents on here with enough space between them to park a bike or car.

"I think ten campers might feel a bit lost on their own on here." Dad laughs. "Shall we say thirty tents maximum? We'll have to get a few bins, a couple of fire extinguishers, make a few signs and get some insurance cover organised and then we're meeting all legal requirements."

"I'll take a few photos and stick something on the TT accommodation forums in a bit and see if anyone is interested. We might be a bit far from the action here." I say getting my phone ready. I take a few pictures and we gather up all the tools and push the mower back down the lane. Dad cleans everything off and puts it away whilst I feed and water anything furry or feathery or green, double check the donkeys and watch them bonding with their baby boy and then head off for a much-needed shower.

Once I'm clean I get to work on Joey's chocolate cake. It's soon in the oven and the cottage smells divine. After supper, I fill it generously with butter cream and Pat's homemade raspberry jam and pipe a very dodgy 'Wel-come Home Joey' on the top then hide it before Dad can take the pee out of my decorating skills or pinch a slice.

With the sound of the North West coming from the TV and Dad snoring in the chair, I clear away everything from the table and set up the laptop. I upload the photos which show the field space, the well laid, even road into the site and the flat parking area, both are a top priority to anyone riding a fully laden motorbike. Then I add some pictures of the scenery and write up a little paragraph to explain where we are and what we will be offering. I repeat it in my basic Spanish, French and German. Craftily, I add a couple of rare old racing pictures of Dad and me to show who owns the place in case anyone remembers us and entitle it 'Blues Cottage Camping'. I hit send and assume we'll get half a dozen enquiries. By the time we switch it off for bedtime we've had three hundred and seven emails from at least fifteen different countries. I'm going to be a bit busy tomorrow. Bring on the madness!

Be careful what you wish for Delilah ....

CHAPTER 17

I wake up raring to go having slept like a log in my cosy, comfy little bed. By half six I've drunk several coffees, read over a hundred emails and started compiling a list. I thought running a camping site would be easy; book them in, show them to a spot and let them get on with it then clean up afterwards, right? Apparently not. Some want one night, some want six nights but would like to pay for five, some want to stay a month! They ask if we do hot meals? Cold meals? Picnics? Can we collect them from the airport? Can we book their ferry? Can we tell them the best route from Timbuktu? Lend them push bikes? Lend them motorbikes? Has Dad still got his 1967 Suzuki Super Six he raced at the Manx? Er, yes he has somewhere but how is it relevant to camping? Put their tents up for them? Taxi them to and from Douglas every night so they can get drunk? Set up a meeting with Michael Dunlop? Arrange a lap on the back of Bruce Anstey?

They want to know; What size are our toilets? What colour are our toilets? How powerful are our showers? What exact temperature is our hot and cold water? How wide is our gate? Where's the nearest spa? Where's the nearest Spar? Do we accept luncheon vouchers? Is our grass real? Do we accept swingers? Where's the nearest brothel?? Do we allow dogs? Do we allow ferrets??? Are we registered with the Camping Club? Are we Vegan Friends? Are we okay with naturists? I smile as I recall Joey's reaction to the first sight of me in my pants and vest, he will be totally incensed if anyone tries to corrupt Wonky by running around in the buff. The list of strange requests and queries is endless!

Dad has to go it alone on chores today. I send best wishes to Nina, kiss him bye and grab my well used notebook, I notice Joey has decorated the front with a pretty little sign adorned with flowers and butterflies saying 'anuva dluby lsit'. I smile and find a clear page. I split it into three. YES, NO, MAYBE, then I think about it some more and do another, simpler list entitled TWO WEEKS and ONE WEEK. I figure if we can get enough 'normalish' folk who want a fortnight it'll save a lot of coming and going. I start to rescan the messages and note down addresses of those who fall into my two categories and don't ask too many odd questions. By the end of the morning I have two more than adequate lists, eye strain, back ache and many symptoms related to caffeine overdose but I have been thoroughly enlightened about what strange and interesting things people from all over the globe expect from a basic camping holiday. At least arranging the insurance is more straightforward and is done with one phone call.

A bark from Jeff alerts me to the imminent arrival of the vet. He's getting out of his Land Rover and I can see through the doorway that he is looking much calmer and more collected today and he's smelling of a rather good, if not a little potent, aftershave too. Dutch jumps up and perches on my shoulder as if to protect me as I go out to meet him. If he finds a one-eyed ginger bruiser, sneezing spectacularly whilst doing an impression of a parrot alarming or unusual he hides it well.

"Congratulations on the new arrival! I'm Ian by the way. I don't think I introduced myself last time." He offers his hand to shake and Dutch snarls quietly as I take it. "How are they both doing?"

I ramble on in a caffeine fueled hype telling him they seem fine and have both been feeding well and relay everything that happened during the birth including how Dutch calmed Giles, how I checked the airways, delivery of the placenta and the baby's first steps. We head over to see them and Dutch jumps from me to Giles and does his donkey whisperer thing again while the vet examines mother and baby unmolested.

"Well you see something new every day in this job!" He exclaims nodding towards Dutch. "Isobel and the baby are really doing very well. Has he got a name yet?"

I laugh. "He's Wonky at the moment but we'll give him a proper name when Joey gets back and we can all take a vote."

"Is Joey your husband?" He asks innocently and Dutch immediately returns to my shoulder looking most indignant.

I laugh and explain Joey is only sixteen and lives here with me and Dad and is the one that has been taking such good care of Isobel and Giles and our chucks and the MSPCA residents.

Ian suggests he might want to train as a vet and says his practice sponsors promising students every year. I tell him I will put it to him when he's back later, I don't mention the fact that he probably hasn't completed a full year of secondary school. We chat a while longer with Dutch as a chaperone and then Ian leaves and I return to my lists.

While I've been outside we've had about thirty more enquiries so before doing anything else I remove all the adverts from the forums. I reply to the first thirty people on my TWO WEEKS list who claim to have ferry bookings at reasonable times and offer them a pitch. I go for some arriving on the Friday afternoon and some on the Saturday morning. This means we're all in and sorted and no-one should be disturbed by late arrivals.

Eighteen reply immediately to confirm and send a ten percent deposit direct to our bank account. Three reply to thank me but say they're now booked elsewhere. I send offers to my next three on the list and cross off the refusals. The three new ones accept and we now have twenty-one pitches sorted. I make a rather impressive spreadsheet to show pitch numbers, the name on the booking, their nationality, how many people are expected, time and date of arrival, mode of transport (currently all motorbikes), if they have paid their deposit and a blank column for when they have paid the balance in full. I have a sandwich to celebrate and take a well-earned walk on the beach with Jeff and Dutch to stretch my aching back and give my tired eyes a rest.

On my return I draft a 'thanks but sorry no room at the inn' email and send it en masse to all of the strangest of the strange folk who enquired about a vacancy. By the time Dad gets home we have full insurance coverage, twenty-six confirmations, twenty-three deposits safely in the bank, an up to date spreadsheet, about a hundred and fifty reserves and a very knackered Dil.

I'm dozing on the chesterfield when all hell breaks loose, Jeff barking Dutch also barking, chickens clucking and donkeys braying; Joey is home! We go outside and he's running up the lane with his rucksack trailing behind. He dives over the fence and gets his fill of Wonky, congratulating a very proud Isobel and Giles, he's allowed to hug them both without repercussions. Then he catches a self-launched Jeff who flattens him and licks him from head to toe. Dutch gives him a sniff and a little head butt of recognition and sneezes over him. When he finally manages to get up he wipes off all the snot and drool and hugs us both and then runs off to check his bike. Muttering that immortal line.

"Got any scran? I'm starvin'!" Dad and I grin at each other, we've missed him so much.

Over sausages, eggs and chips followed by chocolate cake we all catch up and considering we've spoken at length every day we still find plenty to chat about. Anyone passing by would envy our lively, happy, contented, little family and our love filled home.

"Can we all go a ride after tea? Can't wait to get back on me bike." Joey asks.

"I'm up for it as long as there's going to be no reenactments of any races you've watched this week. Especially Paddy Jr's. third place, I don't know how he stayed on at Metropole on that last lap!" Dad tells him. "You fit, Dil?"

"Yeah, definitely, I need to blow some cobwebs away after my day at the office." I laugh. We eat too much cake and then clear away and wash up together, feed and sort the menagerie, grab helmets, gloves and jackets, find extra treats for Jeff and Dutch and leave them both contentedly settled on the rug.

All three bikes starting up together makes a fabulous racket and we head off down the lane with Dad leading the way and me bringing up the rear.

We take a steady ride down past the prison to check Joey is still confident enough to go back into the few vehicles that pass as 'traffic' over here. He shows no sign of having forgotten anything and appears to have gained some tips from Juan and Paddy Jr. He's riding calmly and safely and is fully aware of his bike and his surroundings.

The road is big enough, straight, open and empty so I drop into first gear, lift up my front wheel and wheelie past him and Dad giggling my head off. Very grown up, Delilah! Dad, not wanting to be outdone, goes up on his back wheel and chases me. Joey tries several little bunny hops then makes us stop and teach him how to do it properly. After half an hour he's pretty confident and pulling safe, controlled wheelies to order in first gear and can change into second without dropping the front.

The sun starts going down and I lead the way to Niarbyl where we all lie back on the grass and watch the greatest natural show on earth, a spectacular sunset followed by a million stars. Dad and I point out the different constellations to Joey and name them, telling him stories we remember about each one. He is fascinated, hungrily taking in everything.

He watches me enthusiastically acting out the story of poor, beautiful Andromeda being sacrificed by her vain mother, Cassiopeia then rescued by Perseus who uses Medussa's severed head to turn Cetus, the giant sea monster, to stone and then takes her home to live happily ever after. Dad, lying flat with his hands behind his head begins gently snoring and we realise its way past midnight. We plan lots of daft things we can do to him, like tying his laces together and we're giggling like kids when suddenly he whispers.

"I can hear you two, I'm not deaf and I'm only resting my eyes." We stand him upright and all head on home to bed. We put the bikes in the barn and as Joey goes upstairs, in full on 'Walton's' style he shouts his goodnights to one and all by name and then says, "I've proper missed me bed!"

CHAPTER 18

I rise to a rainy, cold day, the steel grey sky blends into the steel blue sea and with a howling wind raging in from the water; it has all the makings of a perfect excuse for a duvet day. No chance! Despite his late-night stargazing, Dad's up and making bread at half five and wakes me to tell him where I've hidden the yeast, apparently in the larder next to the bread flour is a daft place to put it.

As the weather worsens we're all having a mad panic about Isobel and the baby only having an old awning for shelter. We make a few frantic calls and the lovely Mr. Jeavons quickly delivers twenty bales of straw which we stack into a shelter while we sort something a bit more permanent. He also takes the opportunity to drop off his beloved Manx Norton ready for fixing. A flat pack stable arrives shortly afterwards with no instructions or diagrams and takes us the rest of the day and much hilarity to build up into something like we think it should look.

As soon as we have four corner posts sunk safely into the ground, two wooden sides and a roof on top Isobel abandons her cosy straw shelter, gives a quick snort of approval and leads Wonky inside before we're anywhere near finished so we have to tip toe around and hammer gently so as not to scare them. We also have to contend with the added obstacle of a constantly watchful Giles ever ready in case he gets a chance to take a crafty chunk out of one of us.

It became apparent that Dutch doesn't do rain when he took one look out of the door this morning, grunted in disgust and promptly returned to the comfort of Dad's bed. Jeff, on the other hand, is more than happy to get soaked, muddy and stinky and is busy passing us tools we don't need and generally getting in the way, being goofy and making us smile.

Ricky delivers our camp shower and loo block around lunchtime so I leave the Chuckle Brothers to their own devices and go up to the top field to help him set everything up. He easily reverses the huge trailer through the gate and we do a little bit of maneuvering to get the unit as flat and solid as can be before sorting all of the stabilisers, tethers and steps. Ricky connects everything up and gives me a crash course in how it all works, what to check if it doesn't all work and how to turn everything on and off, refill the water tanks and fuel up the compressor. I ask him a million other questions and he laughs, drops his arm around my shoulder and kisses me on the head.

"Shortarse, if you find yourself knee deep in shit phone us. I'll send someone to fix it." He also offers to bring up a few flood lights later in the week so that no-one gets lost on the way to the loo in the middle of the night and then heads off to his next job after moaning that he's booked solid for weeks and feels like he's hardly seen us.

Nina rings just as I am getting back to the donkey field, to report that she is now safely settled in her own home with Carole fussing over her and to thank us all for keeping everything running smoothly and for taking on Dutch. She tells us Carole has also willingly agreed to take over our MSPCA duties while she's here. I suspect that this is so that she can have a little break away from her patient during the day. I tell them to ring us if they need anything at all and promise to send Joey over as soon as the weather improves so that his Auntie Carole can see how well he's doing and to show them both his bike.

I check up on Jeff and the boys and am just in the middle of updating them on Nina's progress when the phone rings again, it's the vet. He chats away and I tell him what we're up to and that Wonky is doing fine and that Isobel is a great mum and we get onto talking about Dutch and Jeff and the chickens. Out of the corner of my eye I notice Dad and Joey whispering together. I say bye and put the phone in my pocket.

"We think the vet is more interested in our Dilly than our wildlife." Dad looks to Joey for backup and giggles.

"Oh Lord, don't say that I'm not ready to deal with men."

"Is that why ya came over 'ere?" Joey teases innocently. "To ger away from a bloke?"

"Dilly Girl has been running away from men for the last twenty-eight years." Dad announces to the world. "They're lucky if they get a kiss on the cheek."

"Old Man, please refrain from discussing my love life or lack of it, in front of Wonky, he too young to hear talk like that!" I put my hands on my hips in mock annoyance and then have a fit of the giggles.

Now another of my failings has been unveiled there's not much more to say so I offer to go and make some food. They eagerly agree so I go inside, strip off my wet stuff and get a big pan of, previously made and frozen for a day just like today, stew on the stove and put the bread that's been proving in the larder, into the oven. I then take very great pleasure in lighting a fire in our fireplace for the first time.

I artfully arrange the fire irons from the auction so that they are in the order I might need them and then I take time to twist up some pages from an old Motorcycle News, choose some dry kindling from the pile, add a shovel full of charcoal and a handful of wood shavings and strike a match. I say a little prayer of thanks to whichever deity has time to be listening and light the flammable little heap. It catches instantly and mesmerizing flames in turquoise and green flicker and dance before me. I nurse and nurture, slowly adding sticks and logs to build it up to an orange inferno. This gives me time to process Dad's words. He's right, he's always right but I'm not looking to get involved in a romantic relationship now or maybe ever. I'm not even sure I could handle intimacy; it scares the hell out of me!

Dutch comes out of the bedroom to watch me do all of the hard work and then when I've sat and thought for what he deems too long he drops his head and butts me out of the way so that he can relocate from Dad's bed to the rug in front of the roaring fire, he lies flat out and immediately starts snoring loudly. Damn right Dutch, enough contemplation! I go and get on with the food but have to go and move him back a bit when I start to smell scorching fur, I gently shovel him up in both arms and move him back two feet, worried he might panic at me touching him and jump closer to the fire but doesn't even stir. I wash the newspaper print and coal dust off my hands and make some big herby, suet dumplings and add them to the stew. Then l make some hot chocolate, don all my outside gear again and take it out to the boys.

The rain has finally stopped but it's still bitterly cold and windy and they are grateful for something warming. After another half an hour of us all hammering, nailing and felting. Dad declares that the stable is now fully stable and I scatter a thick layer of straw inside and Joey adds a huge, freshly stocked, food bowl to the corner and we tidy all the tools up and take them back to the barn. Once everything is cleaned, dried and put away we all troop inside for a wash and a warm. The fire is roaring, making the cottage really cosy, the stew and bread smell divine. The only thing spoiling the beautiful aroma is the smell of slightly singed cat and very wet dog.

Joey has a warm and admires the fire and goes back into the barn to get showered and changed because he's starving and doesn't want to have to wait too long for food. Dad and I take turns to get showered; Dad goes first and Jeff follows, I assume it's because she's too hot with the fire going and wants to lie in the passageway but it turns out Jeff fancied a warm shower with lots of soapy bubbles. Dad yells me after about twenty minutes to come and coax her out. I find him squashed against the wall inside the shower with Jeff leaning up against him, sitting on his feet, filling the whole cubicle. She has her eyes closed, her head lolled back and a big goofy grin. I manage to tempt her out with a biscuit and discover she also loves a rub with a big, fluffy bath towel. I leave Dad in peace and take a very pretty and fragrant Jeff to finish drying by the fire. She gently shoves over a still snoring Dutch and settles down. Dutch stirs, sniffs her, sneezes loudly and snuggles up to her to go back to sleep.

I finally get a quick wash and then, whilst an impatient Joey sets the table while eating a huge slab of chocolate cake, Dad slices and butters the bread and I dish up the stew. We share our hearty meal and lots more teasing and chatting. We debate Wonky's name and vote to find out his character for a few days before officially christening him. We have a Riding Theory pop quiz and decide to book Joey in for his proper tests as soon as we can because he beats both of us hands down.

With the washing up all done, the fire stoked, a good stock of dry wood and the haunting sound of the wind howling around the cottage we settle down together to binge watch all of the North West racing and practice footage I've recorded throughout the week and are treated to a live commentary from Joey who must have accosted every rider during the week and has loads of little anecdotes and tips they had all given him.

The perfect way to spend a cold, rainy evening.

CHAPTER 19

D ad and I throw on hoodies and head out for an early morning seaside stroll via the donkeys and chucks to check the stable and coop are still intact. Buildings and occupants are all present and correct. The rain is gone and the wind is still strong but promising to blow in some sunshine later. We step onto the beach and are both lost in a wild nest of blowing dreadlocks. We turn into the wind, pull up hoods and tuck all our wild locks away, laughing. We are then treated to the sight of Dutch, leg cocked like a dog, peeing non-stop for a good minute then letting out a contented sigh. He obviously has some camel DNA! Not to be outdone Jeff brings us the biggest tree trunk she can find and jumps around eagerly waiting for us to throw it. I pick up something a little more manageable and they both race off towards the waves to retrieve it.

"I'm really sorry about my big mouth yesterday. I didn't mean to upset you." Dad says as we stroll along arm in arm. "It was out of order but in my defence I worry about you being lonely. Your Mama's only been gone a short while and I missed her company so much before we moved here. You've been alone for a long time. I was even dreading having a double bed again without her to cuddle at night but Jeff soon sorted that." He laughs trying to lighten the moment.

"I really wasn't upset; I need a proper kick in the bum sometimes and it did make me think but everything has gone so well and been so eerily easy so far that I'm not prepared to push my luck any further and I really haven't thought about getting involved with anyone or felt like I want to. I'm contented enough with you and Joey right now. I promise I'll try not to run away if anyone does come along."

"That's good enough for me, Dilly Girl." Dad says, kissing the top of my head.

We walk for miles chatting easily, remembering long ago days on beaches all over the world and reminiscing about some of the scorching TT fortnights we've encountered and others when the rain has been horizontal.

As we return to the cottage we see Joey frantically waving a tea towel at us. We panic and break into a run to see what's happened. Imagining Wonky unwell, the bikes being stolen, Sienna returning...

"What ya lookin' so worried for? I've made breakfast an' its goin' cold an' I'm starvin'." He announces.

We enjoy a more than adequate, well-cooked full English and buckets of coffee and mountains of toast whilst Dutch and Jeff tuck into their own feasts.

"Can we book me tests now?" Joey asks. "I wanna get 'em done, never bin good with tests."

I fire up the laptop with some trepidation expecting some more camping queries. My little pop up tells me I have one hundred and twenty-six unread messages. Deep joy! I bypass emails and go straight online to book a theory test.

"How keen are you?" I laugh. "You can do it this afternoon if you want." He eagerly agrees and we book for half three but agree it might be best not to tempt fate by booking his CBT test before he's got the theory certificate. He runs off to text Nathan and grab his book so that we can test him some more.

I take a deep breath, grab my notebook and prepare to tackle my emails. I scan through without opening any that aren't from a known source or an address on my booking list. The insurance documents have arrived so I transfer them to my new 'TT2020' folder along with my spreadsheet.

We have received two more deposits and an apology and request to cancel as 'the wife has put her foot down' apparently. Although he hasn't asked, I refund his money immediately as I don't want to get involved in a domestic. I don't bother offering his place to the next on the list just yet. We decide it might be worth keeping a bit of space for 'on spec' chancers who arrive without advance bookings. I continue to scan through and stop when I see a familiar name. Dad is looking over my shoulder and spots it the same time as I do.

"Look out! The Germans are coming!" He yells, starts to get excited and runs off to find his phone. The email is from Jurgen, a full on batshit crazy lunatic old friend of my father's. It informs us that he's coming over and bringing his 'bike club'. Before I can reply to the email Dad is happily chatting away to him in what can only be described as 'germlish' on the phone arranging arrival times, planning ride outs, discussing places to watch the racing and promising to stock up on good beer and lots of vodka. He is an 'unusual' man and Dad puts the phone on speaker in answer to Joey's raised eyebrows on hearing a little of the conversation. Jurgen is a very brilliant and very eccentric engineer and very successful bike racer with his own business and many sought after skills. However his English has been learned from watching too many porn movies and his language makes Joey sound positively angelic. Joey collapses in a fit of the giggles when Jurgen signs off.

"Fuck, piss, bollocks and shit! Darling sexy Dylan I must leave you. My bitch secretary says I must talk on the Zoom to the dickheads at NASA they cannot wait for uncle Jurgen, ja? Love you bye."

"How many and when?" I enquire, poised to fill in my spreadsheet, trying not to laugh.

"Ahh. He didn't say how many exactly." He replies sheepishly. "About twenty or so I think and I'm pretty sure he said he'll be here about half three, ahh he didn't say what day actually." I shake my head in mock despair and suggest he texts to find out a little more detail and I put in a provisional twenty-five just in case. We both know from prior experience that plans kind of go out the window where Jurgen is involved.

"Whenever he's comin', I can't wait to meet 'im." Joey grins.

Dad warns Joey not to get sucked into any of his harebrained ideas and recounts the tale of us all skiing stark bollock naked down a black run in Finland in the middle of the night because Jurgen had a theory we could travel faster without clothes and at night because the air was more dense or less dense, I can't remember which. All we proved was that it's too bloody cold to ski in the nude whatever time of day it is.

Jurgen's booking definitely fills all of our vacancies so I've no more work to do on that which may or may not be a blessing. I find some on line theory practice and turn the computer over to Joey, who mutters, swears and whoops his way through test after test until it's time to leave for the real thing. He's nervous but still wants to go on his own bike so that he can relate all the theory to practice on the way and keep his mind off the impending exam. We ask if he wants us both to come, one or neither.

"Both." He replies immediately. "I need you both there."

We all suit up, dish out the dog and cat treats, and set off for the college in Douglas where they have the test centre. We go via the Fairy Bridge to enlist a bit of ethereal support. Nathan is waiting at the college when we arrive to give Joey a bro hug and some words of encouragement then runs off back to work before he's missed. We promise to nip in and let him know the outcome before we leave. We wish Joey the best of luck and send him in with all his necessary paperwork and I root around in my rucksack and produce a huge chunk of smoky quartz to help with concentration and calm any anxiety. He grins and sticks it in his pocket. Then we both wait eagerly, like expectant grandparents, outside on the bench, with a picnic from the corner shop and an assortment of beverages from the nearby Costa to calm our nerves. He comes

out, all smiles, waving his pass certificate, hugs us, does a little jig and steals what's left of the picnic.

"The rock worked great but it wouldn't tell me any answers." He laughs. "I booked me CBT test for tomorrow at ten so we better go an' do some practicin'. Put this safe, Dil." He hands me his certificate and puts his helmet on. Then remembers Nathan and runs into the bank yelling, "I did it!" He gets a round of applause from everyone in the bank, many of whom I recognise from his party, including some of the customers. Nath is really happy for him and arranges to come over after tea for more last-minute lesson time.

We go down to the end of Laxey seafront where its open and quiet and we won't annoy anyone. We set out a course using large stones from the beach and get him to zig zag slowly around them then get quicker, move them closer and do it again, ride in a figure of eight until he's dizzy, then ride it in the opposite direction, emergency stop until his tyre is nearly worn through, make him get off and push his bike safely, have him talk us through some maintenance information and cover everything so that he'll have no nasty surprises.

He finally declares he's knackered and starving so we return the stones back to the beach and head home via the chippie.

By the time Nathan arrives Joey is fast asleep, curled up on the chester-field in a big heap with Jeff and Dutch. He rouses when he hears Nathan's bike and they go and have a quick ride around but are back and watching the North West footage within an hour.

"Mom said she's doing the Tesco run tomorrow while Sarah's at school and to let her know if you want picking up." Nathan tells me. "It'll take your mind off worrying how Joe's getting on." I totally agree and say I'll text her in a bit.

After making everyone hot chocolate and a big plate of biscuits and cakes I head off to bed and leave them to it. When l go to text Sal and set the alarm on my phone I see I have two missed calls from the vet. Oh dear! I start making a list in my head with reasons why I should and shouldn't ring him back. I list an awful lot of reasons why I shouldn't but I'm asleep before I even get started on the reasons why I should.

CHAPTER 20

I'm up early and Joey's up earlier. He's already pottering around the kitchen, getting the coffee on, when I get out of bed.

"Did you get any sleep?" I asked concerned he might be too tired to concentrate all day.

"Yep, slept like a log on the settee." He admits. "Must 'ave zonked out 'fore Nathan left. Woke up 'alf 'our ago with a blanket over me, Jeff on top an' Dutch for a pillow. I smell like a kennel but I feel great. Donkeys and chucks are fed, I'll go and get showered in a minute. Get some scran on I'm starvin'."

Dad comes out of his bedroom looking at his phone and scratching his head.

"Can you make sense of that?" He asks handing it over. It's a text from Jurgen;

'21 schöne Jungs, vielleicht ein paar Damen und ich. Sei am Freitag da, liebe dich'

I laugh. "It says twenty-one beautiful boys, maybe some ladies and me. See you Friday, Love you."

"Oh! I thought it said that." Dad laughs. "I think that's as much as we're going to know until he turns up. Where's Joe? I left him snoring on the sofa last night."

"Getting showered and raring to go." I inform him. "We can head off after breakfast and have a good ride before he needs to be there."

We all start up in unison and I rev up and make some noise. Dad and Joey join in and we set of down the lane making beautiful music together. We stop at the Fairy Bridge say 'Moghrey mie' and leave something shiny for the little folk. Then we let rip and a little imp must have hopped up for a ride on my shoulder because as we go around the Ramsey hairpin he whispers in my ear, I give Dad a nod to check he's good, put my head down and have a full on blast over the mountain like my bum is on fire and don't slow down until I get to Hillberry. I stop to wait for Dad and Joey and The Duchess is pinging and clicking as everything cools down. I'm swinging my legs on the bench when they arrive.

"Very grown up, Delilah!" Dad laughs. "Has that cleared some cobwebs?"

"That was awesome! Me poor little DT nearly blew up trying to catch ya! Could 'ave passed ya on the bungalow but thought I better save some for later." Joey teases.

"He had a bloody good try at catching you." Dad laughs. "The DT must have thought Marley had come back, he always used to wring its neck."

"Have you got rid of all of the madness so that you can be sedate and sensible all day doing your CBT?" I ask.

"Yep, I reckon so. Let's go an' get it done so I can get me full licence."

We head down to Port Soderick and get him booked in. Andy, the instructor is an old acquaintance.

"Oh no! Not another one from the Blue household! Is he a speed freak like the rest of you?" He laughs.

"No he rides like me granny." I tease.

"That's only 'cos she makes me fill me pockets with rocks." Joey shoots back.

"I wouldn't worry if you can already ride like her granny. I recall she was one hell of a racer." Andy tells him with a wink.

We wish him luck and tell him to enjoy himself and report back whenever he can. Dad heads home because he's dying to get at Mr. Jeavons' Norton and I go to Billy and Sal's. We both need to keep ourselves occupied for the day.

Sal opens the door and hands me a coffee.

"I remember when Max and Nathan did their CBTs I wondered round like a loon all day, drove Billy crackers." She confides. "I followed Max around on my bike when she did her full test. At the end the examiner said 'I'm pleased to tell you you've passed and so has your Mum' I've never been so embarrassed." She shakes her head and laughs. "Nathan said he'd leave home if I did it to him. Drink up, get your kit off and we'll go and spend some money. We'll have to go in the car I need a shitload of groceries. Them two eat more than the kids." She nods towards the hallway.

I give the family wolfhounds, the eaters of lots, Murphy and Spudz, a big load of love, leave my helmet, jacket, gloves, bike trousers and buff in a heap on the hall floor, produce my trusty dungarees from my rucksack, empty my coffee cup and we jump in Sal's motor ready to go and cause havoc.

"Thought we could have a mooch around Tynwald Mills then go and look around the antiques shops in Peel if we have time before Tesco. Have you heard off Sienna the slapper? Billy said she's one of the most horrible human beings he's ever met and he knows some strange and unpleasant people." Sal loves a good gossip. "Nath said Joey asked if he thought you'd mind if he changed his name to Blue."

"We haven't heard anything from her and I think Joey would tell us or Nathan if she had tried to contact him. Talking of strange people, guess who's coming to stay for TT?" I steer her off the subject of Sienna.

She has a couple of guesses. "Give me a clue! You know lots of weirdos too." She laughs.

I give her my best German accent. "Liebling, I must lick you all over, ja."

"Oh no! Not Jurgen the perv man?" She giggles. "I better send Sarah to her Nan's when we come over. She'll beat him senseless with all his swearing. She's made a star chart for me and Billy, we get a star for every hour we don't swear. We've had it a week and he hasn't got one star yet."

We park up at Tynwald Craft Mill, a beautiful old mill which is now a very smart department store that sells pretty much anything you could want apart from bikes and bike gear. I'm not a shopper by any stretch of the imagination. I buy essentials from a supermarket on the rare occasion that I venture into one. My two bike T shirts and my hoody are from TTs long past and my two pairs of well-aged dungarees are from Nepal about twenty-six years ago. I've definitely had my money's worth. My 'party' dress, a dungaree pinafore, was actually Max's from when she was about eleven and grew out of it. Needless to say, clothes shopping isn't my forte but I have to admit to enjoying my recent splurges and am well up for today's trip, not least because they have a fab deli and cafe.

"Shall we book a personal shopper?" Sal asks as we get out of the car. "The snooty one here will have a nervous breakdown when she sees you and me. Everyone I've seen her working with are always trying on twinsets and slacks."

"She'll love you, Miss Elegant and perfectly proportioned." I laugh. "She'll have to take me to the children's department."

"We have to at least get a facial, hair and makeup. I love watching all the preened and painted dollies try to control their faces when they see your dreads and you tell them your skincare routine is soap in the shower." Sal has dragged me kicking and screaming to spa days on three previous occasions in the last thirty years or so, one was her hen do. She has never forgotten a single one and recounts the tales to anybody who'll listen.

We enter the shop and are politely accosted by people from various departments offering us the chance to book appointments. We book a hair one. I have to admit my dreads are looking more grey than purple recently and could do with a little tlc. Sal also books us a facial and make-over because she's a sadist. We decline the not so eager offer of the personal shopper experience.

I check my phone and have a text of three thumbs up from Joey so I relax and get into the shopping mood.

"Right we've got an hour before the hairdresser. Where'd you want to start?" Sal asks. "I need some clothes for Sarah because she's growing like a string bean, something nice for Nathan, a few things Max asked me to post over and I need an outfit for the TT Presentation Evening."

"You know I'm a crap shopper! I don't know what I want for who or why, apart from a trip to the deli, I'll follow you round and you can show me how it's done." I laugh.

She grabs a trolley, points it towards the kids' section and we're off. We pick up three lovely Joules leggings and tunic sets in different colours and patterns for Sarah which are all soft and elasticated to grow with her and a couple of not too girly jersey cotton dresses for the summer. Next it's menswear and we both head for the Levis section to get jeans for all of our boys.

We move on and I get some decent waterproof coats, gloves and boots for us all. We nearly froze and drowned putting up the stable. Sal gets a smart blazer, shirt and tie for Nathan to wear for work.

"Hair time!" She announces and promptly changes our direction.

We park up the trolley and walk into a small but well laid out salon with a mature lady and a couple of youngsters all dressed in neat overalls and perfectly coiffed.

"Good morning, ladies." The older one greets us, eyeing me with some trepidation. "What can we do for you today?"

One of the youngsters saves her. "Oh my god! How fabulous! I haven't seen real, proper, full on dreadlocks for ages. I did them as my specialty in college, even went to Jamaica for a month on an exchange at an upmarket hairdressing salon to learn from the best. Please can I do them, I'll be really, really careful, please!" He looks pleadingly at the older lady.

"Have at them, sweetheart!" I tell him before she can reply. "Where do you want me?"

Sal explains very clearly and precisely what she wants done and the older lady relaxes as she's back on familiar territory. She seats Sal in front of a huge mirror and gets to work.

My new best friend pulls my dreads out of their big top knot and appears to have an orgasm. He is so excited. He asks me a million questions about how long they've been growing, how I look after them, what products I use...I hear Sal snorting with laughter from the other side of the room.

"She was practically born with them, never washes them, ties them in a knot on her head so she doesn't catch them in her bike chain and they used to always be a beautiful rainbow but now she just dyes them herself when she thinks it's time to cover up the grey bits!" She informs him. "You should see her Dad's, they've had twenty-five more years growing time and never seen shampoo."

"Do you want them just purple again, Ms. Blue?" He asks handing me a colour chart covered with vibrant, jewelled samples in scarlets, jade greens, violets, oranges, turquoises and golden yellows. I'm mesmerised, my eyes jump from one shade to the next as I stroke the silky samples.

"Oh, good grief! Don't give me choices and call me Dil" I laugh. "What would you like to do with them?" He looks over to see if his boss is listening.

"I'm Alex. This is my idea of heaven; I can't believe it. What I would really like to do is put it back to rainbow colours but it'll take a while to do."

"We need to keep her occupied all day so long is good and rainbow is more appropriate than you know." Sal informs him. "She'll let you do anything as long as you have coffee."

His boss, clearly thinking long time equals more money purses her lips and makes a great show of looking in the appointment book and then sighs and smiles as if she's decided to loosen her corsets.

"You're fine until two o'clock. I can cover everything before then and Lisa can help you if you show her what to do. It's nice to get the chance to be creative once in a while. I have to warn you it will be quite expensive though." She adds. "Go and put the kettle on, please Lisa."

"The cost is not a problem. I'm up for it. If you have the enthusiasm and patience. Go for it!" I smile, sit back and prepare to be transformed.

Alex's face lights up and he's instantly mobilised, collecting brushes, cling film and tools from various drawers. He wraps me up in a huge gown, giggles when my hands and ankles disappear and finds a smaller one, improvises with two disposable plastic aprons hung backwards around my neck to prevent dyeing my back and the salon chairs, Lisa hands me a coffee and we're off. After counting and partitioning my locks they begin mixing divine coloured potions in little black dishes and discussing both logistics and colour combination options. While Sal gets her highlights redone and her already perfectly sculpted bob trimmed I am painted and pasted and wrapped and placated with regular coffee offerings.

"I better go for my beauty appointment." Sal says looking at her watch. "I'll cancel yours and meet you back here when I'm done. "Hopefully your new hair will distract everyone from the state of your eyebrows." She sighs in mock disappointment.

"We can't all be beautiful and elegant like you, Bitch." I giggle. "See you in a bit, enjoy!"

Alex and Lisa continue painting and wrapping for a while until Alex declares me done and asks if I want a magazine while I wait for the colours to take. I decline and reach for my phone to check on Joey. I've got another text with three thumbs up, a funny little screwed up face emoji and IM STAAVIN. He's clearly doing okay. I check up on Dad

and he's knee deep in Norton wiring and happy as a pig in you know what.

"I can do your eyebrows if you want me to." Lisa offers shyly once my phone is away. I agree, let's shock Sal. Once my brows are tamed and my head is deemed to be cooked Alex and Lisa move me to the basin carrying my locks, splayed out on the apron, behind me like a bridal train. After endless washing and rinsing I get to see the finished product. It's perfect! Bright and vibrant and clean and fluffy. The colours complement each other and it looks better than I imagined it ever could.

"Promise you'll come back and let me maintain it." Alex begs when I've paid, handed him and Lisa generous tips, and thanked them all.

"Look at you!" Sal exclaims as she comes to collect me. "That's took twenty years off you. We need to book now for last weekend of TT fortnight so they can sort you before the presentation evening. And bloody hell you've got two separate eyebrows, how did that happen?" I punch her playfully and we rebook and go to find her an outfit for her do. Leaving Alex a very happy man.

She tries on several dresses and looks fabulous in all of them. She chooses her favorite and finds matching shoes and a bag. Because I'm such a skinny little, short arse I don't even look at getting anything fitted but I can't resist getting a leggings and top like Sarah's but in a bigger size, age 10!

Sal shakes her head in despair and drags me towards the petite department.

"You'll be coming to this do too. Haven't you read your invites? They actually emailed them this year. I know you're both on the list and Joey was included too because Meave and Pat volunteered to send them out." She winks.

I confess to not reading my emails recently and tell her all about the camping requirements of our potential visitors. She is doubled up in hysterics by the time we reach the small section of small clothes. I thank the angels for not giving me too much choice but I needn't worry as Sal zips along the row grabbing half a dozen size four dresses and I realise I don't get to choose.

"You don't know how long I've dreamed about doing this!" She admits handing them to me and shoving me towards the changing room. "I want to see every single one on you."

I do as I'm told and put on the first dress. It's awful and frilly and swamps me. I show Sal, she laughs, apologies for her poor choice and pushes me back to try the next one. It's much plainer and fits much better but looks a bit too much like office wear. Sal nods and frowns and sends me back. The third one is in a simple Japanese style. Sal approves and it goes in the trolley. I'm just about to try a fourth one when she comes in.

"Don't panic! I've found the perfect one." She hands me a Michael Kors black Medallion Lace Mini dress according to the label. "Put it on quick." She orders, excited to see. It's very lacy and luxurious and very not my usual style. I feel really exposed but it fits like a glove and looks superb with the new hair. I don't recognise myself when I look in the mirror. Sal is speechless and in tears so it must look alright, she hugs me and runs off to find shoes. I look at the price tag on the dress and have a small breakdown. She comes back with three pairs of what Sarah would probably describe as 'fuckme shoes' and I start to giggle. She reads my mind and starts giggling too.

"Stop it and get your feet in them I'm going to pee myself if I laugh any more!" She approves the second pair and then tells me I need tights and a bag and then we can go to the cafe.

I'm back in my dungarees before she can blink. I grab a pair of black tights and a sweet little black suede rucksack which Sal frowns at but allows as it matches the shoes. We have a welcome feast in the cafe and then buy loads of locally produced goodies from the deli. Sal rings Billy to ask if he can fetch Sarah from school as time is getting on and my phone rings while she's giving Billy his orders.

"I passed! We're done but Andy's gonna take me for a practice lesson for me proper test 'coz I was star pupil." He laughs. "I'm gonna meet Nath from work after if that's okay?"

"Congratulations! Well done sweetheart. Course it's okay. You can do whatever you like, go and celebrate but let Dad know how you've done and ring if you're freaked about riding alone in the dark whatever time it is. The lights aren't the best on the DT. I'm off to Tesco in a bit, any requests?"

"Get me a folder like the nerds 'ave to keep all their paperwork in? I'll give ya the money when I get back." He chuckles. "We need donkey scran as well. I'll be careful. Gorra go, Love ya." Two minutes later Dad texts me lots of thumbs up. Then a photo of a pile of Norton wiring and lots of thumbs down and some laughing faces. He's going to be busy for a while yet. I text him back saying 'Don't forget to eat xxxx' and a picture of my rainbow locks. He texts back immediately, 'nice to see you back my rainbow girl xxxx'

Sal's already heard the good news and passed it on to everyone else before I'm off the phone. She tells me Sarah is sorted and we've got no curfew. We go back to shopping for a little while longer and I get Joey a smart leather document wallet, a normal wallet and a shirt for the 'do'. I buy a couple of soft, furry throws for snuggling up on the chesterfield and some bits for the kitchen. Sal gets the stuff Max has asked for and a few other items that take her eye. We pay up and pile it all into the car.

On the way to Tesco I'm telling Sal about Wonky and happen to mention the vet.

"Not dishy Ian? He's lovely! Pat's been trying to set him up on dates for the last fifteen years." Sal hoots. "He's a really nice guy, always superb when they need him at the farm and he's good with the hounds. The vet in Douglas wouldn't go near them last time we went in. Mind you Spud was trying to mount her from behind the time before." She recalls and continues with her gossip. "His wife ran off with his business partner about twenty years ago. He's pretty much been on his own ever since. He must be worth a fortune by now he never stops working. You need to go on a date with him, it'll do you both good."

"Slow down Cilla!" I giggle. "He hasn't even asked me on a date. He just rang to see how the donkeys were."

I'm saved by our arrival at Tesco's. We fly around grabbing everything we need and everything we want. I get paper plates and plastic cutlery, a ton of loo roll and hand wash and some cheap torches and batteries for our impending visitors. I buy a cheap printer, a ream of paper, a laminator and some pouches, string and a new notebook for my lists and a sketch-book and some pencils for Joey. We're done and back in the car in less than an hour and a half.

"We'll drop off your shopping then back to ours and I'll get my bike out and we can go up the Creg for a pint and show off your hair." Sal announces our evening itinerary.

"Sounds good to me as long as you promise not to try setting me up on any dates." I agree and we head to the cottage.

CHAPTER 21

T T fortnight is almost upon us and the Island is gearing up for the onslaught. Mowers are working overtime trying to make the camping fields big enough to fit in a few more tents by mowing right to the edges. Shops, pubs and cafes are stocking up on basic supplies, take away food and lots of alcohol ready for all the visitors. The kids are getting excited about having time off school, the businesses on the circuit are devising rotas for staff to get in and out before roads close. Those offering room rentals are out buying new bedding and duvets and stocking fridges with bacon, eggs and sausage. Holiday cottages are opened up and aired out and scrubbed clean.

The ladies of the WI and the parishioners are baking and jam making morning, noon and night and finding out their best tablecloths. Contrary to popular belief many TT goers are veterans who are getting on a bit now and much prefer a nice cup of tea and a scone to anything the local hostelry has to offer.

Out on the course everything is being made safe, Marshal's huts are being inspected and restocked, grandstands are being erected anywhere there is a good view and the chance to make a few quid. Signs are being rescued from undergrowth and overgrown hedges and cleaned and re sited to be seen by passersby. Worst of all the lovely no speed limit areas of the Island suddenly have limits.

Down in the paddock and the park hospitality units and the TT village are being built, pop up bars erected, flooring laid, team areas marked out and retailers are setting up their pitches. The famous old score board will be getting a lick of paint too.

I am making signs; PARKING, LADIES, GENTS, FIRES IN THE FIREPITS ONLY PLEASE, PLEASE DON'T FEED THE DONKEYS, PLEASE PUT LITTER IN THE BINS, RIDE ON THE LEFT (LINKS FAHREN).....I'm having the time of my life ..not! Dad is out with Joey helping out Ricky and Billy and I'm preparing for our own personal invasion. I've printed everything in several languages and laminated it and am heading up to attach them to various things when I hear Wonky coughing.

I dive over the fence and run into the stable. He's stopped coughing but is chomping away on his mom and dad's feed. Oh god, he's too young, he'll choke! I grab my phone and ring Ian in a mad panic.

"Wonky is eating Isabel's food! He must have pulled it down to get at it. What should I do?" I'm in a proper state thinking I'm going to have to perform the Heimlich manoeuvre on him. "How soon can you get here?"

"Calm down, Mrs. Blue. It's fine. I can get there whenever you need me to but he's old enough to eat solids and he'll be absolutely fine, trust me I'm a vet." He laughs.

"Really? It's okay? He was coughing." I ramble. "I thought he needed to feed from Isobel for another five or six months. I Googled everything about the birth and totally forgot about afterwards."

"He was probably coughing because he's a greedy little bugger. He will drink from Isobel for a good while yet but he's going to start eating solids too. I'll bring some food round that'll be more suitable for him but don't worry, he's being a normal little donkey."

"Thank you so much, Ian. I was really worried. I need a coffee and a lie down now. Oh, and I'm Delilah by the way. Mrs. Blue was my Mama." I giggle.

"Well Delilah, put the kettle on if you're not too busy and I'll bring this feed over. I can be there in ten minutes."

I move the feed so that Wonky doesn't overdo it and head back to the cottage to put the coffee on. Then I realise I'm still in just my knickers and t shirt and run into the bedroom to throw my dungarees on.

I hear Ian's Land Rover arrive and Jeff goes to greet him. Dutch jumps on my shoulder and disappears under my hair.

"Hi Delilah. Oh wow I love your hair. It's fabulous!" Ian proclaims whilst getting a large sack of food and a salt lick from his backseat. I'm not sure if he's referring to my new colours or the huge ginger idiot nesting in my dreads. Over a cup of coffee and a piece of cake he gives me instructions on feeding Wonky. I listen carefully and write it in my notebook just in case.

I can feel Dutch mooching around on my shoulder and am about to warn Ian to protect his cake but I'm not fast enough, a huge ginger paw extends from behind my ear hooks the butter cream out of the slice he's about to eat and disappears back into oblivion. I try hard but cannot control my giggles. Ian laughs too thank goodness.

"That cat hates me!" He says. "I was really enjoying that and he's nicked the best bit. I haven't had proper homemade chocolate cake for years. All the farmer's wives make me fruit cake, which is lovely." He adds quickly. "But chocolate cake full of jam and cream is best."

"Dutch very definitely agrees with you. Joey would probably agree with you too, he seems to inhale it as soon as it's made. You timed it perfectly this one was only made this morning. So I can actually offer you another slice." He thanks me and wishes he could but says he must go to his next appointment. I wrap him some cake to take with him.

"It was lovely to see you again, Delilah. Maybe we could go for a meal one evening if you're free?"

Oh lord! Stay calm Dil! "That would be really nice but we're having campers for TT so I'm afraid I won't be able to get away from here for a few weeks but let's sort something when it's all over. Don't forget to send a bill for the food." I add trying to change the subject.

"It's a date then. Or it will be. Thanks for the cake." He smiles, ignoring the shop talk, and drives away. A date? Err no. I don't think so but hopefully he'll have forgotten by the time TT is done.

I go back to my string and signs. The campsite is looking absolutely lovely. The old gate has had a lick of bright blue paint and screwed to it is a driftwood sign Dad has made saying 'Welcome to Blues Cottage Campsite'. There is bunting hanging between the trees and loads of lanterns and fairy lights hanging in them, ordered and delivered from Amazon. We have an old marquee, that Nina has given us, erected in the corner in case the weather is unkind. The hedges are trimmed and the grass is mown. The fire pits are built up and full of driftwood, courtesy of Jeff, and there is extra firewood stacked in the corner. We've roped off a big area for Jurgen and his crew to spare everyone from too much exposure. I've made sure we are not expecting any under 25's as I do not want to be accused of corrupting minors.

Everyone has confirmed their arrival times and paid up in full without any chasing or drama. Quite a few have already prebooked picnics for race days which was Dad's inspired idea. Not to be outdone Joey came up with the idea of breakfast supplies packs and has given the chickens a pre order for a regular supply of eggs. We also have a couple of bookings for bike services which no-one thought of but is brilliant and a two man race team from Norway who have booked to camp with us have also asked if they can rent some workshop space to prepare their bike so we're all going to have plenty to do and I don't feel quite so guilty about the price of my hair and dress.

Joey has announced that he is going to take alcohol orders so people do not have to drink and ride and has already been around all of the local takeaways to get menus so that he can offer a collection service for evening meals too. We've told him whatever money he makes is his to keep. He really is a budding little entrepreneur.

Strangely, I'm genuinely looking forward to our guests arriving. I'd usually just want to put on my helmet and get away from any crowds especially strangers. Maybe getting my rainbow back has made me feel a little more visible and given me a boost of confidence or maybe I am just starting to get the hang of how to do 'real life' and act like a big girl. Either way I'm ready to take on the campers and Jurgen and his crew....I hope...

CHAPTER 22

We're all out on the beach really early on Friday morning doing some yoga and having a bit of calm before the madness begins. Suddenly we hear what sounds like a squadron of warplanes coming down the lane. Jurgen and crew were obviously on the night boat. Jurgen is leading the way on a Ducati Panigale V4 25 Anniversario 916 which makes me drool. His helmet is hanging from his handle bar. He's followed by a huge assortment of very expensive and desirable bikes that look as if they are being ridden by the ninja power rangers. They are all in full one piece, all black leathers with black Simpson helmets and dark visors and black boots. They all have matching black throwovers and matching black tents bungeed to their tailpieces. I bet they had great fun trying to get to Heysham last night in the pitch black to catch the 2:15am boat.

Jurgen jumps off his bike when he sees us. "Mein Gott! Fuck! Liebling! You look divine come to Jurgen now I want to.... " I cut him off with a big hug before he can finish his sentence, it's too early to be subjected to the contents of Jurgen's mind. He hugs me tight and smells my hair then buries his head in my dreadlocks and squeals with excitement. Joey is looking like he's not sure whether to laugh or run away. "Do you like my new horsie? She is a pretty bitch, ja?" He asks nodding towards the Panigale. "I chose her for you."

"She is a gorgeous, sexy lady." I reply honestly. "You must let me ride her before you leave."

"Of course you must! Dylan come here my friend." They hug and chat whilst the ninjas all sit in complete silence with their visors down. We introduce Joey who is also hugged and told how beautiful he is but not to worry because uncle Jurgen likes ladies only.

I suggest Dad and Joey go and show everyone to their spot so they can park their bikes and set up camp whilst I go and fill the big tea urn we've acquired from an ad in the local paper. Joey comes to find me after a little while.

"Have the power rangers removed their lids?" I ask giggling at Joe's shell-shocked appearance.

"Oh my funkin' god Dil you need to see 'em. It's like the Rocky 'orror Show! There's gorra be a million quid's worth of bikes there!"

"Funkin? Has Sarah got you on her swear chart?"

"Yep." He grins. "She put me on it last night. Told me 'it will improve my chances in life and I will be taken more seriously if I don't use profanity.' I'm beating Billy already."

"Not exactly difficult, Sweetheart, Billy swears like a navvy with his knackers in a vice." I laugh. "I don't think it's held him back too much. But you won't go far wrong if you take career and lifestyle advice from a four-year-old."

"Billy gets wherever 'e wants 'cause 'e looks like a yeti and on first sight he scares the shi....bejesus out of ya."

"You're probably right but keep listening to Sarah, she talks more sense than most grown-ups and I'm sure she's been here before. Do the Rocky Horror Show require beverages?" I enquire.

"Yep, Earl Grey or Darjeeling if we got any." He collapses in a fit of the giggles.

We made three huge pots of tea; Earl Grey, Darjeeling and good old PG Tips, put milk, sugar and lemon slices on a tray and carry it up to their camp, which is already set up with twenty-two identical black tents all spaced with engineering precision. A very tempting array of bikes are lined up in the parking area.

Jurgen is now wearing some very tight red budgie smugglers and his flip flops, he is toned and tanned, polished and waxed within an inch of his life. For a man in his late sixties he looks amazing. Most of his entourage now look like very well to do middle aged business men on holiday. Shorts, socks and sandals, dad bods and very white skin. Some, however, are younger and more toned. They have long hair tied back in ponytails and are wearing swimming trunks and more mascara and eyeliner than Sienna. I recognise them but cannot place them. They remind me of a rock band. They're here on holiday so I'll not think too hard about who they might be and let them stay incognito.

"I must swim. Come and race me now, lieblings." Jurgen orders after consuming three cups of tea, one of each flavour, and they all troop off to the beach.

Dad looks at me and shrugs. "I'm going back in the workshop. You can go and race him. He'll only sulk when I beat him and his hangers on don't look like much competition."

"I don't think I'm up for taking me kecks off in front of that lot yet an' 'e looks like 'e can do a bit more than the doggy paddle. Anyway I've gorra 'elp Ricky down the paddock in a bit so ya's on ya own, Ma." Joey laughs.

I head indoors to get my swimsuit on and grab some towels. I figure I've got a few hours before anyone else arrives. Me, Jurgen and the silent rock band plan a race for the horizon while everyone else paddles, relaxes on the rocks or does a bit of beach combing. Jeff and Dutch have already introduced themselves to our guests and whilst Jeff is willingly accepting loads of attention and generally showing off Dutch is observing the goings on from a safe distance.

Jurgen is ultra-competitive; it's what makes him such an excellent business man and a damn good bike racer. I am laid back with most things but I do love to race a worthy opponent and can't seem to back down from a challenge. Jurgen has a weird monitoring device on his wrist which makes Dad's Fitbit look like something out of the ark. He informs us we must swim out as far as we can until his alarm sounds and then we must race back to the shore. He sets his alarm and away we go. I take my time to acclimatise as the sea here is never warm.

The band hare off without a thought and one has to return due to cramp after three minutes, another because he is shivering uncontrollably. Jurgen figures out that we swim here quite a bit and follows my lead. I pick up the pace with long, lazy strokes and he swims beside me. We catch up and pass the others easily and they speed up to stay with us. After about fifteen minutes Jurgen's alarm wails and the race is on. I turn around and extend my stroke but still pace myself as it's a long way back. The others take off way too quickly and l know they'll tire before they get back. When we are much closer to the shore l get my head down and glide past the band boys. I catch up Jurgen who is going well but starting to flag a little. He sees me and it spurs him on and we race full on towards the beach. I reach the finish about two meters in front of him. We collapse in a panting heap together on our towels and get our breath back.

"You crazy bitch, I love you so much. You make me work for it. I like that." Jurgen gasps between breaths. The others arrive gasping for air. "Where have you been, you hairy pussies? I am years older than you yet we whup your cute little asses and still look good. You look like Kiss on a bad, bad day! Young boys have no stamina!"

One speaks in perfect English with an American accent and is clearly not a German.

"Yep, you proper whupped our asses Dad. I forgot I was still wearing the bloody make up, that's your fault for making us catch a boat ten minutes after we'd finished the gig last night." They all collapse in a fit of giggles and lay back to recover on the beach.

I raise my eyebrows to Jurgen. "Dad?"

"Ja, ja he is my baby boy. Jurgen is getting on now so my dickhead people wanted to know how many children I have who will try to take my money. I say I don't fucking know I have loved many beautiful ladies. So they try to trace them. Logistics were all wrong with most of them - all fucking dirty liars trying to fuck me, ja. This one I like a lot. I remember his mama from a long, long time ago. She was a singer in Hamburg. I got her a record deal; she was a good girl and I liked her a lot. She went to America. He is a clever boy like his farter, ja, but American. He says he is a singer; he just squeals like a girl but young people like it. He has loads of business brains and his own money and doesn't want anything from me.

I like to hang out with him, he's sexy and cool. I will give him my houses when I'm dead."

"I don't want your houses you crazy old bastard. I've lost track of how many I've got already." He sighs. "I'm Stefan. Thanks for letting us stay and showing us someone can beat him at something. God knows we keep trying." He holds out his hand and I shake it. "This is Emmett and Felix, the 'pussies' over there are Connor and Charlie." He adds waving towards the two guys that didn't finish the race. They wave back and shout 'hi!'

Jurgen's wrist gadget buzzes and he jumps up. "I will go and sleep now and delectable little Delilah will show you how to ride a motorcycle properly." He waves an arm towards the other guys who are happily mooching on the beach. "Leave the silly old gits here they will be happy until dinner, ja."

"Awesome, I can't wait to see this place." Emmett says, clearly from his accent another American. "I'll just go and make myself look a little less crazy." He laughs pointing to his running make up.

I agree to meet anyone who wants to come for a ride out at the front gate in fifteen minutes and run inside to get my leathers on. Dad is happily pottering in the workshop and promises to listen out for any other guests arriving. He opens the door for me to get The Duchess out and leaves it open so that he can be found if anyone who's already here needs him.

Stefan is make-up free and waiting at the gate on a H2 Carbon. "Oh man, is that a real Desmosedici RR? Awesome!"

"You're riding a H2. The Duchess is considerably outclassed." I laugh.

"The Duchess? If I remember correctly the press called it 'The Fire-breather'. I love Ducatis, they are an absolute work of art but they scare the living crap out of me, I've tried a few, it's like trying to ride a wild mustang. They seem to be alive. Hats off to anyone who can handle a full on Desmo."

"She goes easy on me because I nursed her back to life. She belonged to Jurgen and had been seriously used and abused. She was in a shocking state when I managed to rescue her. I'll be forever grateful to him for letting me buy her for about a quarter of what she was worth." I reveal.

"Oh wow! A Desmosedici RR. You've got bigger balls than me lady!" Emmett, also now devoid of make-up, exclaims. Throwing his leg over a BMW HP4. I raise my eyebrows. "It's German darlin', it does what it's told and has lots of cool electronics to save me from myself." He laughs. "The others have flaked out because they have no stamina and the few oldies that aren't asleep on the beach have chickened out because once they saw you beat Jurgen at something they realised they were staying with a force to be reckoned with, apparently it doesn't happen often, so it's only me and Stef you're going to have to wait for. Go easy on us our roads at home are a little wider and a lot straighter." He tells me, putting his helmet on and starting up his handsome beastie. Stefan starts the Kawasaki too and the sound of all three together is sweet, sweet music to my ears.

Without a second thought I head straight to the Fairy Bridge. They park up next to me and are already chatting away, super excited about the landscape and the greenery, the crazy roads, freaky names and quaintness and when I throw in some folklore and superstition they are beside themselves. I have a feeling they may have been to a lot of places but never had chance to really see them.

Once we have given shinies to the little guys, the buggers have cleaned me out lately but have delivered on every wish so I'm not complaining.

"Okay gents, Delilah's Tours is at your service. Do you want the landscapes and culture tour, the TT tour or the see how fast your bike is and scare yourself shitless tour?" They laugh and think about it and jokingly argue with each other.

Stefan asks. "Can we book the two we don't choose today on another day?"

"Yes of course you can. It gives me an excuse to get The Duchess out for an airing and pretend I'm looking after our guests." I sass.

"We've only been here a few hours and I'm having the best time ever." Emmett declares. "I don't think I'm going to want to go back. Can we go for 'landscape and culture' because the guys will get pissy if we do the TT stuff and I need some sleep before I take this baby to warp speed. I've been up since ten thirty yesterday morning, played a full gig, ridden across England on the wrong side of the road wearing a helmet with a dark visor I couldn't see a thing through, been on the slowest, bumpiest and possibly oldest boat in the universe and swum a fair few miles! I'm absolutely knackered but I'm having too much fun to sleep."

"Landscape and Culture it is then, follow me gentlemen." I smile putting on my helmet and heading off steadily towards The Calf which is at the scenic tip of the Island with the added bonus of seals and other wildlife, fun roads to reach it and a superb cafe that Patrick Swayze has sat in whilst filming 'Keeping Mum'. I have always liked the idea that my bottom and Patrick's have occupied the same space, albeit at different times.

I stop off at Cregneash Village on the way down to give the boys a real taste of Manx history. They adore it and take about a hundred pictures of everything. Chatting happily to the volunteers who dress in traditional costume and demonstrate long forgotten crafts and working methods. They get super excited when they are allowed to spin and weave and can barely contain their excitement when they are invited to take charge of a horse drawn plough. Two long haired rock stars in full leathers and bike boots, walking behind two beautiful chestnut shires, ploughing a field really is a sight to behold, there's an abundance of flowing manes. I stand watching, holding three helmets and juggling three phones trying to get some footage on all of them. Their enthusiasm is infectious and I'm having as lovely a time as they are. I finally drag them away and the tip they leave may be enough to buy another plough and several horses.

We get to the Calf and it's really quiet. From tomorrow it will be packed with tourists so I've timed it perfectly. This place would calm the most troubled soul, there is something about the view from here that I find so therapeutic. It's wild and often windy, the sea is turbulent and foreboding and yet the seals play happily in it, showing off to the visitors and to each other. There are lots of hidden crags and coves to explore but it's a little treacherous in bike boots. I show them the views and the seals and take them into the cafe for a cuppa and a late lunch.

They tell me what they want and go to sit by the huge glass window to admire the view. I go and order for us. The young lady behind the counter is extremely excited. She learns forward and stage whispers. "Oh my God! Is that Stefan and Emmett?"

"Nope, they're my mates, Steve and Archie. They get mistaken for them now and again." I laugh. "I don't think they look anything like them to be honest." I shrug then place the order for three lots of fish and chips and two teas and a coffee and leave her looking totally confused. The boys hear and are in hysterics when I get to the table.

"You are brilliant! Do you want to come and be our head of security?" Stefan asks.

The food and drinks arrive and after eating we sit watching the rolling clouds and the swooping gulls as we have another drink and they chat animatedly about everything they have seen so far. They're particularly interested in a large empty house they had spotted and ask me about property prices and tax laws on the Island.

"We better start heading back boys. We're expecting more campers and Steve here can't stop yawning. Sorry guys, I know I'm not great company." I tease, waving a hand at a very sleepy looking Stefan who is stretching languidly.

"Delilah, I apologise, you are delightful company, honey. This place is just so relaxing and it's been a long and eventful day."

"I'll take you back via Port Erin if you can handle a nadgery road and a steep descent." They readily agree and we're off. They make a show of calling each other Steve and Archie on the way out. Using terrible English accents that sounded more like Australian.

"You've dropped your glove, Archie, mate."

"Thanks Steve, I wouldn't be going far without that, mate."

CHAPTER 23

Back at the ranch a lot more tents have been pitched and people are getting settled and barbecuing food. I leave Stefan and Emmett at the field and carry on to the cottage to put The Duchess away.

Dad comes out of the barn as I take my helmet off. "You look like you've had fun." He smiles. Kissing my head he gives me an update on our campers. "We've got five new couples and six guys on their own and they're all sorting themselves and seem happy enough. I've already sold three of the breakfast packs so you'll have to put some more together if you have other orders. I've put Jurgen to work in the barn stripping the top end on the Norton. He's loving it and it's keeping him out of trouble. The racers have rung too, they'll be here in an hour or so. I'm just clearing a corner for them. Joey text five minutes ago to say he's on the way back and starvin'." I laugh.

"Better go and get some food on then. Jurgen, are you eating with us or have you got other plans?" I ask.

"Liebling, Jurgen is gut, danke. I have bought my chef; he is a pervert and a sadist and he will feed me some bird food. Your food is too naughty for me. I must stay beautiful and do not have your clever genes. It is very unfair."

I anticipate that we may have guests so I find my hugest saucepan and start chopping the ingredients for a Bolognese sauce. I can always freeze any leftovers if we do manage to eat alone. When it's on and simmering I put together a few more breakfast packs and in a fit of inspiration as I have a ton of lovely meat from Pat and Will's farm in the fridge, I also make up half a dozen barbecue packs with sausage, burgers, chicken kebabs, steak and lamb chops. As soon as Joey gets in I send him up to the field with them and he comes back sixty pounds richer and with a load of takeaway and alcohol orders.

"Two of 'em want breakfast stuff in the mornin', I'll stick it on ya list. I'll do one beer and food run now and sort the Germans after tea." He grins, scribbles on the notepad, kisses my head, grabs his helmet, a mouthful of cake and my big rucksack and he's gone leaving the barbecue money on the kitchen table. No-one can ever accuse that lad of being work shy! Apart from Joey's take away money which we insisted he keeps despite him being more than happy to hand it all over. We have decided to put all the money we get from the campers in a jar so that we can see if it's all worth the effort at the end of the fortnight. I reach for the jar and add the barbecue money. There's already notes in there from Dad's earlier sales.

A middle-aged couple knock the open cottage door and politely ask if they are allowed on the beach and do we mind if they take some photos of the donkeys. They are both carrying very technical looking cameras and show me some fabulous pictures they have already taken of Jeff being goofy and posing up a storm and Dutch watching the world go by. I ask if they will email me some copies and tell them they're very welcome anywhere on the beach and if they want to take donkey pictures they need to look out for Giles because he's a biter. They thank me for the heads up and ask about the food Joey was selling. I explain what's on offer and they order a breakfast pack for tomorrow and every other morning, a barbecue pack for tomorrow night and picnics for every race day. I write it all down in my faithful notebook which already has preorders from emails and a few extras Dad's written on today as well as Joey's most recent additions. I'm certainly not going to be short of stuff to do and only half the guests are here so far.

I hear Dad welcoming the racers and showing them the workshop, parking up their trailer and then taking them up to the field to set up their camp. Joey comes back smelling like the Chinese takeaway, his pockets bulging with tips.

"We got lots of 'appy campers! I'll go and see to the zoo an' get showered then I need food 'fore I wither an' die!"

"You big drama queen!" I tease. "Donkeys and chucks are already fed, watered and snuggled up for the night. Jeff and Dutch are out on the scrounge but their bowls are full for when the return. Go and get washed and I'll put the spaghetti on. Tell Dad grubs up if you see him."

Dad arrives closely followed by Jeff and Dutch who've clearly been on a barbecue mooch and smell of charcoal, followed by Joey, followed by Stefan, Felix, Connor, Charlie and Emmett, followed by a darling little Japanese octogenarian who doesn't speak a word of English.

"It's your own fault it smells fabulous." Dad shrugs as they all troop in. I better get more pasta on.

"Jurgen's poor chef is having a meltdown so we thought we'd give him a break. He's not used to cooking on a campfire." Emmett laughs. "We we're coming to ask for a restaurant recommendation."

"Chez Dil is the best place in town." Dad tells him with a wink. "As long as you're a meat eater and like spaghetti Bolognese."

"Sounds and smells perfect." Charlie says plonking himself down on the chesterfield.

I quickly chop a load of garlic, mix it with butter and throw some garlic bread in the oven while Joey grates me a big dish of parmesan. We all chat comfortably until it's time to eat. I decide to put everything on the table for a 'help yourself' which everyone quickly does and soon we are all tucking in.

Before and during eating we glean from much sign language, charades and the very limited Japanese that Stefan, Dad and I speak that our little oriental friend, Mr. Tamaki, has actually ridden here on an epic adventure from his home in Okinawa on a twenty year old CB500 via lots of really amazing places and has come over to see the racing as a grand finale before he starts his return journey. His granddaughter had booked our campsite for him as a surprise. He promises to bring his photos to show us all tomorrow night. It looks like he's going to be a regular for dinner.

Stefan and Emmett tell the others about their ride out today and how brilliant it was to go out and not be recognised by hardly anyone and not be hassled at all. They say they cannot go anywhere in the States or Germany without being mobbed and jumped at the chance when Jurgen offered them a camping trip where he said hardly anyone one would have a clue who they were. Felix, Charlie and Connor can't wait to go out now the others have tested the water. They ask if I can take them all out tomorrow. Dad agrees for me before I have chance to speak.

After an assortment of different puddings Joey goes off to get his final orders for the evening and we all head down to the beach to light the firepit, have a well-earned beer and enjoy the last part of the day. I can see the campsite from a distance, the fairy lights and lanterns are starting to twinkle, the fire pits are lit and everyone looks relaxed and settled; Chatting together as couples or in little groups. Jurgen is happily holding court in his part of the camp and waves to us all as we head for the shore.

After Mama Nature has treated us to a stunning sunset of scarlet, ruby, crimson, orange and gold turning to maroons, violets and deep navy blues. Mr. Tamaki thanks us for our company, gives us a little bow and retires to his tent for the night. Joey has rejoined us and is drinking Coke and talking spiritedly to the lads about bike racing in America and why anyone would buy a Harley Davidson apart from an XR750 like Evel Knievel rode.

Dad and I are just sitting back with Dutch, enjoying the idyllic surroundings and the company and chilling; marvelling at the fact that we've got through our first day as campsite custodians without incident. Fourteen more days to go Dilly......

CHAPTER 24

I'm up at five baking bread, cakes and pies and biscuits. They're proving or in the oven and I'm sorting breakfast packs when Jurgen, minus any clothes, sneaks in. "Schnell liebling, I must have a speck sandwich bitte, bitte schon."

I grab the frying pan and get work. I cannot deny any man in need of a bacon sarnie regardless of attire or lack of it. Joey wanders in so I add some extra slices to the pan. He gives me a questioning look.

"He really needs a bacon sandwich." I explain. Dad heads for the shower and doesn't bat an eyelid at a naked Jurgen slicing bread at the table, we've both seen all of Jurgen's worldly goods many times before. I add some more bacon slices to the pan. They all sit around the table shoveling in their sandwiches and arguing about whether red or brown sauce is better.

Jurgen informs us he will be taking his guests for a ride out to several places including the paddock later and double checks his planned routes with us all in case there are likely to be roadworks or closures anywhere. Once the plan is completed Joey goes off to work, Jurgen sneaks back to his tent and Dad goes out to play in the workshop.

I let out and feed the chucks and collect and thank them for the eggs, see to the donkeys and marvel at how much Wonky has grown, kiss Isobel and tell her how clever she is and narrowly avoid a big love bite from Giles. The campsite is starting to wake up and as the first smells of breakfast begin to waft over Jeff and Dutch immediately take themselves off up the lane to see what's cooking.

The racers come down, keen to get at their bike and Dad helps them get it onto the bench and get their toolboxes from out of their van. People start to wander down to collect breakfast packs and to ask about road closures and nearest shops. The lovely photography lady brings down a USB stick so that I can transfer their photos onto my computer. I insist she keeps the money she is trying to give me for the food pack.

Mr. Tamaki arrives, gives me a big smile and little bow and sits down at the table. He is clearly expecting breakfast. I smile and show him an array of choices. He enthusiastically nods a yes to all of his options, so I give him cereal and milk and toast and jam and fry him up a full English. He polishes off the lot, drinks three cups of coffee, gives me another bow and leaves. I like Mr.Tamaki a lot! I wash up, sort all the baking into tins and airtight containers and put the bread in the oven to bake. Emmett comes wandering in, thankfully fully attired, kisses me on the cheek and wishes me 'Good morning'.

"Morning, Emmett honey. Did you sleep well? Want some breakfast?" I ask.

He laughs and sits down at the table.

"Am I that obvious? I truly slept better than I have done in years and I woke up to the most amazing smell of bacon which was pure heaven. This place is unreal. I haven't relaxed like this in .... forever. Stef's Dad isn't half as crazy as he seems."

"It does have an unusually calming effect on people." I agree deciding not to tell him a stark naked Jurgen was sat in the same seat a few hours ago. "Bacon butty or full English? I ask handing him a coffee."

"Bacon butty, please. Your bread is just awesome. And oh my god! How good is that coffee? How long have you all lived here?" I give him a summary of the last few months as I watch the pan and take the bread out of the oven. He is completely astounded. "A few months? Jeez! I was expecting you to say your Dad and grandpa and great grandma were born in this very cottage. I know your family have raced here for decades I just assumed you were Islanders. I've been kind of a TT fan from a very young age but never taken the time to visit until now. You have already made more of a real home here than most people will make in a lifetime!" He shakes his head in wonder.

"Your son is so lucky to have you both and a place like this to grow up in. I'm not looking for sympathy but I grew up in a rich house with everything I asked for but no love or even attention and they definitely had no interest in my career choice. My Grandfather was a stock market man. I only met him once or twice and was expected to call him 'Sir'. I had no relationship whatsoever with my folks at Joey's age. I would have traded for his life any day. He is so confident, clearly loved and has so much love to give. After just shooting the breeze with him last night me and Stef we're saying how together he is and what a great relationship he has with you two and how fucked up and monosyllabic we both were at his age. I heard him take off on his bike this morning singing an old Metallica song and proclaiming his love to the donkeys as he rode past. It really made me smile. Is it too forward of me to ask where his Dad is?"

"I have to take full responsibility for his song choices, I'm usually listening to music and singing along but my repertoire is pretty ancient." I go on to explain how Joey has just kind of ended up here, for which we will be forever thankful and that he's been a real blessing for us but tell him very little of his background. "Was he singing Enter Sandman? It's one of my favourites."

"Yeah, it was Enter Sandman." He confirms. "Oh man! Really? I would never have guessed that. You treat him like your own. You truly have the most beautiful soul." He sighs. "The others take the piss because I am really into spiritual stuff and a great believer in karma and cosmic healing and you guys and this place instantly soothe my whole being. Stef said yesterday he's never seen me looking so calm or having so much fun. I'm usually moody and stressing about everything. It made me realise why I haven't been here before. The right time to come was now. Watching the sunset last night with all of you was the most amazing experience."

"This Island is a magical place. I've moved around a heck of a lot but I've always been drawn back here and I am finally putting down some roots for the first time in many years. Like you say, I just feel the timing is right." I admit with a smile. "Dad and I are strong believers in what Joey jokingly refers to as 'hippy shite', we're down on the beach doing some yoga or meditation or just watching the sun come up most mornings if ever you want to join us. Joey is getting into the yoga and is happy to indulge me when I give him crystals for various situations but he doesn't stay still long enough to learn to meditate yet."

Felix wanders in. "Morning you guys. What's going on here? What time are we going for a ride?"

"Give me half hour or so to get finished off and settle half a dozen imminent arrivals and I'll meet you by the gate. You'll hear The Duchess when I'm ready." I smile, handing Felix a sandwich to go. Emmett gets up to leave and impulsively lifts me off my feet into a big hug.

I hear Felix teasing him and quizzing him as they head back to their tents. "What's going on, old boy? I've not seen you this happy since we played Glastonbury. What have these people done to you?"

Old boy? He can't be more than thirty I laugh to myself. I marvel at how easily bacon sandwiches make a lot of people very, very happy. Unless they are vegetarian of course!

Right on cue I hear the new arrivals heading cautiously down the lane. We are a little off the beaten track and all SAT NAV systems deny our existence so people have to rely on following their instincts or resort to giving us a ring and being talked in. These guys are going on instinct. I walk down the lane to meet them and show them into the campsite, talk them through who, what, how, where and when in my very poor french and leave them to it. Jurgen and the power rangers are just suiting up to go on their adventure and Jurgen is in his element, shouting orders and reeling off the day's itinerary. He waves and blows me a kiss.

We nearly have all of our expected guests here now. The last few will arrive on the slow boat this afternoon. Everyone has plenty of space and there will be room for unplanned arrivals if any manage to find us. I nip into the loo block to check everything is okay and to replace loo rolls and hand soap but it's all clean and nothing is short. I suspect Joey has already checked earlier. I go to update Dad and he ropes me in to sort a fiddly connection on the racers' bike; small hands are a real bonus for a bike mechanic. He says he will get The Duchess out for me while I go and get myself ready. I hear Jurgen and his crew start up and head down the lane with a melodic, roaring wail.

I tidy up quickly, check my notebook to make sure everything is ready for later then pull on my leathers and grab my helmet. I jump on my beautiful steed and head to the field. Emmett, Charlie, Connor and Felix are ready to go.

"Stef is gutted he can't come, he thought he better spend some quality time with his dad. He probably won't see him again for another year." Emmett tells me.

"No worries, I bet he'll have a great day. His dad will show him plenty of places, he knows his way around here. Are we going for the TT tour?" I ask. They all agree so I head straight to Sulby to get us all onto the course. I ride it slowly with The Duchess spitting and snarling and itching to have her head. I pull in at Ginger Hall and check everyone is okay and ready to blow off some steam.

I remind them to stay on the right side of the road, which is the left side of the road and be careful because the locals need a few days before they remember to check for bikes. I tell them to ease off the throttle if they lose focus, use their mirrors, move in straight away if anything wants to come past them and not to worry because I will wait or come back for them if anyone stops. They're all eager to get going so I loosen The Duchess' reins a little. We go at a safe but reasonable speed to the Hairpin. I keep checking my mirrors and they all seem competent enough riders so I take off and let my baby kick up her heels. The traffic is light and we get a superb run.

I pull in at Joey's memorial to wait for everyone and let them see Joey D and the amazing views from up here. Connor is about twenty seconds behind me and Charlie and Emmett a little way behind him followed by Felix. They all park up and pull off their helmets. They are all smiling and hyper. The word 'awesome' is used a lot.

"Lady, you can really ride that beast!" Connor tells me. "I thought I could ride but I barely hung onto your tail and you weren't even trying. I would have been way further back if l hadn't taken your lines."

I laugh. "You all ride really well and you're all here and in one piece which is a bonus. Don't forget I've ridden this course well over a hundred times before. The Duchess can't help herself when we get onto the mountain."

"No fair! I got held up by a truck." Felix wails.

They all take pictures with Joey D, marvel at the 'quaint' mountain train, admire the fantastic views and watch the various nutters whizzing past.

When a group of Americans who have stopped notice the lads and start pointing and whispering to each other we put on our helmets and take off quickly.

We have another wild and clear run all the way down to Hillberry and I stop to let everyone catch up. I check that they want to head to the paddock next and warn them there are speed limits again now. We pootle to the start/finish straight and park up next to Jurgen's beautiful Panigale.

We hear him as soon as we take off our helmets. Then we see him, he's standing up in the grandstand with a captivated audience, recounting a tale of one of his races. He really is a brilliant storyteller.

"See what you're missing? He will always be so much more entertaining and interesting than me." I laugh. "Shall we go up and join them?"

We climb the stairs and Stefan's face lights up when he sees us. Jurgen smiles and waves but doesn't miss a beat on his story. He's speaking German but I remember the race he's reenacting and he's telling a slightly different version to mine but he wouldn't be Jurgen if he wasn't.

I spot Joey, Billy and Rick building up a stage over in the hospitality area and signal to the lads where I'm going. Emmett gets up to come with me. I bet he's thirsty or wants to know where the loo is. I point out Conrod's stand and tell him that's where my wonderful coffee comes from and then point out the toilets as we get to them but he stays with me. He must just want to nose around.

Rick throws a spanner at me. "Tighten that gantry up, Shortarse. I'm sick of smacking my knuckles on it." He points to a lighting set on the floor.

"Daves." Billy acknowledges us but carries on persuading something into place with a big hammer.

"Hi Emmett, 'ow ya likin' the Island? 'Ave ya bought any scran, Dil? I'm starvin'!"

"Meet my extended family, Emmett." I sigh, introducing Billy and Ricky. "They're an ignorant pair of wankers but I do love 'em." I tighten all the bolts Rick's moaning about and get a kiss on the head for my efforts then walk back to the paddock to get them all something to eat. I can hear Jurgen is still in full flow.

"Do you want to head back up to them while I get them some food?" I ask Emmett. "We can all sit down and get something when Jurgen stops for breath."

"I'd rather spend time with you if that's okay? I'll help you carry the food." Emmett says shyly. If he wants to hang around with a little old lady it's fine by me. He's easy on the eye and will save me having to do two trips. We load up with coffee, Coke, pork baps, chips and mini donuts and trail back to the stage. I drop it all in a heap and they swoop in like seagulls.

"Thanks Ma." Joey laughs through a mouth full of bap, shoveling in some chips.

"Dave." Billy acknowledges with a nod. "Coming over yours tonight. Dave's goin' to her Nan's. So I can say fuck and get arseholed."

"Brill, bring beer, we don't have enough to get you arseholed." I laugh and we leave them to it. "See you all later. Love yous."

Emmett and I head back up the grandstand stairs to find the others. Jurgen has finished his performance and they are discussing where to go for lunch. They all eventually decide on the Creg so I call up to check they have room for twenty-two. I ride with them to the pub and then leave them all to it.

"Enjoy yourselves, gentlemen. I'll see you all later. Ride safe!" Emmett is hopping from one foot to the other and looking like he's going to invite me to stay. I take off before he has a chance. I'm not good at small talk and there are far too many people here for me to feel comfortable.

CHAPTER 25

When I get back Dad tells me the last of our guests have arrived and they are all settled and he's written loads of orders on my pad. He looks up towards the field.

"Have you lost something?" He asks, "Didn't you go out with four hairy blokes on rather nice motorcycles?"

"Yep." I laugh. "I've left them up the Creg with Jurgen. He was a far more entertaining tour guide than me. I wasn't even going to try to compete."

I jump off The Duchess, kiss her tank and go to sort the orders and get something on for dinner. I have a strong feeling Mr. Tamaki will be making an appearance and Billy and Sal will probably want something later. Big pot, lots of chopping, loads of lovely spices ....big chicken and vegetable curry, sorted. I make chapati dough and put a big bag of rice on the table to boil later.

I've got fruit pies and crumble and muffins from this morning's bakeathon for puddings and I chop up a fruit salad, check I've got cream and ice cream and make some custard just in case. I put plenty of beer in the fridge and put together the barbecue orders and then tomorrow's breakfast orders. I've just finished when Joey comes in.

"Perfec' timin'!" He grins. "Where's ya rucky? I need to do me grub run." He sweeps up all the barbecue packs, grabs my rucksack and disappears back out of the door.

Dutch and Jeff grace me with their presence for long enough to eat their tea and have a two-minute cuddle and then they're off back to the campsite. They like campers a lot! I fire up my laptop to find that invitation Sal reckons we've got and to put the photos on so that I can give the USB back. I find the invite and print it so that Sal doesn't tell me off. I send 'sorry we're full' emails to the many camping requests without reading them for weirdness.

The photos are absolutely amazing. They have taken some beautiful close ups of all of the donkeys including a fabulous one of Giles about to bite the lens. Wonky looks positively angelic and Isobel looks so proud. They've also taken even more photos of Jeff and Dutch doing their best begging faces, posing, goofing, watching and just being their usual selves. Dutch reminds me so much of someone but I can't think who. There are pictures of all of the bikes lined up and the campsite at twilight with the lanterns aglow and finally some of last night's sunset. I think our photographers have earned themselves free food for the whole fortnight. Dad comes in and we look through them together until Joey comes to join us, he pops the food money in the jar and we go through all the pics again.

I tell Dad Billy and Sal are coming and take the chance to have a shower before dinner. I've just got dressed when Mr. Tamaki arrives with a huge pile of maps and photograph albums and Stefan, Emmett and Felix arrive with beer and wine. I get the rice and chapatis cooking while Mr. Tamaki unfolds his maps, opens his albums and takes us on his incredible journey. We're all so engrossed I burn the first chapati to a cinder and no one notices. Sorry Jeff, the custom is that the dog gets the first chapati but she's definitely not going to want that one! I check the rice and drag myself away from the maps just long enough to serve the meal. I declare that 'dinner is served' and Mr. Tamaki stops immediately and gets himself something to eat. We all tuck in and noisily chat about what he's shown us so far.

Sal and Billy arrive and Ricky and Nathan are with them. I make more chapatis and they all help themselves to curry. Mr. Tamaki resumes his tale and we are entranced. Between us we have travelled to an awful lot of places but Mr. T. has found some hidden gems that we've all missed. His albums are full of azure blue lagoons and cascading waterfalls, empty endless white beaches and all of the lovely, smiling families he's met and stayed with along the way. It gives me a bit of an itch to pack a bag. I see Dad watching me with some concern, he must be able to sense it.

"Looks like we've got some travel plans for the winter, Shortarse." Ricky grins, dropping his arm easily around my shoulder and kissing me on the head. "We'll have to be back for TT 21 though. I've already got stuff booked out." He adds.

Ricky has joined me on numerous previous trips but never instigated one before. Mr. Tamaki must have really inspired him too. We reach the end of the journey to date and Mr. T. gives us a little bow and gets a spontaneous round of applause. I clear away the curry and set out an array of puddings which are quickly devoured. Mr. Tamaki partakes in several desserts, declines the offer of beer, wine or a soft drink, collects his maps and albums and bids us all a good evening and heads back to his tent.

We all spill out of the cottage with our drinks and onto the beach. Billy lights the fire pit and the torches and we all relax and chat together. Sal and I catch up and she tells me all the plans for the presentation evening. She is apparently going to supervise me dressing and put on my make-up. I'm just about to try and wriggle out of it but am stopped by the sight of Jurgen in loud Hawaiian shirt and pristine white slacks heading towards us at great speed.

"Sally, Sally, schöne dame. I have missed you so much. Come to Jurgen now!" He grabs her and is the perfect height to bury his face in her chest. Then he frantically shakes hands with Billy and Ricky. "It's been too long! I miss my big Manx boys so much. Mein Gott! Nathan is a big boy now too.

He is very beautiful like his mama, ja?" He gives Nathan a hug and then drops down dramatically next to the fire. "I have been so busy today; we must all have a rest day tomorrow."

Ricky laughs. "If only! We're going be flat out for the next three weeks. I'll be lucky to see a race."

"Fuck that, Dave." Billy snorts pointing towards Joey and Nathan. "Me and the boys have devised a cunning plan. Well Dave has cos he's clever like his Mam. 'E's written all the work rotas to make sure we'll be in the right places at the right times."

The racers have finally emerged from the workshop and come down to chat with Dad and the photography couple have walked up from further down the beach. Everyone is cheerfully chatting and laughing, discussing and arguing so I wander down to the seashore with Jeff running ahead, a very round Dutch sitting on my shoulder and my beer in my hand. I sit down on my usual rock and watch the waves rolling and the birds swooping.

"What is it you English say? A penny for them?" I turn to see Stefan offering me a fresh bottle.

"Thank you." I take the drink and move over for him to join me. Dutch peers out of my hair, sniffs him, huffs and settles back down. "I actually wasn't thinking about anything for a change." I laugh quite surprised at the realisation. "I'm usually analysing everything, chasing the past, running away from the past or worrying about the future when I sit here. Today I'm just watching waves."

Stefan clinks his bottle to mine. "Here's to watching waves! That's a good title for an album. You looked so peaceful I didn't want to interrupt you but Emmett sent me over. He keeps telling me how amazing you are and that I need to get to know you."

I arch my eyebrow at him. "That boy needs to get out more if he thinks I'm amazing. I'm an old, boring, out of touch, selfish, scruffy little commitment phobe who only talks about hippy shite and motorbikes and runs away at the first sign of trouble." I laugh. "I think he likes what he sees as a family. Poor lad, he said he hasn't had much of a relationship with his Mom and Dad. He doesn't realise we are really just a bunch of screwed up misfits who just 'work' together because this Island has magical powers. It has definitely gotten a hold on young Emmett. You all seem really close as a band, that must be like having family surely?"

"He's not seen his folks since forever. They weren't too impressed with his choice of career or wife and they never even met his kid. The band is our family."

"I'm glad you have each other. It's sad that he hasn't had support from his parents." I sigh. "Mama and Dad have always been there for me. I couldn't have got this far without them. We've always been close even when we were miles apart. Dad's the one that dragged me here and begged me to make a go of it. I was still searching for something that, I have to admit, doesn't exist. I nearly suffocated poor Joey when he first arrived here because I was so desperate for... I don't know what...maybe someone to love?" You're seriously oversharing here Dil, change the subject. "How's it going with your dad? "

"He's a crazy guy but he really has a heart of gold. I was so shocked when the lawyers told me about him. I thought it was just some wily old buzzard trying to get a few dollars out of me. I never even considered that my dad might be German. I knew Mom grew up there but it never occured to me that she could have been pregnant before she arrived in America. Jurgen was being kind when he said Mom was a singer; she performed in the Hamburg clubs and had a bad heroin addiction. Jurgen sent her to America to get clean. He paid for her rehab and her apartment and got her some auditions. She got straight before I arrived and did really well as a backup and sessions singer. She did a lot of voice overs and commercials, they loved her husky accent. She never told him about me or me about him and I never asked." He sighs and continues. "The 'big c' took her a couple of years ago. I don't know why but I suspect Jurgen already knew about me because he knows plenty of details about my career and a few doors opened early on; surprisingly easier than we expected especially in Germany. Many American bands struggle to get a break into Europe, we had no problems at all. This vacation is really good. I'm getting to know him a little but I doubt we'll ever be as close as you and your Dad."

"Jurgen is a good, kind and considerate man, he's extremely intelligent and ingenious even if he comes across as completely bonkers." I tell him with a smile. "He will always be there for you now he's found you. He's been a good friend to Dad and I and helped us through a lot over the years. We have many fond and crazy memories of escapades with him and I wouldn't have The Duchess if he wasn't so generous and I'll love him forever for that."

"Emmett's right, you do have a beautiful soul." Stefan sighs.

"Why didn't Emmett bring his wife and the little one with him if he misses home so much? They could have stayed in a hotel if she didn't fancy camping with a small child. Jurgen wouldn't have minded, surprisingly he's actually great with kids. Billy only keeps Sarah away from him because he spoils her rotten. He bought her a new motocross bike last time he was here."

"Little one? Small child? Hang on how old do you think Emmett is exactly?" Stefan looks at me as if he's just had a revelation. "In fact, how old do you think any of us are?"

"Oh lord, don't ask me that. I am rubbish at guessing ages." I groan. "I don't want to insult you all."

"You won't insult me at all." Stefan insists. "I'll even give you a big clue - two in fact, think about how old my Dad is and remember we live in LA."

"That's no help at all!" I whine. "I don't want to think about it but I'm pretty sure your dad has been sexually active for at least the last half century and I'm ashamed to say I know absolutely nothing about Los Angeles apart from it's mentioned in one of my favorite Chili Peppers' songs."

"Jeez, Delilah, you are such an innocent." He laughs. "Dad was about twenty when he met my mom and I am intimately acquainted with one of the best plastic surgeons in Beverly Hills, she's actually my wife." He laughs. "Charlie and Connor are our kids, my sons."

I am rendered speechless. My little brain is trying to fit everything together and make sense of this revelation.

"No way! You look the same age as your kids! I thought you were a band, all around the same age, mid twenties to early thirties. Oh wow! That means Jurgen is Connor and Charlie's granddad." I giggle. "I bet he's really happy about that but not quite ready to admit it just yet."

Stefan laughs. "I think the boys we're more concerned than he was to be honest but they're fine with it now. Okay, stop stalling, tell me how old Emmett and Felix are."

"Do they also know your wife?" I ask, playing for more time.

"Yes, they know her very, very well, she is actually Felix's godmother."

"So are Emmett and Felix brothers? I know Emmett is going to be the eldest because Felix called him 'old boy' this morning."

"Nope, not brothers but you're right Emmett is older than Fe."

"I would guess they are in their late twenties to early thirties but don't tell them if I'm wrong."

"You are way out." He giggles, clearly liking this game a lot. "Felix is the 'little one', he's twenty-four."

"So was I at least closer with Emmett's age?" I'm determined to get one right.

"Oh honey, you are so funny; Felix is 'the little one' The 'small child'." He makes air quotes with his fingers to exaggerate his point. "He's Emmett's one and only son. Emmett was forty-seven last month!"

"You're joking?" Bloody hell I'm pretty sure I look at least twenty years older than him. Can you introduce me to your wife?" I giggle.

He laughs and hugs me. "You are an incredibly beautiful woman Delilah, inside and out and my wife would tell you so too."

Dutch sticks his head out of my hair and fixes Stefan with a gaze then sneezes and disappears back in.

"He's actually checking my facelift." Stefan laughs. "That cat is the strangest guy I've ever met. I've seen him at the campsite. He's always watching someone or something."

"Talking of strange guys, shall we go back and join the others?" I say, standing up and readjusting Dutch.

"Yeah, Emm will be wanting to know what we've been talking about." He laughs and holds out a hand to pull me up. We head back arm in arm and I can't help but smile when I look around at the group of very special people on our fabulous little beach.

"Are you alright, Shortarse?" Ricky asks, glaring at Stef and looking concerned. "You want another beer?"

"Yeah, honey, I'm more than alright how about you?" I say, leaning down to where he's sitting and kissing him on the head. "I'll go and make some snacks for everyone, you hungry?"

"Always." He drawls and follows me into the cottage to help. "What did the pretty boy want? You looked like you were having a proper giggle."

I tell him what we were talking about and he's amazed.

"He's around the same age as us? Never! We definitely need to invite his wife over next year."

I agree and then we get chatting about Mr. Tamaki's trip and reminisce about some of our own adventures as we plate up sweet and savory muffins and toast and pate and cheese and crackers together with an array of pickles, chutneys, crisps and fruit. We carry the food outside and are mobbed by the vultures.

Jeff brings more wood in exchange for cheesy crackers and Dutch finally climbs down from my shoulder and curls up by the fire. Joey and Nathan are talking bikes, sounds like they're deciding what bike Joe should buy when passes his test. Emmett and Felix are animatedly recounting their run over the mountain to Stefan. Dad, Jurgen, Billy and Sal are catching up on the last few years and the latter are getting steadily hammered.

I sit down by the firepit next to Ricky and lean against his solid side, he drops a big comforting arm around my shoulder and hugs me tightly. I close my eyes and relax, listening to the chatter of my ever-extending family, the sound of the gulls and the gentle lapping of the waves. Life doesn't get much better than this!

CHAPTER 26

Sunday lie in? Not a chance! Campers are down for food and bread and information and tools to sort minor bike niggles. Mr.Tamaki arrives with a smile and a bow and devours another full English plus toast and jam. Jurgen arrives with his clothes on, thank goodness, declares that as today is a rest day he can eat whatever he likes and also tucks into a full English, toast, cereal, muffins and some apple pie and custard left over from last night and then heads to the beach to sleep it off taking a mug of coffee with him. Joey goes off to work and tells me they'll be watching first practice at The Sulby Hotel and me and Dad should try and get there. Dad grabs some toast and tells me he's off to the paddock with the racers to show them where everything is and get them through scrutineering and then he's meeting up with Paddy Mac and the lads to help them out. I tell him Sulby for practice if he can make it.

"It's just you and me, guys!" I tell Jeff and Dutch but they have other ideas and march off to the campsite. Just me then. I have another crazy baking session, put up more food packs, ring Pat and Will to catch up and order more meat, ring Sal to see how her head is; she's fine and far too interested in who Emmett, Stefan and Felix are and what Stefan and I were talking about so I fib and tell her my cakes are burning and put the phone down. I feed the chucks, feed the donkeys, nip up the campsite and clean the showers and loos, empty all the bins, tidy the cottage, change all the beds and put the washing on and eventually plonk myself down on the chesterfield. Wow, I suddenly realise I have time to do what I want.

I get my overalls on, tie my dreads back, stick my cap on and get my spanners out. The Norton engine is sat on the bench and Jurgen has been doing a great job on it. I double check everything and it looks like it's nearly back together. I pour a bit of paraffin in to check the valves but the paraffin runs through so one isn't seated properly for definite. I whip them both out and the valve seats are looking a bit pitted so I find some grinding paste start to regrind them. I'm just doing an impression of a fire starter, twisting one quickly in the seat to smooth it off when Felix puts his head around the door.

"Hi, Felix. Are you okay? Do you need something?" I ask.

"Nope, just nosing around." He admits. "I was coming to get a proper look at your Ducati."

"Have at her. She's there." I point. "Keys are in." This is one of the many joys of the Manx way of life. Keys stay in ignitions and homes are never locked.

"What are you working on?" He asks looking over at the Norton engine.

I tell him what it is and all about its racing pedigree and he listens closely. Then he wanders over to see The Duchess.

"Wheel her out if you want to start her up. She shakes the walls in here and fills Joey's room with fumes." I laugh pointing up to the mezzanine.

"That's Joe's room? Can I see? He said he had a real cool room."

"It's nothing special but I'm sure he won't mind if you take a look." He runs up the stairs and peers in through the doorway.

"That's awesome!"

I laugh "I bet your wardrobe is bigger than that at home."

"I can't remember, it's that long since we've been there." He sighs, half-jokingly.

"Have you been touring for a while? I bet your mom's missing you both." He looks at me as if he's deciding whether to tell me something.

"She moved her new boyfriend into the house last year. She said we were never home and she was sick of being on her own. She got off with a guy she met at the gym. We've not been home because we can't really. We've been staying in hotels mostly." He shrugs as if a weight has just lifted a little.

"Oh, sweetheart, I'm sorry for asking, I thought your Dad loves it here so much because he's homesick."

"I think it's more because this is the kind of home he wanted for us but he was on the road all the time and she was spending everything he made and constantly moaning when he wasn't there and just as much when he was. She was never a homemaker when I was a kid. I saw the babysitter more often than her. I couldn't wait to join him in the band as soon as I finished school and she was more than happy to have me out of her hair. I guess Dad remembers his own childhood and wanted better for me. We're kind of in limbo right now. The two weeks here will be so special and then we will have to move on."

I hug him, partly because I have no solution for him and partly because he really needs a hug. He stays in my arms for a few minutes gathering himself together.

"Wow. Dad and Uncle Stef are right, you have magical healing powers." He laughs.

"It's this place not me." I confess and try to lighten the mood. "You're welcome to take The Duchess for a run but to be truthful she's a handful if you're not going as quick as she wants to."

"She's awesome and I'm honoured that you trust me to ride her but I'll pass. She sounded real angry when you rode with us yesterday. I'd like to think I could handle her but I'm not so sure."

"Where do you keep your bikes when you're on the road?"

"We have bikes in LA but the ones we're on here are all Jurgen's. As soon as he'd talked us into coming here he dragged us into the nearest bike shop and made us choose what we wanted. He's one crazy guy!"

We are interrupted by the photographer lady who asks politely for her food pack as they are planning to eat early and then get a good spot for practice. I give her the food and her USB at tell her how grateful we are for the fabulous pictures. She says she took a load more yesterday and will add them to the stick and return it tomorrow. I refuse to let her pay for the food and she goes away happy.

"Can I see the photos or are you too busy?" Felix asks. "I'll fetch Dad, I know he'll want to see them."

I wipe the grinding paste off the valve and wash my hands. Sorry Mr. Jeavons, I did try to do a bit.

Felix comes back with a smiling Emmett in tow. I turn on the laptop and put the photos on slideshow while I make coffee. I hand Emmett a mug.

"Coffee or Coke, Felix?" I ask.

"Coke, please." He turns to his Dad and teases. "Coffee is for old folks." I immediately burst into a fit of laughter.

"Don't encourage him, he's so rude!" Emmett sighs loudly, giving Felix a look of disappointment. After my talk with Stefan I am now seeing them in a completely different way. The father/son dynamic is very evident. I can't believe I didn't see it before.

"I'm sorry, I can't help it." I giggle. "That was the very first sentence Joey uttered to me."

We look through the photos and I tell them how Jeff and Dutch and the donkeys came to be here and about Wonky's arrival and the chickens and bantams. They humour me by listening quietly and asking questions here and there. My phone pings to say I have a text; You comin Sulby? I'm ordering food X It's from Ricky.

I excuse myself and text him back 'on way in 5. Fish n chips x'

"Where are you going to watch practice? First night is always worth watching." I ask Emmett hoping he will take the hint. They're both really lovely but I want to be with my family for first practice.

"Jurgen has an itinerary for the week but I can't pronounce most of the names." Emmett laughs. "It's Cronky something today."

"Cronk y Voddy." That's a good spot, you'll see plenty of action and there's a burger van there so you can get something to eat and drink too. What time were you planning on leaving because roads close soon?"

Emmett looks at his watch. "In about six minutes." He grins. "Better go, thanks for a real fun afternoon." He bends down and gently kisses my cheek. "I really want to spend some more time with you before we leave."

"Thanks for the chat and the Coke." Felix says and gives me a big hug.

"Thanks both of you for the great company. See you soon. Ride safe."

I grab my helmet and jacket and throw my rucksack on. I shout for Jeff and Dutch and they amble down the lane. I give them treats and tell them I'll be back soon and fire up The Duchess.

I park up at the back of The Sulby Hotel next to Joey's bike and text Dad. He says he's helping the Macs in the pits and won't make it. Joey comes round to meet me with two pints of lager shandy.

"'eard ya comin' from 'ome." He grins handing me a pint. "Gramps's text, 'e's with the Macs."

"Yeah. I just heard, have you bagged a good spot out the front? Rick and Bill are handy for making space." I giggle.

"Yep we gorra table. Ricky's ordered the scran. Come on, I'm starvin'."

It's packed out the front as it always is on practice and race days. It's a popular spot because the road is straight and fast. The bikes come past really close to the barriers at speeds of nearly two hundred miles an hour and take your breath away. I can't wait for Joey to experience it. We sit down and the food arrives. The boys tell me about their day and where they have to be for the rest of the week. The barriers go up across the junctions and the roads are closed.

I love this time, it's surreal. Suddenly the roads are empty and everything is quiet. You can hear the birds singing and usually the TT Radio commentary on the radios in the crowd. Everyone waits in anticipation. It's roughly twenty miles from the start line so you hear them set off on the radio and then it's still and quiet as you wait and then you hear the scream and roar as they approach with the exquisite noise bouncing off the solid buildings that line the roads.

When we hear the first guys set off I tell Joey to go and stand by the barrier. Billy makes a space for him and stands protectively behind him; he knows exactly what's coming. I stand next to Joe and lean back onto Ricky's wall like front.

The first group of bikes come into view and Joey cranes over the barrier to see them coming. As soon as he does they fly past us seemingly inches away. He swears lots and jumps back into a chuckling Billy's waiting arms.

"Good here init Dave?" He grins.

"Good job Sarah's not here with her star chart." I point out.

"Ya could 'ave warned me!" Joey laughs holding his chest.

"Now where's the fun in that?" Ricky asks.

We watch the rest of practice noisily laughing, teasing and tormenting each other and listening to the radio commentary for lap times and speed trap stats. We make predictions on who will be first, second and third in each race next week and wave and scream like loonies whenever Paddy Jr. comes past.

Ricky and I are just messing around as usual, he's busy weaving my dreadlocks in between the barriers and I'm standing on his toes and climbing up him to get a better view. He finds an interesting lump of goo in my hair.

"Dutch snot?" I query.

He sniffs it and rubs it between his fingers. "Nope, grinding paste, coarse grain if I'm not mistaken." Now that's the sign of a real man.

I overhear Billy and Joey talking;

"....yeah, Dave we know...our Mam and the Missus say they'll get married when they finally grow up. The daft twat's followed 'er round the fuckin' world but won't admit why. She's too busy chasing ghosts and he's too saft to kick her arse about it."

"'E better do a Beyonce an' 'put a ring on it'" Joey laughs. "The vet and at least one of our campers is in the queue. Sienna'd give 'er right arm for wha'ever magic she's got an' she ain't gorra clue. Gor enough time an' love for everyone an' everythin' but she don't think she should get any back!"

"Yeah, he's already got an eye on the pretty boys. We'll have to be careful cos she'll do a fuckin' runner again if any of 'em make a move. Gotta keep her here this time, we don't wanna lose her again."

"Oh shit, don't say that, it's took me sixteen years to find me proper 'ome. I can't do without 'er."

Being the dense little person that I am, it takes me a while to realise they're talking about me and about Ricky. Serves you right for eavesdropping Delilah Blue! Now what ya gonna do?

CHAPTER 27

I do what I always do, panic and run like hell! I stay long enough so that they don't know I've heard. They'll be upset if they think I've heard them. Well Joey will. Billy will just tell me it's my own fault for listening. I disentangle my dreads and go and get another round of drinks. I make my excuses after about half an hour. I'm so glad I got to see Joey's reaction to the racing here.

"Oh no! I better go. I bet Mr.Tamaki will be expecting dinner and Dad won't be back until they open the roads so I better go and check on the campers. I'll see you all later. Love you. Ride safe. Enjoy the rest of practice." I jump on The Duchess and ride back to the cottage.

When I get back every single one of our campers is out watching practice, including Mr.Tamaki. I go and have a chat with the donkeys for a while and make sure they're fed and watered then I have a talk with the chickens and the bantams. They give me lovely eggs in return for their dinner and some extra hay but not much advice. I would have thought chickens would know a bit about relationships but they're not sharing. I go and clean out the, already clean, showers again while no one is using them and restock the fire pits.

Jeff and Dutch are mooching around the campsite and come to find me when they hear me banging about. I feel bad that they've got no-one to talk to so we go back down to the cottage so that I can feed them and give them some attention. I can't find anything else to do, my list is all sorted and I can't settle so I head for my rock taking them both with me.

The roads won't open for another hour or so. I wander down to paddle and Jeff runs through the waves around me. Dutch growls at the edge of the water until I pick him up onto my shoulder. I walk aimlessly along the beach trying to get my head straight. So what? So what if the vet likes me? Why is it a problem? He's nice enough, we can be friends. Sal says he's been on his own a while. He must be lonely. Everyone needs friends, even me. Do I? Haven't I got enough friends already?

I am absolutely positive Emmett does not like me, specifically, he likes our lifestyle but he could not be part of it, he's in a rock band and tours all over the world for goodness sake! He's not interested in me at all! He's probably got much younger and sexier ladies throwing themselves at him at every opportunity. Oh, and let's not forget, he's also married!

Ricky, my darling Ricky, is family. What's that awful saying that always makes me laugh, he's 'my brother from another mother'. Rick and Bill truly are my family, my best friends, my brothers, the best friends anyone could have but nothing more.

I'm perfectly fine with relationships, I get on great with them and Dad and Joey and Sal and.....Why the hell was Billy fibbing to Joey? He was winding him up wasn't he? He is a proper wind-up merchant. Bloody hell Delilah! You're getting in a right flap over nothing. Because Dad was teasing me the other day when the vet was on the phone about the donkeys that's made Joey think the vet is interested, Emmett is a friendly guy and Joe has misread him because probably Sienna would say a man fancied her if he was friendly and Billy was just winding him up about Rick. There, sorted! All bollocks and I'm worrying for nothing.

These menopausal hormones are really screwy. I need to find something herbal that'll help with the madness going on in my head. I realise I'm talking out loud and haven't even reached my rock yet. I'm marching around the beach like a crazy woman. It's a good job everyone is elsewhere, they'd think I'm losing the plot. Okay, it's all sorted. No one fancies anyone, least of all me. Dutch looks around from my shoulder, fixes me with a very hard stare, boxes me in the middle of my head with his big orange paw and disappears back into my hair.

Okay ...let's start again. Dad definitely teased me about the vet so Joey thinks..... I go round and round and each time Dutch lets me know he doesn't agree. I give up and go and plonk myself down on my rock. Dutch actually gets down and faces me, glaring in pure frustration. Jeff comes over and sits beside me.

"Come on guys give me some help!" I implore. "What's going on with my head?"

Jeff gives me a big lick on the face and looks at me with her huge soppy head on one side. I give her a big hug and she leans onto me with her wet, sandy coat smothering my face. We sit quietly for a few minutes. I have a little cry but I don't need to. It just makes me feel better.

"Thanks Jeff, that helped a lot. I did just need a hug. You're a very clever girl." I laugh, wiping my eyes and nose on my sleeve and then tickling her behind the ears. Dutch harrumphs like he's really disappointed in me, sighs loudly head butts me in the chin and whacks me in the middle of my eyes as if to say 'Think, stupid!'. I choose not to, Jeff therapy will do fine, this time. It was all stuff and nonsense and I've overreacted. Think about just how ridiculous you're being Delilah! Who the hell would be attracted to you? I laugh at my own arrogance, a vet? A famous rock star? Who are you kidding, you silly old woman? Have a word with yourself!

Jimbob used to describe me as 'weird and wonderful'. He saw something in me that no one else is likely to ever see or be attracted to. We fitted perfectly together, I've found and lost my soul mate. They just haven't found theirs yet, I'm sure they will soon enough. I don't think any of them will have 'weird' on their list of qualities to look for in a potential partner.

I hear some bikes coming back towards the campsite. "Thank you for your patience, guys. I really love you both so much." I kiss Jeff and Dutch and we walk back up to the cottage to see who needs feeding.

I've just made a big bowl of salad and cooked some lovely fresh mackerel when Mr. Tamaki arrives. Dad and Joey come in a few minutes afterwards.

"Okay, Dil?" Joey asks looking really concerned, "Took off like ya arse was on fire. Ya missed some good fly bys."

"I'm fine, darling." I smile. "I was just a bit worried about the campers. Stupid really, they were all out watching practice. I'll stay 'til the end tomorrow."

"Promise?" He asks. "It ain't the same without ya."

"I promise unless we have a major drama here. I'll even bring a picnic if you like." I laugh handing him a plate. "I assume you want another dinner."

"Too right!" He sits down with Dad and Mr. T. and they all tuck in, catching up on their day with chat, mimes and drawings.

I slip quietly back into the workshop, close the door and finish grinding valves. Dad's made the new wiring loom and it's all routed in the right places on the frame. It's not complex as there's no lights or indicators to worry about. It's got a brake light and electric start though so Mr. Jeavons may have had it on the road at some time. I rebuild the head and recheck for leaks. It's fine this time so back on it goes. I reattach the downpipe and am gently persuading the surprisingly sound exhaust back into place when Joey comes in.

"Perfect timing! Pass me that bracket, sunshine." I say pointing to the bench. "I daren't let go of this bugger, he'll never line up again."

He hands me the bracket and the nut and bolt to secure it and holds the pipe in place for me.

"Is it ready for starting?" Joey asks.

"Only if you want to wake the whole campsite and fill your room with poisonous gasses." I laugh.

"Na, not really." He grins. "Are ya sure you're okay, Dil? You 'eard Billy earlier dint ya? I was only jokin' to 'im about you an' Ricky behavin' like an old married couple."

"Don't take any notice of Billy, sweetheart. He loves telling tales and winding people up. I'm surprised Rick didn't punch him. Hopefully he didn't hear him. I'm pretty sure Ricky's got no plans for settling down with anyone, least of all me and I've had my chance already." I change the subject. "Were you off to bed now? I'll pack up and put the lights out down here. I bet you're feeling knackered with all your early mornings."

"Eh, I'm really lovin' workin'. I'm really lovin' everythin' 'bout this place. Why d'ya think ya only get one chance? I'm on me second one already and I'm only sixteen an' me second one is a million times better than the first." He gives me a knowing look, kisses my cheek and goes upstairs to bed.

"Shut up, Dutch." I groan at the silent, fat feline that is looking askance from the workbench.

CHAPTER 28

I'm wide awake at four am so I take the chance to watch the day arrive. Down on the beach its chilly and misty but the wind is moving the clouds on quickly and it's promised to be dry enough for tonight's practice even if we have a couple of showers in the day. I've bought the fishing rod with me to replenish our stocks. I cast my line and, in my head, start planning a picnic for practice tonight. I can test out some of the ideas I have for the race week picnics for the campers. Everything needs to travel well in a rucksack and stay fresh all day so that's excluding lots of stuff unless I buy some cheap cool bags and freeze cool packs or drinks to keep everything else cool. Good plan Dil.

Pat should be dropping off a delivery of fresh meat this morning which will see us to the end of TT fortnight and I'll ring and order some veggie and salad boxes from the farm shop in Peel. I must get our veg patches in the garden planted up. The herbs are doing great. The bits for the bike services should turn up this morning too so I can get those in and done. They are for a husband and wife who had the brilliant plan of putting one bike in for service at a time so they can still go out together on the other one.

As soon as I start to catch some fish Jeff and Dutch appear to check the quality. They share one between them and come back for seconds. Joe comes wandering down the beach towards us.

"Morning, sweetheart. Did you sleep okay?"

"Eh Laa, I always sleep great. That's a magic bed, that is." He grins. "Want a bacon sarnie? I'm just goin' to do one 'fore I gerroff."

"No, thanks darling, I'm good. I'll have something with Mr. Tamaki in a bit."

"We'll be watching from the bottom of Barregarrow tonight so don't be late. Bring food, Billy said there's no scran van there. Ya will come won't ya?" He asks looking worried.

"What's bothering you, darling? I'll be there complete with a large bag of food."

"Feel bad about last night." He admits. "I'm just scared I'll lose ya when I only just found ya."

"Don't be, you daft sod. I'm not going anywhere. I love it here with my kooky new family as much as you do." I laugh looking at Dutch and Jeff eating all my catch. "Even those two reprobates! I'm not going to run away, no one fancies me, no-one wants a relationship with me and everything is fine. Stop worrying it's bad for you."

"Promise?"

"Yes Joey, I really, truly, honestly, hundred percent promise. Stop worrying and go and feed yourself. Take whatever snacks you want for work as well, there's plenty in the larder and the fridge."

He hugs me and kisses me on the head and hugs me some more. Soft lad! He runs off back to the cottage with Jeff and Dutch behind him.

"See ya later, Ma, love ya loads!"

I stay to catch a few more fish to replace those Bonnie and Clyde have pinched then I see Mr. Tamaki on his way down from the campsite. I pack up and meet him at the cottage door.

"Ah breakfast?" He asks looking at me to see if he's said it correctly.

"Yes, breakfast. Would you like fish?" I wave them at him.

"Hai." He gives me a little bow.

We feast on fresh mackerel and poached eggs and bread and butter. He doesn't seem too upset about having mackerel for tea and breakfast. He's such a lovely, happy man. Dad joins us and eats half a loaf of bread and jam. Once he's had his fill and polished off three cups of coffee Mr. Tamaki thanks us and leaves.

"Cheers for rebuilding that head." Dad says between mouthfuls of bread and jam. "Did you check the wiring? Had I missed anything?"

"No and nope. I have every faith in your skills. I don't need to check it." Dad is a brilliant mechanic and I'm really pleased he's been back down into the pits. He was always our chief mechanic when we raced unless he was racing himself. He lost a lot of confidence after Marley got killed even though the crowd and marshals confirmed Marley swerved to avoid a hare that ran out of the hedge and couldn't have done anything to save himself. Nothing was found to be mechanically wrong with the bike. Dad went back to spannering but always wanted me to double check whatever he'd done.

"Is she ready to start up?"

"I suppose so. If you've checked everything." He laughs. "What's up with our Joe? He was muttering something about you leaving yesterday. Are you running off with the band or the vet?"

I groan. "Oh no! Don't you start! Billy has been winding him up about Rick now and you haven't helped with your daft vet comments! I'm not running off anywhere with anyone. No one except you and Joe would want me or could put up with me. I think you've all had too much sun. Let's go and start that Norton."

"Whatever you say, Dilly Girl." Dad shrugs. "Tell us if you're not happy though, we'll sort it together, eh?"

"I'm happier than I've been in nearly thirty years. I'm going nowhere and I'm trying to put down some roots, like you asked me to. I'm contented enough with the company I have. Leave me be you silly old bugger! Come on and get this bike going."

We push the Norton out of the workshop and get the tank back on, connect up the last few pipes and cables, put some fresh fuel in and offer up a prayer to the god of motorcycles. After half a dozen kicks she roars into life. We play about to get her running just right and Dad calls Mr. Jeavons. He revs the bike down the phone.

"Name that tune!" He laughs. Mr. Jeavons is clearly a happy man from the shriek of delight. He tells us he's on his way and puts the phone down. By the time I've dealt with a few camper queries, most of whom have really just come down to admire the Norton, and got the coffee brewed he's arrived with his trailer. We start her up again and he rides up and down the lane a dozen times with a grin that makes the Cheshire Cat look positively grumpy.

"I can die a happy man now!" Mr. Jeavons exclaims.

"We'll hear no talk of dying." I chide. "Dad didn't do all that work for you to go off and pop your clogs!"

"Okay, I'll hang on and put some more miles on her first." He agrees. "Sadly, I'm running out of mates to ride with now, they're all getting old and dying on me. I think that's why I'm getting a bit maudlin. I'm so grateful, I can't believe you managed to get her running again, she sounds even sweeter than I remember. What do I owe you? Do I need to remortgage the farm?" He jokes.

"No. There's no charge at all. It was a pleasure to work on her." Dad says. "You already paid in straw bales when we were having the donkey drama. You really helped us out. Whenever you want a riding buddy I'll be more than happy to come out with you."

Mr. Jeavons looks like he might cry. I'm pretty sure they're happy tears. He pumps Dad's hand for almost a whole minute.

"I've got mates all over the Island with old racers in their barns. You fixing their bikes might give them a new lease of life. I'll be sure to send them all your way." He promises.

"That's good enough for me." Dad replies and helps him to load up the Norton.

Dutch comes out for a nose and Mr. Jeavons is shocked to see him.

"Good grief is that old Ned's cat? There can't be many about that look like him. Bloody hell he must be about twenty years old by now." We introduce Dutch who is now up on my shoulder and ask Mr. Jeavons to fill us in on anything he knows about him.

"He used to hang around in that old farm next door to me. He always seemed to be waiting for someone but the place had been empty for years. Don't know where he came from, he just appeared one day. He got on great with Max, my dog but would never come into the farmhouse. Old Ned came to visit me in the worst of the winter about ten years ago, took pity on him, caught him in a box and took him to his place. He seemed contented enough but Ned said he never really settled, was always looking for someone. Ned loved his company. He named him Seeker, said he was a wise, intelligent soul and spoiled him rotten. Poor Ned died last winter. I went to look for the cat but couldn't find him anywhere. I never thought to ring Nina. I half expected him to find his way back next door. Looks like he's finally found who he was looking for. Don't know why he thought you'd be down at Old Scaard Farm though."

CHAPTER 29

I get all my chores done before I start to bake some meat pies and fruit muffins and sweet and savoury scones and then start putting together a picnic for later. I have no idea where this love of cooking and baking has come from. I seem to have been possessed by Mrs. Beeton since moving here. I've always loved to eat but never been much of a cook. Dad's always made bread and Mama constantly made fabulous meals and cakes. The cooking genes must have finally surfaced. I make some pasta salads with tuna and chicken to see which travel best. Pot up some jam and clotted cream for the scones and a big pot of butter. Make up a cheese board of every cheese I have in the fridge. I freeze some little bottles of pop and juice to try out my cooler theory.

Sal rings to check I'm still going and says she's taking Sarah so she'll pick me up at five. I'm about to argue I'll take The Duchess but she says Sarah wants me to wear my matching outfit and then puts the phone down on me. Eh? Since when did Sarah even care if she or I was wearing anything? Oh well! I can pack more picnic now.

Dad comes in and samples everything on the table and says it's all great and he's coming to watch too if we're having a picnic.

"Mr. Jeavons was happy enough. Hopefully it'll get us a bit more work in. Oh and those service parts have been delivered." He chats whilst stuffing his face. "Weird that he knew Dutch. Perhaps he's here for a reason."

"Everyone knows everyone on this Rock." I laugh. "He's here for a warm bed, lots of food and his best mate, Jeff. Didn't they need you down the paddock today?"

"No, they're fine, I've told them to stop messing with a perfectly good bike." He grins. "I said I'd go down on Thursday if they need me. I want to see a bit of practice with my family. I'm already miffed about missing first night at Sulby."

"Hang on I forgot I've got Joey's reaction to the first bikes on the phone." I mooch in my rucksack and find it for him. It's so funny and we are both giggling and reminiscing about going to places the first time when there's a knock at the door. It's Emmett looking for some barbecue meat.

"Jürgen's chef is cooking some strange eggplant thing; the boys are refusing to eat it. They've lit the fire pit and sent me to find some meat. You sound like you're having fun."

"It was Joey's first time at Sulby." I explain handing him the phone and going to get the meat. "He wasn't quite prepared for the speed and close proximity." He watches and laughs.

"Jeez, that dude knows some bad words! It is awesome though. I was amazed and we were nowhere near as close. Where is this?"

Dad explains how to find The Sulby Hotel and tells him a few more close spots to watch.

"Where's Jurgen taking you all tonight?" He asks.

"I can pronounce it tonight." He laughs, looking at me. "We're watching from the grandstand at the paddock. Are you going to come along?"

"Not tonight, son. We're meeting the mob down at Barregarrow." Dad says. "But we will come with you later in the week."

"Do you want some bread?" I ask handing him the meat. "It's still in the oven I can bring one up in ten minutes. It'll be there before your food is cooked."

"Yes please. That'll make them real happy. I can wait if you want."

"No, it's fine, me or Dad can bring it over. You can get your meat cooking. We've got to come and arrange a service time with another camper." He thanks us and reluctantly leaves.

"That's cruel!" Dad teases. "He wanted to stay and chat with you. He's got his eye on my Dilly Girl."

"Don't start, you stirring old sod! He's a bloody rock star, what would he want with a scruffy little nomad?" I laugh, throwing a tea towel at him. "Go and play in your workshop. Sal will be here about half four." I put everything in the fridge ready to pack, get the bread out of the oven and cut some chunks of butter. I slice the bread and wrap it in foil and head up to the campsite.

The photographer gives me another USB full of photos for which I am extremely grateful. The services are booked for tomorrow and Friday morning. I tell them they should be ready for practice. Jurgen gives me a wave and blows kisses but is deep in conversation with some very corporate looking men. Emmett, Stefan, Felix, Charlie and Connor are joking around by the fire.

"Hey Delilah, how's it going? Cheers, honey." Stefan greets me and takes the bread and butter. The others say 'hi' and go back to watching what's cooking.

"Hey gents! How was practice last night? Did you enjoy it?" I ask.

"It was awesome. I can't believe how quick they go on the first night. They're real crazy guys. We're off to the paddock tonight. Are you coming?"

"I can't tonight, we're meeting Joey and the mob. Where are you watching tomorrow?" He shrugs and looks at Emmett.

"Hillberry, I think." Emmett replies. "Is it good there?"

"Yeah, it's a great spot. One of my favourites. It's where we stopped when we had that run over the mountain. You can see them coming all the way down from the Creg and you can get food, which is always a bonus." I laugh.

"Where you waited for us to catch up, you mean? Come tomorrow and I'll treat you to dinner." Emmett smiles.

"Cheeseburger and hot chocolate. How could I resist? I'll see you guys later. Enjoy your evening. Ride safe."

I shower and change into my 'Sarah' outfit. It's soft and comfy and fits okay, I can't decide if the pretty pastel colours clash with the bright ones in my hair. Accept it Dil, you have absolutely no fashion sense whatsoever, you're wearing an outfit designed for a ten-year-old! I'm just packing the picnic when Sal and Sarah arrive.

"Auntie Dilly!" She dives at me in filthy motocross gear. "I haven't been to school and I played on my crosser all day at the farm. I can do the big jump one handed now and beat Granddad Will in a three-lap race because he's getting old."

"Go Sarah!" I exclaim and high five her. Without a single acknowledgment of my outfit, she runs off to tell Dad and round up Jeff and Dutch. I pack everything in Sal's boot, settle the campsite cleanup crew with treats they probably don't need and grab my jacket. Dad jumps in and we're off.

It's quite a trek from the parking to the best viewing spots so we all grab a food bag each and climb over the fence into the field. We hike down to the bottom and bags the best spot with a big picnic blanket. Joey and Nathan arrive but say Ricky and Billy have had to go and sort a generator down at the paddock and might not make it. After Sarah has interrogated them both with regard to where they've been and how many times they have used swear words, the boys are allowed to settle on the rug. They are about to start on the picnic when Sal intervenes.

"Hang on a minute!" She swats them away. "Let's set it out nicely on the rug." Hmm...We have never stood on ceremony with food. Something fishy is going on here....

I happen to look up at the road and see the vet going by in his Land Rover, he turns into the lane towards the parking area. One minute later he is heading straight for us. Head slap Dil! You've been set up good and proper. Is it just Sal's daftness or is Billy and everyone else in on it?

"Good afternoon everyone. It's so lovely of you to invite me. I usually hide away during TT fortnight; this is a real pleasure." Ian shakes hands with Dad and the lads, Nathan knows him already and introduces him to Joey.

"Ah, you're the gentleman I need to persuade to take over from me one day. Delilah has spoken a lot about you and I hear you're a natural with animals." Joey looks a little confused and I do too, I'm pretty sure a couple of sentences doesn't constitute 'a lot'.

Sal has set out the picnic like a banquet for the queen.

"Food everyone!" She announces in her best Mrs. Bucket voice and Sarah and the boys dive in.

"Hello, Granddad's cow man. Why are you here? Are there poorly cows here?" Sarah asks Ian. I love her logic.

"The only poorly cows are on your sandwich, sweetie. Ian's come to watch the motorbikes like we have." I tell her.

"No he hasn't!" She insists with hands on hips. "He doesn't like motor-bikes, he told me when I said he could ride on mine at the farm."

"He must have come for the food then." I shrug, palms up.

"That's more likely. It is good scran." She tells me and I roll my eyes at Joey who is giggling his head off along with Dad and Nathan.

"I am indeed here for the food and the very charming company." Ian laughs, raising his glass to us all.

We eat, drink and chat and Sal entertains Ian. When the conversation inevitably turns to bikes and racing I remind Dad of the time a bee hit me in the chest coming through this section. I thought I'd been shot. The pain was ridiculous. Dad laughs and recounts the tale to the boys and also the one about when the seagull pooped down the back of my neck. I argue that it was definitely a pterodactyl! Whatever it had been eating ran all the way down the back of my leathers and into my boots. It was gross and it happened on the first lap so I smelled pretty ripe by the time I'd finished the race. We're all giggling at Dad who's telling tales about all of us in various races when Ian asks Sal, "Does Delilah ride a motorbike?"

Sarah is incensed, she jumps up, hands back on hips. "My Auntie Dilly is the bestest and fastest motorbike rider on this whole island. She is the fastest lady round the TT course! How can you live on this Island and not know that?"

"Sarah, darling, Ian doesn't like motorbikes so he won't know about the racing. Not everyone outside of our crazy family has a bike obsession." I explain.

"Well that's just odd. Why would anyone not like motorbikes?" She looks perplexed. "Everyone I know loves motorbikes."

"I know sweetheart, but we're all raving bonkers." I laugh. "Come here, quick! I can hear them coming." She runs over and climbs onto Dad's shoulders to get the best view. Ian comes and stands beside me.

"I'm so sorry Delilah, I'm afraid I've never followed the racing at all. How very rude of me."

"Ian, you don't need to apologise. Sarah has a four-year old's outlook on life, it's not quite as wide reaching as that of a grown up." I laugh. "There is no earthly reason why you would know anything about me beyond the fact that I am crap at donkey rearing."

"On the contrary, your donkeys are extremely well looked after. All of your other pets seem happy too." He counters.

"They're not pets, they're family." I reply immediately without thinking.

"How many pets do you have?" Sal asks. " I bet you bring home plenty of waifs and strays in your line of work."

"I actually don't have any at the moment. I live alone and work all hours; it wouldn't be fair to them." Then, seeing our surprised looks, animals are a very, very close second on our list to motorbikes, he adds. "We have a couple of cats at the surgery and I'm very much planning to get a dog when I get chance to cut back my working hours."

There's a break in practice as someone has broken down and spilled oil on the circuit so we all sit back down and graze on the leftovers. Sarah gets out her notebook and pen and looks us all over. Oh, oh! What's coming...

"Okay, we're going to play Blind Date. What's your name and where do you come from?" She asks Joey, pen poised.

"My name's Joey err...Blue an' I come from Jurby." Joe humours her and grins at me.

"Okay, hello Joey. I can hear an accent there, where were you from before?"

"Dingle, near Toxteth but don't tell the ladies it'll put 'em right off." He laughs.

"Okay, you're funny, girls like that." Sarah tells him. "Tell me what your perfect woman would be like."

"She needs to be a boss cook, not be a meff, 'ave her own bike an' ride like a demon!"

"Ha, that's easy you can marry me or Auntie Dilly!" She tells him. Sal snorts and side eyes me; I think I might meet her definition of a 'meff'. I throw an empty drink can at her.

"That's an impossible choice. Can I marry ya both?" Joey asks, kissing her on the head.

"Nope, don't be greedy!" She tells him. "Okay, Granddad Dylly. What's your name and where do you come from?"

The game goes on, Dad is told he must marry Sarah's teacher because she needs looking after. Sal is told she should marry Billy which is quite convenient. Nathan is told he will shortly be marrying Beyonce which he's quite looking forward to.

"Okay, Auntie Dilly, what's your name and where do you come from?"

"Hello, Cilla. My name is Delilah Tallulah Tinkerbell Rainbow Blue and I come from Jurby."

"Wow, that's a good name, all the boys will like that." Sarah tells me earnestly.

"Who's your perfect man? You can't say Uncle Jimbob because he's dead so you can't marry him." She orders, rolling her eyes. Out of the mouths of babes...

"Patrick Swayze. Oh no I can't choose him either can I. Can I choose Granddad Dylly, he pretty perfect?"

"No! You can't marry your Dad, silly. What good things would you want a man to be like?"

"He needs to be kind and funny and patient and sexy and love my family and all sorts of animals and ride a bike like a demon." I laugh at my own honesty.

Sarah makes some notes in her book. "Okay, I'll get back to you. I have one or two people in mind but I need to find someone just right so that you don't run away again." Hmm, interesting....this kid really has been here before.

"Okay cow man, what's your name and where do you come from?" Ian realises there's no way out and gives in with good grace.

"Hello Cilla, my name is Ian Anderson and I come from Andreas."

"Hello Ian, what would your perfect woman be like?" He pretends he's thinking, rubbing his chin theatrically.

"She needs to be friendly and happy, good with animals even be able to deliver baby animals, cook nice cakes and make super picnics and have a name to remember." We all wait expectantly for Sarah's proclamation, some of us wait a little more anxiously than others.

"That's easy! You need to marry Nana Pat but Granddad Will won't be very happy about it."

We're saved by the bikes restarting. We run back to the hedge and I spend an enjoyable hour explaining to Joey the best line to take through this section and why some guys take different lines, where the bumps are and what slows you down.

Dad chats happily with Ian about the donkeys and his job and camping and building the cottage. Sal is on the phone to Billy and Nathan is sitting a short way away; all giggles and blushes on his phone with a mystery caller. Sarah is busy with her notebook chewing her pencil in concentration and listening out for swear words.

Practice comes to an end for another day so we tidy up what's left of the picnic, which is a little bit of food but mostly empty boxes and bags. We collect up all of our rubbish, fold up the rug and start trudging towards the car park.

This is the worst bit of racing; closed roads mean you can't go onto the circuit until the 'roads open' car comes by. Often we know back roads and can get to most places but this one is a pain so we pack the car and wait. Joey and Nath go off up the back way to meet friends. Joe gives Sarah a big hug.

"Goodbye, my future wife, see ya soon, love ya." He laughs and does the same to me.

Nath hugs us all and tells his Mom he'll be up the Creg if Beyonce calls.

"Ride safe boys, love you." I say as they take off up the narrow lane. The roads open and I say bye to Ian.

"Thank you for inviting me I've really enjoyed myself. Sarah is gorgeous and the lads are so polite and the food was amazing, hands down beat my Shoprite meal for one I had planned. I'll call you later in the week maybe we can arrange to do something together."

"Next week will be really busy. I'll let you know when it calms down." I say, trying to be polite but vague. He kisses both my cheeks and gets into his Land Rover. I jump into the back seat of Sal's car.

"Is there anything you've forgotten to tell me, Sal?"

"Nope, don't think so." She grins knowing she's safe whilst Sarah is in the car.

CHAPTER 30

W e're all eating breakfast and showing Mr. Tamaki some nice spots to go and see on his new map. The Island has loads of beautiful glens with waterfalls and wild garlic and meandering pathways. Spooyt Vane is an amazing waterfall in Glen Mooar. Glen Maye has mesmerizing waterfalls and a walk down onto the beach. There is an abundance of greenery, calming water, soothing woodland and beachside walks on this Rock. Our chat reminds me of at least a dozen places I want to show Joey. Mr. Tamaki polishes off a huge breakfast, thanks us profusely and leaves to go exploring.

"We'll show you all the best glens when TT is done, Joe. Me and Dad'll find some bikes for green laning. You can't beat a ride round the green lanes followed by a picnic in a glen, apart from Glen Helen where you get eaten alive by midges." I tell him. "Jurgen and his crew are going to Hillberry to-night. Can you make it?"

"Sounds boss. Should get to Hillberry easy, ya bringin' scran? Are Felix, Charlie an' Connor comin'? I ain't 'ad chance to catch up with em."

"Yep and nope, we're having carpet burgers off the van. Everyone is coming as far as I know. Emmett is buying." I laugh. "Be careful if you're parking in the field, it gets slippery. Want some food to take to work?"

"Yeah please, got anythin' left from last night? That pasta stuff was boss."

"You're lucky Rick and Bill didn't come, there's a bit left." I put the plastic container and a fork in his rucksack with some fruit and muffins and crisps.

"Cheers ma. Who invited the vet, last night? 'E's a bit of a divvy. Don't think our Sarah liked 'im much." Joey giggles.

"She was a bit rough on him." Dad agrees with a smile. "He was a bit serious though and he's planning to steal our Dilly away. He was asking last night if the cottage was mine or Dil's and whether me and you would cope if she moved out. Not sure about him at all. He seems way ahead of himself with his planning. She hasn't gone out with him and he's plan-ning on moving her into his place." Joey looks as concerned as me.

"Sal invited him and I will definitely be having words about that when I see her next." I growl. "Are you going to stop encouraging me to date now, Old Man?" I laugh. "I only attract strange men."

"Oh, we're only just getting started Dilly Girl." Dad teases. "Plenty more to choose from and we haven't even heard Sarah's suggestions yet. My money's on the American." I stare at him in disbelief.

Joey grabs his rucksack and helmet and kisses my head. "I'll marry ya any day, Delilah Blue. See ya both later, love yas."

Dad disappears somewhere so I get the washing on and chores done in the cottage and up at the campsite then I get my overalls on and start servicing that bike.

It's only an interim service so I do an oil and oil filter change, check and adjust the brake calipers, pistons, cables and levers, see if the wheel bearings are worn, check the state of the chain, re tension and lube it, check the sprocket, check the battery and electrics and see if the tyre pressures are right. I clean and grease everything that needs it and then get to the best bit, a road test. It runs like a dream and feels fine so it goes back to its 'mom'. They are just about to go out so my timing is perfect. The lady thanks me and say they'll transfer payment into my account. A pleasurable way to make £120 and it's not even nine o'clock. I might give them a discount on the second one. Jurgen sees me and comes running over for a big hug.

"Liebling, you are irresistible in overalls. You are coming to Hillberry tonight, ja?"

"Yes, if we have no dramas here. What have you been up to?"

"Meetings, work and planning. They do not leave Jurgen alone. Always pecking at my head. I bring them here for team building and they still want always to work."

"These guys are your work colleagues? I thought they were biking mates."

"Nein, Jurgen must work all the time. I have no friends anywhere but here. I don't like it!" He stamps his foot like a petulant child. "I tell them I am coming here and if they want me to work with them they must come too. They're just lawyers and accountants and dickheads from NASA and damn stupid Government agent men from lots of different places. I make them learn to ride motorbikes and camp in tents. They will do anything for a bit of Jurgen's brain." He laughs bitterly. "I want to retire now. I will stay here and work no more after racing is over. You must choose a house and make it into a home for me and the American boys. You can spend whatever you want. My people will sort the paperwork if you tell them what to buy."

"Wow, okay. Whereabouts do you want to be? Do you want a garden? How many bedrooms? Have you got a rough budget? When do you want to move in?"

"Anywhere is good, everything is close on this Island. I want a garden and garages and a pool and a beach, maybe. I need room for Stefan and his family, ja? and Emmett and his family and me. I want to move in after next week is finished. You can spend five, six, eight, ten million... or more... I have lots." He shrugs and kisses my cheeks. "I knew you could sort Jurgen, danke. I must work more now, love you, bye."

I have never had such a deep, non-sweary conversation with Jurgen and certainly wasn't expecting to have to add 'buying a house' to my 'to do' list today but I'll go and see what I can find.

Back at the cottage I fire up the laptop and look at a few estate agents' sites. I'm sure there's no shortage of empty luxury homes for sale over here. I see half a dozen amazing places that fit Jurgen's very brief, brief. I ring three different agents who are only too happy to oblige when I tell them what I'm looking for. They quickly arrange for me to see three suitable properties today and three tomorrow. My first being just down the road in half an hour. I ring Sal, totally forgetting I'm mad with her about the 'Ian' thing.

"Are you busy? Do you want to come and have some fun and spend a huge about of Jurgen's money? Bring the car and dress business like." I laugh and put the phone down.

I go and put on my plain but posh dress I bought the other day, write all of the names and appointments in my notebook and wait at the end of the lane for Sal. She arrives within a few minutes wearing a smart, navy pin-striped suit. Perfect, let's go shopping!

I fill her in in the car on the way to the appointment. She's totally up for it. We arrive at property number one which is described as an idyllic country retreat with outstanding rural and hill views set in approximately 9 acres of private mature landscaped gardens. The agent greets us as we get out of the car. He looks me up and down with some disdain and heads straight for Sal.

"Mrs. Blue, so lovely to meet you, I'm Arnold, we spoke on the phone. I'm delighted to be able to show you around....." Sal holds up a hand to stop him.

"This is Ms. Blue." She introduces me. "I'm Ms. Parker, her personal assistant." Poor Arnold is now seriously flustered and I'm struggling not to laugh.

"Oh my goodness, forgive me Ms. Blue. Apologies for the misunderstanding. Please let me show you around." He guides us through the huge, imposing front door into a large hallway. "This property comprises of a formal lounge, dining room, informal or second lounge, a fully equipped office, an open plan kitchen leading into a well-appointed conservatory. We have 5 bedrooms, 3 of which are en suite and two further bathrooms......"

I zone out Arnold's spiel, the property is massive and spacious and spotless and it feels totally impersonal. I suddenly realise how difficult this might be. My idea of a perfect home is the cottage; small, cosy, a little shabby, personal and well 'homely'. This place is full of cream leather furniture, cream walls, cream carpets, cream curtains...you get the idea?

Thank heavens I bought Mrs. Bucket.

Arnold is still droning, "To the rear of the property is a full-sized tennis court, a state-of-the-art gym and a temperature-controlled wine store and cellar. There is also a number of outbuildings which could potentially be converted into garages and guest accommodation."

"So there is no guest accommodation and no garages?"

"Er.. no, but plenty of room for both, subject to planning permission, of course."

"Is there a pool?" I ask. "I did say I wanted a pool too, didn't I?"

Poor Arnold is already aware that I'm not showing a great deal of interest and is getting redder and redder.

"I'm sorry, no, but there is plenty of room for a pool but not one here currently. I'm sure planning permission for that wouldn't be an issue." I fix him with my best Paddington 'hard stare'.

"Can you guarantee me approved planning permission and a fully working pool by the end of next week when, as you were informed during our lenghty conversation, we would like to move in?"

"I'm afraid not, Ms. Blue." Replies a very peevish Arnold. "Would you like to see the lounge?" He strides towards a room off the hallway.

"No, I don't think so, thank you." I tell him politely. "I shall only be wasting your time as this property doesn't have a number of things that I requested." Sal looks at him as if he's just beaten her puppy and we stomp back outside to the car. She drives away and we have to stop in the lane because we're giggling so much.

"It's actually quite shocking that you can still get shite service even if you want to spend ten million quid." I say to Sal. "I had a full discussion with that bloke and told him everything this morning. He obviously didn't have what I wanted so thought he'd just show me his most expensive property. Next one's in Andreas, we're close enough to Ramsey so head to Conrod's for a cuppa."

We sit down with coffee and cake and do a bit more research on the next place. It's a sprawling old three storey farm house which has been seriously modernised with three garages that look like aircraft hangers, outbuildings, a pool and jacuzzi, a gymnasium, six en suite bedrooms and two guest cottages. There's land all around including some woodland and spectacular sea views. The only thing missing is a private beach but it has a lake and a pier which looks pretty impressive. It sounds very promising and looks more homely from the photos.

We get there five minutes early intending to have a good mooch around outside but there is already a very nervous young lady waiting for us. She looks as if she should be at school and is wearing her mum's shoes. She approaches at an impressive speed for someone in those heels, as we get out of the car.

"Good morning ladies, I'm Ella. I'm so looking forward to showing you around this beautiful property." She spouts enthusiastically. I'm just thinking oh no, not another one...then she turns around to lead us inside, drops all of her paperwork, falls off her high heels and bursts into tears.

"Oh god, I'm so sorry, I'm so nervous. I've never been in a place like this in my life! I only started this job on Monday. The boss is off sick today and I was in the office on my own. He's going to fire me and probably kill me when he finds out I've lost him the chance of a ten-million-pound sale." She wails, sitting in the driveway, surrounded by paperwork. Poor little darling! I sit down next to her.

"Shall I tell you a secret? I've never been in a place like this either and I sure as heck can't afford one. We're shopping for a very busy but very wealthy friend." She looks up and sniffs.

"Really? You're not going to tell him?"

"Why would I do that?" I get up and hold out my hand to pull her onto her feet. "Come on Ella, me, you and Sal here can go and check this place out." She jumps up and wipes her eyes on her sleeve.

"Please can I put my trainers back on? I'm going to kill myself in these stupid shoes."

She opens the front door and we're in a lovely big hallway with a huge antique mirror on the wall, there's an old-fashioned coat stand and a solid pine dresser. The place is saying home to me already.

"Is this place actually empty?" I ask with some concern. "I did say he wants to move in next week didn't I?" She's really done her homework and replies.

"Oh yes Ms. Blue, that's why I suggested this property. It's got everything you asked for and the owners have moved abroad recently and are hop-ing to find a buyer who will be happy to keep all of the furniture. I figured you wouldn't be able to completely refurnish a place this size in a few days so you'll have stuff when you move in and can change it in your own time. If you don't like anything we can arrange to put it into storage for you. The other property I've chosen for you to view is completely empty but does have all the things you asked for apart from the beach. This one is a little bit nicer too and looks much better on the brochures." I want to kiss her! She's just made my job so much easier.

"You are an angel! Thank you for being so clever. Come on then, show us around and call me Dil."

"To be honest I've never been in here so I don't really know where any-thing is." She shrugs.

Sal hugs her. "Do you want to marry my son? I like you a lot. Let's explore together." She opens a door into a huge living room with a beamed, full height ceiling and a fire place big enough to live in. One wall is completely glass and looks out onto an immaculate garden and a beautiful, huge lake. We all stare outside and go 'Wow!' at the same time. The furniture is brown leather and oak and looks relatively new. A television the size of a cinema screen is mounted on the wall next to the fireplace and there's a panel for lots of state of the art electronic twiddling apparently. The glass wall continues throughout the house which makes it light and airy. The whole place is amazing and really is fully furnished. The beds are still made. It's ideal and I hope Jurgen will like it. I text him to see if he can talk. He rings back immediately.

"Liebling! Have you found our new home? I will zoom you now." He puts the phone down and sends some strange codes on a text. Ella saves us because she knows what he's on about and has the required app on her phone. We 'zoom' him and I turn the phone to show him the garden and lake.

"Perfekt, buy it now!" He squeals, "Where is it?"

"Andreas, less than twenty minutes from us." I run around like a crazy woman, showing him different rooms and views. "There's garages, an indoor pool and jacuzzi and a huge hot tub and another pool outside and you have two nice cottages for visitors you don't want in the main house." I laugh, "And it's fully furnished so you can just move in and haven't got to get anything."

"Delilah, wunderschöner engel! Who is agent? I will tell my lawyer now to send money. Love you, bye." I tell him I'll text the agent's name and number and he's gone. Ella has completely drained of colour and collapsed on a sofa.

"Oh My God! Have I just sold a ten-million-pound house? I can buy a new bike."

"Looks like it, sweetheart." Sal says, "But I'll probably be a little cheaper once the lawyer gets involved. I'd let your boss sort that bit as long as you'll still get your full commission. Did you say bike as in motorbike? You can definitely marry our Nathan."

"Yeah, I passed my test last week. I got the job to save up for a big bike. I think I'll get enough commission to buy one straight off." Ella laughs. "Please introduce me to your son, I'm more rubbish at dating boys than I am at selling houses. Oh no, talking of selling houses you're booked for another viewing; did you want to go and see it just in case?"

"No, thank you. I make most decisions on hunches and feelings and this place feels right. I'm sure Jurgen will be extremely happy here." Ella's phone rings and she has a little panic.

"It's the boss! Do you mind if I answer it?" We insist she does and he sounds like he's a very happy man. He says the price has been agreed and the contracts are being sorted on both sides. She dances are around the room, hugs us both, says thank you a hundred times and then leaves to go back to close up the office for the day. We tell her we're watching practice at Hillberry if she wants to come along. She says she'll definitely be there as her luck in the boyfriend department may improve given her good fortune so far today.

Well, it's not every day you get to spend millions of pounds before teatime!

CHAPTER 31

Sal drops me at the cottage and I find Dad, Jeff and Dutch in the workshop playing with a lovely little KTM.

"What's with the dress?" He looks worried. "Have you been to the doctors?"

"No, you barmy old sod, why would I put on a dress to go to the doctor? I've been spending millions of pounds of Jurgen's money. Who's is the bike?"

"Your Mama always put a dress on to go and see the doctor. I don't know why. Maybe she fancied him." He laughs. "Have you bought him a race team?"

"Nope, a very large house down the road. He's planning on moving in next week."

"That's nice, hope we're his closest neighbours else he's going to get arrested for exhibitionism and indecent exposure within a week. The KTM is yours for green laning, she'll be good with a little bit of work." I kiss him on the cheek, tell him he's the best Dad in the universe and run inside to get my dress off.

I run around feeding and checking everything and take Mr. Tamaki a big cool box containing a chicken salad, bread, fruit, drinks and some scones and clotted cream and jam in case we go on somewhere after practice. Everything is quiet at the campsite which means I probably need to get a move on.

"Are you ready, Old man? We need to get going."

"Yep, Jeff and Dutch are settled. Just gotta get my hat."

We have a slow, congested run over to Hillberry, The Duchess is not amused. We arrive as roads are closing and park up next to Joey and Nathan's bikes. I've got two missed calls from Joey and Ella and a text saying Sal can't make it. We wave to Joey because we can see him, ring Ella and tell her where to meet us and walk down to the front fence. Ella arrives as we do and is swept up in all the multi-national hugs and kisses and hellos without freaking. Jurgen has all his posse with him and she even manages a few words of German, asking how they're enjoying the racing and the Island.

Jurgen gives me a big hug and kisses me half a dozen times. "Liebling, my new home is so sexy and beautiful. It's everything I wanted, you are very clever girl, ja."

"This is the clever girl." I tell him, introducing Ella. "She chose it for us to look around. It is a lovely place, I'm sure you'll be really happy there."

He hugs and kisses Ella. "Bella Ella, danke schon. You are very clever and cute you can come to stay whenever you want."

Ella thanks him, if she's at all concerned that a crazy old German guy just invited her to stay at his house she hides it well. This girl is really going to fit in if she stays around. Then I do see a reaction; her eyes go wide and her jaw drops, I look up to see Emmett, Stefan and the boys heading for us. Emmett sweeps me into a big hug.

"Delilah, I thought you'd stood me up!" He exclaims.

"Carpet burgers and hot chocolate, are you joking? I'm not getting a better offer than that." I laugh, hugging him and then Stef. "Ella, you look like you might already know the guys, this is Stefan, Connor, Charlie, Felix and Emmett and those two over there are mine and Sal's, Joey and Nathan."

"Um... hello." She shakes hands with the band boys shyly then looks up towards the others and smiles. "Oh wow! It's Nathan from school, how are you doing? I haven't seen you in ages." She runs over and hugs him and he introduces her to Joey. Connor, Charlie and Felix join them and they're all chatting like best mates in two minutes. Emmett takes hold of my hand and pulls me a little way from the crowd.

"Let me know when you're hungry, darlin'." He says. "In the meantime sit and talk to me all night. I want to really get to know you before we have to leave." I shrug.

"There's not much to know really, what you see is what you get. I'm not a complicated woman by any stretch of the imagination; a scruffy little wanderer who loves bikes, loves animals, is not so keen on people but have to admit I am getting a lot better at that. I love my family, love being by the sea, love ..."

"That's why you're so awesome! You have so much love for everyone and everything. How many people could just go out and buy a house, no, a home, for someone and choose so perfectly? We went to see it on the way here, Jurgen said Felix and I can stay in one of the guest cottages whenever we want and treat it like our own. The place is exactly what I would have chosen if I was looking. In fact, when I am ready to buy here I'm going to be roping you in to help me."

"I'm pretty sure I haven't bought it and Ella did all the ground work. Sal and I just went and liked it and thought Jurgen would like it too." I say. "To be honest it was a lot easier than I expected. Are you really thinking of buying a place here? Won't it make travelling a bit more difficult?"

"That's another example of how amazing you are, not many people would invite their estate agent out after one viewing." He shakes his head. "It shouldn't make much difference for travelling, the airport is quiet here and we have our own plane. The tax implications of living here are quite favourable according to Jurgen's accountant."

"Sal thinks Ella should marry Nathan, that's how she got invited." I giggle. "That and she's completely lovely and can ride a bike. She's buying her first big bike with her sales commission." We look over at the young-sters and they are all relaxed and chatting together, no-one is hogging the limelight or being left out. It's so good to see Joey at ease in a group with multi-millionaires. They're teasing and jostling and, good na-turedly, taking the pee out of each other.

"It's great to see Felix acting his age. He doesn't get to relax much and only really sees Charlie and Connor. He doesn't have any real friends out-side of our bubble, lots of his old school and college mates back in LA are either jealous of his success or want to bum money from him or both. I hope he'll stay in touch with Joey and Nathan. He commented yesterday that they never let him pay for their drinks."

"I don't think you need to worry about that. Joe thinks they're all great especially Felix, I'm sure they'll stay in contact, him and Nathan are the sweetest, kindest and most thoughtful kids I've ever met but I suppose I might be a bit biased." I grin.

"I love the way everyone just treats us like normal people here. No one is interested in what we are but they're willing to get to know who we are. Even though Ella looked like she'd dropped her bottom jaw when she saw us she's just talking away like she's with her mates now." Emmett muses watching them all laughing together.

"It's a real pet hate of mine when people ask 'what do you do for a living?' as soon as they meet you as if your job defines you." I cringe. "It's as if they're deciding if you're worth talking to. Over here they are more likely to ask who you think is going to win the racing or what you want to drink." I add with a laugh.

I look to see where Dad has gone and spy him deep in conversation with Jurgen and Stef, he looks tanned and chilled, Island life really suits him and I'm so glad he bought us back here.

Suddenly, we hear the bikes coming over the mountain and we all move swiftly to the fence. I climb up to get a good view and Emmett stands pro-tectively behind me as if he's ready to catch me if I fall.

The practice, and ultimately the racing is amazing from here, you can see them coming right down the hill from the top, they're closer together during practice and fighting for the best lines. As they come around the corner from the Creg they pick up speed and race the final sector back to the start and finish line. They are all chasing the ultimate lap time. That currently untouchable hundred and thirty-six mile an hour lap. The course is split into 6 sectors for the racers. This is the final sector. Close enough to the pits to test every component to the limit without the danger of being trapped out on the course and losing valuable practice time if you manage to break something.

Joey comes over and I talk him through the best lines, he's interested and is taking in everything I'm saying, he's going to make a good racer. A group of newcomers flies through taking some very dodgy lines and then it goes quiet, we hear the helicopter take off and red flags come out to signal practice is halted. This is a horrible time; someone has had an accident but we have to wait to find out when and where. Dad walks briskly over to give us a bit of reassurance.

"Paddy Jr. and our campers were in the last but one batch to pass us and the helicopter is heading for the Gooseneck so we know both of them are fine." He looks down quickly as his phone pings. "Mr. Jeavons is up there, says it's a newcomer and he's up and moving. They're airlifting him to Noble's now." I relax and let go of the breath I didn't realise I was holding.

"Must be burger time then." I announce. Emmett holds out his hand and I willingly take it, leading our merry crew to the catering van. The kids ask for hot dogs and burgers and chips and drinks and all get served and go back to sitting on the grass. Dad, Jurgen and Stefan get pork baps and coffees and sit at one of the picnic tables. It sounds like Stefan is being treated to some stories of what they have got up to together over the years. Emmett orders us double cheeseburgers, chips and hot chocolates and leads me to another table.

"You've lost friends here, haven't you? You went so still and pale as soon as you heard the chopper. Your Dad was there before I had chance to react." Emmett asks softly.

"I lost my whole life here." I reply, more to myself that him. "Oh, good grief! That makes me sound like such a drama queen, please ignore me." I shake my head at my overreaction. "We lost my better half and my little brother. Both happened a long time ago and I should have learned to cope with it by now."

"Tell me about them." Emmett says gently. "Please."

"Marley is my younger brother, there's only a couple of years between us. He was a superb rider, really talented. He started racing here as soon as he was old enough and was doing well. He'd done four successful TTs and got onto the podium. He was a favourite to win the lightweight race that year but a hare decided to cross over just before Waterworks and Marley swerved to avoid it and had nowhere to go. I was only a little way up at the Gooseneck, the next corner, holding a pit board telling him; he was leading on lap 2. I heard the crash and the helicopter. I knew it was Marley but I couldn't get to him. He broke his neck badly as he hit the wall and died instantly." I wipe away my tears on my sleeve. I sense Dad watching me so I smile across to let him know I'm okay.

"Jeez Deliliah, that must have been hard on you all. You raced again after that didn't you? It was a brave decision to continue." Emmett says, reaching out for my hand.

"Racing is in our blood. We'd talked as a family about what we would do in the event of one of us getting hurt and always vowed we'd keep going. Mama didn't race much after Marley died but she still rode every day and never asked any of us to stop." Emmett says nothing but squeezes my hand.

The practice starts up again and I am thankfully spared from talking about Jimbob. We walk back to the fence. Emmett stands behind me with his arms around my shoulders. He kisses me on top of the head gently. It feels comforting and I lean back into him.

"Where's the best place to watch another spectacular Island sunset?" He asks.

"Peel, Niarbyl or our beach." I reply.

"Will you come with me to Peel, please? When practice is finished. I want you to myself for a little longer."

Paddy Jr. goes by and we all cheer and wave. He looks like he's making good time and he's smooth around the bend. It gives me a minute to process his request. What's the worst that can happen, Dil? You like him, you have some fun, he leaves, everything goes back to what passes for 'normal' here. I haven't actually been romantically involved with anyone since Jimbob died, ridiculous I know, but getting close to someone else feels disloyal and ... stop it stupid! Have fun, walk away after next week, no harm done. I'm not going to get many chances to meet a famous rock star that likes my company, or anyone else for that matter. He's married so he's not looking for anything more. Life cannot stay on hold forever.

"Delilah, will you come?" He whispers.

"Only if I can have an ice cream." I reply trying to make it sound less intimate.

He kisses my head again. "You can have as many ice creams as you want, little darlin'."

Practice comes to a close and they announce over the radio that the newcomer has a broken wrist and ankle but is doing well. Joey and Felix let us know that they are all going up to the Creg for food if they can get a table and down to Laxey if they can't. I ask Joe if he needs money but he says he's got plenty. I hug them all and tell them to 'ride safe'. Ella gives me a big hug and thanks me for inviting her then runs off after the boys. I notice it's Joey waiting for her, not Nathan. Dad tells me him, Stefan and Jurgen are heading into Ramsey for a Chinese meal and ask if we want to go with them.

"We're alright, thanks. Emmett has promised me an ice cream at Peel." I tell him.

"Definitely can't compete with an offer like that!" He laughs, hugging me tightly and shaking Emmett by the hand. "Have fun, ride safe. Love you."

"Love you too. Ride safe." I kiss goodbye to Jurgen and Stefan and they head off towards their bikes. The very efficient guy, who appears to be Jurgen's right hand man, rounds up the rest of their posse and they take off towards Ramsey. Emmett and I are left all on our own.

Oh God, why am I panicking so much? Sort yourself out, Delilah! You're over fifty years old for heaven's sake, you're not a bloody teenager...

CHAPTER 32

We walk slowly up to the parking field, hand in hand. Emmett lingers by my bike but I shove my lid on quick before he gets any ideas.

"Do you want to go the direct or the scenic route?" I ask.

"However you like, I'll follow you." He sighs putting on his own helmet and walking over to his own bike. The Duchess and his BMW sing a sweet duet as we pull out onto the course.

The roads are bedlam, they always are after practice, everyone is frantically trying to get to a restaurant to honour an optimistically placed booking, to a pub, to meet up with friends or just home after a long day. I turn off the circuit as soon as I can and ride steadily down the beautiful, hedge lined lanes until I get onto the sweeping Peel Road then I let The Duchess loose to have a little fun. I make sure Emmett keeps up and pull into a space opposite the ice cream shop. He parks up next to me.

"You are a crazy lady!" He laughs. "I didn't see much scenery down that last road, it was all a blur!"

"These bikes are not made to go slow." I grin. "It's like using race horses for donkey rides on the beach."

"I think that's something very British but I think I get the idea." He replies.

We cross the road and join the long ice cream queue. Davison's has been here in Peel for as long as I can remember and has every flavour of ice cream and type of cone you can imagine and a huge selection of sweets and chocolates.

"Choose me an ice cream and I'll get us some candy." Emmett says kissing my head and changing to the chocolate queue. He points to the extensive selection. "Anything you prefer?"

"Never met a chocolate I didn't like." I quip. "What about you with the ice cream?"

"Likewise." He replies with a cheeky grin.

I choose my usual for both of us; chocolate waffle cone with sprinkles, one scoop of liquorice, one of banoffee and a fudge stick in the top. Whilst he buys bag loads of chocolates, I pick up a big handful of napkins because I always seem to end up wearing half my ice cream and I wait outside for Emmett.

The sun is starting to drop pretty low as we make our way towards the castle. There are still quite a few people about. Peel is a lively little town with plenty of places to eat and drink. If Emmett is not keen on my flavour choices it certainly doesn't show, he's tucking in and even stealing licks from mine whenever he notices it's dripping.

He is bowled over by the castle and makes me promise to bring him back when it's open so that he can see inside. We walk around to the little beach and watch the fishermen for a while and, when our ice creams are all finished, I lead him up the hill around the back of the castle to find a comfy spot to watch the show.

We settle with our backs against a huge, flat stone and Emmett puts his arm around me, I rest my head on his chest and breathe in the smell of new leather, subtle aftershave and a faint hint of burgers.

"Tell me about him now, Delilah?" He whispers.

"You want our first date to end in snot and tears?" I ask, raising an eyebrow. "Haven't you seen enough of that already?"

"I don't want to make you sad, but if I'm going to have any chance of getting into your heart this is where we have to start. Let me in Delilah, please." He pleads.

We sit in silence for a while, watching the spectacular light show in the sky. Think of it as therapy I tell myself. He will be gone in just over a week and I have a sneaking feeling it's not my *heart* he's trying to get into but don't I always say it's good to talk over big stuff with strangers, they don't judge. I have never spoken to anyone about Jimbob until now but he is right, it stops me moving forward. I don't think he would have wanted that to happen. Okay Dil, take your own advice for once. I take a deep breath and try to be as detatched about it as I can.

"Think Jeff and Dutch." I say with a sad smile. "Jeff is Marley, goofy, loving, wants to please, desperate to make everyone laugh and be happy. A cheeky chancer willing to try anything. Dutch is Jimbob..." I pause for a second at the realisation that this is a lot more real than I planned.

"Go on, darlin'." Emmett urges gently.

"Jimbob was a watcher, a deep thinker. He was so calm and put together even as a teenager. We met him at a Buddhist retreat on Koh Phangan Island in Thailand. We'd gone there while we were travelling for a few months for my eighteenth birthday. Him and Marley hit it off instantly even though they were chalk and cheese." I smile to myself at a memory of them larking around together on the beach.

"He was travelling alone on his motorbike, an ex-care kid with no living family, a real lost boy but he had big plans, his mama was Thai, she'd gone to England on the promise of a better life but found out too late that she'd married a spiteful, violent man, who ultimately ended her life. Jimbob was exploring her homeland then planned to go back to England and set up a workshop." I stop and sniff and root around for my napkins. Emmett just sits quietly.

"During our time there we went on several bike rides together and gradually got to know each other. When we came home, he came too. Marley named him Jimbob, his name was actually Jimuta, which according to Buddhist teaching means 'committed to family and friends, responsible, sensitive and loving with the skill to balance life'. It's a wordy but perfect description of him. He was the kindest, most grounded guy. He did nothing without fully weighing up the consequences. He got into the road racing naturally and he was quick because he was good at reading the road and learning the circuits. Marley and I would always get all hyped up and excited before races, he would be able to meditate and stay relaxed." I stop to wipe my eyes and refocus, looking at the gold and crimson streaks slashing the violet sky. Emmett hugs me tightly and kisses the top of my head but still says nothing.

"We had so many plans together...many are becoming a reality but it feels wrong that he's not here with me. We were going to live here, set up a bike workshop, maybe foster kids, have a family....." I stop to blow my nose, thank heavens I picked up the napkins. This is hard to say out loud and to realise how long my life has been on hold waiting for someone that is never going to return. I've missed out on so many chances; I'm too old to have kids now, that's something I'll always deeply regret. I'm not a pretty person when I cry; I sob and wail and gulp in huge breaths of air, my nose runs and I get a blotchy red face. Maybe this will cool Emmett's ardour somewhat. I laugh slightly at the thought.

"Keep going, sweetheart. You're doing brilliantly." He squeezes me.

"The day he died I was racing too; I'd set off before him and was going well but taking it steady. The weather was far from perfect and there were a lot of damp patches and it was dark and slippy under the trees. Thinking back, he must have sensed something wasn't quite right. He'd been unusually quiet and had hugged us all and told us he loved us before we headed up to the start line. He wasn't normally a demonstrative guy when it came to affection. I knew he loved me but he didn't wear his heart on his sleeve like my family do. I'd just come around Governor's Dip when the race was stopped so I pulled into the pits. It had started raining heavily so I hoped that was the reason but I already knew it wasn't. Jimbob had always hated the rain, he had slid off at the Verandah, the very place that Gilberto Parlotti had crashed back in 1972, the crash that caused the TT circuit to be taken off the main racing calendar. Jimbob had bounced down the mountain side, hitting his head on a large rock which shattered his helmet and his skull. He was almost unrecognisable when we saw him at the mortuary. One side of his face was gone...... We'd travelled through Tibet a few times as it was such a beautiful, peaceful place and he'd said he wanted a sky burial when it was his time to go. I took his body over and stayed there for a few months after the funeral and then just roamed from place to place, coming back a few times a year until Dad called to tell me Mama was ill and asked me to come home."

Emmett rocks me gently in his arms as I cry until I'm completely exhausted. I take another deep breath and clean my face up as best I can although I know I'm still looking hideous. I am so grateful to this handsome, stranger for this brief invasion into my closely guarded life, encouraging me to face my fears like this. I know he'll be gone soon but I will be indebted to him for a very long time after he's forgotten me.

"That's my brave girl." Emmett whispers into my hair. "Are you feeling okay?"

"Yes, I'm shattered but okay." I sigh. "Thank you so much, Emmett."

"Thank you for trusting me enough to share something so painful and personal." He smiles offering me a huge bag of chocolate.

I settle back down on his chest and we watch the sun disappear and let the darkness envelop us. We can hear the muffled sound of people having fun in the town, there's a band on at the Creek and we can hear the beat of the music and the fishermen calling to each other down below on the beach.

"Are you ready to rejoin the world?" I ask when Emmett shivers and I notice it has gone much cooler."

"Nope, I want to stay right here holding you all night. You'll just have to snuggle closer to keep me warm." He lifts me so that I am sitting in his lap and wraps his arms around me. "This is my idea of heaven. You, candy and the sound of the sea. What else could a man want?"

I laugh and relax into his embrace, closing my eyes and listening to the world carrying on around us. Emmett's phone brings us back to reality. He reaches in his inside pocket but refuses to let go of me. It's a text from Felix reporting that they're all back safely and checking up on his Dad. He messages back to say we're in Peel and fine and will be back later. I text Dad too in case he's worried. He sends me back some thumbs up and hearts.

Phones are put away and Emmett wraps his arm back around me, he puts his other hand under my chin and tenderly kisses my lips. I freeze for a second and try to pull away from him. He is gentle but insistent and kisses me again. My body chooses to overrule my head and completely betrays me. I melt into the kiss, feeling sensations I have long ago forgotten. I begin to respond very enthusiastically and everything but this moment ceases to exist. We make out like crazed teenagers for who knows how long. I finally come up for air and wipe my hair out of my face and the fresh tears from my cheeks.

"Oh my life!" I exclaim. "Shall we try that again? It works even better than chocolate and I definitely need more practice."

"Happy to oblige, little darlin'." Emmett drawls.

We continue to play around until way past my bedtime, totally forgetting about the cold and everything else for that matter. When I get the feeling that this is going to get out of hand. I pull myself together and place my hand on Emmett's chest. He reads me instantly and stops. He folds me back into his arms and holds me until our heartbeats slow.

"Delilah Blue, you are an incredibly passionate woman." He whispers shaking his head. "I apologise, I should have a whole lot more self-control at my age."

"Emmett, my darling man, you have done absolutely nothing you need to apologise for I'm just not ready yet. I've got to admit you are one hell of a therapist though!" I giggle, kissing his nose. "Who knew all it would take was an offer of cheeseburgers and hot chocolate."

"Don't cheapen yourself darlin'." He laughs standing up and readjusting his leathers. "I would never have got this far if I hadn't thrown in the ice cream and candies." He holds his hands out to me and I let him pull me to my feet. I'm a little light headed and unsteady and he holds me close until I've sorted myself out. Using the torches on our phones we clamber down the rocks to the beach. We walk hand in hand back down the shoreline to our bikes. Peel is now completely silent and deserted. Emmett embraces me again and I snuggle into him and yawn.

"Are you okay to ride?" He asks looking concerned.

"Yes, if you don't kiss me again." I laugh looking into his eyes. "Oh oh! Too late." He leans down and kisses me passionately, reigniting all of the feelings I had just got under control. "Enough, enough, enough!" I protest, giggling like a silly teenager. "Look the sun is coming up!" I point to the faint glow in the sky.

"Awesome, we can watch the sunrise too. Are you good to ride? We can watch from your beach."

"Let's head for Nairbyl, we'll wake the whole campsite up with these beauties. We can sneak in a bit later when there's more bikes about. You happy following me?"

"To the ends of the earth, Delilah Blue." He winks and puts on his helmet.

I ride really steadily to Niarbyl. Trying to give us both some cooling off time. We arrive as an orange glow is beginning to spread across the horizon. We climb down onto the beach and I show Emmett the fabulous little cottages like ours. These ones were the setting for a film called 'Waking Ned', which I promise to watch with him sometime.

We find another ringside seat and he wraps me back into his arms and we watch as the greatest show on earth begins again.

CHAPTER 33

My phone pings just after 6. 'u wiv emit xxxx' It's Joey. I send one straight back telling him yes and I'm fine and that we'll be back soon.

Emmett's pings. He laughs and shows me, it's from Stefan. 'Are you two STILL playing around? Fair play, old man.'

"Looks like our secret's out, darlin'." He says with a shrug and pulls me into another crazy snogging session.

"We have to return to reality at some time today." I sigh, coming up for air. "Mr. Tamaki will be wanting his breakfast."

"Five more minutes, please?" Emmett pleads, slowly and deliberately unzipping my leathers and slipping his hands inside. I am saved from myself by a car load of fishermen pulling up and unloading noisily in the carpark. Emmett quickly zips me back up and we run back to the bikes, giggling like a pair of idiots.

"Where's that place you love for coffee? Can we go there before we go back?" Emmett asks. I park up on Ramsey corner and we walk down to Conrod's.

"Morning, Dil, we don't usually see you in here this early." Melissa greets us with a smile and starts making my coffee without asking what I want. "What would your gentleman friend like?"

"Whatever she's having is fine." Emmett smiles and heads off to find the bathroom. Melissa leans over the counter and whispers.

"Wow! Dil, where did you find him? He's not a local." I try to play it cool; Mel is an old acquaintance; she's been after Ricky for ages.

"He's camping over at our place; I'm just showing him around."

"Yeah right." She winks theatrically and laughs. "Pull the other one. I heard your bikes come out of Peel about half four this morning and they weren't heading to your place."

I shake my head and roll my eyes at her in mock horror. I grab our drinks and ask for two breakfast sandwiches for now and two more to go. I choose the table in the furthest corner from the counter and sit down.

Emmett joins me giggling. "I think I need a real cold shower."

"Me too if my conversation with Mel is anything to go by. I better go and sort my face out, I'll be back in a sec, watch her, she'll eat you alive." I joke, nodding towards the counter. He grabs my hand and pulls me back to kiss me.

"I'm all yours, little darlin' and I'll be sure to tell her that." I run to the loo in embarrassment, hoping she didn't see us. I am far too old to be behaving like this.

Good heavens Delilah, you slapper! You look a fright. I say to myself in the mirror. I have grass and sand in my dreads my face is glowing and my lips are bruised and swollen but at least I don't look like I spent half the night crying. As predicted, Mel's busy chatting Emmett up when I return to the table. I sit back and enjoy the show.

"So, Archie, how long are you staying?" She asks leaning over to deliver his sandwich and give him a view of her very ample cleavage.

"Just until I've finished my coffee and sandwich." He says with a straight face.

"No, silly, on the Island. Are you here for the racing? My place is on the circuit, you're welcome to come and watch from there." She's not subtle. "I live alone and have plenty of beds, it's more comfy than camping."

"I'm just here to convince Delilah to marry me and have my babies and then we'll be riding off into the sunset." He says with a very serious face. "And I really prefer camping." She looks completely thrown and wanders back to the counter without another word.

"Jeez, she's scary." He grimaces. We eat up and leave.

We get back to the campsite and everyone is up and about. I leave Emmett at the gate and go down to the cottage. Dad comes out of the workshop and smiles.

"Good night, baby?" He asks. "You look tired." I laugh.

"My virtue is still intact. Emmett is a gentleman. I've bought you a sandwich." I hand him the bag. "How was your Chinese?"

"We had a decent night. Stefan and Jurgen are getting to know each other and Jurgen's stoked about moving here, he adores the house... Don't change the subject girly, your virtue is the least of my worries its way down on my list after your head, your heart and your overriding propensity to do a runner at the first sign of commitment."

We see Mr. Tamaki heading down with the cool box. I hand Dad the second sandwich and smile.

"You go and get a few hours kip, sweetheart. I'll sort Mr. T." I kiss him gratefully and head for my room.

Jeff dives on me for a big fuss and then flakes out at the bottom of the bed. Dutch jumps up too and sniffs my face and my hair. He purrs and rubs his head against my cheek then cuddles up next to me and starts snoring. I kiss his head and hold him close. I am asleep in less than five minutes.

I wake to the sound of Joey's DT. He comes in and I hear him bashing about in the kitchen. "You awake, Dil? Want coffee?" He yells. I put my dressing gown on and join him. He hands me a coffee. "We're only down the road so I nipped back for scran. What time did ya roll in?"

"Isn't this conversation meant to go the other way?" I ask, amused by his stern look. Joey laughs.

"I'm hopin' it might do in a few weeks; I really like Ella. I said we'd meet 'er at The Sulby tonight, okay? Ya can bring Emmett; the others are comin'."

"Okay. How about we make a deal? We'll both have some fun and be real careful not to get our hearts broken, eh?" I offer.

"Deal!" He agrees. "Got any cake?"

I make him some lunch and he shoots off back to work. I go and get showered and start my day a little later than planned.

I tick off all the stuff on my 'to do' list and I check on Dad. He's serviced the second bike and offers me the chance to do the test run. He wants to get back to the KTM. I don't need asking twice. I grab my helmet and go for a quick run up past the prison and it feels smooth and the brakes are superb. I park it up at the campsite and the owner is out so I drop the keys inside their tent. Singing loudly to myself, I check the bins and the showers. Someone is using the shower so I turn to leave and as I do a now familiar arm appears around the door and pulls me inside.

He giggles. "Hey darlin', fancy seeing you here." And traps me against the wall by putting a hand up on either side of me. The shower is off and he is wearing a towel, thank goodness. He leans in and kisses me gently as if checking to see if he's moving too fast for me.

"Bloody hell, Emmett, you're insatiable." I laugh. "Can you not behave around here? What will Felix think? I've already just had 'the talk' off Joey."

"Joey really loves you. Felix thinks you're great and hell, Jurgen was most explicit in what he will do to me if I hurt you. I think I love you Delilah Blue."

"This is lust, not love, you daft bugger!" I kiss him again. "Get your kit on, you'll catch your death of cold." He shakes his head.

"Man, I'm enjoying this game. Where are we going to watch practice tonight?" He asks, slipping his hand down the back of my dungarees.

"We can go to Melissa's if you like." He pulls a face and shudders. "If you don't fancy that the plan is Sulby and both of our kids are coming so you'll have to show a bit of restraint." I tell him, extracting his hands.

"Come back to my tent and I'll make sweet, sweet love to you until it's time to leave." He jokingly begs. I put my head on one side as if I'm considering his proposal.

"Err, no!" I giggle and kiss him slowly and deeply. "Gotta go, I've got stuff to do." I slip out of the shower and leave him groaning. Delilah Blue, you're a proper tart! Whatever this man has unleashed is not going back in her box. It is fun though. Dad's got the KTM singing when I get back.

"Try it, Dilly girl. I'm not sure that gearbox will be long for this world." I jump on and ride it down the lane, mucking about doing wheelies and banging it up and down the box to see if it's okay. It seems fine. I notice Emmett and Felix are standing at the gate watching so I ride over.

"You are an awesome woman!" Emmett exclaims. "Felix wants to learn to wheelie like that." Felix grins at me, a little embarrassed.

"Really, or has your dad put you up to it?" I ask with a raised eyebrow.

"No really." Felix laughs. "I scare myself shitless every time the front comes up on my bike."

"Get your helmet and we'll have half an hour." Felix runs down to the tent.

"Can you teach me anything, darlin'?" Emmett drawls suggestively.

"I doubt it very much and I'm not taking this helmet off so you'll be able to behave."

I jump off the KTM and explain the basics to Felix. He rides up and down the lane gaining confidence and willingly following my instructions. His dad doesn't, he whispers and teases and torments like a daft kid trying to get attention. After half an hour Felix is fetching up the front wheel on demand and moving through the gears without dropping it. His dad is applauding and looking really proud and Felix is hyped.

"It's a little harder to control the lift on your big one so take it slow or you'll be flipping it." I warn pointing to the row of bikes parked up.

"I will, I promise." Felix says, handing me back the KTM. "Thanks Delilah you're a great teacher. Are you coming to Sulby later? We're meeting up with Joey and Ella."

"Yeah, we'll be there. See you later." I put the bike away in the workshop and go to find Dad, he's walking on the beach. "Gearbox is good for a while yet."

"Yes, I saw you and Felix testing it." He laughs. "You were always the same as a kid, we'd give you a present and you'd let your brother play with it all day. Where are we watching tonight?" He asks as we walk along, hand in hand, paddling.

"The Sulby, Joe wants to impress Ella."

"She seems a lovely girl, have you had 'the talk' with him?" He asks obviously a little worried about young love blossoming in the mezzanine. I tell him about our earlier conversation and he giggles.

"I don't know why I'm worrying; he's more grown up than the pair of us put together. Oh and talking about playing grown-ups let me know if you and Emmett want the cottage to yourselves any time. I'll pitch the tent up with Jurgen."

"No you won't! I think Emmett is moving way too fast and I'm not going there. I'm having fun. Last night was quite a revelation and it honestly helped me a lot but we just talked most of the night and then were just fooling around like silly kids, nothing more."

"Have as much fun as you want, darling Dilly, you're a beautiful, grown woman with so much love to share and no one will judge you, least of all me and Joey. We just want you safe and happy and here with us."

"You're a soppy old sod and I love you so much. Don't worry about me leaving, I promised you I wouldn't. I'm trying hard to be a grown up and really quite enjoying it." I squeeze his hand. "Have you got any lady friends hidden about on this Rock?"

"I might have." He winks but says no more. "Mr. Tamaki won't be there for tea tonight. He's doing a talk about his travels for a coachload of Japanese tourists from the VJMCC down in Douglas."

"He's an amazing man and I'm sure he'll really enjoy that and so will they." I smile. "It'll be lovely for him to be able to converse without mimes, drawing and pointing at stuff."

"Come on, better get everyone fed and watered before we go. If we get there early enough we can get some food." Dad breaks into a run and we race up the beach with Jeff and Dutch leading the way.

We get to Sulby in plenty of time and I text Joey to see where they are and if they want food. I've just sent it and I hear his bike pulling into the car park. Ella is right behind him on her own bike. Dad goes inside to order all our food and we sit down out the front.

"Billy and Sal'll be 'ere in a bit but Nath's got somat on at work, might get down later. Felix just text to say they're on the way." Joey reports. "'Ave ya bin teachin' 'im to wheelie?"

"Yep, that little KTM is a beaut. Dad's got her purring like a pussy cat."

Bill and Sal arrive and Billy goes straight into the pub to order food and get drinks.

"You're looking good for someone who's been up all night." Sal remarks, kissing my cheek. I don't even bother to ask how she knows.

"You're just jealous!" I giggle.

"Damn right I am." She laughs.

"Dave." Billy kisses my head. "What you bin up to, you slapper? Our kid's bin like a bear with a sore arse all day! I told him to go and get laid so I don't think he'll be out tonight."

"Thanks for airing all the family's dirty laundry." I laugh. "Have you met Ella?"

"'Eard about 'er." He raises his pint to Ella. "Evening Dave, welcome to the clan." He nods at Joey. "You'll not go far wrong with our Dave; the blokes in this family know how to look after their women." Ella raises her drink back and gives Joey a shy but sweet look.

Jurgen, Stefan, Emmett and the boys pull up. Jurgen grabs Sal and loses himself in her chest. Stefan kisses my cheek.

"You look tired Delilah; did you have a late night?" He teases.

"More like an early mornin'." Joey chimes in. "And it wasn't that early. I'd gone to work 'fore she rolled 'ome!"

Dad returns with a tray full of drinks, "Dad, they're all picking on me!" I wail, Emmett is grinning like the cat who got the cream.

Dad's already text Jurgen for their orders and the food arrives and saves me any more embarrassment. We all tuck in and I can see Sal eyeing up Emmett who I'm keeping at a safe distance by sitting between Billy and Dad. I raise my eyebrows at her and giggle. She pulls a face to say she approves and I throw a chip at her. They're just closing the roads when we hear Ricky's bike approaching at a fair pace. He pulls off the road just as the barrier is being put into place.

"Looks like he's been taking his frustration out on his bike." Sal laughs.

"Didn't ya see who was on the back?" Billy asks, shaking his head.

"Oh God, not Mattress?" Sal groans as Ricky comes into view with Melissa hanging on his arm. He greets everyone and goes to get a drink. Melissa doesn't let go of him. Ella tells us she's not watched from here before and I wink at Joey. He's knows what's coming and where to stand to catch her when she jumps. I'm certainly not going to catch Emmett I think to myself with a giggle.

Empty plates are cleared away and I climb up and sit on the edge of the table to see better. Emmett comes and stands in between my knees, facing me.

"You can shift from there when the bikes come, matey. You're blocking my view." I tease.

"Oh, sexy, feisty, little Delilah! I've missed you this afternoon." He proclaims loudly.

"Er, you and Felix we're with me half the afternoon if I remember correctly." Felix holds his hands up.

"Don't get me involved. You've bewitched him. He's been crazy happy all day."

Stefan comes over. "Do I need to pour a bucket of cold water on him? I've never seen him this animated, even on stage."

Billy ruffles my hair. "Our Dave has that effect on a lot of blokes then walks away with no fuckin' clue. 'E must be somat special 'cos I ain't seen her like this in a very long time. Just know we're 'ere." He finishes with a slightly threatening tone.

"Billy, play nicely!" Sal shouts from the other side of the table. He raises his pint to the guys, kisses my head and goes back to Sal.

"He's one scary guy." Emmett shudders.

"'E's not the one you need to worry about." Joey points out knowingly. "'Ave ya met 'is little brother?"

"Don't worry, baby. I'll save you from the nasty boys." I tease, reaching up and putting my arms around his neck. Bad move Delilah! He takes it to mean he hasn't got to behave any more. He pulls me towards him and leans in to kiss me.

"Not in front of the kids!" I tell him firmly but kiss him on the nose to make the rebuff a little gentler.

"Don't worry 'bout me. I need some tips." Joey grins cheekily.

"You guys have fun. It's good to see him smiling. I'll just pretend I don't know him." Felix laughs.

"Well thanks! You pair are no bloody help at all."

"See, we have the blessing of our children, come here and kiss me now, darlin'." Emmett growls and pulls me close. I submit and kiss him long and slow and we get a round of applause from everyone. Well, almost everyone. I think I hear Ricky growl.

The radio announces that the first bikes have left and Joey gets Ella to the barrier and stands right behind her, she's tiny and he can easily see over her shoulder. I poke Billy and point for him to watch. He moves to stand behind Joe just in case he jumps again. I nod for him to look out for Felix as well. They encourage Ella and the boys to lean right out and Emmett looks at me to ask what's going on. I tell him to go and look for himself. He laughs.

"Is this where that clip of Joe you showed me was taken? I'm staying right here with you." The first bikes come into view and they all dive back in amazement as they fly past. Joey stands solid and wraps his arms around Ella to catch her. Billy catches Felix, who is more than grateful and Emmett swears a lot even though he was a little further away. We watch the practice for a while all larking around and chatting and Dad nudges me to see if I've noticed that Joey still has his arms around Ella. That's my boy!

Sal comes over and gives Emmett the third degree and then declares that she approves and kisses him on the cheek. Billy mellows and chats with him about music and his bikes. Ricky stands next to us with Melissa still firmly attached. I lean over and kiss him.

"How you doin, baby?"

"I'm good Shortarse, bin busy, how's you?" He grins.

"Hello Archie." Melissa cuts in before I can answer him. "Fancy seeing you again so soon. Me and Ricky are going for a few drinks at mine afterwards, would you like to come too?" Stef is having a fit of the giggles nearby.

"No, I don't think so, do we Delilah?" Melissa takes the hint and drags Rick away.

"Where are we watching the sunset tonight?" Emmett whispers in my ear, nibbling my earlobe.

"How much sunset did you actually see last night?" I arch my eyebrow. He grins and shrugs.

"Not much. That's why we need to go again tonight."

"I need my bed, I'm an old lady." I whine.

"Bed is good. Your place or mine? How old are you exactly?" He enquires. "Should I be worried about being able to keep up? I'm not as young as I look."

"I'm older than you, you daft bugger and far too out of practice to consider anything more than mucking about. It's been well over twenty years since I played around like this." He looks genuinely surprised but I'm not sure about which part.

"Dil, I'm such bloody idiot, I never even thought. I'm so sorry. I should have realised after what you told me yesterday. I keep pushing you like a stupid teenager. Forgive me?" He whispers softly, checking around to see that no one is listening to us. "What kind of arrogant dick would think they could put everything right in one night?"

"It's all good." I smile. "Last night was a revelation to me and I'll be forever grateful to you for bringing me back to life. I just needed you to know. I'm having the best fun but I don't want to lead you on or mess with your head. Please don't expect too much from me."

"Heard and understood, darlin'." He smiles, wrapping me tenderly in his arms. "Can we go somewhere after practice I need to talk with you, properly apologise."

"There's nothing to apologise for. Will there be more ice cream and candy and fooling around?" I ask.

"Only if you want it, honey."

"Damn right I do!" I giggle. Joey comes over looking sheepish.

"Can I invite Ella to ours? Promise I won't do anythin' stupid."

"Of course you can, darling. You don't have to ask, it's your home but be careful. Take it slowly. I don't want you to get hurt."

"Yas a soppy tart, Ma!" He hugs me. "Are you takin ya own advice? Love ya." He shakes hands with Emmett and says bye to everyone. I see Ricky hugging him and handing him condoms and him arguing that he doesn't want them. I hope he's taken them just in case.

Jurgen invites everyone for drinks at Ginger Hall but Emmett and I slip away after a few goodbyes.

CHAPTER 34

W e're back in the queue at Davison's. I let Emmett choose the ice cream and he gets liquorice and banoffee. We go down onto the beach and I take my boots off and paddle. We walk to the rocks and sit down.

"Do you want a pint?" I ask. "The Creek is a great pub."

"Nope, I want you all to myself for now. I need to talk to you, Delilah. I can't believe what a complete idiot I have been. I must have scared you earlier in the shower and this morning on the beach. I am truly sorry. You bring out the absolute best of the worst in me. I should have far more self-control. My behaviour today was totally unacceptable and I am ashamed of myself."

"Emmett, please stop needlessly apologising. I have more than encouraged your behaviour and thoroughly enjoyed every minute. I just don't want to ... disappoint you. I know this is just a holiday fling and you'll be off back to reality in a week. I'm happy fooling around and having fun but I'm not sure how far I can go with it just yet."

"Do you really think I'm walking away from this?" He shakes his head. "Delilah, meeting you is the best thing that's happened to me since my son was born. I'm not letting you go now I've found you. I will be calling you and flying over every chance I get unless you want to come touring with us? Will you come with me?"

"No, Emmett." I say gently. "This is my home now and I don't want to leave it. You also seem to have forgotten the not inconsequential fact that you're married."

"In name only, my very much ex-partner has made her choice. I knew it was over a real long time ago I just never met anyone so did nothing about it. She can have everything, I don't care. I'll get a divorce, that's easy. I'll buy a place here; we can choose it together. We can look tomorrow." I smile and reach for his hands.

"Emmett, you are a kind, generous, gorgeous, sexy and very understanding man and I am amazed and flattered and extremely thankful that you want to spend time with me but this is moving way too quickly to deal with. Let's not make too many plans just yet, what will be will be. I can't handle pressure and I don't want to put any on you so shall we agree to have fun and go with whatever comes along or is that going to just frustrate the heck out of you and make me a total prick tease?"

"Bloody hell no, you've just made me want to be with you even more now." Emmett sighs. "I promise I will slow down and stop pushing. No, I know that's going to be impossible to keep. I promise I will try to slow down and stop being so intense."

"Okay, that's sorted. Can we fool around now?" I tease. He moves in very hesitantly and kisses me slowly and gently relighting an already simmering flame.

We make out on the beach like hungry teenagers and when it gets a bit too heated we take a walk around to The Creek as I recognise the music that's playing. They're the guys that played for Joey's birthday. We grab a pint and sit down to listen. I completely forget Emmett is in a band and ask what music he likes and whether he plays any instruments. He smiles.

"We actually know so little about each other don't we? I want to spend the rest of my life getting to know you." He puts his arm around me. "I get paid millions of dollars every month for playing a guitar and writing, darlin'. These guys just played one of my songs a few minutes ago."

I giggle. "Oh crap, I totally forgot, sorry. You're just my Emmett when you're here, a very sexy man that rides a fast bike and makes my heart beat faster."

"I'm more than happy just being 'your Emmett' It's amazing how good it feels to get away from 'working Emmett'. I gotta admit I'm missing my guitar a little though."

"Getting you something to entertain those very active fingers might be a good idea." I giggle and catch hold of them as they are about to disappear down the front of my leathers.

The band stops for a break and the guys head outside to cool down. As they pass the table the one at the back spots us. "Hey Dil. How are you? Loving the hair. How's Joey and your dad? We had such a great night at your place. Are you enjoying the show?" He's clearly full of adrenaline from the buzz of being on stage.

"It's really good, my friend here was just commenting on how much he enjoyed a song you played a little while back. He's itching to get hold of a guitar now." I giggle and nudge Emmett in the ribs. He's trying to hide in my hair but groans and lifts his head when I prod him.

"Holy fuck! Is it really you?" He grabs Emmett's hand and shakes it vigorously. "You're my hero, man! The reason I started playing." He flops down in the chair next to us. "Shit! I can't believe this is happening. How the hell did you wind up here?" He looks around frantically to see if anyone else has noticed.

"Don't draw any attention please, man. I'm incognito." Emmett pleads putting a hand on his arm. "I'm Archie if anyone asks." He adds with a grin.

"Oh god, sorry, okay! Sorry, I didn't think." He's ruffled and not quite sure what to do. "Come up and play if you want to. We'd be honoured." Emmett laughs pointing at his leather one piece.

"Not really dressed for it." He sighs. "Are you playing here tomorrow?" Band guy looks devastated.

"No, this is our last night here. Got nothing else for a couple of weeks."

"Perfect, come over to our place tomorrow night after practice. You can all jam on the beach and I'll make some food. It'll draw a lot less attention." I butt in.

"Oh My God, is this really happening? Awesome. Can I bring the rest of the band?"

"Only if I can too." Emmett winks.

"Are you fucking kidding me?" He exclaims very loudly, slaps his hand over his mouth and starts apologising. "You're all here?"

"Come over and find out tomorrow." I point to the guys getting ready on stage. "I think you have to be somewhere else right now." He grins and runs off.

Their second set is really easy to listen to and when they drop the tempo towards the end of the night we get up and have a slow dance before heading for the door. Over the mic we hear. "See you tomorrow Archie and Dil, have a good night." We wave and leave.

We're walking slowly, hand in hand back to the bikes and I'm gently humming a tune and swinging our arms in time to the music when Emmett stops suddenly. He turns to me and takes my face in his hands, looking deep into my eyes.

"You're an awesome woman, Delilah Blue! No pressure but I'm seriously falling in love with you."

"Is this another ploy to get in my knickers?" I ask with a giggle, trying to stop him being so intense.

"Shit, I'm doing it again aren't I? Delilah, forgive me I can't help myself. You just make my every desire come true. I'm just thinking I want a guitar and you bring me a whole damn band. You're amazing! You're ... Shut up, Emmett." He adds with a sigh. I kiss him to make sure that he does.

We get back home at a reasonable hour and Emmett parks up and walks down to the cottage. I leave The Duchess outside, mindful that Ella's bike is still there.

"Coffee?" I offer.

"Can we walk first?" Emmett gestures towards the beach. He's busy stripping off his leathers down to shorts and a t-shirt.

"You now have far too few clothes on for me to feel safe." I tease.

"I had a lot less on in the shower earlier." He grins. "Promise I'll try to behave."

We nip inside to say hi to Dad and I pull my dungarees on and my boots off. I tell him that we're having guests tomorrow night and he's really happy. I grab a couple of hoodies because its dropping cooler and we go onto the beach with Jeff and Dutch as chaperones. I go straight in to the sea and paddle up to my knees, stopping on the way to put Dutch onto my shoulder.

"Come here, darlin' I want to hold you." Emmett groans. I throw him a hoodie.

"Put another layer on and I'll come closer." He quickly obliges. We go to sit on my rock and Jeff runs around throwing seaweed, bringing sticks and being draft. Dutch rubs lovingly against my face and nibbles at my nose. He turns and stares at Emmett long and hard then he sighs, head butts him gently, looks back to me, jumps down and heads for the cottage, taking Jeff with him.

"Did I just get Dutch's approval?" Emmett asks in amazement.

"Looks like it." I reply, equally shocked. He lifts me gently onto his lap and wraps me in his arms. "Okay, time to get to know each other a little more." He says. "Twenty questions, first answer that comes into your head, no passes. Keep me busy and I'll be able to behave for longer. You go first."

"Favourite bike?" I ask.

"Easy, my GS1200 back in the States, she goes wherever I want and I could ride her to the end of the world. My turn. Where were you born?"

"Saint Lucia, I think. How well did you do in school?"

"I was a nightmare and an utter disappointment to my folks and my teachers. What about you?"

"Didn't go very often, was always travelling or racing or working with Dad. Got a degree in advanced motorcycle mechanics and some O'levels but we learnt everything from Mama and Dad. Have you got any brothers and sisters?"

"Nope, only child. First boyfriend?"

"Jimbob. First girlfriend?"

"Amber Feinstein. I was six. Last boyfriend?"

"Jimbob."

He stops to take this one in. "You're not lying are you?" He says in amazement.

"Oi, it's my turn." I laugh.

"Just kiss me now for God's sake I can't keep my hands off you any longer." He groans. "You know everything about me now."

"You said 20 questions. We're only on four! Where's your self-control man?" I giggle.

"That's your fifth question. My self-control is barely under control. Why won't you just put me out of my misery? That's my next question." I kiss him deeply and look into his eyes.

"Emmett, honey, I don't even know your full name."

"Oh lord, Delilah, just slap me. I'm being an absolute dick again." He holds up his hands in surrender.

"Definitely not! You might like it." I giggle and kiss him again. We mess about for a little while longer and then I suggest coffee before we both do something we might regret, although I doubt there will be remorse in his case.

Dad's in bed when we get back and Ella's bike has gone, I have to admit to being a little relieved. I make coffee and we cuddle up on the settee. I feel so cosy and relaxed that I can't stop yawning.

"Emmett, I'm so sorry. You've worn me out. I need to sleep."

"Let me stay here with you please." He begs. "I swear I can control myself. I just want to hold you."

"I only have a single bed, baby. You'll be squashed and uncomfortable. You're not exactly little."

"I'll survive I'm sure." He pleads. "I'll be gone before you wake if that's what you want." I'm far too tired to argue and not even sure I want to. We cuddle down in my cosy little bed and I fall asleep in Emmett's arms.

CHAPTER 35

"Eh Laa, why are there kecks all over the front yard?" Joey shouts next morning as he dumps Emmett's abandoned leathers on the chesterfield. Just as Emmett comes in from the shower wearing my bathrobe.

"Fair play fella, ya gorra give me some tips. I only got to first base an' Ella ran off." He grins his cheeky grin.

"You got to first base?" Emmett giggles. "You need to dish the tips, man. Mine fell asleep on me before I got anywhere near first!"

"I feel ya pain. You've give yourself a proper challenge there. If the ice cream didn't work I dunno what else to suggest. Don't think she'll go for the cross dressing though." Joey giggles, pointing to Emmett's attire. "And if that's ya bag she's not got an extensive wardrobe. I own more clothes than she does."

"In here! Can hear you!" I yell in mock indignation. "Put the coffee on Joe and I might forgive you and make breakfast."

"Already on Mummy dearest." He yells back jokingly. "'Urry up! I'm starvin'."

I pull my dungarees on and go and make breakfast for everyone. Mr. Tamaki is beaming when he arrives. He was such a big hit in Douglas and has been invited back tonight as guest of honour at their annual meal. Dad, Jeff and Dutch emerge and all get fed. Dutch accepts a piece of bacon from Emmett and Jeff scrounges off everyone before eating her own food. Felix wanders in looking for his Dad and happily accepts a sandwich.

"How you doin, Dilly girl?" Dad asks giving me a hug. "What's going on tonight? I'll probably be down the paddock all day unless you need me to do anything."

"No, everything is good. Emmett was missing his guitar so I've invited the band that played at Joe's birthday, they seemed to know who he was, well one of them did, anyway." I joke. "The plan is to mug them and steal their instruments so we can keep Emmett occupied for the evening and hopefully wear him out so that he stops being a sex pest. I'll just go and watch practice at Ballaugh so I can dash back and get some food on before everyone arrives." Felix is highly amused.

"Great, can I invite Ella and Nath?" Joey asks.

"Course you can. Tell Billy as well. Grumpy arse can come too as long as he doesn't bring Melissa, she scares Emmett. I'll text Sal later too I feel the need for some Sarah wisdom."

"Okay. See yas all later! I fed everyone outside already. Love yas." He shouts and he's gone. Dad follows.

"See you all later guys. Enjoy your evening Mr. Tamaki."

Mr. T. accepts another cup of coffee and then leaves with a bow.

"You were up pretty early." Felix teases. "I heard the bikes come back but I must have been asleep before you got to your tent, or did you get lost on the way back?" I kiss his head.

"Thanks, honey. You're a lot more subtle than our Joey. Your Dad did stay here but only on the understanding that he behaved like a gentleman."

"And did he?" Felix asks.

"I've no idea, I slept like the dead 'til Joey woke me up this morning." I laugh. Emmett gives a huge mock sigh.

"You're losing your touch, old boy. Sort yourself out, Dil's a real keeper." Felix tells him. "Have you got me a bass for tonight? I can't believe how much I miss playing. Gotta go and tell Charl and Conn. Thanks for breakfast." He wags a finger at his Dad. "Behave yourself!" I pour us another coffee and sit down at the table.

"I think we're alone now..." Emmett starts to sing. "There doesn't seem to be anyone around..."

"Bugger off and find someone else to play with. I need a shower and I've got a huge list of chores to do." I groan.

"I can help with chores and the shower. I can scrub your back." He replies.

"Thank you but no. Go and treat Felix to an ice cream in Peel and see what that Beemer can do. You could take him to Murray's Museum, or down the road to the transport museum, they've got some cool stuff, I think you'll both really enjoy it."

It finally gets through his very thick skull. "Okay, you need a break don't you? I'm getting heavy again."

"I'll still be here later, sweetheart. I've no plans to run off with the postman."

"One more kiss? Just a little one? Then I promise I'll go, and Delilah, thank you for trusting me last night it meant the world to me." He adds softly.

My god he's a smooth operator. I melt into his arms and we are really in deep when Stefan bangs on the door frame and coughs theatrically.

"Perfect timing! Take him away now, please before he persuades me to do something I'll hate myself for." I beg Stefan, laughing. Emmett doesn't take his eyes off me.

"Stef, I am in love with this woman, she does things to me I can't explain."

"It's lust, not love you sex pest." I groan.

"Come on, you horny old buzzard. Jurgen is taking us for a trip down to where Delilah took us the other day, The Calf is it?" Stefan queries.

"Calf or The Sound." I reply. "Technically the little island off the end is The Calf. Enjoy yourselves, a rip on the bike will do you good. I'll see you both later."

"You're invited too." Stefan says.

"Thanks but I think we both need a 'time out' I'll see you all tonight. Ride safe."

"I'll have a few words with him." Stefan sighs. "Come on you tart, where are your leathers? You need to cover that up!" Emmett looks down, laughs and picks them up and leaves, blowing kisses from the doorway. I take a deep breath and sit down at the table. Dutch jumps up and looks at me.

"What have I got myself into?" I ask him. "Am I being a complete idiot?" He holds my gaze as if considering the questions, then shakes his head slowly and gently head butts me, rubbing my tears away.

I pull myself together and get showered. I bake loads of goodies for tonight and put in the bread Dad has left proving. I make up some more food packs and plan the picnics. I scrub the cottage, change the beds and give The Duchess a bath and polish. I spend some time with the donkeys and get a huge bruise on my bum from Giles because I stupidly turn my back on him to cuddle Wonky.

I start to sort the garden and organise what's going to be my veggie patch, planting some carrots, cabbage, cauliflower and onions and strim the weeds that are sneaking back in at the back and the front. I tidy the beach up and Jeff helps me refill the fire pit ready for tonight and I fill the torches with oil. I want it to be perfect tonight and I'm really looking forward to it. I ring Sal to see what she's up to and scrounge a lift to get some drinks in. She's over in twenty minutes.

"Fill me in, how's it going, have you been up to anything yet?" She demands.

"It's going much too fast and it's way too intense and I don't know how I'm stopping myself from getting into serious trouble." I admit.

"Why would you need to stop yourself stupid? You're both consenting adults." She sighs. "Bloody hell Dil, just shag him it'll do you the world of good. Look at the state of you, you seriously need to get laid!"

"Thanks for that advice, Claire Rayner." I laugh. "Can we go and buy beer now?"

"I only tell you because we love you and we want you to be happy." She offers to soften the blow. "Oh and how's Joey doing with lovely little Ella?"

"First base, apparently. What happened to wanting her marrying Nathan?"

"Don't tell Bill but I think our Nathan might be batting for the other team." She confides with a giggle. "He's been chatting on the phone a lot and it doesn't sound like a girl on the other end."

We buy plenty of drinks and snacks and unload it all back at the cottage. "Thanks, sweetie." I kiss Sal bye. "See you later." I go and have another shower and check everything again ready for tonight. My phone pings and I realise Emmett doesn't even have my phone number. It's Ian, the vet asking how I am and if I can join him for a late lunch on the Sunday after TT. I send a quick apology explaining that I'll be going to the Presentation Do. Then it hits me that Emmett and all of our campers will all be gone by then and everything will have returned to normal. I'm just contemplating this when my phone pings again. It's the band guy asking if yesterday really happened and if they can come and set up before practice starts. I happily tell them to come over whenever they like.

They arrive in half an hour and I leave them to get set up.

"We've bought all our spare stuff just in case." The guy explains when I see how much they're unloading. "I'm Dan by the way. I forgot to introduce myself in all the excitement yesterday."

"Hi Dan. That's really kind of you. The boys are going to be really happy to see you, they're all pining for their kit." I hear the bikes thundering down the lane. "Sounds like they're back already." Dan goes into panic mode and runs around like a headless chicken. "Calm down, sweetheart. They're just normal human beings. They won't thank you for being starstruck. Just treat them like your mates and that's what they will be by the end of the night."

"Okay, thanks Dil." He calms slightly and then Felix scares the crap out of him when he makes a spectacular entrance by doing a massive wheelie and dropping the front about a foot from us.

"Impressive honey!" I giggle as he takes his helmet off. "I see you've been practicing."

"Yeah." He grins. "Had a few hairy ones but I've got it now. Dad's just gonna get showered, he stinks." He drapes his arm around me and kisses my head and then notices Dan and the van. "Is the band here already? Awesome!"

"Dan, Felix, Felix, Dan." I introduce. "Dan close your mouth and find Felix a bass and he'll be your best friend forever." I laugh. They go off onto the beach together and I go back inside to get ready to go and watch practice. I'm just about to come out of the door when a gorgeous smelling, freshly showered and very sexily dressed Emmett blocks my way. My heart skips several beats.

"Where do you think you are you off to, little lady?" He drawls suggestively. "We need to be making up for lost time."

"Felix!" I yell. "Come and show your father a guitar, quickly." Emmett shakes his head and laughs.

"Why are you so completely immune to my charms? That's my best John Wayne impersonation."

"I'm really not." I confess. "That's why I'm yelling for your son to save me." He folds me in his arms just as Felix comes running over.

"Put Dil down and come and meet these guys." Felix suggests. Emmett has other ideas and I am picked up in a fireman's lift and taken to the beach too. "I believe you've already met my Dad, the caveman and Delilah, his lovely woman." Felix laughs as the others look on in awe. "Can anyone lend him a guitar so that Dil can have some peace?"

My phone rings and Emmett takes it out of my pocket.

"Delilah can't come to the phone right now I'm busy doing unspeakable things to her."

It's Joey. "Fair play, soft lad. When you're done can ya tell 'er practice is off, too much fog, not enough marshals. I'm at the paddock so me and Dylan'll start back in a bit. Ask Felix to look after Ella if she gets there before us." He relays all the messages and shoves the phone back in my pocket.

"Put me down, idiot. I can go and get my kit off." I say, meaning my bike kit.

"I'm up for that." He drawls and starts back towards the cottage with me still on his shoulder. Stefan and Jurgen are walking across, chatting.

"Isn't it lovely to see the children so happy." Stefan laughs. "You do know Delilah is going purple, don't you, Emm?"

"Don't care what colour she is, she's a slippery minx and I'm not letting her go." He replies, not slowing at all. We get inside and he finally puts me down but keeps me wrapped in his arms.

"Emmett, let me breathe, honey." I plead. "I need to get my leathers off." He grins sheepishly and backs off, hands up in surrender.

"Am I being an over enthusiastic dick again?" I smile in response.

"If it's any consolation I did really miss having you around today. Regaining control of my senses was quite a letdown after the intense few days we've had."

"You are a special lady!" He sighs. "Need any help with your zip?"

"NO! And be warned my four-year-old goddaughter will be here later and I really will be upset and angry if you try any stupid stuff whilst she's here."

"Delilah, darlin' what do you take me for? I promise I will behave... when she arrives." He adds reaching for me and pulling me into another mind-blowing kiss.

I escape long enough to change and actually take time to choose what to wear, putting on new skinny black jeans and a white, fitted t shirt. I let my dreads down and they cascade right past my bottom and I slap on a little make up.

"Eh Ma, ya look proper grown up!" Joey exclaims as I walk into the kitchen. "I'm gonna get showered. Ella's on the way."

Dad's already out on the beach, sitting with Jurgen. He takes my hand and squeezes it gently, smiling.

"You're looking rather lovely, my darling daughter." I stay by him, watching the others jamming and laughing and sharing ideas and stories. Emmett is engrossed in conversation with Dan, he's showing him a riff and explaining a technique. We hear one of the other band guys ask Charlie if Jurgen is their manager.

"Man, I wish he was; he'd be brilliant at it. He's my Grandpa."

Jurgen looks so proud and gets a tear in his eye. I kiss him on the head and slip back into the cottage to sort food and drinks. I hear Ella's bike arrive and she pops her head in the door.

"Hi sweetheart, how are you doing? Joe's just getting showered, he'll be down in a bit. Do you want a drink?"

"Hi Dil, you look nice. Yes please, have you got a Coke?" She asks and adds shyly. "Are you okay with me staying over tonight?"

"Yes, sweetie, you can stay whenever you like but please be careful and don't break my baby's heart else I'll come after you." I tease.

"We're taking it really, really slowly and I do like him a lot." She replies earnestly then adds. "Whose leathers did I fall over out the front when I left last night?" We both dissolve in a fit of giggles.

"What ya plottin'?" Joey asks, kissing Ella gently on the cheek.

"I was getting lessons in self-control from Ella." I joke offering him a Coke or a lager. He takes the lager and grins. "Go and join the others. I'll bring some food out in a while. I know I need this advice more than you but just be mindful when Sarah's about. Help me out if Emmett gets over excited."

"Loud an' clear, Mama Bear!" Joey replies with a salute.

Sal and Billy arrive along with the whirlwind that is Sarah, she dives into my arms.

"Auntie Dilly, you look posh. I still haven't had to go to school and I've been baking with Nanny Pat and I made motorbike cakes. They're really good. Where's Joey? I've saved the best one for him." She plonks a Tupperware container on the table, jumps down and runs off to find Joey with a cake in her hand. Clearly hoping to show him she can cook and is therefore an excellent marriage choice. The container is full of muffins generously iced in an interesting Kawasaki green butter cream and with little rice paper motorbikes on the top.

Billy walks in carrying a huge case of beer. He looks me up and down and whistles.

"Fuck me, Dave, somebody's lucks in. I 'ope our kid don't turn up; 'e'll 'ave 'eart attack."

"Hello to you too, Bill." I laugh as he lifts me off the ground in a huge bear hug.

"Bloody hell, Dil, I ain't seen you in a pair of jeans that actually fit you since ... ever! This man's having a really good effect on you. Go girl!" Sal says as Billy puts me down and she sees me. "Good god, you're even wearing warpaint. It's a shame you haven't mastered the art of wearing shoes yet." She adds looking down at my bare feet and sighing.

CHAPTER 36

The party is getting going as I head outside with drinks. Almost everyone from the campsite has found their way down. Jurgen's crew all look relaxed and appear to be getting along great with each other. The teambuilding is clearly going well. They're discussing work and laughing and slapping each other on the back. The photographers are busy snapping everything that's going on and it reminds me I still have photos to look at. The racers are sharing a bottle of vodka with the French guys. Paddy Jr. and Juan are chatting with Dad and Joey. Sarah looks like she is interrogating poor Ella. Emmett is still busy with Dan and another lad from Dan's band. He looks over in my direction, does a double take, then looks again. He blows out a huge puff of air and beckons me over with his finger. He puts down the guitar and pulls me onto his lap.

"Wow, you are a real sexy lady." He whispers in my ear. "You look gorgeous, little darlin'. What are you trying to do to me?"

"You scrubbed up pretty nicely so I thought I'd make the effort too." I snuggle into his neck, smelling subtle aftershave and clean hair. "I'm not really sure what the plan is to be honest." I giggle nervously. "Total seduction seemed like a good idea when I was dressing but now must admit I'm getting a little scared."

"I'm up for total seduction but you're in charge, darlin'." He breathes into my hair. "Tonight'll go exactly how you want it to, I promise. No pressure, no stupid stuff."

"Who are you? Are you going to marry my Auntie Dilly? You look nicer than the cowman. I like your hair. Can I be a bridesmaid but not wear a dress? Do you like motorbikes?" I pull a very inquisitive Sarah onto my lap on top of Emmett.

"Hi sweetie, this is Emmett. He is definitely much nicer than the cowman and yes, he does have very lovely hair, doesn't he? He likes motorbikes, he can ride really well, not as good as you yet but he's doing okay. I don't think we have any plans to get married just right now but you can definitely be a bridesmaid and wear whatever you like if we do. Emmett meet Sarah, my goddaughter." Emmett kisses her hand theatrically and shows no sign of panic over her wedding suggestions.

"Good evening Miss Sarah, pleased to meet you. What would you like to wear when we do get married? I'll buy it for you." He adds.

"Dunno, I'll have to have a think, maybe a Wonder Woman outfit." She tells him and thinks a little more. "I don't think Auntie Dilly has a dress either. Are you going to buy her one too? She'd look funny in a dress." She giggles.

"Should I get her a big dress like Cinderella when she goes to the ball? And some glass slippers?"

"Nah, Auntie Dilly can't walk in high heels. She'll fall off them and hurt herself." She laughs. "My Dad says she's more of a bloke than he is! Buy her some bike boots and she will probably marry you then."

"Thanks for the great advice, sweetheart." Emmett says, trying desperately to keep a straight face.

"I think I like you a lot and you smell very nice. I'll put you on my list for Auntie Dilly. I can give you some motocross lessons if you want and you can have one of my cakes."

"I like you a lot too, honey." Emmett smiles. "Cake and motocross lessons would be awesome. What's your list about?"

"I need to find someone to marry Auntie Dilly. Uncle Jimbob is dead and I never even met him and mommy says she really needs a man. Joey was going to marry her but he's got Ella now and I like her, she's alright and she has agreed to share and I don't even like the cowman much, he's not no good for Auntie Dilly, he can't even ride a bike! He doesn't even like them! Who doesn't like bikes? He could marry Nana Pat but even she likes bikes and Granddad Will wouldn't like it probably." She's speaking so seriously and Emmett is nodding and agreeing in all the right places. "It's really good you're here because I've only got one person on the list. It's been very hard work." Sal comes over before he has chance to ask who but I suspect I already know.

"Hey Emmett, is my youngest giving you the benefit of her wisdom." She laughs, scooping Sarah up. "Come on baby let's go and raid Auntie Dilly's fridge."

"Oh jeez, she's the most adorable kid in the universe." Emmett smiles. "Do you wanna come shopping for bike boots tomorrow? I'll buy you a dozen pairs if it'll get you to marry me. Who is the cowman?"

"A four-year old's logic is sometimes all I need to put everything into perspective" I sigh happily. "My bike boots have another twenty years of life in them and trust me you do not have to worry yourself about the cowman. If Sarah disapproves it's going nowhere. I'm pretty sure you're safe on the marriage thing too, I don't think you're allowed to be married to two people at the same time."

"Who is my competition then? Who's the mystery man on her list?"

"Who knows?" I say putting my arms around his neck, taking the opportunity for a quick snogging session whilst she's indoors with Sal and the chance to avoid answering that question.

"Darlin', you drive me wild." Emmett laughs, coming up for air.

"Want a drink or something to eat?" I ask. "I'm going to sort some food and grab a bottle." He lets me go without any silliness.

"A beer please, darlin'. I'll eat later. I want to play for a while." I feel his eyes on me as I walk away.

I set a ton of food out on the table and plate up a load to take outside and grab two beers sticking one in each back pocket. I drop off a plate of food with Dad and one with Joey.

"Nice one, Dil." He offers it to Ella before tucking in.

"Plenty more on the table." I yell as I head for Billy. "Grubs up, Bill!" I say handing him a plate. He slings his other arm over my shoulder and pulls me close.

"What yow plannin', Dave? Yow gonna piss off with 'im when 'e goes?" He points his bottle at Emmett.

"Nope, I'm gonna behave like a complete and absolute tart and then wave him goodbye next Saturday." I reply. "That's the plan, right now."

"Ya sure? I ain't seen yow even interested in a bloke since Jimbob. It's good seeing ya 'appy but what the fuck's goin' on?"

"I have no idea, Billy. I think coming back here just made me realise life is passing me by and like Dad says Jimbob isn't coming back in his previous incarnation and he probably wouldn't want me to wait around forever. Knowing they'll all be leaving next week kind of makes it easier; a bit of an experiment to see if I still have a heart." I admit.

"Don't run, Dave. Wherever 'appens. Stay." He kisses my head.

"That's the plan, hun." I sigh, leaning into him for a big hug and feeling safe. "Having fun and going nowhere."

"Sal's took Dave to me Mam's so yow can cavort like a hooker for the rest of the night and we can get pissed an' 'ave a shag in peace." He laughs. "Enjoy yerself, don't get 'eadfucked... Do one thing for me."

"Whatever you want, babe."

"Let our kid take you to the shindig Sunday. He just needs his fix and he might chill the fuck out. This is killin' 'im." He nods his head towards Emmett again.

"I gotta get it out of my system." I shrug. "I'll be there Sunday and he'll be gone. Our Rick's got plenty of very willing ladies to choose from."

"That'll do for me. Ain't got a fuckin' clue 'ow much 'e wants yow, 'ave ya?" I open my mouth to argue but have nothing to say. "Dave's fallin' an' all. Must be somat in the air round 'ere." He points to Joey with his arms wrapped gently around Ella, swaying to the music.

"Sal had her pegged for Nath. She's lovely."

191

"I'm pretty sure our Dave's on the other team but don't tell his mam. Who's the blond kid that's got an MV?"

"Connor. Why?"

"He's bin round our way 'til pretty late most nights." He winks.

"You and Sal need to talk." I sigh.

"About what? Talking wasn't what I had in mind." Sal asks, putting her arms around Billy's waist. "Give me my husband back you hussy. Go and play with your own sexy man. I've got serious plans for mine tonight. I've been watching you for some tips." She giggles.

"Teams." I say. "You need to talk about teams and you've got more game than I've ever had or will ever have, you tart!" I smirk and kiss her on the cheek and leave them in peace.

The guys are playing some seriously good music. I don't want to distract Emmett so I sit down with Dad and The Macs and chat about how their TT is going so far and how the bike is running, talking through some different set ups. Then I light the fire and the torches and go to grab another drink. I think Bill pinched my last two. Emmett appears behind me as I reach into the fridge.

"Where have you been my beautiful woman? I need you close to me and I'm pretty sure you promised to get me a beer an hour ago." He laughs.

"I'm sorry, sweetheart. I got sidetracked and you were playing some serious stuff so I didn't want to disturb you." I say, offering him a bottle.

"Come and sit with me now, please? I want to share the music with you."

"I can't believe how much this has calmed you down." I smile teasing him. "You really didn't need me at all, did you? You just needed a guitar. You'll have forgotten who I am by tomorrow."

"Has Sarah gone home?" He asks, looking around then taking the bottles from me and putting them gently on the table.

"She's gone to her nan's, why?" He pins me up against the fridge, growls and proceeds to demonstrate how much self-restraint he has been showing. Its rather a lot! Oh dear, there go my plans. I'm willingly jammed against the fridge with my legs wrapped tightly around Emmett's waist, sucking his face off, when Stefan saves me from myself once more.

"Hey, you two, you're blocking the access to the beer and I'm pretty sure it'll be getting warm too! We're gonna try playing a few requests. What's your ultimate killer tune Delilah?"

"Faithfully." I reply immediately, without thinking. "Shit no! Don't play it I'll cry like an idiot."

"Well it's certainly an appropriate choice." Stef laughs looking at Emmett who is looking at me strangely, he must know it, surely. "Come on, Captain Caveman, put the sexy lady down, we need strings." Emmett puts me down but holds onto my hand tightly and collects our beers on the way out.

"Request time, ladies and gentlemen." Dan announces. "Who's going to kick us off?" Dad does.

"How about Bad Company? Feel Like Making Love." They play a superb rendition to much cheering and whistling. Jurgen requests Child of Babylon by Whitesnake and it sends shivers down my spine. Emmett doesn't take his eyes off me as he's playing.

"Something heavier and newer!" Charlie begs from the drums.

"What's that one Dil's always singing about Never Never Land?"

"Enter Sandman." I laugh. "It's about as up to date as my musical knowledge reaches but It's older than you Joey."

"Be good to 'ear what it's s'posed to sound like." He quips back.

They do it a damn sight more justice than I ever have. Then we're treated to some Scorpions, a beautiful, heart wrenching version of Desperado with just Stef singing and Emmett on guitar.

"Can we have some DC, now?" Billy yells and we get a complete montage.

"Come on Dil, your turn." Dan says.

Emmett plays the first few chords of Faithfully. I shake my head rapidly pleading with my eyes for him to stop, thankfully he does and goes straight into a rendition of 'Why, Why, Why, Delilah'. I can't stop giggling.

"How about some Chili Peppers? Under the Bridge or Give it Away or Californication."

"An excellent choice, ma'am." Felix drawls and we are treated to some seriously good guitar and bass playing.

"More Whitesnake, Is this Love." Sal shouts next.

"Dan, it's all yours, man I need to hold my woman for this one and possibly the rest of the night." Emmett yells, putting down his guitar.

He holds me close and we sway to the beat as he sings softly to me and I can feel his fingers playing the chords up and down the base of my spine. Look out Dil, you're getting in way too deep!

They drop the tempo and anyone with a partner gets up to smooch.

"Okay, last one guys, it's 3am and some of us have work in the morning. Well, in three hours actually." Dan groans. "This one's for Dil, so hold her tight, Emmett." He steps back and Stefan steps forward and with his hauntingly beautiful voice and no backing whatsoever sings the first few lines of Faithfully by Journey.

Emmett has to hold me up, my legs turn to jelly. Don't cry, don't cry! Too late. I'm pretty sure I now look like Emmett and Stefan did the day they arrived, mascara everywhere. I've got my face buried in Emmett's chest, lost in the song. I feel him reach over and take the mic and he gently lifts my chin. Looking directly into my eyes, he sings to me like no one else is there, not letting me go...'loving a music man ain't always what it's supposed to be...Oh Dil *please* stand by me. I'm forever yours, faithfully....I think I've just died and gone to heaven. My whole body is tingling, that weird feeling when you've had way, way too much coffee and you're buzzing. Inside my head any last vestige of self-control and doubt is gone I'm pretty sure I will be giving in to Emmett's advances tonight. I can't fight it any more. He finishes to a massive round of applause and kisses me gently and wipes away my tears. Bless him, he kicks me out of my stupor and stops me making a complete fool of myself.

"Was it that awful, darlin'?" He jokes.

"You win, take me now." I laugh, shaking my head in amazement.

Everyone helps the guys pack away their stuff and then drift off back to their tents or home. Dan shakes hands with Stef and Emm and thanks us for a surreal night.

"Come back next week and we'll do it again." Felix says, giving him a bro hug. "We've had the best time! I'll text you tomorrow." Dan looks like a very happy man as they drive off. "I'm away to my bed, enjoy the rest of your night guys." He hugs and kisses me and hugs his Dad. "Night Joe, night Ella"

"We're goin' up. Got work in a few hours." Joey says with a yawn. "Bin a great night! Love yas." He leads Ella to the barn. Bill and Sal come over for a hug.

"Fair play Dave, I gotta admit ya makin' a real effort. I'd shag ya if yow sung to me like that!" Billy grins, shaking Emmett's hand. "Just remember she might still run yet, so tread careful. She's a very unusual kind of special this one." He looks at me closely, checking I'm okay, hugs me and they leave. Dad, Jeff and Dutch come out of the cottage.

"Me and the guys fancy a night under canvas." He smiles, kissing my head and heading for the campsite. We are alone. Oh shit! Stop panicking Dil!

CHAPTER 37

I start to tidy away the plates and bottles and Emmett stops me. "That can wait until the morning." He says gently. "Come here, please Dil."

"Do you want to walk on the beach?" I ask, stalling for time.

"If that's what you want to do, darlin'." Emmett smiles indulgently, taking my hand. "Whatever happens next, I just need you to know tonight has already been truly amazing. Thank you."

"You're thanking me? Emmett are you crazy? I invited some people over! You turned it into one of the most special nights of my life and possibly Dan's too I think." I reply trying to lighten the situation.

"Playing has become a job." He shrugs. "Tonight was freedom and fun and the chance to go back to how it used to be. It really was good to see Felix and Charlie playing with no pressure and you even chose one of his favorite songs without even knowing it. You make magic happen, Delilah Blue!"

"I didn't want the night to end." I confess. "There's at least a dozen other songs I wanted you to play. Did you get to play your favourite?"

"Yeah, didn't you see the look on mine and Stef's face when you asked for it?" He laughs. "We both love that one. It's been the soundtrack to our lives. Come on then, more getting to know each other. What's your all-time top five?"

"Tough one, you go first!" I say. "I can't put them into order it depends on what I need at the time, music helps me through stuff."

"Okay, I'll make it easier... next favourite Journey track?"

"Open Arms!" We both say at the same time and laugh.

"Chili's?"

"Californication." I reply.

"Bizkit?"

"Their version of Behind Blue Eyes."

"Let's go old school..... Floyd?"

"Numb."

"Who?"

"Behind Blue Eyes."

"Meatloaf?"

"Gotta be Paradise by The Dashboard Light!" I grin. "I wanted to be Ellen

Foley. She was so sexy and sleazy and tough."

"Delilah you are truly my soul mate! I will not tell you what I wanted to do to Ellen Foley as a young man. I can demonstrate if you'd like me to? Come here and kiss me now!" He demands with a laugh, sitting down on my rock and holding out his arms. "I will sing you anything you want if you just let me hold you."

"I'm scared, Emm." I finally admit when I'm safely in his arms. "I don't know if I can do this. I'm going to be a real letdown to you."

"Stop thinking and go with the flow, darlin'. You will never do anything but amaze me." Emmett kisses me deeply and slowly and runs his hand down my spine. I tense and panic and he stops straight away. Bloody Hell, Delilah what is wrong with you?

"Relax, little darlin'. You're totally in control." Emmett whispers into my hair. "We're doing this your way. I can handle it wherever it goes. Those showers have got a really good cold setting." He adds with a wry smile.

"Emm, I'm so sorry, I can't handle pressure. I know it's me putting it on myself and not you and I know I've pushed you to the limit. I don't think I want this to end and it will as soon as I give in."

"Why the heck would it end? Delilah, this is just the start, you crazy woman! The start of a very special and very long journey to paradise" He giggles at his cheesy line. "Come on darlin', it's late and you're getting a bit overwhelmed by all this, it's been an intense evening, let's just go to sleep and I can hold you all night. I'll be content with that, I swear."

We head back to the cottage hand in hand and I feel like a complete failure. I really am disappointed in myself. I've led this poor man on so badly and he's still being kind and gentle with me. What the hell is wrong with me? He's sexy and gorgeous and does things to my body and my mind that I never knew were possible and I have enjoyed every second of it and gone back for more. He's shown restraint when I've asked, been compassionate and patient throughout. I made the poor guy lie with me all night yesterday with no payback. He is an angel! Sort your bloody head out Dil! You know this is the very last hurdle, why do you not want to jump it?

"Shit! Stop Emmett. I need to come clean!" I stop him and he turns to face me looking seriously concerned.

"Dil, what's wrong, darlin'? Talk to me please. I need to know so I can fix it." I take a very deep breath; okay this is it Dil...

"You know I told you that my first and last boyfriend was Jimbob..."

"Honey, I don't need to know that you have some kind of casual relationship with Ricky. I've seen how relaxed you are around him and much he wants you whenever he's near. Technically I'm married Delilah, I'm not going to judge you."

I laugh. "Err no, I most definitely don't. I love him to pieces but it is purely platonic. Ricky is my safety net and I am a challenge he thinks he wants to conquer but has never really tried. He makes me feel like I could play around if I wanted to, makes me feel more 'normal'. I was telling the truth, Jimbob was my first and last man before you. I've been running away from relationships ever since."

"You don't have much experience? Do you really think I care? It makes you even more special. Darlin' I'll take it as slow as you want. I'm looking forward to working on that with you."

"Jimbob was a pretty devout Buddhist..... We weren't married....." It takes him a second for it to sink in.

"Ah... I see... jeez... okay, even less experience than I thought?" He raises an eyebrow in question. I nod. "No wonder Billy is so protective of you. Wow! As I said you never do anything but amaze me, Delilah." He doesn't seem to know what to do for a second then he folds me into his arms and just rocks me gently. You've done it now you cowardly idiot, he knows what a complete freak you are now. He's going to make excuses the first chance he gets and run a mile. No, hang on that's what I would do! Now's your chance Delilah, take it for heaven's sake!

"Kiss me, Emmett, please...make me feel like you have done so many times over these last few extraordinary days and nights. I promise I won't stop you. I want you so much it scares me." He obliges immediately. Kissing me deeply and taking my breath away. He picks me up and carries me into the cottage and sits us down gently on the settee. He takes me to the edge of reason just by kissing me and stroking my spine, then stops.

"Shower?" He asks. I nod, praying he doesn't put me down because I'm pretty sure I will be unable to stand up. He carries me into the bathroom, turns on the shower and then puts me onto my feet. "Arms up, baby." He smiles and gently pulls my t-shirt over my head. I'm just in a euphoric daze. He takes a breath when he sees I have no underwear on, I've never had anything that warranted a bra but I instinctively cover myself with my dreads. He pushes them back over my shoulders, doesn't touch, just looks, sending me into total frenzy. I panic slightly when he goes for the button on my jeans. He stops immediately and backs off, pulling off his own t-shirt to distract me. It works...he is a work of art ..toned and tanned, sculpted, without an ounce of extra meat on him. I realise I had done my best not to look when he copped me in the shower before. I put my hand lightly on his chest exploring with my fingers. He shivers at my touch.

"Dil, you're driving me crazy" He whispers. "Are you okay?"

"Emm, okay doesn't really cover it. I couldn't honestly find the words right now but I definitely don't want it to stop. I have a feeling I'm going to really enjoy whatever is coming next." He turns me around so that I am leaning on his chest with his arms around me and he undoes my button and zip slowly and carefully then quickly slips off his own jeans and hops into the shower giggling.

"Come on in, darlin', the water's lovely."

I tear off my jeans and dive in. We spend lots of time slowly exploring each other's bodies and getting soapy and slippery. He traces his fingers carefully around all of my tattoos, fascinated by their meanings and the stories behind where I got them.

"Where the heck is this bruise from?" He asks looking at my left buttock. "My god, I haven't done that to you have I?" He asks in a panic. "I forget you're so tiny and fragile. I get carried away."

"I might be little but I'm as hard as nails, honey. That's a love bite off Giles." He looks confused for a second. "The donkey, you twit." He shakes his head.

"Now I'm jealous of a donkey. Are you clean enough gorgeous? Want to hit the hay?" We dry each other off with big fluffy towels and I lead him to my little bed. He doesn't question my choice. Pulling back the duvet and jumping in, he cuddles me up tight.

"You're so brave and beautiful my darlin' Delilah." He says. "We can just sleep now if that's what you want. We've got the rest of our lives to ...." I cut him off with a kiss.

"Keep going baby, something tells me this is going to be the best bit."

"I'll try my best to make it memorable." He smiles, turns me onto my back and disappears down the bed.

"Oh, good grief Emmett!" I squeal as my toes curl and my whole body tingles.

He reappears, looking concerned. "Don't you like that?"

"Bloody hell, yes! Do it again!"

"You're in charge." He grins and gets right to it.

When he comes back up for air I kiss him softly on the chest and down his ribs and his stomach and ...

"Woah, darlin'. Time out!" He groans, putting his hands under my arms and tugging me back up to look into his eyes. "This is going to be over far too soon if I even think you're planning to do what I think you are." He laughs. "I know I said you're in charge but you're getting pretty adventurous and it's been quite a while for me too. I've only got so much self-control; you're driving me wild. You can do whatever you like to me later but right now let me take the lead sweetheart, please. Trust me."

"I'm all yours, baby, do your thing." I giggle. He turns me onto my back, throws the duvet onto the floor and, after pinning my wrists above my head with one hand so that I cannot touch him, he slowly and deliberately kisses every single inch of me sending my senses into a complete frenzy. My entire body feels like it's fizzing. Holding his weight above me with one arm, he gently guides himself inside me. He groans and lets out a growl like a caged bear. I gasp and he stops still, looking into my eyes, checking I'm okay.

"Don't stop, Emm." I plead.

He takes me to a place way beyond paradise. I lose all sense of time and reason. Oh my God Delilah why have you waited so long? This is better than cave diving. It's like freefalling without a parachute! One hell of a rush!

Emmett growls again, it's more of a guttural howl this time and a million fireworks go off inside my body and I completely lose my head. He slows and collapses on top of me. I can feel our heartbeats crashing together. He rolls us over so that I am on top and holds me tightly whispering softly into my hair.

"Are you okay, little darlin'? I'm sorry I couldn't hold on any longer, you make me lose my mind." I wipe away my tears and laugh.

"I know I have no previous experience but I'm pretty sure five hours is more than adequate and I'm more than satisfied. I'm spent. My whole body has no idea what's just happened to it but I'm definitely gonna need to try that again really soon."

"Give me half an hour or so and I'll gladly oblige, darlin'." He drawls and we fall into a deep, dreamless sleep our bodies completely entwined.

I'm awoken sometime later by Emmett making slow and beautiful love to me. No pressure, no athletics just slow, gentle, sleepy love. It feels so amazing. I just relax completely and let him guide our every move. It is beyond bliss. I have never felt so out of control in my life and it feels unreal. I eventually drift back into sleep and am awoken a second time by a big dribbly lick on the head and a full-on attack from a very happy Jeff.

"Coffee, darlin'?" Emmett smiles handing me a mug.

"Thank you, baby. Can this day get any better?" I sigh taking a sip of coffee made to perfection.

Emmett gestures to the mug. "Did I get it right?"

"Spot on. You're a genius."

"Not exactly. I've been on the phone to your Joe for twenty minutes, I couldn't even work out how to turn your fancy gadget on! He gave me a walkthrough."

"That's proper love, that is." I tease. "You can stay for a while."

"Honey, I'm hooked. I'm going nowhere." He leans over and kisses me. "Fancy a rip on the bikes later?"

"Sounds like a plan but I'm not sure I can even stand up right now." I laugh. "I need all my wits about me to wrestle with The Duchess and quite frankly, I have been ... Errm... I think the technical term is, 'shagged senseless'." Emmett dissolves into hysterics and shakes his head in awe.

"I'm pretty sure I love you, Delilah! I'm actually a little scared of what I appear to have unleashed."

"Scared is good. We can work on that." I tease.

"Get dressed before I do something unspeakable to you that I will not regret in any way whatsoever." He laughs, throwing my t shirt at me. "We need to go face the music."

"Not sure I'm ready to share you just yet." I groan. "Wanna try out that thing you're not going to regret first?" He does and there are definitely no regrets on either side.

CHAPTER 38

I t's way past lunchtime when we finally emerge from my little bed. I've got half a dozen texts. Dad telling me everything is sorted for the day and he's at the pits and to join them later if we want, Billy, Sal and Joey checking I'm okay. Dan thanking us again for last night, the vet inviting me to dinner a week on Tuesday and another from Billy from ten minutes ago 'ok? ansa 4 fuksake'. I send him a quick one back 'better than ok xxx'

"You ready to face the world now, my beautiful darlin'?" Emmett asks, taking my hand and leading me out into the sunshine. We walk on the beach to clear our heads and check my legs still function correctly then I start to clear up the bottles and plates from yesterday.

Felix wanders down. "Good evening both. Man, you guys must have been really tired last night." He teases looking at his watch. "Are we going to be watching some practice later or are you two still sleepy?"

"I'm pretty sure you and Joe are related." I laugh. "Have you ever been to Liverpool?" I ask Emmett with an arched brow.

"Not that I recall, ma'am." He drawls. "Almost positively sure this is the only one I'm responsible for."

Felix groans. "Oh hell, I'm not sure I wanna spend time with you if you're this happy, it's frightening."

"You have no idea, Son." He laughs. "I will apologise now because I'm gonna be embarrassing the heck out of you for the foreseeable future."

"Thanks for the heads up. Do I need to warn Joe too?"

"That might be a good idea." I smile. "Moving swiftly on... Dad asked if we wanted to go down to the paddock for practice. We could go in a bit and get in a run over the mountain but the traffic won't be too clever so no pissing about, or we can watch from wherever you like."

"Paddock is fine, I've developed a bit of a thing for those hot pork sandwiches." Felix replies. "I'll text Joe and go and let the others know."

"I'll clear this lot and meet you at the gate in twenty minutes." I tell him. "Take your Dad with you or else I'll be late."

"Come on, old boy, Stef is beside himself, he's been pacing round like an expectant father for the last three hours." Emmett grins and reluctantly follows him.

I finish tidying up, feed the donkeys and chucks, give Jeff and Dutch loads of cuddles and treats, watching Dutch carefully but getting nothing but head butts, purrs and love. I have a quick shower, put on my decent bike jeans, a clean t shirt and a bit of make-up, grab my leather jacket and fire up The Duchess.

I stop at the gate to pick everyone up but don't take off my helmet, I suddenly realise they all know what I was up to last night and I'm more than a little embarrassed even though they don't know the half of it.

Despite earlier reservations, I am now in the mood to ride and I need to clear my head of everything that's happened before I become overwhelmed. I focus on the road and ride like a maniac over the mountain, carefully dodging what little traffic there is. Jurgen is right behind me and I can sense his enjoyment of the thrill of the chase, Emmett and Stefan are almost keeping up, Felix is way back fooling around and pulling wheelies despite my 'no pissing about' suggestion and the others are riding sensibly in a small group behind him. We pull up at the paddock and the bikes are hot. Dad comes straight out to meet us.

"Is the devil chasing you Dilly Girl?" He asks. "We heard you coming over the mountain."

"Jurgen made me do it!" I reply with a big grin, taking my helmet off. Dad hugs me tightly and laughs.

"Jurgen, are you leading my daughter astray?"

"Nein, I think you must speak with Emmett about that." He replies. "Delilah was definitely in front and you know men will chase her. You must try this baby before I leave, she is a pretty nice ride." He says patting the Panigale.

"I'll ride her back home later if you promise not to abuse The Duchess."

"I can't promise that she's like you, Liebling, she makes me do bad things."

Joey and Nathan pull up beside us and come over. Joey gives me a quick hug. "'ow was ya coffee, ma?" He grins.

"Perfect. Did you get to second base?"

"Nah, I did a Dil on 'er and fell a kip when she was in the shower." He shrugs. "But she was still there s'mornin' and Emmett's put me right on the shower thing." He grins optimistically.

Emmett hears as he comes up behind him. "That's my boy!" He laughs. "Come here, my crazy little speed demon." He drawls at me.

"I'm off, Felix already warned me." He rolls his eyes and takes off after Nathan and the others.

I notice Nathan and Connor are pretty cosy. "Emm, has Connor got a girlfriend?" I ask casually.

"You do not miss anything Delilah, you already know the answer to that, don't you? Billy doesn't know does he?"

"Yep."

"Shit. Should we be worried?"

"Bill's a pussy cat."

"Okay, not the first word that comes to my mind when I see him but I'll take your word for it."

"It's all good. Feed me now, baby!" I giggle. "I seem to have worked up quite an appetite today."

"Darlin', come and get your strength up 'cos the day ain't over yet." He holds out his hand and we head to the food vans. We eat everything they have to offer and go and find seats up in the back of the grandstand, away from everyone else. Well, Emmett finds one and draws me into his lap.

"How's my girl?" He asks. "No smart mouth, the truth."

"Emm, I could not be happier, truthfully. You have taken me on the most amazing journey to places I have never been and whatever happens next I will never forget you and always be grateful for the time you have shared with me." I kiss him gently. "You are the best thing that has happened to me in a very, very, very long time. I get that it will all end soon and I can deal with that."

"Dil, why do you keep saying it's going to end? I'm not letting you go now I've found you."

"Emmett, sweetheart. Our lives are on parallel lines. You love it here because it's so far away from your normal life. You can be someone else here. It's not real is it?"

"Don't say that. This is absolutely where I belong. I have enough money to stop working. I don't ever have to leave here. Just say the word and I'll stay."

"No Emmett, I can't do that. I saw you play last night; music is your life; you'll be lost without it and what about Stefan and the boys? This isn't just about me and you. I would never ask you to stay or put pressure on you to change anything. You know what I think about pressure."

"Darlin', can we agree to disagree right now? I'm not risking anything with you, I know you're a runner. We'll have the best time of our lives, make fools of ourselves, embarrass our kids, get to know each other and see if you can teach me to ride like a demon and I'll share a few of my skills with you ..." He grins.

"Now who's the smart mouth?"

"Kiss me, gorgeous woman! No more talk of endings." He crushes his lips mine and makes me almost forget our conversation and leaves me wanting so much more. The sound of the bikes starting up kicks me out of my stupor.

"Auntie Dil, can I talk to you?" It's a very worried looking Nathan, Connor is hovering a little way behind him.

"Any time sweetheart, you know that. What's up?" I ask patting the chair next to me. "You want Emmett to make himself scarce?"

"He's fine, he knows."

I take both his hands in mine. "Nathan, my beautiful boy, do you honestly think Emmett knows something about you that I don't?"

"He's told you?" He's not sure whether to be relieved or feel betrayed.

"Emmett didn't say a word. I promise." I look at Connor to make sure he's heard too. "Your Dad told me."

Every bit of colour drains from his face. "He knows? ... How much?"

"What bike does Connor ride?" I smile. "You know your Dad's gonna notice an MV pipe. He knows everything he needs to."

"He's okay with it?" Nathan looks at me in amazement.

"He's cool with it, darling. He loves you and he always will. You know that."

"Mom?" He asks.

"Didn't know about Connor last night but your Dad's probably told her by now. She does know about you. They didn't know that each other knew. I dropped a real big hint that they should talk last night."

He throws his arms around me and hugs me tightly. "Joe said you'd sort it, thank you."

"I didn't sort anything, Nathan. Talk to them but don't worry, it'll be an ordeal for you but they'll be fine."

"I know, I'll talk to them, I promise. It's a big ask but can you tell Uncle Rick if Dad doesn't?"

"Ah, yes. I can see why you'd wanna avoid that one. It might be an interesting conversation." I cringe, Ricky has occasionally voiced extremely homophobic views, especially when a lady he picked up in Thailand turned out to be a man. "Leave him to me, darling. I'll talk to him."

"Thank you. I owe you one."

"If I've gotta tell Rick you owe me more than one!" I laugh. "You're you sweetie and we all love you and we will love and accept whoever you choose to be with, don't ever doubt that." He kisses my cheek and takes off with Connor to get a drink.

"Delilah, you are one hell of a woman!" Emmett tells me yet again.

"He's the one with the guts, Emm. I can't imagine how hard that was for him. Poor baby."

"You made it so much easier for him. Is his uncle going to freak out?" He asks.

"Rick's a puppy dog, same as his big bro." I laugh.

"He's a scary, big ass predator and he wants my girl." He sighs.

"Rick doesn't do commitment sweetheart. We would have happened a long time ago if we were going to. We just enjoy the game."

"No more playing with other boys, you're mine now. I'm gonna fulfil your every need."

"You'd better buy yourself a plant hire business then and be prepared to jump out of perfectly good airplanes into large holes in the ground and free climb big chunks of rock and fix punctures in the middle of the jungle. Ricky will always be in my life, he's family, get over it. Have I mentioned your wife at all?" I kiss him to soften the blow.

"Heard and understood." He laughs when I let him up for air. "What did I hear Joe call you yesterday? He's right isn't he? You really are a 'mama bear', family is everything to you even when they're not blood. You'll fight for them."

"You're getting to know me, Emmett, my darling." I shrug. "You'd fight for Stef and Connor and Charlie, wouldn't you? And I know you'd kill for Felix."

"Yeah, I guess so but I love your passion, you've got real balls."

"Now you know that's not true." I tease. "I wasn't exactly brave last night; I was a right state."

"Delilah, darlin' I wouldn't change a second of last night for all the money in the world, would you?" He looks concerned.

"Yep." I giggle. "It wouldn't have ended for another three weeks at least. I was having too much fun to let you go."

"Your place or mine tonight?" He grins.

"I can't keep kicking Dad out of his home." I groan. "Can you control the growling and howling if we stay in the tent?" I giggle.

"I do not growl and I certainly don't howl." He laughs.

"Trust me, honey, you do." I shrug as he lets out a low growl and smothers me with kisses. Dad comes up to sit with us to watch the bikes and pick my brains about brake shoes for Paddy Jr.

"Have you eaten?" I ask him.

"Yeah, Meave bought us a box of goodies earlier and I've had a pork bap. I'm fine. Think we're going to eat on the way home. I'm gonna stay up with Jurgen again tonight, okay?"

"No Dad, I'm not turfing you out of your own home. We're camping tonight."

"Dilly girl, getting to see you so happy is worth a million nights in a tent. I like sleeping under canvas. It's what I want to do so no arguments." He sees Paddy Jr. pull in and runs back down stairs.

Stefan comes up next and kisses me on the cheek. "Hi gorgeous, is he looking after you?"

"Nope, he's teaching me some really bad habits and our kids won't come near us." I reply.

Stefan and Emmett dissolve into hysterics. "We're going for a meal afterwards at The Hawthorn, me, Dad, your dad and the kids. Are you coming?"

"Did Joey and Felix say we can?" I ask.

"Only if you're not going to, and I quote, 'take your kecks off and shag on the table or howl' I think Joey's words were or 'suck each other's faces off while we're eating'."

"Is that a request from my Son?" Emmett laughs.

"Yeah. I think they're long lost brothers. Didn't we play a gig in Liverpool about seventeen years ago?" Stefan muses with a grin. I look at Emmett and arch that eyebrow again.

"Don't you start, Stef. Dil accused me of being his father earlier."

"Must be something in it then." He grins. "Nathan's been to see you hasn't he? Whatever you said meant the world to him. He looked like a different kid when he came from talking to you. Connor said you were an angel. Thanks, I remember what hell Connor went through. He's never been quite so smitten with anyone until he met Nath."

"Nathan is one of the kindest, gentlest and most generous, patient young men I have ever had the pleasure to know and I love him dearly. Is he going to get hurt when you all leave next week?" I ask seriously.

"I don't think so." Stefan replies. "I think he might come with us. If he doesn't then between Connor and Emm the plane is going to be getting plenty of use."

"Thank you for being honest with me. Were there any other caveats to us joining you to eat?" I enquire with a grin.

"Only one, you have to let me ride The Duchess. I'll treat her with more respect than Dad." He grins a cheeky grin like Joey and I agree.

Practice is done and we head back to the bikes. Emmett grabs me for a quick snog before I put my helmet on.

"Father, what have you been told?" Felix places his hands on his hips in mock annoyance.

"That I can't take my kecks off and shag on the table or suck Delilah's face off while you're eating" He replies. "Are you eating? No! So put your helmet on and bugger off!"

"Jeez, you're impossible!" Felix laughs.

I talk Stefan through some of The Duchess' more quirky quirks and throw my leg over the Panigale.

CHAPTER 39

The Panigale is so easy and smooth compared to The Duchess but the journey is too short and the traffic too rubbish to put it through its paces.

"Can I ride her home?" I ask Jurgen as we park up. "She's got potential but I couldn't try her out."

"Of course, Liebling. She is beautiful ja, Kawasaki's have no soul." He sighs gesturing to Stefan's bike. "I think it will improve though if I can chase you back."

Stefan gives me back my keys. "She's one scary son of a bitch!" He exclaims. "She dares you to push then kicks your ass! I have never ridden anything like her. I'm pretty sure she growled at a car that was blocking her way back there."

"Yeah, she does that a lot." I smile. "Hang on to the keys if you want. I'm going to give the Pan a proper workout on the way home."

"I might swap with Dad or your dad. I don't have a death wish." He grins.

"I'll ride her back." Felix offers cheekily.

"I have no desire to lose my only Son, even if he is a cheeky pain in the ass." Emmett says. "Every safety aid known to man is fitted to your bike. You have only just been able to turn the wheelie control off because Dil taught you to handle it. You will not throw your leg over that scary thing ever! Even if Delilah says you can."

"Aw, Dad!" Felix whines. "I'm not a kid!"

"Get Delilah to take you on the back tomorrow, you'll get a feel for it." Dad suggests. "She's not a tame beastie like yours. Even I have to be in the mood for her."

"Will you?" Felix begs me. "Tomorrow?"

Jurgen giggles. "Dylan, you are cruel. He is a young boy; he will embarrass himself, ja?"

Dad realises what he's talking about. "That's not what I meant." He laughs. "Dil wouldn't do that to him!"

"Your daughter? She will not be able to resist." Jurgen replies.

I'm only half listening and too busy thinking about food. "Yep, if you get up early enough we can have a clear run."

"It's a date!" Felix grins, giggling when he sees his Dad's face.

We all head for the pub door and Emmett pulls me back asking Felix to order us both the biggest steaks on the menu.

"Oh heck, I'm so sorry Emmett honey, I won't take him if you don't want me to." I say, concerned that he's just told him no. "I shouldn't have done that."

"Done what?" Emmett looks confused for a second. "Oh him? Darlin' scare him shitless; it'll do him good. I wasn't holding you back for that. I trust you to take him on any bike." He gives me a really cheeky smile. "If I've gotta behave for an hour or so I need a fix. Come here and let me suck your face off!" I happily let him drag me into a dark corner of the car park.

We get drinks and sit down. Joey one side, Felix the other. "We're the decency feds." Joey informs me with a grin. "Behave yerselves."

I playfully shove him off his chair. "Where's Bella Ella?"

"Some family thing, she might come round 'ome later if it's okay?"

"Joe you don't have to ask, darling, you know that. Just be careful please, I don't wanna be a 'grandma bear' for a few years yet."

He laughs and hugs me. "You'll be a really boss nan but don't worry I've got plenty more stuff planned before becoming a dad. That's about twenty years from now I reckon. I wanna 'ave done stuff I can tell me kids about. Ricky an' Bill keep warnin' me an' all, I ain't daft."

The food arrives and we all tuck in and spend the evening having fun, putting the world to rights, noisily chatting about music and bikes, catching up on Jurgen's retirement plans. Nathan looks so happy and relaxed and I notice he's holding hands with Connor under the table. Emmett is also up to something under the table, he is worse than a teenager! I giggle and squirm as he squeezes my knee and walks his fingers up my thigh.

"What's he up to now?" Felix asks rolling his eyes.

"Grown up stuff, you wouldn't understand. I'm not breaking either of your rules." His Dad teases him.

"I am a bloody grown up, I'm twenty-four." He laughs "Jeez, I behave more like a grown up than you! I bet you'd be more scared on the back of Delilah's bike than I will."

"Enlighten me Son, why would that be?" Emmett laughs.

"Easy! You're a control freak." Felix shrugs. "You will have to let Delilah take total control. You won't handle that."

"It's 'ell of a rush an' I know she went real careful with me on the back." Joey chimes in. "Me 'ead went light and me eyes rolled when she opened 'er up. Pretty sure I was unconscious for a second or two."

"Okay, I'll leave the BM here and go home on Dil's pillion if you like." Emmett rises to the challenge.

"Don't count." Joey says. "She's ridin' Jurgen's Pan back. The Duchess is somat else. Paddy Jr. took me on 'is race BM and it was boss but nothin' like The Duchess."

"Okay, tomorrow morning. You're on. Wanna go first or second?" Emmett challenges Felix.

I get up from the table with a giggle and a sigh. "Far too much testosterone here boys, I'm going to get a drink and talk to my Dad."

Dad and Jurgen are animatedly recounting the tale of testing nighttime skiing speed theories to Stef, Connor, Nathan and Charlie. I'm sure Nath has heard it once or twice before but he's clearly enjoying Jurgen's story telling style. I shiver involuntarily just thinking about it and they all laugh at me.

Eventually, another lovely evening comes to an end and we're kicked out of the pub at closing time.

"Who riding what where?" Dad asks as we get to the bikes.

"Have you got the minerals to take The Duchess again?" Jurgen goads Stef. "Or do you want your carbon zombie back? If I am going to chase Delilah, I need a worthy steed." I send a pleading look to Stefan over Jurgen's shoulder.

"I'll take her but I'm racing no one. I'm just pootling home like a little old dude." Stefan concedes taking the keys.

Dad laughs "Give us the keys, she will give you hell if you try that with her. You take mine, let your Dad take yours and I'll get The Duchess home." I blow him a big kiss and am about to put on my helmet when Emmett stops me.

"Hang on one minute there little lady, restrictions are lifted, the kids have finished eating."

Felix shakes his head and starts his bike up. "Come on guys. See you both in the morning!"

"Night boys, ride safe. I'll give you a ten second head start, Jurgen. Past our turn off and one lap and back to the campsite." I tease. They all take off.

"Ten seconds?" Emmett asks.

"Kiss me, honey, you're running out of time." I giggle. "I wanna try this baby out then I'm all yours. You can howl and growl at me all night long."

"You can bloody well wait for it now! It might make you ride faster." He laughs pulling on his helmet.

"Emm, it's pitch dark and you don't know the roads be careful, please. I'll warm the bed if I'm back first. Ride safe." I take off after Jurgen.

The roads are deserted and the bike is amazing. It has every electronic gadget under the sun and is the smoothest, most forgiving bike I have ridden in a long time. The brakes are razor sharp, the suspension firm and the tyres have superb grip. It still has both soul and character it's like The Duchess after ten years at the most refined finishing school. It drifts round bends too and that's a really neat trick.

I take a cheeky short cut and come out just behind the others and zip past the kids easily. Felix takes chase but scares himself on a damp patch and shuts off. I pass Stef who's giving Dad's old Kwak a gentle leg stretching and catch up with Dad who's letting The Duchess do her thing. We race for a few minutes and I can hear him talking to The Duchess, telling her to behave. He moves over as we reach the hairpin, he knows I will race as fast as I can past all the ghosts and heartache. He likes to shout 'hi' to Marley and Jimbob, I still can't even look at either spot.

I'm thinking of nothing, Jurgen is in my sights, the road is completely clear and the moon is almost full and it's bright. I hope this baby's been run in because she's about to get a thorough thrashing. I hare up the mountain mile and drift around the Verandah. Jurgen sees me and gets his head down. I'm right behind him as we pass the Creg and I manage to get by him coming round Brandish and down to Hillberry. We slow a little down to the start/finish line as there are still a few cars about and neither of us want to get knocked off or stopped by a jobsworth police officer. Bray Hill is clear and we take off again but then have to ease off past the Crosby as there's still plenty of movement in and around the pub.

Once we get to the crossroads we know we're pretty safe so we dice and play past Glen Helen, ride through Cronk y Voddy at close to three times the recently sign posted speed limit and bounce off the jump at the bottom of Barregarrow. We both give it loads of pipe through Kirk Michael and the sound echoes off the houses. I'm in the lead at Ballacrye Jump then have to slam on the anchors at Sulby crossroads to head for the campsite. The lanes are narrow and Jurgen can't pass me. We slow right down and coast back home. I park up the Panigale with a big grin and pat her tank.

"She's pretty impressive." I tell Jurgen.

Everyone else starts to arrive and Dad parks up The Duchess with the other bikes. I say goodnight and me and Emmett head for the cottage. Joey comes up behind us on his bike and parks next to a waiting Ella.

"Why are you out here, honey? The door's always open." I laugh, kissing her, hugging Joe and going inside.

"Shower and bed?" Emmett smiles.

"Nope, just bed! I'm planning on you making us both extremely hot and sweaty and stinky so let's shower afterwards." I reply. "And I'm pretty sure we've got an early start in the morning so you better get on with it."

"You're the boss, darlin'." He grins, kicking off his boots and climbing out of his leathers at quite an impressive speed. I've just removed my jacket when he scoops me up and drops me onto my little bed, pulls off my boots and my jeans. "Arms up!" He orders and removes my t-shirt. I'm still buzzing from my ride so I'm just going with the flow, no fear, no hesitation.

"You are an exquisite creature, Delilah." He tells me as he kisses me softly all over.

"I need to talk to you about the morning, Emm." I say. "About the pissing contest you got into with your son."

"Why? Will you not be able to control yourself if I'm pressed up against your sexy little body with my arms wrapped around your tiny waist?" He jokes licking me and making me shiver all over.

"Er, it's not me and you I'm worried about." I sigh. "Is Felix a thrill seeker?"

"Yep, he gets that off his Dad." Emmett jokes. "Just scare the crap out of him, he'll get over it."

"That's just it Emm, it doesn't scare the crap out of you. It has a very different effect on your body." He's not quite following. "Did you ride your bike too fast when you were Felix's age?"

"Still do now!" He grins.

Okay we're getting somewhere. "Why? Think then even more than now. Be honest."

"It gave me a hard on!" He laughs at the realisation.

"What would have happened if you weren't the one holding the bars? The ultimate thrill, no control?"

"Ah" He smiles. "Growling and howling?"

"Yep! You got it. Marley would never get on the back of my bike or anyone else's once he hit puberty said he had no control over his body if he did. I still get emails and letters off pervs and weirdos from every corner of the globe offering me money for pillion rides. For some reason, riding pillion on a fast bike turns grown men on, now what's it gonna do to Fe? I need to know so I can deal with it. Dad was talking about a quick blast over the mountain but you two have psyched each other up for something far more."

"Whoops, that's not an ideal situation is it." He muses, licking me from my stomach to my chin. "Shall we think about it in the morning? I'm a little busy right now and this is not really a discussion suitable for the current situation." I hit him with the bed pillow and he pins me to the bed and makes me squirm some more. Then he gets us really hot and sweaty and stinking like a pair of feral cats. He starts howling at about four in the morning and the next thing I hear is Felix loudly whistling 'Californication' as he walks past the bedroom window. He comes into the cottage and yells.

"Are you two decent? It's time to ride."

"Shit, Emm. I smell seriously funky." I laugh. "Go and feed your baby while I get showered and have a word with him please."

"And what am I supposed to say to him?" Emmett cocks an eyebrow at me. "By the way Son, don't fall off Delilah 's bike while you're...." I cut him off with a kiss.

"Just warn him to stay away from me when we stop at Hillberry and make sure you're there to catch him. He'll thank you for it later."

I grab my robe and zip to the bathroom. "Morning Felix, give me five minutes to shower. Get the coffee on."

Toast and coffee devoured we set off. Emmett on the back of The Duchess, Felix on his own bike.

Emmett is not a very good pillion even riding slowly. I stop for a breather and to get fuel in Ramsey.

"Do you really wanna go for it?" I ask him. "Can you stay still and focused? It's like riding with Jeff on the back at the minute."

"Yep, after last night's conversation I can't wait to try it." He drawls. "You turn me on when I watch you ride normally. Come to think of it, you turn me on whatever you're doing actually." He says matter of factly.

"Felix don't try to keep up, honey. We'll stop down at Hillberry and wait. Take your time, learn the road. It'll make the ride easier and more fun for you. Emm, you need to stay very still, wrap your body around mine and put your hands on the tank and your head on my back. Don't move, don't look up and don't try to lean the bike anywhere. Got it?"

"Loud and clear, little darlin'. I'll try my best but I'm a bit taller than you." He laughs.

I start off steadily, scared he will do something daft but he's following the rules. The Duchess thinks this is a great game and fights to go faster. I let her have her way and the run is perfect, lightning fast and smooth. I almost forget Emm is on the back, he is so well behaved. I pull up at Hillberry and take off my lid. He launches at me, crushing me into his extremely hard body and kissing me savagely, nearly breaking my teeth. He takes more than a few seconds to regain control of his senses and only stops trying to mount me when Felix pulls in. I quickly move out of his reach. Emm sits himself down on the bench, he is shaking his head and grinning like a maniac. "Wow! What a rush! That was so intense. You weren't exaggerating last night were you?"

"What's up old boy? Can't you handle the speed?" Felix teases. "Come on, my turn."

"Ground rules?" I glare at Emmett and leave them to talk.

We go all the way around at a sensible pace and Felix is okay apart from trying to look over my shoulder quite a bit. I stop down at Ramsey. "Okay, same as I told your Dad, stay very still, wrap your body around mine and put your hands on the tank and your head on my back. Don't move, don't look up and don't try to lean the bike anywhere. What did your Dad tell you to do when we stop?"

"Get straight off the bike and sit on the bench because I'll feel dizzy." He rolls his eyes. "Give it everything you've got Delilah, I can handle it, you really won't scare me. I'm afraid it takes a heck of a lot to impress me."

I was going to go easy on him but that was a proper challenge. I shake my head ruefully. The Duchess roars back into life and I think a few fairy folks jump aboard just for the mischief. How the hell did you get yourself into this, Delilah? You stupid, thrill seeking, idiot. Oh well, too late to back out now, I shrug to myself. Why can't you just mellow into middle age? You're old enough to know better....

Felix stays really still until I feel his head roll back slightly and he suddenly grips me tightly. He's blacked out for a second I remember what a weird feeling it is, I slow fractionally and he shakes his head slightly and loosens his grip. Tapping me to say he's good. My crazy gene takes over and I let The Duchess almost reach her limits. Felix starts to get a little fidgety as we near Windy Corner and is writhing about as we come down to Hillberry. I pull up and Emmett peels him off the back of the bike and I just take off again and go for cold drinks and breakfast pastries.

Felix is looking reasonably composed, if a little shell shocked, when I get back ten minutes later. I hand him a Coke and his danish. "Get some sugar in you before you get back on your bike and we'll go back because roads will close at ten."

Emmett grabs me when I try to hand him his food from a distance and pulls me close. "He's okay, don't look so worried." He says softly into my ear.

"Don't tell me anything and don't mention it again, ever!" I whisper back. "I'm pretty disgusted with myself right now."

Stefan pulls up. "What did I miss?" He asks, looking around at us all. I give Emmett a warning look. Felix, bless him, comes over and puts his arm around my shoulder.

"You missed Delilah giving me a lesson in humility that I will never, ever forget." He laughs.

I share my vanilla crown with Stefan and tell him we're heading back to grab picnics and see where we'll be watching the first day of racing because we've already had enough excitement for one day even though people are only just getting up for work.

CHAPTER 40

We get back in plenty of time for me to sort everyone's packed lunches and wish them all a brilliant day. The weather is already superb and promises to stay good for all six laps of the superbike race and hopefully for the side cars afterwards. Roads close at ten but racing doesn't start until twelve. Jurgen has booked VIP tickets at the Creg for his crew so doesn't need any food and heads off early as breakfast is included in the package. Stefan and Charlie, Connor and Nathan go with them. Emmett and Felix had already decided to come up to the mountain the back way a little later with me, Dad, Joey and Ella.

Felix goes back to his tent for an hour's kip and Emmett goes to get a well needed shower. Joey and Ella wander into the cottage whilst I'm making a few cakes and pies for us to take later. Joe dunks his finger in the muffin batter.

"Yum, are ya puttin' chocolate stuff on 'em?"

"Yep, if you want chocolate stuff, my little ray of sunshine." I smile. "What frosting do you want on some muffins Ella?"

She's floating around with a daft smile on her face. "Eh? Er what? Ham please."

"Good grief, Joe, what have you been doing to the poor girl, she's lost her mind?" I tease.

He grins sheepishly. "I'm pretty sure she like's orange and lemon stuff. She 'ad about eight of 'em the other night."

I put the baking in the oven and make a pile of bacon and sausage and egg sandwiches. Joey and Ella sit down to eat, Dad, Jeff and Dutch join them and then Emmett reappears looking and smelling gorgeous. He realises there are no seats he can reach at the table, picks me up out of my seat and sits down on it, putting me in his lap like a small child and grabs a sandwich.

Dad laughs, "That's what I used to do with her when she was little."

"She still is little." Joey chimes in. "How was Fe's ride s'morning?"

"Explosive!" Emmett giggles as I glare at him and elbow him in the ribs.

"She didn't?" Dad looks at Emmett eyebrows raised.

"Yeah, she did."

"He got mouthy, I'm not proud." I add mortified. Cutting Joey off before he can speak. "Don't ask Joey, you don't want to know, darling."

"Bugger! I owe Jurgen twenty quid now. He said she wouldn't be able to help herself." Dad tells Emm and they burst into giggles like a pair of stupid kids.

Change the subject quick Delilah. "Ella, How did your suitability interview with Sarah go?"

"She's a real beaut isn't she?" She smiles. "I was given preliminary approval as long as I accepted the fact that I had to share Joey with her if she was sad because he can always make her laugh and if she gets her crosser stuck in the mud in the winter and her grandad, dad and uncle Rick are busy. I also have to share him with you if she can't find anyone suitable. How did Emmett do?"

"Jury is still out on several counts but she did offer him a few tips." I say looking directly at him and raising an eyebrow. I go to climb off his lap but he engulfs me in a huge hug and tickles my ribs. "Let me go you twit, or else Ella's ham muffins will be burned." I squeal.

I rescue the baking and make a big bowl of frosting. I go to the pantry to grab some cocoa, choc chips and fruit and Joey, Dad and Emmett all dive in the bowl and eat half of it.

"Right, that's it! Bugger off all three of you while I sort this food out otherwise the racing will be over before we get there."

They go to play with something Dad's working on in the barn whilst I make more frosting and Ella makes sandwiches.

"Are you okay, sweetheart?" I ask Ella when they're out of the way.

"Really, really good." She smiles. "I like Joey a lot, he's funny and kind and gentle and patient. Thank you for inviting me to Hillberry and for letting me into your crazy home with your wonderful family. I am so happy right now." She hugs me and laughs. "Oh and by the way Jurgen's place has all gone through. He should be able to move in by Wednesday. I dread to think how much the lawyers have made from moving that quickly. Two big American corporations have rung to ask me to find houses nearby for them, Jurgen has stuff in his head lots of people want. My boss thinks I'm brilliant right now."

"Jurgen's head is a complete mystery to me and I hope it stays that way." I shudder. "Go and grab Joey's rucksack and we'll get this lot packed up."

She goes and Emmett reappears with a cheeky grin. "Am I allowed back in yet? I'm missing you."

"We're just going to pack the food then we'll get off. Do you think Felix will still want to come?" He smirks at my unintended pun and I punch him playfully. "Will he want to stay here or watch the racing? Are you going to wake him up or shall I ask Joey to?"

"Ask Joey I have other plans right now." He tells me suggestively.

Ella brings the back pack and I ask her to go and wake Felix. Emmett immediately sweeps me up and carries me into the bedroom, kicking the door shut with his foot. He growls as he deposits me on the bed.

"Right my little maker of mischief, I've had a very, very cold shower after my ride this morning and it hasn't worked. I need a serious seeing to otherwise I will not be held responsible for my actions during our family picnic."

I emerge from the bedroom having been fully educated on the concept of the word 'quickie.' I have a lightning fast shower, pack everything, share out the rucksacks, kiss Dutch and Jeff and give them treats and fire up The Duchess. Felix and Emmett join us at the campsite gate and we head up along the beautiful back roads through Tholt y Will and past the reservoir and park up at the top of the road.

We climb over the fence and hike a little way up the grassy banking so that we have the best view of the bikes heading towards us and then all the way up the mountain mile. The sun is smiling down on us, there's not a cloud in the sky and the scenery here is unreal. We throw down all the picnic blankets, tune into Radio TT on my phone and lie about relaxing and teasing and chatting. I talk to Joey about getting up here somewhere with a pit board for Paddy Jr. on Monday and he's completely up for it. We discuss lines and angles and bits to look out for as markers. He's clearly taking it all in, asking relevant questions and putting it all together with other parts of the circuit we've discussed before.

Dad and Emmett are flat out on the blankets, arms up behind their heads, relaxed smiles on their faces, both snoring gently. I take a picture on my phone. It's my perfect screensaver. Felix is chatting with Ella and I hear her ask about when and where their next gig will be. I move away quickly, I don't want to know, don't want to think that this time next week will be their last day here. Mine and Emmett's last day together. The TT fortnight is always a pause on real life for me but this one has been like spending time in a truly alternate reality…. Hang on Delilah! This was meant to be a bit of fun. Therapy, a stepping stone to move on. You aren't falling in love are you? You stupid tart! God woman, can't you get anything right?

I'm leaning on the fence waiting for the bikes to pass by wrestling with my stupid thoughts when Dad joins me. "What you plotting, Delilah Blue? I can hear the cogs turning from up the hill. Going somewhere?"

"No, Dad. I'm going nowhere. Just having a little chat with myself about next steps. I've taken some pretty big ones this week, solved a lot of issues and got over a lot of hurdles and now I'm doing what I always do, building a bloody load more!" I sigh.

"If you want to leave with him I get it, you have my blessing, sweetheart. I only ever wanted to see you happy. I know you'll be back often enough and Joey'll keep me company."

"What's Emmett's last name, Dad?" I ask.

"I've no idea, why?"

"Neither have I." I say. "I know nothing about him and this isn't real. He'll be gone next week and you, me and Joey will get back to normal."

"Bollocks, Delilah! I couldn't even pronounce your Mama's name properly in the fifty odd years we were married. It didn't stop us loving each other! She may have been named Mizuki but to me she was my Suki Suzuki. I was a little sad that we could speak barely a word of her mother tongue when Mr. T. arrived but she chose not to teach us and we have to respect that. Stop building walls where there aren't any. You don't have to crush everything that makes you happy, you deserve to be the happiest girl in the world! Whatever you decide to do I'll be here but don't expect any sympathy if you're behaving like a petulant child." He laughs, kissing my head and hugging me tightly. "What was it your Mama used to call you? Chihiro, 'seeker', what are you looking for baby? Isn't this it?" He whispers holding up his arms to make me look around me.

"It's pretty damn close. Just in my perfect world it's TT fortnight forever, no one knows him apart from us and him and Felix never have to leave."

"Stop thinking Delilah and get doing." Dad sighs. "Have fun today and think about tomorrow, tomorrow."

"Loud and clear!" I laugh, kissing his cheek and run over and dive on a still sleeping Emmett.

"Wake up you lazy bugger, I can't have worn you out already? What you dreaming about?" I giggle. He wraps his arms around me and rolls quickly over so that he is on top of me. His haunting deep blue eyes wide open.

"Hello, beautiful. I wasn't sleeping I was recharging and working on a song and dreaming about you, of course."

"You're such a smooth operator! You know just what to say to keep me coming back for more." I tease.

"I'm fully restored and running on all cylinders now. Would you like me to demonstrate by wrapping you in this blanket and doing some extremely naughty things to you?" He asks suggestively.

"Very much so but the race has started so I'm afraid you're too late honey. You snooze, you lose!" I kiss his nose, jump up and run back down to the fence to watch the bikes come past on their first of six laps.

He saunters down to stand behind me and throws his arms around me. I notice Joey watching him and mirroring his moves with Ella. It makes me smile. I hug him tightly around me. "Emm, you have made me so happy. Thank you. Don't stop doing what you do."

"Happy to oblige, little darlin'." He drawls and kisses the top of my head.

We behave like normal grown-ups for a few hours; chatting about the racing, cheering on our favorites, having ten pence bets between us all about who's going to be leading at each sector, pit stop lengths, distances between riders in specific sectors. Between us, Dad, Joey and I fleece Emmett, Ella and Felix for the grand total of £3.80.

Felix appears to have completely recovered from my stupidity this morning and is smiling and relaxed. I'm not sure whether I should apologise to him or pretend I'm unaware of what happened. I take the easy option; total denial. He seems to also have that special Joey trait of moving straight on without any drama. The race comes to a brilliant climax and we are all screaming our support and clapping on the guys as they pass on the final lap.

"I'm starvin'" Joey announces as the radio plays footage of the podium presentation. "Crash the scran, Dil."

We empty all of the food out of the rucksacks and dive in. Felix and Joey roll around play fighting over the chocolate muffins. One of them gets a muffin, the other one tries to take it off them. Dad and Ella happily share the St. Clements ones without any issues. I muse that this is another of the many things I don't know about Emmett, he's eaten everything I've put in front of him without hesitation.

"What's your favourite flavour?" I ask pointing at the madness going on.

"Delilah." He replies with a grin so I am still none the wiser. Is he deliberately not telling me stuff or am I just having a menopausal paranoia attack? I can feel Dad's eyes on me. Definitely the latter, stop being a bloody idiot, Dil! Emmett must sense my frustration. "We're on the road and eating garbage most of the time. Your home cooked, real stuff is the best food we've both tasted in years, in forever actually. We can't get enough of it or you and I can't tell you a favourite of anything until I've tried them all. Ask me in another twenty years, darlin'." He smiles.

"I can tell you mine." Felix giggles as he continues to wrestle with Joe. "It's definitely these chocolate ones right now but I'm open to trying new flavours every time you're baking."

"There's white chocolate and strawberry ones over there and some lemon meringue ones too." I point to a container and Emmett, Felix and Joey dive on it. "Save me one you bloody gannets!"

"You need to try them orange an' lemon ones Ella's got, they're alright." Joey tells them.

Ella eyes them up with some suspicion. "You can all piss right off!" She giggles, hugging the container closer.

I sit back and watch my ever-growing little family with a regretful smile. Why did I run for so long? What a waste. I am a great believer in Karma and I don't regret my travels and have many amazing memories of the last twenty-five years but I'm starting to wonder why she made me wait so long to get to this perfect place in my life and why it'll all be snatched away so quickly. She really is a bitch.

Emmett comes to sit next to me. "You're doing that zone out thing again. Where's your head at, darlin'?"

"I was having a little chat with Madame Karma." I reply. "I'm just trying to work out how I got here. What I've done to deserve so much happiness all of a sudden and why now? I'm trying to get a heads up on what's coming next but I don't think I really want to know."

"That's strangely similar to a discussion I had with her whilst lying holding you in your cosy little bed the other night." He says earnestly.

"Did she give you any clues?" I ask.

"Yeah, she told me I'm not getting any younger and to stop questioning it and make every single second count because it really is the beginning of something very, very special." He smiles.

"Thanks, Emm." He draws me into his lap and I kiss him tenderly. "You and Dad always have the answers I need to hear." I sit quietly wrapped in his arms for a little while, saying nothing just enjoying the peaceful feeling of belonging.

"What we doin' for Mad Sunday?" Joey asks.

"What's Mad Sunday?" Felix's ears perk up.

"Is it actually a thing?" Emmett asks. "I've heard about it but wasn't quite sure it was real."

"It's usually carnage and is not quite so special now that the mountain is one way all fortnight rather than just on the Sunday like it used to be. You can do whatever you want, babe, but to be honest I'd rather you take Dad or me if you do wanna get involved. It can get pretty dangerous up here especially if the car guys come out to play. We usually go down to the Sprint at Ramsey, lots of bikes and noise but less risk of death." I tell Joey.

"And don't let Jurgen talk you into anything, especially if it involves removal of clothing. There's a chance it will become an annual event." Dad giggles knowingly.

I shake my head. "Not this year, I promise. I'm old enough to resist his challenges now." Dad and Emmett both look at me with raised eyebrows.

"Dylan, don't leave us hanging, tell all!" Felix begs.

"Mad Sunday has traditionally always involved a lot of crazy idiots flying over the mountain and a load of other silliness mainly down on Douglas front. It's a lot tamer and health and safety conscious nowadays. The Purple Helmets are still riding around doing their daft stuff and there's organised stunt shows and good bands playing. We used to make our own entertainment back in the day and the law happily joined in." Dad recounts fondly. "We all used to ride up and down the front doing wheelies and burn outs, bouncing the bikes of the rev limiters, drag racing, all sorts of stupid shit. Dil, Marley and Jurgen were winding each other up all week with the challenges getting wilder each day. By the end of Wednesday Marl and Jurgen had to completely shave their heads because she's beaten one at a one handed wheelie challenge and the other in a blindfolded drag race. Suki was beside herself when Marley's dreads came off. She challenged them all to a Kendo Tournament and kicked their arses then told them they had to ride down Douglas Front in just their boots on Mad Sunday. I insisted they had to wear their helmets too. Dil and Jurgen continued to do it on Mad Sunday for twenty years almost every year and there were more and more people joining them every year but for the last ten years or so they've changed it to the last day of racing instead and managed to keep it a little more low key."

"Thanks for sharing that Dad!" I groan.

"Can we join you this year?" Felix asks with a giggle. "That sounds like a perfect finale to this crazy show. I can honestly say I have never had such a memorable vacation in my life. We'll definitely be here every year so we can continue the tradition with you from now on. We are going to buy somewhere over here aren't we, Dad?"

"That's the plan, Son and I know of a really talented estate agent." Emmett replies loudly, knowing full well we're all listening. "But Delilah hasn't quite come round to the idea yet so let's give her a little while to get used to it."

The side cars come roaring down the hill, stopping the conversation from going further. We run to the fence to watch. Felix stands close. His phone rings and he looks casually and the looks again. "Jeez, it's Cherry! I thought she'd forgotten we exist."

"Tell her we don't." Emmett snarls. "What's she want?"

"Dunno, don't care, I'm not even answering it." Felix laughs, putting his phone firmly back into his pocket. "Oh man, I just realised, you've sent that thing haven't you?"

Emmett's phone rings a minute later but he doesn't even take it out. He hugs me tightly and whispers in my ear. "Don't worry darlin'. I know what she's calling for now. She'll have just received some paperwork courtesy of Jurgen's lawyer, that she probably won't like much. She can call him about it if she needs to but I'm sure it was pretty self-explanatory."

"Is Cherry his ex?" I ask assuming poor Felix was being stalked by an old lady friend.

"No, his mother." Emmett scowls.

CHAPTER 41

Dad insists he's going to be camping again tonight but right now we are all sitting around on the beach by a blazing fire, enjoying a drink and each other's company. Jurgen is blissfully happy that our tradition is once again growing and has easily roped in Stef, Emmett, Felix and Charlie. Nathan and Connor are being very non-committal and Joey is adamant that he's not taking his kecks off in front of anyone. Jurgen is also looking forward to moving into his new place.

"Oi!" I joke. "You've booked until Saturday. You're not going to do a runner and not pay are you?"

"You must chase me Saturday night if I do." He winks theatrically. I laugh, he hasn't paid nor will I expect him to, friends are always welcome.

Dad is telling more tales to Stef and the boys and he looks so chilled. It's lovely to see him stretched out on a blanket with his arm around Jeff, chatting happily.

Emmett is deep in conversation with one of the guys that follows Jurgen everywhere. "Who's Emm talking to?" I ask, being nosy.

"Hans, my lawyer man. He's the best, ja. Papers will be through very, very quickly. Like my beautiful new home. Bella Ella where is your new steed?"

"I haven't got paid yet." She explains. "And I can't decide what bike to get, there's too many I like. We've looked at the MT07 and the 650 Kwak but now I like that F800 BM Felix has, he let me try it I hope you don't mind and I want to try a 799 Monster too."

"Tell me which one you want and I will get them to send it here tomorrow and I will pay." Jurgen tells her.

"That's really sweet but I can already afford it with my savings and the commission I will get from selling you your new place. You are technically buying it anyway." She smiles.

"You are family now! I can buy you presents. I will get you a Ducati tomorrow. All beautiful ladies must ride red Ducatis, you can ride it with us on Saturday night." Ella looks astounded and is about to refuse again.

"You're wasting your breath, honey. He'll not take no for an answer." I tell her, kissing Jurgen on the head and going inside to find more bottles.

Emm and Hans are still deep in conversation. I offer them drinks and Emmett absently draws me onto his lap and continues talking.

"No, nothing else! She can have the house she's in and the place in the Hamptons. Sell the three apartments and give the money to Felix; he says he doesn't want to keep them. We're keeping the place in Whistler.

We love skiing and I know Dil likes it too and Fe loves the Maldives when we ever get chance to get out there so keep that. I want all of our studio equipment and our instruments and our bikes and cars shipped over here, Jurgen says they can go to his place though lord knows what I'm gonna do with the Hummer and the RV on these roads. Dil can drive the Corvette, it'll suit her." He laughs. "She knows the prenup was cast iron, she's entitled to nothing but getting plenty. I refuse to give her a monthly payment. She can have one lump sum and then never ever contact me again. Felix can choose what he wants to do. She's still his mom even if she doesn't behave like it and he's a grown man."

Hans advises him he has seen the prenup and he thinks Emmett is being too generous. Felix comes over to sit with them and I go to move away. Emmett holds me tightly to stop me getting up.

"Emm this isn't my business. I shouldn't be listening."

"Yeah, it is darlin'. We want you to be part of every bit of our lives from now on. Don't we Fe?"

"I honestly can't imagine you ever not being here now Dil." Felix says leaning over and hugging me tightly. "Did you say we're keeping the chalet? Dil, you'll love it you can ski out of the front door onto the best black runs. You can do it clothed or unclothed because it's really private too." He teases me then turns to his dad. "I heard my name mentioned. What have I done?"

Joey must have seen me struggle to get away and he casually comes over to make sure I'm okay.

"How well can you ski, Joe?" Felix asks genuinely. "You'll love it at Whistler."

"Eh? Never bin skiin' in me life." Joey laughs. "Funny innit, Dil. I've forgot me life before I came 'ere. Me an' Felix rap for hours about everythin' 'e's like the big bro I never 'ad but we're from diff'rent worlds ain't we?" He turns to Felix and Emmett. "Before I adopted Dil an' Dylan an' was kind of reborn on me sixteenth birthday. Sienna, me ma was a crackhead hooker and me Da was a dead smak 'ead. So I didn't get to do a lot of skiin'." He giggles.

Felix looks shocked for a second, pulls himself together and then shrugs. "No worries, you'll pick it up easy, little bro." Emm squeezes my hand and returns to the original conversation with Felix, not remotely bothered that Joey is still sitting next to me.

"I was saying you didn't want the New York apartment or the other two, we've never even seen that bloody place in Paris she bought, but we do want our stuff out the garage and the studio. Is there anything else you want?"

"Only the dogs and the horses." Felix says wistfully. "But that's not possible is it?"

"Sorry Son, I thought about that but I can't see a way around it. Taking three Dobermans and four stallions on tour isn't going to be happening and Jurgen's happy to have them but he will still be travelling quite often so it's not practical. I don't want to buy anywhere else until everything is sorted and Delilah has got her head around the fact that she's going to be stuck with us for the rest of her days."

"Eh Laa, can't we 'ave 'em 'ere Dil, I'll sort the stable bit out down the bottom. I can look after 'em. I like 'orses. I always wanted an 'orse."

"They're amazing!" Felix interjects. "Midnight is a crazy beast, Luna is easy to ride, he'll always look after you. Dad has Seraph, he's a softy and Angel who is the devil incarnate. Can you have them Dil, please? I really miss them."

"I don't know if there's enough room here, darlings. You and Joey'll have to check tomorrow." I smile, giving in easily. "Why didn't we get kids that want skateboards and BMX?" I shrug, palms up, at Emmett.

"Shit, my skateboards, I want those!" Felix laughs. Hans makes a note of it.

"She's not entitled to any royalties or anything to do with the band at all. She can change her name back too I don't want her to keep my name." I look at Felix in case he's upset by anything being said.

He puts out his hand to hold mine. "Dil, don't worry about me. Dad's my family. She's never been very motherly. She told me not to call her mom when I was nine."

I'm horrified, Joe says it to me jokingly now and again and it's the best feeling in the world. Joey realises what I'm thinking. "Ya don't 'ave to give birth to be a mom. The best ma's choose their kids once they've grown up when they already know 'ow fucked up they are an' still love 'em."

I laugh. "So I'm unofficially your mama now then, am I?"

"Face it Dil, you've bin me ma since you came out ya tent that first morning in ya vest and knickers."

"I can sort that too." Hans informs us seriously.

"Sort what?"

"I can make you his mother, officially."

"Sorry Hans, he's just kidding. He humours me because he knows I love to smother him and control his life and pretend he's my baby. He's sixteen, he doesn't need an official guardian."

"I might want one though." He replies sheepishly. "What would it cost?"

Hans actually laughs. "I'm making a pretty penny from Jurgen and Emmett. I'll do it for you for free. I'm having a brilliant time here and I'll do it to pay for my vacation. Do you want me to go ahead with it?"

I look at Joey and he looks at me. "Your call sweetheart, you know I'll be a constant source of embarrassment, be overbearing and go on about you riding safely and keep giving you advice when you don't need or want it but I will be more than honoured and I'll be proud of you and love you until the day I die and beyond."

"Yep, that's all the reasons why I want it made official. Them an' the fact that ya can't get away from me then, ever." He grins. "Do it, please." He tells Hans. I dissolve in a flood of tears and we hug each other and everyone embraces us.

Dad comes running over concerned. "What's up Dilly girl?" I fall into his arms and he holds me tightly.

"You're about to become a Grandpa." I tell him, he looks confused for a second. "I'm officially adopting Joey. Hans is going to sort it." Dad is over the moon, hugging us both, then everyone else and running over to tell Nathan and Jurgen and Ella and the others.

"Emmett I'm so sorry. We just completely hijacked your conversation with Hans, I hope he's not charging by the hour." I giggle. "We got carried away. I can't believe what has just happened. Can my life get any better right now? I keep thinking I'm going to wake up soon."

He kisses me affectionately and looks into my eyes.

"I couldn't be happier for you both darlin', he's an awesome kid and you are a great mom already, why not make it official? I hope there's still room for me and Felix to join the family."

"Emm, you're already both family, my beautiful, patient man."

"You're more of a mom than Cherry has ever been." Felix adds. "You've already fixed me more food than she has in my whole life, you taught me how to wheelie and definitely gave me one hell of a lesson this morning, even if your methods are a little unorthodox, I'll forever think of the consequences before I smart mouth." He laughs hugging me.

Some fizz arrives from lord knows where and we toast each other and everything and anything until late into the night.

We all start to turn in Dad and Jurgen hug and kiss me and go off to their tents. Dad says Felix can have his bed if we're not using it. Hans shakes hands very formally then gives me a big hug.

Nathan is so happy for us. "Can I tell Mom and Dad?"

"Of course you can sweetheart. How are you? Have you told them your news?" I enquire gently.

"Yeah, Dad asked if he could ride Connor's bike and Mom asked if she'll get free gig tickets." He laughs. "Sarah said it was good because apart from Beyonce, she's only got Ella on my list and Joey got there first." I hug him tightly and wish him goodnight. I know he's staying in the tent with Connor.

Joey and Ella and Felix come into the cottage with us and I make hot chocolate and toast.

"Felix, honey. Dad says you can have his bed tonight if you want it."

"Are you to safe to be around?" He asks.

"You're good once 'e starts 'owlin'." Joey laughs. "They're quiet after that." He hugs me. "Night, Ma. See ya in the morning."

"Don't start me crying again." I smile.

"Ya better get used to it. I got a feeling Fe'll be callin' you it an' all soon enough. I love ya, Mama Dil. A lot. Thank you." He kisses my cheek. "Come on Bella Ella, it's bed time." She hugs me and Emmett and Felix and they're gone.

Felix goes to get into my little bed. "Other one's yours, honey."

"Nope, Dylan said you have to have the big bed tonight. Night Dil." He goes into my room taking Dutch with him.

Emmett comes out of the bathroom as I'm standing, open mouthed, in the middle of the kitchen. "What's up darlin'?"

"Your child and the cat just stole our bed." I tell him.

"We get the big bed? Awesome!" He giggles. "Do we need a shower first?"

"No, I feel a bit freaked about Felix being in the next room." I tell him honestly. "And about doing 'stuff' in my Dad's bed."

"That boy sleeps like the dead, darlin'." He replies. "But I totally get it. Come on, let's just get some sleep too. It's been another epic day."

We climb into the big bed. My head is buzzing with the revelation that I've just become a 'mama'. Another thing I can cross off my list of regrets.

Emmett folds me into a warm embrace and kisses me gently. "Goodnight, my beautiful girl. I love you so much and I want us to ...."

Despite all of the excitement and everything whizzing around in my brain, I relax in his arms and I'm asleep before he's finished his sentence.

CHAPTER 42

The breakfast table is as crowded and jovial as ever. Dad and Jurgen are affectionately arguing over past races, Ella and Joey are loved up and cuddling on the big chair together, Mr.Tamaki is devouring his body weight in food whilst teaching Charlie some rudimental Japanese, Nath and Connor are tentatively making plans, Stef, Felix and Emmett are catching up on their meeting with Hans. Jeff and Dutch are mooching for treats and I'm singing softly to myself whilst cooking the entire contents of the fridge.

I look around in wonder at my little slice of heaven. I am still convinced it's all a beautiful meditation journey and I will have to wake up on my rock on the beach soon. I'm almost daring to believe Emmett might not evaporate into thin air after next Saturday. Ridiculous I know, but it was Felix asking to bring the dogs and horses that made it a little more real. I'm not pushing though; I'll not say anything if they don't mention it again.

"What ya singin', Mama Dil?" Joey yells, "Sing it louder!"

"It's one Dad used to sing to me a lot, an old Bob Marley one. Don't think I wanna show myself up in front of present company." I giggle. "I'm way out of my league. You can't even identify what the song is half the time."

"That's 'cos they're old not 'cos ya sing bad. I like ya singin'."

"Come on Dil, let's hear it." Stefan teases. "I've heard you singing to yourself loads. It always sounds good."

"I wouldn't subject you to my singing whilst people are eating." I say, turning back to the pans.

"Liebling, are you backing down from a challenge? You owe Emmett a song, ja? I will tell things I know if you do not sing now."

I sigh in resignation. "I'll get you back Joey Blue!" I stay by the cooker but I look Emm in the eyes and take a deep breath and start singing Is This Love? The line 'We'll share the shelter, of my single bed' had made me think of Emm and I. After a couple of verses Emmett takes pity on me and joins in and then everyone joins in too including Mr. T. We almost finish the song and Dad comes over and takes my hand. "Don't worry about a thing... and we all join in with a rousing rendition of Three Little Birds and then Stef and Connor come back with 'No Woman, No Cry,' and we're off again. We finally collapse in a big heap of hugs and tears and giggles after a finale of 'One Love'. The cottage is well and truly filled to the rafters with noisy but melodious love.

Stef gives me a hug. "That's put me to shame, honey. Do you want to come on tour? You have a beautiful voice."

"I would run away screaming as soon as I saw the stage. I don't know how you do it." I laugh. "I just looked at Emm and pretended the rest of you weren't there and I know and love all of you. A room full of strangers would scare the crap out of me. I'm so in awe of the fact that your kids can do it so confidently at such a young age."

"You get used to it." Stef shrugs. "They grew up with it because I took the whole family everywhere with me. So they were running around the stage as toddlers. Kim, my wife didn't work while they were young."

"Was she working this fortnight? Can't she come over for a few days? You can have a bed if she's not up for sleeping in a tent."

"We agreed I'd come and get to know Dad but I might send the plane to get her later if she's free. She's dying to meet the boy who's bewitched Connor and the woman that has stolen Emmett's heart and she's more than happy sleeping in a tent. She was wild that she missed our jam the other night."

"I really hope she can come; I'm pretty sure Dan and the guys will be up for an encore."

"Really? Can you get them back for next Friday night? That would be awesome. She'll not hesitate if I promise her that."

I grab my phone and call Dan. "Do you wanna come back and play with the boys on Friday?" Dan says lots of rude words which I take to mean yes. "See you after the racing?"

"They'll be here. I better start writing my request list." Stefan hugs me and grabs his phone, wandering off as he's dialing.

Emmett comes over. "What are you two up to?"

I wrap my arms around him. "Sorting a woman for Stefan and writing my play list for you and the 'Blues Campsite Beach Band' for next Friday."

"They're coming back? Awesome! After that impressive performance just now you're going on the set list this time, darlin' and Stefan already has a perfect woman."

"Err No, that's not gonna be happening ever. Stef's going to get his wife over if she's free."

"Delilah, you are amazing! You'll love Kim and she'll love you. Have we got plans for today or just chilling?"

"We normally go down to Ramsey Sprint a bit later. I wasn't sure if you needed to see Hans or anything so I told Joey I'd let him know in a bit. He dashed off somewhere with Fe and Ella."

"Pretty sure they're down the back sorting the stables." He grimaces. "Sorry darlin', Felix and I come as a rather large package."

"I wouldn't have it any other way." I smile. "If they're too rough I'll get Paddy Mac over, he'll soon get something up fit for your four-legged friends. If there's not enough room we can open up both fields and they'll have to bunk up with the donkeys. I hope Felix isn't going to be disappointed. I'm not prying and tell me to butt out if you want to but is his mom going to be reasonable? I don't want him getting his hopes up if she's not. I know he's not a baby but I don't want to see him hurt."

"Delilah, nothing I do or say is private as far as you're concerned. I'm not anticipating any issues, especially with the dogs and horses. She might fight over the houses but Hans seems pretty impressive so far. He can deal with it all. She's had enough off us already. I'm doing this to protect Felix. She's taken too much of what we both work hard for."

Stefan comes back looking really happy. "Where are the kids? I've got good news for them. She'll be here in the morning." He goes off to find them.

"Why now, Emmett?" I ask. "I need to know I'm not the reason. I couldn't bear it if Felix ever says you split from his mom because of me."

"Sit down, Delilah Blue, I will tell you the story." Emmett smiles, guiding me to a blanket on the beach and falling down next to me. "Barely three weeks ago today, we were sitting in a hotel suite in Munich after a gig. Well, I wasn't sitting, I was stalking around the room, screaming into my mobile at my accountant because the poor guy had rung to warn me Cherry had been enquiring about Felix's Trust Fund. My parents never met Fe but they did leave him a massive amount in trust for when he turns twenty-five; that'll be in six months. He also told me she was looking at buying an apartment in Rome. She's always bought property when she's bored, stupidly, I've just let her get on with it. Property is a good investment and buying it keeps a little back from the taxman. I do have the good sense to insist they are always registered in my name. The Trust Fund was the final straw. We already knew she's moved her personal trainer into the LA house, one of Felix's 'friends' took great delight in calling to tell us about that a long while ago. The press had a field day with it too. We stopped going back between tours or stayed with Stefan and Kim when we did, just visiting the stables when we knew she was away. Poor Stef never got a break from my moods and rants and stressing." He stops for a breath and shakes his head.

"Anyhow, I'm screaming into my phone and this crazy little German guy arrives. I knew about him but we hadn't met. Stef had met up with just him a few times before and wanted us all to meet him. I felt bad that it was important to Stef and I was fucking it up. I finally get off the phone and pour myself a large scotch. Stef introduces me and Jurgen looks me up and down and says 'Can you ride a motorcycle? You are broken. I will take you to Delilah, she is broken too, you will fix each other' and then carries on talking to Stef and the kids as if I'm not even there. I pace around the room some more and Stef tells me I really need to sort my shit out. I settle to listen to them planning the trip over here. I say if Felix can come with them, I'll go back and sort the divorce and everything while they're here. Felix tells me it's about bloody time and he'll be glad when it's all over and he can have his normal Dad back. Jurgen tells me I have to come here and he will bring his lawyers to sort everything for me. He absolutely refused to take no for an answer. So, here we are and I will be forever indebted to that 'crazy little German'. Never in a million years would I have envisaged myself in a tiny cottage full of love being sung to by the most beautiful soul in the world." He kisses me tenderly.

"Another one I owe Jurgen." I laugh. "Are you sure you're not being pushed into anything? This place makes you forget reality."

"Dil, I've never been more sure of anything in my life, darlin'. I should never have married her. Everyone told me she was wrong for me. My folks, Stef and Kim all tried to talk me out of it but I was arrogant, pig headed and stubborn and she'd told me she was pregnant and I wanted a kid more than anything. She'd lied. She got pregnant with Felix later because we were falling apart and I'd talked about separating. She didn't want him and complained about losing her figure all through the pregnancy. She made Kim do a load of surgery on her weeks after the birth. She barely held Felix and I started taking him on tour when I could. Kim was always there to look after him. Cherry used him as a bargaining chip to get whatever she wanted. They never really bonded at all. He has the same relationship with his mother as I did with mine, which was the opposite of everything I wanted for him. We'll all be happier when this is over. She'll have enough money to do as she pleases, Felix will have closure and I will have my sanity and you can drive me crazy in a completely different and wonderful way without ever having to think about all of my baggage."

"I'm not going to argue with that." I smile. "Thank you for being so honest and open with me."

We are snogging on the blanket when the kids come running back from the stables.

"Ew must you do that?" Felix laughs. "The stables'll need new doors but there's enough room there." He tells us. "I'm more than happy to pay for the work if you're okay with it. Even Ella says she'll help with mucking out."

"I'm fine with it, darling. I'll see Paddy Mac tomorrow because I'm pit crew so I'll ask him to come over and get it sorted." I stand up and look at the weather forecast on my phone. There's a text from Rick 'sprints on wanna run?'

"Who fancies an afternoon wearing out back tyres?" I giggle and text back 'hell yeah xxx'

We round up Dad and Jurgen and Stef and the boys and ride down to Mooragh Park in Ramsey. The sprint is an eclectic mix of weird and wonderful 'run what you brung' bikes. It's been running for decades watched over by the mountain and the sea. It's an Idyllic spot. You just sign in, get a quick safety check, pay and get a number then join the queue. You get put into a class based on the size of your bike. This is just an 1/8 mile drag sprint down the prom. Everything runs, from mopeds to turbocharged full drag beasts. 5.72 seconds is the current record. The waiting line is quite long so we join it and leave the bikes. I notice Rick's, Billy's and Sarah's bikes ahead of us.

"Wow, do they let kids run? That little dude must have some balls!" Emmett exclaims pointing out Sarah's trick little drag bike, built by Billy, in the queue.

"Three guesses who it belongs to." I laugh as Sarah comes flying over to us in her fab little red one-piece leathers and ear defenders.

"Auntie Dilly!" She dives into my arms. "I've smashed my time from last year already." She looks at Emmett in his leathers. "Hello Uncle Emmett. Are you running?"

"I'm going to give it a try, honey. Any tips?" She holds her arms out to him so that he will take her from me and hold her and whispers some things in his ear, kisses his cheek, then runs off to hug Joey who's just behind us.

"Good tips?" I ask.

"Yeah." Emmett laughs. "She told me to leave all of my electronics switched on, warm the back tyre properly, don't panic, drop the clutch gently and not be sad when you beat me."

Billy is following her and grabs me in a big bear hug. "Dave! Yow good?"

"I'm better than good hun. Where's Sal?"

He holds me at arm's length and checks me all over to make sure I'm not lying. Then acknowledges Emmett with a big smile.

"Somewhere about. Our kid is an' all an' Mam an' Dad." He says. "Where's our Dave? 'E ain't bin 'ome for days."

"He's been staying at our place. He's proper loved up. It's really sweet. He's about somewhere, they've both signed up to run." I smile.

"Watch Dave, I need a piss." He says nodding his head towards Sarah.

"Will do. See you in a bit."

"How many ice creams have you had today?" I ask Sarah as we pass the van.

"None yet. Do you think we need one?" She replies. "Uncle Emmett might be too worried about his run and have a funny tummy like Nathan used to."

"How are you feeling about taking your turn, honey? Too scared to eat ice cream?" I tease.

"I think I can probably handle one." He laughs and buys us all huge cones. We stand by the barrier and watch everyone run. The noise, the smell and the atmosphere is intoxicating. We're guessing times before they set off. Ricky comes to the line, gives us a chin lift and salutes when he sees us, heats his tyre, sends up clouds of acrid, burning rubber, drops his visor and takes off like a scalded cat.

"Uncle Ricky is going pretty fast so far today." Sarah comments. "Daddy is doing rubbish."

Rick comes back down the return lane as Billy comes to the line. Bill takes off and Ricky comes to the barrier.

"Come on Snot Monster, you're up next." He takes Sarah from me and kisses my cheek to say hello. He brings Sarah's bike to the line, checks her boots, gloves, zips and helmet and gives her a thumbs up. She throws her leg over and he puts her visor down to keep the smoke out. She heats her back tyre evenly, pulls in the clutch, selects her gear, gives it a handful of revs and waits for the lights to go green. She wrings everything out of the little engine and does an amazing run.

"Jeez!" Emmett exclaims. "It's not just you I need to worry about beating me. She is unreal."

Sal appears at his side and grins proudly. "I've always said she's Dil and Jimbob's kid. Oh shit, sorry, that wasn't very appropriate was it?"

"Sal, you don't need to tiptoe round me. I'm a big boy." Emmett laughs putting his arm around her shoulder.

Sarah comes down the return lane to a massive round of applause and takes it all in. She parks up back in line and runs over to get her results from the double decker bus that serves as HQ. closely followed by her doting Dad and uncle.

"Smashed it!" She shouts, running over to us, waving her timing slip.

Rick is right behind her. "Read 'em and weep, Shortarse. Parkers vs Blues, losers buy the beer." He giggles waving his own time at me and lifting me over the barrier like he did with Sarah so I can get ready to run.

"Me, Dad and Joey? No fair, Parker! Sarah's got way more experience than Joe."

"Yeah but we've got Bill and he's riding like a complete twat. Nathan doesn't count either, I don't know who's bike he's riding but it ain't going well." He laughs.

Emmett climbs over and Dad and the guys appear from the other side. Dad, Nathan and I give them a crash course while we're waiting in line.

Like everything that involves an element of danger the adrenaline kicks in as you get closer to the line and the kids are all starting to buzz. Dad goes first and I feel for his poor old Kwak as he shows it no mercy. Joey can't wait any longer and does the same to his poor little DT, lying flat out on the tank to get up all the speed he can muster. Nathan's up next and he's on Connor's MV. He's not used to it and spins up when he launches so loses loads of time. Charlie puts in a good run and Stef and Jurgen do too.

It's my turn. The Duchess loves to drag but it's pretty impossible to keep both tyres on the tarmac. I heat the back tyre so that its properly sticky, pull the clutch in, smack her into gear and lean as far forward as I can to keep the weight on the front end then launch. She growls and snarls and lifts about a foot then drops and grips and goes like a rocket. It's a superb feeling but over too soon. I wrestle her out of warp speed to round the hairpin and cruise back to the back of the queue as Felix flies past in the opposite direction on his run. I rejoin the line and go over to cheer Emmett on. He does pretty well for his first run and comes back as hyped as the kids.

"Man, that's a rush!" He grins, taking off his helmet and pulling me in for a passionate kiss.

"This adrenaline stuff really turns you on doesn't it?" I giggle, trying half heartedly to extract myself from his crushing embrace.

"Yeah, it appears so." He laughs, shaking his head at the revelation.

"Remind be to take you base jumping if things ever get stale." I tease. "That really is real next level shit."

"Things will never get stale, darlin' but definitely put it on our 'to do' list. I need to try everything with you."

We go back to chat with Sal for a bit and Pat and Will are with her. They give me loads of love and hugs and I introduce Emmett to them.

Pat stands back and looks him up and down. "Are you treating our Delilah right?" She asks.

"Trying my absolute best Ma'am."

"Are you going to stick around after the madness is over?"

"That's the plan. My son and I will be here until the end of time if Delilah will have us. We were making some plans for the future just a few minutes ago."

"How are you getting on with Joey?"

"Dil thinks I may actually be his father. He's a great kid." Emm laughs.

"He'll do, Will. I like him." She tells her husband and hugs Emmett.

Jurgen brings the Panigale to the line and attempts to break the sound barrier. It is impressive to watch.

Ricky puts in another blinding run as does Sarah. Joey gets a bit carried away and goes off line losing seconds. Dad does a brilliant run as always and Billy puts in a really good time too. Nathan does loads better on his second run. I jump back on The Duchess and let her rip. It's a superb run and I get back as Emmett gets onto the line. I blow him a kiss and watch him put in a pretty good run. I'm ready for him when he gets back this time. I jump on him, wrapping my legs tightly around him and 'suck his face off'.

Nathan does another decent run on Connor's bike and I seize the chance for a bit of treachery. Ricky is on the line. I go over and as I'm dropping his visor for him I lean in close, smile sweetly and mention that the MV belongs to Connor, Nathan's boyfriend. Delilah Blue! That's cheating! Rick completely buggers up his start and puts in a bad time. He comes back in shaking his head and laughing.

"You bitch, that's playing real dirty."

I smile sweetly again and kiss his cheek. "Sorry Rick, I didn't read the rules." He picks me up and throws me over his shoulder, smacking my bum. He drops me down by Emmett.

"Can you keep your bloody woman under control." He groans.

"What did you do to deserve a spanking?" Emmett laughs. "Are you making mischief?"

"I took the opportunity to tell him Nathan's news." I shrug.

"You didn't? Oh my god Delilah you did deserve a spanking. That's not playing fair. Sorry Ricky, man, I don't know what gets into her."

"You better get used to it if you're sticking around." Ricky tells him. "She's a real fucking hellcat when she wants to be. She rides with the devil, this one." He kisses my head and stalks off, still chuckling to himself.

We run all afternoon and our tyres are looking well used by the end of the day. Pat invites us all around to the farm for late Sunday dinner. Jurgen and Stef and the boys thank her but decline as they have a table booked elsewhere. Nathan goes with them after hugs and kisses for everyone. Ricky treats him the same as he always does and is polite and well behaved when he says hi and bye to Connor. Sarah is fast asleep on her dad's shoulder, worn out from all of the excitement. We put her bike back onto the pick-up and follow on to the farm.

Food and company is excellent as always. Emmett, Felix and Ella are made to feel part of the family immediately. Sarah recharges and takes the kids outside to motocross after a huge dinner. Emmett, Dad and I relax and we all talk rubbish until Pat gets up to make supper and Sal and

I join her to help.

"He's a nice lad, Dil." Pat says. "He's got lovely manners and he's smitten with you. Are you happy?"

Sal laughs. "Look at the state of her, Mam! She's more than happy." We make a mountain of sandwiches, salad and cheeses and plonk it all onto the table and everyone dives in.

Ricky pulls a load of timing slips out. "Come on then Shortarse, who won?"

Bill throws his and Sarah's slips in and Dad puts in his and Joey's. "You had loads more runs than us!"

"Top three from everyone counts then." Ricky declares. "That takes out your cheating."

"I wasn't cheating, I was relaying very important family information." I counter with a giggle.

We sort through and add up and the Parkers win overall by 0.3 of a second. Me and Dad concede with good grace. Joey did brilliantly for his first ever sprint.

We talk together until the kids have been asleep on the sofas for hours and we've put the whole world to rights. Then we gently wake all of our babies and head home.

CHAPTER 43

I wake in my little bed entangled with Emmett. He's asleep and I take the time to study his beautiful face. He looks so relaxed. His hair is fanned out across the pillow. He is tanned and unlined, he has dark stubble appearing, the sexiest eyelashes and as I trace my finger lightly across his sensual mouth it curls up into a smile.

"Morning little darlin'." He says without opening his eyes. "Have I got time to show you how much I love you before we get up?"

"That depends on how long it's going to take." I laugh.

"All day. I think I can do all day at least." He replies.

"Kim's coming soon and I'm pit crew for Paddy Jr. this afternoon so you better get started now." I tease, kissing down his chest to his taut stomach.

"I'll have to revise my time calculations if you get any lower, lady." He growls.

Dad is making breakfast when we emerge and hands us both a coffee. "Morning! Toast, bacon or the works?"

"Just toast please, Daddy darling. I ate a mountain at Pat's last night" I say.

"The works if you're cooking for you too. I need to keep my strength up." Emmett laughs.

"I'm cooking for everyone that's gonna head over when they smell the bacon." Dad replies happily.

I take the opportunity to deliver all of the days picnic lunches and check the site, the donkeys and the chucks. As soon as I get back Joey wanders in.

"Mornin' Family. Sprint was boss. Where can I get a new back tyre? I'm starvin'."

"I'll pick one up later. I'm going down the paddock in a bit. Are you gonna do a pit board for Paddy Jr?" I reply and Dad hands him a full breakfast. "Where's Bella Ella?"

"Work. She'll be back for tea when roads reopen. Yeah, I can do a board, Rick's give me the day off 'cause we need to go round and empty all the bogs later, gorra meet him about half eight tonight. Where d'ya want me? D'ya want Nath or Felix to do another one?"

"Another what?" Felix asks parking himself at the table and happily accepting a plate from Dad. "Thanks Dylan. Morning guys."

"Sulby Bridge or The Gooseneck, whichever you fancy. Wanna be pit board crew or are you staying around here to see Kim, Felix?"

"Pit board but can you check that my back tyre is still legal before I go anywhere." He laughs. "We need to do more drag racing real soon. Motocross was fun too. Sarah is awesome!"

"She's going to be a future TT winner without a doubt." Emmett adds.

Mr. Tamaki arrives with Stefan and Jurgen. Emmett and I vacate our seats to make room.

"What time is Kim arriving?" I ask Stef.

"She'll be landing in an hour or so. I was planning to pick her up at the airport but she's going to get a cab or probably a rental now, she's got some excess baggage." He says cryptically, looking over at Emm and Felix and putting a finger to his lips.

Hm, that doesn't sound good. Emm seems completely oblivious. "I need to get showered. Back in a minute." I kiss Emmett and run off to the bathroom.

Excess baggage? Oh my god, she's bringing Cherry with her isn't she? I bet they're closer than Emmett's let on and she's coming to talk him out of the divorce. Oh well Delilah, it's been fun and you're just gonna have to face facts. He's not yours to keep. He never was. You knew you'd have to let him go sooner or later. I stay in the shower a while hoping they will all be gone when I come out.

Joe's still at the table. "Ask Paddy Mac about the stable, Dil will ya?"

"I'll see how busy he is sweetheart." I promise and rush back to my room. I doubt we'll get to see the horses now.

I get my stuff together as quickly as I can. I don't want to be here when they arrive. I can hide down the paddock and won't be able to use the phone in the pit area so can legitimately stay incommunicado.

"I'm off down the paddock, Dad. See you later. Tell Joey that Paddy Mac will leave the boards and numbers with the sector marshals. Remind him to charge his phone or take a radio." I say as I jump on The Duchess.

"Will do, I'll either be down later or go with Joey. Ride safe." He says, looking at his watch, probably wondering what the rush is. "Love you."

Emmett is by the campsite gate. I stop briefly to tell him where I'll be all day, remind him roads close at ten and tell him to have fun and say 'hi' to Kim for me. I make a point of telling him that my phone will be off all day. I kiss him passionately, realise it might be the last time, tear up and put my helmet on quickly. He looks a little confused but I don't think he's realised that I've guessed that Kim is bringing Cherry and I'm sure he doesn't know about it himself yet. It's not my place to tell him, if there's a chance of saving his marriage I don't want to stand in the way. Well I do! But I won't.

I have a run over the mountain to empty my head. It works only whilst the throttle is wide open and then thoughts come flooding back. Stefan is just looking after Emmett and Felix. He must think there's a chance they might reconcile, maybe the lawyer said something? Why wouldn't Emm mention it this morning? How would he know? He slept in my bed; he wouldn't have seen Stefan until the same time I did. Felix wants to do a pit board is that to get out of the way? Surely he'd want to stay if only Kim was coming? Does he know? Oh shut up Delilah! Whatever happens will be for the best. Accept you've had the time of your life and you knew it would end.

Enough now Dil! You can't go into the pits with a head full of crap. If anything happens to Paddy Jr. because you're not concentrating you'll never forgive yourself. Put it in a box for now you can unpack it later, or not.

I head down to the tyre guys to order a new one for Joey. They promise to get it here by lunchtime. Then I walk over to Paddy Jr's garage.

"Morning gents. How are we feeling?" I ask pulling on my fireproof overalls and switching off my phone.

"Hey Dil, perfect timing. I'm having a mare trying to get this pad in." Juan replies and I immediately get stuck in and forget the outside world. We check and double check and triple check everything. I tell them Joey will have a board for them and I'll let him know where later. I don't mention Felix in case he gets side tracked.

Superstock rules have been updated recently and rear wheel changes are now banned during pit stops and we aren't allowed to 'tinker' with the engine like we always used to. Before the new rules we would play with cam timings and change the head gasket but now it can't be touched, it has to stay like a sealed engine from the showroom.

The lads have increased the power a bit with better fueling via a kit ECU and fitted a race air-filter and a full race exhaust. The brakes and the suspension have also had a few tweaks. Everything needs to be spot on and working to perfection before Paddy Jr. gets to the start line. We fit the pit lane speed limiter and mess and fine tune until we're happy then get it to scrutineering to get it passed as fit to race. Nothing left to do but wait now. We'll measure out our fuel allowance just before the start. We head for the food vans to grab some lunch.

Superstock is the last race of the day, starting at quarter to three and lasting four laps with one quick pitstop. Road racing is really physical and you need to keep your strength up. It seriously drains your energy if you're too nervous to eat beforehand. Paddy Jr. has no such worries, he eats like a horse! We have pork baps and chips and doughnuts and coffee and then an ice cream. Juan turns his phone on and it goes crazy with pings for texts and messages and missed calls. He starts to read them.

"Joe says put your phone on." He tells me.

Reluctantly, I turn it on and it pings. I have several missed calls all from Joey and Emmett. Joey has sent a picture of Dutch looking like he is about to make serious trouble 'butch batin 4 the blus oo let the bogs out' and some dog emojis and kisses.

The next one is from Emmett. 'Answer you phone, please. Has Joe told you who's arrived? I'm so sorry no one told me apparently your Dad said it was fine. Don't blame Kim she just wanted to make Felix happy. X'

Another one from Joe 'fone me xxx'

One from the vet 'wondering if you can make time for a drink on Thursday evening?'

Last one is off Ricky 'u n Dyl goin Sundy? Wanna lift? Xx'

I realise Juan is already on the phone to Joey organising pit boards and relaying the information Paddy Jr. needs on them. Joey tells him Felix and Nathan will do the Sulby Bridge one and he'll go up to the Gooseneck with Dad because he knows the back roads better. I yell to him that I've sorted his tyre and for them all to ride safe. He yells back thanks and wishes Paddy Jr. loads of luck. I turn off my phone and put it away; I'm not ready to face anyone else right now and I don't need to. Joe's sorted and I know where Dad is too so it's all fine.

I walk over to grab Joey's tyre before I forget and we head back to the garage to sort fuel, get everything in place for the pit stop and for Paddy to get his leathers on. The ten-minute warning is announced and there's a crazy flurry of activity. Everyone starts heading up to the start line and getting into their set off order. Racers go off individually at ten second intervals. Paddy is number twelve. We get the bike in place, put it on the paddock stands and stick tyre warmers back on. You don't want to be wailing up Bray Hill with a full tank of fuel and stone cold tyres.

One-minute warning, this is it. We are now at the mercy of the Gods; the gods of speed, of weather and of all things mechanical. Tyre warmers are off, visors, helmets, zips and gloves checked, last minute advice and declarations of love are given. We slap Paddy Jr. on the back and get out of the way. He gets a really clean start and now we can do nothing but wait and listen to the commentary. He's not planning to pit until the end of the second lap so we stay by the wall and watch the action.

The weather is ideal, it's dry and warm but cloudy and the sun isn't going to catch you out with blinding rays as you come out of sheltered sections. The atmosphere here is totally unique. Everyone in the pits are either chattering noisily or rushing around sorting stuff or waiting anxiously for their racer to go or for news of their progress. Those who have already raced today or won't be racing until later in the week are now winding down, relaxing and having fun. Down in the paddock the rock music is playing and you can smell barbecues getting started.

Peter Hickman currently holds the lap record for Superstock. He put in a blistering time of 16 minutes and 50 seconds on a BMW which is pretty phenomenal on an essentially stock road bike. With rule changes this year I don't imagine this will be broken but I can guarantee everyone on the circuit will be trying their best to get close. Paddy Jr. is going to have to nurse that back tyre round if he still wants grip on the final lap. We hear the times from the first sector at Glen Helen and he's doing fine, clearly no mechanical issues to worry about. By Ballaugh Bridge he's started gaining on the guy in front.

Juan goes out of the pits area to ring Nathan and then Joey to make sure they're in place and have the board ready. He comes back and says they're all set. Timing at Ramsey tells us Paddy's gained a little more and more again at The Bungalow. We get into a space with a good view of the gate so that we can run like maniacs into the pit if he does pull in unexpectedly. He sails by us looking like he means business. We make sure again that everything is to hand for when he comes in. Many races are won and lost on superb or disastrous pit stops. All he needs is a dash of fuel, maybe new tear offs and a drink it should literally take seconds.

Timing announcements confirm he's making brilliant time and when he pulls in he's happy and his visor is fine, he takes the drink I offer and leans back so we can get the fuel in quickly then we move and he's gone, it's all down to him now. The pit lane is filling up so we move back to the wall. Two more laps and it's all over, nothing we can do here but wait. Come on Paddy Jr. get home safely and quickly. Timings continue to improve and two of the top guys are forced to retire, one with electrical issues on lap three and the other running out of fuel less than a minute from the finish line on their final lap. Lap three is smooth and by the middle of lap four Paddy is in third place but is only half a second up on the bike in fourth when we hear his final time at Cronk ny Mona so it's going to go right down to the wire. He crosses the start finish line with no idea if he's third or fourth but they direct him in to the winners' enclosure so third it is! We run over to congratulate him. He parks in his allotted spot, burns out his back tyre, gives me and Juan big hugs and gets dragged into an interview by the radio bods. All the Mac's arrive from every direction and there is much hugging, kissing and cheering as Paddy Jr. climbs the steps to the podium.

I sneak back to the garage to clear everything away and get it ready to go back into the van. When it's all neatly sorted and waiting I don't bother to remove my overalls, grab my helmet and jacket and Joe's tyre and go for a coffee. I sit at one of the picnic benches and watch the world go by. I can't put it any longer so I turn my phone back on. There's a dozen missed calls, mostly from Joey. I ring him back straight away. He's buzzing.

"Eh Laa, he came round 'ere like a mad man. Dunno 'ow 'e read 'is board!"

We chat for a few minutes and Dad says they'll leave the boards with the marshals for the Macs to collect on the way home and then head back as soon as roads open and pick up Nath and Felix on the way. Neither of them mention our new visitors and I don't ask. Dad does say we only need to feed ourselves and Mr. Tamaki because everyone else is sorted.

Emmett has sent more texts telling me to answer the phone. The latest one says. 'Congratulations, just heard results on radio. No excuses now, call me! Xxxxxx.'

I text him. 'Just packing up. I'm cool with whatever's gone on. I'll be back later what time are you going out to eat? x'

He rings and I send it straight to answer phone. He texts. 'Stef's booked something, you're all invited. PICK YOUR BLOODY PHONE UP DELILAH!!!!'

It rings again. I turn it off and put it back in my pocket. I better head home and face the music. I don't really want to make a complete idiot of myself with a snot and tears performance in the middle of the paddock. I wave good bye to the Mac's, tapping my non-existent watch and shrugging to say I need to go when they beckon me back, and head across the park to The Duchess. The roads are still closed so I make my way home by riding down to Douglas front, past the ferry port and along the back roads.

I turn The Duchess off at the top of the lane and coast down to the cottage. Most of the bikes are out except for Stefan's, Charlie's, Connor's and Emmett's. I put my baby straight into the workshop and go inside quickly. I've just put the coffee on when Dutch arrives and jumps on the table. He eyes me up and sighs. I squash his beautiful face gently in my hands and kiss his head. "Thanks for the support earlier gorgeous, Joe said you made your feelings known. I suppose Jeff's best mates with everyone already is she?"

Suddenly. I am aware of Emmett standing quietly in the doorway watching me, looking exasperated and a little sheepish. "Delilah, darlin' why won't you answer your phone? Do you enjoy driving me crazy? I've missed you so much and I really need to apologise again."

I take a sip of coffee and a deep breath and try hard to be normal. "Hi Emm, want a coffee? I'm not able to have my phone on in the garages. I did warn you this morning and you don't have to apologise for anything, whatever it is I can deal with it I'm a big girl now. Have you had a good day?"

"No, my girl wouldn't talk to me and my best friend's wife brought uninvited guests. I'm still trying to work out if the two are connected. Felix was so happy though; I wish you'd seen his face."

I change the subject. "Did you get chance to watch the races or listen to the commentary?"

"Yeah we went up to Sulby to watch for a while but I didn't want to leave our new arrivals unsupervised for too long."

"Where are they now?"

"They're down on the beach with Connor and Charlie. Wanna come and meet them?"

I'm just about to make an excuse when Joey, Dad and Felix come bowling in.

"Where's my babies? I'm missing them already. I can't believe they're here!" Felix hugs and kisses me. "Thank you Dil, it means so much to me, only the horses to sort now."

I'm starting to realise what a complete idiot I have been, yet again.

Emmett laughs. "They're on the beach. I was just going to introduce Dil, she hasn't even met them yet or agreed that they can stay."

Felix grabs my hand tightly and drags me outside like an excited child. He stops by the fire pit and whistles loudly and Jeff runs up the beach followed by three huge Dobermans. I collapse into a complete fit of tears and laughter. Delilah you stupid, stupid tart! That'll bloody teach you. Just communicate and stop making up worse case scenarios at every opportunity.

"They can stay forever." I announce before they even reach us.

CHAPTER 44

I am formally introduced to Odin, Thor and Loki. They are sleek and muscular and beautifully marked and have docked ears and tails, making them look almost cartoon like. All are perfect gentlemen and respond quickly to commands but are also soppy and cuddly and slobbery. Felix and Joey roll around the beach with them whilst Connor and Charlie go off to get showered and ready for their night out. I sit down on the blanket and Emmett sits next to me. He puts his arm around me and pulls me onto his lap.

"Talk to me Delilah, I've been so worried all day. You took off all of a sudden and seemed upset. Why wouldn't you call or answer your phone?" I laugh, shaking my head at my own stupidity.

"Emm, baby, I've been asking myself that for the last ten minutes. I'm such an idiot and I get scared and run away a lot. Half the time what I'm scared of isn't even the truth I've just made it up in my stupid head. I had convinced myself Kim had bought your wife with her when Stefan mentioned 'excess baggage' this morning. I never for one second thought he meant something as wonderful as the dogs."

Emmett holds me tightly. "My poor darlin' Delilah, do you not listen to a word I say to you? Why ever would you think such a crazy thing? We are done, finished, over. Papers have all been signed and served."

"I'm stubborn and stupid, Emm, just accept it and kiss me." I sigh, shaking my head again at my own idiocy.

We are making up for the lost day, I'm sitting astride Emmett with my legs wrapped around his back, he's undone the zip on my overalls and we are snogging like teenagers when Stefan and Kim come over. I'm filthy from being in the garage all day, my hands are black, I stink of exhaust fumes and my dreads are wilder than ever. Kim is stunningly beautiful and spotlessly dressed in a white shirt and blue jeans. She giggles when she sees us, a huge mass of hair and legs.

"Emmett, honey, put her down and introduce me."

Stef replies with mock disgust. "Get used to it, he can't keep his hands off her and she's been busy all day so he's gotta catch up. They only come up for air if Delilah feeds him or if she hears a motorbike."

"Thank you for that lovely introduction, Stef." I laugh, extracting myself from Emm's embrace and hastily pulling down my t-shirt and re zipping my overalls. "I apologise for both my appearance and my manners. I was going to get showered and changed but Emm can be very persuasive."

"I love you already!" She exclaims and hugs me tightly.

"Kim, darling, you're going to get filthy! I'm covered in oil." I warn, hugging her back.

"I don't care. I've been dying to meet you. The boys have been telling me more and more every day and I couldn't stay away any longer. I'm so sorry about the dogs. It was stupid not to ask first. I took so long sorting passports and vet's certification I just got carried away with the idea and convinced myself you wouldn't mind."

"Don't worry about it, they really and truly are more than welcome."

Felix, Joey and the dogs join us. Felix looks like it's Christmas day. He grabs me, picks me up and swings me around. "Delilah, you are an angel!" He sings.

"I've got nothing to do with it." I squeal. "It's all Kim's doing not mine." He finally puts me down and does the same to Kim.

"Did you ask Paddy Mac about the stable?" Joey asks.

"Oh shit! I forgot." I say grabbing my phone and ringing him straight away. Wherever they are there is much celebrating going on but I shout loud enough to be understood. Paddy Mac says he'll be around in the morning. I tell Joey and get another hug off him and off Felix.

"Anything for a quiet life!" I giggle and Kim hugs me again.

"You are so special! Please come and eat with us I want to get to know you so much. You too Joey."

"Thanks but I'm spendin' the night cleanin' bogs." He laughs. We hear Ella arriving on her beautiful new Ducati, courtesy of Jurgen. "Are we 'avin' scran 'fore I go, Ma?"

Ella comes round to us and hugs and kisses everyone including Kim and the dogs. Then announces that her bike is perfect and she's 'starvin'.

"What time are you leaving? I need to get showered and feed my babies. I don't want to show you up or hold you up." I laugh.

"We're going in half an hour or so. We can wait."

"Okay, take Emm away with you now and I should be ready in time." Emm grabs me and kisses me.

"Don't make me leave you again Delilah, I've missed you so much today. I really love you!" He exclaims, being a dick, Stef drags him back up to the campsite with Kim giggling behind them.

Felix comes in with Joey and Ella. "I'm hanging here with Joe and Ella and the dogs if that's okay. I don't wanna go out. Dad won't mind. I'll keep El company when Joe goes to work."

"Do whatever makes you happy, honey. Do you want feeding too then?"

"Yes please." He grins.

I dig a huge Bolognese sauce out of the freezer and put it on to heat. I throw some pasta in a saucepan and have a quick shower while it cooks.

Joey has already grated a bowl of cheese when I get back and Ella is stirring the sauce.

"Kim's got a rental car by the way." Felix says. "You won't have to ride tonight."

"I doubt they'll be room for all of us." I laugh.

"Connor, Charlie and Nathan aren't going because they're watching a band somewhere else. There's plenty of room. It's only you, Dad, Kim, Stef and Jurgen."

"Where's Dad?" I ask Joey. "Tell him grubs up unless he's coming to the restaurant."

"He knows and he's got other plans for later." Dad laughs as he comes in. "I smelled it cooking. Where are you off to? Kim's wearing a pretty fancy dress."

I dish up plates full of food for everyone, including Mr. Tamaki who arrived with Dad.

I nip outside seeing if I can get a glimpse of Kim so that I can dress right and not show Emmett up. He's just walking down looking smoulderingly gorgeous in jeans and a shirt. I'm still in my bathrobe but I run barefoot and dive into his arms wrapping my legs around him like a child. "God, why are you are so sexy? Can we just go to bed now?" I whisper into his ear.

"Nope, you've made me wait all day so now you can suffer." He grins. "We're going in the car if that's okay. I came to help you get dressed." He drawls running his fingers down my spine.

"Unless you wanna make love in the lane I suggest you stop that now." I tease. "What should I wear? I think Kim well and truly outclasses me when it comes to being a lady. I don't wanna show you up."

"Delilah, I will never be ashamed to be seen with you. Wear whatever you like. I'm happy enough with you in your bathrobe, your overalls or your birthday suit." He replies carrying me into the cottage and through to the bedroom. Stopping to say 'hi' to everyone on the way and stealing a slice of garlic bread. He dumps me on my bed and opens my drawers.

He throws a pair of white cotton knickers at me. "That's a good start." He quips. "Do you own any sexy under wear?"

"What do you think?" I sass. "I dress out of necessity and for comfort. Sexy underwear has never been high on my priorities list. I don't really have the required assets either." I add, looking down at my nearly flat chest.

He sighs and mooches in the next drawer finding the dress from my shopping trip with Sal. He opens the bag and unwraps the tissue paper from around it.

"You can put that back." I laugh. "I bought it whilst under the influence of Sal. It's going back to the shop on Sunday. It's too short and way too expensive. There's a smart dress in the other drawer if I need a dress."

He holds it up and sucks in his breath. "Put this one on right now!"

"No, Emm. It's too much. I look like a grand-a-night hooker in it."

"Let me be the judge of that." He drawls, unzipping it and ripping off the labels so that I cannot return it. "Arms up, darlin'."

"Emmett!"

"Don't Emmett me, darlin'. Just do as you're told. Arms up!" He laughs.

I put it on and he turns me around to do it up, then back to face him. "Oh my god Delilah you look beautiful!" He exclaims. "It fits you like a glove."

I pull the front up and the back down and pout. "It's too low and too short. Have I got to wear my 'fuck me' shoes too?"

"Whatever they are the answer is almost certainly yes." Emmett giggles. "I need a pee I'll be back in a minute."

I dig out the tights, the shoes and the bag, sort my hair and put on a quick lick of makeup.

"Ready." I say throwing my purse and phone into the bag as he comes back in.

"Wow! I'm scared to touch you. You look amazing. Like an exquisite china doll." He exclaims holding his hand out to me. "Come on quickly or I'm going to make us really, really late."

Everyone at the table looks at me like I've been abducted by aliens.

"Fuck me, Mama!" Joey exclaims with a whistle.

"You look absolutely gorgeous." Ella says punching him.

"Wow! Lost for words." Felix says. "You're a lucky man." Dad just kisses my head and smiles. We hear the car pull into the front and Emmett leads me outside.

Jurgen jumps out and opens the door for me. "Mein Gott! What have you done to Delilah? Liebling, you look simply divine!"

We jump in the back of the car and Stef gives me a loud wolf whistle. "Delilah! You still continue to amaze me in many good ways." He tells me.

"You certainly scrub up well, honey." Kim laughs. "It would take me a week to transform from mechanic to out of this world gorgeous and you did it in half an hour and fed the family."

I cringe with embarrassment and Emm puts his arm around me. "Stop now all of you she's not used to this formality and soppiness. I just had to force her into this dress. She's not too impressed with me so don't make it worse."

"I have known Delilah over forty-five years and I have never seen her wear a dress for anyone before." Jurgen concurs. "You are very special to her."

"Forty five years? You knew her before she was born?" Kim asks confused.

"I wish! I was seven when Dad and Jurgen first met and became very firm friends. He's been leading me into bad ways ever since."

Kim takes off her seat belt, turns around and looks at me like Dutch does. "You are not over fifty years old! You have the body and facial features of a small child! Why is my life so unfair?" She giggles. "Stef thought you were in your thirties when he was telling me about you on the phone. He was worried that you were too young for Emm then couldn't stop laughing when he found out you thought him and Emm were the same age as the kids."

I laugh. "I am lucky enough to have a strange mixture of really good genes. Mama never really aged and Dad's not looking bad for nearly eighty." I reply.

"Jeez, I thought he was the same age as my Dad and he looks a decade younger than he should!" Stef exclaims.

We're eating at The Abbey in Ballasalla which is a highly commended restaurant that I've been to once before, a very long time ago, for afternoon tea with Sal. It's very smart and I'm a little uncomfortable before we even get inside. It's not a place I would choose to eat; not because of the food, which is amazing, but because I feel like I don't belong. I'm just going to let everyone else take the lead and stay as quiet as possible.

We are greeted by a maitre'd who shows us to a private table. Emm must sense my anxiety, he squeezes my hand "Relax, darlin'." He whispers. "Have I told you that you are the most beautiful and the sexiest girl in the whole world?"

"Stop it, you're making me worse." I giggle nervously. "This place is a bit posh for me, I'm feeling well out of my depth. I don't want to show you up."

"Not gonna happen, darlin'. I couldn't be prouder than I am when I'm with you."

Once we're all seated Jurgen orders some bottles of extremely expensive champagne and they bring over menus. I take a drink and shudder involuntarily. It's bubbly and sour and bitter, nothing like the stuff we were drinking when I agreed to adopt Joey. Emm laughs at me and grabs a passing waitress. A pint of lager and blackcurrant appears seconds later. I smile and drink far too much of it to steady my nerves. I am amazed at how vulnerable I feel when out of my comfort zone. I'm lost when I'm not surrounded by my family or messing with bikes.

"Stef was telling me about your Bob Marley breakfast sing along yesterday. He says you've got a real good voice. I so wish I'd come over with them all right from the start. Connor is clearly head over heels in love with Nathan and I can see why already. Charlie is looking more relaxed than I've seen him in ages. Felix has been transformed into an entirely different kid. I don't know what's happened to the smart mouthed, distant one I saw last time? Don't even get me started on Emmett." She sighs looking at him fondly. "He was in a constant state of a seething rage. Now look at him."

"Delilah cured some of Felix's sass." Jurgen laughs and with Emmett's input and Stef's confirmation, proceeds to tell her the whole story. I want to curl up and die. She is in absolute hysterics.

"You're an enchantress, honey. You've put a spell on everyone." She smiles, taking my hand. "Connor told me you were brilliant with him and Nathan too. Said you sorted his folks and his scary uncle."

"I didn't sort any of them. His mum and dad both knew but hadn't told each other." I feel the need to defend Sal and Billy.

Emmett jumps in again and tells her what I did to Rick. "You are making me sound like such a right evil witch." I groan. "Ricky is, near as damn it, my brother and my best friend. I know what I can get away with." I explain to Kim.

I try to steer the conversation away from me. "How did you sort the dogs so quickly? I would have thought they'd have to go into quarantine or something."

"They aren't allowed to leave your place for a little while I'm afraid." She frowns. "Ian, the vet that met us at the airport, said he knew you very well and was happy for them to be isolated at your place. He'll be over to check them every week. He seemed really keen to have a reason to come by, said he'd check every day if I wanted."

Emmett raises his eyebrows in interest. "Do you know this vet?"

I shrug. "He's Sarah's cowman."

"Jeez, Kim! Trust you to find the vet that wants to marry my girl." He shakes his head.

"He wants to take me on a date, not marry me. I'm sure one date will be enough to put him off." I reply with a smile.

"Your dating days are over, darlin'! You are well and truly spoken for." Emmett growls.

The starter arrives and we tuck in. The food is fresh and tasty. Jurgen tells Kim all about his new place and promises to take her tomorrow. He's pretty sure he'll own it by Wednesday. Then he tells Emmett that Hans has served all of the divorce papers this morning with their list of conditions and insisted they reply within twenty-four hours.

Kim asks if I mind them talking about Cherry and I tell her not at all, I'm happy to just sit back and let them all catch up. It's clearly not what she meant and she launches into a huge tirade of abuse. She really is not on Team Cherry.

"I texted her to tell her I was fetching the dogs for Felix, I didn't tell her they were coming here, and to leave them at the stables so I could get them. I wanted to check the horses and chat with Tiff, she's the stable girl, about getting them too when we could. She asked how Felix is, she's really pining for him. She'll sort everything that end when you're ready here. Anyhow, Cherry turns up late, looking like she's been in the beauty salon for a week and is about to take part in a fashion show, goes to kiss me like we're still friends. I'm thinking I want to punch you in the face but I need to wait until everything is signed first." She laughs. "She tells me how lonely she is and how much she misses her boys and tries to get me to tell her where they are so I ask where her personal trainer is. She looks stunned, goes a lovely shade of red, lets the dogs out of the car and drives off as quickly as she can. I wish I'd been a fly on the wall when those papers arrived this morning."

Emmett kisses her. "You're an angel Kim, thank you."

"You're a jerk!" She laughs, batting him playfully. "How many times did we tell you not to marry her? It's got to be costing you a pretty penny to get rid."

"I'm a stubborn idiot, I know." Emmett sighs. "But it's okay now because I've found Dil and she's even more stubborn than me." He then tells them I've avoided him all day and why. Thanks Emm!

"She certainly didn't look like she was avoiding you when we met." Kim giggles. "You were, according to the boys, 'sucking her face off.'"

"Yeah." Emmett grins. "We do that a lot unless people are eating. We've been banned from doing it when there's food about."

Stefan is beside himself. "Delilah, I am so sorry. I never thought about that for a second. Man, I feel awful now. How could I do that to you? I suppose I thought your Dad might have told you but I doubt you'd even have seen him. How can I make it up to you?"

"Don't worry about it, Stef, really. It's my fault for being stubborn and stupid and not asking. The dogs have more than made up for it and we're fine now. I run and hide when things get heavy. Emm is starting to get used to it now. He just nails me down until I tell him what's going on in my head."

Jurgen pats my hand. "Poor Delilah has been running and hiding too long now. Emmett will make it all better for you."

The main course arrives and Emm has ordered us steaks again. They are succulent and tender and melt in the mouth. He orders me another pint too. They chat amiably for the rest of the evening and I happily listen. Jurgen tells us his retirement plans, Emmett and Stefan tell Kim more about our jam session and about the week of practice and the racing we've seen so far, drag racing and ploughing with the shire horses. She makes us promise to take her everywhere.

"You're going to run out of days." I laugh. "There's racing Wednesday and Friday. That doesn't leave you much time."

Jurgen sighs at me like I'm a bit simple. "Liebling, Have you forgotten I will have my new home by Wednesday. We do not have to leave on Satur-day any more. The bean counters and work obsessed can go home. Jurgen is staying and Stefan and Kim and everyone who wants to can stay with me too. Kim is staying for a month at least."

"We're not touring now until mid-September and we can set up a studio at Dad's place to write." Stef adds. "Emm will work much better if you're nearby."

"Bloody hell! I just imagined TT will end and everyone would leave. I was trying not to think about it until I had to face it." I say without thinking. "I am such an idiot!"

Emmett looks at me like I am completely crazy.

"Delilah, what in the world would make you think I am leaving you on Saturday or any other day ever? I will travel when we're working because I have to but I'm going to be here any other time. Did you really think I was going to dump my dogs and horses on you and just expect you to look after them? Do you not listen to anything I tell you? I know we agreed to take it slowly and Felix and I can live in Jurgen's cottage until you get used to the idea of us being a permanent thing and choose a home for us."

I just sit still and silent letting this information sink in. Emmett is not leaving; Felix is not leaving. Jurgen will be here forever. I can't speak. I just look at Emm. He pulls me into his lap and wraps me in his arms.

"Apologies everyone I am going to have to break some rules." He sighs and kisses me for several minutes. The others just laugh and continue chat-ting and drinking. Emmett wipes my tears away and tells me again what an idiot I am.

Sweets arrive and I go to move but he keeps me in his lap and eats with one hand, holding me tightly with the other and feeding me spoons of ice cream.

"That's what we can do tomorrow." He announces. "Peel Castle and ice cream. You up for it Kim?"

"Yeah, definitely. Count us in." She replies. "Do I have to get on the back of a bike? It's been a while."

"You can travel however you want." Emm says, "But we'll be on our bikes, following a leather clad Delilah is a real pleasant experience. That's the next thing we need to ship over." He laughs. "My GS!"

"I think we might need to speak to Paddy Mac about extending the cottage and barn as well as sorting the stables. We're running out of room already."

"We could build a place on the beach." Emmett says. "Plenty of room there. You could wake up looking at the ocean. You'd love that."

"I would love it but that's not the ocean, it's the Irish Sea you twit! It gets as rough as hell in the winter."

We stay chatting long after our meals are eaten. Making plans for the coming weeks and discussing how many rooms in Jurgen's place are already spoken for.

The staff start to get a bit antsy so we leave. Kim gives me a big hug as we wait for Stefan to fetch the car.

"Are you okay darling? Is Emmett moving too fast for you? He's fallen hard and he can get a little intense. Talk to him if he gets OTT. He wouldn't want to do anything to intentionally hurt you. Please don't hurt him. He's waited a long time for you to come into his life."

"I'm still reeling from the revelation that he's not going to be leaving Saturday. I have spent so much time psyching myself up to handle it and a lot more time trying to avoid thinking about it." I admit. "I'm still in shock. I keep thinking he'll suddenly realise what a screwed-up creature I am and run for the hills."

"Trust me honey, you're stuck with him for good now. He doesn't give most people the time of day. You are a revelation." We jump in the car and head home.

"Do you want a bed for the night? Me and Emm can camp."

"No, thank you darling. I can't wait to sleep in the tent. I love it." Kim giggles. Stefan parks up at the campsite and I hug Jurgen and thank them all for a lovely meal and we hug Stef and Kim and arrange to meet up in the morning for our trip to Peel.

Emmett piggybacks me to the cottage. "Wanna walk on the beach?" He asks.

I take off my shoes and strip off my tights and leave them by the door with my bag and we walk down to the sea. I paddle along in the waves.

"You're doing it again, Delilah!" Emmett scolds. "Just when I think we're good you lose it."

"Emm my head is spinning, baby. I'm trying to process some pretty heavy stuff right now. I want to just hold you and make love and forget about everything but I need to face it, not run."

"What's got you so worked up, Dil? Talk to me."

"You're staying. Are you staying? Is this all real? Why me? I'm a complete screw up. How can I keep you happy forever? You'll be bored and disappointed in a few weeks. Emm you're gorgeous and sexy and funny and patient and kind and let's not forget, rich and famous. I'm no one. I was so completely out of my comfort zone tonight. I can't even dress myself properly!" I wail.

He wades into the water fully clothed, picks me up and carries me to my rock.

"What else can I say to convince you?" He asks as he paces back and forth running his hands through his hair in frustration. "You look beautiful tonight and I am the proudest man on this earth. You were fine in the restaurant and did nothing wrong. If this meltdown is because I put you in a dress I promise I will never ever do it again. Me and Felix and Kim and Stefan and the boys already love you to pieces because of who you are. You amaze, fascinate and frustrate the hell out of me every minute of every day and make me lose control of my senses. I don't give a fuck what you're wearing to do any of it. I have fallen totally and utterly head over heels in love with you and I want to spend the rest of my life getting to know all of your hopes and fears, likes and hates and the screwy stuff that goes on in your head! I will keep trying until I learn how to sort it and then I will slowly but surely make you trust me and love me and we will both grow old together. Right, rant over. You now need to repeat all of that back to me so that I know you have heard and understood." He growls, dropping down next to me.

"Oh okay. Do you want all of it or just the highlights?" I giggle. "Emm I'm sorry, I'm falling in love with you and it's scaring the shit out of me."

"Am I going anywhere?" He prompts.

"Not until September." I reply.

"Wrong answer, Delilah!" Am I going to leave you ever again?"

"No?...Emm you can't promise that."

"I can and I am! Am I going to work on this relationship and be patient?"

"You're already doing that."

"Do you believe I love you more than anything else in this world and beyond?"

"No...not yet but I'm trying to get my thick head around that bit."

"Do you want me to stay, Delilah?"

"More than you'll ever know." I whisper.

"Come here then, please let me hold you." I move quickly onto his lap and wrap myself around him like a spider monkey, forgetting all about my dress. He holds me tightly and we kiss violently, both desperate to connect. Emmett puts his hands onto my thighs and pushes my dress up past my bottom. He undoes his jeans and slides them down and sits me back down on top of him.

"Make love to me, my darling Delilah." He begs leaning back on the rock so that I am sat astride him. I willingly oblige and we hungrily devour each other until we are completely drained.

When we finally get our breath back Emmett kisses my head. "Okay, what have we learned today? He asks. "I've learnt that I shouldn't try to dress you. It freaks you out."

"I like it when you undress me." I sass.

"Doesn't count you already knew that." He scolds.

"Okay, I've learned that I need to ask before I run."

"Perfect, we're getting somewhere. I now know If I keep going on long enough you will talk to me."

"I've learned you're not leaving on Saturday and I like making love outdoors in the moonlight! Can we go to bed now?" I tease.

"One more." He replies. "How much do I love you?"

"More than lots?" I ask.

"That's my girl!" He laughs and carries me indoors for bed.

We are greeted by wall to wall Doberman's and Felix fast asleep on the chesterfield. Someone has already covered him with a blanket and I tuck him in and gently kiss his head. I go to go into my bedroom and there's a note on the door 'Use big bed'. We have a slow and sleepy shower together and crawl into the big bed. I'm not sure about Emm but I feel totally mentally and physically exhausted.

CHAPTER 45

We are woken by the smell of bacon and the sound of Dad gently singing 'Wishing Well'. I turn over and find Dutch lying on Emmett's pillow. He unceremoniously climbs over Emmett's head, butts me affectionately and rubs his face against mine then jumps down to follow the smell of breakfast.

"Is that a sign of how the day is going to go?" Emm sighs. "Trampled by family members before I'm even awake."

"I can make it better if you want." I tease. "Today is going to be a great day. No stupid stuff, no panicking, no freak outs. I'm gonna be totally devoted to you! Wanna demo?"

"Yes ma'am." He drawls and I kiss his chest, down his ribs, across his stomach and. ..the door opens and we are flattened by four stupid dogs, one of which is being ridden by Dutch, followed by Felix with two cups of coffee, Joey wearing my shoes on his feet and my tights on his head and Dad with breakfast. I hastily throw on a t-shirt Dad has left by the side of the bed and we are happily engulfed by dogs, kids and Dad while we all enjoy breakfast butties in the big bed. I look across to Emmett, shrug and sigh and mouth 'later' suggestively to him. He smiles ruefully and is treated to a big lick on the face from Jeff while Loki drools all over him waiting for some sandwich.

"Did you sleep alright?" I ask a yawning Felix.

"Really well! That sofa is amazingly comfortable. I must have dropped off watching TV with Dylan. I'd still be spark out now if it wasn't for this lot."

"Kim told me someone was asking after you." I tease. "Who's Tiff?"

"The wonderful woman that looks after the horses." He blushes. "What was she asking?"

"How you are. Ask Kim, she spoke to her when she fetched this lot." I gesture at the three dumbos sitting on us.

"I see you're coming round to my way of thinking with the cross dressing?" Emmett giggles at Joey who's still got my shoes and tights on.

"Eh laa, I dunno 'ow women wear stuff like this. Me feet a killin' me already." He laughs. "I fell over 'em by the front door. It's 'appenin a lot round 'ere lately."

"Are you lot coming to Peel Castle? We're going to be tourists for the day." I ask.

"Us men 'ave gorra work." Joey grins. "We're checking everythin' that's out on the course while we can get at it. Fe's comin' to 'elp."

"I'm bonding with my extended family. The scary brothers!" Felix giggles. "Is it true there's a third one?"

"I've got at least one job coming in." Dad announces. "Mr. Jeavons' mates are starting to call up thick and fast and yes, there's a third one, Chaz, the big brother, he's even bigger that Bill and Rick, sure Pat said he's away running some training course."

"We haven't seen him for ages, I ought to text him to see when he's back. Oh shit! Paddy Mac is coming about the stables." I remember.

"I'll be here." Dad says. "Who needs to fit in where? Is there anything else we need him to look at? Like a big extension for the dogs and another mezzanine room for Felix?" He asks raising an eyebrow. "The poor lad can't be expected to sleep on the sofa indefinitely."

I laugh. "Four horses at least in the stables. You and Paddy Mac can sort the details between you. Emmett fancies an 'ocean view' so ask him what he can put up on the beach for us. Felix, honey do you want a cottage room or a space like Joe's?"

"One like Joey's please. I'll pay for everything and the stables. I'm pretty sure I've got shit loads of money somewhere that I never get chance to spend." He says, looking to his Dad for confirmation.

"You have got a few million dollars here and there, Son." Emmett replies. "In fact you can pay the vet bill for this lot." He adds smiling at Loki who is fast asleep on top of Thor, on top of him.

"We'll be next door neighbours." Joey grins.

"Anyone home?" Yells Kim from the doorway.

"In here!" We reply in unison. Her and Stef come in and laugh at the inter-esting family scene.

Stefan shakes his head in wonder. "I see the dogs have settled in, are you having a John and Yoko day? Joey, why are you wear...?....I'm not even going to ask. Did we smell breakfast?" He turns to Kim and shrugs. "This is what I mean about this cottage and these crazy people, honey. It gets weirder every day yet this is their idea of 'normal'". Dad smiles and gets up to make some more breakfast. Joey finally removes my shoes and tights, kisses me, the dogs and Dutch and goes to raid the larder and fridge for 'work scran'. Felix heads for the shower taking the dogs and Dutch with him.

"Go and have breakfast guys." I say to Kim and Stef. "We'll be ready in a minute now we can actually move."

"Take all the time you need. I'm gonna try everything on the menu." Kim giggles, closing the door as she leaves.

"Where was I before that brief interlude?" I ask Emm diving on top of him.

"Hang on there, little darlin'." He pulls me up to look in his eyes. "Did you all just agree to let me and Felix move in and plan to completely rearrange your home to accommodate us?"

"Yep, I reckon we did. It appears that family meetings in bed are the best way to get stuff sorted." I reply.

"You amaze and astound me once again, Delilah Blue! Yesterday I thought you were about to run and I wake up to plans for a home on the beach....you are never, ever going to get boring or predictable."

"Have you got time to explain that 'quickie' thing again before I get dressed?" I ask in reply, pulling off Dad's t- shirt.

"Be the least I could do under the circumstances." He grins.

I zip across to my room and pull on my 'Sarah' outfit under my one piece and grab my helmet. "Where's my bag, Joe?" I yell. He throws it at me from the table and I empty my phone and purse into my rucksack. "Cheers, sunshine, have you found enough work scran?"

"Yeah, Mama Bear, got plenty. Ya need to do some more bakin' soon though."

Emm emerges from the bedroom in just his boxers, stretches, yawns and grabs himself coffee and a chair. Kim is still happily munching on toast and jam and chatting away to Mr. Tamaki who is also tucking into breakfast.

Felix appears with a towel wrapped around his waist giggling his head off. "Odin just ate my shorts whilst I was in the shower! Can you go and get my jeans out of the tent, Joe please?" Joey runs off up to the campsite and comes back with his rucksack. "Cheers, bro." Felix laughs wandering into my bedroom to get dressed.

"Stef, you're right, it is like being in an episode of the Walton's!" Kim exclaims with delight. "You truly are a family already."

"We're a little closer to the Addams family than the Walton's if you ask me." Dad replies, handing her more toast and coffee. I pour me and Emmett another coffee and we share his chair. Dad kisses the top of my head and hands us both toast. Felix comes out fully dressed.

"Ready bro? We gorra go!" Joey asks, kissing me and stealing a piece of the toast I've just buttered and covered in jam. "See ya later, love yas. Enjoy ya day. Ride safe!"

"Love you too, my darlings. Ride safe!" I reply as Felix kisses Kim then hugs and kisses me and steals my last piece of toast as he follows Joey out the door.

"Laters fam, love you all." He laughs with a mouthful of toast. "Have a fun day."

I share Emmett's toast whilst Kim and Stefan watch on, shaking their heads in amusement.

"Delilah, I can honestly tell you, and Stef will back me up on this, that in all my years I have never seen Felix that happy or relaxed or ever behaving like that with Cherry. I definitely never saw him kiss her voluntarily." Kim says. "And don't get me started on Emmett! I can hardly recognise him."

Emmett hugs me tightly and smiles, happy that Kim has noticed.

"Fe appears to be learning a lot of bad habits from his newly found little brother." I sigh. "Stef and I are still trying to work out if Emm is Joey's real father."

She dissolves into a fit of giggles. "Oh Emm, no wonder you're both so happy, she is beyond adorable."

We finish breakfast and wish Mr. Tamaki a good day. I clear the table and Emm and I wash up while Kim and Stefan go to get their bike gear. Dad hears a van arrive and goes out to meet and help unload his next job.

Emmett leans over and kisses me gently. "We're you listening carefully to Kim? Dil, she's not just blowing smoke up your ass. Felix means as much to her as Joey does to you."

"Heard and learned." I reply kissing him back. "You need to get some clothes on, baby or else we're going to get sidetracked again."

We grab helmets and I fire up The Duchess, kiss Dad and tell him to have fun and give Emm a ride up to the field to get his own bike.

"Oh good lord Delilah! Is this 'The Duchess' the boys keep referring to? She sounds like a real beast and you're so dainty and tiny. How can you possibly handle her?" Kim exclaims having clearly forgotten the story the boys were telling her last night. Thank goodness.

Stefan laughs. "Would you like to go pillion on Delilah's bike honey? I'm sure she'll ride really carefully with you."

Emmett shakes his head in mock horror as he climbs off to get onto his own. "Kim I strongly advise that you do not get on the back of Delilah unless you are prepared for the ride of your life. She has two speeds and warp is the slowest!"

"That sounds like a challenge, boys. Maybe Delilah can bring me back later. I better get used to being on a bike again first, it's been a while."

"Later would be good, honey." Stefan smirks. "We don't have any plans for tonight yet do we?"

"I don't think so." Kim replies completely oblivious.

"Are Jurgen or the boys coming?" Emmett asks.

"No, Dad's gotta work and the boys went off somewhere with Nathan earlier. It's a double date, bro. Me, you and our girls." He replies with a grin.

"Perfect, go Dil. We'll follow you."

"Straight there or scenic route?"

"Scenic!" They all reply. I head to the Fairy Bridge. I figure the little guys have well and truly earned some shinies the last few days. Kim, being a true lady, has no money on her so keeps taking it off me and the boys and gleefully placing it in between the stones.

"Murray's is one minute from here do you want a quick look?" I ask. "Kim might be bored. It's a load of old bikes."

"Is that the place Joey was telling us about when we first arrived?" Stefan asks.

"Maybe, he's been there with me."

"Yeah. Let's go. We won't stay long." Stef replies looking at Kim.

"I'm just your passenger, honey." She giggles. "Take me wherever you want to."

We arrive at Murray's and Peter greets me with a big hug. "And is this the young man the whole island is currently talking about?" He laughs, shaking Emmett's hand warmly, then greeting Kim and Stefan.

"Sounds about right." I shrug.

"Coffee or the five-cent tour?" He asks.

"Tour for the boys, Kim and I will raid the biscuit tin and go and kiss the donkeys."

He leads the way into his Aladdin's cave and the boys follow willingly.

"Sorry, is that okay?" I ask Kim realising I've just made the decision for her. "That was a bit presumptuous of me."

"You've read me to perfection, honey. I love whatever makes Stefan happy but I have no real interest in motorbikes. I haven't been on the back of one since the boys first passed their tests and we used to ride together so that I knew they were safe. Donkeys are a whole different matter, your three are the most adorable things especially the baby. Connor said he's called 'Wonky'."

"Afraid so." I grin. "Giles, Isobel and Wonky. The poor darling was going to get a proper name when we'd all decided what suited him but Wonky has kind of stuck now. Watch Giles if you fuss them he's a bugger. I still have a bruise from days ago."

She laughs. "Yeah, on your bum. Emmett shared that with me the first time I went to see them yesterday."

"Good God. Is nothing sacred." I look to the heavens.

"He can't help himself, honey. You have become his world. He talks about nothing else." She says taking my hands. "He loves you, Delilah, very much."

"The feeling is mutual." I tell her and take her through the museum to meet the resident donkeys before this gets too deep.

The boys reappear awestruck and smiling. Emmett hugs me. "Pete's been showing us a bit of 'Blues' history. You have quite a considerable and impressive racing pedigree and have been extremely modest about your past achievements. I thought I knew a fair bit about the racing but our coverage must be really limited."

"Pete, what've you been up to?" I sigh. "You haven't bored them to death with the photos and the trophy cabinets have you? I bought them to see the bikes!"

"They didn't even know you're still the fastest woman around the course. This young man needs to know what a prize he's bagged." Peter tells me proudly.

"He's no idea what he's taking on, Pete." I reply rolling my eyes. "He appears to be sticking around to find out though so he must be tougher than he looks."

We say our farewells and return to the bikes. Emmett grabs me before I put my helmet on. "Emm, I'm sorry. I wanted you to see the bikes not a load of ancient crap about my family."

"You are so humble. We've just had a superb time looking at photos of Jurgen, your grandma, you, who I might add are even sexier now than you were then, your handsome dad, your beautiful, tiny mom, your brother and Jimbob all racing and winning trophies. I now know you are very modest and you have your mom's build and eyes and cheekbones. Do you even know what pictures he has?"

"Yes, Emm. They're mine." I smile sadly. "I don't know what possessed Pete to show you."

He hugs me tightly. "Of course they are! God, I'm an idiot!"

I can hear Stefan telling Kim about the pictures they've seen and the trophies with our names engraved on them. "Are we ready for the Castle? Or at least the ice cream." I ask. Emmett reluctantly lets me go and I kiss him gently before I put my helmet on. "Old memories make me sad Emm, I gave them away a long time ago. I'm making new memories now, it's time to be happy and look ahead."

"Come on my fragile angel, let's go back to the ice cream shop and I'll buy you the biggest licorice and banoffee cone they have."

I pull on my helmet and make some noise to clear my head. I ride across the middle of the island on quiet roads and open up The Duchess wherever I can safely do so. Emm keeps up pretty well and we slow and wait when we lose Stefan. I find myself on the plantation road; it's long and straight and usually empty so I put my head down and let The Duchess do her thing. I'm just slowing when I see a police man step out and point a speed gun at me. Oh bugger! Then I see a very, very big police man put out his hand and wave me in. I jump off the Duchess, take off my helmet at lightening speed and dive into the arms of the big police man.

"Chaz man! When did you get back? We we're only talking about you this morning."

He squashes all of the air out of me and sits me on his hip like I'm a child.

"Get here baby girl! Let me look at you." He pushes my dreads back and looks at my face. "I've been hearing so much gossip. Are you really settling down at last? Mam's already chosen her wedding hat. I've been stuck over in Ireland. It's my first day back today. I came out to watch the new lads work. You just made it worth it."

Emmett is sitting on his bike looking bewildered. Stefan and Kim have just pulled in. The young police man also has no idea what's going on.

"Come on! Don't be shy. Get your hat off mate." Chaz says to Emm slapping him on the back. "Let's see who finally tamed our wild child. You better look after her else we'll come looking for you." He half jokes.

Emmett reluctantly removes his helmet and Chaz gives him the once over then gives him a big bear hug whilst still holding me. "Welcome to the family, bro."

"Emmett meet Chaz, Billy and Ricky's big brother." I smile hugging his neck.

Chaz turns to the young copper. "Right lad, let me explain something. We don't give Delilah tickets ever. She'd have bought the whole Island three times over by now if we did." He laughs, shaking his head. "This is, for all intents and purposes, my little sister and she can ride as fast as she wants on my Island, okay?"

"Yes, Chief Inspector, Sir." He replies.

Chaz sits me back astride the Duchess. "I'll see you soon, little sis. Have a lovely day. Ride safe. Love you."

We arrive in Peel and I park as close to the ice cream shop as I can. The boys pull up next to me.

"Oh my god! I thought you'd both lost your licenses for sure and then see Delilah wrapped around a very important looking police dude like a spider monkey!" Stefan exclaims, "What the hell was going on? He didn't look like the kind of policeman that you should offer sexual favours to in order to get off a speeding fine."

"It appears that Delilah is more than best mates with the Chief of Police over here." Emmett explains. "She just keeps on amazing me. What would you have done if that little guy had given us a ticket?" He asks me.

"Phoned Chaz and told on him." I giggle. "Come on I just saved your ass. You owe me ice cream."

I strip off my leathers and leave them thrown over my bike and hang my helmet on my mirror. "Won't they get stolen?" Kim asks.

"Nope, no one will fit in them and if they do go missing they'll be back at our place before tea time." I laugh. "Are you going incognito guys?" I ask as they put on caps and sunglasses. "Are you Steve and Archie again now?"

Emm squeezes my hand and twirls me around looking at my outfit. "Yeah, we are in disguise. You look like a tiny doll." He smiles. "How many ice creams do you want?"

We all get ice cream and walk down to the sea. I take my boots off straight away and paddle. Kim joins me. "Oh wow, that's cold!" She exclaims but stays in and tells the boys to get their boots off and come in too. They're too lazy to undo them and stay on the sand so Kim and I do our best to soak them by kicking up the water. We get to the end of the beach and climb up the steps to the castle entrance, pay the entrance fee and go inside. Emmett corners me in the dungeon and whispers all the ways he would torture me if I was his prisoner, most of them sound really quite fun. I'm not sure he's got the gist of torturing. We all run around behaving like silly kids, climbing on walls, trying to lift cannon balls and when I run up some stairs in a tower and stick my head out of a window Emmett quotes;

"But, soft, what light through yonder window breaks? It is the east, and Juliet is the sun...."

Kim interrupts him with her best impression of Joey, elbowing me playfully, "Hey, la, ya boyfriend's back." And we all burst into a rendition of Dire Straits' Romeo and Juliet, draw far too much attention to ourselves and eventually collapse in a fit of giggles on the grass.

"I've not laughed so much in years!" Kim squeals, gasping for breath. Emmett wraps his arms around me and kisses me. "Hey Steve, can we try some of this snogging too?" She giggles climbing onto Stef's lap and wrapping her arms around his neck.

"I don't see why not, honey." He drawls, kissing her gently at first then getting the hang of it quite quickly. "Hm, I think I might need a lot more practice at that." He announces when he finally lets her go.

"Yes, it does need a little fine tuning." She teases.

We explore every inch of the castle, spontaneously bursting into song now and again and mucking about and making fools of ourselves. I demonstrate some yoga moves, which the others try to copy. I throw Emmett and Stef to the ground several times with some martial arts demos and prove I can still do a pretty impressive backflip. Kim tells me all about how she met Stefan and Emmett which amazingly was at medical school when they all started training to be doctors. The boys dropped out when the band began taking up too much time. Kim finished her training, married Stef and fitted in working around touring schedules and having the kids. Cherry was also a medical school dropout but they all agree she was only there to find a rich husband.

Emm and Stef just lie back on the grass in the sunshine, chilling and smiling as Kim and I chat together, getting to know each other. They add bits of extra information here and there but mostly let Kim talk. Her stomach suddenly rumbles loudly.

"Oh my goodness! There's something in the air over here that makes me constantly hungry." She says. "I ate more at breakfast than I usually eat all day. I shall be as big as a house by the time we leave."

"I've been doing a really fun exercise that keeps it off." Emmett drawls. "I've been eating like a horse and not put an ounce on." He dives on me and rolls over so that he is on top of me, grinning. "Do I feel any heavier, darlin'?"

"Get off me, fat lad!" I giggle. "Kim needs feeding." He tickles me until I am struggling to breathe then kisses me and gets to his feet holding out his hands to help me up.

CHAPTER 46

We leave the castle and go to the little outside cafe right next door for fresh kipper baps and chips and sit up on the wall, looking out to sea, watching the boats coming and going.

"You need to treat Kim to one of our beautiful sunsets." I remind Stefan. "If this weather keeps up tonight's will be pretty impressive."

"Another double date?" Kim asks. "I haven't had so much fun since the kids were born. We've been too busy playing mom and dad. The boys are right, this place is magical. Delilah is like Peter Pan." Stefan and Emmett immediately break into a raucous chorus of Enter Sandman and attract some more unwanted attention.

"Okay, Archie! Steve! Apart from 'Never Never Land, where would you like to go next? Do you want a pint at the Creek and a mooch around here; the museum is good, another castle, a ride, more scenery; there's a beautiful glen and waterfalls just down the road, more ice cream, go karting or does Kim want some shops? If we go to Castletown there's a castle and shops."

My phone pings and I get a cryptic message from Sal. It's a picture of three big antique beds saying 'which one does Emmett like best? Xxx'

I show Emmett. "Sal's losing the plot. Please choose a bed for her."

He looks. "That big sexy, cream scrolling metalwork one." He says. "Who's it for?"

"I have no bloody idea, maybe Nathan?"

"Why is she asking me and not you?" He asks.

"Because she knows Sarah already has more idea of style, coordination and home furnishings than I ever will, Sarah must be busy." I offer in reply.

I text her Emmett's choice then she replies with 'cream, white or sky blue?'

I ask Emmett who shrugs. "You're on your own there, honey."

"Shall we say white? That seems like a safe answer whatever the question is."

"Sounds like a good plan."

I text 'white' and she sends back kisses so it must be right and we hear no more from her. "Have we decided what next?" I ask Stef and Kim.

"Archie and I want a pint, a mooch around, possibly more ice cream and then some full-on heavy snogging up on that hill over there." Stefan giggles pointing to the hill next to the castle.

"I'm with Steve." Emmett grins.

"I'm happy doing whatever but I want to do all of the other things too real soon." Kim smiles. "And I don't think I can drink a pint. Maybe a white wine."

"Delilah can sink pints like there's no tomorrow." Stefan laughs.

"That's because I was dragged up by hippies. I'm actually not usually much of a drinker at all. Emmett has driven me to it this week." I muse. "Kim is a real lady and can drink whatever she bloody well wants to. Come on my darling, I will get you wine." I tease, holding out my hand to Kim. She takes it and we walk up to the Creek, arm in arm, checking out the boats in the harbour and the menus in the restaurants while the boys follow on behind, chatting happily.

I order a round of drinks and spot Dan sitting having a drink with one of the other band members. They yell 'hello' and come over to check we're still on for Friday, meet Kim, accept the offer of a pint and then leave us in peace. We go and sit outside on a table by the museum. We drink up and look at the brilliant maritime statues outside then Kim can't resist a look inside at the rest of the exhibits. We get engrossed in the stories and the history and spend a good couple of hours looking around.

As with all well set out tourist attractions the gift shop is on the way out and Kim drags Stefan towards some exquisite Celtic silver in a glass cabinet. Emm hugs me, looking over Kim's shoulder. "Can I buy you a present too so that you to remember today?"

"You don't need to buy me presents, Emm. I won't ever forget, it's been a fab day and it's not finished yet. This TT has definitely been unforgettable."

"Please let me. I want to get you something special." He pleads.

"If it makes you happy, my sweet man. I'm not going to argue." I sigh kissing his cheek.

"What would you like? Can I buy you jewellery?"

"It's a lovely thought but I will break it or lose a chain Emm, you know what a clumsy mare I am."

"If it's a ring you'll be okay." He says, testing the water.

Kim points one out. "That is just perfect for Delilah." It's a tiny Celtic silver open knotted band with a little blue stone set in the centre. It is absolutely lovely.

The assistant comes over with the cabinet keys. "Is there something you want to look at? She asks. Kim points out some dainty silver earrings she wants and Emmett asks for the ring. "You better try that one, it's really tiny. Mind you, it could have been made for you." She smiles looking at how small I am.

Emmett takes it out of the box and holds up my left hand looking at me with a raised eyebrow trying to gauge my reaction, he slips it on the third finger. It fits perfectly. Kim hugs me tightly and hugs Emmett too. Being a complete idiot I do not realise the significance of Emmett's choice of finger and think Kim may need to lay off the wine as she's getting a bit over emotional. The shop assistant gets teary too as the boys pay for their purchases. She must be on good commission.

"Thank you, darling it's really beautiful." I say, kissing Emmett.

"We can get you a different one if you prefer." He says. "It's not very conventional."

"Why would I want a different one? You just chose this one and it's perfect."

He picks me, swings me around up and hugs me tightly. "I love you, Delilah!" He shouts at the top of his voice.

We race each up the hill and collapse in a heap at the top. The view is a spectacular 360-degree panorama. Kim gets out her phone and starts taking photos of the scenery then goes to take one of me and Emmett wrapped around each other. I freeze and Emm feels it straight away. "Happy memories." He whispers into my hair. I loosen up a little and let Kim take her photo. Then take the phone and snap some pictures of her, Stef and Emmett together.

"Right, let's have another go at this snogging thing then we better go and see what all of our kids and dogs and Dads are up to." Stefan laughs, enfolding Kim in his arms. We mess about like teenagers for half an hour or more. I'm sitting astride Emm holding his arms above his head and teasing him with tiny kisses around his earlobes and his neck and stroking my fingertips down his ribs, laughing at his frustration at being unable to move. He lets out a huge growl and turns us over so that he is on top and kisses me hard making my head fizz and my toes curl. "Stop being an imp, Delilah! You know I'll get you back."

"I'm counting on it." I giggle, as I pull him down to kiss me again. He starts to do that chord playing thing down my spine. "That's playing dirty! I think we better go home before I disgrace myself in front of friends."

"Don't mind us." Stefan giggles from the other side of the grass verge. "We're having our own fun. I don't think Kim wants to go back just yet."

"Jeez, Delilah, look what you've done to my best friends. They were grown-ups when we set out this morning."

"You're wasting time Emm." I tease as he starts playing spine chords again and gently singing along..."I could stay awake just to hear you breathing...." Stefan joins in and Kim and I get beautifully serenaded.

Then they both have a fit of giggles and lunge at us for another snog.

We get hot and bothered and far too carried away and I call 'time out' before clothes start to be removed.

"Come on my lost boys we need to head home before we get arrested for lewd acts in a public place."

"Could Chaz get us off?" Emmett laughs.

"Yep but he'd make sure the whole bloody Island knew first." I reply with a wink. "You pair have already drawn plenty of attention today. Do you really want some gonk with a mobile to sell video footage of our sexual exploits to the media?" I ask jokingly.

"Man, that would be superb exposure." Stefan replies. "You need to do our publicity as well as vocals and our security, Dil. It's strange because we've all just relaxed and not thought about media or security or anything since we arrived. Tiny would have a breakdown if he saw us."

We get back to the bikes and I pull on my leathers. "Wanna go over the top?" I ask pointing towards the mountain.

"Yeah. Honey I'm coming on the back of you so be gentle with me." Kim says.

"Are you sure? Emmett does strange things to my body and I have to ride pretty quickly to clear my head. I'm not good at slow and The Duchess is not good at gentle."

"I trust you." She says, climbing up behind me.

"Stef, are you okay with this?" I ask.

"Yeah, I'm looking forward to getting her back home." He laughs.

Emmett kisses me and kisses my hand by my new ring. "Ride safe, my gorgeous girl."

I take it steady out of the town and Kim is light and relatively still. I get onto the Peel road to head for Kirk Michael. I wrap Kim's arms tightly around my waist and tell her to keep her head down. I see Emmett giggling as we pass him at warp speed. I make lots of noise through Kirk Michael and take it at a pretty fair pace through Ballaugh and Sulby then slowly into Ramsey and up to the hairpin. Kim is fine and I tell her to tap me if she's had enough. Then let The Duchess loose.

I will never, ever tire of this sensation. My whole body is alert, my head is clear of everything but the road ahead and the sound of the bike. I feel alive and out of control but completely and absolutely in control at the same time. It's impossible to describe.

I don't even look in my mirrors to see if the lads are keeping up I just keep going until we get to our little lane. Jurgen greets us at the gate. "Is the devil chasing you again, Liebling?" He asks. "We heard you over the mountain."

"Just blowing off some steam." I smile. "Chaz is home, I saw him this morning."

"Ah, you are free to ride like a crazy bitch now, ja?"

"Yep." I shrug and realise Kim is still wrapped around me. Emmett and Stef pull in and she rallies round and takes off her helmet but doesn't climb off.

"Stef, you need to carry me, honey. I don't think my legs will work anymore." She giggles. "Thank you Delilah, that sure was one hell of a ride."

"I'll go and sort some food, head over when you're ready." I tell everyone. Emm jumps on the back of me.

"I'm coming with you. We have unfinished business to attend to, little darlin'." He drawls.

As I pull out of the field Paddy Mac and four of his lads come out of the cottage in their truck. Wow, that's brill I bet they're dropping off some plans already on the way home from another job. They wave and smile but don't stop. I park the Duchess in the barn and strip off my leathers and boots. Sal's car is here. Sarah dives at me covering me with sandy, sticky kisses.

"Come and see what me and Mommy and Granddad Dylly and Uncle Paddy have done. We've made you a 'Love Shack'."

She jumps down and grabs both our hands, dragging us onto the beach. Just a little way down from the fire pit is a large wooden cabin, painted with sky blue and white stripes, facing the sea.

Inside is the huge cream antique bed made up with lacy, white, cotton, bedding and little frilly curtains. There are multi coloured fairy lights all around and candles in jars. Sarah has collected some pretty shells and stones and arranged them by the door. Dad has made a driftwood sign saying, 'The Love Shack' and mounted it over the door.

I am completely lost for words; I hug Sal and Dad and Sarah and cry lots. Emmett just stands staring with a daft grin on his face then does the hugging but not the crying. I put my hand out to stroke the bedding and Sal squeals. "Oh my God! When did you get engaged?" She grabs my hand and studies my ring. "It's perfect, very you." She concludes. They all hug us again and congratulate us. I look questioningly at Emmett hoping he'll explain it's a misunderstanding but he just smiles and shrugs. Sarah announces that she can cross me off her list now and she'll have another think about her bridesmaid outfit.

"Felix can have your bed now until the mezzanine is done and Paddy and the boys will be back Monday to sort that and the stables." Dad grins. I hug him again and wipe my tears on his t shirt.

Joey and Felix pull into the front and they come around to us followed by all the dogs and Dutch. "Fuckin' 'ell! Where'd that come from?" Joey exclaims. Picking up Sarah for a hug and apologising to her for his language.

Sal is chasing out all of the dogs she had just herded into the cottage before the boys arrived. "Right, I better go and feed Billy. If you're home I suppose he is too."

I thank her again and strap Sarah safely into her seat. "Come over Friday night we're having a party."

"An engagement party?"

"No, definitely not an engagement party! There seems to have been a missed communication somewhere." I say looking at my beautiful ring. "Emmett and I need to have a talk. He has a little explaining to do about how that happened."

"It's brilliant! He's a hell of a catch and he loves you to pieces. Stop fighting Dil and enjoy it." She chides. I shrug and wave them goodbye.

There's a line of boots by the cabin door and the boys are all sitting up on the big bed, watching the waves, when I return. I shed my boots, jump up and snuggle in between Dad and Emmett. The view is perfect. They couldn't have chosen a better spot.

"Dad this is way beyond amazing, thank you." I sigh, hugging him tightly.

"A fitting engagement present for my beautiful girl and her wonderful fiancé." He replies, kissing my head.

Felix and Joey look at each other then at us and Felix grabs my ring hand to confirm.

"Don't get too excited boys." Emmett halts them. "I have completely hoodwinked poor Delilah. I'm pretty sure she had no idea of the significance of that finger when I chose to put the ring there."

"Too late, it's there now." Joey laughs. "I bet she can't get it off."

"No, it's meant to be so it'll be stuck on for good now." Felix joins in with the daftness. He tries to remove it and can't. "See! When's the wedding? We can have it here, on the beach."

"Slow down Son." Emmett chuckles, putting his arm around Felix. "Give Dil some time to think about it first. She wasn't even aware she was engaged until ten minutes ago when Sal told her." He looks at me with some concern. "Please don't spook her. Let us have some time to talk it all through first. Technically she's not engaged anyway because I didn't propose to her."

"Well get on with it, man!" Joey scolds. "There's a queue round the Rock after 'er!"

Emmett takes my hand in his and looks deeply into my eyes. "Delilah Tallulah Tinkerbell Rainbow Blue." The boys are all prompting him, saying my name with him. "I have totally and completely fallen in love with you and all of your crazy family. Will you please do me the very great honour of agreeing to be my wife? Marry me, Dil, please." Felix nudges him. "And Felix." He adds.

I am stunned into silence I just gaze into Emmett's eyes. Dad elbows me gently in the ribs. "Answer him, Dilly girl." He urges, tearfully.

I look at Joey and Felix, they are both anxiously awaiting my reply. "What do you think boys? Are you ready for this?"

"Yes!" They all scream at me.

I look at Emm. "Having fully consulted with my family and yours, it appears the answer is most definitely yes!" I laugh, throwing myself into his arms. "Today has been quite eventful."

"It's not over yet." Emm drawls.

"Eh Laa! Is this place soundproofed?" Joey groans.

"Come on little bro let's go and spread the good news." Felix suggests, hugging us all and climbing off the bed.

"Okay, big bro!" Joe replies with a cheeky grin, doing the same. They race off with the dogs in pursuit.

Dad hugs us both tightly. "I'm so happy. There couldn't be a more suited couple or a more perfect proposal. I love you both very much. I better go and get some food on and some beers in the fridge because I have a feeling company is coming."

"We'll come and help." I say moving to get up.

"No you won't. You'll stay here and talk everything through with your future husband otherwise this will completely overwhelm you and you'll be freaking by supper time." Dad suggests firmly.

"Thanks Dylan. You don't know how much I appreciate that advice." Emmett sighs with relief, knowing I will listen to Dad.

He closes the door as he leaves. I lean in to kiss Emmett.

He puts his hand on my chest to stop me.

"Talk first, Delilah. Then I will kiss you all night long and forever more." He promises. "Come on, tell me what's going on in your head."

"Everything and it's all weird in a good way." I reply. "I'm in shock, still have no idea what you see in me, still can't believe you just asked me to marry you, don't even know if you legally can marry me, we have a new space of our own... Emm I'm freaking!" I laugh. "But it's 'way beyond over the moon happy' freaking not 'run away screaming and scared' freaking. What happened to us taking it slowly, no pressure and not making any plans?"

"Our families had other ideas? I don't know how it all happened, Dil. I'm not usually so impulsive but this time I've never been more sure in all my life. Everything has just been in the right place at the right time, even that little ring. We can fight Karma, my little darlin'. Are you sure you're totally okay with it all?"

"If I say yes can I have lots of kisses?" I tease.

"Only if you're being totally honest." He sighs.

"You'll have to bear with me while I get my head around it all but yes, Emm I am very, very, happy. I love you and am more than willing to spend the rest of my days with you. I can handle everything as long as you are my Emmett here on the Island. Please don't ask me to tour with you or do anything away from here until I'm completely ready for it and I don't mean change your life for me. I just mean leave me here and I will be waiting when you return."

"We can definitely work with all of that." Emmett smiles holding his arms out, I fall into them willingly and we just lie quietly.

Emmett's phone pings. It's Stef, 'are you ever coming out or is it safe to come in?' Emm jumps up and opens the door. They hug and Stefan congratulates him and tells him how pleased he is. Kim climbs onto the bed and embraces me.

"Honey, you are perfect together. You will make each other so happy. Come out and have a drink, everyone is already celebrating." She hugs Emmett and he picks her up and twirls her around. Even he had tears in his eyes now.

Joey grabs me in a big cuddle as soon as I step onto the beach. "This year's gerin' better an' better ain't it, Ma? Are ya okay? Me an' Fe kinda pushed that a bit."

"I'm fine sweetheart, we're a family it should be a group decision. How about you? How do you feel about having rock stars as your dad and big brother?"

"Fuckin' ace!" He grins. "I've got the perfect family. The best road racers on me Ma's side an' some seriously good musicians on me Da's. I'm lerin' us down a bit ain't I?" He frowns.

"Joey, trust me when I tell you, the road racing world is going to know your name soon enough." I say, standing on tip toe and kissing his head. "Unless you choose a completely different path. We'll all be proud of you whatever you do. We already are." He grins and we hear Ella's bike coming. "Are you and Ella okay?"

"We're real cool, I ain't gonna do an Emmett any time soon though so don't panic."

Emmett comes up behind me and puts his arms around me. "What have I done now? I just heard my name."

"Nothing bad baby, it's all good. Wanna drink?"

Hans comes over and congratulates us. "I have some good news for you all. Joseph's mother has signed everything. She asked for money and I told her the laws with regards to bribery and how much time she could expect in jail if she attempts any form of blackmail or extortion so just let me know if she tries to get in touch." He tells Joey. "You are now officially Joseph Blue. I've taken the liberty of sending for your paperwork." We thank him profusely and hug each other. "I also have divorce news; she contested the first offer so I took yet more of a liberty of removing the offer of the house in The Hamptons and suggesting that we just went to court on the grounds of her committing adultery. She's signed everything and the house in The Hamptons is still yours. Presently, you have six months to remove your belongings from the LA property. All of the non-disclosure agreements were signed too so she can't make money selling stories. We have a few minor details to finalise but you are now completely free to marry Delilah whenever you choose."

Emmett shakes his hand. "Hans, you are a miracle worker. Thank you so much. Can you help with getting everything over here?"

"Yes, of course. It will be my absolute pleasure."

Jurgen comes to congratulate us. "Didn't I tell you?" He says to Emmett. "You must always listen to Jurgen, ja. What shall I get you for a present? Do you want the BMW? Delilah will have the Panigale."

I start to object but he kisses my cheek. "Do not argue with uncle Jurgen, Liebling, I know best."

Everyone comes to congratulate us and we eventually get a drink and light the fire and the torches. Dad has heated a huge pan of chili from the freezer and made a mountain of rice. So we all tuck in and talk and laugh until the sun goes down in spectacular fashion on our little piece of heaven.

After much hugging and kissing everyone finally leaves or heads off to bed. Joey does his Walton's thing. "Night Grandpa, night Ma, night Pa, night big bro, night Dutch, night .... ". Felix laughs and does exactly the same on his way to my little bed followed by the dogs and Dutch.

"Are we gonna christen this new bed then?" I ask and Emmett sweeps me up and carries me, bride style, into our cosy little love nest illuminated by fairy lights and flickering candles.

He drops me onto the soft bed and gestures for me to put my arms up. I do so willingly and he removes my top then he lifts me under the waist and removes my leggings. Then he kisses me from my ankles all the way up my body slowly and deliberately driving me into a writhing frenzy. When he gets to my lips he looks into my eyes and giggles because he knows he's driving me nuts. "Hello, my future wife. How are you feeling?"

"Right now? A little sexually frustrated." I groan.

"Ah, should I stop? Shall we have five minutes to find out what's new in our lives right now?" He smirks, slowly removing his own clothes.

"Would you like to be a battered husband?" I ask raising an eyebrow.

"Bloody hell, Delilah. You have no idea how much I love you, darlin'." He exclaims burying himself deep inside me.

We test our new bed to within an inch of its life. The sun is coming up by the time we finally climb under the covers and I drift off to sleep with Emm gently singing to me. 'Lying beside you, here in the dark...'

CHAPTER 47

We wake to much chattering and excitement outside. I can hear Stefan talking to Felix. They're both giggling. I hear snatches of conversation ... "Be interesting to see how the new chilled version takes it.." .... "We'll just hide behind Dil....She'll calm him.." "You can tell him..." Emmett obviously hears them too, groans and pulls on his jeans. I put my top and leggings on and Emmett opens the door. The dogs pile in.

"Okay, let's have it!" He growls holding out his hand to take an iPad from Stef and sitting down on the front step. I look over his shoulder at a news headline;

'Still Sensationally Smouldering and Sexy but No Longer Surly and Serious!' The story goes on... *"Seeming to give confirmation to long circulating rumours that the marriage of Emmett Wright, 47, fiercely private guitarist of rock band Era, is really over, in a rare public appearance he was yesterday seen and heard behaving in a very casual and relaxed manner, bursting into impromptu song, having fun and playing around with band mate and best friend Stefan Fischer, 48, and Stefan's wife, eminent plastic surgeon Kim Fischer and a very colourful and agile mystery lady.'* The pictures were of us at Peel Castle doing yoga, chatting on the grass, me doing Ju Jitsu moves on Stef, me wrapped around Emm kissing, Emmett lying over me and tickling me, us walking up to The Creek, Kim and I arm in arm and Emmett picking me up when we came out of the museum. The story went on...*'the mystery young lady is obviously already well known to the Fischer's as they appeared to be very close. He was later heard loudly declaring his love for her as they walked along the road. Has adorable but unapproachable Emmett finally found the real Mrs. Wright?'*

Emmett hands it back running his hands through his hair in frustration. "Fucking hell! Is Kim okay?" He asks Stef.

"Course she is, she loves that photo of her and Delilah, she's going to call them for a copy." He laughs.

Emmett looks at me. He is barely controlling his anger. "Are you okay, darlin'? They'll do their best to find out who you are now. Don't worry, we'll get this sorted out." Felix moves close to me, I'm not sure if he's planning to protect me or hide behind me. I just burst into an absolute fit of the giggles and Emm relaxes slightly and smiles and Stefan and Felix start nervously giggling too. "What's so funny?" He asks grabbing my hand and pulling me onto his lap.

"Bloody hell! I'm marrying 'Mr. Wright'!?" I say in complete amazement. Kissing his nose and giggling again. "Chill, baby the pictures aren't unpleasant and the story isn't untrue, apart from the bit about me being a lady, so why worry about it? Come on, shower and breakfast, roads close at ten." I stand up and hold my hands out to him. He takes them and stands up embracing me as he does.

Stefan turns to Felix and sighs. "Crisis averted. We can go and tell everyone it's safe to come out now. See you in a bit guys."

Emmett puts his hands on my shoulders and holds me at arm's length, looking at me closely. "Talk Delilah!"

"I'm marrying Mr. Wright." I reply. "Why would I be even remotely worried?"

He sighs. "I can't believe you agreed to marry me and didn't even know my name. You are a very wondrous creature Delilah and you are such a calming influence. If I'd seen that a fortnight ago I'd have had a screaming fit. Did you see poor Felix hide behind you? I'm still mad but you made it easier to bear."

"What do you want to do? We can lay low here and I can ask Chaz to keep out the snoopers or we can just carry on enjoying our life and they can carry making tomorrow's chip paper." I smile.

"God you are a perfect woman! Come back to bed now." He growls.

"Nope, I stink and I'm starvin' and I need a wee." He kisses me deeply and does his best to persuade me that his plan is better but then smells bacon cooking and finally relents.

We head into the cottage and I go and get showered while Emm chats with Dad. I sort all the picnics and put some barbecue packs together for later and take over cooking breakfast. Jurgen comes in all animated and asks Emmett if he wants Hans to sort the press issue. I tell him to save the money it's not worth it. Jurgen laughs. "They are good pictures, ja? I like the one with you kicking Stefan's ass."

I hand him a bacon sandwich. "Is it moving day?"

"Ja, Bella Ella will bring the keys later and we can all be in by tonight."

"Our campsite will seem empty." I sigh. "I'll miss having you all here. Joey will too I'm pretty sure he's made a small fortune fetching your guys booze and take aways."

"He's been a really good boy, ja. When the bean counters and brain pickers fly home he can have one of those motorbikes. What would he like?"

"Jurgen, honey, he's not passed his test yet and I think he's made enough this fortnight to buy his own."

"He will pass easily. He can choose later. I cannot give presents to Ella and you and Emmett and not to Joey and Felix."

"Oh heck! What did I do?" Felix asks arriving from outside somewhere.

"Nothing sweetheart, Jurgen is giving away motorbikes like there's no tomorrow." I kiss his cheek and hand him a sandwich.

"Can I buy mine, please?" He asks Jurgen. "It's got too many great memories to let it go now."

"Nein, you cannot buy it. I will give it to you now as a present." Jurgen tells him.

"Wow! Thank you so much." Felix exclaims, genuinely touched.

"Where are we watching?" Dad asks. "Joey went to work really early, they're hoping they'll be done by lunchtime. He said to text and say where we are."

"Conker Trees?" I suggest. "I'll make a picnic."

"Good call, Dilly Girl, haven't been there in ages. I'll let them know."

The itinery for the day is 10.00am roads close,10.30 one lap solo warm up, 10.50 a one lap sidecar race, 11.45 the lightweight race over 4 laps and finally the second four lap super sport race of the week at quarter to three. So plenty of action and the weather is still holding up.

Suddenly, Thor, Odin and Loki go into full on guard dog mode and stand in a line in front of us all, growling and alert. A very worried looking Ian, sticks his head in through the doorway.

"It's only me, I came to check that your new visitors were okay."

They are still in full attack mode, it's impressive to see. Emmett very quietly says. "Stand down." They return to stupid soppy pets.

"Teach me that, Emm. It's cool." I say in awe. "Come in Ian, would you like a coffee?"

"Yes please. Oh my, you weren't joking when you said you'd be busy were you?" He says as Stefan, Kim and the boys wander in too.

Emmett moves next to me possessively. Kim gives us both big hugs. "Are you okay Mrs. Wright?" She teases. "Love that picture of us and how is Mr. Sensationally Sexy Wright? I thought there'd be thunder clouds until bedtime. You are a dream Dil." She suddenly recognises Ian. "Oh hi, how are you? What do you need to check on the dumbasses? Do you need more blood?" She asks gesturing towards the dogs who are now sharing sandwiches with Felix and Charlie and Connor.

Ian stands looking a little overwhelmed by the madness that is our usual morning. "No, no. I only need to check they're still here and not unwell or behaving oddly."

"Odin ate Felix's shorts and Thor is being permanently ridden around like a horse by Dutch and they all appear to have a sock fetish. Does any of that constitute odd behaviour?" I ask handing Ian a coffee and realising I am still in my very losely fastened bathrobe.

"Err, sorry, Dil, I meant to tell you Loki ate your shoes too. The sexy ones

Joe was wearing. I'll buy you some more." Felix adds.

"She has no further need for 'fuck me' shoes so save your money, Son." Emmett interjects.

Ian smiles at me. "No, that all sounds perfectly normal for this house. Talking of horses, Mrs. Fischer happened to mention bringing over some stallions too. Do you have a date for their arrival?" I shrug and look at Emm. He shrugs and looks at Dad.

"According to Paddy Mac, stables should be sorted by next weekend along with a shower room for you two and the mezzanine for Fe." Dad informs us.

"A week on Monday." I inform Ian and Felix whoops and jumps up to kiss and hug me. "Can we do the same with them as the dogs?" I ask when he finally puts me down. "They'll need to be exercised though; can we ride on the beach? It is technically our property."

"Yes, it should be fine as long as you have all of the correct veterinary certificates from your vets in the States."

"I'll call Tiff and get it sorted." Kim offers.

"It's okay, honey. Felix can call her." I reply, winking at Fe.

Ian gives the dogs a quick check over and asks how the donkeys are. I walk out with him and we make our way over to see them.

"You didn't mention you were planning to bring over the dogs and horses at the picnic the other day. Was it a spur of the moment decision?"

"Yeah, I seem to have found myself making rather a lot of those recently." I smile. "Wonky is doing brilliantly, do we need to change his food or give him anything extra now?"

"No, he's looking really handsome. Just keep doing what you're doing."

Emmett comes stalking over to fetch me with all the dogs in tow. "Roads close in twenty minutes, darlin' and you haven't even got any clothes on." He says wrapping his arms around me and kissing my head to suggest ownership.

I laugh he really is as vulnerable as me. "I'm coming, gorgeous. Go and find my bike jeans please. I think they're in the pile of ironing I still haven't gotten round to.

"Delilah, you are about to marry a multi-millionaire. Why do you still only have one pair of jeans? You could have a hundred pairs." I whisper gently so that only he can hear me.

"Stand down, Em!" His face clouds for a second and then he giggles and shakes himself.

He holds out his hand to shake Ian's. "Thanks so much for sorting the dogs and, in advance, for the horses. We really appreciate it. Excuse me,

I need to go and attend to Delilah's extensive wardrobe he laughs and kisses my head. He walks away and mutters something to the dogs who go back into full guarding mode with Dutch joining in. "I'll get you back, Mr. Wright." I yell as he goes into the cottage, chuckling.

"It is true then?" Ian asks. "I must confess I saw the news this morning and recognised you immediately. I knew who Mrs. Fischer was but didn't connect it with her husband's band until I saw the photographs."

"A heck of a lot of stuff has happened over the last week and a half." I admit. I would really appreciate it if you didn't tell too many people although I'm pretty sure it's already round the Island by now."

"My lips are sealed." He smiles. "I'll be back later in the week to check the dogs and pick up the details of the horses if that's okay?"

"It's fine, thank you." I go to kiss his cheek and Odin rumbles loudly. "Ah, I better not do that had I until I've worked out how to switch the dogs off. Emmett appears to be a little over cautious right now." I sigh. "See you soon, Ian."

I go back into the cottage with my armed escort. "He's gone, can you call off the troops?" I laugh.

Felix looks at me like I'm bonkers. "They know you're family, they'll do whatever you tell them."

"Stand down!" I say in my best stern voice and they turn immediately back into lolloping idiots. "Right, where's your Father? We need to have words." Felix points to the bathroom.

I open the door quietly and he's singing to himself in the shower. I sneak in and am about to steal all of the towels when an arm grabs me and pulls me inside. "Hello my little imp!" He grins.

"Hello, my overzealous future husband." I reply raising an eyebrow. "What was all that about?"

"Darlin', I'm sorry, didn't I mention I get crazy jealous and totally obsessive and possessive? Not some of my better traits I admit. I'm a dick sometimes get used to it." He shrugs with a cheeky Joey grin.

"I love YOU, Mr. Wright!" I tell him. "Get used to it."

"Touché! Have we got time for a quickie?" He drawls.

"Do your thing, honey. We're already late." I jump into his arms and wrap my legs around him and he leans me against the wall in the shower.

I leave my soaking bathrobe hanging in the shower and pull on jeans and a t-shirt from the ironing basket.

"I really am going to buy you a wardrobe full of sexy underwear and expensive clothes." Emmett tells me when he sees me search the basket for knickers, fail to find any and then go commando.

"And where are we going to put it?" I ask. "You need to downsize honey and actually you owe me some bloody expensive shoes. What can I wear with my hooker dress on Sunday now? Oh, and Felix told me how to switch the dogs off so you can't pull that daft shit again either!" I rant jokingly.

"Okay. You win. New shoes and nothing else." He shakes his head in exasperation. "Come on, we're late. Er no, hang on a minute. Where are you going in your hooker dress on Sunday?"

"The TT Presentation Do. I'm going with Dad and Joe and The Parker massive."

"Are you?" He asks raising an eyebrow.

"Yes sweetheart. I am. Dad always loves it; he meets up with loads of old mates and Joey will get to meet a lot of the sponsors and racers and he can pick their brains for tips. I'll be coming home to you and if it helps I won't wear the hooker dress." I add with a smile.

"We'll talk about it later. When I'm not in attack dog mode." He concedes. "I'm not quite so easy to turn off."

I throw together a picnic and fill another rucksack with drinks and blankets and go to find everyone. They're chatting on the beach and inside the workshop.

"Are you ready to go?" Dad asks. "Everything okay?"

"It's all fine Dad. I may have inadvertently agreed to marry a Rottweiler but I'll get him trained soon enough." I sigh.

"That's my girl. Give us those rucksacks and go settle the zoo."

I go back inside check there's no more stuff for the dogs to eat apart from treats. Grab my helmet and jacket and we all head off.

We park up, find a good spot, call Joey to tell him where we are and spread out the blankets and settle down. Emmett is really on edge, watching everyone with a phone nearby. I pull him back so that he is lying with his head in my lap, looking up at me. He looks intense and on edge, his jaw is clenched tightly.

"Relax, my darling man. Close your eyes and Dil will make it all better." I soothe, kissing his forehead. I begin to give him an Indian head massage and he slowly melts under my touch. I continue to massage him even as I am chatting to Kim and soon he is sleeping like a baby but I don't stop.

"You are so patient with him, Delilah. You're just what he needs. The news thing would have been a nightmare without you to ground him. Stef couldn't believe how quickly you bought him down."

"It's all new territory for me and I can imagine how it would be a pain sometimes. The biking press are only interested in the bikes so they were never really that intrusive. There was a bit of morbid obsession when Jimbob and my brother both died but they were still quite respectful and now it's only a few of the old boys that remember me. Whoever took the photographs isn't local because they would know who I am just because I live here and everyone vaguely knows everyone. Chaz text earlier to ask if we wanted someone to watch the house but I said we're good. I have a feeling my 'minders' will turn up shortly though. The story just showed us all happy and having fun. That can't really do any harm to the band can it?"

"Honey, it's you he's worried about, not the band. He has some pretty devoted female fans, several he's had to take out injunctions against, who may want to hurt you or do something stupid. You saw a demonstration of his obsessive behaviour with the vet this morning. You gave him no reason to behave like that other than the fact that he loves you and wants to keep you safe. He won't ever let anyone hurt you."

"What do we do about this story then? Do I genuinely need to be concerned?"

"I'd say confirm it all and announce the relationship publicly then the media have nothing to find out but it's entirely up to Emmett and you. Emm's got no skeletons in his closet, have you?"

"She hasn't even got a fucking closet." Emmett replies for me opening one eye. "Google her. It's interesting. I especially like the picture of her riding an elephant naked. She was a sweet kid." I take my hands away from his head. "Don't stop darlin', you are working magic with your hands and I love hearing you talk." He groans, so I continue to massage.

"When and why did you 'Google' me? Are you a stalker? The elephant incident was a personal protest a very long time ago. Jurgen is to blame for that photo."

"About a minute after I first saw you. I was absolutely mesmerized. I wanted to know everything about you and could hardly find a bloody thing." He admits.

"Emmett you are a very strange man." I sigh, turning back to Kim. "Are you looking forward to moving into Jurgen's place? It's absolutely amazing. I'll be round to swim whenever I get chance.

"We can have a swimm..."

"Shut up Emmett!" I order. "I've agreed to marry you not your money." He just sighs and shrugs.

"Oh Delilah! You are so perfect for him." Kim laughs.

Joey turns up. "Eh laa, me Mam and Dad are all over the papers doin' hippie shite and snoggin'!" He laughs.

"Yeah, sorry about that, Son." Emmett grimaces.

"Don't sweat. They got some nice piccies. Ya look real 'appy."

"See, stress head! You need to be more 'Joey'." I tell Emm, kissing his head. "I told myself I needed to be more 'Joey' a little while back that's how you managed to get through my usually impenetrable fortress."

"Then I am forever indebted to Joey." He smiles.

"Talking of debts, I need to ask Joey where my only pair of shoes are." I giggle.

"Oh shit, Dil, that was my bad. I'll get ya new ones."

"I'm teasing sweetheart. They're only shoes. It doesn't matter. Emmett can replace them it was his bloody dog that ate them."

"Technically, it was Felix's dog. Odin and Thor are mine. Seriously though, we do need to do something about clothes. We only bought a rucksack full; the dogs are working their way through stuff at an alarming rate and someone keeps getting me all hot and sweaty."

"Yeah." Felix joins the conversation. "I'm reduced to nicking Joe's underwear and socks already."

"The washing basket is by the bathroom. Just throw your stuff in there and I'll wash it." I laugh. "I'm going to the good shop on Sunday with Sal, you can come and have a mooch around while I get tortured." Emm raises a questioning eyebrow. "Hairdressers then the beauty parlour. Sal is a sadist." I explain.

The radio announces the start of the race, avoiding any further discussion about Sunday. We make our way to the fence just as Sal, Billy, Sarah and Ricky arrive.

Sarah launches herself at me. "Auntie Dilly! You was on the telly just now having fun with Uncle Emmett and this lady." She points at Kim. "Hello lady."

"Hello, honey. What's your name?" Kim replies.

"Sarah Delilah Parker. What's yours?"

"Pleasure to meet you Sarah Delilah Parker I'm Kimberly Katherine Fischer."

"You talk funny like uncle Emmett and uncle Stef and Felix and Charlie and Connor, he's my brother's boyfriend." Sarah informs Kim.

"I'm Connor and Charlie's mommy, darling. Stefan's wife."

"Oh, you're family then!" Sarah reasons, holding her arms out to Kim for a hug. Then seeing Joey and flying into his arms.

"I see you've just been 'Sarah'd'." Sal laughs as she hugs me and warmly addresses Kim. "I'm Sal, Nathan's mom. It's great to meet you." They embrace and chat. I run to Billy and dive on him like Sarah did to me.

"Ey up, slapper what yow bin up to?" He laughs hugging me tightly. "Yow was on telly. We thought a bit of family security might be a good idea."

"Do they know who I am yet?" I ask.

"Nah, they're just showin' the same shit over an' over."

Emmett comes over tentatively with his hands raised in surrender. Billy hugs him enthusiastically while still holding me. "Dave! Yow din't waste any time, fair play! Welcome to the family."

Ricky is cooler but very civil. "Congratulations both." He smiles, shaking Emmett's hand and taking me off Billy like a small child to hold and hug. "It's good to see you so happy, Shortarse." He whispers into my hair. "I'm still gonna be watching him, though."

"I wouldn't want it any other way, baby." I say, hugging him tightly and kissing his head.

We hear the bikes approaching and conversation stops. I stand with Emmett behind me, his arms around me and Ricky and Bill standing sentry either side and feel as safe as I ever could. I talk Joey through lines and tactics and point out things to look out for. He listens as carefully as always. The racing is excellent and we're soon betting our ten pences and Emmett has lost all of the tension and angst from earlier. Kim is well into betting but has no money as usual so bets with Stefan's, then Dad's, then Jurgen's. She gets so excited and makes us all laugh. Race one over, we sit down to eat, putting Sal's picnic with ours so there's more than enough.

Emmett smiles fondly at me as I offer him a sandwich. "Feeling better, baby?" I ask.

"You truly have magical powers, Delilah. You soothe my very soul. Who'd have thought having your minders here would make me so much happier too?" He replies. "Come here I need to hold you." I climb onto his lap and steal a bite of his sandwich. "Imp!" He laughs.

"You keep telling me what's yours is mine." I shrug, stealing another bite. "Are you going to include sandwiches in our prenuptial agreement?"

"Darlin', you are the most unmaterialistic person I have ever met in my life! I'm not even gonna waste my money on a prenup."

CHAPTER 48

"**W**hat else are you planning on bringing over because we really do need to talk logistics." I enquire.

"The cars, the bikes, the horses, guitars and basses and the studio stuff. Jurgen says we can set up the studio at his in one of the garages so the instruments will go there too. He says we can park the cars and bikes there as well. I'll just leave one home for you to use every day. If that's okay? I just had a thought, do you even like cars? Do you even drive?"

"I love anything with an engine that makes a good noise and goes fast and I drive like I ride, honey." I reply with a cheeky wink.

Ricky is listening close by and we hear a sharp intake of breath. "I'd advise you very strongly never to get in a car, no, actually, a vehicle of any description whatsoever, with her. At least, in theory, you can jump off the back of her bike. Dil driving the Road of Bones in anger because they messed up at the docks and took our bikes to the next port, is not something I ever wish to repeat. She thought she was Colin McRae on amphetamines. I'm pretty sure she broke several of my ribs as well as my hips and my spine! I would have got out and walked it but she wouldn't even slow down enough for me to bail out. The suspension on the truck was nonexistent and the brakes glowing red and completely fucked when she finally stopped."

"Oh shit! That sounds scary and painful. Thanks for the heads up, Rick." He laughs. "Maybe we need to rethink the car thing."

"Mitigating circumstances, your honour, they lost The Duchess! And he is a total drama queen." I plead. "Come on, Emm, don't be a spoil sport! You can at least tell me what you have even if I can't play with it."

"If you've got a Shelby. She'll marry you this afternoon." Rick teases me. "Won't you, slapper?"

Felix joins in with the teasing, pretending to be a car salesman. "What would be your preference, ma'am? If money were no object what are your absolute must haves?"

"Easy, a '66 Shelby Cobra 427 Roadster 500 hp V8 with a 4-speed box. White with a blue stripe preferably. But I'm also quite partial to a second gen. Dodge Charger, a black one, or an early Corvette, a white and red '63 Stingray would be nice."

Emmett grins. "We might be able to do some business here, little lady. You may have to compromise on your colours and move a couple of years either way but otherwise we can meet that list." I am both impressed and lost for words.

"You're a braver man than me if you're gonna let her near any of that list." Rick groans, shaking his head. "Let me know when they're coming and I'll get off The Rock."

Felix pipes up. "There's also another Shelby, the GT 350 and the GT40 and my good old Trans Am I learned to drive in. What are we going to do with the Hummer and my pick up?"

"Get them taken down to the Hamptons, I suppose, or sell them. They're not much use over here" Emmett shrugs.

"I'd hide your Trans Am kid. She blew one up when we were over in the States a while back, d'ya remember, Dil? The rental guy was not happy."

"Oh my god, yeah I did didn't I? I thought he was going to shoot you!" I recall, giggling. "Where were we going? Don't I still owe you money for that one?"

"Probably." He sighs dramatically. "We'd just done that fucking mental free climb at Yosemite. You were so hyped you blew the car up. Fuck only knows how much innocent machinery could have been saved if only you'd discovered the joys of sex earlier."

"Ricky! Stop now or I will tell them about that 'lady' you picked up in Thailand." I threaten.

"Which one?" He smirks. "Shortarse, you know I have far more on you than you do on me."

Emmett is shaking his head in wonder. "Ricky, man, me and you are gonna have to go for a few beers and you can tell me more stories."

Ricky laughs. "Do you really wanna know what you're taking on? You might be better staying in the dark. Just be mindful, she rides the Duchess everywhere because it's the only bloody thing we've ever managed to make 'Dil' proof."

"Tell us some more stories, Ricky, please." Felix begs.

"Er, No! Rick." I warn. "I do not want to be known for having the shortest engagement in living history."

"Tell 'em why she went to jail in Bangkok, Rick." Joey suggests loudly from over by the fence.

I do a double take. "How the fuck does he know about that?" I glare at Ricky.

"He begs us for stories all day long." He shrugs. "Everyone wants to know what their mam got up to when she was little."

"Mine still is little." Joey grins. "I know all ya secrets, Mama Dil!"

Ricky laughs watching my face for a reaction. "Joey, son. We still ain't even told you half of 'em yet! Remind me to tell you about that Yosemite trip and about skydiving in Belize, tomorrow."

"Will do." Joey replies.

"Come on Ricky man, you can't leave us hanging! How did Delilah end up in jail in Bangkok?" Felix groans. "What were you even doing in Bangkok?"

"Base jumping. She's a freak."

"Isn't it really built up and busy and full of buildings and people?" Felix asks.

"Yep! We were going off the skyscrapers." I laugh. "Your Dad's going try it one day."

Ricky looks across at a slightly alarmed Emmett. "Don't do it, man, if you survive the jump she will break you afterwards, she was so hyped that I could not control her. I gave her a joint with enough stuff in it to floor a rhino and she smoked the lot and was still off her tits wild. We went into a bar and she was doing her spider monkey thing, wrapped around me being super sexual and having no idea what vibes she's giving off. I deserve a medal for all the shit she's put me through. That trip cost me a fucking fortune in hookers."

"Too much information, Rick." I interject. "If you must tell this story to my future husband and Son can we just have the PG version, please."

Joey grins. "I got the whole story, blow by blow, everythin' you did to this guy. Felix can 'andle it."

"Rick, you must have a fucking death wish." I growl under my breath.

He just laughs and squeezes my thigh affectionately. "Anyhow a big nasty looking punter in the bar mistook her for trade and went to cop a feel. He grabbed a handful of her ass and she went batshit crazy and basically castrated the guy and put him in a coma. Then she got arrested and carted off to jail. Turned out the bloke was quite a high up foreign diplomat. I had to get the bloody British Consulate to help me get her out. Thank fuck he didn't wanna press charges when he finally woke up in hospital two days later. The bastard had a wife and three kids back home. I was out of my mind, worried sick about her and when I went to pick her up she was absolutely fine, just really pissed because she'd missed three days base jumping!" He automatically leans over and kisses my head. "Crazy Bitch!"

"Okay, we need to rethink the cars and the offer to go base jumping." Emmett muses. "And we definitely need a boy's night out."

"You two are never going to be left alone together. Ricky knows far too many incriminating stories about me." I assure him.

"That's exactly why I wanna get him out." Emmett grins.

The racing resumes and we go back to watching and betting and analysing lines. Emmett is getting on far too well with Ricky and now I can hear

Billy adding his two pennies worth. Oh well, it was good while it lasted. He'll be running for the hills by teatime, Dil!

"Come on Speedy Gonzales. Tell me about the proposal." Sal demands coming up beside me. "You didn't hang about once you found what you wanted, did you?"

"It'll all be off soon; Rick and Bill are telling tales." I laugh. Then tell her about how everything went down. She interrogates me until she has every last bit of information then smiles. "You are still coming Sunday, aren't you?"

"Definitely hair and stuff. The boys wanna come too for shopping but I'm still working on him for The Do. He's a bit freaked about me going without him at the minute."

"Right, well I'll go and get that sorted right now!" She says, marching off.

Sarah runs over and jumps on me announcing really loudly. "Auntie Dilly, that man over there just offered me sweets to tell him what your name is. He's a stranger and that's wrong! I told him to Fuck Right Off!" Ricky and Billy have got hold of him before Sarah has finished her sentence. Two police officers appear from nowhere and the man is taken away immediately.

"Clever girl, Dave!" Billy kisses Sarah proudly. "What did 'e say to ya, bab?"

"He asked my name and I said I don't talk to strangers then he asked Auntie Dilly's name and I told him to Fuck Right Off!"

"Good girl." Sal says, hugging her tight. "Uncle Chaz will sort him out."

Ricky is going through the guy's phone. He's got a dozen pictures of me massaging Emmett's head and chatting to Kim and others of us betting and giggling together. Ricky looks in the phone contacts and finds a couple of numbers for the shitty press element. The guy must just be a freelance chancer. Ricky growls and heads off towards the police car.

Emmett's jaw is clenched again I pull him down onto the blanket. "Emm don't cause a scene, please. You'll scare Sarah. The guy is going nowhere and neither are those photos. It's done and finished okay?"

Sarah comes over and offers us her bag of sweets. She takes one look at Emmett and hugs him. "Don't worry Uncle Emmett, Daddy and Uncle Rick and Uncle Chaz and me have got it all under control. Have you got time to discuss my bridesmaid's outfit?"

Emmett hugs her back tightly. "I have all the time in the world baby, what were you thinking?"

"I want my hair done like Auntie Dilly and some purple dockers and maybe a red dress with a cape, I think. Should I draw you a picture?"

"Definitely, I want to get it exactly right for you." She hops up to go and get her crayons and book then plonks back down in his lap. He looks over at me and his eyes are full of unshed tears. I leave him to be Sarah'd and check Rick hasn't committed murder.

He's talking to Billy and Dad and Joey and puts his arm around me automatically as I join them. "Bloke is just a druggie twat from one of the hostels in Douglas looking to make a few quid for his next fix. Ain't even got any credit on the phone. He'll be in court in the morning and probably Jurby Jail before lunchtime." He kisses my head, holding me protectively. "You okay, Shortarse?"

"Yes honey, thank you. I was just a bit shaken because the bastard used Sarah to try to get to us."

"He's lucky she didn't put him on his ass." Billy laughs. "He definitely didn't try to touch her or she'd have decked him. Ya know that because yow taught her to do it."

Stefan comes to see if everything is okay. I can hear Kim talking with Sarah and Emmett. Ricky tells Stef it's all sorted and not to worry and he relaxes, thanking them both for dealing with it. Saying that hardly any other spectators even turned from the racing so we didn't attract too much attention. Stef and I join Emmett and Kim to see how Sarah's outfit is looking. Kim has hijacked the sketch pad and is busily drawing the most exquisite portrait of Emmett and Sarah. Sarah is mesmerised. Her eyes are wide in wonder. "Look Auntie Dilly." She whispers, pulling me to sit next to her and Emm. Emmett puts his arm around me and raises a questioning eyebrow.

"All sorted, don't worry." I whisper watching in total amazement as Kim begins to add me to her picture.

Stefan smiles at his wife. "Oh no! Who gave her paper? She'll be at it all afternoon now." He wanders off to stand with the boys. We sit in silence for a little while as Kim makes magic and when it's done Sarah drags her away to show Billy.

"She's an incredibly talented artist." I say to Emmett. "Does she draw often?"

"All the time if she's got a pad and pen." He replies. "There's amazing drawings all over their place, she can't help herself. It's kind of her 'security blanket', like my guitar and your Duchess. That guy must have spooked her a little."

"How was your talk with Sarah? Did she sort you out? I'm so sorry, I wasn't much use. The fact he tried to use her really unsettled me. He was just a junkie after fix money, hadn't even got any credit on his phone. He'll likely be locked up by lunchtime tomorrow."

"You have an extraordinary family, Delilah. They will protect you better than anyone in this world and you already told me that. I don't know why I don't just relax and let you sort everything like you seem to always do."

"There is something you can do for me." I say.

"Anything you want, baby. Don't even ask about Sunday I know you will be safe and Ricky loves you but respects your choice. Man, he's far stronger than I could ever be, you must have put him through absolute torturous hell over the years, darlin'. I feel for him but I know you will come home to me. I had no right to say you can't go. I was being a dick again and I'm sorry."

"Wasn't even thinking about that." I shrug. "And yes, it appears I have unwittingly helped to keep the world's prostitution industry buoyant for almost the last three decades and I definitely do not want to think about that."

"You want the Cobra?" He shrugs, palms up.

"No you bloody idiot. I just want you to suck my face off!" He grins and pulls me down on the blanket crushing his body against mine and kissing me hard.

"Delilah, you make me so happy. I can't wait to see you on the horses and driving the cars. It'll be so good to have you to enjoy them with."

"You're still gonna let me in the cars even after Ricky's warnings?"

"Yeah, I love you that much." He teases. "Anyhow if you break them you can fix em, can't you." He adds kissing be again.

"Can I do a full race tune on the Charger?" I can't resist asking.

"Can we make out in the backseat when you're done?"

"Yep, and several times before I start and whilst I'm working on it if you're happy getting oily." I reply.

"Can we have wild and crazy sex on the Stingray hood?" He replies.

"Most definitely, I'd be very disappointed if we didn't." I counter.

"The Cobra?" He raises an eyebrow.

"On it, in it and under it, baby!" I drool.

"What are you two up to?" Felix asks dropping down next to us.

"We're negotiating, Son." Emmett sniggers. "It's real fun."

"Well if we're negotiating who has the best guard dogs, Dil wins hands down and I bet hers don't eat underwear either." He smirks.

"I'm learning Dil pretty much wins everything hands down, Son. Even if I think I'm winning it's only because she's letting me."

"Are we still news or has something actually happened in the world?" I ask.

Felix checks his phone. "Looks like you've already been relegated. Some rapper is running for president whilst having a mental meltdown."

"See, Emm? Drama all done, nothing to stress about. We're chip paper already." I sass. "Are you taking me and our beautiful boys for dinner this evening to celebrate our engagement or have Rick and Bill scared you off now with all their bollocks?"

"Delilah, if he chickens out, I will propose to you. You are just awesome!" Felix giggles. "I can't wait to hear more stories about you."

"What were Sarah's words earlier? Oh yeah I remember now, you can just Fuck Right Off! Son." Emmett replies putting his arm around Fe and playfully pretending to beat him up. "Proposing to your step mother is seriously wrong. Especially when you're younger, fitter and far better looking than me. It's a good job I had the foresight to buy the Cobra."

"Don't come crying to me when she breaks it." Fe sasses back.

"Okay, that's it. You two are not playing with Rick again, he's a really bad influence." I laugh, wagging my finger jokingly at them both.

Sarah drags Kim back over and drops in my lap. "Auntie Kim draws nice pictures. Is Uncle Emmett better now? Have you seen my bridesmaid's outfit? Are you getting married on Friday? It won't give us much time to get my hair done."

Kim sits down in between Emmett and Felix, smiling indulgently at Sarah.

"Auntie Kim does draw amazing pictures doesn't she? Uncle Emmett is fine, you mended him because you are a clever, gorgeous girl. I haven't seen your bridesmaid's outfit because Auntie Kim ran off with your book and I'm pretty sure we are not getting married this Friday although judging by how this week has gone so far I won't rule it out." I laugh, looking at Emmett. "We'll make sure you look perfect before we start anything. Did you draw your picture before auntie Kim stole your book?" I ask giggling at Kim's indignant face.

Sarah shrugs. "Nope not really, I couldn't decide what I wanted on my head. Uncle Emmett said I could have flowers or a crown but I think a Batgirl mask would be good."

"Definitely a Batgirl mask, honey. That would be just perfect! Purple dockers, rainbow dreads and a Batgirl mask. I think I will wear the same as you."

"We need some clothes too, silly." she giggles. "How about a full Batgirl outfit?"

"Awesome! I definitely want to get married dressed as Batgirl. What should Uncle Emmett wear?"

"A Batman outfit, of course." She replies as if I'm a bit simple.

"Who can Auntie Kim be?" I ask watching Kim hanging onto Sarah's every word.

"She can be Wonder Woman if she wants to. I was going to be Wonder Woman but then I'd have to wear a skirt." She rolls her eyes in horror. "Will Auntie Kim mind wearing a skirt?"

"Oh, I don't think so, she's very ladylike. Shall we ask her?"

"Auntie Kim would you like to be a bridesmaid with me? You can be Wonder Woman if you don't mind wearing a skirt." Sarah asks. "I'll show you what you have to do so you won't have to worry."

"I would absolutely love to be a bridesmaid and Wonder Woman, sweetie." Kim replies, trying not to cry. "I'll happily wear a skirt for you."

"What can Felix and Joey and Charlie and Connor be?" I ask as Felix is frantically prompting me.

"Power Rangers or Ninja Turtles, I suppose." She replies after a little think.

Joey's listening too now. "Eh laa, I always wanted to be a Power Ranger."

"Me too!" Felix exclaims. "I was always pretending to be the red one."

The wedding outfit discussion continues until Sarah falls asleep in my arms. I gently hand her over to Emm and start packing up the picnic.

"Delilah, other than Joey, have you ever thought about adoption?" He asks, looking lovingly at Sarah. Stroking her wild hair out of her eyes.

"I know she tells everyone Sarah's mine but I don't think Sal will sign that one over no matter how many millions you have." I giggle.

"I'm being deadly serious, Delilah. I always wanted to have a dozen kids. It's one of my biggest regrets."

"Me too, it is my biggest by far. Poor Joey never stood a chance." I reply with a sad smile. "We were gonna buy the big farm next door to Mr. Jeavons' place and foster or adopt a shed load. Mama and Dad always fostered and Jimbob had been in care, we wanted to make a better life for as many care kids as possible. It turned out Karma had other plans for me. I've never been in the right place until recently and Joey came along at the perfect time."

"How about now?" Emmett asks quietly.

"Who knows? Madame Karma is up to some really very seriously, freaky weird, fucked up shit right now, Emm." I reply with a sad smile.

Sal comes to reclaim her beautiful daughter and puts an end to the conversation. "Wedding plans are sounding pretty advanced." She laughs. "I'm not sure I can find enough Super Hero costumes by Friday though."

"We are not getting bloody married on Friday! Let me get my head around being engaged first." I tell her clearly, making sure Emmett is listening too. "I'm still waiting to hear his big plans for taking me and the boys out tonight to celebrate."

"It's already planned. The boys and I have decided on Peel chippie and then The Creek for a pint. Okay?"

"Man, you really know how to show a girl a good time." I laugh. "It sounds perfect."

CHAPTER 49

W e get home and park up. I nip up to the campsite to deliver food packs, empty the bins, clean the showers and check there's enough firewood. Jurgen's little black tents are all being neatly packed away and they are all getting ready to move to his new place. It makes me feel really sad. Ella arrives to deliver the keys and they go off, in convoy, to get settled. I hug them all before they go. "Liebling, do not be sad, I am a few minutes away. I will be here forever now, ja." Jurgen laughs at my tears.

Emmett is busy talking with Hans. I stay away. I need some headspace. I collect a pile of dirty washing from a grateful Felix and go and put it in the machine. I feed the donkeys and the chucks, put a steak and ale pie in the oven for Dad and Mr. Tamaki later and then call the dogs to go for a walk on the beach.

I paddle aimlessly, with Dutch on my shoulder, while the dogs run in and out of the sea. Dutch puts out a paw to wipe away tears I didn't realise were falling. "It's been an eventful TT so far, babe." I tell him. "What am I bloody crying about now? I've got pretty much everything I've ever dreamed of and lots I'd never even knew I wanted. I have my fabulous Old Man; my rock and my voice of reason, the most amazing Son, a kind, patient, caring man who wants to share his life and his own son with me and is teaching me some very neat tricks that make my body incredibly happy and the most loyal family in the universe. Somehow I've acquired a brand new Panigale, three more mental dogs and have been promised that beautiful horses and my dream cars are arriving shortly. Why am I sad? Which bit of that is bad or upsetting? None of it! They are clearly happy tears and I need to get a grip." Dutch rubs his head against my cheek and gently bites my nose in agreement. "I'm going to marry, Mr. Wright, dressed as Batgirl, what more could a woman want?" I giggle, hugging Dutch tightly.

Emmett appears looking worried. "I wondered where you'd gone, you disappeared."

"Can't exactly lose me. There's not many rainbow haired scruffy little hippies wandering around with four dogs and wearing a cat on her head." I tell him with a shrug.

"Did I spook you earlier? I'm really sorry. Holding Sarah just made me yearn for more kids. Isn't it funny, the happiest moments always seem to highlight the biggest regrets?"

"Emm sweetheart that is sadly not something I can give you, as much as I want to. You're still young enough to have more children but you'll have to find a younger bride. I won't stand in your way. I really do understand that desire very much."

"I can't physically have kids any more that you, Delilah. I had a vasectomy twenty years ago. Cherry insisted, she wanted no more kids after Felix. I asked you about adopting not having babies. You're doing that thing again where you make up your own version of the conversation, you exasperating woman. I only thought about it when I was watching you today with Sarah and Joe and Felix. You are a perfect mom; funny, caring, mindful, nurturing and soothing. You looked ready to launch at Ricky for oversharing in front of the boys." He grins. "I wasn't talking about next month, maybe not even next year, I'm making long-term plans, we've got a lifetime ahead. You're a real mama bear. I just want to see you with more kids someday. Our kids."

"Emm, I don't know who sent you or what I've done to deserve you but I truly love you more than anything." I wrap my arms around his waist and lean my head on his chest being careful not to unseat Dutch.

"Are you really marrying me dressed as Batgirl?" He asks.

"You don't wanna marry Batgirl?" I tease.

"On the contrary. I'm a little concerned about whether I will be able to keep my hands off you long enough to get through the ceremony." He replies, picking me up and striding back up the beach.

"Put me down you sex pest I've got a pie in the oven and washing that needs hanging out!"

"My needs are greater than yours right now I'm afraid. Listening to Rick telling stories about you was doing me some serious damage earlier." He tells me, depositing me on our bed, gently reseating Dutch on Thor's back. Shouting to Joe to check on the pie and closing the door, he quickly undresses himself and me and makes my world spin a whole lot more.

We lie in each other's arms each lost in our own thoughts. "Where's your head at, baby?" I ask after watching his sleepy expressions slowly change from confused to concerned to smiling and back again.

"I was just riding the roller coaster that is my life right now." He replies. "I can't quite believe it's all real. Everything is moving so fast and so perfectly I keep thinking something is going to derail it."

"Welcome to my world, Emm." I smile. "That's my head at least twenty times a day. It's so scary finally getting everything I've ever dared to dream of. I just start to get my head around one amazing revelation and another comes along. I've been sent a lifetime of happiness in less than a fortnight."

"Well explained, darlin'. That's exactly how I'm feeling. What do we do about it?" He enquires.

"Enjoy the ride?" I suggest.

"Yeah, good plan." He grins rolling on top of me.

Half an hour later I reluctantly disentangle myself from my beautiful man and throw the tunic top from my Sarah outfit back on, lord knows where the leggings have gone. "Come on gorgeous, our kids are gonna need feeding."

The pie is sitting on the table with a couple of slices already missing. I peg out the washing on the line and look across to the campsite. It's a little empty without Jurgen's regimented camp. I sigh, another TT is coming to a close. Don't start Delilah! Eyes forward from now on. You've already spent too much time in the past.

Felix comes into the garden all smiles. "I rang Tiff."

"And?" I prompt.

"She wants to fly over with the horses, to check they're okay."

"And?"

"Can she stay a while? She's really lovely and I'll pay for her board."

"Felix, sweetheart, I know this is a lot for us all to get our heads around but right now I'm pretty sure this has just become your home so there is no reason why you would have to ask permission for anything here, least of all inviting a friend and you certainly don't need to pay for their keep. It'll be cosy but we'll be fine. Your room should be sorted and you can't possibly make any more noise than your Father. We're all coping fine with the madness now, what difference will one more make?" I reply. He hugs me and grabs his phone to call her back.

"You are an angel, Delilah Blue!" Emmett laughs. He's obviously been listening from the back doorway. He's leaning against the cottage wall, arms folded, wearing just his jeans, barefoot and looking smoulderingly sexy and handsome. "Joey and Ella have had the same idea as us, Felix is going to be on the phone for hours, your Dad has gone over to Jurgen's new place. All is right with the world. And you look too darn good in that outfit. Come here and misbehave with me right now. I'm not hungry yet, we can work up an appetite together."

"You are bloody insatiable and irresistible!" I giggle, jumping up and wrapping myself around him like a spider monkey.

"It's your fault for being so goddamn sexy." He groans turning around so that my back is against the wall and reaching for the button on his jeans.

"Don't even think about it!" I growl. "Fe could walk around the corner any second."

"He'll just turn around and walk back the way he came. He's a grown man now. He's been found in far more compromising positions." He giggles and recalls. "He was only fifteen when he first discovered the joys of Tiff. One afternoon and I caught them in the stables working their way through a copy of the Karma Sutra."

I'm so engrossed in his story I don't realise what he's up to until it's too late and he starts to move slowly and with perfect rhythm making me totally lose control and forget about being sensible.

"Jesus, Emmett you are such a bad influence! I can't believe we just did that." I shake my head; we're slumped against the cottage getting our breath back.

"Delilah, you are so funny. You are bloody fearless. Why is daytime, outdoor sex so wrong?"

"I don't know." I laugh. "Maybe because the sex thing is so new to me. Or maybe it's because you are in control and not me. I instigate all the stupid shit I usually do so there's an element of control. You make me lose all sense of reason. My body is far too eager to bend to your will without listening to my head."

"Sounds like I've got you right where I want you my little imp." He says. "But the truth is my body is doing what it does because you make it do crazy things. I've been able to get by fine without much sex until I met you and now I'm worse than a horny teenager." He starts singing an old Kiss song to me. "I was made for loving you baby... you were made for loving me..." He leans over and pulls me across his lap and starts playing the guitar solo on my spine.

"Eh Laa, what yous two up to now? Are we goin' the chippie? I'm starvin'."

"I was practicing my finger work but now I'm starvin' too, Joe. Round up Bella Ella and Felix and we'll get showered and go eat." Emmett laughs putting his hands under my armpits and standing me up.

We quickly shower and set off for Peel making plenty of noise, all revving engines, pulling wheelies, doing burn outs and generally being irresponsible and pratting around. We park up and Felix insists on a photo of us all together with the bikes, grabbing some passing holiday makers and using his charm to get them to take several lovely ones. He sends them to us all and I set one up as a new screen saver.

"Can I send one to Tiff? She was asking what everyone is like."

"Course you can darling unless you think it'll scare her off." I smile.

"She's pretty bomb proof." He replies. "Isn't she Old Boy?"

"Who, Tiff? Yeah, she'll fit in fine." Emm assures him.

We get fish and chips and sit down on the little beach by the castle. When we're finished eating, Joey rescues a floating beach ball and we indulge in a strange game of Anglo-American football with me, Joe and Ella vs Emm and Felix but no real rules, lots of physical contact and much snogging between me and Emmett despite being on opposing teams.

"Okay, it's two all next goal is the decider. Losers buy the drinks." Emm announces. Felix has the ball and I rugby tackle him to the ground and sit on him, tickling his ribs, Emm comes to rescue him, Joe comes to rescue me and we end up in a writhing heap. I quickly pass the ball to Ella and she scores in an unmanned goal.

"Ha! We win! You're buying boys." I taunt. Emm picks me up easily and throws me over his shoulder.

"Come on family, pub time!" He announces, grabbing his shirt on the way.

We manage to find a table outside and Joey and I go in to get a round with Felix's money. Dan's there again and waves hello, shouting 'See you Friday!' We get Cokes for Joey, Ella and Felix and a pint for me and Emm and Joey carries the tray back to the table with me running interference because it's so busy. I give Felix his change and kiss his head in thanks for the drink and sit down on Emm's lap. We clink glasses and spend a relaxed night taking the piss out of each other.

Felix begs Joey. "Come on Joe, tell us some more of the tales Ricky has told you about Dil." I inform Felix I know what he used to get up to in the stables.

He laughs. "At least it's a little more private than the back garden, Mom."

"Oh my good god!" I beat up Emmett.

Felix smirks. "Ha! Lucky guess, I saw him standing by the wall when we were talking. He looked like he wanted to devour you. I could feel the vibes. I didn't see anything at all."

Ella giggles. "We heard plenty. They were right under our window and your dad really howls."

I beat up Emmett some more. "And you want more kids?" I say raising an eyebrow.

"He's selling you a dream, Dil." Felix laughs. "He's firing blanks. Cherry was so disappointed with me she got him neutered."

"I'm pretty sure the only thing she was disappointed about was having to share your dad, especially when he loved you so much more than her, darling." I assure him. "I'm way past childbearing age. We were going to just buy a few off eBay." I joke.

"Awesome!" Felix and Joey say together. "Can we have a little sister like Sarah?"

Emmett grins and squeezes me affectionately. "Now look what you just walked right into."

"Bugger! Anyone want another drink?" I shake my head in submission. Felix and I go for more drinks and when we return Joey and Emmett are telling Ella all about the new wedding plans.

"Who can I be, Dil?" She asks.

"Whoever you wanna be my darling. Are you going to be a bridesmaid or do you want to just stay with Joey?"

"Oh Dil! I'd love to be a bridesmaid." She jumps up and hugs me.

"It's going to be so far removed from a normal wedding I'm not sure how its gonna work. We'll just wing it or do whatever Sarah tells us." I laugh.

"I know how it's going down." Emmett drawls. "You're gonna turn up dressed at Batgirl and I'm gonna get a major hard on, tell the rabbi to get a move on and then drag you off into our love shack and consummate the marriage while everyone else eats the buffet."

"Too much information for the children, darling." I sigh. "Changing the subject, Ella you could be Catwoman?"

"Eh Laa, that'll do nicely." Joey drools.

"He really is yours, isn't he?" I groan at Emm, rolling my eyes.

Felix returns to his earlier request. "Come on Joe, Dil stories."

Joey is an angel and tells a few tamer ones which I know would be far more graphic if Rick was telling them. Sadly they all end with Ricky in a whorehouse of some description.

"Is that why you and Ricky split?" Felix asks. "You must have been together a long time. Did you mind him going with prostitutes?"

I spit my beer all over the place in astonishment.

"Felix, you've got the wrong end of the stick there, baby. Me and Ricky have never been a couple, we're just best mates. We've never been romantically involved with each other. His choice of sexual conquest was no business of mine and I should add, their frequency is very recent knowledge."

Emm laughs. "That man has an iron will. I don't know how he survived so long."

"Subject change now, Emm please." I beg quietly.

"Did Jurgen speak to you about a new bike earlier, Joe?" Emmett asks and I squeeze his hand in thanks.

"Yeah, he's a crazy man." Joey laughs. "I'm 'avin' that RSV4 Hans was riding."

"You bloody well aren't! You'll kill yourself!" I go into full on 'mom' mode.

Joey giggles his head off. "Got ya! I'm 'avin' one of them MV F3's. It's a 675 and we can put a restrictor on it."

"You little shithead! You nearly gave me a heart attack!" I scream.

He gives me a cheeky grin. "When we goin' green lanin'? 'Ave yous got off roaders already?" He asks Felix.

"Nope, we're bringing road bikes over but my off roader is miles too small now. I had it as a kid. We can go and buy some."

"What ya bringin'?"

"Dad's GS12 and he's got one of Gard and Keanu's Arches which is real cool."

"Got any Harleys? Rick says they're Dil's favourite." Joey teases looking for a rise from me. "She's killed a lot of Harleys. Didn't ya throw one off a cliff somewhere, Ma?"

"I'm gonna kill Ricky!" I say through gritted teeth.

"Maybe we'll move the Harleys to the Hamptons with the Hummer, the RV and the pick-up." Emm suggests. "We're already set up here with Jurgen's gifts."

"Probably a wise choice." I agree. "That Arch sounds pretty interesting though. Talk dirty to me, honey. Tell me more." I turn so that I am facing him, straddling his lap.

Emm grins, pulling me tightly into his groin. "It's a KRGT-1 with bespoke Ohlins/ARCH suspension front and rear, BST carbon wheels .... " He doesn't get to tell me anymore.

"Get a room, you two!" Felix groans.

"You wait 'til Tiff gets here, I'm gonna give you so much shit. We're gonna be stark naked and shagging on the lawn when she arrives."

"How is that going to be different from now?" He sasses.

"Is Felix getting a smart mouth again, darling?" I laugh arching an eyebrow.

"Yeah, he is." Emm laughs, putting his arms around the boys. "Come on, enough family stuff. I wanna go home and whisper sweet nothings to my woman about piston sizes and big bore kits."

We drink up and Ella jumps on Joey for a piggyback. I jump on Felix and we race down the harbour as Emmett strolls behind happily shaking his head at his crazy family.

We go back onto the beach for one last paddle before heading home. I walk hand in hand with Emm while the kids lark around. "I like family night. We need to make it a thing." I tell him.

"Whatever you want darlin'. I will make it happen and thanks for what you said to Fe earlier, you were spot on, Cherry was jealous of him."

"No kid should ever think they're a disappointment to their parents." I say. "She sounds a little insecure. Can I have a Lamborghini Huracán?" I joke.

"Are you going to blow it up?"

"Probably." I shrug.

What colour would you like?"

"Yellow. Can I ride your Arch?"

"Nope, not a fucking chance my little Harley killing imp." He laughs, kissing me hard.

We get home and the dogs swamp us and Dad makes us all hot chocolate and cheese on toast and tells us about Jurgen's move. In true Jurgen style he arrived, took off all his clothes on the drive and dived in his swimming pool. Stef, Kim and Charlie were well settled in the main house and Connor and Nathan in one of the cottages. Stef had asked what we were doing tomorrow.

"Castletown and Laxey, I think." I say. "Emm, can you text and let them know? Ask what time they wanna meet up?"

"Are you coming with us?" I ask Dad.

"Nope, I'm having far too much fun in the workshop. I've seen everything this Rock has to offer a million times." He kisses my head. "You go and enjoy yourself, Dilly Girl. I'm happy staying here and playing with my tools."

"Can you keep an ear out for some green laners for Fe and Emmett?" I ask.

"Already on it. Gonna look at a couple tomorrow afternoon." He smiles.

"Thanks, Dad. You definitely have to be Superman at the wedding." I laugh.

"Ordered me tights already, girl!" He replies.

We wish goodnight to everyone and head off to our beautiful, big bed. Emmett lights the candles and pulls back the duvet. Climbs into bed and pulls me over to sit on top of him.

"Well my amazing woman, it's been another fun packed and educational day, I've learned rather a lot about my family today. The same cars turn us on, you've put poor Rick through hell for decades, you're a criminal, your family is one hell of an effective security unit, the vet is no competition for me, you don't like Harleys, you do like daytime, outside sex but get a guilt trip afterwards, you like family nights, I'm marrying Batgirl dressed as Batman, with mini Batgirl, Wonder Woman and Catwoman and the Power Rangers in attendance and Superman will be giving you away, oh and our kids want a little sister....What do you know darlin'?"

"That I'm going to murder Ricky Parker." I smile through gritted teeth. "Other than that, I think you pretty much summarised everything else extremely accurately. Although I could add that you're a really bad influence and that you're mean because you won't let me play on your Arch or blow up your Harleys and a chicken because you won't base jump with me."

"You ended up in jail, Delilah! In Bangkok!"

"I've been to jail in worse places." I shrug.

"Don't even tell me! You scary woman." Emmett shakes his head in despair. "I'm marrying a psychopath."

"I'm fine now, I've discovered sex." I tell him. "Want me to show you some?" I ask, kissing his chest and slowly moving down his body.

"You are unreal, darlin'." He laughs dragging me back up the bed and kissing me passionately.

CHAPTER 50

"Eh Laa, me Mam an' Dad are in the news again." Joey laughs as we go in for breakfast.

"Great, it wasn't when we were in the garden was it? Dad, give Emmett a bacon sarnie quick so he doesn't have a meltdown." I laugh.

"Shit, you don't care, so why should I?" He sighs, sitting down and drawing me onto his lap. "Come on then, Son, let's hear it." He sighs.

Joey tries to read it and stumbles over the words. "Too many big words there for me, laa." He concedes. "You read it, Ma."

'A Wright Family Night? Following recent speculation about beautifully built Emmett Wright, 47, the fabulous, elusive guitarist of world-renowned rock band, Era has again been seen with his mystery lady and this time they appeared to have bought the family along. Emmett's son and fellow band member, Era bass player Felix Wright, 24, who has been blessed with his father's good genes and was looking tanned and lean is also usually very camera shy but was clearly very relaxed in the company of his Dad's new lady friend and another handsome young couple. They ate fish and chips on the beach before playing a very rowdy and physical game on the sand where the boys had removed their t-shirts to use as goal posts and all looked toned and extremely sexy. Although the Wright's seemed to have lost the game they were so good natured about it that Emmett's lady got a lift to the local pub where they definitely looked to be having plenty of laughs and intimate conversations together. There were public displays of affection from all. They finished their night off with a piggyback race and a romantic stroll on the beach. How and why has Emmett kept this relationship secret for so long? It looks to be well advanced. A source has confirmed that his divorce from Cherry Martinez has now been finalised. Maybe this is why he's chosen to go public now? So who is the new potential Mrs. Wright? Whoever she is she's clearly making him a very happy man!'

The pictures show us playing on the beach, me sitting on top of Felix, us all piled on each other, me, Joey and Ella celebrating Ella's goal, Emmett grinning with me thrown over his shoulder, a few of snaps of us sitting chatting at the Creek, me and Emm kissing, me kissing Felix's head, me punching Emm and laughing, Ella and me hugging, Emm with his arms around Joey and Fe, Joey and Ella kissing and Felix piggybacking me with Emmett smiling behind us.

"Have you had sex with this reporter at some time? She's very complimentary and clearly likes you a lot." I tease Emm.

"Not that I'm aware of." He drawls. Felix comes out of his room, half asleep. "Morning Son, have you ever slept with a reporter?"

"Er, not knowingly. Why? Did we make the news again?" He grins coming over to join us. "Wow, nice pics, love that one." He points to the piggyback one. "Dad looks so chilled."

"Peel seems to be our place to be watched. We'll just have to be a bit more mindful when we're there." I say.

"I'm being more 'Joey' like you told me." Emmett replies, laughing. "I don't give a damn. Gotta agree the pictures are great though."

Felix's phone pings. "Stef's out the front asking if it's safe to come in."

Emmett picks me up, puts me back on the chair and goes outside to meet them. I get up and add some more breakfast to the pan.

Kim looks as beautiful as ever and Stefan looks well rested. "How's your new digs?"

"Apart from the small fact that my father-in-law seems to be permanently naked, it's really lovely."

"He does that a lot; you'll get used to it." Dad tells her.

"Want breakfast?"

"Yes please, honey." Stef replies kissing my cheek. "I see you got papped again. How come he's so calm about it?"

"I've put a spell on him." I laugh.

"I think you really have, honey." Kim replies.

Joey grabs his helmet and a pile of food I've just put on the table for him.

"What 'ad I gorra ask Rick about? Belize and Yosemite?" He gives me a cheeky grin hugs and kisses me.

"Tell Ricky he's a dead man walking!" I growl.

"Will do, love yas!"

"Love you too, little shithead, ride safe."

Kim is giggling her head off. "You guys are so close. What's Belize and Yosemite about?"

Emmett groans. "You know I said she has no skeletons? It's becoming apparent there's a whole crypt out there somewhere."

"No there isn't. Jurgen and high up policemen are very useful in certain circumstances. The elephant pic is still there because Jurgen likes it. The whole story is long gone." I wink.

"Oh my god, don't tell me." He groans again. "You should have heard some of Ricky's tales yesterday, Stef. It turns out my future wife has led quite an eventful life. She needs a calming influence and a family to keep her out of mischief."

"We're going to be shopping for a new addition soon." Felix tells them.

"Me and Joe want a little 'Sarah'."

Dad gets excited. "Are we gonna foster again? Want me to ring some of the agencies? I bet the Liverpool guys would love to see how Joey is doing now."

I look at Emmett and roll my eyes. "We need to have a chat about the definition of 'long term plans', darling. Shall we let Paddy Mac do his thing first and get all the logistics sorted, we've run out of beds here already."

Stef shakes his head at Emm. "Bro, you sure don't do things by halves, do you? You've found the perfect woman and got the perfect family in just over a week. I'm so happy for you."

"Dysfunctional, unhinged, bonkers, delusional.. there are a lot of more appropriate words than 'perfect' that come to mind." I laugh. "Anyhow the wedding is off, he won't let me ride his Arch."

"Honey, Kim and I will buy you your own as a wedding gift if you go through with it." Stef offers willingly.

"Don't you dare! I'm just kidding. He's not getting away now. I've waited far too long for Mr. Wright to come along. Arch riding negotiations are underway, he'll come round, he can't resist my charms." I inform him with a grin, kissing a grimacing Emm on the head.

"Those photos are lovely again, aren't they?" Kim says. "Are you going to formally announce your engagement now?"

I shrug. "What difference will it make? All those that matter already know."

Felix whistles. "It's not doing us any harm sales wise." He announces, looking up from his phone. "Downloads are through the roof! We need to take our tops off and play on the beach more often, Old Boy, it's good for business."

"Are you coming sightseeing Fe? We're going to Laxey to see the big water wheel and Castletown to the castle."

"No, I'm gonna hang out here with Dylan if that's okay? Bike shopping and playing with tools sounds like fun."

"Be glad of the company." Dad smiles.

"We brought the car by the way." Stef says. "Dil can drive, she knows the way."

Emmett and Felix both burst into laughter. "I strongly advise you to retract that offer. She's apparently not very mechanically sympathetic."

"Well, that's an understatement." Dad agrees. "Rick's been bringing you up to speed, has he?"

"Parker is really going to suffer!" I growl. I clear the table, wash up, grab my bag and change into my dungaree dress and a t-shirt and my purple dockers and tell Dad and Felix to have fun.

I shout directions from the back seat and we park in Laxey right near the huge water wheel. We pay the admission fee and look around. It's really interesting, I've been loads of times but I love the history and the wheel is a real feat of mechanical engineering.

"Are you coming up to the top?" I ask, pointing to the narrow steps up to the middle of the wheel.

"Yeah." Stef grins. "Race you!" We fly up the steps with Emmett and Kim in hot pursuit.

"Watch the bar!" I yell, coming up to the lintel across the stairway that is head height for most people but I pass beneath it easily. Stef looks up at just the right time to dodge it but it slows him a little and I duck under his arm and win.

The view from the narrow walkway at the top is so impressive and Kim spots the train coming down the mountain. "Can we go on that?"

"Yes, the station is just over the road." I tell her. "We'll go over from here if you want. The cakes alone are well worth the trip up to the top."

There's another older couple already on the walkway who got quite excited when we all burst out of the top of the steps giggling and gasping for breath. The gentleman tentatively raises his hat in greeting.

"I understand congratulations may be in order." He says in a very American accent, looking at me and Emmett. "We don't mean to intrude but we've seen the papers and you really do look so happy together. We're big Era fans, have been for a real long time." His wife nods enthusiastically in agreement. "Our daughters both walked down the aisle to one of your songs."

Emmett's face clouds and I squeeze his hand tightly. "Play nicely, Emm." I whisper. Stef shakes hands with them and says 'hi' and lets the guy take a photo of him with the lady. They are beside themselves with joy. He waves the camera at us.

"Can we, please? I promise on the life of our children and grandchildren that it will go nowhere but in our personal album."

Emmett smiles in acceptance and puts his arms around me. "Do you know my fiancée, Miss. Delilah Tallulah Tinkerbell Rainbow Blue?" The couple go wild, shaking our hands and congratulating us.

"I knew I recognised you. You're one heck of a racer ma'am." He says respectfully and they take their one photo and then leave us in peace. Wishing us a long and happy life together.

"Jeez Dil, you are a witch! That poor guy would have gone over the railings if you hadn't been here." Stefan exclaims.

"I'm being more 'Joey'." Emmett tells him.

"Can I ride you're Arch yet?" I ask.

"Nope." He laughs. "You're still not going near it."

We go back down the steps a little more sedately and continue looking around until Kim's stomach rumbles. "Did you mention cake earlier?"

The electric railway is Victorian, running regularly up to the top of Snaefell from the quaint and immaculately kept Laxey Station. It peaks at 2,036 feet above sea level and boasts that on a clear day you will be able to see all of the Seven Kingdoms: England, Ireland, Wales, Scotland, the Isle of Man and the kingdoms of heaven and the sea. We take in the amazing view and I point them all out whilst we consume our combined body weight in home made cakes and drink hot chocolate full of cream and marshmallows.

Catching the train back down we attract a bit too much attention in the tightly packed wooden carriage by breaking out into a loud rendition of 'Crazy Train' led by Kim, probably due to a massive sugar rush.

I navigate to Castletown once we're back to the car and we have a sing along to everything that comes on the radio. Castletown is the old capital of the Island and Rushen Castle dominates the centre of the town. It's a lot more intact than Peel Castle with plenty of rooms and stairways and ramparts to explore and history to immerse yourself in. The guys all love it. Emmett and I are snogging on the ramparts and his hand is just about to disappear up my dress when somebody approaches us.

"Is this your mystery lady, Mr. Wright?" He nervously asks.

"Nope, I make out with complete strangers all the time." Emm drawls, not even looking at him. "Who are you and why do you need to know?"

We look up to see a skinny, geeky looking lad not much older than Joey. He's wearing a smart shirt and tie and looks petrified. "I'm Andrew Ellis." He holds out a hand to shake. "I work for the Manx Independent, well I'm currently doing an apprenticeship with them. Is it at all possible that I could interview you, please?"

"Nope, fuck off!" Emmett replies.

Young Mr. Ellis looks as if he might cry. "Okay, thank you for talking to me." He starts to walk away.

"Emm, what harm can it do? He's a local lad and once the full story is out then there's nothing to find out so they all go away. My skeletons are well buried and you have none. He's only Joe's age, give him a break."

"Delilah, you are such a strong persuader." He laughs. "He's got five minutes but you better not leave me alone with him. You can do the talk-ing. If he says one stupid thing I will deck him."

"Give me a second to coach him in Emmett wrangling." I laugh. "Don't let him run away, Stef."

"Andrew, hang on. Come on down to the grounds for a minute. Kim and I want to interview you first."

His face lights up. "Okay Dil, er sorry, Miss. Blue."

I laugh. "This may seem a daft question, Andrew but if you already know who I am why are you asking?"

"At least three huge reasons." He admits. "Nathan's Dad and his uncles. That and probably half of the Island will lynch me if I write anything without first having your blessing. That's before adding in Mr. Wright's well documented temper with reporters." Kim is shaking her head in amazement.

"Everyone knows who you are, I was at Joey's sixteenth. Which was a hell of a party by the way. I went to school with Nathan and Ella. I've met Connor a few times since he's been over here too, Mrs. Fischer. Him and Nathan dared me to ask Mr. Wright for the interview."

Kim hugs him. "Oh, you poor boy, well you can just tell my Son you were brave enough to do it."

"What's you angle for the story, Andrew? Emmett is not going to answer silly or private questions, he'll lose his temper with you if you want to get gossip or write a nasty piece." I ask. "And I would prefer if you kept Joey's name out of it I don't want Sienna turning back up."

"I value my life too much to upset the Parkers. I'd have to get the next boat off the Island." He tells us seriously. "I just wanted to write a nice, feel good story. Too much news is bad and sad already. I kind of want to for- mally announce your engagement if I can."

"Show us your questions and we'll decide if they're okay."

Kim and I read the questions and cross out the more banal ones. Kim reads one and laughs. "My Son has had a hand in writing these hasn't he?"

I start reading a few questions for me. "Yeah, Nath has been involved too."

"Don't answer anything you don't want to. I promise I will send you the final copy to approve before I submit it." Andrew offers.

Emmett and Stef come over. "What do you think, girls?" Stefan asks.

"Your Son dared him." Kim laughs.

"Felix?" Emm growls.

"No, Connor and Nathan have been making mischief this time."

"You're a friend of the kids? Not really a reporter?" Stefan asks.

"Yes, I am a real reporter but I'm only just starting my career. This would help me so much."

"We get to see the story before it goes to press. You say no whenever you like and he knows my attack dogs will be activated if he upsets anyone. He's very aware of The Parkers." I assure Emmett.

"Come on then, let's just get it over with." He sighs, throwing himself down on the grass and pulling me into his lap. Stef and Kim join us and Andrew sits down, opens his notebook and grabs his pencil. Connor and Nathan come strolling across the lawn.

"Hello, shithead. You lost a bet." I sigh at Nathan.

He drops down beside me and kisses my cheek.

"Hey Auntie Dil. I didn't bet. I've seen what you can do with Uncle Rick and he'll rip people's arms off if they look at him funny, Emmett's a push-over for you." He giggles, narrowly avoiding the playful slap around the head from Emm. "Connor just lost fifty quid."

"Serves him right." Kim says. "Okay Andrew, let's have some questions."

"Is it true you're engaged and if so when and how did you propose? Joey and Felix said it was brilliant." He adds, without realising.

"How about you tell me what you know and I'll tell you if it's right." Emm laughs, kissing my head.

"They said you bought Dil, can I call you Dil? A ring at Peel Museum." I nod to tell him it's fine. "That you got home to a surprise beach house your Dad and Nathan's mom had sorted and proposed on the big bed inside it with Joey and Felix and Dil's dad there too. Joe said they helped you out a bit."

"Don't forget the four dogs and Dutch the cat were also present to witness." Emmett smiles. "And Sarah helped with the beach house."

He writes frantically. "Can I describe the ring in the story?"

"If you like." I hold out my hand and he tries to sketch it quickly. Kim takes his book and draws it perfectly. Emm takes time during the break for another snog.

"Wow, thanks Mrs. Fischer. Can I have my book back now? Okay, are you having an engagement party and have you set a date for the wedding? Can I tell people the wedding plans? They sound unreal."

"Do they?" Emm asks. "Why?"

"Is it true you're all going to dress up as superheroes and marry on the beach at Dil's place, where you had Joey's party?"

Emmett shakes his head in amusement. "Apparently."

"Joey hasn't told you how the ceremony is going to go, has he?" I collapse in a fit of giggles and Emmett kisses me to shut me up."

"So have you set a date?"

Nathan interjects. "Don't say Friday, Mom will have a complete break-down."

"Engagement party is Friday. Oh, shit! That's tomorrow isn't it? We haven't set a wedding date but it won't be too far away. Our long-term plans only usually extend to a week." I tell him arching an eyebrow at Emm.

"So, a week tomorrow then?" Stefan teases.

"Who knows?" I shrug. "Stuff kind of happens. I'm just along for the ride. Depends how far along we are on Arch riding negotiations."

"Emmett's got an Arch? No wonder you agreed to marry him!" Nathan exclaims.

"Spoken like a true Parker." I laugh. "FYI shithead, I didn't know until after I'd agreed."

"Last question, I'm hungry!" Emm announces. "Make it a good one."

"Will you be taking up permanent residence on the Island?"

"Dil's heart and her family are here and I wanna be wherever she is so it looks like it, son." Emmett smiles, kissing me again. Me, Nath and Kim shed a happy tear.

Emm stands up and throws me over his shoulder. "Come on, woman, where can we eat around here?" He asks striding toward the gatehouse.

"There's a nice place just around the corner by the square. Put me down Emmett the blood is rushing to my head and I'm probably flashing my knickers to the whole world."

He sits me on the wall in the square. "You are unreal, Delilah! That's the first reporter I have spoken civilly to in the last thirty years."

"I don't think young Mr. Ellis is representative of your average reporter." I laugh. "I think you can safely say your record is still unbroken."

He pulls me tightly into him and kisses me hard.

"You do real bad things to my mind and my body. I'm turning into a pussy and whatever the male equivalent of a nymphomaniac is."

"A satyr." I tell him. "What's wrong, Mr. Wright." I tease nibbling his ear and kissing his neck.

"That's not helping here, Delilah." He laughs rubbing himself against me to highlight his problem.

"Think about something scary ... like me riding your Arch?"

"That vision does not scare me one bit. It has very much the opposite effect."

"How about me in my overalls with the zipper half open, wearing that sexy underwear you keep promising to buy me, bending over the bonnet of your Cobra with a spanner in my hand..."

"Stop it you bloody imp!"

Stefan, Kim and the boys join us after saying bye to Andrew.

"Well that wasn't your most conventional journalistic interview." Stef observes, patting Emmett on the back. "Well done, bro."

Emmett grins. "Dil says that one doesn't count. He hasn't quite got the hang of it yet, has he?"

"He was a sweetheart and I'm going to be making sure Connor doesn't welsh on his bet!" Kim adds, raising an eyebrow at Connor. Nathan jumps in to support him.

"In our defense, Andrew is absolutely desperate to become a journalist, he was a year below me in school, in Ella's year. He ran the school paper and was great but he's lost a bit of confidence since he started work because he didn't get kept on at his first placement. This story will do him good, the world needs optimistic journalists. I wouldn't have gone along with it if I didn't think Auntie Dil would save him."

"Okay, you're forgiven. Let's eat!" Emmett sighs adding quietly to me. "If I can't satisfy other urges."

"What like seeing me in a Batgirl outfit, astride my new Panigale..."

"Stef, give us the car keys, bro. Dil's left her phone. Order us whatever looks good. We'll be five minutes." He takes the key and drags me back to the car.

"Emmett, what are you planning exactly?"

"You know darn well what and it's your fault." He growls. "Stop winding me up!"

"Emm, having quickie sex in a hire car in the car park is not really practical or grown up."

"And your point is?"

"No point. I'm totally up for it, just saying." I shrug.

He grins, undoing his jeans and pulling me onto his lap in the backseat, facing him.

"Sorry darlin', I am a desperate man and you're the only one that can save me."

We get to the table as the food arrives and drinks are waiting for us. While we're all chatting after the meal is finished Nathan's phone pings and it's an email from Andrew with our story.

Nath reads it to us all;

"Today, I was granted a very exclusive interview with Mr. Emmett Wright and his gorgeous fiancée Miss. Delilah Blue. Yes, you read it right! They graciously

took time out of their snogging session on Castle Rushen ramparts to answer a few questions for me. I have the honour and their blessing to confirm they are officially engaged!

The ring is intricate Celtic Manx silver with a very apt blue stone which was purchased at Peel Museum. Not your usual tasteless blingy diamond but they're not a couple that follow the herd. She is a renowned rainbow dread-locked, motorbike racer and TT winner from the Blue racing dynasty. A well-known and well loved, adopted local. He is possibly the world's greatest guitarist and, I might add, honest and funny and friendly and only a little scary.

Literally flying in the face of tradition they are planning a Superhero themed wedding on the beach with just the close friends and family that are so important to them both. The Fischers were with them today.

The proposal itself was a family affair with Emmett's son, Felix, and Delilah's son and father present along with all of the family dogs and Dutch the cat. It took place on a big bed in their newly erected beach hideaway which was a surprise present for them from Delilah's Dad and her best girlfriend and goddaughter.

Three of the dogs have recently arrived from the States and belong to Emmett and Felix hinting of possible plans to stay on the Island. When I asked Emmett whether he would be taking up permanent residence on The Rock he replied, and I quote; "Dil's heart and her family are here and I wanna be wherever she is so it looks like it."

He concluded by striding off in search of food with tiny, elfin-like Delilah slung romantically over his shoulder. They truly are a beautiful, loved up, un-conventional couple and a perfect match.

I had to wait for several kissing sessions to cease in the course of this interview. I know I am not alone in wishing them a long and happy life together!"

Emmett is giggling his head off. "There's not much in there I can object to really, is there? Tell him to go for it."

"He says can he use Kim's drawing? He will give her credit for it."

"Of course he can." She smiles.

We stop off on the way home to pick up booze and food ready for tomorrow night.

CHAPTER 51

S enior race day. The big one. Roads close at half nine. The second side-car race over 3 laps is at half ten and the big boys' race, the Senior over 6 laps at quarter to one. I'm awake really early and leave Emmett peacefully sleeping while I indulge in a proper yoga session.

Naked, I stretch out all of the knots and kinks as the sun rises, bringing with it a beautiful day. I settle down on my rock, not to meditate but to take stock of the fortnight. It's been one heck of a ride.

Bloody hell Delilah, how did we end up here? You finally popped your cherry at the grand age of fifty-two. You're engaged to a rock star. He genuinely gets you, accepts all of your faults and flaws and weirdness, wants to be with you. What's going on with our heavenly cottage? We've outgrown it already and we're talking about more bikes, cars, horses and kids.

Somehow, I now have two amazing sons who have bonded like true brothers and are ready to welcome a little sister. Dad is in his element, surrounded by both family and friends with a workshop full of jobs. Joey has someone special too, lovely Ella is family already, they're young and it may not work out but they will always be close. Jurgen, the crazy German, is now our neighbour with enough spare room for everyone. Ricky's stories have been a bit of a revelation. I never once thought I was causing him so much frustration but he's kept coming back for more and even tried to instigate a trip last week. He's a bit of a worry, I love him dearly and want him in my life forever but I'm a little confused. I'm going to try and talk everything through when I get chance.

I am truly blessed and I thank all the gods and stars and angels and Madame Karma for my current situation. I am saluting the sun when Emm appears, barefoot, bare chested and sexy as hell. He leans against my back with his hands on my hips, as I bend from the waist and kisses me passionately as I stand and lean back, arms stretched above my head.

"Morning, my future wife, do you know that you're not wearing any clothes? Are you ready for the 'Blues Wright' engagement party? I don't know how the heck I got here but I honestly could not be any happier."

"I was just thinking the exact same thing, Emm." I smile. "Do we have to consummate our engagement or is that just the wedding?"

"Yeah, definitely. It's the law. Before, during and after the event." Emmett giggles, and my rock is christened again. I run into the sea afterwards and swim a long lazy stroke to take out the last of the knots. Not exercising properly for a fortnight, unless wild sex sessions count, is doing my body no favours at all. Emm stands on the beach for a second then strips off and chases me. We swim side by side for a while then turn back.

Joey, Felix, Dutch and the dogs are on the beach when we start to swim back in. Jeff, Loki and Odin swim out to us. Thor stays on the beach with Dutch on his broad shoulders.

"Eh laa, why are there kecks on the beach? Can't you twos keep ya kit on?" Joey groans. We walk out of the sea, laughing. He puts his hand over Thor's eyes. "Don't look laa, that's the picture they should 'ave put in the paper. It's like the porno version of James Bond."

"Is Andrew's story out already?" I ask. "We're you two involved?"

"Yeah, kind of." Felix offers vaguely.

Emmett pulls his jeans back on and Joey takes off his t-shirt for me.

"How exactly were you involved, Son?" Emm enquires.

"Might have given him a couple of pictures." He shrugs. Emmett takes him by surprise and picks him up easily, carries him out and throws him into the sea.

"How about you, Joe?"

"Knew nothin' 'bout it." He grins. "Never even met the kid."

Andrew's story is online on the newspaper's website. It is word for word what he sent us. The pictures include Kim's drawing of the ring and another divine drawing of me and Emm entwined, a mass of hair, legs and dreadlocks, both are credited to Kim. A beautiful photo of us walking on Peel beach holding hands, deep in conversation with a superb sunset behind, one of us all by the bikes, my screensaver. Several from the last band visit; me sitting on Emm's lap while he plays the guitar, Me slung over his shoulder talking to Jurgen and Stef, us seriously making out against the fridge, Emm singing to me and us singing a duet in the cottage, us snogging at the sprint and me sitting astride him on the picnic blanket.

"Nice, apart from the fridge scene." I laugh, hugging a soggy Felix.

"That's Stef, not me. I didn't witness that carnage, thank heavens!"

Emm shakes his head in amazement at the treachery of his best friends and family. "Traitors left, right and centre." He sighs.

There are already thousands of comments, most are wishing us well, a few jealous trolls saying they would treat Emmett better and a few pervs sharing what they would like to do to me, but on the whole positive.

"Sales are unreal, Old Boy. You showing your human side is doing us no harm at all. September dates are all sold out already. Who's coming tonight, have you sent invites?"

"Nope, have you?" I laugh.

"I've invited Ella's ma an' da." Joey pipes up. "Everyone what matters just turns up. It's a weird thing 'ere. Even Andrew'll be 'ere." He sees Emm raise an eyebrow and quickly adds. "Whoever 'e is. Where we watchin'? I gorra tell Rick an' Billy. They're comin' to tell Emm more stories."

"In that case I'm not telling you." I grin. "Let's go and get some scran on, I'm starvin'."

Are ya puttin' ya kit on first?"

"Nope, I'm being more Jurgen. Don't forget you've gotta all get your kecks off tomorrow night." I laugh throwing his t-shirt at him.

"I'm up for it." Felix laughs stripping off his soggy clothes and hanging them over Loki. "Come on, bro. It's very liberating." Emm shrugs and follows suit.

"Eh laa, I've never took me kit off in front of anybody." Joey says embarrassed.

Felix holds his arms wide showing off his taut, tanned,muscular body. "Have you got anything I haven't?"

"Ah, fuck it yas all tapped." He groans, removing his boots and jeans.

"Jeez Joe, what ya worrying about? You're hung like Angel, Dad's stallion and ripped like you're about to do an iron man challenge!"

"I told Rick them jonnies was too small an' 'e laughed at me." Joey shrugs.

"Don't you worry Son I'll take great pleasure in letting telltale Parker know his condoms aren't big enough for my little boy." I say hugging him.

"Gerroff me Ma, you're starkers!" He moans.

"We barely dressed at all when I was a kid. Unless we were going out on the bikes." I tell him. We all walk into the cottage naked.

"Is it washing day?" Dad asks with a smile.

"We're being more 'Jurgen' today." I inform him, kissing his cheek.

"You'll all be needing bacon sandwiches then, I assume."

"Ja!" We all yell in unison.

I get the coffee on and fetch a load of baking ingredients out of the larder to get some extra stuff ready for later. I mix some muffin batter, make some pastry and make a chocolate sponge batter for Joey. The gannets all eat half the mix as usual before I get it to the fridge. Then I make a big picnic and fill the rucksacks and get all the food ready for the campers for the last time this year. Sal arrives with a huge pile of food and decorations.

"Are we saving our clean clothes for tonight?" She laughs at us all eating breakfast in the buff.

"We're practicing for tomorrow." Emmett tells her.

"Oh god. I forgot that's tomorrow. Our Sarah can't wait, she can't decide if she's going pillion or if we've got to take her bike. Are we going from Jurgen's? And thanks for giving Andrew a break." She says, kissing his cheek.

"No idea, we'll see Jurgen in a bit I expect, or tonight. Are you coming to watch?"

"Nah, I'm going to organise you an engagement party to remember. Have you even invited anyone?"

"Yep. Both the bands and Ella's mom and dad and all the Parkers." I reply, winking at Joe.

"You didn't invite any of the Parkers you cheeky mare, I did!" Sal swipes my head.

"But I knew you would." I giggle. "Is Sarah at Pat's?"

"They're busy making food for later. They'll be over to help in a while. The lads were going to watch at Sulby Bridge, they're doing a couple of pit boards."

"I was thinking there too but your man and Ricky are doing their best to frighten my future husband away."

She laughs. "Dil, you know Ricky will never tell your worst ones, he values his life too much. They'll never find those bodies now anyway."

"Thanks Sal, that helps a lot! Emmett's jaw has just hit the table, you bitch."

"Anytime, slapper." She grins, kissing me and dancing off out the back with her box of goodies. "By the way I've told everyone they can camp by the way. You've got loads of room in the field. God knows where the DJ is going to set up though now your shag shed is in the way. ..."

"Give us your clothes Fe, I'll put them back in the washer." I say as Loki appears still draped in them. "Where's your wet jeans Emm?"

He shrugs at me. "On the beach somewhere." He takes Fe's off Loki and shows Odin, telling him to 'seek' and he disappears and returns with them a few minutes later.

"That's cool, Jeff just sticks her head on one side and licks you if you ask her to do anything." Dad laughs.

"These three cost a fortune and never get to do much at all but they can do plenty. At least they're actually with us now." Emm sighs rewarding Odin with some bacon. "They can do security tonight, give Rick and Bill a night off."

"Is Chaz coming, Sal?" I yell.

"Supposed to be. What ya wearing?"

"Ain't even thought about it. My jeans and a t-shirt, I suppose."

"God Dil, you're a lost cause!" She comes back into the kitchen just as Joey gets up from the table and stretches. "Bloody hell, Joey! What have they done to you? You look like Jason Momoa with extended extras."

"Bill and Rick expect me to shift the same stuff as them and Ma keeps feedin' me." He shrugs in reply, pulling his jeans back on.

Felix goes to his room to get dressed and I clear the table and grab t-shirts out of the ironing basket for Joe and me and put the wet stuff on to wash. Emmett goes off to dress too.

"Well I've definitely seen worse views first thing in the morning." Sal comments, watching him leave.

"He is pretty darn sexy, isn't he?" I grin. "I'll be back in five minutes." I laugh, chasing after him.

He's sitting on the edge of the bed about to pull his clean jeans on. "Hang on one minute there, sexy. This girl has urgent needs."

We head down to Sulby Bridge after letting Stef and Jurgen know. Bill and Rick are already there with a space saved for us all. I set out blankets and drop everything down. Bill gives us all big bear hugs and Ricky grins at me.

"Ready for some skeletons to be dug up, Shortarse?"

I launch at him and quickly and easily put him down on his back. As the others watch in amazement, apart from Bill who's seen it all before. I've got my knee in Rick's solar plexus and my elbow in his throat. My face is right over his.

"One word, Parker and I will ensure you never father children." I growl, glaring at him for a long second, kiss the top of his head and let him up.

"Remind me never to piss off my psychotic future wife." Emm says to Bill.

"That's just brothers and sisters playin'" Bill tells him. "'E loves it. Knows 'ow to get a rise out of 'er. 'Ave yow lot bin 'ere less than ten minutes? I owe 'im a fuckin' tenner if it was."

"Fraid so, bro."

"Bollocks!" He laughs. "Thought she'd be a bit more in control now she's discovered shaggin'. Ain't she started with the rough stuff on you?"

"Nope, she's enthusiastic and very keen but I think she's like AI she learns from you until her abilities outweigh yours. She's already instigating more and more risky stuff, wound me up enough to go for it in the hire car in a car park yesterday."

"Fuck man, you've got the measure of 'er already. You're perfect for 'er." Bill slaps him on the back. "Ya know where we are if yow need any trainin' tips."

"I appreciate that, Bill. She is an enigma. It's gonna be one hell of a ride. I keep thinking I'm in control but I'm not at all, am I?"

"Not even close, Dave." He laughs.

Rick slings me over his shoulder and walks over to Bill and Emm.

"Tenner, bro." He grins at Bill, shaking Emm's hand. "Morning bro. Ouch! You fuckin' bitch, don't bite me! Do you want your hellcat back or shall I chuck her in the road?" He laughs smacking my backside and putting me down next to Emmett.

"Cheers Rick, have you got some more stories for us then?" He laughs wrapping his arms around me. I'm not sure if it's to protect me or Ricky.

"Plenty, bro. Give 'er five to get 'er 'ead on right and it's Jackanory time." He pats my head like I'm a puppy. I snarl.

"Who we doin' boards for, Bill?" Joey asks.

"17 and 38" Billy says. "Get the numbers on, son. Other way round, Dave, three first." He adds patiently.

My baby is dyslexic. I've had my suspicions for a while. I'll have a chat with him when the madness is over. We can try a few things that might help if he wants. Marley and a few of the kids we fostered were dyslexic. It's a classic cause of truancy and behavioural problems in school. If you can't understand what people want from you how can you deliver? Joey is such a people pleaser. It must have been hell for him. I watch, overwhelmed with love for him as Bill hands him letters and numbers. He's grown in every way since the day he arrived. He's relaxed and easy in the company of his ever-growing family, he's tanned and broadened and looking nothing like the skinny, wary kid that arrived, that fateful morning, with Nina and the donkeys. I was amazed in more ways than one when he took his kit off this morning. He would not have had the confidence to do that a few weeks back. Nothing fazes my handsome, lovely boy.

"What you smiling at, darlin'?" Emm asks watching me carefully, following my eyes.

"Joe, I love him so much it hurts." I sigh. "He's such a beautiful kid. How did my life get so good?"

"Don't ask just accept it, Dilly girl. You deserve it." Dad says, patting my knee.

Stef, Kim, Jurgen and the boys arrive. Obviously in the hire car from the amount of stuff they are carrying. Stef immediately holds his hands up in submission.

"Sorry bro, I couldn't resist." He laughs. "Story was sweet though."

"Judas!" Emm replies with a grin. "You've just missed a demonstration of Delilah in anger. It was impressive. You're lucky she's okay with soft porn being fed to the press."

Stef raises an eyebrow. "You haven't pissed her off on your engagement party day, surely man?"

"Nope, and I will not be pissing her off ever after her display just now. Ricky was winding her up and she had him on his back with an elbow in his throat and a knee in his ribs before I could blink. She snarls better than Odin."

"Ahh, sorry I missed that." Stef looks at me. "Are you better now, honey?"

"Yep, I'm good. Rick is a dick and my knee was in his solar plexus, far more effective and painful than the ribs."

"See what I mean?" Emm shrugs.

Kim drops down next to us and hugs Dad, me and Emm. Nath sits down to chat with his dad and Joe and Charlie and Connor catch up with Felix.

"Kim, that drawing was so lovely. Can I have a copy, please?" I ask.

Jurgen is super happy about his new home. "Liebling, if I had looked for a year I would not have found a more perfect place, ja. It has everything Jurgen needs and room to bring over my toys too. Did you know I have a helipad in the garden? I will bring my whirly bird over. Do you want to learn to fly it?"

"Yeah, I was hoping you would bring it. We saw the pad from one of the upstairs windows." I say. "How's the pools?"

"The best. You must come and try."

"I will as soon as the sea gets too cold." I tell him. "Sal asked if we're meeting at your place tomorrow."

"Ja, we will ride and have a house warming party. Party all weekend; yours tonight, mine tomorrow, Pavillion Sunday. It will be a good weekend."

The sidecars come flying down the straight. They are superb to watch, jostling for places on the narrow roads

and scrubbing off speed for the bend over Sulby Bridge. I wanted to try sidecar racing a long while back but no one would agree to be my passenger. "Wanna try this, Joe? D'ya reckon you could hang on?"

"Easy! Shall we do the Southern this July?" He replies enthusiastically, coming to stand with me.

"We might need a bit of practice, it's harder than it looks and I'd rather build our own. We'll go for the Manx in August."

"Can I race a bike and passenger in the sidecars?"

"Yeah, long as we've sorted all your licenses and you've got enough races in." He drops his arm easily around my shoulder.

"How ya doin' Mama Dil? Ya ready for this commitment stuff?" He asks, genuinely concerned. "Things move pretty fuckin' fast round 'ere."

"Fast is how I like it, darling. I've had a few wobbles but they were over daft shit that's all been sorted. Emmett has the patience of a saint." I laugh."I honestly couldn't even imagine being any happier. How about you? You seem to be coping well with an overbearing Mama and the American invasion."

"Ma, I thought I'd be dead before I got to where I am right now. I'm in 'eaven!" He smiles, kissing my head and hugging me tightly.

"Friends yet?" Ricky asks putting his arm around both me and Joe.

"Nope, fuck off, dick!"

"God, I love it when you talk dirty to me, Shortarse. It's nearly as good as when you get rough with me."

"You're a fucking masochist, Rick!" I laugh, shaking my head.

"Yep, can't get enough pain and humiliation." He drawls.

"Talking of pain, you've been supplying my baby here with something that is not fit for purpose." I raise an eyebrow at him.

"Their purpose is to stop him making babies. Would you rather he got her up the duff?" He shrugs.

"I'm very happy you gave him condoms, thank you for that. I just wish you gave him ones that are big enough." I giggle.

He looks at me. "Too small? You're joking, they're large. I use 'em!"

"Too small." I confirm.

"Fair play, son! I'll get you some XL ones on the way over later. He said they were too small. I explained they gotta be tight to stay on. I just thought it was because he wasn't used to 'em."

"Thanks, honey." I lean up to kiss him, forgetting I'm mad with him. "Me and Joey are gonna start sidecar racing."

He groans. "I'll give a 600 engine about a ten-minute lifespan in your hands but at least I know you won't try and kill yourself while he's in the chair."

CHAPTER 52

The sidecars come around for their second lap and Joey is asking about lines and movements, why some lean right out of the chair and others lean forward, others over the wheel. He has an amazing eye for detail and understands complex explanations quickly. He's going to make a good racer. By the third lap he's repeating it all back to me and pointing out who's doing what and why even reasoning what they could do to make quicker times.

We break out the combined picnics and settle on the blankets. Jurgen produces several bottles of champagne and a huge, and very professional looking, engagement cake with little figures of us together, making out on the Duchess.

"Jurgen, that's far too nice to eat." I laugh.

"Nonsense, my chef is so happy to have a kitchen. We have another one for later and mountains of food to bring over." He replies, popping a champagne cork. "Congratulations! Fuck it, I forgot glasses." He sighs, drinking from the bottle and passing it around. I take a swig and screw up my face, it's definitely not something I'm ever going to acquire a taste for. The cake is yummy though and everyone soon sees it off.

"Okay can we have some stories about the happy couple?" Felix asks.

Charlie starts us off. "Does Dil know Emmett has a crazy psycho stalker?"

"Nope, tell me more." I reply.

"She's completely insane and turns up at every gig. She always takes off most of her clothes when we play one particular song. She has a tattoo of Emm on her left breast and swears undying love to him constantly on all the fan sites and forums, claims she was married to him in a former life. Tiny's had to remove her from dozens of hotels where she's been running round the corridors yelling for Emm. She got into his room once. Scared the crap out of him."

Emm shakes his head in embarrassment. "I've got an injunction against her. She should stay away for a long while."

"When did you last see her?"

"About three months ago. When we were in Germany. She disappeared after the injunction was served but they assure me it's because she's locked up."

"What was Dil's first brush with the law?" Connor asks.

Dad answers. "Would have been when she was three. I caught her getting ready to take my day old Triumph Bonnie for a joyride in the middle of the night. Her first official one was when she got stopped testing one of her race bikes on the M5 at four in the morning. She was doing 148 mph but as she was only eleven at the time they couldn't ban or fine her. Little bugger had got our Marley on the back too."

"Eleven? When did she start racing?" Kim asks

"She was winning trophies in drag racing and moto crossing before she was four, competitively track racing at seven. She was practically born on a bike; she's got oil for blood. She'd ridden across five continents before she was officially old enough to have a licence." Dad says proudly.

"Jeez, my Mom is wild. Come on Stef. You must know plenty of stories about Dad before I came along." Felix urges.

"He was always pretty intense and focused on his music even when he was a kid. He's only become a reprobate since he's met Dil." Stef laughs. "We had a brief crazy drugs phase at medical school and first few years the band took off. Him and Kim did get kicked out of school for letting all the animals out of the research lab. The place was overrun with rabbits, rats and monkeys for days. Then I married my beautiful wife and we had the kids and late nights and drug fuelled parties became a distant memory."

Kim giggles. "Jeez, we did. I forgot the monkey thing. We we're boring really weren't we? Apart from Emm's few, well documented, reporter incidents and his big fights with Cherry especially the one at the hotel when the Superbowl was on. Because the kids were with us most of the time we were doing all the theme parks and sightseeing. You were performing, eating or asleep."

Felix perks up. "What fight with Cherry? I don't ever remember her being with us anywhere apart from on a few vacations and all she did then was lie on a sunbed and ignore us."

Stef laughs. "They had some epic fights before you came along, Fe. They'd realised they didn't like each other much and mostly avoided being in the same country once you arrived. She knocked him unconscious with a champagne bottle less than ten minutes before we played the interval at the Superbowl. He still played completely concussed. He couldn't see anything. We took him straight to the hospital after the gig, thought she'd broken his skull. We banned her from touring with us after that."

"Why did she hit him with a bottle?" Felix asks and Stef looks at Emm, a little uneasy at answering his question.

Emmett nods to give Stefan an okay. "It was before you we're born Felix. They'd only been married a few months. He was treating her like a princess because he thought she was pregnant then he found her in the players' locker room hot tub getting jiggy with several of the players. She told him she was never pregnant. He said he wanted a divorce, so she hit him with the bottle."

"Good riddance to her, cheating bitch. I'm only keeping her number in my phone so that I don't accidentally open a call from her. Over to you again then Ricky." Felix shrugs. "Let's hear some more about the bride."

"Hang onto her then." He warns Emmett. "How about Colombia?" He grins at me.

"Okay, that didn't involve prostitutes that I know of or me going to jail." I consent, relaxing in Emm's arms.

"We'd been free climbing at Chicamocha Canyon for a few days and this real shifty bloke, like a merc, thought he was Rambo, had taken a proper liking to her. He was hanging out at the hostel we were staying at but didn't look like he belonged in a cheap doss house. He'd got a load of armed guards with him constantly. I tried to avoid him as much as possible, everything about him felt dangerous. There was all sorts of nasty shit going on over there in the early nineties. She was getting back every night high as a kite from the climbing and kept being drawn to his psycho vibes. She kept on chatting away to him completely oblivious of the fact that he got a massive hard on and looked at her like he wanted to eat her every time he saw her. He kept rolling her some top grade, super mellow spliffs and giving her really good coke which she just gave me because she wouldn't know good coke from Ajax." He sighs.

"I asked around the village and was told he was one of the biggest drug barons in Colombia, laying low 'cos he had a large price on his head and some even more dangerous guys than him on his tail. He caught up with me in the bar one night when I'd finally got her to settle and gone for a well-earned pint. He literally offered a truck load of cocaine for her, making it very obvious that it wasn't up for any negotiation. God knows why I didn't just take his offer; I would have been set up for life. I went back to our room and woke her. We packed our shit up and left as soon as we safely could, which meant the middle of the night. Thankfully I'd got extra cans of petrol that day because we were planning to move on. She wanted to just use it to set fire to the place but I convinced her to leave quietly. We were riding 'El Trampolin De la Muerte'."

"That translates as The trampoline of death. That doesn't sound very safe." Kim comments.

"It's a steep twisty dirt track just outside Equador up mountains and through a load of stinking hot jungle, there's landslides all the time and great chunks of it have fallen away. We planned to get over the border as quick as possible. We rode that deathtrap trail through the jungle in the dark knowing there were about twenty armed henchmen following us. She was in her element. Thought she was a flat chested version of Lara Croft." They all laugh and I lean over to punch him.

"She's riding like a demon over everything in her path, then she gets a bloody puncture and we know we can't risk riding on it or putting a light on to fix it so we have to pull the bikes off the trail and mend it in the pitch black and something fucking bites me, doesn't it? We had no idea what it was and I don't wanna risk moving in case it was something venomous or anything and I pass out once it starts moving around my body, so she decides she's gotta suck out whatever is in it just to be safe. So we're hiding in a bush with the bikes, she's on her knees sucking my groin and the goons all go flying past within two feet of us. She doesn't even flinch. We gave them ten minutes head start then followed them right to the border. Thankfully I'd got a pocket full of really good coke so we managed to easily cross a little way up from the official gates and rode through the night until we got to Riobamba. We found out later her admirer was Fidel Castaño and he was hiding from Pablo Escobar! Good job we moved on before *he* caught up with him."

"It was the top of your leg, not your groin, dickhead!" I laugh.

"Jeez, Delilah. You're crazy!" Charlie exclaims. "Weren't you even scared?"

"Of Ricky's groin? No, there's not much to scare you down there." I deadpan. "I get scared about everything except scary stuff. It's not my fault I'm weird. Stupid things just seem to happen to me. A lot." I shrug.

"What's the story behind Dil's naked elephant ride?" Emmett asks Jurgen.

"Ah, that one did involve me going to jail." I sigh.

Jurgen is very happy to become the centre of attention. "My favourite photo in the whole world. She looks like Mowgli from the Jungle Book, ja? We were all in Laos. We'd gone there after racing in Macau. There were some idiots selling elephant rides and Delilah wasn't at all happy about how they were treating the fantastic creatures. They were chained up and made to carry fat, lazy tourists in the boiling heat. They didn't have fresh water or hardly any food. She kept feeding them in the night and picked all the locks on their chains, put a flaming rag in the fuel tank of the owners' jeep to create a diversion, jumped on the bull elephant and led them all off into the jungle to live a long and happy life. She got locked up for a few days and I had to pay a fine and a few bribes when we eventually found out where they were keeping her."

"How old was she?" Connor asks, looking at the picture on the internet via his phone. "She looks like a kid."

"Thirteen?" Jurgen looks to Dad for confirmation.

"Not quite, eleven or twelve I think. Her Mama knocked out several policemen and high up officials that week, didn't she?" He smiles fondly at the memory.

The racing starts and spares us from more stories, though I suspect more will be told this evening.

This is the race everyone wants to win; the bikes may look standard at first glance but they are far from it. They are very much purpose built for this race. The mechanics give their riders as much braking, suspension and engine improvements as they possibly can. This is not racing for amateurs. The average lap record is almost 135mph which is beyond amazing when you think of how many bumps, bridges, obstacles, tight bends and hairpins there are on this 37-and three-quarter mile circuit.

We sit up on top of the bank, there's no fencing here at all. There's a long run of built up banking and some temporary grandstands. It's just down from the Sulby Glen Hotel so it's on a long straight that goes to a ninety-degree bend and then off past Ginger Hall and a bumpy ride up to Ramsey. Bill and Joey get the radio tuned in clearly so that they can hear timings and set the boards up. Emmett sits up on the bank and pulls me onto his lap.

"Hello my beautiful girl. I just had a thought are we gonna be the Blue-Wrights or the Wright-Blues?"

"Dunno, hadn't thought about it." I admit. "What do you wanna be?

"Blue-Wright I reckon, ladies should always come first." He replies.

"Well this one definitely always does." I laugh, kissing him passionately.

"Don't start darlin', I'm saving myself for tonight. Our official engagement night should be special."

"Emm, we've already had sex three times today. Am I really that crap at it that you don't remember?"

"Before breakfast doesn't count." He informs me. "You are always perfection but I wanted to blow your mind tonight."

"Emm, honey. You blow my mind every single time you touch me! Don't forget everything is new to me."

"Our life together isn't going to be anywhere near as exciting as your earlier life." He sighs. "What if you get bored of me?"

"Emmett, I've wasted a big chunk of my life looking for something that didn't exist because I was running away from pain and loss. I've done some really stupid shit in my time and although I've not regretted a single thing I've done and it's all made me who I am. I do regret how long it's taken to find you. I'd be dead a dozen times by now if Ricky hadn't turned up to stop me or save me, lord knows I've tried to find enough ways to die! In my screwed-up head I had no reason to live. I reasoned that everyone had someone so no-one needed me. It was only when Mama died and Dad was alone I rejoined the real world. Now I've got you and I've got a life way better than I ever dreamed of. I can't imagine wanting to be anywhere other than here with you, Dad, Joey and Felix. I am never going to be bored or yearn for excitement or run away." I assure him.

"It wasn't ever really fun that I was looking for it was a way to stop the hurting. Listen carefully to all of Ricky's stories and you'll realise how close to self-destruction I was. You and I already have a whole load of new stories to tell, happy stories, our adventures together and with our family. Emm, I love you so much and I promise you now if I thought for one second this wasn't going to work out I wouldn't be going through with it. I've come up with every reason to run away and none stand up to scrutiny. You are stuck with me for life now if you still want me."

He wipes his hand across his eyes. He's crying. Oh god I've made him cry. I hold him tightly and rock him gently. "Are you okay baby? Are you having second thoughts? I get it if you are. I know I can be a bit of a handful. We can wait a while longer if you want to." I whisper into his hair.

He wraps himself around me. "Delilah, I have never been more sure of anything or wanted anyone more. I want to marry you right this second and never ever let you out of my sight, my beautiful, fragile, little angel. I cannot think of living my life without you in it now. I wasn't sure if I would be enough for you."

"This is a whole new trip for all of us but as long as we keep talking we'll survive and thrive. I think we're doing okay so far. Don't you?"

"I really, really, love you, Delilah Blue!" He laughs through his tears. "Yeah, we are doing more than okay, I'd say. Have you got any requests for tonight?"

"Yep, be happy, enjoy yourself and rock my world."

"You know what I meant! Song requests."

"I love anything you play darling, just watching you play makes me happy. If you asked me what's gonna be 'our song' at the wedding? I don't know yet. So many songs have made memorable times even more special during the last two weeks. 'Faithfully' is the one for me right now but I don't wanna hijack Kim and Stef's song. Maybe I need to expand my musical knowledge to include anything written in the last twenty-five years." I laugh. "Especially stuff from these Era guys I keep hearing about."

"It's already 'Is this Love' for me." He sighs. "I couldn't believe it the day you sang to me. No one has ever done that. It made me fall even harder for you than I already had and I love the fact thatyou do not give a toss about my job or our music. I'm just Emmett to you, not the guitarist or the rock star. You have no real interest in money at all do you?"

"I will sing to you whenever you ask my darling man. Singing is good for the soul, Dad always says. Maybe not knowing anything about each other helped us get to know one another better. Would you have been so keen if you'd heard Rick's stories before we met? Money has always just been a means to an end for me. If I want something I work to get the money to buy it. I love exotic cars and fast bikes but I've always been happy just to see them and never dreamed of owning them and sure as hell don't feel jealousy for anyone that's worked hard enough to own something special. The Duchess is my only real possession. Dad also always made it clear to us that memories are the only things you can take with you wherever you plan to end up; whether it's Nirvana or the Pearly Gates or the depths of Hades."

"Your Dad is a very wise and wonderful man." Emm smiles. "He's bought you up to be a wise and wonderful woman."

"Okay, enough soppy stuff now. We're missing some damn good racing here." I kiss him and turn around so that I can see the road clearly. The leaders are all pretty close, close enough for pit stops to make a huge difference. We listen to the radio to see who's are good and who loses valuable seconds and their current place. Something as simple as not hitting the pit lane limiter soon enough will give you a heavy time penalty. I never mind who wins, they're all heroes for taking part, but I do have a soft spot for Manxman Conor Cummins and not just because he sells the best coffee and bread pudding on the Island.

The more recent arrivals are extremely impressive though and everyone has had to up their game this year which is making for some nail-biting action. Good weather usually means records are broken and the weather is perfect again today. It's been a great week of racing with no major accidents which is always a huge blessing.

We get the ten pences out and have fun betting on times and lap winners and overall top three and top five. I win a bit but then Kim loses it all again making wild bets and getting over excited.

We yell and scream and cheer as they come howling by on the last lap and then the racing is all over and the TT course falls silent again until August when the Classic takes place.

I win a pound from everyone for naming the top five winners correctly. Joey wins fifty pence from everyone for naming the top three.

"Eh laa, that reminds me, the jar in the kitchen is too full to get any more cash in."

"Yeah, I noticed it was getting full up the other day. What shall we do with it?" I ask.

"We could give it Neenaw." He suggests.

"That's a brilliant idea, sunshine. We'll do that."

"She'll be over at ours later with Carole for the party." Dad tells us. "Joe can give it her then."

"Have you chosen something sexy to wear for tonight?" Kim asks as we're packing up the picnic stuff.

"I haven't even thought about it. I don't have any dress sense at all. I'm so glad Sarah suggested a super hero wedding, shopping for a bridal gown would have scared the crap out of me. What do you want me to wear later, Emm?" I ask.

"I'm not going there, darlin'. Last time I tried it you had a meltdown." He replies. "Wear whatever makes you happy."

"I'm being serious Emm. Everyone keeps asking what I'm wearing like it should be something special. My hooker dress is the only 'dressy' thing I have and it's a bit over the top for a beach party and I've got no shoes to go with it now and we probably ruined it having sex on the rocks."

"You in jeans, a white t-shirt and barefoot drives me wild every time baby. You're not you if you dress up. But if you do wear a skirt it means I can get at you much quicker and easier should any emergencies arise." He grins cheekily.

Kim giggles. "I actually bought you some gifts over with me but then thought you might think I was rude. And I certainly didn't need to buy your affection at all when I arrived, you welcomed me with open arms, literally. They're in the car, shall I send Stef to get them? They can be engagement presents. If you like them it'll solve your outfit dilemma."

Stef appears a few minutes later with several pretty bags and a big smile.

"You'll get used to her shopping habits, honey. She's not judging or implying anything; she just loves to buy gifts for everyone. If she sees something she thinks you'll like she has to get it." The bags contain two gorgeous little cotton miniskirts, a white one and a pale pink one and matching pink and white t-shirts. Some short lemon coloured, lacy cotton dungarees and some very sexy Daisy Duke denim shorts and a bikini top. There's also a pair of little diamante embellished sandals and some tiny diamond earrings with a delicate necklace with a 'D' hanging on it.

"Oh, Kim, they're all just perfect. Thank you so much. How did you choose so well without even seeing or meeting me?"

"The boys kept sending me pictures of you and telling me stories. I worked out you were tiny but couldn't tell properly because you were either in bike gear or baggy dungarees or Emm was always wrapped around you. He'd sent a picture of you from the back sitting on a rock talking to Stef and I went off that. I chose casual stuff because you sounded like such a tomboy. I'm really glad you like them. It was nice to shop for girly things for a change. I got you an 'E' to go on your chain too, just in case. Would you like it?"

"Yes please!" She gives it to Emmett and he hugs and kisses her and puts it onto my chain and the chain on me.

"I can get you a 'J' and an 'F' too, now that I know how important your family is to you." Kim adds, smiling.

I jump up and hug her tightly. "Thank you, thank you, thank you, Kim, you are an absolute angel. My dressing up crisis is almost averted but now I have too many choices."

"White t-shirt and pink skirt, please." Emm drools. "Or the other way around, I'm not fussy. Those shorts are not for public viewing until I learn to control myself, though."

CHAPTER 53

The cottage has been transformed. There are balloons, fairy lights and lanterns everywhere. A huge banner says, 'Congratulations Emm & Dil. Happy Engagement.' Dan's van is already here and they're setting up on the beach. Luke, the DJ is back too and waves excitedly when he sees us all arrive. Sal comes out to meet us, all smiles.

"Have you had a good day? Food is sorted and Jurgen is sending loads more over in a bit, barbecue is lit, firepit is full, music is setting up so I'll go and get showered and changed and pick Billy up. Go find Sarah for us."

I go onto the beach and don't need to look; she comes flying at me and dives into my arms.

"Auntie Dilly! We've made more green motorbike cakes and we got some chicken and some burgers and some sausages and some fruit and we made some sandwiches and put up the fairy lights and put some blankets down for everyone to sit on but we will be dancing not sitting most of the time so I left some dancing space. Does Joey remember the shark dance?"

"Wow! It all looks absolutely brilliant darling. I think Joey will remember the shark dance. You will have to teach it to Ella and Felix and Uncle Emmett though. But you need to go and get daddy now, Mom's waiting for you."

"Okay, I'll teach everyone when I get back. See you in a while." She hugs me and runs to find her mom. Emm and Felix are chatting with Dan and the band so I go to grab a coffee and a shower.

The cottage is full of food and drink and three beautiful bouquets of flowers. One is from Jurgen and the other from Stef, Kim and the boys and the third is from Dad, Joey, Felix, the dogs and Dutch and the donkeys and the chucks. The whole place smells heavenly. I sit down with my coffee and empty the rucksacks, washing empty containers and putting everything away. Dad comes out of the shower with a towel wrapped around his waist.

"Thank you for the lovely flowers. Want coffee?" I ask and he nods and sits down at the table with me.

"My little Dilly girl is finally engaged to be married." He sighs contentedly. "I'm not going to ask if you're happy because I know you are. It's been a long time coming but you've finally got the life you deserve and I wish you everything that you wish for yourself and more, my precious child. Mama and Marley and Jimbob will be here in spirit tonight and will want you to have the best night of your life. You've got an exciting journey ahead of you. No more looking back now, Dilly Girl; there's no need." He finishes his drink, hugs me tightly and goes to get dressed.

I go to get a shower and steal Emm or Felix's razor to shave my legs so that I don't look like a cactus in my new skirt. Emm wanders in, drops his clean clothes on the floor and gets into the shower with me.

"Don't touch me Delilah, I'm saving myself for later." He demands playfully when I start to soap his back.

"You are kidding aren't you?" I plead." You just got in the shower with me."

"Nope, it's killing me but I'm totally saving myself for later. Is that my razor you're shaving with?"

"Might be...You going to resist even if I put on my cute new Daisy Dukes?" I tease. "And leave the top button undone..."

"Yep." He sticks his fingers in his ears, closes his eyes and sings loudly so he can't hear my teasing." I kneel down and start to kiss downwards from his hips.

"Stop it now you imp!" He hauls me to my feet, opens the shower door and throws me out. "Go and get dressed you little demon. We have guests arriving." He giggles. "And don't use my bloody razor to shave your legs."

"What's yours is mine, honey!"

I open my underwear drawer and find a bag similar to Kim's earlier gift bags. It contains some extremely sexy lingerie and few pairs of lovely, lacy knickers. I select the pair that covers the most. My skirt fits perfectly but is a little shorter than I would usually wear and the t-shirt is very fitted compared with my normal baggy ones but both are soft and comfortable. I put on some make up and wrestle my locks up into a high ponytail, put in my sparkly little earrings and put on my sparkly, flat sandals. I look very grown up. This is it Delilah. Are you ready to be a responsible adult and a significant other? Hell yeah! Bring it on.

Emm, fresh from the shower, smelling and looking as sexy as hell, opens the door as I am about to walk outside. He whistles in appreciation, herding me back inside, holding me at arm's length and drinking me in with hungry eyes.

"Delilah, you look beautiful, darlin'. You are too hot for words. Did you find your present?" I lift my skirt to tease him. "Stop it, I need you to be serious for two minutes." He groans. "I will ask one more time and then never again. Are you absolutely sure you want to marry me?"

"Emmett, I've never been more sure of anything in my entire life." I reply honestly.

"Come on, let's go and make some music before I lose control. I can't promise I'll be able to last all evening without a taste of you."

"I'm counting on it." I laugh. "It's your daft rule, not mine. I'm feeling very grown up and very sexy and am a very desperate woman right now." He pulls me close and presses his body against mine, his hand easily finds its way up under my skirt and he kisses me with real passion. My head swims and my whole-body tingles and Sarah flings the door wide open.

"Auntie Dilly! Uncle Emmett! I'm back!" She dives on us. Emm lets me go immediately and runs interference while I sort myself out. "Come and see all the food we bought. Nanny Pat and Granddad Will are here. They've got a card for you." She grabs our hands and leads us outside. Then sees Nathan and Connor and runs off to talk to them.

So many people are here already. They hug and kiss and congratulate us. The last of our campers are here and several ask if they can book again for next year. The photographers hand us a gorgeous, framed photo of Emm and I, almost in silhouette, walking hand in hand on our beach at sunset. The dogs are all around us and Dutch is sitting on my shoulder.

"Oh wow! It's perfect. Look Emm. Thank you so much! Thanks for all of your brilliant photos this fortnight. I've deliberately saved the last ones to look at when everyone is gone to stop me getting sad when TT is over."

"Are you going to be taking campers for the Manx GP?" They ask. "If so, can we book? We've made a fortune on our photos this year. We sold as many wildlife ones we've taken on the beach, as racing ones this time. Please don't think we'll sell or share any of people, we don't ever do that."

"I haven't even thought as far ahead as next week yet." I reply. "I think we'll open up for Manx but I'll email and let you know as soon as we've all had chance to sit down and make some plans."

"We have had the best time ever. We were all saying earlier on the site, we don't know whether we should recommend the place to everyone or keep it secret."

"Let's keep it secret, shall we?" I smile. "We prefer it that way."

Nathan grabs me next, picking me up and swinging me around. "Congratulations, Auntie Dil! I know you're going to be really happy. I love you so much. Enjoy your party!" Connor hugs us both too and they go off hand in hand to chat to Luke, the DJ.

Ella arrives in the car with her parents, looking lovely. She's wearing a pretty little dress and has her hair and make-up done. Joey runs over to welcome them. I drag Emm over to say hello.

"This is me Ma, Dil and, according to rumours, me Da, Emmett." Joey laughs. "This is Ken and June, Ella's folks."

"Hi, lovely to meet you. Ella never stops talking about you all." Ken smiles, shaking hands with Emm. "Joey is a real credit to you both, a proper gentleman. Ella has never been so contented and settled. Congratulations on your engagement." They hand us a bottle of fizz and a card.

"Thank you so much. Ella is an absolute angel too. We've all fallen in love with her." Emmett tells them. "Sorry she landed up in the news the other day. It's a bit of an occupational hazard, I'm afraid."

"Don't worry about it." June says. "Her Grandma was so excited about that; she woke us all up before six in the morning. The pictures were lovely, you all looked really happy."

Felix comes wandering over. "Hi, Bella Ella, looking good!" He hugs and kisses her.

"This is me big bro, Felix." Joe introduces everyone.

"Hey, great to meet you, Ella is a dream. She's keeping Joe on his toes. Can I just steal Dad for two minutes? Dil, you look and smell divine." He adds with a hug. They go off to sort music and Joey takes Ella and her parents to get a drink and some food.

Mr. Jeavons arrives with a couple of his old mates on their bikes. "She rides like a dream now." He smiles at his Norton as he climbs off and introduces me to his two companions. One is on a 1970 T120 Triumph and I tell them about Dad's earlier story of my attempt to steal his when I was three. Dad appears and takes them all off into the workshop.

Nina and Carole arrive next, Nina with just one walking stick already. Joey runs to them, hugs Nina gently and picks Carole up off her feet.

"Good Heavens, Joey! What have they been feeding you? You've grown a foot in height and width wise since I last saw you. Delilah, he looks like a man! He's really filled out."

"He is a man." I laugh. "How are you both?"

"Really good. Nina is getting around fine, she's been into the kennels the last few days, haven't you?"

"Yes, I'm doing well. I can't wait to see your new arrival." Joey takes them over to meet Wonky.

Andrew arrives with another young man, both looking casually smart. "Hello Dil, Congratulations, I've been offered so many jobs since I got your story, thank you." He hands over a card and a huge giftbag.

"You've got an exclusive on the party too, as long as you let us read it first." I shrug.

"Oh my god! Really? I promise it will be all good and respectful."

"Some of my friends can get a little out of hand. I don't want to read about any of that, please, especially when one is the Chief of Police here." I laugh, knowing Jurgen will have his kit off soon and Sal and Billy will probably be having wild sex by the fire and Chaz will be rolling joints to share with Rick and Dad.

"I take it The Parkers are here." He grins. "I promise you can read it and change anything you're not happy about. Sorry, I got carried away, this is my partner, John." We hug and John thanks us for giving Andrew our story.

Next to greet us is Ian, the vet and a lovely, smiley little lady who is busy admiring the dogs and giving Jeff loads of fuss and kisses.

"This is Vicky, she's just joined us to help manage the practice for me." Ian tells us. "She couldn't wait to meet your pets...er family."

Vicky gives me a hug. "Tell me who is who. They are all gorgeous. Ian already warned me that they're working dogs but I really want to cuddle them all." She reaches to touch Thor but he backs away and curls a lip in warning. "Oh my, they are impressive." She laughs.

"You've just met Jeff." I smile, gesturing to the big dope that is now following Dad. This is Thor, that's Odin and Loki. They won't hurt you but they won't let you near them when they're working. Dutch is about somewhere and Ian can show you the donkeys but watch out for Giles." I can tell that she is desperate to fuss Thor who is eyeing her suspiciously. "Stand down, Thor." I say quietly and he turns back to stupid and she hugs and kisses him happily.

Emm comes over and shakes his head at me in mock frustration. "What's the point of having guard dogs if you keep deactivating them, Delilah?" He laughs. "Stand, Thor." And the playful mutt is gone again.

"This is the scariest one of the lot, Emmett." I introduce him to Vicky and they shake hands.

"Is it true you have some horses flying over too? I've seen the paperwork in the office." She is a woman after my own heart, more interested in four legs than two.

"They should be arriving a week on Monday." Emmett tells her. "Ian will have to come over so you're welcome to come and meet them."

"She's a doll ... Who invited him?" Emmett giggles as they walk away. "Get me beer, woman. I'm going to play with Dan's toys." He smacks my bum playfully and heads back on to the beach.

I finally make it into the cottage and find Kim and Sal chatting away. They both approve of my look and Sal hands me a couple of bottles of beer.

"Everything's under control in here, go enjoy yourself." She orders. I hug Pat and Will on the way out.

Stef, Jurgen and Hans arrive on the Panigale and Joey's promised MV and Hans' wonderful RSV4 and park them by the workshop.

"Happy Engagement, Liebling." Jurgen says, pointing to the bikes then disappears into the workshop with Hans, after Dad. Stef walks over to the band with me. He looks over at Emmett laughing with Felix and Dan, messing with a guitar.

"Delilah, honey you have turned my oldest and best, but usually stressed and miserable, friend into a very happy, relaxed and contented man. Thank you. I know you will both be extremely happy together." He hugs me and kisses my cheek. "And you look divine, by the way." I hand Emmett a bottle and he puts an arm around me so I can't wander off again.

"Stay here for five minutes darlin'. I'm missing you." They continue chatting about running orders while the DJ plays some good music. Emmett is listening to the songs and playing the chords absently on the base of my spine as he talks with Dan. It's sending me wild. I try to hold his hand to stop him and he realises what he's doing, grins at me, and does it more. I bite his ear gently and kiss his neck to distract him. "Give me five minutes gents, my fiancée needs some attention." He laughs, picking me up so that I wrap myself around him.

He carries me down to our rock and sits down with me in his lap. "Hello, my sexy girl. Are you getting squirmy already?" He teases, running his hand up my bare thigh. "The party is only just getting started, you've got hours to wait yet."

"Can I divorce you on the grounds of sex deprivation before we're married?" I groan. "I have a lot of years to make up for."

"Nope, and really we shouldn't even be having any sex at all until after we're married." He teases more, his hand getting higher up my thighs. "In fact I might do that."

"Emmett Wright you are a cruel and heartless man. Remind me again why I love you?" I laugh. His fingers reach their intended destination and with the lightest of touches my insides do somersaults and I lose my head and turn into a shuddering heap.

He whispers into my hair. "You love me because I have magic fingers, Delilah."

"Oh my god, I do don't I?" I smile. Loki and Odin come pounding down the beach.

"Can you survive another half hour without giving off your weird sexy vibes that are enough to goad any man into pleasuring you?"

I sigh a contented sigh. "Maybe twenty minutes if you're lucky." I tease as Loki stands about two inches from my face and Odin does the same to Emm. "I think the dogs are trying to get our attention." I giggle.

"Yeah, I reckon Felix has sent them to fetch us." He stands up and holds his hand out to me. "Come on we're missing our party."

"Go and play with the boys, baby. I'll go and find more beer." I say, kissing him and moving away once we get close to everyone.

"I will come and find you if you're not back in ten minutes." He promises.

Sarah is leading half the guests in a full-on rendition of 'Oops upside your head' with everyone sitting on the beach, waving their arms around. Rick is at the front of one line and grabs me as I pass, picking me up and plonking me down between his legs and holding my wrists, moving me in time to the actions.

"Does this bring back memories?" He laughs. "It's been a few years since I heard this one."

I can't stop giggling; I can't remember the moves and keep going back as Ricky comes forward and nutting him in the chest. Sarah is not impressed so I relax and lean into Rick and just let my body go with his. Then she gets us doing the Cha Cha Slide, The Floss to Katy Perry's Switch, makes us Whip/Nae Nae to Watch Me, then do all the actions to The Shark Song finishing us off with the Time Warp. I have no breath left from jigging around, singing and giggling by the time we're done and drop onto Ricky in a heap on the beach. Sarah jumps on top of us.

"That was good. Let's do it again!" She squeals.

Ricky puts his arms around both of us. "I think I need a beer first, bab." He laughs, kissing Sarah on the head. "Go and tell him he forgot YMCA."

"Oh yeah!" She runs over to Luke.

"How you doin, Shortarse? Looking a bit too sexy in your big girl outfit." He says to me. "Are you finally ready to settle down at last?"

"Yep, I am. Ricky baby, thank you for always being here for me, for saving me from myself a million times and for sharing so many good times and making the bad ones bearable. I love you so much." I kiss him, carefully, trying not to give him the wrong idea.

He holds my upper arms and easily lifts me up off him. "Give me a fuckin' break, Delilah, please! There's only so much I can take. Do you want a beer?" He stalks off to the cottage.

Great, why do I have to fuck things up all the time? Billy is manning the barbecue so I go over for a cuddle and a burger.

"Yow screwin' with our kid again?" He asks throwing his arm around me.

"Yeah, but I didn't mean to. I was just saying thanks for being so great, he called me Delilah so I must have really pissed him off."

"Bab, rollin' 'round in 'is arms for 'alf 'our then lying on top of 'im and kissing 'im isn't sayin' thanks, it's bein' a full on fuckin' prick tease. Give 'im a break!" He sighs, kissing my head. "You ain't got this sex stuff under control yet. Stick with your Dave until you've got it sorted. 'E'll look after ya."

"Okay." I agree. "Tell him I'm really sorry." He gives me two burgers and I pick up two beers and go to find Emm.

"Thanks darlin'. Did you have a good dance? What's wrong?"

"Billy told me off." I shrug. "Said I've gotta stay with you and behave."

"Can you stay with me and misbehave?" He asks.

"I don't see why not." I reply, kissing him and climbing into his lap.

We eat our burgers and Stefan makes a lovely speech wishing us a long and love filled life together and thanking everyone for coming to celebrate with us. We get a huge round of cheers and applause and the guys, minus Emm, play a medley of cheesy but brilliant, songs, ending with 'Everybody Needs Somebody' in full Blues Brothers style. We clap and whistle and cheer.

"Okay, let's get down to some serious playing!" Stef laughs. "Hand him over Delilah, we need him for a while." Emm kisses me passionately, tells me to behave and picks up his guitar and they start as they mean to go on with 'Seven Nation Army'.

Ricky holds out a bottle to me. "Peace offering." He shrugs. "Sorry, Short-arse. This is harder than I thought but it's not your fault."

I take the bottle, desperate to hug him but careful not to. "Rick, darling. I am so sorry. Bill just gave me a right bollocking. I'm so used to holding and kissing you I don't think. I can't live without you, baby, but I'll try to tone it down a bit."

"Like you keep saying, I'm a masochist bab, I can take it and I'll keep coming back for more." He smiles a sad smile, hugging me tightly. "It's great to see you so happy."

"Emm is a good man but I'll always need my family." I tell him, honestly. "Just talk to me if I'm getting too full on but please don't ever leave me."

Chaz saunters in and I dive on him like a spider monkey, he is totally immune to my charms. He hugs and kisses me and dances to the music, with me on his hip like a child. Sarah comes running to join us and he puts her on the other hip and continues to dance. "Hello, my two favourite ladies in the whole world. Are we having fun?"

"Yeah, I've been teaching everyone lots of good dances and Auntie Dilly and Uncle Ricky had a fight and Daddy told her off but they're all better now." She doesn't miss a thing this kid.

"Is he still suffering?" He asks me.

"Yep, and I keep trying to make it better and just make it worse." I sigh. "Hormones are a little out of control right now, on both sides I think."

"You'll get through it. You know he'll go to hell and back for you."

"I just wish he didn't have to. I don't know how to fix it."

"Stop trying. Enjoy your party. He loves seeing you happy as much as he hates it. Your man seriously knows what to do with a guitar!" He exclaims watching Emm play. Emm nods a greeting at Chaz and smiles fondly at me and Sarah in his arms. Dad joins us and chats for a while catching up with Chaz. "I need to meet the latest editions to the family. I hear your youngest is going to be taking after you both."

I laugh. "Joey is going to be a racer without a doubt. My other beautiful boy is the bass player there, Felix." Fe sees us and his eyes widen in recognition, he waves eagerly and mouths 'hello Chaz'.

I send Odin to get Joe and he appears in a rush.

"What's up Ma? Dog said ya want me. It's like bein' in a Lassie film." He laughs. Sarah holds her arms out to him and he takes her and kisses her head without thinking. "Hey little sis, 'avin' fun?"

"I wanted to introduce my handsome Son to Chaz." He suddenly notices a big bear is holding me.

"Eh laa, great to meet ya. I've 'eard loads about ya." He shakes his hand enthusiastically, without loosing Sarah.

"Likewise, son. Everyone keeps telling me you're a tamer version of your new mam with the patience of your granddad so you're gonna be a good 'un."

Joey kisses my head proudly. "Tryin' to be."

"He's got a lot more sense than I'll ever have." I smile. Emm gestures that he wants another bottle. I leave Chaz, Joe and Dad chatting and jump down to get some drinks. Sal is standing by the barbecue cuddling with Billy and Kim is busy sketching everyone. She's bought her own pad today.

I grab half a dozen bottles out of the fridge and as I close the door I feel a familiar hand on my bum.

"Have you missed me, baby?" Emm drawls, taking the bottles and putting them gently on the table. "I have a feeling we've been here before." I dive into his arms and we reenact the last meeting here. Things get very heated and we move into Felix's room for a bit more privacy. He leans me against the door. "Jeez, Delilah. Just watching you dancing, having fun and even talking is sending me crazy. You are irresistible."

"Have you forgotten you were saving yourself for later?"

"Nope, it was a stupid idea, I can't concentrate and you're frustrating the hell out of Ricky, so I changed my mind." He shrugs.

"Do you want to know how much I want you right now?"

"Yeah, show me." He growls. I undo his jeans and drop to my knees. "Oh no you don't! I have got to play again in five minutes." He lifts me up and holds me against the door gently guiding himself inside me and moving in perfect rhythm until I lose my mind. "You are the most amazing woman in the universe. Come and sing with us."

"Good god no! Emm. There's about a hundred people out there. Stef and Dan's guys are doing a superb job already."

"Come on try it, it'll give you a buzz." He pleads. "It's nearly as good as sex." He laughs.

"I'll stick with the sex thanks." I grin as we hear a large furry head banging on the door to get our attention. "Your audience awaits." He kisses me hard and does up his jeans. Grabbing my hand and our bottles, we head back outside.

"Have you had your fix, bro?" Stef asks over the mic. "Is Dil up for a few tunes? How about a duet?"

"Nope, not a chance." I yell. Two minutes later I've got a mic in my hand. We muck about singing Sonny and Cher stuff and 'I was made for loving you' The Kiss song we were singing in the garden. Then I get a bit braver and go for Leather and Lace, the old Stevie Nicks/ Don Henley duet and then make Emm cry singing 'Is this love?' to him again. Then we both end up crying, by singing 'Open Arms' to each other. I hand the mic back to Dan. "You show them how to do it properly, honey."

"Wow, that was impressive, Dil. Do you wanna job?" Dan says over the mic.

"I'm okay thanks, I'm going to be a kept woman, I've managed to bag myself a bloke with a few quid." I yell back and everyone laughs and claps.

"What about Dylan?" Stef asks.

"I'll save it for the wedding, which will probably be next week, knowing these two." Dad shouts back to much more laughter and agreement.

"Okay it's request time. Who wants what? Make it good guitar stuff else Emmett's gonna wander off again." Dan announces with a grin.

"Sweet Child o' Mine, for our Sarah." Sal requests, then Grandad Will is taking her home to bed.

They play it followed by 'My Sarah' the Thin Lizzy song and Hall and Oates' 'Sara Smile'. Then Emmett gives me a big grin and starts playing 'Enter Sandman'. A very sleepy Sarah basks in the adoration, gives everyone hugs and kisses goodnight and is carried by her Uncle Chaz to the car and off to Never Never Land.

"More Chili's, Fe." I yell to Felix and we get a medley of mine and Felix's favourites.

"Sweet Home Alabama." Chaz requests and I dance with him.

"How about some Hendrix?" Billy yells and Emmett's playing sends shivers down my spine.

"Okay, the kids are moaning about playing old stuff now." Stef laughs so

they can play their own for a bit, I need a drink and Emm needs a fix."
Him and Emmett come over and the kids begin to play some 21 Pilots
with Connor taking over the mic.

Emm throws himself down and wraps himself around me. "You're quite a
performer. Tell me you enjoyed it"

"Not half as much as watching you play Hendrix." I drool. "But it was fun."

"You have got a really good voice, Dil and you work the stage or the beach
in this case." Stef adds with a smile. "You wanna do some more?"

"I think I'll leave it to you guys. Thanks for letting me have a go but I'll
stick to singing in the shower and when I'm doing the housework." I tell
him.

"It'll get you in the end, you'll find it harder and harder to resist." Stef
laughs. "Where's Kim? Ah, she's there, I'll see you in a bit."

"Talking of things getting harder and harder... " Emm grins, pressing
himself up against me. "Shall we stroll on the beach?"

"I don't think sex on the beach is a good idea with so many people about,
honey."

"Where's your sense of adventure gone, darlin'? Are you getting sensible
now you're settling down?" He teases.

I laugh. "Oh my god, I might be. How did that happen?" He takes my hand
and we walk down to the sea. I take off my sandals and paddle in the cold
water. Grounding myself.

"I like being engaged. When are we getting married?" He asks, kissing my
engagement ring.

"I'm just waiting for Sal and Sarah to tell me." I reply. "Who knows? Could
be tomorrow? I think Sal is looking to order the tightest, sexiest Batgirl
costume she can find."

"Can't come soon enough." He sighs.

"Are we still talking about the wedding?" I tease, raising an eyebrow.

"Stop it, you torment. I'd just got myself back under control. Come here
and let me do bad things to your beautiful body." I run to him and put my
arms around his waist.

I laugh." That should be our song. 'Bad Things' from True Blood."

"I can't even remember how it goes." Emm says.

I sing the first verse to him quietly. " ....But before the night is through.....I
wanna do bad things with you...."

He smiles and sings the second verse back to me.

"That's it. The programme was full of sexy vampires. Proper soft porn. I
loved their accents." I recall. "Now we're officially engaged, can I ride your

Arch?" I ask with a cheeky grin.

"Are you going to blow it up?" Emm replies patiently.

"Well this is progress." I tease. "How about I solemnly promise I will try not to?"

"That's good enough for me, my little imp." He smiles, kissing my head. "We need to get it over here for the wedding, Batgirl riding my Arch will really make me wanna do bad things."

"Talking of doing bad things, have you bought me all the way down here under false pretenses?" I arch an eyebrow. "The dogs will be rounding us up any minute and you're a wanted man." He slips his hand under my skirt and my body melts to his touch. "Baby, I don't know about you needing a fix, you are turning me into an addict. I can't get enough of you. An hour without you touching me and I'm rattling." I sigh.

"I am going to be here to fulfil your every need to the end of our days, my future wife." He tells me, kissing me hard and sending my head and body into another dimension.

"I really, really, love you!" I tell him.

CHAPTER 54

T he band are playing some Imagine Dragons and the kids are all dancing or listening. Turns out I actually do know a bit of more modern music than I realised due to always having the radio on. They notice me dancing and play 'Hey There Delilah' by the Plain White Ts. I laugh and wave to them. The firepit and lanterns are lit, and fairy lights are twinkling everywhere. Stef and Kim are smooching on the blankets. Ella and Joe are dancing, Ella's folks are chatting with Jurgen.

Dad and Carole and Jeff are looking very cosy, is Carole his mystery lady? Nina is in deep conversation with Mr. Jeavons and his mates, with Dutch sitting close by. Our campers are chatting and drinking and dancing. The Parkers are laughing and messing about together round the barbecue, getting wasted. The Macs are all here with girlfriends and wives, drinking and teasing each other.

"Congratulations Delilah and Emmett! Paddy Mac jumps up and embraces us both in a big hug. How'd you like your 'love shack?' We'll get some plumbing to it so you can have a bathroom and make a start on your stables on Monday, then get your mezzanine done."

"Paddy, you're heaven sent." I smile. "Do you think stables will be ready a week on Monday?"

"They will be done way before then." He laughs. "Are you expecting visitors?"

"Emmett and Felix's horses are coming to live with us. Four stallions by all accounts. Oh, I forgot, Meave has horses, doesn't she?"

"Meave, did you hear that?" Paddy shouts his wife. "Four fully equipped boys are on the way over."

Meave squeals with excitement. "New blood on the Island. Are you planning to breed?"

Emmett starts a very animated conversation about breeding and Arabs and Spanish Purebreds, Friesians, American Quarters and dams and sires. It all goes way over my head but Meave is hanging onto his every word. I leave them to talk and discuss the week's racing with Juan and Paddy Jr. then head inside to grab us some food. Stef has had the same idea and is piling food onto plates for himself and Kim.

"Come and see Kim's drawings. She's done some lovely ones of you singing with us."

"I'll grab some more bottles to put in the fridge and then I'll be out." I go to the back door to get beer from the boxes and Odin, who obviously drew the short straw and has been allotted to watch me, goes into full alert and snarly mode. I look out the back and see a shadow moving about by the chucks pen. Emm and Joey come running in with the other dogs, they seem to have some kind of telepathic link, Emm sends them off to get whatever is lurking out there. Billy, Chaz and Ricky come around the side of the cottage.

"What's going on?" Chaz demands.

"Not sure yet. Dogs heard something. They've gone to see what they can find. It's probably just some journo trying to get pictures." Emmett tells him, then runs his hand through his hair in exasperation as the dogs proudly present their findings. "Oh fucking great! It's my stalker! Delilah be careful, please. Chaz, I have an injunction against this woman, she's mentally ill and totally obsessed with me. She was armed with a knife last time she was arrested. I was assured she was still safely locked up in a mental health facility only a few days ago."

As she gets closer I notice she is completely focussed on me and looks very 'Miss Havisham'. She's wearing a long white dress and is a bit dishevelled from hiding in the bushes and being dragged around by the dogs, she's wild eyed and wearing just one shoe. Chaz is on the phone to somewhere asking for the men in white coats. Emmett moves to stand in front of me. Rick laughs.

"Emmett, mate. She's the most dangerous out of all of us. Just let her loose and your stalker problem will be solved." Emm sighs, smiles and relaxes a little. The dogs stop her a few feet from us and move into a protective line between her and us.

"Try and keep her talking, they'll be here to get her in a minute." Chaz says.

"What are you doing here, Rachel?" Emmett asks. "You're not well, you should still be in the hospital."

She replies to Emm but continues to stare at me.

"I saw the news, I had to warn you, she is a witch. She has bewitched you and will enchant you and then break your heart."

"She sounds pretty sane to me." Ricky deadpans.

"Look at me, Rachel. I am very happy to be bewitched. Isn't it my choice who I spend my life with?" Emmett asks trying to get her attention off me and not to laugh at Rick.

"But I will make you happier, weren't we always happy?" She whines. "You swore to be faithful to me in our every lifetime."

"Rachel, I have never had a relationship with you. We were never happy and we were never together. You know I have been married to someone else for a long time." This seems to upset her a little. She snarls which makes the dogs snarl back.

"In our last lives we were together always. We were happy." She insists, glaring at him. "She said you were never happy with her because you wanted to be with me. You divorced her to be with me."

"I divorced because I wanted to bring an unhappy and unhealthy part of my life to a close and begin a proper, loving and caring relationship with Delilah and give my Son the family he deserves. You were never in my plans. That man you loved wasn't me, Rachel. It never has been. We're not together in this life and we never will be."

She seems to calmly consider all of this, standing with her head on one side, like Jeff.

"If we cannot be together in this life, then we must be together in the next life." She sighs. I see the glint of the knife a millisecond before Thor does. She draws it slowly up her arms from wrist to elbow, opening up her own veins then launches herself at Emmett. Thor and I flatten her at the same time. Thor takes the knife out of her hand by biting her wrist and I hold her down to stop her from moving and when I can see she no longer has the weapon, throw her onto her front and put my knee in between her shoulder blades so that she can't get up.

"Get this straight right now, lady. Emmett is not yours and never will be and if you ever come anywhere near him or any of my family I will not be held responsible for my actions. And if I've got blood on my party outfit I will not be impressed." I snarl into her ear, looking down and noticing blood on my new skirt. "Okay, get this woman treated and out of here, now before I do her some real damage." I hand her on to Ricky and Bill.

The hospital guys are standing watching the show from the side of the cottage and run over to wrap up her arms and take her away. Chaz carefully puts the knife into a plastic bag for evidence and says he'll sort all the paperwork in the morning. I stand down Thor, check him over, grab a cloth to wipe all the blood off his face give him loads of fuss and praise them all.

Emmett is looking shell shocked. "Are you okay, Emm?" I ask, hugging him.

"Yeah.... did a crazy woman just try to kill me?"

"I would say that's a fair assessment, Dave." Billy laughs. "Why ya worried? She'll kill for yow and we'll kill for 'er. The crazy bird didn't 'ave a chance."

"Come on I think we all need a beer." I say, taking Emm's hand. "Have you got any good stuff Chaz? Emm might need it." I sit him down at the table and get us all a beer and Chaz rolls him a joint. "Smoke that honey, it'll help." I hand Joey a beer. "Thank you sweetheart."

"What for?" He laughs, folding me into a big hug and kissing my head.

"You did all the work."

"You were there, that means a lot."

"I'm gonna go see if Ella's okay." He says and leaves us to sort Emm.

"I'm gonna go and see to my missus." Billy laughs.

"Well you'll certainly have some stories to tell your grandkids." Ricky chuckles, shaking his head. "Give us that joint if you're not smoking it." Emmett is staring blankly into space. He takes a deep drag and hands it to Rick.

"You'll have to give statements tomorrow, if we get her done for attempted murder she'll go away for a very long time." Chaz tells him. "I'll call somebody to get the evidence and takes off whilst dialling.

"Emmett, honey are you okay? Do you want me to get Stef or Felix for you?" I ask, sponging down my skirt at the kitchen sink.

"No, I just need you." I sit in his lap and put my arms around him. "Why did you do that, Delilah? You could have been hurt. I can't bear to lose you."

"Emmett she had a knife, she was going to hurt you and I couldn't bear to lose you either, my darling man. I'm not going to stand by and let someone take away the best thing in my life, am I?"

"You really would kill for me, wouldn't you? Bill wasn't joking."

"For any of my family." I confirm.

Felix comes flying in. "Joey just told me. Are you both okay?"

"Your Dad's a bit spooked but he's not hurt. Thor saved him."

"Delilah, saved me." He corrects me. "The crazy bitch had a knife again and Dil still didn't hesitate. She's an amazing woman."

"Good job you're marrying her then." Fe says, hugging us both. "Come and play some more, it'll help you relax."

"Yeah, it will, come on baby." I coax, standing up and holding out my hand.

He gets to his feet and follows us outside. There's a bit of a buzz as the word of what's happened gets around. Emmett and Felix pick their guitars back up and Stef checks Emmett's okay and then runs over and checks me.

"Get him playing, Stef. He's a bit freaked, take his mind off it."

He hands me the mic and I start singing 'Bad Things'. It's in a really deep key and Stef sings with me to get the lower notes. It works an Emmett sings back giggling. I hand back the mic and they play some excellent stuff that gets everyone up and dancing.

Ricky holds me closely and we sway to the music. "You okay, Shortarse?

Didn't break a fingernail or anything?"

"I'm good, sweetie. Didn't even break a sweat. Pissed about getting blood on my new skirt though." I laugh. "Do you think Emm's okay? I'm a bit worried about him."

"If he needed proof of your love and loyalty he just got it in spades. He'll be alright, you'll look after him."

"Thanks Rick. Don't get mad with me but I need to tell you how stupid I am for not realising you had feelings for me. I've been so hell bent on destroying myself for so long, I was totally self-absorbed. Now I've discovered the sex stuff I know I put you through sheer hell. It was never my intention to hurt you and I am truly, truly sorry."

"Dil, it's my own fault. You could have lost control with me a hundred times but I always stopped you because, to be honest, I was scared you'd hate me for it and I'd lose my best friend. I'm glad you're happy now, I'll never let you go. I know you love me but I also know you're in love with him." We hold each other tightly until Chaz cuts in.

"Okay, little hellcat?"

"Yeah, Chaz. I'm fine. Do we need to go to the station in the morning?"

"'Fraid so. It'll go to court, whether she's crazy or not, that was attempted murder."

"He's got an injunction against her. She's supposed to be locked up already. I will kill her if she comes near us again."

"She won't, you won't see her again. You know we do it properly over here."

"Thanks, Chaz." I rest my head against his huge, solid body and relax into the music.

Dad comes over and holds me tightly. He doesn't say anything, just dances with me in his arms. When the song ends I go back inside for more beer, taking the dogs with me just in case. I take the bottles over for the band and Emmett blows me a kiss. I settle down on the blanket with Kim to watch them play. He looks more relaxed but he's lost in his thoughts, letting the music soothe him.

"He's okay, stop worrying." Kim says. "Two more songs and he'll be looking for you. They're playing their normal set. Stef is trying to give him something familiar to focus on. He's working through it all in his head." She smiles.

Two songs later, him and Stef join us on the blanket and the DJ retakes control of the music. Emm wraps me in his arms and holds me so tightly I can barely breathe. "Emm." I whimper. "You're crushing me."

He giggles and eases off a little. "Sorry, darlin'. I can't get you close enough."

"Want a head massage?" I offer.

He lays back on the blanket, taking me with him. "No thank you. I just want you close to me." Wrapping his whole body around me, how he does when we sleep. I close my eyes and relax into him.

We wake a little while later with a blanket over us and the dogs standing guard. The tempo of the music has dropped.

"Morning sleepy heads." Kim smiles, handing over a gorgeous sketch of us fast asleep.

"Oh, wow, Kim that's amazing. How long have we been asleep?"

"Only half an hour or so. You just needed to recharge after all the excitement. Go and have a walk on the beach and then come back and rejoin your fabulous party." We get up, stretch out and do as we've been told.

"Didn't I say we'd be making plenty of our own stories." I joke.

"You did, darlin', but that one wasn't quite what I was expecting." He sighs.

"Get used to it. I appear to attract trouble." I laugh. "You have to trust Chaz; she's sorted and gone now for a very long time. We have to go to the station in the morning and then it will be over."

Emm is still processing it all. "I've tried to help her. I paid for her to have medical help three times. I'd even done the psychology training on how to talk to her. They keep failing her. They promised she was safely locked away and didn't tell me she'd left the facility."

"She's got something going on up there if she can get herself all the way over here in a couple of days. Where did she get the money?" I question.

"I don't know, darlin'. I was wondering that too." Emm replies.

"Shall we just forget about it and let Chaz's boys do all the thinking." I offer my hand. "We'll follow Kim's orders and enjoy the rest of our engagement party."

"Delilah, you just saved my life. I'm not going to forget that."

"Oh, stop being so dramatic." I laugh. "She was aiming in totally the wrong place to kill you and was about to pass out from blood loss. Chaz would have just folded her in half if she'd got past me and Rick and Bill would have dismembered her if she'd got past him. You're totally irresistible to women, especially crazy ones. I'm sure I'll have to save you a dozen more times before we're too old to move."

"You are the most amazing, crazy woman I have ever met. Don't ever leave me, darlin'."

"You're stuck with me 'til the end of time, Mr. Wright. Are we going back to this party or what?"

"Kiss me first."

"Whatever you say, honey."

"Hello, Old Boy. Did you have a nice nap?" Felix laughs when we get back by the cottage. "Grab your guitar for a couple more before Dan and the guys have to get going. Any requests Delilah?"

"Behind Blue Eyes and Comfortably Numb, maybe?" I shrug.

"Yeah, nice choices."

They play both of my choices and then some real soppy ones for everyone to smooch to. Dad's dancing closely with Carole, Ella's mom and dad are smooching as are Joey and Ella. All the Macs are up and cuddling, Ian and Vicky are looking cosy, Andrew and John are wrapped together. Bill and Sal are practically, or probably already, having sex over by the fire pit. Chaz is dancing with Pat and Jurgen is swaying happily with Nina. I put my arms around Rick's waist. "Dance with me, honey?"

"If I must." He rolls his eyes in horror. We move easily together to some superbly played Nirvana and some classic Clapton finishing with "Wonderful Tonight'.

Dan rounds off the night. "Folks, another fabulous night at Blue's Beach must come to an end. I've got half an hour to get to work! We can't say it hasn't been eventful, not many engagement parties include a gatecrasher who wants to kill the future groom. We're hoping to be invited back for the wedding in a week or so and I'm sure everyone still standing will join us in wishing Delilah and Emmett the best life together." Everyone claps and cheers. "They want to say a huge thank you to Sal for making it all happen and everyone for their help, kind wishes and cards and gifts."

Emmett interrupts. "See you all soon for the wedding! Thanks Dan and the guys for keeping us supplied with instruments and letting us play support."

Dan bows as everyone claps and cheers again, then looks at his watch. "I'll come and get this lot later, gotta go." He runs off and jumps in his van.

We all start to clear away and people drift off. Emm and I hug all the Parkers they go off to their tents.

Ella's folks thank us for an excellent night and ask if we're okay with Ella staying.

"She's welcome to stay anytime." I assure them. Joey and Ella kiss us goodnight and see her parents off before heading to their bed.

The TT campers all go off to get a few hours kip before they have to pack up and get their boats. The band wrap everything up so it's ready to go into the van and they get off in their car, promising to collect it all later.

Luke the DJ is all packed and leaves after saying his goodbyes. Andrew promises to send us a copy of his story before tea time and thanks us again for letting him have the exclusive. We finally get showered and to our bed about half six in the morning. Someone has put a beautifully scented bouquet of flowers by our bed and sprinkled rose petals on the duvet and placed my sexy baby doll lingerie on the pillow. I put it on and give a very sleepy looking Emm a twirl.

"Jeez, I thought I was too tired to move, but apparently I'm not any more. My future wife is too darn sexy for words."

"Want some slow, sleepy, easy sex?" I tease. "Because I know I do."

He holds his arms open and I fall into them and we meld together, moving in perfect harmony until we are completely spent and both fall into a deep, dreamless sleep.

CHAPTER 55

S omeone lets the dogs in to wake us about ten and leaves us with two choices; get up or get flattened and licked to death.

I pull my Daisy Dukes and bikini top on, because I can't find any other clothes, and go to get breakfast. I get to the door and an arm pulls me back and orders the dogs outside.

"Do you think I'm letting you leave this room dressed like that?" Emmett asks with a raised eyebrow. "Not until I've had my wicked way with you, anyway."

"It better be a quickie, I need a wee, I'm starving and we've gotta be at the copshop in a bit."

"Trust me, darlin', in that outfit it will be." Emm growls.

We finally get to the kitchen and Carole is busy cooking breakfast for an assortment of bodies who must have camped last night.

"Fuckin' hell, Dave. I thought I was too hungover to get a 'ard on, what the fuck are yow wearin'?"

"Good morning to you too, Bill." I sigh, kissing him. "Blame Sal and Kim, they keep dressing me. Someone has hidden my old faithful dungarees."

Sal giggles. "The dogs ate them."

"Liar!" I hug her. "Thanks for a really special night, sweetie. You did us proud."

"You've got a mountain of cards and presents. I've piled them up on the hearth."

"Shall we save them for later?" I ask Emmett and he agrees, gratefully accepting breakfast from Carole and drawing me onto his lap. Dad hands me coffee. "I love you, Daddy." I smile.

Joey and Ella appear, Ella is wearing one of Joe's t shirts as a dress and looking really cute. "I forgot to bring some clothes to change into." She explains. "Mom's already text me, they had the time of their lives. What was Chaz and Ricky smoking? I'm pretty sure they were giving it to her and Dad."

"Damn good stuff. Your mam was a scream." Ricky tells her walking in. "Fuckin' hell Shortarse, stop wearing big girl clothes, these jeans are tight enough already."

"Blame your sister for feeding my dungarees to the dog." I reply.

"Carole, I apologise. My family are a bunch of heathens and filthy perverts with no social skills, apart from Joey, he's a gentleman."

"Them johnnies better, Son?" Ricky asks Joe with a smirk.

"Eh laa, they're fuckin' brilliant, ain't they Ell? I've still got some feelin' in me dick this mornin' them others were cuttin' me blood off."

"Ahh, I spoke to soon there, Carole. I apologise for my Son too." I laugh.

"I love your family, Delilah. They are all brilliant." She replies with a smile. "Seeing Joey so happy and relaxed is such a treat."

Chaz appears, fresh from the shower. "Sounds like too much fun going on in here. Fuckin' hell, bab. Don't you dare go up the station in that get up. All of me blokes and half the lasses will be sneaking off for a crafty wank."

"Dad...Pat...as patriarch and matriarch of this family you should take responsibility, why am I apologising to Carole?' I wail in jest.

"Discipline was Will's job." Pat laughs. "I just fed 'em and cleaned up after 'em."

"I blame your mother." Dad shrugs. Carole is giggling her head off.

"I give up!" I hold my hands up in surrender. "Joey, have you seen your new toy out the front?"

"Yeah, it's boss. Can I ride it to the fed shop?"

Emmett laughs. "Think about that for a second, Son. You're asking if you can ride an uninsured bike, you're not even legally allowed to ride on the road to a police station accompanied by the Chief of Police. What's the answer gonna be?"

Joey looks around at us all and we reply in unison. "Hell, yeah!"

Emmett looks at us all as if we're completely insane.

Chaz slaps him on the back. "No point being in charge if you can't be naughty now and again. Saddle up boys, let's get this shit done with. Get some fuckin' clothes on first, our Dil, you slapper." I grab my jeans out of the washing basket, peel off my shorts, and put them on. I put a t-shirt over my little top and I'm ready to roll.

I talk Joey through controls and gearing and not getting throttle happy and we ride in convoy down to Douglas via the mountain so that Joe can try out the MV. He is a totally natural rider and is stretching its legs within minutes. I know he can follow my lines safely so I let the Duchess loose. He stays on my tail without much effort. I'm not going warp speed but I am being consistent and not slowing for bends, seeing what he can do. He's good. We slow into Douglas and park up in the station car park.

"Eh laa, it's fuckin' boss! It's so easy to ride." He's full of adrenaline, all hyped up.

"Ya gonna be a fuckin' racer, Dave." Billy grins.

"He's smooth, Shortarse. Kept right on your lines." Rick adds.

"Yeah, we'll sort his race licence now TTs done." I smile.

Hans is waiting for us when we arrive. We go into the station and Chaz goes into grown up mode, ordering everyone about, getting statements all taken at once so we're not here all day. Joey comes in with me so that he knows what to expect and to wait for me to go in with him. The officer is lovely and gets the statement done quickly. He doesn't ask too many questions, just listens and records, then reads it all back to me verbatim.

"Do you want me to do Joey's now or do you want a break first?"

"Are you ready, Joe?" I ask. "Shall we get done then we can go and play?"

"Yeah."

The officer puts on the recorder and goes through the routine. "Please state your full name."

"Joseph Dylan Marley Blue." He looks at me and grins. I'm so proud I could burst.

"In your own time and your own words can you tell me exactly what happened yesterday evening?"

"We were avin' me Ma an' Emmett's engagement party and the dogs went off on one 'cos there was somat out the back. Emmett sent 'em to fetch it an' they bought a woman back. Uncle Chaz phoned somebody an' told Emmett to keep 'er talkin' an' she was ramblin' on about bein' with Emm in another life an' somat about Cherry tellin' 'er 'e wasn't happy with 'er cos 'e loved this Rachel woman. Anyhow she went mad, cut 'er arms with a big knife an' flew at Emmett. Thor, the dog, and me Ma decked 'er. Thor made 'er drop the knife an' me ma 'ad a word with 'er. Then they took 'er away an' we got on with the party."

"Can you clarify who Cherry is for the record please?"

"Cherry is Emmett's ex-wife, 'e's just got divorced. I s'pose she set the crazy woman loose." He shrugs.

Oh my God. He might have something there. I heard her mention 'her' and 'she' but didn't think about it.

"Ms. Blue, you look like you've just remembered something. Would you like to add it to your statement?"

"She didn't mention Cherry by name but referred to 'her' and 'she' and why Emm had divorced. Emm and I wondered how she had the funds to get here and the address but I never put the two things together." I admit. It's added to my statement and we're free to leave.

The others are waiting outside for us. Chaz hugs us all and says he's off to chase up some American coppers and find out who sprung Rachel.

I hold Emmett tightly. "I think our Joey may have just answered that one."

Chaz raises an eyebrow. "I'm just gonna look at all the statements, see if any of us heard different stuff. I'm gonna see this Rachel woman later."

"Ask her about Cherry. I wasn't listening carefully but she did seem to mention her as if they'd spoken."

"Yeah, I heard that, strangely Ms. Martinez wasn't home when they sent people over last night. Did they get all possible addresses from you, Emmett?"

"Yeah, Hans says he'll handle it all so they've got his details."

"Good man, see you all tonight for Jurgen's shagfest." He laughs and hugs us all. "Ride safe. Love you."

Ricky and Bill go off to start collecting all their kit in. Joey promises to go and help in a little while. We call Felix and Dad to let them know how it went and tell them we're having a ride for an hour or so. Dad's happy spending the day with Carole and seeing off the last of our campers. Felix says he'll meet us at Hillberry. We get there quite quickly and sit and wait on the bench.

"Chaz's fed shop was alright." Joey states. "Was they okay with you, Emm?"

"Yeah, Joe, they were really good. No waiting around or unnecessary questions. Hans is an absolute dream. He just kept saying that he'd take care of everything and writing himself little notes. If I hadn't met Delilah I might have thought about marrying Hans." He laughs.

"He is heaven sent." I smile remembering Joey proudly stating his newly registered name.

Fe comes down from the Creg like his arse is on fire and pulls in giggling. "I love this place and I love that bike." He proclaims. "You guys are all pretty neat too." He adds with a grin. "How's the bike little bro?"

"Eh laa, it's proper boss." Joey tells him. "Try it in a bit. Where we ridin' Mama Dil?"

"Over the South Burrule down the A36. I reckon. We'll go down to Port Erin then if you're feeling confident enough we'll go up the nadgery road to The Sound, okay?" Everyone agrees so I have a quick snog with Emm whilst Joey shows Fe round his bike, and then get my helmet on and lead the way.

The south of the Island is beautiful. There is a large plantation and loads of countryside walking, green laning and mountain biking areas. The hills and farmland seem wild and sweep down to the sea, it's isolated and desolate here in the winter time. You can see coast all around and dotted here and there are ruins of buildings from another time, towers and follies. The roads are flowing and empty and relatively safe so ideal for Joe to get a proper feel for his new steed.

The Duchess loves this undulating, rollercoaster road. I just relax and go with the flow, keeping Joey and Felix in my mirrors. I stop down at a layby at the bottom of the hill just to look at the views, breathe in the freshest air in the world and warn the boys the road is narrowing.

"Jeez, it's so peaceful here. Where are we?" Emm asks.

"Near Mr. Jeavons' farm." I point out the buildings.

"Is that all his? How's he manage it on his own?"

"No, half of it is another old derelict farm. It's the one Jimbob and I were dreaming of buying."

"Does it make you sad to see it?" Emm asks hugging me.

"Not anymore." I say, a little surprised. "Wistful, but not sad, it was another lifetime, Emm, maybe I'm living there in another dimension."

"Do you want us to buy it? We'd have room for everyone plus new additions there." He offers.

"Thank you, darling. I really appreciate the thought but no, it's not part of our life any more than your home with Cherry and the Macs have got enough to do at our place already."

"Talking of her, do you think she was behind yesterday's visit?"

"Emm, I really don't want to speculate. I didn't think it at all until Joey made his statement. Let Chaz and Hans sort it."

"Can we swap bikes for the next bit?" Felix asks.

"It's just skinny, busier villages for a bit. You'll have more fun if you swap on the way back but you can if you want. Who wants The Duchess?" I laugh. "We're going up that road off the back of Port Erin, Emm. I bought you and Stef down it, coming back from the Sound."

"That really steep, twisted one? Let Felix ride her." He laughs.

We stop down in Port Erin for a drink and a paddle then head over to The Sound. I warn the kids to keep their front wheels down and remember its two-way traffic and there's no room for two vehicles. The back road is incredibly steep, blind and tight. I lead and Emm brings up the rear. The kids struggle a bit with their gearing but both keep control, I'm impressed. There are a lot of interesting words coming from both of them all the way over the hill. It's a good job Sarah isn't here with her swear chart.

The Sound, devoid of all the TT visitors is emptier than it has been, making parking easy.

"Eh laa, that's a fuckin' scary road!" Joey exclaims. "I'd be better on me DT up there."

"I'm well impressed with both of you. It is a rough one." I smile.

"Aren't you impressed with me?" Emm pulls a daft sad face. "I did it too!"

I kiss him. "Extremely, darling. Being at the back is the hardest. Come on I'll treat you all to lunch." We pick a table outside and throw our jackets and helmets on it. I go and get menus and drinks with Felix.

The same girl that recognised Emm and Stef is serving she looks at Fe then does a double take. "You can't fool me this time." She says. "I've seen you all in the papers. Hello Felix. I'm a huge fan."

"Great, does that mean the drinks are free?" Felix sasses. I slap him round the head and pay for the drinks. We come out giggling and Emm asks what happened.

"Your Son is trying to use his charm, good looks and fame to get free shit." I sigh. "I smacked his head."

"He's about to be half yours so you need to take some of the blame." Emm tells me.

"The half with the smart mouth is definitely yours." I laugh.

Felix is telling Joey. "Jeez. She really whacked me one. She had to stand on her toes to do it. I never saw it coming."

"It's nice to 'ave a Ma that gives a toss 'bout what ya do, init?" Joe comments.

"Yeah, it's awesome." Felix laughs, rubbing his head. Everyone decides what they want to eat and I go to order it. The girly brings everything out to our table and smiles at Emmett but doesn't comment.

We chat about last night but only the fun stuff and the kids tease us for falling asleep. My phone pings and it's Andrew sending his story.

'As the very honoured, exclusive on scene reporter at the much anticipated Blue-Wright engagement party, words cannot describe the event. From the warmest of welcomes from the happy couple themselves. I have not witnessed a happier pair in a long while, to the amazing food, a very raunchy engagement cake and naturally, out of this world music with Era playing, of course, but with local Peel band 'Edge'. There's no starstruck behaviour with Stefan Fischer happily sharing vocals with James Cassidy and Emmett Wright letting Dan Evans show us what he can do on vocals and the guitar. Delilah joined them for a few songs proving without doubt that she is pretty darn good at everything. Local DJ Luke Kneen was also keeping the party flowing with floor filling dance tunes. The bride to be, her best mate, her cute goddaughter and numerous guests performed a very impressive and enthusiastic dance medley ending with the Time Warp. Luke said. "I love these guys they are so much fun and always so generous and welcoming."

There was a moment of drama when Emmett's well-known stalker Rachel Schwantz arrived without an invite. She was quickly dispatched and the party continued into the very late hours of this morning. I for one had an amazing night in a perfect setting with some seriously beautiful people, inside and out, and wish this very special couple a long and happy, adventure filled, life together.'

"He's never going to get a job with Private Eye but that is real sweet." Emm sighs. "I didn't see the cake, did you? I also didn't know the guy in the band is called James."

"Nope, on both counts. Didn't know the name of their band either." I shrug.

The kids giggle. "Wanna see a picture of the cake?"

"Yeah, I think I might." I say. Felix hands me his phone. The cake is a recreation of the fridge scene. A big fridge with figurines of me and Emm making out against it. My legs are wrapped around him and he's holding me up by my bum. There's even a dent in the fridge. "Oh man, why didn't I see that? it's amazing! He must have done that from that photo Stef took."

"It tasted fab." Felix tells us.

"Are we all happy with Andrew's story then?" I ask.

"Nah, let's do our own." Joey grins. "What 'appened first?"

"Okay, I'd just got dressed and was showing Emm my new underwear when Sarah burst through the door...."

"Loads of people I'd never seen before in my life squashed, kissed and mauled me." Emm adds. "And someone invited that vet guy..."

"Dad and Dil nearly broke the fridge again and went off for a quick a shag in my room...." Fe grins.

"Me girlfriend's ma got off her tits with me uncles..." Joey recalls.

"A mad woman turned up to kill us all..." I giggle.

"Me ma decked the crazy woman ..."

"I had a complete breakdown and the Chief of Police gave me some seriously good weed...which Rick stole..."

"Dad and Dil went off down the beach for anoher shag...." Fe sasses.

"Me Ma an' the band sang and played some good tunes..."

"Rick had a meltdown and Bill gave me a bollocking..."

"Dad and Dil had a little nap because they're old now..."

"Sal and Billy were having sex by the firepit..."

"Enough!" My sides are aching and my food is cold. "Eat your food and go help Rick and Bill. I'll tell Andrew his version is fine. I need to get back and straighten out our place. Oh, and be advised Jurgen's party will be very 'grown up' tonight. Not many clothes will be worn, there will be male and female escorts there and it will be an eye opener so let Ella know and be prepared. Just let me know if you're freaked and we'll leave."

"Jeez! Really?" Emmett exclaims.

"Have you seen Caligula?" I ask with a raised eyebrow. "Jurgen is completely debauched."

"Didn't Sal say Sarah was going?"

"Only for the ride out. They're ordered to behave until she leaves."

"Can we join in?" Felix asks. "I was just thinking about asking the waitress out, I'm that desperate. I haven't had sex for weeks and everyone else is getting more than their fair share. I don't think I can hang on 'til Tiff gets here."

I look at Emm, he shrugs. "That half is definitely yours."

"Thanks for your support, honey." I laugh. "You're a grown man, Fe. You can do whatever you want as long as your Dad's okay with it. The escorts are all high end, clean and police checked. Just wrap it to be safe, please. They'll have plenty there. Both of you, absolutely do not take anything unless Dad or the Parkers gives it to you. Stay close to us or them if you do take anything. Spliffs and coke only, if you must try something. Do not take any pills!"

"Will do and won't do, Mama Dil!" Felix salutes me. Joe copies him. I check Emmett is okay with me giving orders to Fe and he smiles and salutes too.

"You can do whatever you like, Emm. You're a big boy." I giggle.

I find a pen in my backpack and make them both sign a napkin saying 'thanks for lunch. Emmett and Felix Wright' and leave it on the table with a tip.

"Where are Bill and Rick?" I ask Joey. He texts them.

"Paddock then yard."

"Okay, are you coming back for your DT or can I trust you on the MV? We'll book your test on Monday. You'll walk it."

"I'll take it easy, promise."

"A5 to Douglas it is then." I put my helmet on and Joey and Felix swap bikes. I nod to Emm to see if he wants to try The Duchess. He thinks about it then shrugs in agreement and hands me the BM key. I throw my leg over and turn off all of the electronic gadgets. "It's like putting stabilisers on a downhill mountain bike" I sigh, shaking my head. "Wrong."

Emm takes a deep breath and fires up The Duchess. I lead the way, blowing kisses and shouting 'Fastyr mie' to the fairies as I go over the bridge. Joey does the same. We get to the paddock and drop off the boys. Rick and Billy are out the front collecting up all the barriers. They laugh at Emm as he dismounts and shakes his head in disbelief.

"Alright there, Dave? She's as wild as 'er ain't she?" He nods at me.

"I have never ridden anything like her in my life!" Emm whistles. "She is ... focussed."

"That's one way of putting it." Ricky grins. "She's fuckin' possessed. Did ya notice she growls at shit in 'er way?"

"Yeah. I did hear that a few times." He agrees.

"Well, you ain't dead, Dave. She must like ya." Bill slaps his back.

"I've bought you some back up crew." I tell them. "Don't work 'em too hard Felix wants to save his energy for tonight."

"You an' me both, son." Rick laughs in agreement. "We ain't had a Jurgen shagfest for too long."

"See you later kids. Are you taking the Duchess all the way?"

"Er, no. Give me my keys and turn all my stabilisers back on." He says.

"Wanna ride before we go back?" I tease. Nodding to the paddock. "The grandstand'll be empty."

"Nope, you can get home and put those shorts on so that I can be a perv and then take them straight back off you." He informs me, starting up his bike.

CHAPTER 56

We get back to an empty camping field and an empty cottage. It makes me feel a little sad. I look down the beach and see Dad, Carole and the dogs walking in the distance. I put on my shorts and take off my t shirt and stand in front of Emm with my hand on my hip.

"Shall we open our cards?" I tease.

"Get here, now." He groans. I jump onto his lap, astride and facing him, pull off his t-shirt and rub myself against his groin, tormenting him and kissing him lightly on his shoulders and down his chest, scratching his back gently with my nails.

"How far away is your Dad?"

I shrug. "He might be back in five minutes."

"You are such a risk taker!" He picks me up and strides outside to our space, shutting the door with his foot. "Come on then my little imp, do your worst. I'm all yours." He laughs, throwing me and then himself onto the bed. I undo his jeans and peel them off and start to massage his feet. Then I kiss him slowly all the way from his ankle to his groin, then up his hips and his ribs. "God, Dil. I surrender. Let me inside you now!"

"Nope, I'm taking control for a change. I'm going to make you feel how you make me feel. Hands off!" I hold his wrists together above his head. Then I kiss him hard, sucking on his bottom lip.

"Jeez, Delilah. Let me go I need to touch you."

"Nope. I'm busy." I giggle, teasing and torturing him until he's squirming like I always am and then I let him take control. He sits up and throws me across his knee, admires my shorts then smacks my bottom hard.

"Ouch, what's that for?" I groan.

"Lots of things." He tells me. "Wearing that outfit, being a tease, making me wait... the list is endless." He smacks me again and slips his fingers inside my shorts and sends me crazy. "What are you plans for tonight's party?"

"Oh, I might hook up with a male escort or two and then a female one or maybe both together, shag Rick and Hans, cavort naked in the Jacuzzi.... "

"Do you want another one?" He asks, showing me the flat of his hand.

"I'm going to stay with you, stupid, and keep an eye on the boys. Emm, I know I'm inexperienced and pretty frustrating at times, if you want to play with someone with a lot more game than me I won't be worried about it. Please don't think it would spoil our relationship. I'm pretty sure you'll have been to similar parties in your line of work."

"Delilah, you never cease to amaze me. You're telling me you're fine with me shagging prostitutes at a party your friends and your Dad will be attending?"

"Yeah, why not? They'll be knee deep in the hedonism, especially Dad. You could just get a blow job. You're too scared to let me do it yet, aren't you?"

He sighs. "No Dil, I'm not scared. I'm just delaying that pleasure until we have time and privacy to take it slow. You make me happy a million other ways right now."

"Ha, you're scared!" I laugh.

"You scare me every time, darlin'." He admits. "I'm scared I will lose control and hurt you. You're so tiny and you make me want to be so rough."

"I can handle rough, baby. I'm a lot tougher than I look. Anything goes tonight, I mean it. I might actually enjoy watching you have fun." I muse. "I could pick up a few tips."

"Jeez Dil, stop it!" He groans, removing my shorts and burying himself deep inside me.

I emerge from our room on a euphoric high, leaving Emmett to rest, and I start to clear away last night's debris. Bless Dad and Carole, they have already collected the washing up. I find all the empty bottles and cans and fill three black bags. I move the band's stuff to the front of the cottage so they don't have so far to carry it all. I shake out the blankets, refill the fire pit and go into the cottage to find it already neat and tidy, coffee on, washing up done and washing hanging on the line.

I admire and smell all of the beautiful bouquets and read the attached cards. I notice the gorgeous photo our campers gave us is already hanging on the wall. Then look at the huge pile of gifts and cards on the hearth and the chesterfield but save them to open with Emm. I pour a coffee and he appears in the doorway with a cheeky smile.

"I missed you, darlin'. Pour me one too, please. I need caffeine. You wear me out." I hand him mine and make another. He looks around at the immaculate cottage. "You have been busy."

"Not me." I admit. "It was spotless when I came in."

"That's so sweet. Shall we open all these gifts?" He asks. "Lord knows where we're gonna put everything."

"It'll mostly be drinkable or edible, I suspect." We open bottle after bottle of champagne. "Well we haven't got to buy any for the wedding now. Do you actually like the stuff?"

"I can drink it but it's not my first choice." He laughs, saluting me with his coffee mug. "Have we got anything left to eat? I'm starving." I go to the larder and find the remains of our engagement cake. The figures are still intact and look so good.

"Do you want to eat me or yourself?" I ask. Emm comes to see what I'm looking at.

"They're amazing! Cut us some of the fridge bit." We eat huge slices each then get back to the presents.

Sarah has made us some colourful friendship bracelets with tiny D and E initials on beads, which we lovingly tie on each other. Sal and Billy have bought us a large assortment of heavy-duty sex toys.

"Oh wow! Have they got instructions?" I ask picking one up and studying it. "I don't know what half of them are for."

"Don't worry I'll demonstrate later." Emm grins.

Rick has bought us a year's supply of coffee and 'Mr. Right' and 'Mrs. Always Right' mugs which makes us smile. I go and wash our others and refill the new ones. "There you go Mr. Wright."

The Macs have enclosed an IOU in their card. 'IOU one stable block. Will be there to deliver on Monday Love Paddy, Meave and the family xx'. We're speechless.

Chaz has got us his and hers wristwatches, engraved on the back with 'Emmett & Delilah, together forever and yesterday's date. Emm lets out a whistle.

"They are pretty special!" He takes his current watch off and puts his new one straight on, admiring it. "That man has superb taste. Fe will be crazy jealous when he sees it."

"He has very expensive taste. Should I be worried about losing it?"

"They won't have been cheap, honey." Emm confirms, putting mine on my wrist. "You probably don't wanna be wearing it when you're elbow deep in oil and grease."

Pat and Will have made us up a huge picnic hamper full of meats and cheeses and freshly baked pies and cakes and homemade jams, pickles, wines and cordials. "Now that's my kind of present!" I whoop, digging in, sharing a huge sausage roll with Emm. I empty the hamper into the fridge and larder to keep it all fresh.

"Who's this one off?" Emm waves a gift bag at me.

"Andrew, I think." He opens it and it's an intricately carved, wooden memories box complete with copies of all of the newspaper stories the photos he's used in the stories plus a few extra ones the kids must have given him to print out. "That is so special." I sniffle, wiping my eyes.

Nina and Carole have sent us a really cute little silver ornament of a leggy, wonky, baby donkey. I stand it on the hearth.

Kim's sketchbook is next. She's decorated the front with a big heart and 'Emmett and Delilah's Engagement Party' and the date. The drawings are exquisite with so much detail, she's captured everything and everyone. I sit wrapped in Emm's arms and we go through picture after picture of the night progressing; from us greeting the guests to Emm, relaxed and laughing with Felix and Dan, the band playing together, me, Sarah and Ricky doing the Time Warp, me and Emm singing, me and Stef singing, us down by the sea, us fast asleep, Dad and Carole and Jeff, Joey smooching with Ella... They are the most perfect gift. Tears are pouring down my cheeks as I kiss Emmett. "She is a truly amazing and talented lady." I tell him.

"There's more from them here too. She said she got bored at the airport waiting for their slot." He hands me more bags. They're full of clothes for us both. A few pairs of jeans, t shirts, soft cashmere sweaters, more lingerie, a bottle of Emm's aftershave, a subtle perfume for me, swimming costumes, silk shirts, bottles of Cognac and whisky, designer sunglasses.... "Jeez, I think she's emptied the duty-free shops." He laughs. Holding up a powder blue t shirt with 'I am the real Mrs. Wright' emblazoned across the front. "This is some of the cheesy merchandise they sell on tour. It's finally found its rightful wearer." He hands it over and I put it on. In the bottom of the bag, wrapped in tissue are the F and J she promised for my necklace. I show Emm and he undoes it and threads them on for me. "Last ones are for you from the boys."

"They already got us flowers." I say pointing to the huge bouquet. "They shouldn't waste their money on me."

Emmett laughs. "Dil, buying you gifts is not wasting money. Get used to it because I am going to buy you everything you ever wanted."

"You're too late, babe I've already got way more than that." I smile. The boys have bought me the necklace, earrings and bracelet that match my engagement ring. They are exquisite, so dainty and unique and made by a true craftsman.

I tidy away all the wrapping and packing and Emm cuts us more cake and pours more coffee. We start to open the cards. The dogs and Dutch come flying back in and give us loads of fuss. Dad and Carole arrive a few minutes later and I've already cut them cake and made them drinks.

"Thank you so much for all of your hard work. The place looks lovely and thank you for our little donkey he's gorgeous." I say hugging Carole.

"Delilah, it was my pleasure. I really miss having a house full. I hope you didn't mind me putting the washing on."

"Good grief, no." I laugh. "I'm getting really lazy around here, Emm is a bad influence. Did the campers all get off okay?"

Dad grins. "Eventually, I don't think they wanted to leave. We won't have to advertise next year. They just need to fetch the showers and we'll be back to normal. Have you opened your cards? Love the mugs, were they off Rick?"

"Who else would it be? Nope, we were about to start on the cards." I show them all of our fabulous presents. We open the cards one at a time taking turns to read them out. I recognise Dad's writing on an envelope and inside is a card with an idyllic beach scene, some paperwork falls out when I open it and I read it carefully. "Dad, you can't do this." I whisper.

"Can and have." He shrugs. "Hans is a handy man to know. It makes real good financial sense and there's no duties to pay when I eventually pop my clogs. I can't do that for at least seven years else it's null and void so stop worrying before you start." I hug him so tightly he taps out. He's given me the deeds to the cottage and they are all in my name. "There's green laners in the workshop for you all too."

"Dad you are the best, thank you." I am still in shock.

"Right, I better get Carole home if we're off to Jurgen's in a bit he says, rubbing his hands in excitement. Have we got a lid that'll fit her? She wants to try the bike." I hand her mine but it's too small. I get Joe's old one from the passage way. It fits fine and so does his jacket. I hug her and thank her again. Emm does the same. "See you in a bit then." Dad says and off they go.

"Emm I can't believe Dad has done that. We need to put those papers and Kim's drawings in the memories box before the dogs eat them.

"Right we need to talk about tonight, lady." Emm says seriously, sitting me down. "Stef has just text me saying there's some weird stuff turning up at Jurgen's place."

"I did warn you. Surely you've been to plenty of sex and drug fueled parties, you're a rock star for heaven's sake, isn't that what you do?" I ask.

He laughs. "Not since Felix was born. Jeez! I am starting to sound like an old man. Your Dad is well up for it, why am I panicking?"

"Are you concerned about what I might do?" I ask. "I've been going to Jurgen's parties and similar ones since I was twelve and I was still a virgin when you met me. Anything that goes on is consensual and no one is forced or coerced into anything. I drink beer, swim naked, play games, get involved in a challenge or two, eat loads and laugh at the antics of my family."

"But now you know what you're missing." He states.

"If the urge arises and you know darn well it will. You'll be there to give me everything I could ever need. I will not have sex with anyone but you. That said, I'm not going to stop you from doing whatever you want with whoever you want. Dad and Mama used to have the time of their lives at parties. It didn't do their marriage any harm at all."

"Delilah, I can't believe you're saying this to me. You are unbelievable.

Cherry would screw around behind my back and then scream blue murder if I looked at another woman."

"Emm we're old enough and secure enough to weather pretty much anything and be honest with each other. You appreciating another woman won't faze me at all. I love you and have decided to spend my life with you. That doesn't mean we stop being us. What did you do for sex after you and Cherry split? You didn't become celibate. You say you were always angry and frustrated. You would have needed a release from that. It wasn't playing your music because you've always had that. The most obvious one is sex."

He looks shocked at the direct question. "How do you know me so well? Yeah, I used call girls. No attachment, no heart break just business transactions. I was scared to get attached again after I made such a disaster of my marriage and until you literally swam into my life I wasn't attracted to anyone enough to make the effort to get to know them."

"It takes two people to make a marriage, darling. If she wasn't willing to try you hadn't got a hope of it ever working. Don't beat yourself up. Our marriage is going to be long and filled with fun and family and love because we're going to try hard and communicate. Did you like using call girls is this why you're worried? Tell me Emm, what's on your mind?"

"Blow jobs." He laughs. "I stop you because I associate it with hookers. It's demeaning for you do it. You're my angel and my princess, you don't have to do things like that."

"Thank you for being honest. Now we've got a starting point the only way is forward, or downwards." I add with a giggle.

"Delilah, I love you; you are amazing and beautiful and perceptive and patient and sexy as hell. Whatever you lack in sexual experience you more than make up for in enthusiasm. Let's go get showered and get ready for this party." He picks me up and heads for the bathroom. Grabbing Kim's bags so that we can dress afterwards.

An hour later, everyone is home, dressed and ready to go. "Joe, does Ella know what she's letting her in for? Have you talked it though?"

"Yeah, Mama Bear." Joe laughs.

"What's the rules, Felix?"

"No pills, no bareback, stay close. I've got it."

"And no sticking your face in anything. Chances are someone has already been there!" I add.

"Ew, that's good advice, thanks Mom." Felix grimaces. Emmett and Dad are giggling their heads off.

The addition of the MV and Ella's Ducati do no harm to our family soundtrack as we travel the short distance to Jurgen's.

The place is lit up like Blackpool Illuminations and the courtyard is already busy. There are a number of very scantily clad waiting staff offering trays of drinks and nibbles and greeting guests. I see Chaz and dive on him. "Hey up, bab. You alright?"

"Raring to go. Can you keep your eye out for the boys for me? They've got rules and one of 'em is stay near us or you lot."

"No worries, little sister. Can they have a bit of somat?"

"No pills. They should be okay with weed or coke. Just make sure they're going easy. More worried about Felix than Joe."

Emmett comes over. "Any news?"

"Yeah, your ex-wife has been arrested at The Hamptons and is being charged, most probably as an accessory to attempted murder. She did visit Rachel more than once and had long conversations with her. She took in the newspapers and showed her pictures of you all. We have proof she paid for the plane tickets to get her over here. Rachel is in a secure unit being assessed but she will be charged as soon as we can."

Emm is stunned into silence. He stands still and stares into nothing. Felix and Stef come over, concerned. "What's up Old Boy? You scared?" Fe teases.

Emm rejoins the world. "Cherry set Rachel on us. She paid her airfare."

"Jeez, we should'a seen that coming. Is she off to the pen?"

"Already there, awaiting charges." Chaz clarifies quickly. "Rachel is away as well. There's nothing to worry about."

Stef gets drinks from a passing waiter and hands them both to Emmett. "Drink those, bro. Then let's party!" Emmett does as he's told.

I squeeze his hand. He looks at me and smiles. "It's a good job I'm never going to divorce you. If she's capable of that I don't even wanna think about what you might do to me." I laugh. He's back with us.

Jurgen appears on his balcony with a microphone. "Good Evening my kinky darlings! Are you ready to ride?" He blows a whistle and everyone runs to their bike and peels off their clothes. Emm looks around him in amazement. Joe, Felix, Ella, Dad, Stef, Kim, Connor, Charlie, Nathan, Sal, Billy, Rick, Sarah, Chaz, Hans and me and several others all stark naked apart from boots and helmets. Jurgen comes striding proudly towards us shedding his clothes as he walks towards a new Ducati Diavel. All the other party guests are cheering.

"Watch you don't get that caught in your spokes, Son." Ricky shouts to Joey, laughing. Sarah comes running over.

"I'm coming on the Duchess, Auntie Dilly." She climbs up behind me and we all follow Jurgen out onto the road. We do a steady lap to much waving and honking of horns then ride down to Douglas front and mess around for half an hour, doing drag races, wheelies, stoppies and burn-outs. Then head back to the party. Sal collects a sleepy Sarah and whisks her off to her Nan's.

"Are we puttin' our kecks back on?" Joe asks.

"Up to you sweetheart. There are no rules apart from mine." He shrugs and confidently saunters toward the house naked, holding hands with Ella and fooling about with Felix who has also opted for no kit.

"They have very beautiful bodies, ja? Confident, proud boys. You are a good mama, Liebling." Jurgen comments.

"They are pretty special but I can't take the credit for any of it." I reply.

"Yeah, you can." Emm tells me. "Their confidence comes from knowing they are loved and cared about."

Jurgen offers us a huge tray of cocaine. "No thanks, you know its wasted on me." I laugh. Emm declines too.

We find Stef and Kim, who already has her clothes back on, sitting out the back.

"Oh my lord, what is going on here?" She exclaims. "Stefan's father is a very unusual man. Emmett honey, I have never seen Felix so relaxed and comfortable. I don't think I've seen him get naked since he's been old enough to dress himself. Him and Joey are completely at ease and me and Stef are hiding in the corner." She giggles.

"We had a test run yesterday morning and they were told what to expect and given a few guidelines." Emm explains. "Delilah may be extremely unorthodox in her parenting methods but they sure do work well."

Ricky hands me a joint. "Try that on 'em, Shortarse. It might loosen em up a bit." He looks across to Joey who's chatting with Nathan and Connor. "Joe wasn't lying about needing XL was he? Can't believe he's that same skinny little scally that turned up a few months ago."

"You and Bill are responsible for the muscles, making him lift and shift heavy stuff all day."

"He's a grafter, alright. It's paid off. I'm gonna get laid. Enjoy yourself." He kisses me and wanders toward the house.

I get a light off a passing waiter, take a deep drag and offer it to Emmett. He looks at me like I have two heads.

"Hippy parents. What can I say?" I shrug. "If you think me smoking a spliff is the strangest thing you'll see this evening you're in for a bit of an eye opener, honey."

"I've never even seen you smoke a normal cigarette." He says.

"Nor will you ever, they're disgusting." I laugh. "Try it, it's really mellow."

He takes a drag and passes it to Stef and Kim and soon they are all giggling like naughty schoolkids. "God we are so out of practice with the partying." Stef laughs. "When did we get so old?"

"Are you coming for a swim?" I ask.

"I haven't got my bathing costume on." Kim giggles.

"Neither has anyone else." I reply, heading for the pool.

CHAPTER 57

T he pool is huge and surrounded by mood lighting, waterfalls and large double sun beds. Huge piles of fluffy towels sit on a bench. There are tables and chairs and waiting staff hovering attentively to get whatever anyone requests. I ask for a round of drinks and grab a table. I love people watching and this is a good spot for it. The hot tubs are already full of noisy, cavorting bodies but the pool is relatively empty. I run and dive in swimming lazy lengths, letting the warm water soothe me. Emm watches while talking with Stefan. Kim gets brave, strips off and dives in she gets in sync with me and we swim side by side.

"Thank you so much for our amazing gifts, especially the sketch book. We will treasure that forever."

"I'm really glad I didn't bring a sketch book tonight." She shudders.

"Jurgen is an eccentric man but he is also kind and generous and thoughtful and would do anything for his friends and family. No one gets hurt or mistreated at his crazy parties. Everything is consensual and a chance to go wild safely and without being judged. You can just swim all night or sit drinking, relaxing and chatting, no-one will bother you." Felix dives in on top of us. "Apart from family." I add, laughing.

His eyes are wild and he's giggling his head off. "Who's given you shit?" I demand.

"Ricky." He tells me. "It's really good stuff. I'm getting up the courage to go and get laid."

"Want me to come a pick you a nice lady?" I laugh.

"Yeah." He grins. "Will you come with me?"

I slip out of the pool and hold my hand out to him. "Come on then, sunshine." Fe jumps out and walks with me, holding my hand like a small child. "Back in a min." I tell a stunned Kim.

We go into the house and Jurgen is holding court in the huge hallway. "Liebling, what's your pleasure?"

"What delights do you have that Felix can sample?" I ask. He smiles widely.

"Walk this way and take your pick." There are loads of beautiful young ladies and gents relaxing in the sitting room. "Hello, my darlings, who would like to play with this handsome boy? Jurgen asks. There are several very keen takers. "How many would you like?" He asks Felix, Fe looks at me and shrugs like his Dad.

"Two or three?" He nods and shrugs again. I choose two. "No more coke for at least three hours. Condoms ladies please. Have fun sweetheart." I leave him in their very capable hands and return to the pool, ordering drinks on the way.

"Where've you been?" Emm draws me onto his lap. "I was enjoying watching your sexy little butt as you were swimming. Where did you take Felix?"

"To get laid. He's as indecisive as you." I tell him. "Little bugger is full of cocaine he needs to sweat it out before he gets back on his bike. I've left him in the capable hands of two lovely ladies."

Emmett laughs. "Delilah, darlin' you are my kind of weird. Are you getting horny? I think I need a fix. I'm surrounded by people getting off. Even Stef is trying to get Kim to agree to a quickie in the pool."

"I'm ready and willing. Where do you want me, baby?" I tease. "There's private rooms upstairs or massive grounds or the garages or right here, right now." I squirm playfully in his lap, daring him.

He moans loudly. "Jeez, Dil. What are you trying to do to me?" I lift myself a little and do it to him again. "Stop it, you demon!" I lift to do it a third time and he's ready and impales me, everything around us ceases to exist. He howls and is less controlled, a little rougher than usual. I like it a lot. I jump back into the pool to cool down afterwards. He follows me, looking really hungry. I keep swimming out of his reach, swimming under the water, touching him and teasing him. He catches me and clamps his hand around my wrist. "Stay still, you tease! I'm gonna put you over my knee in a minute." He pulls me to him and I wrap my legs around his waist and kiss him hard. He responds equally hard and lowers me onto himself. We move slowly then get more and more frenzied, desperate to pull each other closer and deeper. I cry out loudly and he howls again.

I swim a few more lengths trying to calm myself down and regain control of my wayward body. Emm watches, waiting to pounce again.

"Having fun, bro?" Stef grins at him. "We haven't fooled around like this since before the kids were born. It's liberating."

Joey and Ella appear to touch base. "Hey Son, where have you been?"

"Eh laa we've bin in the house gettin' some lessons off the brasses. They showed us some good tricks. What ya bin doin'?"

"Shagging your Ma in the swimming pool!" Emm laughs.

"Fair play, thought I 'eared ya howlin'. Where's Fe?"

"In the house somewhere, working off a coke rush."

"Fuckin' twat." Joey says affectionately. "Drugs is for mugs!"

"I'm starvin'." I announce. "Shall we go and find some food?" We walk around to the huge barbecue terrace. There are refrigerated tables and hotplates full of food. I recognise Jurgen's chef and we go over to thank him for our engagement cakes and the food he sent. He is in his element here, fussing over huge joints of roast meat and sending out trays and trays of ornate nibbles. He stops shouting orders when he sees us and runs around his counter to hug us all.

"Congratulations on your engagement! I had so much fun making those cakes. The kitchen here is excellent. I have space to work." He piles up huge plates of food and hands them to us. "Eat, eat, enjoy!"

We do, everything tastes wonderful. "What are you up to next?" I ask Joey and Ella.

"There's loads of games going on around the back. We're going to join in. It looks fun." Ella tells us.

We have a game of naked croquet with Nathan, Connor, Charlie and a pretty little lady he's taken a liking to. Emm and Joey keep cheating and whacking everyone's ball off the lawn.

Emm spots the mechanical rodeo bulls and bucking broncos. "That I've gotta try." He whoops. "If you can ride that for a minute I'll let you ride Angel when he gets here." He challenges us. There are several options to try, all well-padded for the inevitable fall. Some have reins others have poles sticking up on which you can impale any part of your anatomy in order to hold on. We all opt for reins so have to go in twos. Me vs Emm, Ella vs Joe, winner vs winner. I conveniently forget to tell them I've held the record here since I was fourteen. The actual world record according to Guiness is two minutes and fifteen seconds. My record here is one minute forty-two.

"Any tips?" Joey asks me, carefully watching those going before us.

"Relax, move with it, use your body to balance and don't try to ride it just go with it."

"Got it." He grins and him and Ella take their turn. Ella does a respectable twenty-six seconds but can't stop giggling and loses her concentration. Joey is focussed and learning, anticipating each move. He manages just under a minute and gets his name on the leader board.

Me and Emm are up next. I'm already regretting the huge plate of food I ate an hour ago. Rick comes over with a pretty little oriental girl.

"Show 'em how it's done, Shortarse." He laughs and kisses my head. I take a deep drag from his spliff and jump on.

The reins lull you into a false sense of security, you're better not touching them. I stretch my spine loose and sit down flat, leaning forward slightly. Emm suddenly clicks. "You've done this before, haven't you?"

"Yeah, a couple of times." I reply with a wink as the countdown starts. I hold Emm's gaze as we buck and twist and I wave my arms in the air to keep balanced. I can see he's enjoying the show and he's looking pretty good too. We both go over one minute then I start to use dirty tactics. I can hear Ricky laughing as I stretch my arms above my head seductively and stick out my tiny chest and start shouting what I'm going to do to Emm when we're done. It works, he falls off, shaking his head in disbelief. I stay on another ten seconds afterwards and then jump off.

"Cheating little imp!" He scolds and throws me over his shoulder, smacking me hard on the bum. "I should have seen that coming. You play dirty."

"How many times have we warned you, man?" Rick laughs.

I stretch my arm down Emm's back and gently scratch at the base of his spine, teasing and biting at his sides. He puts me down and wraps his arms around me. He takes a drag on the joint Ricky offers him. Dad saunters across the lawn, he looks way beyond relaxed, his rangy body languid, even his dreads are hanging lower than usual, He doesn't look a day over forty.

"Have you worn all the ladies out already?" I laugh.

"Giving 'em a breather." He replies with a cheeky grin. "Came for a swim, some food and to check my family is all good. I've just seen, or rather heard, Felix. He's a howler like his Dad. What are you up to?"

Emm covers his face in mock embarrassment. "She is playing real dirty and driving me to distraction. It's no wonder I keep howling."

"That's my girl." Dad smiles. "How you two doing, Joe?"

"Eh laa, this place is boss, we're 'avin' a great time. We're just gonna 'ave the buck off 'tween me 'n Dil."

Dad grins. "You do know she's held the record on that since she was a kid, don't you?"

Emm raises an eyebrow. "You forget to tell us about that, darlin'?"

"You never asked." I shrug. "Come on then, Joey Blue, let's see you take my crown. I promise I'll play fair." Dad and Ricky instantly start playfully making bets.

The guy in charge of the broncos joins in, hyping up the crowd. "Okay, ladies and gentlemen. It's the bout of the night. Youth and enthusiasm versus experience and treachery. Broncos stop at two minutes if you're both still on it's a draw. No other rules apply. Mount up!"

I kiss Emm hungrily and jump on my leather and steel steed. My head automatically goes into competition mode and I block out all distractions and await the countdown. Joe watches and copies me easily. Rick yells. "Ella's up the duff!" I laugh and hear Ella slap him and shout that she most definitely isn't. Joey starts laughing too. We both pull ourselves together as soon as the bucking begins. I get into the zone, thinking and seeing nothing, just feeling. One minute passes and I hear Joey start swearing but he's not been unseated. One minute thirty is called and I'm starting to writhe about to keep my core tight enough.

Joey is swearing again. "Relax, Joe, nothing mechanical can ever be in charge of your head." I yell and he stills and regains his composure. Focusing on my voice. He's fine for a few more seconds.

"Talk more, Ma!" He yells. "I'm losin' it!"

"We're nearly there, Joe. Just relax your brain and tighten your stomach muscles. I think you're about to beat my record, honey." The crowd start counting down from ten, nine, eight seven .... The Broncos slow and we are given a huge round of applause. We jump off and take a bow.

"Eh laa, me bollocks are black and blue. I'm gonna sit in the pool and cool 'em down." We all follow him over and dive in as he lowers himself gingerly into the shallow end. Dad and I swim together in comfortable silence. Emm sits chatting with Ricky and his lady, Stef and Kim.

"Well I can't keep the ladies waiting any longer." Dad grins after eating a plateful of goodies. "See you later, family."

"We're coming with you; I've got an itch that needs scratching." Rick smiles, following him. I climb onto Emm's lap and find Stef and Kim have very much mellowed from earlier and Kim is well and truly in the swing of it, sitting on Stef's lap and kissing and teasing him as he shoots the breeze with Emm.

"Hello, my sexy little cowgirl." Emm greets me. "Do you need a buckle bunny?"

"A buckle bunny? That's not an English one. I need a translation." I raise an eyebrow.

Him and Stef laugh. "They're the starstruck ladies that hang around rodeos trying to get off with the cowboys who ride the bulls and broncos. Cowboy groupies." Stef explains. "Technically he's a buckle buck, I suppose."

"I definitely need one of those. Do they provide lots of hot sex?"

"Yeah little darlin'." Emm drawls. "That is their primary function. You have to drag me away and use and abuse me."

"I'm sure I can manage that." I decide, jumping off his lap. "Walk this way." He winks at Stef and says he'll catch him in a while. I head to the quiet parking area.

Emm lets out a breath. "Really? Here?"

"Why not?" I shrug, draping myself over The Duchess like a complete slut and giggling.

"God, Dil you're so fucking sexy." He bends me over The Duchess's seat and takes me very enthusiastically.

"Are you ready to go in the house?" I ask when we've got our breathing back under control. "I want to check Felix is okay. We haven't got to get involved in anything."

"Do you wanna get involved in anything?" He asks with a look of interest on his face.

"I just want my man to know I'm willing to try anything with him because I trust that he will keep me safe." I tell him, holding his gaze. "Are you hearing me, Emm? This circus probably won't be back until next TT and I don't want you to regret missing out on anything."

"I will look after you, always. Let's go and have a look around, shall we?" He holds out his hand.

We walk in and I see the lady Felix was with. "Where's my Son?" I ask.

"Fast asleep, third room down." She smiles looking at Emmett with keen interest. "Is this his Dad? Is there anything else I can do for you both?"

"Maybe later." I reply and head off. Fe is tucked up cosily in a huge bed, sleeping soundly with a huge grin on his face. Emmett and I curse not having our phones on us for a photo. Smile adoringly at him and each other and creep out, closing the door.

"How's it all work here then?" Emm whispers.

"Simple." I explain. "Ladies and gents are downstairs in the lounges. You can chat and choose. If doors are closed up here you stay out if they are open you can join in. There's themed stuff like BDSM dungeons, roleplay dress up rooms and anything you can think of."

"I didn't realise it was that intense." Emm admits. "It's an impressive set up."

"Jurgen doesn't do anything by halves. He's set parties like this up wherever we've been." I tell him. "What do you want to see first?"

"We could go and roleplay our wedding night?" He offers. "Will they have Batman costumes?"

"Sure they will somewhere unless Sal's nicked them." I giggle. "Do you think we need a dress rehearsal?"

"I just want the real thing; for you to officially be my wife."

We head upstairs to the top floor and find a strip bar with pole dancers. We order a drink and Billy and Sal stroll in. Sal and I chat to one of the dancers who teaches us several moves and then a slow, sexy routine to the classic 'Girl, you'll be a woman soon' from Pulp Fiction. My core muscles are gonna be complaining in the morning. Sal chickens out but I perform it for Emm and he is very appreciative. Billy smacks me playfully around the head and calls me a slapper.

"We need a pole installed on the beach right now." Emm informs us.

"I'll get some for the wedding." Sal promises. "Batgirl on a pole will do wonders for a beach full of blokes in tights. You need to come with us to the beauty salon next door. I'm going to get Bill waxed. I'm just getting him pissed enough so that he doesn't deck anyone." She explains. "That bush needs a serious trim."

I look down and shrug. "You up for some gardening, Emm?"

"I'm definitely up for that, darlin'." He grins.

In the beauty parlour they hand us a menu board with all of my waxing choices. I am intrigued and way out of my league. "Pick one hun, you spend far more time down there than I do." Emmett laughs and chooses something. The lovely lady is gentle and efficient. She asks Emmett if he wants jewels or piercings. He's keen on a piercing until she tells him it'll take up to six weeks to heal, meaning no sex. He tells me I can have it done when they go on tour. Thanks Emm!

Billy is not impressed with his 'crack and sac wax' he sounds like he is being tortured and the air is blue. We can't stop laughing and mine is painless because I'm so distracted.

Emm gets a quick tidy while we're there because he wants to show a bit of solidarity for Bill.

Rick sticks his head in the door. "Is this the torture chamber?"

"Yes it fuckin' well is!" Bill yells. "My missus is a fuckin' sadist!"

"Where's you little lady gone?" Sal asks, unconcerned about causing her husband great agony.

"Broke that one." He shrugs. "Was off to find another one when I heard him screaming. He looks around, cringes and walks away.

"We're goin' to the punishment room next and I am gonna whip your arse!" Billy informs Sal loudly.

"Ooh, yes please!" Sal replies.

"Where's that?" Emm's ears prick up. "I know someone who deserves a proper spanking." She tells him it's the other side of the bar. Thanks Sal!

We leave Billy and Sal to their fun and Emmett heads quite hastily to the other side of the bar.

"Will this involve me in pain?" I arch an eyebrow.

"Most certainly but I'll make it better afterwards." He growls. "You've gotta admit you deserve it after the rodeo stunt and it is a serious fantasy of mine."

The area is separated into private rooms which each contain an array of whips and paddles, a cross on the wall with hand and ankle cuffs, a padded bench and a few other freaky bits of apparatus. He takes his time to choose his weapon of choice then arranges me face down leaning on the bench with my feet on the floor.

"Jeez, Dil you're too sexy and I'm way too horny!" He enters me roughly and forgets completely about why we came here. He's barely in control and it's amazing and over in an intense few minutes. "Okay." He grins. "I might have a little more self-control now. Bend over that table, lady." I do as I'm told willingly. He spanks me hard about five times and then loses control again.

"I like this spanking stuff." I giggle when he howls and I writhe in ecstasy, after being taken on another out of body experience.

He kisses my head and groans. "I'm not very good at it am I? We need more practice."

"We've got all night." I shrug. We practice for a little while longer then go back to the bar for a drink. Emm nips to the bathroom.

Chaz is there looking as relaxed as Dad did earlier. A beer in his hand, a very sexy lady with her head in his lap and a handsome man massaging his shoulders.

"I've missed Jurgen's shagfest." He sighs. "Is Emmett embracing the concept?"

"Yeah, he's starting to get the hang of it all." I laugh. "I might have a closet dominant on my hands. It's funny coming to the dark side myself after all these years of just watching everyone else have fun. I haven't lost my skills on the broncos but Joe's matched me already."

"He's a good lad. He's gonna be one hell of a racer." Chaz muses.

Emm returns and raises his drink in salute to Chaz and thanks him profusely for our gifts. I go to play on the poles again and leave them chatting. A sleepy eyed Felix wanders in and smiles when he sees us. He tries to copy my moves on the pole giggling then goes to get a drink and joins his Dad. Chaz has moved on.

"Hello Old Boy, are you getting into the swing?"

"I've been up to plenty while you was having a nap." He replies.

Fe laughs easily. "Those ladies Dil chose certainly knew what they were doing. I've been thoroughly used and abused. Where's Joe and Ella?"

"They were outside in the pool when we came in. We've been having a bronco tournament. He's as determined to win as Dil, I think he's destroyed his nuts." Emm grins.

"Against Dil? Did he win?" Fe looks surprised. "She doesn't give in without a fight."

"They drew. Joey and I won the croquet. I have no idea what the rules are but we definitely won." Emm tells him with a smirk. I can feel him watching me wrapping myself around the pole.

Hans arrives. "Hello, my friends, Delilah, you are very graceful, a pleasure to watch." Then goes straight back to business. "Ms. Martinez has admitted to her visits and conversations with Rachel. I've taken the liberty of withdrawing your original settlement offer based on this knowledge. The divorce papers were already signed so you are legally divorced. Her lawyer and I were still in talks over the finer details. You are divorced and she is now entitled to nothing whatsoever. Rachel is being evaluated in a mental health facility but will probably be tried as sane and put away for attempted murder." Emmett thanks him for the update and shakes his hand as he gets up to leave.

Felix grins. "Are you the first rock star in history not to get taken for a fortune in a divorce?"

I walk over, laughing. "You haven't seen Hans' bill yet. He's good but I bet he's not cheap."

"I don't care, he's been a bloody godsend." Emm shakes his head. "I'll happily give him everything I was gonna give her."

"What time is it?" Fe asks then notices his Dad's new timepiece. He whistles in admiration. "When did you get that? It's the one I wanted for my twenty fifth."

"Chaz bought them for engagement gifts, Dil has one too. Nice eh? It's nearly half three. What time does the circus close, darlin'?" I shrug.

A barman, we didn't even notice was there, politely coughs. "Entertainment ceases at approximately five a.m. Is there anything I can arrange for you? I can call any area from here."

"Shall I get my ladies back or get or try new ones?" Felix queries. "They were very good."

"They'll all be very good, Jurgen handpicks them all." I tell him. "Do you want to go back down and choose yourself now your head is a bit clearer."

"Come with me again, please." Fe gives me a cheeky grin. We thank the barman and head downstairs back to the lounge. Felix's original ladies jump up looking keen.

"Hi Felix, have you recharged your batteries?" One smiles, looking Emmett and then me up and down, she adds. "I'm very happy to provide a service for your whole family, you're all very beautiful."

"Thank you but no." Emm replies. "My wife is more than enough for me."

Felix looks a little freaked by her suggestion and decides to go for someone different. She wishes us a good night and we follow him toward his newly acquired targets. The ladies' faces light up when they see him and very willingly follow him out of the lounge.

"Do you want to sample the goods?" I ask Emm as he looks around the lounge.

"No, darlin'. My girl is streets better than all of these put together." He smiles, kissing me gently. "Let's go and find Stef and Kim, get a coffee and then go home to bed."

"Coffee and bed sounds perfect." I take his hand and we head outside.

CHAPTER 58

W e all sleep in late. My phone wakes me at half nine. It's Sal reminding me of my hair appointment and other tortures she has booked. She arranges to pick us up in an hour. "Did you still wanna come to the shop or has Kim fully replenished your wardrobe?" I ask Emm as he tries to drag me back under the duvet. He doesn't have to try too hard I have at least half an hour.

"I'm coming with you. I miss you if you're not here. Felix wanted to go too. He's running out of clothes. Not sure about Joe and Ella."

"Did you enjoy your evening?" I ask, snuggled up with my head on Emm's chest.

"Yeah, but I don't wanna do it too often." He admits. "I think I like you all to myself." He strokes my cheek. "We definitely need a pole here though." He adds. "I'd get you a bronco too but Midnight and Angel will be here in a week and they're gonna give us a run for our money. I bet even Seraph and Luna will be a handful, it's so long since they've been ridden by anyone but Tiff."

"I can't wait. The wilder the better." I reply honestly.

We rise at a leisurely pace and get showered together while the coffee brews. I knock Felix's door and ask if he's coming with us. He's up and ready before the bacon butties are cooked. Dad will have stayed over at Jurgen's. I go and say hello to the donkeys and the chucks and give them loads of food, treats and love.

It seems overly quiet with no campers preparing for their day but I am proud that our first successful TT venture is done. Although, I feel that I almost didn't have chance to enjoy it because of everything else that has gone on this fortnight. I empty the bins, tidy the last few bits of firewood and clean the shower block one last time.

I send the dogs up to rouse Joe and Ella. Joey comes down, walking like a cowboy.

"Mornin' sweetheart. Did you wanna come shopping?" I laugh, giving him a hug.

"Na, I'm gonna grab some of that scran then get back in me pit." He grins, following me into the kitchen and chatting while I cook then gratefully accepting a big plate of sandwiches.

"I hear you were crazy enough to join Mom in a bronco challenge." Fe laughs. "Two minutes? Are you insane?"

"Eh laa, me bollocks'll never be the same again!" He groans. "Enjoy your shoppin'. Get us some socks, dogs keep eatin' mine." He pads back to bed, taking the plate full of sandwiches, coffee for Ella and all the dogs and Dutch with him.

Sal comes in and helps herself to coffee. "God, my head is throbbing." She winces taking a huge mouthful. "Oh, heck, that's better."

"How's Bill after his waxing?" Emm enquires.

"Looks like a dog with mange." Sal sighs. "He only let them do half a job then threatened to rip their heads off."

Alex and Lisa are ready and waiting at the hairdressers and greet me like an old friend.

"Delilah, hi. Congratulations on your engagement. All of your media coverage has shown off your hair so brilliantly." Alex gushes. "People on all the forums have been asking where you get it done."

"That's great, you can set up as a dreads specialist. Can you recreate it with non-permanent dyes for my little goddaughter? She wants to be a rainbow dreadlocked bridesmaid."

"Yes, of course we can. We'll just use chalks or spray colour so it'll wash straight out. When do you need it done?" I shrug and look over at Emmett, he shrugs and looks over at Sal.

"Since when did I become the wedding planner?"

"Since day one when you told me I was engaged." I reply.

"Give me a couple more weeks." She laughs. "I'm still in search of a few XXL super heroes. I can't find anything to fit Chaz or a bodysuit long enough for Bill." I agree to let Alex know as soon as we have a definite date. He and Lisa get to work and Emm and Felix go off for a mooch. Sal gets a trim and then goes to keep them company and no doubt help them spend some money.

"I'll be back for you in a bit. I've booked us facials and full body massages."

"Sounds like hell." I grin. "See if you can find me some more 'fuck me' shoes, the dog's eaten mine. And tights, please." Lovely Lisa sorts my eyebrows again while my colours are taking and I am done so much quicker this time. I thank them, pay and rebook. I and am leaving as Sal and the boys come to meet me.

"Hello, my pretty rainbow girl. I've missed you." Emm grins. Sal is pushing a trolley full of heaven knows what.

"Your men are well into shopping. You're gonna need another extension on your place."

I roll my eyes in horror. "Did you find me some shoes for tonight?" I ask, looking at the huge pile of merchandise. "What time is torture? Have we got time to eat first?"

"Three pairs at least and about six dresses to go with them. Half two and hell yes, I'm starving!" Sal replies, heading for the cafe.

"I don't need any more dresses. I've got two." I groan. "When am I going anywhere to wear dresses? They just take up space. You were supposed to be shopping for yourselves, not me."

"Don't worry about that." Sal laughs. Shovelling homemade pie in her mouth and waving her fork at me. "They've shopped for everyone they can think of. I won't need to buy anything else for Sarah for a year. They're the shopping companions I always wanted you to be. I'm going to borrow at least one of them every week from now on. We've already put one trolley full in the car."

"Have you got more money than sense?" I ask.

They both shrug together. "Yeah. We got lots of money." They giggle. I keep forgetting. "Thanks to Hans and Chaz I've got more than I antici-pated right now so I'm celebrating." Emm adds. "I can't exactly break the bank in here. Stop worrying about money Dil, we've got plenty."

"Come and buy me everything they have to offer in the deli and I'll stop whining at you." I sass.

"Deal." We leave Sal and Felix at the table and go and fill a basket with meats and cheeses and olives and pickles and pies and flavoured breads and every manner of deli fayre. Emm growls when I go to pay. "I'm buy-ing, put your purse away. We need to get a bank account over here. I'm gonna get Nathan to sort it then you and Joey can have cards and spend what you like."

"An Island bank account makes good sense but I don't need to get at it, thank you. I've got enough, in fact more than I need thanks to Mama and Dad." He looks at me in amazement.

"You are my fiancée and about to be my wife. I think I can trust you with my bank details, Delilah. I want to share everything with you, provide for you. Why are you so bloody independent?" He runs a hand through his hair in frustration.

"Years of being bloody independent, maybe?" I smile. "I'm sorry honey, I love you to the moon and back but I can't lose all my idiosyncrasies in a fortnight and one thing I never ever want to argue about, in this lifetime or our next, is money."

"Okay my exasperating little darlin'. How about you let me get you a card and you keep it in your purse and never use it?" Emm offers. "Or you can use it to buy me presents." He adds with a cheeky grin.

"If it makes you happy. Go for it." I sigh. "I am grateful, it's just a little overwhelming. Are you coming for a massage? I bet there's room if we ask nicely."

We are all welcomed and accommodated at the beauty parlour and the massage is fabulous and relaxing. Felix and Sal both fall asleep and snore in harmony. Emm and I get a facial too and my nails are painted to match my hair.

"Are you looking forward to your night out?" Emm asks.

"To be honest two nights of fun has been more than enough. I'd rather stay home and go to bed straight after tea." I laugh. "It'll be good for Joey, though, and Dad loves it. Do you wanna go and I'll stay home?"

"Felix and I are going for a meal with Stef, Kim and the boys. We'll only be two minutes away, call me if you're tired and I'll come and get you."

"Thanks baby. That's worth more than all the money in the world." I tell him honestly.

"Was there anything in the store, anything you want?" He winces when he realises what he's saying. "Did you need anything?" He amends with a grin.

"Socks for Joey and Ella could probably use a bathrobe even though she looks really cute in Joey's t shirts."

"Felix got Joe's socks and a load of t shirts, jeans, trainers, hoodies and lord knows what else. Shall we go and get a robe then come back here for the sleeping beauties?" We choose a cuddly pink robe and some cute cotton pyjamas and I let Emm buy Ella, Sal and I lovely soft velvet lounge suits, perfect for leisurely breakfasts or wandering on the beach with the dogs. I get Sal the designer handbag she was eyeing up last time we were here too. We collect Sal and Fe and get back home. Joey and Ella are on the beach with the dogs and come to help us unload the car.

"'Ave ya bought the whole fuckin' shop?" Joey looks at the boot full of bags and boxes.

"Pretty much, little bro." Felix grins. "Half of it's for you. I've had a great time." We pile it all on the chesterfield, drink coffee and share the deli nibbles while we unpack the bags, it feels like Christmas. I have more shoes than a centipede, lovely black suede sexy boots and some ridiculously expensive designer trainers, really sexy grown up, thin knit woolen dresses, a couple of little sundresses, stockings, tights, socks and a softer than soft dressy, leather jacket in the same deep blue as Emmett's eyes. Joey has a complete designer wardrobe and can't believe it. Ella loves her bedtime snugglies and Felix has bought her some tops and trainers too. He's bought himself plenty of new kit and so has Emmett.

Sal thanks us for a good shopping day and all of her and Sarah's gifts and goes off to get ready for tonight. She says Rick will pick us up at half eight.

"Gramps phoned 'e's gonna meet us there." Joey lets me know.

I look at my watch. "Two hours to fill before I need to get ready. My bed is calling." I yawn. I collect up all of my amazing presents, say my warm thank yous and head off to our bed. I've just about managed to find space for everything when Emm joins me.

"Want me to keep you company?"

"Always." We make slow, sleepy love then fall asleep in each other's arms until my alarm tells me I need to get ready.

The Presentation event is always fun. Past and present riders, team bosses and the corporate bigwigs rub shoulders with marshals, independent racers, scouts and everyone TT needs to run as seamlessly as it does. It is a great celebration and I will enjoy it. I head to the cottage and Joey is outside saying bye to Ella. She's back to work and normality in the morning so off home for an early night too.

"Night sweetheart, see you tomorrow. Love you. Ride safe." I say as I go for a shower.

I throw some make up on and go back in my robe to dress. "I've got too much choice now." I wail. "What shall I wear?"

Emm throws knickers and tights and one of my soft, cosy dresses and my new boots at me.

"I think it's getting cooler these might be warm or is it one of those places that gets hot and stuffy?" He asks waving a sundress at me.

"It's usually quite chilly actually their air conditioning is impressive. I'll go with your original offer." I decide. He does up my necklace from the boys for me and I change my earrings to match. The heather blue dress clings softly, stopping mid-thigh. The boots are knee length with a small heel. "I feel like a grown up again. Does it look okay?" I ask.

"You look beautiful, Delilah." Emm smiles. "You are beautiful. Can we spend the day together tomorrow, just you and me?"

"I don't see why not. Unless Paddy Mac needs labourers, I'm all yours. What's on offer? Does it involve ice cream? We can't spend the day in bed if they're going to be working on our bathroom." I think of all the ways I would like to spend the day with him.

"Haven't decided yet." He shrugs, pulling on a cashmere sweater and jeans. "Just want you all to myself for a few hours at least. I'm sure ice cream can be factored in."

I grab my bag and stuff my phone and purse inside. I hear Ricky's Ranger pull up and we walk around to meet him. Joey comes down looking very James Bond in a grey suit, white shirt and navy tie.

"Looking sharp, Son." Ricky whistles. "You've scrubbed up well. You look alright an' all, Shortarse." He adds with a kiss to my head. "What you got planned with your bit of peace, Emmett?"

"We're going for food with Stef and Kim. They'll be here in a few minutes.

I better find Fe. Enjoy yourselves. Look after my girl." He kisses me gently, whispers 'behave' in my ear, and waves us off. We pass Stef and Kim in the lane and wave our hellos.

The Pavillion is pretty full when we arrive and are shown to our table. Dad, Jurgen, Sal and Billy, Pat and Will are settled and enjoying each other's company. Once the room is seated and the doors are closed the waiters begin to serve a traditional, formal three course meal; soup, huge slices of roast beef, mountains of veg, Yorkshire puddings, roasties and mash, followed by rhubarb, cherry or apple crumble with ice cream, cream or custard. As soon as the plates have been cleared away the MC wastes no time beginning to rattle out all of the awards and prizes and achievements. We are treated to raucous taunting and tormenting during speeches and plenty of good-natured banter. All of the formalities are completed quickly to avoid eating into serious drinking time.

TT fortnight is intense and fraught and although these guys wouldn't want it any other way tonight is a release of all of the pent-up frustrations and emotions they have all been subjected to during the last two weeks and all of the planning beforehand. They will relax for a week or so and then start planning again. Although there are lots of different committees for the many motorsport events that take place on this tiny island every year many overlap and include the same kind and generous people willing to freely give their time and knowledge year after year.

One of the organizers of the Jurby Festival comes over to our table and grabs a vacated seat. "Hello to our latest Island residents." He directs his greeting to me, Dad and Jurgen. "Are you going to be around for The Manx? Can I put you down to ride in the parade laps?"

Dad smiles. "Of course you can. Can we have better weather this year? Last one was bleak." We all shiver at the memory of howling rain and biting wind from the last August we had attended. It was more like the middle of December and we were frozen through to the marrow.

"Sun's going to shine on us all this year." He proclaims optimistically. We chat for a while about their plans for the festival this year and Jurgen happily agrees to get some of his past race bikes over in time for the show. Some of the old racers come over next and there's lots of reliving past races, teasing and gentle arguments.

I leave them to it and go and find Joey. He's in the middle of a very animated conversation with Andy, the instructor. I get closer and he's telling him about the bucking bronco events of last night. Andy is wide eyed with amazement. "Are you telling stories, Joey Blue?" I interrupt with a smile.

"Hi, Delilah. Congratulations on your engagement. Are you well?" Andy asks. "I've missed Joey this fortnight. Every time I've seen him he's been too busy to chat."

"Back to normal now for a few weeks, or as normal as it gets at our place."
I reply. "Has he told you about his new baby?"

"The MV? Yes, ideal for his test."

"When can we book him in? He's keen to get started on the race scene, we
need to get his license and get him some experience so he can race next
Manx and then TT afterwards."

"We're back to working all hours from Monday so I'll book the first one I
can get for him. He's going to get through fine, he's a natural rider." Andy
announces proudly.

"Thanks Andy." Joey and I say in unison.

"Do you want a drink, Joe? I was going to coax the moths out of Ricky's
wallet." I ask.

"Yeah, Coke, please. Who can I talk to about racin' 'ere?" He quizzes, looking around.

I laugh. "Take your pick, baby. Everyone here will have something you
can learn. Sit with Dad and Jurgen for a bit. You'll be pretty impressed
with the company they keep." He willingly follows my suggestion and I
go to find Rick. He's talking at the bar and easily drops an arm over my
shoulder and kisses my head.

"Yo, Shortarse. Wanna drink?"

"Yep. And a Coke for Joe."

The man he's talking to is familiar but I can't place him. He raises his
glass in greeting. "Someone here has the willpower to drink Coke?" He
smiles. "Can I sign him up?"

"My Son." I smile. "He's yet to be seduced by the dark side."

"Your son? I wasn't aware you had children, Delilah." The man states.

"He's a recent acquisition." I laugh. "But he's a Blue through and through."

"Does he ride like a Blue?" The man's interest is peaked and I remember
where I know him from, he's a local business man who runs a few race
teams as hobbies and tax write offs. He's been instrumental in starting
the careers of several successful sportsmen and women.

"He's a natural rider but isn't racing yet. We're going to get all his licenses
and everything sorted now TT is done." I tell him.

"No one has taught him any bad habits yet? Sounds interesting. Can I
meet him?"

"Yeah, of course. He's sitting over with Dad and Jurgen." I point him in the
right direction. I make frantic hand signals to Joey to give the man his
time.

Ricky laughs. "You shameless hussy, are you selling your kid to the first bidder?"

I punch him playfully. "I am not! I want Joey to get as much experience and opportunity as I can find. He wants to race. You know he deserves a chance to at least prove he can ride to someone who can open doors for him."

"I'm teasing Shortarse. I just collared him on purpose to tell him about Joe, myself."

I kiss his nose. "Thank you. I'll take these drinks over then I'll be back." I drop off the tray with a smile and go back to Rick. I snuggle into his solid side and relax under his comforting arm, drinking beer and falling asleep to the sound of him chatting with Billy and Sal.

A buzzing wakes me, it's a text from Emm. 'Having fun, beautiful girl? xx'

I send him one back. 'Was having a nap. Xx You woke me. XX"

'Are you sleeping on a table? xx'

'Nope, on Rick xx'

'Should that concern me? xx'

'Nope, middle of room, fully clothed, with Sal & Bill here too xx'

'Okay. We're home bed feels empty without you xx'

'Looking forward to seeing you and our bed. Probably leaving shortly. Have you tested any of our engagement toys? Xx'

'Don't think we have enough batteries! Xx

'I'll text when we're leaving to give you time to make hot chocolate xx hot chocolate and sleepy sex is what I need right now xx'

'I'll be waiting with both. Look out for paparazzi. Stef's sure he saw one of the nasty ones earlier xx'

'okay x love you xx'

'Love you too xx'

Ricky looks under his arm at me. "Okay Shortarse?"

"Yeah, really tired. Emm said there's a nasty reporter about. I haven't seen anything, have you?"

"Not been looking to be honest." He shrugs. "You ready to head home? I gotta be up early in the morning."

"Yep, I'm beat. All the partying and late nights are catching up on me. I think I'm getting old." I yawn.

He hugs me and kisses my head tenderly. "You're just finally learning how to relax." He laughs. "Sex is a pretty good cure for most stuff, ain't it?"

"Yeah it's great." I sigh, dragging myself from his arms. "I'll go and find

Joey and Dad." They're still chatting away and are happy to stay to the end and get a ride back with Jurgen or Bill and Sal. I say night to everyone and Ricky and I leave.

We just walk out of the door and someone shouts my name. We are blinded by a flash and a weaselly man, in a badly fitting suit, shoves something towards us.

"Are you cheating on Emmett already, Delilah? Who's this? Does he know you're a cheating little bitch?" Ricky knocks him out cold with one swift punch. We take the recording device he was pushing at us and the camera he is carrying and his wallet so we can tell Chaz who he is and leave him on the pavement in the recovery position.

Ricky calls Chaz when we get in the van and I look through the pictures. He's taken them through the window or skylight with a long lens, they're grainy and unfocused but show me chatting and kissing Ricky on the nose, cuddled up against him, laughing with him and walking out with him. Chaz comes out to us and retrieves everything and a police car arrives and the man is loaded into the back.

"You're keeping the boys and girls on their toes, little sis." Chaz grins. "They were only moaning earlier it was gonna get boring again now TT is done. You and Emm have made their year already, junkie chancers, mad women and attempted murder and now they can spend the night talking to this piece of shit." He kisses me through the open window. "See you soon, sweetie."

Ricky drops me off at home and declines the offer of hot chocolate. I kiss him and thank him for the ride and the reporter. "Night Ricky, love you."

"Love you too, Shortarse. See ya soon." He drives off.

My sexy Emmett, topless, in loose board shorts, which are hanging dangerously low on his hips, is making drinks and watching tv. The dogs and Felix are snoring peacefully on the chesterfield in a big heap. Dutch has Dad's armchair to himself.

"Hey gorgeous, how was your night?" He smiles.

"We just met your reporter friend." I tell him, dropping my bag on the table and kicking off my boots.

"Oh shit! Are you okay? He's the nasty bastard that took me to court for assault. He writes vile rubbish. I barely touched him."

"Oh dear! He's going to be wanting to take Ricky to court then." I giggle.

"What happened?" He raises an eyebrow.

"He called me a cheating bitch, Rick knocked him out, Chaz's boys shovelled him up and took him to the police station." I shrug.

"Delilah, will you ever cease to amaze me?" Emm shakes his head and hands me my drink.

"God, I hope not." I laugh. "I haven't got much else going for me."

"Darlin', I will never, ever tire of you. Everything that has blighted my life you are just laying waste to without missing a beat. Can we go and get married tomorrow? I don't want you to get away."

"Do you wanna incur the wrath of Sarah and Sal?" I question.

"Nope, not that brave." He admits.

"Didn't think so, me neither" I smile. "Okay then, I've got the hot chocolate, what else did you promise would be waiting?"

"Walk this way for some sleepy sex, honey." He turns off the tv, throws a blanket over Felix and holds out his hand to me.

CHAPTER 59

T he Macs are here in full force before seven the next morning. I pull on my super soft lounge suit, leave Emm snuggled up and get the breakfast butties going. Felix must have made it to bed as he's no longer on the sofa. Dad comes out of his room and I kiss him and hand him coffee and breakfast.

"Thanks, Dilly Girl. I need that. No more parties for me for at least a week." He states, holding his head.

"How was last night? Did Joey find plenty of people to talk to?"

"He worked the room like a right pro." Dad smiles at the memory. "Had half a dozen fighting to offer him trials. We took a lot of numbers and he told them he needed to discuss it with you before he committed to anything."

"Good lad." I say proudly. "I'll just take these butties out and feed everyone." I head down to the stables and find Felix already here helping out. He takes a sandwich and gives me a hug. "Morning sunshine, you're keen."

"I can't wait to get the horses and all our stuff over here. It's so good to finally have a proper home. I woke up in a pile of dogs on the sofa again this morning. I didn't smell too good but I felt great. They weren't allowed in Cherry's house and I'd have been moaned at for days if I even put my feet on a sofa. I feel like I can actually be a kid here even though I'm too old now."

"You are never too old to be a kid Felix. Don't let anyone ever tell you different."

"Morning Delilah!" Paddy Mac comes to get a sandwich. "Wonderful party, we all had such a great night. I didn't know you were such a little songbird. Is there no end to your talents?" He teases.

"It's shocking what copious amounts of alcohol will make me do." I laugh easily. "Do you need a hand with anything?"

"No, we're all sorted here. Felix is supervising this end and Joey is over helping to dig your footings for the pipework for your shower room. Do you want us to reinforce all of the fencing?"

"Felix is in charge." I laugh. "He's paying for this round of upgrades. Including the stables. We can't accept that as a gift it's too much. It's enough that you're making the time to do it." Paddy Mac waves his hand as if to brush my words away.

"Yes, please reinforce the fencing, Paddy. Angel is a real wild one, he'll be testing for weak spots within ten minutes of arriving and Midnight will be jumping them if they're too low. They're all so beautiful Dil, you're gonna love them."

"I can't wait to meet them, honey, and Tiff." I smile. He blushes slightly. "Are you and Joey home today? Your Dad and I were going for a ride out in a bit."

"Yeah, we'll help out all day. Joe's waiting for a call about his test." Emm arrives looking all sexy from sleep. "Hey Old Boy, how high should we have these fences?"

"Six feet should keep them in." He replies. "How's it going?"

"Joe, Ella and me have already scrubbed them out and taken off all of the rotten wood. Paddy's boys are going to re-roof it and then they're fitting new woodwork and maybe adding another couple of stalls nearby."

"They're efficient guys, they've dug the footings and started putting us a bathroom in already." He reports.

"I did tell you they're the best builders in the universe." I tell him, winking at Paddy Mac. "Dad's here if you need anything, he'll be in the workshop. We'll be back later."

"No worries, enjoy yourselves."

Dad is already tinkering in the workshop by the time we've got our kit on. We admire the bikes he's found for Emm and Felix. I kiss him bye and tell him we'll all go green laning later in the week.

"Where you taking me, sexy man?" I ask.

"I have no idea, darlin'. I just wanted you all to myself." He sighs. "Where would you like to go?"

"Do you want to ride, sightsee, walk, eat or just sit and watch the world go by?"

"Yeah, all of those." He grins. "We need ice cream in there somewhere too."

"Okay baby, follow me." I have a crazy run over the mountain and then go down the back lanes beside The Creg to Laxey. We park up by the cafe and go for a walk on the beach, down to the sea and follow the waves down to the rocky cove. Apart from two lone dog walkers we have the whole place to ourselves. This is what I love about this Island you can always find space to breathe.

"How is my fiancé today?" I ask swinging his hand as we walk. "Is it too quiet for you now all of the racing and parties are done?"

"Nope, I've been wanting time with my girl to myself with no interruptions or commitments for days now. This is bliss." He stops, holds my face and kisses me deeply. "I want to get to know all of your hopes and dreams and wishes and start to make some future plans with you."

"Oh no! What future plans? Your future only extends to next week." I roll my eyes and smile. "Are you bringing over an orphanage full of kids by Friday? If you are you better let Sal know so she can sort them all a wedding outfit."

He laughs. "If I did it wouldn't faze you at all, would it? That's why I love you so much. You see life as one big adventure."

"It certainly has been so far and I wouldn't change much of it. What about you? Where do you wanna be in ten years' time?"

"Work wise, not touring so much but still writing and performing once in a while at festivals or charity stuff. Home wise, Joe and Felix might have given us grandkids by then and we'll have some younger kids of our own. The dogs will be toothless and have puppies and their puppies will have even more puppies, the stallions will have fathered half of the Island's equine population. Our little cottage will have been extended another six times. Isobel, Giles and Wonky will have been joined by a dozen more donkeys and Dutch will still look exactly the same." He stops to take a breath. "Oh, and we'll be having parties on the beach every TT and taking in campers. Felix will have his own band and Joey will have ten TT trophies at least and your Dad will be managing our race team."

"Not really thought about it much then?" I giggle at his detailed account.

"Never stop thinking about my future with you now. What's your ten-year vision?"

"Ten years ahead is too scary to plan. Karma always steps in and completely fucks up anything I have mapped out so now I just go with the flow." I shrug. "Bring on whatever your heart desires, darling and I will embrace it as my own. If you're happy I will be."

"We need some plans together. I need to know this is real." He pleads.

"We've already got a few in place haven't we? Stables, bathroom, mezzanine, horses, cars, bikes, your studio, wedding? Not 'long' long term I admit but already in motion."

"Yeah, we don't hang about do we?" He grins a lopsided grin. "When is our wedding?"

"Dunno, pick a day and I'll tell Sal." I shrug. "She'll sort it whatever we tell her. She can work miracles."

"I can't wait too long; I don't want you to have second thoughts."

"Not gonna happen. I can't think of a single reason why I shouldn't marry you and can give you plenty of reasons why I should."

"Tell me some, please." He begs.

"You're patient, kind and understanding and accepting and thoughtful and generous and intense and bossy and possessive. You play heavenly guitar, have magic fingers, sing like an angel, treat Joey and Felix the same, cope with all of my weirdness and you are as sexy as hell and you make my body and my brain go wild constantly and are the only thing that has ever made me lose control ...There's lots more if you want them." I giggle.

"Stop there, my head is getting too big to get my helmet on." He smiles. "I need an occasional bit of reassurance that the last fortnight has really happened. It's been so intense. I just wanted to have time to talk with you."

"Do you want to talk about the big stuff or just pretend we're a normal couple?" I ask with a knowing look.

"Everything, I suppose. Where do we start?"

"Coffee and a sandwich at the cafe?" I offer. It seems as good a place as any and the little seating shelter is looking welcoming and devoid of people. We order and settle on a picnic bench in the corner looking out at the panoramic view of Laxey coastline. "Okay, shall we start with a summary of the fortnight and then pick out the discussion points?"

"Yeah, sounds like a plan. Shall I go first?" He offers. I nod in agreement. "Right, I've met the woman of my dreams and claimed her for my own in almost every way possible, got engaged and will be married within a fortnight, hopefully before, dressed as Batman. I've got divorced and have all of the paperwork to prove it and I don't appear to have given my ex-wife anything and as an added bonus she is currently incarcerated awaiting trial for being an accessory to attempted murder. The stalker that has plagued my life for decades has tried to kill herself and me and been taken out of action by my amazing lady and her equally impressive family. Felix and I have moved into a tiny cottage on the beach on a tiny Island I knew nothing about but now can't bear to leave. We have a real home for the first time in our lives. My Son has the loving, caring mother and family I always wanted for myself and him and we have the possibility of extending it in the future, the cottage and the family." He adds with a grin.

"I've attended a full-on sex fest without any issues or repercussions and reconnected with my best friends whom I had started to take for granted. All of the presents and rewards we have bought ourselves to make the touring and working mean something we are actually going to have the time to enjoy and family to share them with. Thanks to you, I have rekindled my love of playing and mellowed beyond all recognition especially with regard to the media and the one reporter I have wanted to hurt for ever has now got his just desserts. I'm pretty sure I've missed a ton of stuff there but it's a beginning." He lets out a huge sigh.

I kiss him. "Well done, baby. That was impressive. Now for the hard bit;

how do you feel about it all?"

"That's not hard. I am unbelievably happy about pretty much everything but there's probably a couple of bits we ought to discuss, I suppose." He adds. "I wasn't exactly shocked about Cherry but I kind of expected she would just take the money and run. I didn't think she would even know Rachel was still obsessed with me. We're already divorced, what's she got to gain from me being dead?"

"Control of Felix, control of his Trust and ultimately everything because everything you have would all go to him anyway? That or she has a nice insurance policy on you." I offer.

"Oh, shit, yeah, of course she does. How could I be so bloody naive. She was already after Felix's money and she knew she was only getting a tiny fraction of what we have even though it was more than enough to live comfortably until the end of her days. She had got us both on some hefty insurance policies too come to think of it. She's never been satisfied with anything; I should have known she wouldn't settle for what she was offered."

"Well it's backfired on her big time." I laugh. "She has nothing at all now, not even her freedom and she is going to have to spend whatever she does have on a good defence lawyer if she wants to get out of prison. I'm sure Hans will personally want to take up your side and be more than a match for anyone she can find."

"Yeah, I'm just gonna leave it all to Hans I don't want to see her ever again. She can't deny any of it Hans has CCTV evidence of her sitting with Rachel and they're looking at the newspaper together. The only good thing to ever come from her is Felix." He shakes his head as if trying to get rid of his thoughts.

"Wanna talk about the other crazy ladies in your life or do you want to move on and blow Cherry out of your head?" I offer.

"I want to hold and kiss the one and only crazy lady that matters to me and then we'll move on, metaphorically and physically." He replies, standing up and holding his arms out to me. I willingly jump into his embrace. We cross the road and sit on the low wall, watching the waves and making out like hungry teenagers. He still makes every nerve in my body tingle and my brain fog just by touching his lips to mine.

"Where to next?" I ask when I can bear to disentangle myself from his warm and wonderful body.

"Back over by where we got stopped and down past Mr. Jeavons' place. I loved that road through the trees and then over the moors." He suggests. We remount and I lead the way at a brisk pace. The ride is a good one, the views are amazing and there's very little traffic anywhere. I stop just down from Jeavons' Farm to show Emmett The Raad ny Foillan, The Way of The Gull, it's a superb coastal path. We walk a little way along it to one of my favourite views. "Wow! That's awesome." He exclaims looking down at the rugged coastline and sea views. "Can we do the whole path?"

"Not today honey, it's just under a hundred miles long, it goes around the whole Island." I laugh. "But we will do it and we can wild camp which means you can howl all night and start rumours about hounds on the moors. It's quite tough in places and bike boots aren't ideal walking footwear on slippy cliff tops."

"I can't wait. Shall we do it for our honeymoon? This place is so peaceful. I can't get over how different it is everywhere on this tiny Island."

"It would be the perfect honeymoon." I agree, hugging him. "Close to home but feeling miles away."

"Are you sure? We can go anywhere you want. We could go over to the Maldives but we'd end up taking Fe and probably Joe and Ella."

"I'm happy with hiking and camping. Can we do the Maldives when it's cold and horrible here and we're all fed up with dark nights? I'd love to go skiing with the boys too." I add not wanting him to think I'm never going to leave my little haven.

He smiles and his face lights up. "Yes my gorgeous girl we will dive and swim, snowboard, ski and play in the snow and relax in the sunshine. You will be treated like a princess and never have to endure an English winter."

"Sounds like heaven." I tell him and it really does. I know I will get itchy feet eventually but from now on I have a real home to return to so travelling for three or four weeks at a time will be enough for me.

We reluctantly draw ourselves away from the cliff edge and return to the bikes. "Want to see Port St Mary? You've not been there yet." He follows me to the pretty little coastal village and we climb down onto the rocks and settle in a secluded little cove to watch the waves crash against the huge stones on the shoreline. Emm draws me into his lap as he sits himself down on a flat rock and leans back against the solid old seawall.

"I love you, Delilah Blue, shall we get married this Friday before the horses arrive?"

"We won't be able to walk around the whole Island and consumate our marriage in two days!" I giggle.

"We could do it before." He replies. "We haven't exactly done anything by the book so far, have we? We can start our honeymoon tomorrow and get back in time for the wedding."

"I can text Sal and ask." I offer, getting my phone out of my bag. I've got a message from Joey. ' tset tmora xx'. I whoop in excitement. "Joe's got his bike test tomorrow."

"Brilliant! Can't honeymoon tomorrow then, we'll be too busy having a family celebration when he passes. Chippie and The Creek again?" He asks, smiling.

"Sounds perfect. I like family nights." I text Joe to tell him he'll do fine and we'll be celebrating tomorrow night then text Sal about Friday and she immediately replies. 'Chaz's costume not here til Saturday at the earliest. Can do next Friday or Saturday. What's the rush? Are you pregnant? lol Xxx' I show Emm and he rolls his eyes.

"Next Friday it is then." He announces. "Horses will be here and settling in and we'll have a bathroom so we won't have to leave our cabin for a week. Is a week long enough to consummate our marriage?"

"Don't think a lifetime will be long enough." I tell him. "I will never get enough of your kisses or your sexy body." I start singing 'I can't get enough of you' by Kiss to him.

I text Dan and Luke to check they're free Friday and then tell Sal once they've confirmed. She gives me the okay and tells me to book Sarah a hair appointment. I ring straight away and book one for Friday morning, school will cope fine without her. Then, I text Dad, Joey and Felix and Emm texts Stefan.

Dad sends back thumbs up and kisses. Felix and Joey ring us to ask why we're waiting so long and give us an update on the building work. Stables are done and they are just treating the wood, the fences are up and the bathroom is well underway with all the digging finished. We tell them it's family night tomorrow and they're more than happy with the idea.

Stef rings next to ask where we are and tell us a huge car transporter and a truck have just turned up at Jurgen's with what looks like some of Emmett and Felix's stuff from the States. We tell him we're on the way over.

We arrive at Jurgen's place to find the ever-efficient Hans supervising the unloading of various vehicles, goods and equipment into different garages. He smiles and shouts hello but is too busy to come over. Kim gives us both a huge hug and offers to make us lunch. I follow her inside while the boys watch Hans and catch up.

"How are you? Have you settled in?" I ask as Kim moves around the kitchen looking in fridges and cupboards.

"Yes, the house is lovely and we've got everything we need here and we're getting to know Stef's Dad. You were right, he is eccentric but very kind and generous and one of the most intelligent and interesting people I have ever met. We have sat up all night talking. He did so much for Stef's mom and seems to have known about Stef for quite a while but not intruded because she was still alive. Chef has gone back to Germany today to get everything he wants from his other kitchen." She adds by way of explanation as she continues to search the fridge. "Do you want pasta or shall I make us some sandwiches?"

"Liebling, how wonderful to see you, come and swim with me." Naked Jurgen comes into the kitchen and kisses both my cheeks. "Your wedding is Friday, ja? Lots of nice toys have arrived for you all."

"Not this Friday, next Friday." I confirm. "Unless Emm realises what he's letting himself in for and runs for the hills beforehand."

"Do you want lunch, Dad?" Kim asks and Jurgen looks like he might burst with happiness.

"I must swim one hundred lengths first, come Delilah, set me a fast pace." I shrug at Kim and follow Jurgen out to the pool, stripping as I go.

We dive in and swim a very brisk hundred lengths with Stefan and Emmett joining us part of the way through. Kim brings out some towels and sets lunch out on the poolside table. We eat lunch hungrily, wrapped in the big fluffy towels and the boys fill us in on what's arrived.

"The studio equipment is nearly set up in the room above one of the garages along with the instruments. Felix is gonna be so stoked to see his old basses and his drum kit. I've forgotten we had half of the stuff that's arrived. Hans is a miracle man. There's a couple of cars and bikes too." Emmett tells us, looking at me with a teasing grin. "Hans has even got Felix's skateboards, BMXs and ramps sent over."

Stef laughs. "Don't keep Delilah in suspense, you know what she's waiting for." I lean forward in anticipation.

"The Shelby's, the GT40, the Dodge, the 'Vette and Fe's Trans Am are here and my GS and The Arch." He finally puts me out of my misery. "If you eat all of your dinner I will let you play with our toys." He giggles, kissing my head.

"That's just cruel." I laugh. "It's a good job lunch and the company is fabulous." We chat for a while, Jurgen is so pleased with his new home and has vowed to not work at all for at least three days each week and is insisting that anyone who does want to work with him comes here. Stef admits he's been writing and can't wait to get into the studio. Kim is enjoying her break from work and spending time with Charlie, Connor and Nathan.

Hans comes to join us and accepts the offer of lunch.

"Everything from the house in LA you asked for is here or in transit, Emmett. The other vehicles have been moved to The Hamptons. You can keep the house or put it up for sale, let me know what you want to do, I can put all of Ms. Martinez 's belongings into storage. Jurgen, your requested items from Germany will be here at three thirty. The horses are all ready, most of the paperwork is in place and the flights booked. I have news on Rachel. They have moved her to Rampton Secure Hospital in England and the trial will start in two weeks. Both will plead guilty by all accounts and hopefully it will all be done by video link so no-one will have to attend and it will be over quickly and cheaply."

"Well she certainly won't be wandering out of Rampton any time soon." I tell Emmett. "It's about as secure as you can get."

"That's comforting to know. Have you any idea how long they will keep her there, Hans?"

"Eight years at least. She tried to commit murder whichever way they look at the case so very probably much longer or even indefinitely if they deem her criminally insane. Ms. Martinez should expect to get a minimum of three and a half years, more if you want me to make it difficult for her. I will get a restraining order on her so that she can't come near you or any of the family or try to contact you."

"Check with Felix first, please." I request. "I don't want him to think we're stopping him from seeing his mom."

Hans smiles. "It was Felix that asked me to take out the order. He wanted to keep you all safe. Your reporter friend has a broken nose and a fractured cheekbone. When he's released from Noble's he will be escorted off the Island and will not be allowed back here. He is not planning on pressing charges since he met Chaz."

"I thought Cherry got the LA house?" Emm queries.

"She signed all of the divorce paperwork before we'd fully negotiated everything. Then she set Rachel loose and anything we had agreed was null and void. Your prenup was a good one. She's only entitled to anything she can prove was purchased with her own funds. She didn't have any income so she can only claim gifts and clothes. The properties and vehicles are all in your name only."

"Jeez, this day keeps getting better and better. Thanks Hans, you are a miracle worker." Emmett exclaims then turns to me. "Are you ready to see the motors, sexy girl?"

I jump up, excited. "Yep."

"Are you gonna get dressed?" He asks pulling on his own jeans.

"Nope, can't wait that long." I giggle. "If you have some of Mr. Shelby's best work to show me a towel is fine. I don't want to scratch anything with buttons or zips."

CHAPTER 60

Everything has been hidden away in the cavern-like garages. Emm leads me inside one and closes the door. It's dark and I can barely make out anything. He snaps on the bank of lights and the first thing I see is the Shelby Cobra, it's blue with a white stripe, I can live with that. I can feel myself drooling as I reverently stroke the bonnet and down the curvy wings and flared arches. The side exhausts are deeply chromed and polished to a mirror finish and all of the other shiny parts are the same. Emmett opens the driver's door.

"Wanna try it out for size, ma'am?" He asks, gesturing to the front seat. I unconsciously drop my towel and ease myself into the beautifully crafted, well-worn leather. The cockpit smells so masculine. The wooden steering wheel is a work of art and the clocks reflect one of the best motoring eras, stylish but only essential dials are mounted in a leather covered dash. Lap belts and the iconic roll bar are the only nod to safety.

Emmett drops himself into the passenger seat next to me.

"Emm, its gorgeous." I whisper, as I absent mindedly caress the perfectly shaped gear stick, my eyes raking over the long front view, following the stripes down the hood.

"Jeez, Delilah, come here and do bad things to me now. I don't think I've ever seen anything so erotic in my life!" Emm growls and I turn to see him appraising me with hooded eyes. I carefully climb onto his lap and he lets out a huge groan. "Shit, why did I get dressed?" He grumbles, fumbling urgently with the button on his jeans. We make love frantically with lots of giggling and groaning and banging of knees and elbows.

"Oh dear, I haven't even seen under the bonnet yet." I giggle.

"Do you wanna?" Emm raises an eyebrow. "I'm very much looking forward to bending you over one of those wings." I happily oblige by undoing the bonnet catches and both the engine and Emm's show of appreciation are very, very impressive. We eventually collapse in a big heap on the spotless garage floor. "Think we better save The Arch for another day?" Emm laughs, pulling me into his arms. "I can't get enough of you, darlin'."

I look to my left and see a black 1971 Dodge Charger RT 440 V8. I crawl slowly towards it on my hands and knees, giving Emmett a lustful look over my shoulder. He growls deeply and follows me. We seriously test the springs on the huge back seat. Emmett hasn't howled this loudly since I met him. I'm starting to think he may be a werewolf.

"Shall we spend our honeymoon in Jurgen's garage?" I giggle.

"Right now I'm not sure we're even gonna get out in time for the wedding." Emm drawls, looking at me like he wants to eat me and reaching over for the Charger's bonnet catch. "Come and see what I've got under here for you." We fool around some more until I completely lose my senses and Emmett is howling again.

I look across the garage and take a sharp intake of breath. "Oh my god!" I exclaim. "You have Christine." A 1958 red Plymouth Fury is sitting in the corner.

"Yeah, I totally forgot she was still in the garage. I learned to drive in her."

"A strange choice. Did you manage to pick up many girls in that?"

"Yeah, plenty." He grins. "Lots of weirdos and freaks. Exactly what I was looking for at sixteen."

I laugh. "You've not lost your taste for weirdos."

"Delilah, you are the weirdest and most wonderful girl I've ever met, exactly what I have always wanted. I've been searching for you my whole life."

"Have you had enough excitement for one day?" I ask, my head resting drowsily on Emm's chest. We have just relived his teenage years in the front seat of 'Christine'. I have lost all sense of time but our stomachs just started rumbling loudly and I'm starting to get chilly. "Where did I leave my clothes?"

"No idea, darlin', you were already naked when I jumped in the pool. They must be somewhere between there and the kitchen. Shall we head back in that direction and retrace your steps? Can't ride starkers again."

"Nope, it's going a bit cool now." I shiver. We climb out of the Plymouth and I stretch languidly. "Thank you for an extremely enjoyable afternoon. I like your taste in cars. Can we come back and explore the other garages tomorrow? It'll take my mind off Joey's test. Otherwise I'll be tempted to do a Sal."

"It's a date." He agrees enthusiastically. "What did Sal do?"

"Followed Max around on her bike for the whole of the test." I explain. "Nath made Bill lock her up for his."

"Oh yeah, we should definitely all go on Joe's test with him before we come back to the garage. I know he'll want us there." Emm grins.

Holding hands, we wander back to the pool and I find my clothes neatly folded on the table, courtesy of Kim I'm sure. I dress and we go back into the house.

"Evening guys." Stefan smiles, turning away from the TV programme they're watching. "Had a good day? Did you hear that pack of wolves earlier?"

"Yeah, heard that." Emm laughs. "They must be in the woodland at the back of Jurgen's garages."

"It's great to see, and hear, you're so happy, bro." Stef says genuinely.

Kim smiles in agreement. "Would you like some food before you leave?"

"Thank you so much but no, we'd better get back and see how the Mac's are getting on and feed the kids." We hug and say our goodbyes warning them we'll be back tomorrow and I haven't even seen the Arch yet.

Back at home the boys are looking dusty and tired after an honest day's work.

"Hey kids, how's it going? Had fun?"

"Yeah, The Macs just left. The stables are all done and waiting. The smell of paint and everything will be gone by the time the guys arrive. I'll get the bedding and stuff in on Sunday." Felix tells us.

"Got ya bog an' shower in." Joey adds. "The lads are comin' tommorra to sort Fe's space."

"Jeez, they don't hang about, do they?" Emmett smiles.

"Go and get washed you stinky pair and I'll get some food sorted." I giggle as Fe smells himself and wrinkles his nose up. Joey hugs me and rubs his mucky, sweaty body over me.

We all sit down at the table to huge plates of lamb tagine and rice. "Guess what's arrived at Jurgen's place?" Emm asks.

"What? The stuff's here already!" Fe exclaims excitedly.

"Cars, studio and your skateboards and BMX. Not sure what else, Dil and I got sidetracked." Emm laughs.

"Will Jurgen mind if we go over later? I want to see what's there." Felix looks excited. "It'll take Joe's mind off his test too." He adds.

"Eh laa, I ain't worryin' 'bout it." Joey shrugs, adding. "Are ya all comin' with me?"

Dad laughs. "Do you want us to?"

"Yep, all of ya." He admits with a grin. "It's 'alf nine in the mornin'."

"We'll be with you." I promise. "Jurgen won't mind you going over tonight. Stef'll be glad to have an excuse to get back in the studio."

"Ya gonna teach me to play somat?" Joey asks.

"Yeah, will do. You'll soon pick it up." Fe offers.

"Your drum kit is there."

"Awesome!" They say together looking at each other.

"Have you been to check out your bathroom?" Dad asks me.

"No, not yet. I came in and started dinner. I'm saving that pleasure for later. I'm really looking forward to not having to run to the cottage for a wee in the mornings." I giggle.

We continue to chat and catch up over dinner. Dad tells us he's got several jobs on the go. Mr. Jeavons' friends have bought him a couple of their old race bikes and he's got a few other jobs via word of mouth. He's really enjoying being elbow deep in oil and grease again. He blushes slightly when I ask about Carole and says he'll invite her for Sunday lunch soon.

"The wedding is a definitely a week on Friday. Dan and the guys can make it, and Luke, and Sal reckons she can be sorted by then."

"Cool! Has Sal got our outfits?" Felix asks.

"Not sure, you'll have to call her but I imagine she's got it all under control. She was just waiting for something for Chaz. He's not exactly standard size." I explain, then open the oven, take out a pie, and ask. "Who wants apple pie and ice cream?" I get a chorus of 'me'. I dish up generous portions for everyone and we tuck in happily. "How's Tiff? Is she looking forward to coming over? How long can she stay?"

"She can't wait. She's lonely at the stables on her own. She said there have been reporters and media crawling all over the place, with the dogs not being there, they're getting a bit pushy. Angel has bitten and kicked several that have gone snooping in the stables so we kind of need to get him here before he kills someone. She hasn't got to go back for anything. Her folks actually live in Ireland so she'll be closer to home, not that she ever goes home. She can stay indefinitely so long as everyone is okay with her being here." Felix fills us in.

"Shit! Poor girl, I didn't think about the fact that she'd be on her own and vulnerable without the dogs. I'll get some protection organised for the rest of the week. Is Tiny still on vacation?" Emm groans, grabbing his phone and calling Hans. Two minutes later its sorted and Hans is sorting some security and trying to move the flight to an earlier date. "Shall we just put the LA house up for sale? I don't want to go back there at all and everything we want in it, that we haven't already got, can be moved to the Hamptons house." Felix agrees without hesitation and goes off to call Tiff and let her know what's going on. Emm calls Hans again to get the house sale underway.

"Now we can definitely cover Hans' bill. The LA house is worth at least eighteen and a half million dollars according to Hans, and he reckons he can sell it within a month." Emm tells us and Joey lets out a whistle.

"Eh laa, drinks are on you tommorra." Emm smiles and tells Joey he can have whatever he wants, whenever he wants it and he's going to sort bank cards for us all so we can get at his money. Joey shrugs. "I'm good Emm thanks, got more than I ever wanted already."

"Jeez, you and Dil are impossible." Emm sighs. "You're both getting cards whether you want them or not. If we don't spend it the taxman will take it away. Dil, you can use it to pay for the bills and food shopping at least."

"That reminds me we never counted up the TT jar and took it to Nina. Grab it Joe, let's see how we did." Dad tactfully changes the subject, knowing I won't willingly accept Emm's money. "See if there's enough to keep a donkey for a week." Joe gets the jar and tips it onto the table. It's full of ten and twenty pound notes. Joe's been doing beer and takeaway runs every night on top of our breakfast and barbecue packs and although Jurgen's chef was feeding his guys healthy meals they were still all indulging in the occasional cheeky late-night snack and giving generous tips. Joe counts it carefully into hundred-pound stacks and then into thousands.

"Fuckin' 'ell there's over five grand 'ere!" Joey exclaims. "She can buy a dozen fuckin' donkeys. We can take it over to Neenaw after me test in the mornin'. Can ya resist bringin' somat else 'ome if ya go in there?" He asks looking to me.

"Depends on who they've got in." I shrug. "Can't help it if they want to join our crazy crew. We've got plenty of room for more chickens." I add.

"When we gettin' more kids?" Joey muses. "Little bed's spare when Fe's room's done."

"Maybe we can look into it after the wedding." Emm says with a raised eyebrow.

"We'd better offer Tiff the option of the little bed first rather than expecting her to just sleep with Felix." I add.

Joe laughs. "Fe and Tiff are bothered ya won't let 'em to shack up soon as she gets 'ere." Felix walks back in and smiles when he hears the conversation. He shrugs in agreement with Joey.

"That's sorted then." Emm laughs. "New kid after the wedding. If everyone else is ready for it. Do you want me to bring the Dodge home tomorrow for Family night? We'll all fit in it and everyone can have a drink. You're coming too aren't you, Dylan?"

"Yeah, I'm not going to miss it again." Dad smiles. "Dil, can you have a look at the wiring on this Gixer in the shed later?"

"Yep, course I can. Are you going back to Jurgen's with the boys, Emm?"

Emmett face lights up at the idea of getting into the studio. "Yeah, I might go and have a few hours with Stef."

"Sorted, I'm all yours Old Man." I tell Dad as I wash up, Joey dries and Felix puts everything away. "I'll go and check out our new bathroom and then get my overalls on. Is Ella coming over?"

"Nah, she's out with 'er mates. She'll be 'ere for family night tommorra."

Once everything is tidied away Emm and I go to look at our new addition to our little cabin. Despite the fact that the Macs have been working all day, everything is spotless and the beach looks almost untouched. Inside the previously empty little room is now a double length shower, a tiny corner sink and our own loo. Heaven! It's all sealed and floored with that rubberized stuff, like a wet room. I laugh at the thought that it'll be perfect for washing the dogs.

"Paddy Mac is pretty damn high on my 'perfect men' list." I state.

"Is that so? Who else is on that list?" Emm asks with a raised eyebrow.

"You and Dad." I tell him with a grin. "And the boys of course."

"You ready, Old Boy?" Felix shouts. "We're off to Jurgen's now."

"Yeah, coming." Emm kisses me and tells me he loves me and promises we'll christen the shower as soon as he gets back and is gone. I listen to the bikes go off down the lane with a smile. Well Delilah, how the heck did you get so lucky? I choose not to question anything at this moment. I test our facilities, pull on my overalls and head for the workshop with dogs and Dutch in tow.

Dad is already working on an amazing old BSA café racer which looks like someone has started as a project and got out of their depth, there's wiring everywhere and the tank is sitting at a very odd angle. Dad already has the engine out on the bench.

"Can you just get that last bit of the loom in on that Gixer, Dilly girl? I can't get my fingers in without smashing up my knuckles." I cheerfully settle into the task with Dutch supervising from my shoulder while to dogs run upstairs to snuggle down on Joey's bed. "I don't know about you, Dilly, but I feel like I've finally found my forever." Dad sighs as he works next to me on the BSA engine. "It's took a while but in the last few months everything seems to have fallen into place. I haven't been this contented since you and Marley were kids. It's wonderful to have you with me and see you every day and I love spending time with Joey and Felix and Emm. I have a family again. I didn't think I'd get another chance before I popped me clogs."

"It does all seem to be falling into place right now." I agree. "I'm trying to enjoy it without questioning it. I certainly never could have dreamed any of this would happen when we arrived here. I'm feeling the same, like I finally belong somewhere. How long have you been seeing Carole?"

"Since she came over, I suppose. I went to help out at MSPCA a couple of times while Nina was just out of hospital and we hit it off straight away. She's in the same place as I was, widowed and missing her family, she's fostered and always had a house full. She really wanted to take on Joey but was selfless enough to realise he had a better chance over here away from Sienna. She's tried her best with that one but the little mare just uses her and takes the pee. They're not actually blood relatives, Carole fostered her when she was pregnant and helped her out when she first had Joe. She's helped her out quite a few times over the years and again recently for Joey's sake but had already asked her to leave before we invited her here, so was really grateful that we got her to come over and then fate intervened and she got to look after Nina and we got to look after Joe. She cried so much when she saw him at your engagement party. She couldn't believe how happy and settled he was with us and what a confident young man he's become. She's not stopped going on about how great you all are and how lucky I am since she stayed over."

"She's lovely and has been so kind to Joey, Nina and Sienna, the ungrateful little madam. Has she got any plans for when Nina is better? Does she need to go back to Manchester?"

"She's weighing up her options at the minute. I would like her to stay over here and get more involved with us but I was taking it slow. We're not exactly normal, are we? Also, you are the lady of this house and I don't want anyone to change that." He grins. "I think she's asked an estate agent to give her some ideas on sale or rent options on her place and Nina has said she can stay there as long as she wants. You know Nina's place is big enough for two people to live there and never see each other if they didn't want to. She has a married son but they live in Australia. They've asked her to go and live over there but she doesn't really want to."

"Nope, I admit we're not the most conventional family but she wasn't too daunted by the party or breakfast with everyone at their worst the other day. We've still got plenty of room to extend here if you want to move her in, I don't mind at all, we can build you a separate bungalow if you want your own space. The Macs appear to be more than up for whatever we throw at them. You being happy is more important to me than anything. Invite her to family night tomorrow then she can get to know us some more."

"And you being happy is most important to me Dilly Girl. We're both doing great right now aren't we? I like to see you running the house and taking care of your family, you'll just let her take over and go back to being a kid again if she moves in here." He laughs. "She asked to go another ride on the bike, I'll take her for lunch again when she's free but I'm not offering any more than dates and companionship yet. I want to spend time with you and your new family before I get wrapped up in another serious relationship. We're just enjoying each other's company and having a bit of fun." He changes the subject to stop me prying further.

"Sal seems to have everything under control for the wedding. I rang her earlier to see if she needed me to do anything but she said she's just waiting for a couple of costumes and everything else is sorted. You need to go and sign some papers this week I think. She said she'd send you a 'to do' list in a day or so."

I giggle at the idea of a 'to do' before 'I do' list. "She has been an absolute angel. I need to get her a huge thank you present."

"That's something you can buy on Emm's card." Dad smiles. "Humour him with the money thing, Dilly. A man likes to feel like he can provide for his family."

"Yeah, I'm struggling to get my head around the fact that my future husband has more money than god's dog." I sigh. "You need to come and see the cars he has, they're pretty impressive."

"I am looking forward to getting under the bonnet of that Charger. Is it standard?" Dad replies.

"It's absolutely untouched, looks like it just came off the production line." I confirm. "It's just begging for a full race tune. He might bring it back tonight."

We carry on shooting the breeze and working until we hear the boys coming back and can instantly tell Emm has bought the Charger home. It sounds superb. We open the big doors so that the light floods outside and Emmett pulls in close so that Dad can have a good look under the bonnet. I head inside to make hot chocolate and snacks whilst they play.

"What ya makin', Mama Dil?" Joey asks, reaching over my shoulder and stealing some cheese after planting a big kiss on my head.

"Hot choccie or there's beer or Coke in the fridge and some crackers and stuff. Want pate, cheese or sliced meat?"

"Yep, all of 'em. I'm starvin'. 'Ave we got any cake?"

"There's loads in the larder. How was your night?"

"Boss, bin playin' drums an' there ain't no neighbours to complain." He grins. "Emm an' Stef were writin' new stuff. It's cool to watch 'em work."

"Are you ready for tomorrow?" I ask handing him a plate full of crackers and slices of cake and mugs of chocolate.

"Cheers Ma, love ya. Yeah, I'm ready. Be good if I know ya all there."

We head outside and everyone dives into the snacks and grabs a mug. I wander over with a torch to check the donkeys and go down to look at the new stables. They are looking very smart and the fences are all new and pretty high. I have a feeling the latest editions to the family may be a handful. I'm leaning on the fence daydreaming when Emm appears at my side.

"What are you thinking about, darlin'?"

"Looking forward to meeting our next arrivals." I tell him honestly. "And just thinking about how blessed I am. How was your evening? Shall we go and test our shower before bed?"

"They're gonna be wild when they get here." He shakes his head at the thought. "Tiff is a good girl but she'll not have ridden Angel, he's too unpredictable. If she's been at the stables alone she'd have been crazy to ride him. She'll have ridden the others but they'll still be in need of a lot of schooling if we're going to convince people they're worth breeding with. Meave was sure we'll have a queue around the Island but they won't want to risk damaging prize mares. I'm with you on the life's good page, we've been writing tonight and it was coming so easy for me and Stef, we couldn't get the ideas down quickly enough. Shower sounds perfect, I smell of sex, exhaust fumes and swimming pool chlorine."

CHAPTER 61

We're all up early and buzzing with excitement about Joey's impending test. I cook a huge breakfast and everyone tucks in. Joe's showing no sign of nerves and eats his bodyweight in sausage, bacon and eggs then drinks a rare cup of coffee. I feed the dogs, donkeys, chucks and Dutch and then we go for a walk up the beach with the dogs as they'll be home alone for a few hours. Although, I expect The Macs will let them out for some fuss. We all mess about throwing sticks for the dogs and seaweed at each other, collecting driftwood, splashing in the rockpools and skimming stones. The perfect way to start the day.

We get back to the cottage to find Ian, the vet waiting for us. "Morning everyone. I've got the paperwork for the horses. They appear to be arriving tomorrow now." He informs us. "I just need to sign off the fact that the stables are suitable and then check on them when they arrive at the airport. I needed to just check the dogs too but I can already see they're fine. Can I see the stables?" Felix and Joey let out a huge whoop and start dancing with the dogs.

"Hi Ian, no problem, come on down." I reply, walking in the direction of the back paddock. "How's Vicky? She's really lovely."

"She's good thank you." He blushes. "A godsend at the practice, the place has never run so smoothly or been so tidy and organised. I don't know how I did without her. She asked if she could come and see the horses when they're settled."

"She's welcome any time." I tell him. "We're getting married on the beach a week on Friday, you must both come."

"Wow, that soon? Congratulations, yes we would love to come. Your engagement party was an amazing night. We both really enjoyed it and it convinced Vicky that the Island won't be too quiet and boring for her to stay. She certainly wasn't expecting to be made so welcome by everyone or meet so many interesting people in one night." He gushes as he looks around the stables and is suitably impressed. "These are more than adequate." He announces. "The fences and gates are perfectly secure. I'm happy to sign everything off. I've already had a few enquiries from some local breeders about your new arrivals. I must say their lineage is extremely exciting. I'm looking forward to seeing them in the flesh."

"Me too." I admit. "Emm thinks they'll need a bit of time before they can start meeting the ladies though. The stables are Paddy Mac's work and he's had plenty of practice putting up Meave's very impressive yard."

"The Macs are certainly the first one's I recommend for any building work. Don't worry about the stallions being wild you seem to be pretty good with anything on four legs. I have no doubt they'll be doing whatever you tell them within a week or two." He laughs.

"I'm not so sure about that, Giles still takes a chunk out of me at any opportunity." I shrug.

"There's always an exception to every rule." Ian grins. "Oh and given the time difference it will be quite late tomorrow when we all arrive. I'll call when we leave the airport."

"Is it all okay?" Felix asks as soon as we get back to the cottage. "I can get the food and bedding in later this afternoon. It's all on the way now. I just called to get it dropped off early." He picks me up and swings me around. "Tiff and the boys will be here tomorrow, Mama Dil! I can't wait."

"You better warn her she's going to have to share the little bed for a few days until your space is finished." I tell him.

"Dylan's already offered to swap." Fe smiles. Ian looks at us as if we're a little too bohemian for his liking and not quite right but doesn't comment apart from to tell Felix that everything is fine.

"Get ya kit on, Ma." Joey yells. "We gorra get off now." I apologise to Ian for the fact that we have to rush off as Emm hands me my leathers and helmet and I start to strip off my lounge suit and pull on my one piece. Ian says hasty goodbyes to us all and jumps into his Land Rover. "Ya keep scarin' the shit out a that bloke." Joey laughs.

"I think we all do. Come on boys let's go and get Joe legal. Are you coming on the Duchess Emm?"

"Yeah, I stupidly left the BM at Jurgen's last night." He grins, pulling on his helmet. "Dylan's offered me a load of other options from the workshop but I want to be close to my woman, be gentle with me." He climbs on, gets far closer than necessary and puts his hands on my chest, making me laugh.

We head for the test centre and Andy is waiting outside. He smiles when he sees us all. "I see it's going to be a family affair."

"We couldn't stay away." I admit. "We won't get in the way."

"It'll be good to have the company." He says. "We're just waiting for two other guys and one is a dreadful rider so I'll be glad to have you with us. Can you remember all of the test maneuvres?"

"Yep, I think so." I say reeling them all off to him.

"Perfect. I'll assess Joey and the older guy and you can watch the crazy kid." He grins handing me a headset. "He won't pass in a month of Sundays."

"Cheers Andy." I say unenthusiastically. A little Repsol liveried Honda 125 comes screaming towards us in completely the wrong gear and bouncing off the rev limiter. "I assume this one is mine?" I get a smile and nod in response.

I keep my helmet on and get the lad set up with his headset and explain to him how the test is going to go and what I will be looking for, what I expect and what will constitute a fail. Andy does the same with Joey and the other gentleman. Emmett stands back and watches me. We move to the bikes to start the tests and Emmett pinches Felix's bike and Fe jumps on the back of him.

They all go off at the front with Andy and I follow a little way back with my new charge. I give him a quick   refresher on his gears as he seems to have completely forgotten where they are and how and when to use them. His language makes Joey sound like a saint. I talk to him for a little way to help him relax and he actually remembers to use his clutch at least twice. I also have to remind him to take his foot off the back brake several times because he's using it as a footrest.

Despite the fact that all he has to do is follow the others, and Dad and Emmett are being model pupils, he still manages to get in the wrong lane at the first roundabout we approach and when I advise him of this he tells me it's fine because he can just cut across the car at the side of him. I let him know he will fail immediately if he does so and he swears a lot more. I suggest he goes right around and then places himself in the correct lane and he actually does so without further drama.

His next obstacle is a T junction on a slight hill. Joey and the others handle it without hesitation and a small gap opens up between us all. Even though I clearly tell my guy to not worry or try to keep up with them, he tries to launch himself out of the junction without looking properly and would have been flattened by a quarry wagon if it wasn't for the fact that he stalled due to being in the wrong gear yet again. Andy must have thought Christmas had come when he saw me this morning! I point out that this is a serious fault and if he doesn't start to concentrate properly, listen to me and follow my instructions fully he may as well call it a day and go home as he will fail. He swears a lot more and then tells me this is his fifth attempt and he needs to pass as he uses his bike to get to work every day.

I am shocked by the fact that this is not actually his first time riding a bike at all. He promises he will listen from now on. We do okay for the next ten minutes and catch up with the others. I get a little optimistic and suggest we try an emergency stop which results in a stoppie with the back wheel a good six inches off the ground and copious amounts of swearing. He obviously knows it's not acceptable.

Once all the maneuvres have been attempted there's an element of free riding and Andy is leading the guys up to the mountain. My man takes this as a sign that he needs to do something drastic and suddenly starts to chat me up and offers to take me to dinner if I pass him. I advise him very clearly that I will not be bribed and that I think that he is far too dangerous on a bike, for himself and everyone else on the road. I ask how many lessons he's had and he admits he's lost count. He also admits to having already been involved in several accidents, three of which re- sulted in hospitalization. I gently tell him he needs to stop now before he meets his maker. He swears a lot more and concedes that I'm probably right. I suggest he sells his bike and buys a bus pass. He tells me we're two minutes from his house so he's going to head home and thanks me for my advice. He asks me to tell Andy he'll return the headset in the morning. I wish him well and let him go.

I catch the others up and Andy has let them go for it on the mountain so I let a very hot and unhappy Duchess loose and howl past them all. Joey soon gets on my tail and proves without a doubt that he is a capable, nat- ural rider. We get back to the test centre and I inform Andy that my man had a change of heart about his test and he thanks me for talking some sense into the kid. He also tells me how impressed he was with Joey and that Emmett and Dad had passed too.

We all congratulate Joey and Andy gives me a phone number to call, ad- vising me that the guy is a team owner looking for new lads and admits he hasn't seen anyone who can ride like Joey in the last ten years. He says he will call this man and let him know we may be in touch. We thank him for everything and go off for a celebratory ride to Peel for ice creams.

Emm is back on my pillion. "Why did you run away? Did authoritative me scare you?" I giggle when we pull up.

"Nope, very much the opposite, darlin' but as you had a radio on I didn't think I'd be helping if I came and told you how turned on I was. The kid was having enough problems without having to listen to pure porn in his helmet."

"I'm no longer wired, you can tell me all about it now." I tease, wiggling my bum in his lap as he climbs off the Duchess.

"Later, darlin'. I will definitely tell you all about it later." He growls, leaning in for a kiss. "Licorice and banoffee?" He asks, adjusting the front of his leathers as he gets into the queue.

"Of course." I hug Joey again. "Well done, baby. I knew you'd walk it. Andy gave me another number for a team guy."

"Fuckin' boss." He grins and hugs me back, lifting me off the ground. "We got a load from the 'do'. Can we go through 'em all later? Gorra text Ell, Rick an' Bill an' Nath. Get me a chocolate one." He nods toward the ice cream shop before walking back over to the beach and getting out his phone.

Once we've all got a cone we walk down to the little beach and sit down on the rocks.

"We're all yours for the day, Joe. What do you want to do?" I tell him.

"I'm happy back at 'ome 'elpin' the Macs get Fe's space done. We're still comin' down 'ere tonight ain't we?"

"Yeah, shall we book a table at the Creek or do you want chippie?"

"Book us a table. Let's 'ave somat posh." He laughs.

"Posh? Want the Creek or shall we do the fancy one round the corner?"

"Will we freak 'em out if we all turn up?" He giggles. "Bill, Sal an' Ricky'll come an' Nath an' Conn. Will Stef an' Kim come?"

"Probably, I can book it on the phone." I shrug. "Can you read the number from here?" Felix looks across and reels the number off and I ring and book for fifteen or possibly more." They seem happy enough with the booking and say they'll be fine if there are extras and will keep the upstairs room free for us. Emm calls Stef to invite them and Jurgen and Hans and the boys. They tell him Jurgen and Hans have gone over to Germany for a couple of days but they'll happily come along. We let everyone else know when and where and then Dad remembers the money for Nina in his pocket and we head for the MSPCA to hand it over.

Carole and Milly are both there and the café is really busy. Joey and I wash our hands and grab aprons to help out. Dad takes Felix and Emmett to find Nina and for a look around.

"Use your charms to rehome some babies and we get a vote too if you find someone to come home with us." I shout as they head outside. Felix turns to give me a cheeky grin.

I make at least two dozen sandwiches, pour a load of coffees and teas, cut a shed load of cakes and take a mountain of orders and then finally the rush is over and everyone drifts away. I mix a huge amount of muffin batter and fruit cake mix and pop them in the ovens so they have some for selling tomorrow. Joey cleans all the tables, wipes the chairs down and mops the floor. Carole gives us both huge hugs and thanks us for all our help. She congratulates Joey on his test and asks why we came by. Right on cue, Nina comes bustling in, tears in her eyes and a handful of cash. She draws me into a huge embrace and then holds her arms out to Joey who picks her up gently and hugs her.

"I don't know how to thank you all, it's a vast amount of money. Thank you so much. It will go to very good use I promise you."

"We know it will. Joey worked hard and insisted you have it all. Hopefully we'll make as much next TT. What are Dad and the boys up to?"

"They are all using their good looks and powers of persuasion to get a few of my residents rehomed." She grins and we're treated to a rare giggle. "Young Felix is a real charmer. Everyone is coming out of the café fed and happy and then getting accosted by three very attractive men. The few that manage to resist the American charm are being bewitched by Dylan's most beautiful Caribbean lilt. We can't lose."

"Oh my goodness Nina, I have never heard you speak like that." Milly laughs. "Carole is a good, or maybe a bad, influence."

Nina shrugs. "You cannot deny they are all very fine specimens. If Joey goes out too we'll have no one left to rehome by tea time. There are several lonely ladies who'll happily take the men home as well as a furry friend."

"No one is having my man!" Carole growls untying her apron. "Come on Joe, help me fight 'em off." Joey grins and follows her outside.

"Really, thank you so much for everything." Nina says earnestly. "The money is a godsend, all of your love and support has meant that Joey has grown into the most humble, generous and confident young man and your help whilst I was in the hospital was really appreciated. I don't know what I would have done without you all."

"You're a trooper, Nina. You'll always find a way." I tell her. "Are there any male shoppers out there that might feel left out? I can show the boys how it's done." She laughs and tells me there are at least three and one is looking for a big dog.

I walk down to the kennels and smile when I see my family; Felix and Joey are giving their full attention to a little girl who looks about three. They are carefully helping her to hold all of the rabbits and guinea pigs, one by one. Dad is talking a very smart and well to do looking lady into taking on a couple of Persian kittens and Emmett is being licked to bits by a huge puppy whilst being chatted up a very giggly young lady. I spy a quiet, mature gentleman down by the kennels where the older dogs are kept and go over to see if I can help.

"Are you looking for anyone in particular?"

He looks a little unsure. "Err, I don't really know. I lost my wife a few months back and everyone keeps telling me to get a dog so that I will go out and get exercise and meet new people. I think it's a good idea but I don't know which is best. I've never had a dog before. My wife was allergic to furry animals."

"Okay, we'll take our time and have a look to see who you like and who likes you, shall we? What sort of home do you live in? Do you have a garden?"

"The house is big and we have a huge garden and it's all fenced so it should be safe." He tells me. "I think I want a big dog, and a grown up one, not a puppy."

"Do you like walking?"

"Oh, definitely. I go walking most days, a dog would be good company, wouldn't it?"

"They are brilliant companions but they do need a bit of looking after. Walking every day, feeding and grooming and then there's vet bills if they get ill. They also need somewhere to stay if you're going away and don't like to be left home alone for too long."
"My children said they will help out for holidays, not that I have any planned, and my grandchildren will want to be involved too. I work from home so they won't be alone often."

"That sounds great. Come and meet a our residents." I smile leading him

411

into the clean, bright kennel area. He looks into the rooms as he makes his way down the row. "If you see one you would like to meet tell me and I'll get them out for you. You're under no obligation to take any. Don't rush, just take your time."

"How will I know which one is right?" He asks looking a little worried.

"You'll know, trust me. Animals often pick their owners rather than the other way around."

"Do you have a dog?"

"I have four dogs, a cat, three donkeys, chickens and some bantams and four horses arriving any minute." I tell him with a smile. "Most of them came from here." He stops suddenly and his eyes meet the huge brown eyes of a beautiful German Shepherd. They look closely at each other for a long moment and I can tell it's love at first sight.

"This is the one, isn't it?" He states.

"Looks like it. I'll get her out to say hello." I open the door and slip on the lead hanging nearby. I take a quick look at her notes. "This is Lily. She's just four years old and her owner sadly passed away last week. She's fully house and lead trained and can live with other dogs and cats and is fine with children. We still advise you to take everything carefully and be vigilant especially with any little ones."

"My grandkids are over twelve and will be very gentle." He is on his knees with his arms around Lily and she has her eyes closed and is resting her head on his shoulder. "Can I take her now? Can you sell me a bed and some food and treats too and a lead and some toys?"

"She already has a lot of stuff that came in with her. We try to send them with familiar things. She has a lead and collar, her bed and some toys and we can sort some food in the shop." I take a note of what she is currently eating. "Are you happy for someone to come and do a home visit in the next day or two?"

"Yes, yes, of course, any time." He takes the lead from me. "Come on, sweet girl, let's go home." I introduce him to Nina so that she can sort the paperwork and I go and get all of Lily's belongings and food.

I'm just returning to find another willing victim when Felix and Joey come over to me with matching cheeky grins. "We want you to meet someone." They drag me over to the rabbits and there is a Flemish Giant the size of a dog. He looks like the rabbit equivalent of Dutch; a real bruiser and a bit knocked about with chunks out of his ears and fur missing in several places. Despite this he comes bounding out when he sees us and pushes his head against the mesh to rub against Joe's face. "Can we?" Felix pleads.

"What's his name?" I sigh, tickling him behind the ears.

"We've named 'im Frank." Joey grins. "The owner bought 'im in 'cause he's been beating up 'er Yorkshire Terriers and takin' 'imself for walks. Emm an' Dylan're okay with 'im."

"Did anyone bring a rucksack or do we need to go and get the car?" Dad appears behind me and waves his rucksack. "Thought we might need it. Is Frank joining the Clan?"

"Looks like it." I smile. "Get in the bag, Frank." He very happily climbs in when Dad holds it out to him. It's quite a snug fit.

Nina announces that Felix has won the afternoon by rehoming four kittens, three rabbits a guinea pig and a little terrier. Emm and Dad have managed four cats, two kittens, two puppies, a rabbit and two rats between them. Pretty impressive work all round. Nina is more than happy and insists we take Frank without leaving a donation.

The Macs are doing a sterling job when we arrive home and the dogs are out and 'helping' as I suspected. We let Frank out to meet everyone and him and Dutch hit it off immediately rubbing heads affectionately, Jeff licks him from ears to tail and Odin gets a swift kick in the nose for sniffing his bum. "He's going to fit in fine." Dad laughs as they all disappear onto the beach.

"How's it going, Paddy? Need a hand with anything?"

"We're all good but you must start that Dodge up for us to have a listen in a bit and the boys might be getting a little peckish." He replies with a wink. I go and put the kettle and the coffee on and get some sandwiches and cakes sorted.

The floor for Felix's room is already down, the plasterboard walls are going up along with the insulation, the electrics and some lights and heating.

"Are you going to sort your bed and furniture Fe, or do you want me to do it?" I ask as he stands there grinning at the room taking shape.

"I'm on it. Meeting Nath and Connor in Douglas in a little while so that I can order everything before they close. Nath knows the furniture shop guy. Me and Joe are just going to get the bedding down in the stables then I'm off but I'll be back to get ready for family night."

"It's going to be extended family night, I think."

"Perfect either way. I love this family however it comes." He kisses my head and makes his way down to the paddock. I let Paddy know the keys are aready in the Charger if he wants to play and he runs over to it like an excited child. I take a walk down the beach with the zoo and then go to get showered and ready for our meal.

CHAPTER 62

I'm just putting on some of my new sexy underwear, including black stockings and suspenders, when Emm comes into the bedroom. I smile and ask if he likes them.

"Jeez, Delilah, we're going to be late again. Come here, quickly!" I giggle and willingly do as I'm told. He wraps me in his arms, pulls me onto the bed and demonstrates how much he likes. Once we've had our fill of each other I put one of my lovely soft woolen dresses on and a spray of my perfume Kim bought for me, slip on my boots and I'm ready to go.

Despite offering Frank the clean and cosy kennel and safe run next to the chucks, Dutch and the dogs sprung him immediately and he is obviously planning on being a house rabbit and roaming with the pack. We leave them all lounging on the sofa, chair and beds.

We pile into the Charger; Emm and Dad in the front, me, Ella, Joey and Felix in the back and arrive just in time to meet up with everyone pulling up outside the restaurant.

Sarah flies into my arms. "Auntie Dilly, you look funny in a dress. I told everyone at school about the wedding and my teacher says she wants to come and I have got to take lots of pictures to show my class. Can I invite my teacher? She's lonely and I need to get her a man to marry. I've put her on my list, she might like Uncle Ricky if he behaves himself but he's probably too old for her or maybe Charlie might like her. She is nice and very pretty but a bit strict and a bit boring sometimes, like when she wouldn't let me take my crosser or the dogs to school, but maybe that's just because she's sad and lonely. I told her I'd ask if she could come because there would be lots of fit men for her to look at but she can't have Daddy or Uncle Emm or Uncle Stef or Joey but she can look at them because Mommy says they're all sexy and 'ripped' and there's no point looking at our Nathan and Connor because they love each other too much to be bothered about her. I can tell her not to look at Uncle Emm if you want me to but she'll probably look anyway. What do you think?" She finally stops for breath and does a 'palms up' shrug at me.

Emm, Stef and the boys are hanging on to her every word. Kim is smiling at her like she is an angel. Ricky is laughing his head off and Sal is rolling her eyes.

"You can invite her if you want to my darling if you don't think our crazy family will be too scary for her. She can look at Uncle Emm because it's really hard not to look at him when he's so lovely but if she touches him I'm going to have to have a serious word with her. I think she'll love Uncle Ricky because he's funny and kind and cuddly even if he is a bit old he'll be able to make her laugh a lot, especially if he takes off his clothes, but if he doesn't fancy her we'll find someone else. She'll have to dress as a superhero and she's has to like cake and be okay with dogs and cats and donkeys and big horses and rabbits."

"You haven't got any big horses or rabbits." She states, looking puzzled.

"Yep we have. Uncle Emmett and Felix's four horses are coming tomorrow and Frank the rabbit came to live with us today. Joey's got some pictures on his phone for you."

"Awesome! I'll tell her tomorrow. Can I ride the horses?" She squeals and dives into Joey's waiting arms. "I might be a horse lady when I grow up."

Emm hugs me as we all enter the restaurant. "Please can we have a Sarah real soon. She's fearless, can she ride?"

"Honey, Sarah is one of a kind, there are no more like that anywhere in the world. Yep, she can ride. Sal takes her every weekend."

We get crushed from behind in a Billy bear hug. "Daves. Yow won't want one when you're trying to 'ave a shag an' it keeps interruptin'." He comments. "'Er latest 'I want' is an 'orse an' I reckon 'er teacher'll be reportin' us to social services if she comes near your place an' sees us in full swing."

"We'll just get her teacher too drunk to remember what she saw." I giggle. "She'll have to get used to us all if she's marrying Rick."
"Shortarse, I ain't marryin' nobody and I'm pretty sure she ain't much older than our Nath. Sarah told me about her on the way here and the description didn't really get my dick hard. A kid who dresses like my Mam isn't high on my 'I want' list." He deadpans. He leans down to greet me and bite his nose then kiss his cheek. "And don't go thinking you got away with that 'clothes off' sass either. I'll get you back."

The banter and the teasing continues as we all get seated. The restaurant could not be more friendly or accommodating. They have laid a long table and all fifteen of us sit down, well fourteen do and Sarah is flitting from chair to chair getting hugs and cuddles, gossiping about her schoolfriends and her family and I hear her describing her teacher in detail to a very interested Charlie. I nudge Emm so he can listen.

"She's taller than Auntie Dilly but so is everyone, not as tall as Mommy, she's not fat but not skinny, she has nice big boobies and a nice bum like Ella's and she dresses a bit like my Nanny Pat but I think that's just for school because she wore skinny jeans and a t shirt when we went on a trip to the wildlife park, that's how I know she has boobies and a nice bum. Her hair is long and blonde and wavy. She has her own flat in Ramsey right by the sea and lives on her own with a cat called Tom. She works very hard and doesn't go out much. She likes music because she puts it on in the class lots and she sings okay too. She likes children, except for Jack but nobody likes him because he's nasty and spiteful and he says very bad things to her. Daddy would smack him in the mouth if he heard him. If she does come what superhero could she be?"

Charlie thinks for a second. "How about a Powerpuff Girl? She could be Blossom or Buttercup or Bubbles. You could definitely be a Powerpuff Girl. I think you might already be one but it's a secret so we don't know." Sarah looks confused but intrigued so he sits her up on his lap and finds her a cartoon on YouTube on his phone. She's enthralled and stays watching with Charlie, discussing all the superpowers she has, until our food arrives.

Rather than having to wait for everyone to choose from a menu the restaurant offers to bring us a tasty array of everything and there are plenty of starters, mains and desserts to dig into and the drink flows very freely. Everyone toasts Joey and congratulates him on passing his test.

I go to chat with Sal about my 'to do' list and Billy won't move so I sit on him. He puts his hands on my legs and feels my suspenders and then takes great enjoyment in pinging them every few minutes. Emm just encourages him with a laugh and then starts chatting with Stef about getting back into the studio. It's great to see how relaxed and understanding he is becoming about my odd relationship with Billy and Ricky.

Kim comes to ask if she can help with anything for the wedding. Dad and Rick are talking bikes and the kids are all catching up. Sarah is fast asleep in Felix's arms; he is laughing at a huge chocolate ice cream hand print she's left on his new, white t-shirt. God, I love my bonkers, ever growing family so much.

We sort most of the wedding stuff; food, flowers, cake, decorations, altar, seating and drink then Sal asks what sort of ceremony we want.

"I have no idea. I'm sure Emmett mentioned a Rabbi during one discussion but I don't actually know if he was serious. Does he follow a religion, Kim?" She says none that she's aware of he's more into spiritual stuff. "I'll talk with him later and let you know. Do we have any options currently? I was probably envisaging a handfasting performed by a druid, an ethereal fairy lady or someone dressed as Elvis; a humanist ceremony. What was his first wedding like?" I ask, remembering he's done it all before.

"Certainly nothing like this one will be." Kim giggles. "It was a rush job in Vegas as he thought she was pregnant and wanted to do the decent thing and she realised she'd found her meal ticket and didn't want to let him get away. There was only Stef and I and some of the band and the crew there. His parents weren't speaking to him by then and I don't know anything about her family but none of them were there. Everyone I know was against the idea of him marrying her and didn't really want to attend. Turns out we were all right. Thank goodness Stef made him get a prenup." She shrugs. "Even Elvis was booked up so they got some old drunk who could barely stand. I think he could probably argue it was never legal to begin with, as he got all of the wording wrong and missed bit chunks of the legal stuff out. It sounds like Karma has caught up with Cherry so there's no point worrying now."

I'm quite surprised to hear this, I don't know why but I'd imagined he'd had a huge white wedding and a lavish party for hundreds of friends and family and loads of media publicity and magazine spreads. Now I feel a bit bad for talking him into our current crazy plans. Come to think about it, we haven't seriously discussed it at all. I make a mental note to sort this later. Glancing across the table I can see him engrossed in a discussion with Stef, Connor, Charlie and Nathan. He doesn't look unduly worried about our impending nuptials or anything at all for that matter; he's calm, smiling and giggling and describing something with his hands. He senses me watching him and gives me a huge grin and blows me a kiss.

"Ma, what name did Andy tell ya earlier?" Joey yells. He's discussing his recent offers with Ricky. A sound idea because the Parkers know everyone and can tell us if these people have enough funds to run a team. I join them and get another suspender twang as I leave Billy. Of course, Ricky thinks it's a great game and immediately joins in. I punch him playfully and then find the name and number. Ricky says the guy does indeed have more money than sense but no mechanical knowledge and not many connections. Joey shows him more names and numbers in his phone and Rick confirms at least three are worth calling back. I make a note so that we can call as soon as Joe wants to.

"Can you sort loos and showers for the wedding, please? Everyone can camp again and I have a feeling it might still be going on through Saturday. Dan and the band have booked time off work so they can stay 'til the end."

"Sal's already given me my orders. I'll bring everything over next week." He replies.

"Where's Chaz?"

"They sent him off somewhere for work again. He'll be back for ya wed-

418

din' bab, you know he wouldn't miss it for anything."

"Who you coming as?" I ask. "You going to be your favourite superhero?"

"Of course, who else would I be?"

"I remember us going to see the movie when it came out. I laughed so much I nearly peed myself."

"You did. You also nutted the bloke sitting in front of us because he was recording it all on his phone and told you to be quiet." He recalls.

"He was rude!" I giggle.

"Happy days." He says, kissing my head and pinging my suspenders again. "Now look at ya? All grown up and dressed like a big girl with a house and a husband and kids and responsibilities."

"Yep, don't quite know how that all happened." I sigh contentedly, looking across the table with nothing but love for everyone around me. "But I've never been so happy. I just hope it doesn't all come crashing down, given my track record, I know it eventually will but I'm enjoying it while it lasts."

"Don't jinx it Shortarse, it'll last this time. I reckon you've already had your share of shite."

"I hope so Rick, I don't think I could ever come back from losing this."

"Not gonna happen. He loves you more than you know and would give up everything he has if you asked him to. Your Dad's even more chilled than usual and loving having you around. The boys are doing great and you're here with us now so we can keep a proper eye on you, on all of you." He nods his head towards Emm.

"You two reminiscing again?" Emm asks picking me up, sitting on my chair and putting me on his lap. "Want some more drinks? Stef's just ordering."

We eagerly order two more pints and I tell him about the cinema trip we were remembering.

"Come on you've gotta tell me, who's the superhero?"

"Guess." I laugh. "Which superhero is most like Rick?"

"The Incredible Hulk?" He shrugs. I shake my head. "Thor?" I laugh outright at that idea. He has a few more guesses that we tell him are wrong. "I have no idea, honey. Tell me."

"Deadpool." I giggle.

Emm rolls his eyes and groans. "How did I not get that? He's absolutely you, just a little less built."

"What we doin' for your stag do?" Ricky asks. "Wanna go over to the mainland for a couple of days? Or Dam? I ain't bin there for ages."

"Hadn't even thought about it to be honest." Emmett admits looking at me. "You mean Amsterdam?"

"Yep, I love Amsterdam. Can we go there?"

"No Shortarse. It's your future husband's stag do. You ain't invited." He turns to the rest of the table. "What you reckon men? Amsterdam for Emmett's stag do next week?" Stef, Dad, Felix, Billy, Charlie and Joey shout a unanimous 'yeah'. Nathan says he should be able to get time off and Connor looks more willing on hearing this.

Emm shrugs, "Looks like I'm going to Amsterdam, darlin'. You okay with that?"

"Yeah, I'm completely fine with that, you don't need my permission. You'll have a great time with the boys. Have you been before?"

"Nope, heard about it but never been. Stef, text your Dad, see if he can join us. What about Chaz?"

"Already on it." Stef replies, waving his phone at us. "Texting every guy we know."

"What do the girls get to do?" Sal yells.

"Muck out horses and donkeys, plan weddings, do loads of cooking and booze shopping and walk dogs, cats and rabbits." I reply.

"Wow! Can't wait. That doesn't sound fair." She groans. "They get to cavort with strippers, shag prossies and eat happy brownies and we get to shovel shit!"

"You can take the plane wherever you want as soon as we get back." Emm offers with a laugh, adding quietly to me, "I will not be partaking in the shagging of prossies."

"Okay then, that sounds more like it." Sal concedes. "I can probably get used to having a private plane at my disposal."

"Does that mean you will be involved in the happy brownies and the strippers?" I ask, raising an eyebrow.

"Yeah, I might get involved in some of that." He grins. "Be rude not to if the boys have made such an effort to organise it."

"Totally agree, babe. I'd be doing exactly the same if I was there." I admit.

"You are heaven sent, Delilah. I can't believe how easy going and relaxed you are about everything." He kisses me deeply.

"Blame it on the hippy parents. I've had a very liberal upbringing." I explain, grinning at Dad, who raises his pint in salute and acknowledgement.

The restaurant manager, or maybe he's the owner, comes to the table with two huge cakes. "We know you have just got engaged, we saw the news in the local paper, and understand that you are also about to be married so we would like to add our congratulations. Compliments of The Boatyard."

Everyone claps and cheers and we gratefully thank them and order coffees and nightcaps before all diving into the cakes.

Sarah wakes up, she obviously has the same inbuilt cake detector as Joey. She hugs Felix and tells him he's very comfortable then climbs up onto my lap which is still in Emmett's lap and wraps her arms around his neck.

"Hello Uncle Emmett, you look very nice tonight. Have you got some cake that I could have, please?" She asks, wide eyed and innocent. I see Emm just melt as he cuts her a big chunk off each cake and hands her the dish. She grins widely, jumps off us and trots away to torment Joe with her winnings."

"That's my girl!" Billy laughs. "She soon twigged how to work you." I laugh too because I was thinking the exact same thing. Emm grins, knowing he's been played and admits he'll fall for it every time, is power-less to resist and will give her whatever she wants.

"Don't let her hear you say that." Sal groans. "She'll write you a list, a very long and expensive list. Her own pony is currently top priority."

We finish up our drinks, food and coffee. Emm pays the bill and we all head outside to our cars and bikes. We all hug and say our goodbyes and Rick says he'll sort all of the accommodation and everything for Amster-dam and let Stef know what's happening.

We jump into the Charger and head home. Dad drives and Felix sits in the front. Emm sits in the back with me on his lap and Ella cuddles up on Joey's lap. The sound of the Dodge in the dark, quiet night is amazing, we all wind down the windows to listen; me and Joey hanging our heads out of the windows like dogs. When we see the huge full moon we both start howling. Everyone in the car dissolves into a fit of the giggles. Emmett slips his hand up my skirt and twangs my suspenders. We journey home via the scenic route and sing and howl when we're not listening to the roar of the engine and the note of the exhaust pipe.

"I love family nights; immediate and extended ones." I announce once we get home and are all saying goodnight and being flattened and slobbered and nibbled by the released menagerie. Emm and I take a walk down the beach with the dogs, Dutch on my shoulder, Frank on his. I've kicked off my boots at our steps and walk in my stockinged feet. "You looking for-ward to your stag party?" I ask, giggling as Frank nibbles on his hair and wraps awkwardly around his neck.

"Yeah, I think so. Actually, yeah, I really am. I know it'll be fun and I'll be safe."

"What did you do on your last one?"

"Nothing, didn't have one. My first wedding was a very last minute and very bad decision based on a complete lie."

I think about this. "Did you forget how really bad that decision was when you proposed to me after less than a fortnight?" I ask with an arched eyebrow.

"Delilah, darlin', I was never more sure of anything in my life when I proposed to you. I wanted to make you mine the second I met you. As soon as I saw you I was hooked. I couldn't stay away. Stef kept warning me to be careful and slow down or else you'd think I was a stalker but I couldn't help myself. I was so relieved when Kim came over and told me I was right to go for it, even though I was too deeply in love to change my mind by then. Then Sal saw your ring and gave her blessing and the boys encouraged me to make it official. I knew I wanted to be here, with you, always, from the very first time I walked into the cottage."

"I blame the smell of breakfast and fresh bread on a lot of things." I smile. "Sal asked what sort of ceremony we wanted earlier and I didn't even know if you followed a religion."

"Did that upset you?" Emm looks concerned. "We've got our whole life to get to know each other. I don't have any strong beliefs apart from the inevitability of the intervention of Madame Karma. You aren't having any second thoughts are you?"

"Good Lord, No! We're one hundred per cent getting married." I laugh. "I just realised that you've willingly gone along with my kooky madness and given Sal free rein with regard to how the engagement party went and how the ceremony is going to go and had no input. I told Sarah she could bring her teacher without even asking you. I just thought you might be feeling a little rail-roaded about now. How did you see your perfect wedding going?"

"Darlin', marrying you as Batgirl while I am dressed as Batman, on our own private beach surrounded by the most amazing and genuine family and friends, far outweighs any dreams I've ever had about my ideal wedding, which I can truly say, I never even thought about. Isn't dreaming about your wedding day just a girl thing?" He replies honestly, adding a cheeky grin. "And you know full well that I would give both you and Sarah the moon. Inviting her teacher is not an issue at all."

I laugh. "Maybe it is a girl thing but I have to admit I'd never thought about it either and I just followed Sarah's lead with the superhero thing,

I can't take the credit for the idea at all. Do you want a humanist ceremony? Maybe a handfasting?"

"I am going to love every second of whatever the day brings. I will willingly take part in everything Sarah, you or Sal have planned. Is that bad? Did you want me to be more involved in the planning?"

"I'm not really involved either, if I'm honest. I'm leaving it all to Sal." I shrug. "I just felt bad that I have done that without even asking you."

"Don't ever feel bad about just telling me how stuff is going to go. It's another of the many things I love about you. You always surprise me in a good way so I'm happy to be led by the nose in whatever direction you want to go. I have already had some new and pretty fabulous adventures with you that I didn't expect and I know Amsterdam for my bachelor party is going to be another experience that I will not forget."

"How Felix, Stef and Kim can claim you're a stress head and a control freak is beyond me. You are chilled and mellow and so easy going."

"It's you that has made me this way. You have bought out the carefree side of me that they hadn't seen for a very long time. Are you happy to let Sal carry on with the planning or do you want me to be more involved?"

"I'm more than happy to leave it all to Sal. It makes it more fun when we haven't a clue what's coming next." I yawn.

He smiles and holds out his hand to me. "Come on, my soon to be wife, it's way past your bedtime." We deposit all of our furry companions back in the cottage and hear grunts from Felix and Dad as they get flattened by their arriving bedmates.

"Thanks, parents!" Felix calls out. "Great night by the way, we need a Sarah." We giggle and head for bed.

I'm lying in Emm's arms with my head on his chest. "Are you looking forward to the horses arriving?" I ask.

"Yeah, but I feel a bit bad about leaving you to look after them. You'll have Tiff to help out though."

"Tell me about Tiff. What does she like to do and eat? I feel bad that all the boys are going to run away to party when she's come all this way."

He thinks about it for a second. "She's a female version of Felix but with an Irish accent."

"Really? Sounds adorable. Explain more."

"She's got a smart mouth but she's eager to please and really easy going. She works hard and is brilliant with the horses. You'll get along fine, you won't be mucking out, she's still going to be doing her job when she gets here."

"I'll help out. I've got plenty of time. I'll need something to keep me busy while you're all away. Sal will want to ride too if that's okay. "

"You do whatever you want to my beautiful woman. I'd be more than happy if you came with us."

"As much as I would love to come we have a lot of dependents that need looking after." I giggle. "Hi Tiff, we're off on a drug and shag fest, good luck with the horses, don't forget to feed the dogs, cat, donkeys, chickens, bantams and rabbit......"

"Ah... put that way I see what you mean. I'll miss you and ring you every ten minutes."

"Every ten minutes is a little excessive." I say with a smile.

"Fifteen?" He shrugs.

I yawn and stroke his chest. "Whatever makes you happy, baby. Definitely videocall me when you've been on the brownies, that I need to see. Night, night Emm. I love you so much."

CHAPTER 63

"Yo Ma, feed me now! I gorra 'elp Rick an' Bill so they can get next week's work done 'fore Emm's rave." Joey kisses my head and he leans over to steal the toast that's just popped up. "Oh, an' I ain't gorra passport. Can ya sort it?"

"I can certainly try, sunshine." I laugh. "It may be a little short notice."

"Ring Hans, he'll sort it." Emm offers. "Want me to do it?" He picks up his phone and calls without waiting for a reply. "Joe look this way and don't smile. I need some photos for Hans." Joey tries to be serious and I tickle him, keep pulling faces and distracting them both until Emm threatens to set the dogs on me and Felix gets up and holds me in a big bear hug with my face buried in his chest so that they can get some sensible pictures. Emm sends them to Hans and says it should be sorted before they go away.

"Is yours in date Dad?" He goes to check his passport is still valid and confirms it has two years left on it. "Have you got any jobs you need a hand with? Anything you've promised for next week?"

"Got a couple on the go but the should be ready in time, thanks Dilly Girl."

"Gorra go." Joey announces, grabbing the rucksack full of food I've just packed. "Ta, Ma. I'll be back to 'elp with ya furniture later, Fe. Love yas"

"Ride Safe. Love you too." I smile as Dad, Emm and Felix shout exactly the same words at the same time as me.

"What time is your furniture arriving?" I ask as I hear The Macs pull up in their truck and get more bacon and sausage from the fridge.

"I told them as late as possible so probably around half four. Horses should be here around half seven I think so it shouldn't be too hectic until then."

The Macs are herded into the cottage by the dogs who then proudly show off the newest member of their pack to those who missed his arrival.

"Morning guys." Emm greets them, pointing to our new resident who is sprawled on the chesterfield. "Meet the latest edition to the family, Frank."

"Don't look like we're going to need to build him a hutch anytime soon." Juan quips as he tickles him behind the ears. "Does he know he's a rabbit?"

"Nope, totally thinks he's a dog." Fe replies. "We need to get my room done soon, sharing a single bed with at least two Dobermans, a cat and a rabbit is going to kill the romance for me and Tiff."

"Where do the rest sleep?" Paddy laughs. "Don't worry, son, we'll have you sorted today."

"The rest sleep with Dad." I tell him. "Dutch sometimes comes in with us if we promise we're going to behave. Who wants bacon and who wants sausage?" I hold up two huge plates of sandwiches which soon disappear.

The Macs, Felix and Emm go to get the mezzanine sorted, Dad to get on in the workshop and I visit the donkeys and chucks to muck out, serve breakfast and get cuddles, then I clean the cottage, sort the washing and ironing, do a bit of gardening, bake a mountain of sweet and savoury goodies and precook a load of meals for the freezer, the smell of which brings everyone down for lunch. I feed them and wash up, finish the cooking and baking and finally stop for a rest. I like being a housewife I laugh to myself as I collapse on the sofa with a coffee and a muffin still warm from the oven.

I check my phone and Sal has sent a message thanking us for last night and asking who she needs to find to marry us. I ask her to find us someone to perform a handfasting ceremony preferably teetotal and under ninety. She texts back 'M or F?' I reply that I have no preference. She sends back 'you're too easy' and a smiley face. I'm just going to reply when I hear a van backing into the driveway.

Outside I find a huge furniture van and a couple of brawny delivery men. "Felix Wright?" One asks. "Where do you want this lot?"

"No, I'm not Felix." I laugh. "I'll get him." I yell upstairs and Fe comes down.

"Perfect timing. We've just finished clearing everything up. This way guys, please." They pull a king-sized bed out of the van and follow him up the stairs.

"Fe, did you buy a duvet and bedding?" I shout after him.

"Oh shit, no!" He groans. "I'll go in a bit."

"They'll be shut. What colour bedding d'you want? I'll go now."

"Dil, you're an angel. Any colour, I'm not fussed but not flowery. I forgot pillows too."

I grab my purse, jump inthe Charger and race to the shop before closing time. I choose an expensive down duvet and some masculine cotton bedding including a blue and white striped duvet cover set and some blue cotton sheets then an extra set of white sheets and a black and white duvet cover set and some pillow cases. I get Joey a matching duvet set too as I don't want him to feel left out. I buy half a dozen different bed pillows as I have no idea if Fe likes them soft, firm or somewhere in between. I buy Emm a lovely toiletry travel set for next week and some more bath sheets then head back to the car when they start kicking out for closing time. When I arrive home the Macs have packed up and left and the furniture van is gone too.

Emm greets me at the car. "You look you stole your dad's car." He laughs as he sees I've got the chair pulled forward as far as it will go and two of the new pillows shoved down my back and one to sit on.

"Do we need to get you a booster seat?"

"I've just bought you a present. I don't think you deserve it now." I growl, in mock indignation.

"I totally deserve it I've been a very good boy. I'm sorry darlin' I couldn't help myself. Come and see Felix's room and then I'll make it up to you." He winks. I throw the duvet at him and giggle. "You better make it real good after that comment, Mr. Wright."

The room looks great. The bed is already put together and Emm and Joey are busy assembling wardrobes and bedside cabinets. Felix remembered a lamp too.

"What bedding do you want on?" I show him the bags.

"Either, they're both cool. Thanks Mom." He drawls cheekily, kissing my head.

"Black one's sexy. I like it" Joey states.

"Thought you might. I bought you one too." He hugs me and takes the linen to put in his own room then returns to help Felix. I make the bed with the black and white and it looks very manly.

"How come they get man's stuff and I get lace and frills?" Emm moans jokingly.

"I got theirs, Sal got ours." I offer in explanation. "If you want black, we'll have black next time. These could really have done with washing first but I'm sure Tiff won't complain after her epic journey, she'll be too knackered to notice anything." Felix looks mortified and then slightly disappointed and we all burst out laughing.

"Don't look so worried, Fe. She'll have missed you so much she'll forget how tired she is. Anyhow girls like sleepy sex so you'll be fine." Emm reassures him and looks to me for confirmation of the last statement. I smile and nod in agreement.

Once everything is in place the room looks great. I get him some towels out of the linen box in Joey's room and we head down for food and to await the arrival of the horses.

We tuck into chicken and broccoli lasagne and eat a mountain of garlic bread then devour a massive fruit salad, I chopped earlier, with ice cream. I warn them to save some lasagne and fruit for Tiff, for later but am too late and I'll have to find her something else. We're just finishing the washing up when Ian and Vicky arrive. Ian looks fraught but Vicky is as bright and cheerful as she was at the party. "Everything okay?" Emm asks, looking concerned.

"Yes, everything is fine." Vicky smiles. "Your boys were a little wild in the plane. They'll be fine when they get to kick their heels up. They are all amazing. I haven't seen such big stallions up close before. Angel is a sight to behold. Your groom is lovely too, very professional and she has the patience of a saint."

The horsebox pulls in and much kicking and whining and snorting can be heard from the back. A curvy young lady with a huge mop of curly red ringlets jumps down from the driver's seat and slams her hand on the back of the truck and yells. "Give it a motherfucking rest Angel, we're here now, you fucking psycho, chill baby!" She walks around the front of the truck and sees us all standing there. She stares at Emmett for a long second as if she's expecting a bollocking. "Oops, you didn't hear that did you? Hello Mr. Wright, I'm really sorry, it's been an extremely long and interesting journey." Her eyes dart to Felix and her face lights up but she's unsure of how to behave in front of everyone and just stays glued to the spot.

"Come here you daft tart!" Fe laughs and she jumps into his arms and bursts into tears. "Give Dad the keys and we'll get you fed and sorted." He carries her inside the cottage, handing over the horsebox keys as he passes.

Emm backs it in through the paddock gates and opens the back door with some trepidation, two huge horses trot out happily and whinny in recognition at Emm, nuzzling and fussing over him. Vicky stands on the fence, watching eagerly whilst Ian half-heartedly helps out from a safe distance. The inner stall in the horsebox is looking a little misshapen and Emm puts his head inside and talks soothingly to the occupant then leads out a sulky looking strongly build lad who kicks and throws his head around as soon as he is outside the box.

Emm smiles and heads back in for what I assume to be Angel. We hear plenty of squealing, kicking and choice language and then a jet black, super sleek and super-fast missile launches out of the vehicle and bucks like a crazy bronco all around the field then races to the perimeter and gives the fence a good booting to test its strength. He flies to the opposite fence but stops abruptly to glare at Ian. His ears twist back and his eyes narrow and he lets out a serious snort or disapproval. Joey pushes Ian out of the way as Angel aims a brutal kick in his direction, missing by inches. Ian runs and jumps over the fence to stand by Vicky. Angel chases him with serious determination but stops when he sees Vicky, eyes her up as if he's flirting, sniffs her and rubs his head against hers.

"Eh Laa! 'E likes Vicky." Joey pants. "'E's a ladies man."

We approach cautiously and Vicky is cooing gently at him and kissing his nose. "Can he have a polo mint?" She asks. "He is amazing."

"Be careful he doesn't take your fingers with it." Ian warns her. "Do you think we should give him another sedative?"

"Yeah, he can have a mint and no, I think he's already a little unhappy that you gave him a sedative." Emm laughs. The other three come over to see what they're missing and Emm introduces us to each one. They all accept fuss and mints and kisses from me, Dad, Joe and Vicky whilst Emm quickly runs his hands over them all to check they haven't damaged themselves in transit. Then go off on a crazy lap again when they see Felix and Tiff approaching with buckets and sacks.

Midnight and Luna nearly flatten Felix as he gets into the paddock, they shove him with their noses and bump up against him in recognition, desperate for his attention. He hugs and kisses them and offers carrots and whatever else he has in the sack for them. They both eat hungrily and Ian nods his approval.

"They seem to have travelled well." He announces. "Keep an eye on them and if any develop a cough let me know straight away. I'll be back to check them in the morning." Angel and Seraph go over to mug Felix for the treats and he swears as Angel takes a crafty bite of him. Vicky tears herself away and I walk her and Ian back to their car.

"Do you ride?" I ask on the way and Ian looks at me as if to say, 'are you seriously going to ride any of those?' I laugh. "I can't wait to take them down the beach."

Vicky is more excited about the idea. "Yes, I've ridden since I was tiny. I was planning on getting a horse over here as soon as I'm settled but I'm only renting a little apartment at the moment because I wasn't sure if I'd like the Island or the job. I've been down to the riding stables Ian recommended but the horses were all a bit too docile. I totally understand why but I like a more spirited mount, a bit less predictable."

"What are your thoughts on the place now?" I ask.

"Doesn't it just draw you in?" She sighs. "I can't think of anywhere else I'd rather be."

"It does tend to get under your skin. Just look at how many bodies we've accumulated, human and furry. You haven't met our other new edition, Frank the Flemish Giant." Hearing his name, Frank sticks his head and front paws over the half door.

"Oh my gosh, he's huge!" Vicky laughs, tickling his chin then dissolves in giggles when she looks over the door to see he's standing on top of Loki and Thor. I let them all out for Vicky to fuss and for them to go down to see the horses now they are a little more settled but I scoop up Frank as I don't want him to get accidently trampled.

"The boys are away on Emmett's stag do next week so I'll probably need a riding buddy if you're up for it. Emm will be a lot happier if I'm not riding alone. I'll get you the number of the place Sal and Sarah ride too. I know they have all the reprobate horses from the MSPCA. Speak to Meave Mc Donnagh as well, she's got a big stable but she's a breeder I imagine she can always use an experienced rider."

She throws her arms around me happily, then gives me her number. "Thank you so much I will get in touch with her. Ring me anytime I would absolutely love to ride one of your new editions." I thank Ian for his time and wave bye to them both then rejoin the boys.

The dogs and horses seem equally happy to be reunited and are all running around the paddock together. Jeff appears to think she also knows them all and is joining in. Dutch is sitting on Dad's shoulder, keeping well away from the madness. I look over at Tiff and she is swaying and looking more than a little exhausted.

"Felix honey, Tiff needs her bed before she falls asleep against that fence post. I think the horses had a much easier trip than she did." She smiles gratefully at me and Felix grins and leads her inside. "Night, both. Sleep well."

"Night fam, love you all!" Felix shouts back.

Frank climbs up onto Emmett's shoulder to observe the goings on in the paddock without showing any desire to join in. We all lean on the fence and watch for a little while longer and I tell Emm that Vicky wants to come and ride.

"Awesome, she can keep you company too, and possibly out of mischief." He adds with a smirk. "I know I can't trust Sal or Ella to do that."

Joey laughs. "She'll get involved in anythin' Ma does. She loves 'er to bits. They'll all say Sarah made 'em do it if it's bad anyway." He shrugs. We laugh and I punch him playfully.

"You know them too well, Son." Dad says. "Are we going to try and get the crazy horses in the stable or leave them free tonight? I've checked the weather and it's going to be warm and dry but they're used to LA so it might be cold for them."

"Gonna leave them out, they seem happy enough." Emm says. "I'll get their blankets out of the horsebox and put them on just in case." Moments later he hands me, Dad and Joey a beautifully soft, warm blanket each with names embroidered on them. "You can have Angel's; he likes the ladies." Emm winks at me.

"Thanks, honey." I laugh as I unravel it all to make sure I can throw it on in one quick movement. I approach Angel and he seems willing enough to tolerate me. I talk gently to him and stroke his neck as I put on his coat. As I'm doing up the buckles he decides to taste my dreads and nibbles quietly at my head until I'm finished. "He must have jet lag, that was easier than I anticipated." I muse as we head back to the cottage.

"Wait 'til you try to put a saddle on him." Emm replies.

"Ya makin' supper? I'm starvin'" Joey asks. "An' I just saved the vet's life so I should at least get cake." I happily provide supper and cake for my growing boy and the rest of my family, leaving a covered plate on the table in case Fe and Tiff emerge.

Next morning I plan get to know Tiff and the horses a little better. I pull on my daisy dukes and a vest top and head for the paddock. I'm impressed to find Tiff fully, and very smartly, dressed and already grooming Luna at half six. She's almost as tall as Sal but much more curvy. She has her gorgeous red hair pulled back into a neat chignon and is dressed in riding boots, jodhpurs and a big thick fleece. She has a pretty face and a cute sprinkle of freckles across her nose. She looks a few years older than Felix. She hears me approaching and stands up straight. "Good morning Mrs..er... Oh lord, what do I call you?" She looks really nervous.

"Whatever Felix calls me is fine, sweetheart."

She looks at me a little confused. "Lix calls you Mom whenever he's talking to me about you. I don't think I should be calling my new employer 'Mom'." She giggles.

I laugh. "Delilah or Dil is fine. We don't do formal here but expecting you to call me mom is a little much."

"Oh, okay. Mr. and Mrs. Wright were always very formal. In fact, I didn't even recognise him for a minute when I arrived. I hadn't seen him for quite a while but he looks ten years younger than the last time and he wasn't growling. He looked dead sexy. Lix said he'd mellowed beyond recognition now he's cut ties with Queen Bitch but I didn't believe him. Oh my god! I'm doing it again, I'm so sorry Mrs... er Delilah I should not be sharing my very personal thoughts about Mr. Wright with you. I'm sorry for being so unprofessional. I kind of feel like I know you from chatting on the phone so much with Lix. He talks about you all constantly. Please don't sack me on my first day."

"Tiff you really need to relax, my darling. We're so laid back here we're almost horizontal, including Emmett. I've heard plenty of stories about his 'growliness' but we've fixed him now and I totally agree, he is dead sexy." I laugh and her cheeks colour. "I hope you like it here and please know that you will be treated like a member of the family. We are a freaky family and might take some getting used to but don't ever feel that you can't speak to any of us like that or speak freely about anything at all."

She lets out a huge sigh and hugs me. "Lix said you were amazing, thank you."

Emm joins us with the dogs in tow. He's looking super smoulderingly sexy in jeans and no shirt, his feet bare and his hair wet from the shower.

"Morning my gorgeous girl, those shorts drive me wild." He growls at me then remembers Tiff is here. "How are you feeling, Tiff? Are you two getting to know each other?"

Tiff checks him out and blushes again and giggles when she sees me doing the same. "I'm good, Mr. Wright. Thank you so much for allowing me to travel over with the boys and for letting me stay. Please let me know when you want me to move out and I'll start looking for somewhere nearby."

"I think Felix might have something to say about that." Emm smiles at her. "He's just had a whole new room built and furnished so he can have you here and have his wicked way with you forevermore." She blushes deeply.

"Emm stop it." I chide. "She's used to grumpy, formal Emmett, you're embarrassing her."

"Oh, Tiff, I'm sorry baby. I'm a whole new me and we are definitely no longer formal or grumpy." He throws his arms around me as if to reinforce his words. "In fact we all behave like lunatics in this place and spend lots of time behaving like sex crazed teenagers, you'll get used to it, and hopefully like it a whole lot more than LA. Call me Emmett and thank you so much for getting them all here in one piece. I don't imagine it was a walk in the park and I am very grateful."

She giggles and loosens up a little. "Lix has told me a few tales but I must admit I thought he was exaggerating."

"You'll probably find he was toning them down." Felix laughs as he saunters towards us and picks me up in a big hug. "I can't believe everything I ever wanted is all here. The horses, the dogs, my girl, a happy Dad, a little brother, a real Mom and even a super chilled Grandpa."

I kiss his head and smile. "We have all found the perfect blend of crazy here, haven't we?"

"Tiff will soon chill out once I've had a few nights to work my magic on her." Fe grins and she blushes again. "I was going to give her a taste this morning but she was up and gone before I woke up."

"Well take her away and give her a proper welcome but feed her first there's plenty of breakfast still warm in the pan on the stove. Give us that brush, Tiff. We can finish the boys off." I say.

"Are you sure? I can come back and finish when I've eaten."

"No you can't. We are off to bed for the rest of the day. I've waited long enough." Felix giggles bending forward and throwing her over his shoulder.

She smacks him on the back and hisses. "Lix don't make me lose my job on the first day."

"Not gonna happen, baby." He tells her, smacking her bum. "You're here for the duration."

"Actually who are you and what have you done with my moody, serious Felix?" She squeals with laughter.

"That's my boy!" Emm grins. "Don't forget to feed her first."

We work side by side, grooming Luna and Seraph as they happily graze on hay nets and Midnight and Angel charge around with the dogs in hot pursuit.

"Have we got a tack room?" Emm asks eyeing the pile of saddles and bridles in the back of the horsebox. "We need to find somewhere for that lot and move this truck out of the way."

"Yep, in the new bit over there. I think. Who's truck is it? We better knock the dents out Angel's made."

"No need, it's ours, Hans bought it and had it delivered to the airport for when Tiff arrived."

We start unloading and find a perfect tack room with hooks on the walls and saddle racks, feed bins and shelves for polishes and other bottles and a bigger shelf for blankets and coats and even a boot rack.

"Paddy is a dream." Emm sighs as he drapes saddles and hangs ropes and harnesses and bridles then empties a bag of bottles and tins onto the shelf. I bend right over the saddle he's just hung so that I can reach to put some boots on the rack in the corner. I hear Emm let out a loud moan.

"Don't move, Delilah, stay right there. I have something for you." Before I can stand he's behind me with his hands on my hips and I can feel exactly what he's got for me pressing into my backside. "You in those shorts is one hell of a turn on." He groans and we are loudly christening the tack room when we hear a polite cough and find Ian waiting outside.

"Good morning both. Isn't it a lovely day?" He greets us. "I've come to check the horses. Has there been any worrying signs, coughs or lethargy?"

"No, they seem to be fine. They're eating and drinking and running around without looking unhappy." I tell him. "We've groomed Luna and Seraph and we didn't see any marks or scratches or swelling. We were about to attempt Midnight and Angel but we got a little sidetracked unpacking stuff in the tack room."

"Do you want me to check their temperatures?" He doesn't look too enthusiastic about the idea.

"No, don't bother, they're all good." Emm assures him. "We'll call you if we have any worries." We walk Ian back up to his Land Rover and Felix chooses that precise moment to confirm the rumours that he does, indeed, howl just like his Dad. Ian takes off like a rocket and Emm and I can't stop laughing. Dad sticks his head out of the workshop when he hears us. "See, I told you."

Once we've pulled ourselves together, Emm gives me a seductive look. "Now then, where were we?"

"Grooming Angel and Midnight?" I offer.

"I don't think so. I think I was shagging you senseless in the tack room." He growls.

"Oh yeah, I remember now." I giggle. "Shall we head back down there?"

"I'll go wherever those shorts go darlin'."

"Bed then. Just in case anyone else drops by to meet the horses."

"I'll head them off if I hear anyone." Dad promises. "See you later."

CHAPTER 64

A few hours later we get peckish and I go in search of food whilst Emm showers, I resist the urge to join him or else it'll be tea time. I make a huge tray full of sandwiches and a hearty veggie soup so that everyone can help themselves as and when they emerge from wherever. Emm and I are just losing control against the fridge again when a sleepy Felix and a wide-eyed Tiff come in.

"I don't know how that bloody fridge still functions." Fe groans. "Parents, put each other down please, we have company." He turns to Tiff. "See I was not exaggerating. He can't leave her alone in those shorts. It's like living in a hippy commune here."

"Food is on the table, pretend we're not even here." Laughs Emm, making no attempt to loose me. I tap out with a giggle and he reluctantly puts me down.

"Is everyone groomed?" Felix asks.

"Nope, we did Luna and Seraph and then your father led me astray in the tack room. I'm going to tackle Midnight and Angel when I've eaten some lunch and worn him out but I'm struggling with the wearing him out thing. He's getting worse."

"Serves you right for wearing those daisy dukes, you complete tart. The whole family have warned you about those, even the Chief of Police." Fe deadpans. I smack him playfully upside the head.

Emm growls. "They make me wanna do bad things to you." Me, Emm and Felix burst into the True Blood song and Tiff bursts into a fit of giggles.

"Oh lord, what have I walked into? Your dad is a sex fiend and I can't even imagine you ever speaking to Queen Bitch like that she'd have had a heart attack." She stops speaking and slaps her hands over her mouth, looking at Emm.

"Cherry?" He asks with a grin and a raised eyebrow.

"Yeah, sorry." Tiff grimaces. "I keep oversharing."

"It's a good name for her. Believe me, I've called her far worse. You certainly won't upset me by bad mouthing my very ex-wife. Have you had a hard time in LA since we've been gone?"

"No, not really, she's left me alone apart from dropping off the dogs whenever she's gone away, which was most weeks, to be fair. She bought her fitness trainer up to the stables a couple of times to show off the boys but he seemed to be more interested in my butt so she didn't come back with him again and I think he's been gone a while now. She bought a couple of people there recently who looked like buyers. I did let Mrs.

Fischer know. She came over once in a while to check everything was okay. I've been a bit lonely but Maisie has been up to help whenever she was out of school. It got a bit scary when Mrs. Wright was arrested and the press and media were everywhere but it was fine as soon as those security guys arrived. The 'for sale' sign was up before I left and I'm sure there'd been several viewings."

"Good riddance to the place. It was never a real home." Felix comments, kissing my head. "This is a real home. Not normal but very real."

Joey, Billy and Ricky fall through the door pushing and shoving each other playfully. "Fuck me Shortarse, you've bin told about them shorts." Rick groans making a big play of adjusting the front of his jeans as he kisses my head. "We've bought ya bogs for the shag fest."

"Daves." Billy grins, bear hugging me. "Feed us now. Fuck, yow smell like you've already bin 'avin' a shagfest."

"It's the shorts. He has no control." Fe sasses.

"You can talk, Bro." Joey smirks. "You smell worse than Ma."

"Will you all just shut the fuck up, please!" I groan. "Say hello to Tiff, who is now a complete wreck and will be booking the next flight home which means Felix will stop talking to us all and I'll have to look after the horses."

"Dave." Billy greets her with a salute of his coffee mug.

"Good Man, Felix my son, she's a looker." Ricky offers after studying her carefully.

"'As 'e bin 'owlin' all mornin'?" Joey asks. "Me an' El might 'ave the little bed tonight."

"They both have. I reckon it's linked to that full moon." Dad laughs as he joins us. "Are you lot scaring poor Tiff?"

"She's not going anywhere. I've got hand cuffs and everything." Felix shrugs.

She slaps him playfully. "You weren't exaggerating, were you?"

"Nope, can you handle it or shall we get our own place and disown them all?"

"I think I can get used to this kind of crazy." She grins.

"Good girl!" Emm says. "Just give them back all the sass they give you."

"Billy, Ricky and Joey." I offer by way of introduction. "Joe's an angel when he's not with these two but they are a bad influence on him. And this handsome fellow is my Dad, Dylan."

"Hello er....family." Tiff gives a little wave to everyone.

"See, she's getting it already." Felix says proudly.

"Well she won't be gettin' it next week." Rick smirks. "I've booked the hotel and Stef's booked the airport space and we'll be there and partyin' from Monday lunch and home on Wednesday night. Kim and Sal can take us to the airport. She ain't comin' else Emm won't get on the plane." He points his sandwich at me.

"The bachelor party? Lix did warn me. I can spend some time getting to know Delilah and all the girls."

"That won't end well." Billy states matter of factly. "Dave better cancel all leave for his boys."

Tiff looks a little confused so Dad explains. "Chaz is the big brother to these two. He's Chief of Police on the Island."

"So Lix wasn't joking about your 'shorts warning'?" She giggles at me.

"Nope, but it wasn't official. It was just banter." I smile.

"Bollocks was it!" Joey intervenes. "'E's banned 'er from goin' out in public in 'em. Is 'e comin' next week?"

"Yep, flyin' over on Tuesday and then comin' home with us." Billy tells him.

We carry on in our usual way whilst we all eat lunch and start on the cakes and muffins. Tiff seems a little overwhelmed and I can't help but think how surreal it must be after living and working in LA and being treated like an employee one minute and then suddenly being welcomed into the family. She must be feeling pretty confused.

"Right, I'm off to get the guys groomed, who's helping?" I announce when lunch is done.

"We're gone, got shitloads to do, ta for the food." Billy replies and he, Rick and Joey take turns to pick me up like a ragdoll and squeeze the life out of me, slap Felix and Emm on the back, salute Dad and take off for the afternoon.

"I'll come and help, I should be doing it any way. It's my job." Tiff says.

Felix pretends he's hurt and pulls a very sad face. "What? You don't want to spend the afternoon with me?"

"I don't want to lose my job." She groans.

"Tiff, sweetheart, your job is more than safe. A day or two off after the last few months you've had is the least we can give you. Stop worrying, things happen very differently here, not at all like LA. You're not expected to work all hours or clock on and off. Do what needs doing whenever. We're not going to be keeping tabs on you." Emmett tries to explain. "We'll be in and out of the stables but it's to enjoy the horses not to check up on you."

"That's settled then. Emm is on grooming duty with me and Felix can show Tiff around or take her back to bed. Dodge keys are in the car if you want to go out or there's a helmet somewhere to fit Tiff if you're going on the bike. Can you ride a bike, sweetheart?"

"No, only a horse." She laughs. "I've never even been on a bike."

"We'll soon change that. Come on Mr. Wright let's get back to work." I hold out my hand and Emm takes it and follows me with a mock sigh. "You know where we'll be if you need us."

"Making out in the tack room?" Felix sasses.

"Damn right Son." Emm growls.

Angel is distracted enough by my dreads and, according to Emm, my shorts, to stand still enough to be groomed and given a good check over. He seems fine and has fared much better than the horsebox which has some pretty impressive dents. Midnight isn't quite so happy with Emm and bucks and weaves about, biting and snapping at the brush then instantly rolling around in the dirt as soon as he's released.

"There's gratitude for you." Emm laughs.

"Can we take a ride down the beach? They all seem like they have excess energy to work off."

"I don't see why not, my beautiful girl. If you can get a saddle on any of them we'll give them a run." I grab two saddles from the tack room and hand one to Emm. He looks at the markings on it. "This is Seraph's. That's Angel's. You might want to get Luna's instead."

"Spoilsport." I giggle, heading back in to find the right bridles.

"Up to you baby but he really is a handful."

I gently approach Angel with his bridle and he eyes me suspiciously but he allows me to put it over his ears and do it up without much more than a snort. Emm already has Seraph ready and waiting to go and is watching me with interest. Talking quietly all the while to Angel, I gently place his saddle on his back and lean down to buckle him up. He snorts and butts me playfully in the head with his hind quarters.

"Oi shithead! You can pack that in now." I laugh and he does it again. I tighten the girth, drop the stirrups and lead him out of the gate to Emm and Seraph. Emm looks suitably impressed.

"Ready to roll?" I ask as I haul myself up and I throw my leg over, a very tall, Angel. He instantly bucks and drops his back and tries to unseat me but it's quite a half-hearted effort and he soon calms enough for me to urge him forward.

"Delilah, there is no end to your talents." Emm shakes his head in wonder.

"I'm light and small, he doesn't see me as a challenge." I explain as we walk up past the front of the cottage and onto the beach.

"Jeez, Delilah, you really are a witch." Felix exclaims as we meet them walking on the beach. Tiff looks like she can't quite believe it either.

"I haven't ridden him for weeks. I was too scared on my own."

"I'm about to gallop his legs off so he'll be happy." I laugh heading down to the shore so that there are no big rocks to avoid. "Want to stretch your legs, Angel?" I whisper. He doesn't need any more encouragement that a little nudge in the sides. Wow, he moves like the wind and he is so smooth and sure footed, taking long, even strides. I lean into his neck and enjoy the ride. He dips in and out of the water and I get splashed and can taste the salt on my lips. I pull him up as we're nearing the next bay and he slows into a canter and then down into almost a walk. He's foaming and steam is coming off him and he's panting, shaking his head, bobbing and kind of dancing around on the sand. Emm isn't far behind and Seraph is looking equally well used. Emm is grinning like a happy child who's just discovered a long lost favourite toy.

"He is very impressive." I smile. "Like The Duchess but no gears or clutch. He likes to be in charge but he's really responsive." I say rubbing my hands lovingly down his foaming neck. "How's Seraph?"

"He's still a sweet and gentle boy, do you want to swap over and carry on around the bay?"

"If you want to. I'm good with this handsome devil but if you want to try him out I need to find a soft spot to dismount, it's a long way down."

"Stay up there if you're happy, you look very, very sexy in those shorts and that wet t shirt. I like watching you on Angel although it is making my riding a little uncomfortable." He laughs, making a show of adjusting himself.

"Emm, you are a great big perv! I love you so much. I've got to admit this is a real adrenaline rush. Want to take it slower to the next bend and then I'll race you back?"

"You're on, baby." We ride, side by side, Angel butting Seraph and jigging about playfully, throwing his head around carelessly. The beaches are deserted apart from the wildlife and the sky is clear and pale blue with a few fluffy clouds floating lazily overhead. All in all, a perfect day. We turn at the agreed spot and I immediately let Angel have his head.

"No fair, we weren't ready." Emm yells from behind us, laughing. We both thunder down the sand at full speed, pushing the boys to their limits. It's a real head rush. We slow up our blowing mounts and walk them, foaming, steaming and flaring their nostrils back to the cottage and find a frustrated looking Ian, and excited looking Meave, with Paddy in tow and two policemen.

"Oh oh! Busted!" I giggle at Emm. Angel is not at all impressed with the welcome party and rears right up onto his hind legs, kicking out. I laugh and get him back under control.

"Delilah Blue. I might have guessed." The policeman sighs. "I see you've progressed from two wheels to four legs. We've had reports of a runaway horse, a child on a runaway horse, a man chasing a barefoot gypsy girl stealing another horse, a wild horse swimming from Ireland and my personal favourite, the ghost of Black Bess and Dick Turpin. Should have guessed you'd be involved as soon as barefoot gypsies got a mention. I assume that everything is legal and you're not horse rustling."

"Nope, just letting off a bit of steam." I explain. "How you doing Deano? Haven't seen you in ages."

"I'm great Delilah, thanks. How's your Dad? Congrats on the engagement too, Chaz said you'd finally found your man."

"Dad's great. He's in the workshop, go and say hello. He might put the kettle on for you." I gesture to the door.

"Will do, see you later." They wander off towards the barn. Emm is talking to Ian so I leave them to it.

"Hey Meave, Paddy. Everything okay? You didn't get a call too did you?"

"Yes, apparently two of my horses were being ridden down your beach at a dangerous speed. I wish they were mine." Meave laughs eyeing up Seraph and possibly Emm. "I guessed who it was but wanted to come and see them. I was just waiting for a good excuse."

"You're welcome anytime, you know that. Come down to the paddock. Angel needs sponging down. He's goes like the wind. I've got him a bit hot and bothered."

She follows us down, admiring Angel as we walk. "Oh gosh Delilah, he is one amazing stallion, absolutely stunning and very spirited. I have no idea how you are riding him barefoot. What's his name?"

"This is Angel, that's Luna and Midnight and Emm was riding Seraph."

I dismount and kiss Angel lightly on the nose. I remove his saddle and grab a bucket and sponge and gently wipe him over then remove his bridle and let him run off to see the others. Meave walks to them and checks them all out.

"When are you looking to start breeding?" She asks me excitedly. "I have some mares coming into season that will make the most perfect foals with your boys."

"I know nothing about it but I'm pretty sure we'll be in trouble with Ian if they breed during their quarantine time." I grin. "You'd better ask Emm and Ian."

Emm comes strolling down, leading a very chilled out Seraph. "The vet got a call about horses being ill-treated on the beach. I told him they weren't complaining and are both built for speed. Said you we're calming Angel down." He laughs. "He's gone now. I told him he doesn't need to knock when he comes to see them for check ins, to just come down here. Hi Meave, how do you like them?"

I sponge down Seraph whilst Emm and Meave chat. As soon as I take off his bridle he ambles over to his friends looking calm and relaxed.

"I want to breed with you as soon as possible, you gorgeous boys." Meave announces and then giggles and blushes. "That did not sound right but you know what I mean. What are your stud fees?"

"The vet says we can get away with ten days quarantine so you can try introducing one to a mare then but I warn you they're all untried so it might be a nightmare. We don't want any payment; you'll be doing us a real favour by seeing how they perform. You'll be risking the mares."

"I'm really looking forward to it." Meave admits. "First foal will be yours, as thanks and as our wedding gift to you."

"That's too generous, Meave. There's no need to do that."

"I insist. Right, where's Paddy gone? He took one look at Angel rearing and shot off into the barn somewhere. We'll get off and leave you in peace."

"Probably in the workshop with Dad. Oh, did Vicky from the vets call you? She was looking for some riding opportunities. I think she's got plenty of experience."

"Yes, thank you so much, she's coming over later to see us. See you next week if we don't see you before. Bye both." She goes off in search of Paddy Mac.

"Shall we take Luna and Midnight now?" I ask, raring to go.

"No, you don't get to have all the fun." A freshly showered Felix and Tiff come into the paddock, smiling. "We'll take them now. What did the police want? Kinda killed my vibe, five-o storming in below my room and demanding tea."

"Just came for a laugh and obviously a decent cuppa, they had gotten a few calls about us going at full pelt down the beaches but you should be safe now. Deano is a close mate of Chaz's. They trained together. I've met him loads of times. He'll let the station know to head off the rest of the curtain twitchers." They tack up Luna and, a very excited, Midnight and go off on their ride.

"Come here my little barefoot gypsy. I wanna do lots more really bad things to you." Emmett beckons me over to the tack room. "I nearly flattened that very unwelcome welcoming committee. I was so wound up after chasing you along the shoreline, one of my many fantasies involving you was happening right before my eyes. Maybe we need to stop half way to relieve my urges next time."

"And how are you going to keep Angel and Seraph busy whilst you have your wicked way?" I ask.

"Never thought that far ahead." He grins. "Wasn't really focusing on the practical side of my plans. Delilah, stop delaying the inevitable and come here now you little imp." I saunter towards him with a huge smile on my face and we spend a very inventive and enjoyable hour or so before we hear Fe and Tiff returning.

"This is the perfect place to ride." Fe exclaims. "We just went for miles without seeing a soul it's so private and peaceful."

"We went miles without seeing another soul and then returned to find the police, the vet and a local breeder waiting for us." I point out. "You may not see anyone but they will see you. That's the amazing thing about this place. They have a saying, if you want to know what you've been doing, ask your neighbour."

Tiff is giggling. "Oops, I hope they didn't see everything we've been up to on the beach."

Emm's eyebrow raises and his lips twitch. "How'd you manage that with the horses in tow? I need a logistical solution, especially if we're getting visitors as soon as we get back to the cottage."

"We went off to the left past your cabin. There's the remains of an old breakaway a little way up, it's really solid. Not sure it'll hold Angel for long though." Felix offers willingly. "Mind you he looked pretty compliant with Mystic Mom."

"He is definitely a ladies man." Emm shakes his head in wonder.

"He's a complete bugger when I go near him and will happily try to throw me without a second thought." Tiff sighs. "He clearly doesn't think I'm a lady."

"He's probably still sedated and jet lagged." I reply. "He might be a different boy once he gets aclimatised. And I'm pretty sure being a lady probably isn't anywhere near as much fun as not being one." We all laugh and they sort the horses whilst we head to the cottage to make some food.

Our evening meal is a very long and leisurely, family affair. Tiff is well rested and much better able to cope with us all and she and Ella hit it off immediately. We tell tales long into the night. Moving to the comfy seats and lighting the fire when it starts to get chilly.

Once we're all yawning and starting to doze, I make hot chocolate and then we go off to our respective beds after Joey has made Felix promise that he won't be howling. If he does do any howling I certainly don't hear it because after all of my exercise during the day I sleep like the dead.

CHAPTER 65

N ext morning we are awoken by Tiff screaming, Dad yelling for the dogs, Felix banging our door and mine and Emm's phones ringing simultaneously.

"Morning Delilah, It's Deano. We've had a dozen reports of wild horses walking killer dogs on your beach and a few more about attack dogs walking escaped horses and a couple about a vicious giant rabbit riding a scary dog. Know anything about it?" He laughs.

"Not yet, but something untoward is going on outside our door so I imagine we're responsible again. Sorry Deano." I reply.

"Don't worry, honey. We're loving it down here. Ring if you need us." I say bye and Felix throws himself on the bed dramatically and tells us.

"Someone's stolen Angel and Midnight and the dogs. I thought the dogs were with Gramps and he thought they were with us but they didn't run in for breakfast so we realised they're missing."

"Don't panic. They've apparently all gone for a walk on the beach." I giggle. "From what Deano just said they should arrive back here any second now."

"Yeah, the vet just rang too and it sounds like you're right." Emm confirms. "He's had similar reports." We get up without bothering to dress. Poor Tiff is beside herself.

"Oh my god Mr. Wright, I am so sorry. I know we locked the gate properly I remember checking it after putting their coats on but I did leave them outside. I should have stabled them. Oh god, It's all my fault."

"It's okay sweetheart, stop worrying, they're here now." I point to the crazy little circus ambling down the beach. Dutch riding Thor and Frank riding Loki with Jeff and Odin bringing up the rear behind Midnight and Angel. We stand and take in the surreal sight for a few seconds.

"I'll go and get their head collars or we'll never catch them." Tiff panics.

"Don't bother. They got out somehow let's just wait and see how they get back in." I tell her, already having my suspicions.

As we watch they all greet us happily. Angel gives me an affectionate blow in the neck and pushes me in the chest while the others get lots of fuss and attention and mild scolding from everyone else and then the merry band continues to the paddock where Loki lifts Frank, who leans over the gate and slides the inside bolt across and then the outside bolt and Odin opens the gate to let the boys back into their field.

"Well that's something you don't see every day." Dad laughs. "Somebody had better go and buy a couple of padlocks. Who wants breakfast?"

"Me. I'm starvin'" Joey grins, putting Frank up onto his shoulder and high fiving his little bunny paw. Tiff looks like she's finally released the breath she's been holding since her scream and now just looks drained.

I put my arm through hers. "Come on sweetie, a bacon sandwich will make it all better. Wherever they'd gone they wouldn't have got far and no one would be able to get them off the Island."

"I was so scared. I just kept thinking how many more times can I fuck up in my first days here? The tally keeps rising."

"You are doing a great job of fitting into our happy world of madness and are most definitely not responsible for the reprobate rabbit, who appears to be the instigator of this jailbreak." I giggle.

We all eat plenty and have a laugh about the morning's entertainment. Joey and Ella take off to work, Felix and Tiff go off to sort the horses and Dad to get on with his jobs in the workshop. I try to stifle my laughter when Emm lines up the dogs, Dutch and Frank in front of him and gives them a stern talking to about the dangers of going off on their own and the importance of following quarantine rules. They are all listening intently, heads cocked to one side. Jeff is periodically licking his head.

"I think a trip to the hardware store in Ramsey might be slightly more effective, baby. Are you coming? We can go to Jurgen's afterwards and you can show me more of your toys." I wink. He cuts short his lecture and a big grin spreads across his face.

"I'm ready." He announces. "Are we going now?"

"Don't want to kill your enthusiasm, my darling man, but you're still barefoot and only wearing your boxers. We kind of missed the 'getting dressed' stage of the day in all the chaos." He looks at me and I'm just wearing the hoodie Joey had handed me when I went out naked and shivered at the chilly morning air.

"I love this alternate reality we now inhabit." Emm grins. "Poor Tiff, hopefully she was too traumatised about the horses to notice."

I laugh. "Trust me, Tiff is having a good look at you whenever she gets a chance. She's certainly not going to be upset by the sight of your almost naked body. In fact she was probably disappointed you had anything on at all."

He shakes his head. "Jeez Delilah, I don't wanna know that. I'm old enough to be her dad and you know I'm a one-woman man."

"Appreciation of the perfect male form is normal. You really don't want to know what Sal wants to do to you, especially after she saw you leaving that morning in the kitchen when we were all in the buff."

"No, I definitely don't want to know. I love her but she's more scary than

Billy. She would eat me alive. Don't ever leave me alone with her. What do you wanna do with my perfect male form?" He asks in a suggestive voice, raising his eyebrows and holding his arms open in invitation.

"Take it to the hardware store." I reply with a shrug and he looks surprised by my unusual resistance to his charms. I giggle and add. "We might need to go via the shower and bed in whichever order you fancy."

His cheeky grin returns instantly. "Bed, shower then Ramsey and Jurgen's. Sounds like a good plan." He holds out his hand for me to join him. "If you're a real good girl we can go to Conrod's for coffee."

We finally reach Jurgen's at around half past two in the afternoon. Stefan and Kim are up in the studio. Kim is happily sketching in the corner and Stef is wearing headphones and twiddling with knobs and buttons on an editing desk. I creep up behind him and poke him in the ribs like a naughty child. He jumps a mile and the headphone jack comes out of its socket. Instantly filling the room with the most beautiful melancholy song, Stefan's haunting voice accompanied by an acoustic guitar. The sound reminds me of the sea and literally brings tears to my eyes. "Wow. That's amazing." I sniff, wiping my cheeks with my sleeve.

"Glad you like it. We're playing around with some new and different stuff." Stef kisses me and grins. "It's going to be on our next album; Watching Waves."

"Good title. I might just buy that one." I giggle.

"You can probably have a free one because I stole your words and you know a couple of the guys in the band." Stef laughs. "That and we might want your vocals on one or two of the tracks."

I look at him in complete bewilderment. "What?"

"We've been playing around with a melody but we think it needs a female voice. Kim's sung it with us and it does definitely sound better but she can't hold a tune in a bucket so it's not an option."

"None taken!" Kim huffs jokingly from the corner.

"I wouldn't have a clue what I'm doing. I just sing for fun."

"So do we darlin'." Emm replies. "You don't have to do anything other than feel it and enjoy it."

"Okay. I'll give it a go but can't promise anything." I shrug.

Stef gets excited and starts looking on his computer for something. He presses a button and I hear a soft beat and a haunting melody and get ushered into a corner in front of a microphone and relieved of my jacket and bag. Stef hands me a piece of paper and Kim smiles and shrugs in answer to my 'what's going on?' look.

Stef laughs at my utter confusion and turns off the music. "Sorry honey,

I'm getting a bit ahead of myself here, aren't I? Let me get some levels, sing something sad, anything at all."

I think about that and quietly begin singing Back to Black. All three of them just stand still and stare at me then Stef starts frantically twiddling knobs.

I get totally distracted and start giggling. "What's up? Is it that bad? You look like I did something wrong."

"You sound amazing!" Kim gasps. "You are so talented."

I laugh. "Says the most sought-after plastic surgeon in LA who can draw like da Vinci."

"Gotta say it, we are damn lucky dudes." Stef grins to Emm. "Our ladies are both gorgeous and talented. We could retire tomorrow and be kept men for the rest of our lives."

"Sounds like a plan." Emm laughs, smacking him on the back. "What else have you got for my girl because I was on the way to introduce her to the Arch?"

"Couple more songs please." Stef begs. "I really wanna get this track down and once you're in the garage we won't be able to tear you away for hours."

"That predictable, eh?" I sigh.

"Yep, unless I want howling on the track I'll be quitting as soon as you two head down there." He replies with a silly grin. He shoves me gently back to the corner. "Sing something with high notes. I wanna see where I can go."

I laugh, look deeply into Emm's eyes and start to sing, 'Lovin' you is easy 'cause you're beautiful...Makin' love with you is all I wanna do....' I sing it to the end and a teary Emmett folds me in his arms.

Kim wipes her eyes. "That was so beautiful, Delilah. Stef needs to play with what he has in mind a little more because you can do way more than he had planned. I wasn't expecting Minnie Ripperton."

"Her Mama sang that all the time didn't she Liebling?" Jurgen smiles sadly from the doorway.

"She did, and much better than me." I reply.

"Nein, you sounded perfect. It was a treat to hear it. I saw the bikes so I bought coffee." He puts down a tray of mugs and plates of cakes, petit fours and biscuits. "Chef is trying new creations for your wedding, taste and I will tell him what you say." We all dive in and groan with delight at the heavenly flavours.

"All perfect, make lots and lots of them all." I laugh as Jurgen waits for our feedback.

"Yeah, I second that." Emmett grins. "Especially that orange and lemon one. Ella will love it."

"One more song, Dil then I'll let you go." Stef gets us back to business. "I need an ocean themed song. Anything that comes into your head."

Jurgen smiles and begins singing 'The Skye Boat Song' "That's another one her Mama sang to them." He looks pensive then grabs the tray and heads off back to the kitchen.

I go back into the corner and Stef plonks himself back in front of his knobs. I start singing 'Ocean Eyes' my modern music knowledge isn't much but I do love Billie Eilish. Joey told me to listen to her a while back and her voice is so beautifully sad I adored it. When I quite can't remember the words I go back to old school and start singing 'Echo Beach' and finally 'Octopus's Garden' and 'Yellow Submarine' which Kim and Emmett join in with. "I can't think of any other ocean songs." I giggle.

"Well my girl certainly has a varied repertoire." Emmett shrugs at Stef.

"I'm impressed, how do you know Billie Eilish songs? Thought you were strictly old school."

"Joey recommend her. I just love her sound and her lyrics."

"It's kind of the sound I was looking for." Stef admits. "I'll play about some more with it now. Will you come back with Emm in a day or so?"

"I'll get her here, bro." Emmett promises. "Can we go and play now?"

"Yes children, go have some fun." Kim says in a teasing mummy voice. "We'll see you both later."

Emm grabs my hand and we run down the stairs and into the previously unexplored garage. He snaps on the lights and I see a slightly battered Trans Am which makes me smile. "Felix's equivalent of my Christine. I don't even wanna think about what's gone on in there." Emm shudders playfully. He points to my right. "Here's another from the Shelby stable you might like."

It's a GT500 but not a classic, It's a 2017 Super Snake fiftieth anniversary in white with the familiar blue stripes.

"Oh, that's very pretty." I purr. "Pull the bonnet, baby. I think I'm going to like what's under there. Didn't they only make a short run of these? Seven hundred and fifty brake?"

"Yeah, they made five hundred. This one is number sixty-nine." He chuckles, pulling the bonnet catch.

"Interesting choice." I giggle.

"Happy accident. Had no idea when I ordered it. Needed to spend some money so I bought this and The Arch. I've never even driven this. I'm ashamed to say I forgot I'd got it. Hans clearly took our list of what we wanted from the house as a rough guideline, thank goodness. He says there are several containers of other items we probably wanted on the way over that he put on a ship to save money. Can't wait to see what's in them." He comes up behind me and puts his hands on my hips. "Did you just hear anything I said, my little imp?"

"Eh? Er yeah, what?" I offer in response. "Sorry, what did you say handsome? I was too busy drooling over this pristine V8." I playfully wriggle my bum into him and it's game on.

A gorgeous, classic red Stingray is sitting in the corner and I slink over to breathe in that intoxicating old car cockpit aroma. I sit in the driver's seat singing 'Little Red Corvette' and running my hands over the leather. "A '66? Real classic. Mr. Wright you have lots of very desirable motors." I whisper. "I just love those sexy side pipes and the knockoff wheels."

Emm talks dirty to me about 425 brake via 11:1 compression, Holley four-barrel carburetor, aluminum manifold, mechanical lifters, four-hole main bearing caps. I cut him off with a fierce kiss when I can't take any more.

We eventually make it over to the GT40 and discover a curious little note, in Hans' neat handwriting 'smells unpleasant inside. Suggest valet.'

"Oh man, I hope a skunk didn't get in the garage." Emm groans. I cautiously open the door and we are assaulted by the smell of a mixture of really strong expensive perfume and equally strong cheap aftershave. "Jeez! That's far worse than skunk." Emm wrinkles his nose and shuts the door. "I think we just found out which car Cherry's been driving."

I pat it's bonnet affectionately. "Well she'll have had no trouble bagging men if she's been driving this baby. We should leave the windows open, it'll soon clear."

"Not until we're ready to leave. That disgusting smell will seriously affect my continued performance." He says with a shudder.

"I highly doubt anything will, you're insatiable. Any idea where our clothes went?"

"Don't know, don't care." He smiles, holding out his hand for me. "Can I interest you in a '66 GT350 in ivy green with white LeMans stripes?"

"I think you probably can, Mr. Wright." I reply with a purr. He opens the door to the 350 and I can tell he's driven this one much more than the others. "Is this a favourite?"

"Yeah, I think so. I've had it a long while and it was always my 'go to' when I opened the garage. Don't know why, she's a bitch to drive." He adds with a grin.

"You like a challenge and it suits you." I smile as I take in the huge, highly polished, wooden steering wheel with the Cobra motif in the centre and study all of the clocks, loving the attention to detail and the real crafts-manship that seems to be sadly absent from modern day cars.

"Wanna feel how good the springs in the back seat are, darlin'?" Emm drawls after watching me for a while. "There's not a lot of room back there though."

"Be rude not to." I giggle, climbing into the back and then shrieking when I sit on the cold metal lap belt catch.

"Need me to kiss that better?" Emm asks, climbing in next to me.

"My butt should be as hard as nails after riding Angel yesterday." I say. "I'm surprised I even felt that."

"Your ass is perfect, like the rest of you." Emm teases as he grabs a hand-ful to prove his point." We doze in the back of the Mustang for a while, wrapped in each other's arms.

The sound of the garage door opening rouses us. Stef is standing in the doorway looking for us. "Emm? Dil?"

"We're here. What's up?" Emm shouts back, getting out of the car.

"Sorry to interrupt your fun, bro. Fe's been trying to get hold of you. Angel has thrown Tiff. Nothing major, don't panic. Your Dad's taken them to the hospital, he thinks her wrist is broken."

"Poor Tiff." I go off in search of my clothes and Stef laughs.

"Lost something, Delilah?"

"It's some weird thing that happens around him. My clothes keep disap-pearing." I shrug.

"Have you gotten to see the Arch yet?" Stef asks.

"Nope, saving that 'til last." Emm smirks. I hand him his jeans and he takes his phone out of his pocket and looks at the half dozen missed calls from Felix. He rings him back and Fe tells him they're on the way home and Tiff has a cast on her wrist and a couple of bruises but she's okay. "We're at Jurgen's. We'll be heading home in about ten minutes. See you there."

"Why did she try to take Angel out? She knows he's an unmountable shit-head." Stef asks.

"Little Delilah Doolittle here was riding him like he was a gymkhana pony yesterday." Emm says. "They must have thought he'd be okay." Kim appears behind Stefan.

"Oh my goodness Delilah, he's a scary beast. I hope you took it really slowly and you at least made her wear a helmet and a back-protector Emmett."

"Not exactly. She was barefoot and in her daisy dukes and rode him like she rides The Duchess." He gives Stef a huge cheeky grin. "It was damn hot, man, never seen anything like it."

Stef lets out a low whistle. "Wish I'd been there to see that." Kim smacks him playfully.

"There's also the fact that he was taking orders from a rabbit earlier." I add to change the subject. We explain the high jinx of this morning and they cannot stop laughing.

CHAPTER 66

We get back to Dad looking after a very tearful and apologetic Tiff. "I'm so sorry Mr. Wright. I wanted to get them all exercised to make up for the time I had off yesterday. Angel was compliant when I groomed them all and he was reasonably calm when I saddled him. I thought he'd be okay. He's not hurt, he didn't knock himself on anything. I'm so sorry. I can still work and I'll pay for the medical treatment."

"Tiff, all that matters is that you are alright, sweetheart. No one is mad at you." I hug her to prove it. "What did the hospital say? We don't pay for medical stuff directly over here so don't get worrying about that."

"I have fractured my wrist but it's not too bad and it wasn't very swollen so they put this cast thing on and I have to go and get it checked in seven days. They gave me some pain meds. The bruises are no worse than I've had before. I hadn't even got up on him when he bucked. I'd got one foot in the stirrup, I fell backwards and put my hand out to save myself. Luckily I got my foot out before he took off up the paddock."

Poor Felix comes from the shower looking as white as a sheet. I hug him tightly. "Are you okay, Fe?" Emm asks.

"Er, yeah. I think so. I just keep thinking about what could have happened if Tiff hadn't managed to get her foot out before he bolted. It was stupid of me to let her try to ride him."

"You're both okay so stop going over should haves and could haves." Dad soothes. "Tiff's made of tough stuff. She'll soon heal."

"Poor Midnight didn't get out either. We got him all tacked up then had to go off to the hospital."

"Emm and I will take them both in a minute. You just rest and stop worrying." Emm raises an eyebrow but says nothing. I kick off my boots, hang up my coat. put my helmet away and drag him down to the paddock.

"After my busy day I'm not sure I can cope with sitting in the saddle for long." He giggles. "I'm not sure about letting you ride Angel and I'm definitely not up for it."

"Just a quick one, I promise. I'm happy riding Angel if he'll let me on him."

We saddle up and Angel is skittish and dancing around but only butts me and chews my hair. I mount him quickly so he can't get me like he did Tiff. He drops his back and kicks up his heels but I just indulge him. It's a fantastic feeling to be in control of such a huge beast. "Come on shithead, behave yourself." I laugh, urging him forward. He prances up next to Emmett. Midnight lunges at him and they shove each other around before settling as we get onto the beach.

"This is a much fairer race." Emm grins. "Midnight's mummy and daddy have an extremely impressive racing pedigree."

"I can't deny he's a beautiful boy and does look like he'll be fast but Angel is a psychotic loony so he'll still be faster."

"Game on, darlin', game on!" Emm yells as we take off down the beach, riding hell for leather, side by side. I lean forward with my cheek resting on Angel's silky neck and enjoy the amazing feeling of being carried at such speed with the sound of hooves thundering in my ears and the sea spray sticking to my eyelashes.

"Where's the finish line?" I shout and Emm points to the rocks at the end of the bay. We're neck and neck all the way and cross the imaginary finish line too close to call. We slow to a canter and then a walk and I pat a snorting, blowing Angel as he strides around, full of adrenaline and does a few crazy little excited bucks. Midnight takes a huge bite of his bum and he bucks and weaves some more. "We'll call it a draw, shall we?"

"Yeah, for now but we'll have a rematch tomorrow." Emm agrees. "Come on, my crazy lady. I need a shower and some supper." We have a steady canter back and Joey is just getting in from work.

"When ya gonna teach me to ride?" He asks as he kisses and pets a snorting, prancing Angel. "I wanna go on this big boy."

"You might want to rethink that. He's broken poor Tiff's wrist today." Emm tells him. "Luna or Seraph are a safer bet for a first ride. They're both pretty placid."

"Where's the fun in that?" Joey asks, winking at me. "Is Tiff okay?"

Emm smacks him playfully around the head. "Tiff's fine and you are as daft as your mother."

"Yep, that's me. We got any scran? I'm starvin'."

"We'll just sort these guys and I'll come and feed us all."

"Boss, I'll go an' get washed up."

We see to the horses and get slightly waylaid in the tack room then I get some food sorted while Emmett showers. Tiff and Fe are cuddled up on the chesterfield, watching tv surrounded by dogs, Dutch and Frank. Joey and Ella join them and they tell them about the day's excitement. I make a loaf of garlic bread and a couple of pizzas, a huge bowl of spaghetti and a Bolognese and a carbonara sauce and grate a mountain of parmesan. I put it all on the table for everyone to help themselves. Emm and Dad appear by magic as they always do when food is served.

"Did Angel behave for you?" Felix asks when we're all seated at the table.

"Delilah appears to be able to handle him whether he's behaving or not." Emm tells him. "I suggest we just let her deal with him for the foreseeable future or at least until Crazy Joe has had a couple of rides on Seraph or Luna." Joey nods in agreement.

"I'll take you out tomorrow, bro. Are you working all day?" Felix offers.

"Nah, only 'til half one. Ricky's on a promise, wants to gerroff early."

"Is he building up his stamina ready for next week?" I giggle.

"Dunno, I'll ask 'im tomorra." Joey grins. "Expect 'e'll text ya an answer."

We talk rubbish, light the fire and all settle in front of the TV. Felix insists we watch back to back episodes of Breaking Bad until we all fall asleep. Emm wakes me and we go off to our bed after covering everyone up.

We sleep in late and there are no dramas occurred or occurring, when we finally emerge from our big, cosy bed. I head for my recently neglected rock and indulge in some yoga. Emmett saunters down with coffees and a handful of danish pastries.

"Continental breakfast on the beach, ma'am?" He smiles, handing me my mug and a vanilla crown.

"You really know how to make me a very happy woman." I sigh contentedly.

"I know lots of ways to make you happy." He grins and wiggles his eyebrows at me. "Do you wanna come and see my Arch?"

"Yep. Is Stef gonna make me sing again?"

"Possibly, probably...yeah, he's been texting all morning sending ideas and lyrics. Talking of phones yours went earlier." He pulls it out of his back pocket. Sal has texted me. 'Got a registrar for legal stuff then handfasting will be performed by a sexy druid, ok? Xx' I inform Emm who looks as intrigued as I am and I reply that a sexy druid sounds great. I have another text from Rick. 'haha fuck off shortarse got more stamina than youll eva av xxxx I laugh and show Emm.

"He wishes. You're like the energizer bunny."

There's a missed call from the police station too. I ring back and get Deano and put it on speaker. "Hi, it's Dil, got a missed call, is everything okay?"

"Hey Delilah, it's all quiet. We only had two calls late afternoon yesterday about you riding. Oh, and a call about a Rastafarian drug dealer in a big American car. We're getting a little bored." He laughs. "Got any other plans that'll cheer the boys and girls up here?"

I laugh out loud. "That would have been Dad taking Tiff to the hospital with a broken wrist. We'll all be riding again later. Felix is going to teach Joey. We might get some more American cars out to play or even Emmett's Arch if I can sweet talk him."

"Great we'll start a book on all the calls now. Enjoy yourselves. Stay safe."

"Man, I love this place." Emmett sighs, wrapping his arms around me and looking out to sea. "Everyone is so real and everywhere is beautiful."

"You're very poetic this morning, baby." I chuckle. "Is The Rock getting under your skin?"

"Darlin' it, and you, have taken over my whole body and soul! I can't imagine ever leaving here again for any longer than I have to. It feels like home. The Island, the beach, the cottage, the family, the animals, and most of all, you...it all feels like home. Does that make sense?"

I kiss his cheek gently and rest my head on his shoulder. "Yep, totally. Couldn't be anywhere else from now on."

"Have you planned a bachelorette party with the girls?"

"Nope, maybe we could go back to The Boatyard for a meal. I'm hoping Sal's too busy with the wedding plans to organize a hen night. I must transfer her some money. I bet she's spent a pile of her own."

"That's gotta be our first job this morning, Nathan's bank to sort an account. Come on gorgeous girl we've got lots to do today."

"Nath's manager is a bit of a dragon she might not let you near him."

Emm strides into the bank like he owns the place. I hang back to watch the show. A smartly dressed lady in an expensive suit makes a beeline for him. "Mr. Wright, what a pleasure to see you here. I read that you were on the Island. I'm Ms. Quayle, the manager. How can I help you?"

"Is Nathan Parker here? I want to open some accounts with him."

She looks confused. "Nathan is only a junior clerk here, I'm the manager. I can take care of whatever you need."

"I need to see Nathan to open me some accounts for my family."

"I can sort that with you, come this way, Mr. Wright."

"I would like to deal with Nathan please."

"He's working on the counter right now. I am much more qualified to deal with your request."

I can tell Emmett's patience is wearing thin so I step next to him and put my hand in his. He sighs deeply. "Lady, I want to open an account with Nathan Parker at your bank. I was planning to deposit at least ten million dollars, if you won't let me deal with who I want to I will take my business elsewhere. Are we clear?"

Her eyes widen and she sucks in a breath. "Nathan! Come and attend to Mr. Wright immediately." She yells in a shrill voice.

Nathan appears and hugs me and Emm. "Hi Auntie Dil, Uncle Emmett, what's up?" His manager's eyes widen a little more.

"We're good Nath, how's you and Con?" Emm asks. "Hardly got chance to chat at the meal. You are coming to my bachelor do next week aren't you?"

Nath grimaces and looks at his manager. "Can't have the time off, too short notice apparently. I'm trying to talk Con into joining you though. I'm really sad I'm missing it. Jurgen was going to get the helicopter over so that we can maybe join you for one night and I can get back in time for work."

"Con knows where the plane is too. It's not a long flight. You have to come for one night at least, family's not complete without you two, son."

"Aw, Uncle Emm you're turning into a big softie!" He hugs him again. "Did you want to open your account?"

Ms. Quayle is now showing all kinds of emotions from angry to trite to shocked to downright impressed. "I didn't realise your leave request was for such a special occasion, Nathan. I will revisit the rota and see what I can do. Is Connie your girlfriend? I've not really ever spoken to you about your family."

Nathan rolls his eyes at me. "No, we don't speak about anything that isn't work related. My family come in every week to do their business and personal banking and my partner is a member of Emmett's band."

"He's also my godson, Connor." Emmett adds with a challenging look at Ms. Quayle. She has the decency to look embarrassed with herself.

"You can use my office, Nathan." She gestures towards a door to the rear. "Would you all like coffee?"

"Auntie Dil might, she's a coffee fiend." Nathan laughs, elbowing me playfully.

He sets up an account for Emmett and transfers some money into it from elsewhere then Emm tells him he wants extra cards for me, Joey and Dad and one for Felix in case he ever loses his own or gets stuck anywhere. Nathan is super-efficient and gets everything done quickly and without fuss.

"All done, I'll get the cards to you as soon as they arrive and put Auntie Dil's married name on so we don't have to change them again. Thanks for getting the dragon to hopefully give me the time off I don't want to miss Amsterdam."

"How do you feel about her now knowing about your private life?" I ask.

"I think it'll do her good. Might make her realise we're people here not just minions for her to boss about. Think she was shocked at my impressive connections." He giggles.

We leave the office and Ms. Quayle is hovering outside. "Is everything okay? Has Nathan been able to deal with all of your requirements? I've re-jigged next week's rota and you can take the days you requested Nathan; I wouldn't want you missing an important family event."

"Thanks, Ms. Quayle. That's really kind of you." Nathan says genuinely. "Got to get back to work. See you later, fam!" He hugs us and disappears.

Ms. Quayle looks slightly worried about being left alone with us. "Er, well thank you so much for your business. If there is anything else we can help with don't hesitate to contact me...or Nathan." She adds as an afterthought.

"We will do and thank you for letting Nathan have the time for Emmett's stag do, it wouldn't be the same without him and Connor there. Our family is very close and time together is important to us."

She looks at me as if she's only just noticed I'm there. "Are you really Nathan's aunt? I had no idea. My brother used to have posters of you on his bedroom wall when we were teenagers. He thought you were amazing."

I cringe at that information. "I'm Nathan's godmother. I actually delivered him. He just calls me 'auntie' because he always has done. It's a sign of respect within our family." I don't add that he also does it to tease as he knows it makes me feel old now he's a grown man. "We better be going, thanks again." I say as Emm is already dragging me out of the bank.

"Where do I get hold of some of those posters?" He asks with a raised eyebrow. "And tell me the story about you delivering Nath. I didn't know about that either."

"There's still loads we don't know about each other but I think we've covered most of the important stuff." I smile. "I delivered Nath in the back of Billy's old truck because Sal was a stubborn tart and wouldn't go to Noble's when her contractions started coming every couple of minutes because we were having a curry and she didn't want to leave until she'd had her lychees for dessert. To be fair, she did all the hard work I just yelled encouragement, caught him when he shot out and kept Bill from fainting and Ricky from puking. The posters I have no idea about; prob-ably something in the old TT programs or an ancient MCN. I think Ms. Quayle just wanted to share a family story so that we didn't think she was a completely heartless bitch but didn't want to admit to having pos-ters of you all over her own wall."

"Ha Ha very funny. Nathan's arrival sounds like it was a fun evening." He laughs then screws up his face in sadness. "Felix arrived via elective caesarean. She had no interest in carrying him any longer than necessary or having a natural birth. I didn't even get to hold him until he was two days old."

"I very much doubt he or Nath remember their arrival into this world and both are pretty fine adults so don't beat yourself up about it." I smile.

"You always know the right thing to say, thanks darlin'. At least we got Nath his time off to come next week. Ready to make some magic in the studio?"

"Not sure about that but I'm ready to admire your Arch and maybe take the Cobra for a run over the mountain if we have time."

"We'll make time, gorgeous." He kisses me passionately before he pulls on his helmet. "Well depending on how impressed you are with the Arch, that is." He adds with a cheeky grin.

Stef is already busy in the studio when we arrive and has loads more stuff set up than before. "Hey both, ready to play?" He talks me through what he's looking for and gives me the words but also has them karaoke style on a laptop screen. He and Emm sing and play the beautiful, sad song about a lonely lady waiting on a beach for her long-lost lover. I listen to them for a little while then tentatively join in. Connor and Charlie sneak upstairs to watch and then join in with an oboe and a flute. Not what I expected at all but the sound is so haunting and so perfect I can feel tears on my cheeks. We sing and play over and over changing words and sounds and pitch and volume until Stef is finally happy and announces that he's got plenty to work with.

"We good, bro? It's Arch time." Emm giggles, rubbing his hands together with excitement.

"Yeah, go. Have fun. Thanks Dil, that was superb just the sound I was looking for."

"I really enjoyed being part of it. Thank you. By the way Connor, Emm sweettalked Nathan's boss into letting him go next week."

"Awesome! Cheers guys. Can't wait. By all accounts it's a very open-minded place."

"That's one word for it." I smile. "Nathan has been with me and his mom before but he was only a kid. We took him to the Anne Frank Museum because he was totally fascinated by the story when he studied it in school."

"Yeah, he was telling me about rollerblading in the park with the gay guys."

"That was a good day. We skated for hours. He didn't want to stop. Then he invited them all to dinner with us. It was an hilarious evening." I laugh at the fond memory of two of the guys in their tiny shorts and crop tops, patiently holding hands with Sal as she screamed and swore like a navvy all day because she couldn't stand up and the others racing with Nathan over and over because he was so desperate to be as fast as they were or teaching me and him cool dance moves and rollerblading tricks. "You need to all go skating in the park next week." I tell Emm.

"You wanna marry Batman with a broken leg?"

"Least I'll be able to catch you if you decide to run away from the altar." I giggle.

"Not gonna happen, darlin'. The running or the skating. Come on, time's a wasting." We say bye to everyone and I eagerly follow him down the stairs. "Okay, are you ready?" He grins as he throws the cover off the Arch. I take a sharp breath in. It's an absolute work of art. I drop to my knees to study every part of it. The engineering work is so precise. A perfect billet aluminum subframe and swingarm and the distinctive S&S V Twin engine, Ohlins shocks, carbon fibre wheels....The lines are all clean and flowing and I love the 'unfussyness' of the design, the fact that I can see daylight through it. It's also been custom made to fit Emm's body. So when I very reverently throw my leg over it, everything is in the wrong place for me which makes him smile. "Oh dear, you'll have to get measured up for your own."

"Will Keanu personally be measuring my inside leg? I think I might enjoy that rather a lot."

"Maybe you won't be getting one after all." He growls, pretending to be wounded by my confession. "He's a real cool guy, not letting you near him. You'd love him."

I playfully drop my bottom lip and hold out my arms to him. "Come here my baby, I'll make it up to you. You know there's only one man for me, forever more." He needs no further invitation and our clothes somehow end up in a heap on the floor and we spend a good while worshipping the Arch and each other's bodies.

"Who needs Keanu when I have you?" I ask when I've finally regained my senses. He wraps me in his warm embrace and kisses me softly.

"Hungry? little imp." He grins as my stomach lets out a huge rumble. "Shall we take the Cobra down to the Sound cafe?"

We dress and Emm pulls the gorgeous beast out of the garage. It sounds wonderful, deep and throaty and growly. The roads are pretty clear but we have quite a sedate drive over the mountain, enjoying the noise and smell of the car and taking in the beautiful scenery. Our lunch is a relaxed affair, watching the seals play on the rocks, followed by a little way down another small section of the Raad Ny Foillan.

We drive back into Cregneash Museum village but this time we continue

459

up the bumpy road to 'The Chasms' which is part of the Raad and consists of heather strewn walkways and huge rugged formations on the dangerous coastline including dramatic slashes in the rock with the roiling sea smashing below. We sit on a flat slab and watch a Peregrine and a Hen Harrier hunt on the hillside and the Shearwaters bob and dive in the waves.

"How lucky are we to have all of this beauty on our doorstep and the time to enjoy it?" I marvel with a contented sigh as I snuggle into Emmett's side.

"It is a blessing, darlin', without a doubt." He agrees. "Are we still camping for our honeymoon or do you fancy something else? We need more plans now as most have already happened again."

"What's with the plans, baby? Does it make it more real for you or is it so that you don't get bored and always have something to look forward to?" He thinks about it for a long moment. "Not really sure. Definitely not the getting bored thing." He concludes. "Maybe I want to be sure you'll be here always and by making plans it'll mean you stay with me."

"Emmett, darling, I am marrying you on Friday. I will make that commitment only once and only to you, until the end of my days. I promise faithfully that we will never be apart for longer than necessary and will always do as much as we can together as a couple or a family. I love you so much I can never be without you. My plan is to do everything in my power to make you happy and content and never feel any regrets."

"I think I might just follow your plan. Sorry, am I getting overbearing again? I can't handle the thought of you not being here forever."

"Stuck with me for always now, Emm. Plans are already in place for your stag do and the wedding, honeymoon can be whatever you want as long as it involves lots of sex and more sex." I giggle. "Meave is keen to get on with the breeding, I want to get Joey set up with a team before the Manx GP in August, Southern 100 racing is on in July, we could offer camping for neither, either or both, you've got an album to write, I'd like to build a sidecar outfit and race tune your Charger but I can do that whilst you're on tour to keep me busy, everyone is keen to look at the fostering or adoption options, I'd really love to ski around Christmas time if we can. That's all going to keep us busy for a little while. What do you want to do before the end of this year?"

I notice how his face screws up slightly at the mention of fostering. "We could just spend our honeymoon in our love shack with a 'do not disturb' sign on the door." He gives me a cheeky grin. "I'm looking forward to Amsterdam but wish you were coming; can we not do camping for Manx? I want you all to myself because I'll have to go away in September and I think you kind of missed out on lots of TT because you were so busy with taking care of everything and everyone else. I really do want more kids with you and I get that the fostering is a sensible option to start I'm just not sure how I'll feel about giving them back when the time comes." He admits.

"I get that completely, Emm but I'm a bit worried that you're all asking for a 'Sarah'. Our Sarah is a result of her very unique upbringing; she's been nurtured, loved and indulged by everyone she knows for all her life. She has never been alone or scared or seen anything traumatic. No child available for fostering or adoption will have had that chance of even a small taste of that. I don't want to take on a kid who has a massive example to live up to and doesn't even know it. It will hurt them, you, Felix and Joey."

"Shit! I never thought of it that way." He rubs his face in a pensive way. "We have kinda set the bar high, haven't we?"

"Couldn't get any higher if you tried." I shrug ruefully. "We should all sit down together and have a proper family discussion before we make any final decisions; Dad can tell you more about the realities of fostering and what to expect and we can look into adoption once everyone is a bit more open minded."

"You talk so much sense, darlin'. It's a good job one of us has some grasp on reality. I feel like I can have whatever I want whenever I want it right now because all of my dreams have suddenly started to become truth. I need to rein it in a bit, don't I? The more I have, the more I want, I'm like a greedy kid and I'm not stopping to enjoy what I've got right now."

"I have to admit sometimes I feel like I'm not living up to expectations."

"Jeez, Delilah, don't ever think that. You exceed every one of my expectations in every way possible. You show me something new every day and make me really stop and think. I need that and I need you more than you'll ever know. You need to tell me when I'm being a dick, I'm sure we already had that discussion."

"You just sometimes seem to be in too much of a hurry to move on to the next attraction or distraction as if you're worried it's going to disappear if you don't grab it right now."

He sighs deeply, dropping his shoulders. "Yeah, that's exactly how I feel, like it's just all going to end; like one day I'll wake up and everything will be gone."

"Life has all become a tad surreal recently. I think we all need some time to adjust to our new 'normal' before we subject an already damaged child to it. Let's face it, honey our 'normal' isn't going to be anything they've witnessed before." I smile and hope Emm gets that I'm not being a bitch, just a realist.

He loosens up a little. "Can't argue with your logic, little darlin'. We aren't exactly a conventional 9 to 5, 2.4 kids, family unit. We've all got enough love for some extras though."

"We have, in spades, my big softie. It's going to happen sooner rather than later but please give me a little time to enjoy you and Felix and Dad and Joey and even Ella and Tiff, I barely know Tiff yet."

"You're always right, Mrs. Wright." He giggles. "I'll stop pushing and be more mindful and appreciative of what I already have. Now come here and kiss me so that I know you don't think I'm a complete jerk."

I willingly fall into his open arms.

CHAPTER 67

We arrive home to find a very unhappy Angel stomping around alone in the paddock. "Oh crap! Has the rabbit sprung them again?" Emm laughs.

"Fe was going to take Joey riding. I guess Tiff has gone too. I'll saddle up Angel and go and find them. He looks like he's feeling a little bit left out."

"Okay, darlin'. I'll go and catch up with your Dad and then get some dinner started." He wraps his arms around me for a long, slow kiss. "Thanks for today, I've truly enjoyed it and thank you for talking some sense into my thick head once again. Tell me next time I'm moving too fast."

"I don't ever want to change you, my sexy man." I reply. "I love you just the way you are."

"Me too, darlin', you're my perfect woman but that's partly because you point out my flaws and make me rethink my arrogant ideas and suggest a different angle. You've opened my eyes to a whole new world and I really do need to slow down and savour every part of it. Never stop talking to me, Dil. I promise I will always listen to you."

"Only if you promise to tell me to shut up when you've heard enough." I reply.

"Not gonna happen, I can't get enough of you, baby." He bursts into our Kiss song once more then kisses me again and strides off towards the cottage after issuing a quiet warning to Angel to behave himself and look after me.

I attempt to tack up a very bossy, arrogant Angel who, despite Emmett's plea, does his best to avoid both bridle and saddle even though he's desperate to get out. I drop the saddle over the fence. "Okay, shithead. We'll go bareback if you let me put the bridle on." I bargain with him. He gives me a 'Jeff' look which makes me laugh so much I manage to throw his bridle on while he's listening to my giggles. I climb up the fence and throw my leg over him, give him a second to adjust to me being aboard, kick my boots off and guide him up to the cottage. He dances and struts, kicking out his back end. Emm and Dad are outside the workshop discussing the merits of the Cobra. Dad smiles and gives Angel a quick tickle on the nose. Emm's eyes widen at the lack of saddle.

"You are one crazy mama!" He shakes his head. "Ride safe."

I love his easy use of our family salutation. "Did they go left or right, Dad?" He points to the right and I urge Angel into a canter to find the kids. I'm looking forward to seeing Joey riding. It's an excellent way to improve balance, core body strength and being able to react to the unexpected; all useful skills for a bike racer.

I see Felix and Joey walking steadily down the shoreline. They look so chilled and are good-naturedly laughing and teasing each other. I marvel that these young men from such outwardly different worlds have so much in common and have become brothers in every sense of the word. I slow Angel to a walk and eavesdrop for a few seconds.

"Where's the clutch, Bro? Need to get into second gear." Joey is easily moving about on Luna, gently patting his neck and loosely holding the reins.

"You sure?" He's pointing to Tiff ahead of them. "She's been riding since she could walk and look what Angel did to her. We better take it slow; Mama Bear will smack me upside the head if her favorite son gets broken."

"Eh Laa, she's got no favorites, she'd kill for both of us ya daft twat. Anyway, Angel is a fuckin' psycho, Luna's a pussy cat and Ma'll think I'm a wuss if I ain't tearin' down this beach like me arse is on fire within an hour." They laugh and bump fists.

"True that, Brother." Felix replies. They finally notice me following them and move over to accommodate Angel. He decides he's pissed at them for leaving him behind so he bumps heavily into Midnight, pushing him sideways into the waves to douse Felix with sea spray and then bites Luna on the bum making him rear up and whip around in shock.

I swat him gently on the neck. "Behave, shithead! You're out now, stop being a dick." He snorts in reply and prances around like a circus performer. The boys laugh at his showing off. "Oops! Sorry about that Fe." I giggle as Angel snorts a load of snot down his nose and shakes it purposely at an already wet Felix.

"No you're not." He laughs, shaking himself like a dog. "Did you forget you needed a saddle?"

"Nope, shithead here, couldn't stand still long enough for me to put it on."

"You're a crazy mama."

"Apparently so, that's exactly what your father said." I reply as Angel rears and decides to be a bucking bronco before splashing in the sea and soaking us all.

"Come on, Ma. Stop fuckin' around an' show us 'ow to make this baby go faster without killin' meself."

"I talk him through the basics and Felix takes over whenever Angel jigs off. I hate trotting so I talk him through cantering and galloping and stopping. "Ready to try a canter? Watch where Felix puts his feet in the stirrups and his body in the saddle. I'm a rubbish role model because I've got no stirrups or saddle and Angel only does what he wants, not what he's told."

Tiff rejoins us on Seraph and gives me a wide-eyed look when she sees me. Fe nods to her. "Yeah, Dad and I already told her she's crazy. She just laughs at us."

"How can you even stay on him, Delilah? He's like a bronco. I'm an experienced rider but I admit he scares me. He's too unpredictable."

"I'm little so he just thinks I'm just a bit of an irritation that can be tolerated and he knows I'll let him run and that's what he wants to do. He's not unpredictable at all; you know he's going to play up every way he can." I shrug as he dances and whickers in agreement, pawing the sand as if to say, 'come on, let's go.'

"Joey's ready for a canter so stay close to him, please. I know Angel will just go off like a rocket the second I give him his head."

Tiff raises an eyebrow, clearly thinking we're way ahead of usual riding lesson protocol but doesn't comment on this. She's starting to accept our strange ways.

"Okay, you get that side Lix, I'll stay this side. Ready Joey? Relax and go with Luna, he'll look after you." He nods and they take off down the beach in a line. Joey looks calm and in control. He is constantly checking Tiff and Felix and adjusting his body, trying to find the most comfortable approach for him. Luna is behaving impeccably, taking long, even strides, being mindful of his rider.

Angel, on the other hand, is being the devil incarnate; he's pulling and straining and throwing his head from side to side in pure frustration, stomping and snorting and writhing his body. I hold him in check long enough to make sure Joey is safe and shout a warning that I am going to let Angel set his own pace. I lean over his neck and whisper in his ear;

"Come on then my Angel, show me what you've got." He needs no further encouragement and, just like The Duchess, does a pretty impressive standing start. We thunder down the beach, in and out of the surf. The feeling is almost unique, like we're in perfect harmony, my mind empties of everything but the beach ahead and the sense of total freedom. I get this same sensation on a bike but the fact that Angel is a beautiful living and breathing creature heightens it more. At any second he could choose to stop or change direction, we have to trust each other, be in tune.

The boys and Tiff catch us up so Joey obviously doesn't have any issues with riding. The huge grin on his face tells me he's loving it. We turn back towards the cottage and Angel is finally calm enough to ride side by side with the others. "What do you think, Joe? Like four legs as much as two wheels?"

"Dunno yet." He shrugs, patting Luna affectionately on his neck. "It's a bit less predictable. Got more control of me bike. All good though."

"Plenty of transferrable skills. If you can control something alive that is way bigger than you then a piece of machinery shouldn't give you any trouble at all."

He thinks about that for a short while. "Yeah, I get that. I wanna go on Angel next time."
I throw my head back and laugh. "That's my boy! Better wait 'til he's got a saddle on."
"This whole family is crazy." Tiff mutters under her breath.
"You're part of it now so get used to it." Felix replies. She looks a little surprised, then embarrassed and then a big smile spreads over her face.
"You can be the sensible one that tells me and Joe off when we get too stupid."
Joe rolls his eyes playfully. "A bossy big sis, just want I always wanted."
Tiff laughs. "If my Mom could hear you and see me now. She'd not believe her eyes. She always told me I needed to grow out of playing with horses, it was only for little girls and would leave me lonely, broke and miserable. I might not be rolling in money but I'm definitely not short of it, I've got a gorgeous man and his crazy family to keep me company and I'm sure as heck happier than I've ever been."

"Do you speak to your parents? Fe said they were only across the water, in Ireland." I carefully try to pry a bit more information from her. "How did you end up in LA?"

"I went over at fifteen to do a summer vacation job at a stables belonging to one of my Dad's friends. I stayed on after the summer and never returned to finish school. I couldn't bear to leave the horses and Mom and Dad weren't too keen to pay my airfare back anyway. I ended up at The Wright's when they bought horses from the stables and needed a groom. Mr. Wright was willing to give me a chance even though I was so young. I think lustful, teenaged Lix may have had something to do with that." She giggles. "We hit it off straight away and I loved having a little stable of my own to run and I worked damned hard to keep it perfect. Then Queen Bitch started to be even more unbearable to them than she had been and wasn't going away as much when Lix and Mr. Wright...er...Emmett came home and their visits got less and less frequent. I just worked and stayed out of everyone's way. I recently got the vibe from Lix's calls that they weren't going to be returning to LA any time soon and had just reluctantly started to look for other jobs when Mrs. Fischer came over to check I was okay and then she suggested I was expected to come over with the horses I couldn't believe my ears."

"In my defence," Felix adds. "I never mentioned her coming over because I just assumed that she would be. We were moving everything we wanted from the LA house and she was definitely on the list."

"Fe, she's not and object!" I sigh and shake my head. "A bit of respect, please."

"It's fine, really. They'd already been so kind and I totally get that Lix was getting used to being here himself. His phone calls conveyed how happy he was and how much he wanted to stay. I was so pleased for him. He spoke about you and his Dad and Joey and it sounded like he finally had a real family. His mom treated him in very much the same way as she treated me." She quickly checks with Felix to make sure she's not said too much and he just nods in agreement. "I still haven't spoken to my folks; they don't know I'm so close now." She adds, remembering my original question.

"You could invite them to the wedding if you want to see them." I offer. "No pressure though, sweetheart, it's up to you, or if you want to go home to see them we can spare you for a few days. Whatever you decide, we can work around it."

"Delilah, you are so lovely! I'm not close to them and I think I'd like to stick around here with your happy, non-judgmental, family for a while before subjecting anyone to my folks, including me." She adds with a sad smile.

"Ya part of the family now, big sis." Joey grins, slapping her on the back. To her credit she doesn't look overly concerned by the statement.

Sal and Sarah are waiting when we get back. "Well, hello, boys." Sal coos at the horses. "We came over to meet the latest editions."

Sarah takes one look at Angel and raises her arms. "Up, Auntie Dilly." I shift back slightly and Sal hands her up to sit in front of me. Angel does his usual dropping of his back end and prancing. "He's silly. I like him." Sarah giggles as she hugs his neck. "Hello silly Angel. Can I ride him to the end?" She points down the beach. "I want to see how fast he can go."

"Okay, baby. Tiff this is Sarah, my goddaughter and Sal, my best, and only, girlfriend." Sal rolls her eyes at me. "Billy's wife and daughter."

"Hello, Sarah, Hi Sal." She smiles and waves. "Lovely to meet you both. Do you want to ride?" Tiff asks Sal, as she dismounts and offers Seraph's reins. "He's pretty worn out from chasing the crazies but I'm sure he'll not mind a little bit more beach time. My wrist is aching now I need some painkillers."

Sal mounts easily and gives Seraph some fuss. "Hey handsome." She turns to me. "Have I just happily plonked my child on the psycho horse?"

"Yeah, he's a little unhinged." I grin. "You riding or just talking?" I take off down the beach and she chases after me shouting abuse and laughing. Sarah's squeals of joy drown out her mother's curses.

Once we're back and the horses are settled, fed and comfortable we head inside for coffee. Emmett is at the kitchen table, looking at his phone. Sarah dives on his lap and slings her arms around his neck.

"Hello Uncle Emmett, I've just been riding on Angel with Auntie Dilly. He's a silly boy but I like him a lot. My teacher is going to come to the wedding but only at the night time because she can't pretend she's poorly and have the day off like I'm going to. She doesn't even know what super-hero she's going to be yet and I told her I'm already exhausted thinking of everyone else's so she's on her own." She rolls her eyes at him to highlight her exasperation. Emm gives her an understanding squeeze. "It's a lot of responsibility, you know? I think Mommy and me will need a big rest when all of this is over." Desperately trying to keep a straight face, Emm looks at Sal who gives him a palms up shrug.

"Sarah, darlin' I don't know what we would have done without you and your mom sorting everything for us. I think I'll have to buy you both really special presents for being so brilliant." Sal nudges me and winks.

Too late he realizes he's been played again. "Oh that's very nice, thank you Uncle Emmett. Were you thinking of something special like a pony? Your horses are very lovely but they're very big my sides hurt already from riding Angel. I would like a brown and white pony with a pretty long mane that I can put ribbons in. I don't think your big boy horses will like wearing ribbons, do you?"

"A pony for you, huh? I think you have a point about ours being a bit big for you and I'm definitely not brave enough to put a ribbon in Angel's mane. Auntie Dilly probably could though because he likes her. What about your Mom? She's done nearly as much hard work as you have. What would Mom like?" Emm can't help himself. "Would she like a pony too?"

"Nope, she wants a fast, red car with a roof that comes off. A Frari" Sarah tells him with wide eyed innocence.

"Okay then, princess, we'll get that sorted before I go to Amsterdam." Emm promises.

"Don't be a daft twat, Emm!" Sal laughs. "We don't want anything. Miss cheeky knickers rides every weekend at the stables. She doesn't need her own pony. She's trying you because me, Bill, Rick, Chaz and even her Nan and Granddad have already told her no."

"There's plenty of room with the donkeys." I shrug. "If she wants a pretty one I don't think putting her in with the boys is a good idea."

"Don't you fucking start, Dil. She's too young to look after a bloody pony." Sal growls. "There's room up at the farm but she'll soon get fed up of the grooming and mucking out." She points to her chest. "And muggings here will have to do it all. Will and Pat have enough to do."

"Tiff can look after her and I've got plenty of free time. It won't be any more work. I have to muck the donkeys out already." I offer. "The boys will be more than willing to help out too if it makes their little princess happy."

"Pleeeaaase, Mommy?" Sarah bats her eyelashes and holds her hands in a praying gesture. "I promise I will help Auntie Dilly and come to ride and feed her every day after school and clean up all her poo. Pleeeaaase."

Emm gives Sal an apologetic look. "It's fine with Dil and me. If you say it's okay I'll find her a good one. I'm sure Meave can recommend something."

Sal drops her shoulders in surrender and laughs. "Don't moan at me when she's round here all the time or not here at all in the arsehole of winter because Billy and I can't be bothered to get out of bed. You're both too soft for your own good. I'm taking zero responsibility for it at all. And for fucks sake DO NOT buy me a Ferrari."

Emm grins and kisses Sarah's head. "I think mom just said you can have a pony, baby." She stares, wide eyed again, at him as the news sinks in then she hugs him tightly and peppers his face with kisses before running off to tell Joey and Felix, yelling behind her. "Thank you, thank you, thank you, I love you all sooooo much."

I hand Sal a coffee. "Sorry, babe. He can't help himself. She's Emmett kryptonite."

"You're as stupid as he is." She bumps me with her hip and thanks Emmett with a kiss on the cheek. "Nothing to do with me. No responsibility for it. All your problem. Going to save me a fortune in riding fees." She reiterates each point with a bump of her hip against mine.

"You staying to eat?" I ask, looking in the empty pans Emm has placed purposefully on the stove. "Emmett's cooking apparently."

She laughs. "No thanks, hun. Billy will be home in a bit and the spoilt one needs a bath and it's already past her bed time. Not that she's going to sleep now. She's got school in the morning. God help her poor teacher, she'll be talking 'pony' all day." She swills her coffee mug in the sink, kisses us bye and goes in search of Sarah.

"What you cooking, sexy man?" I ask, straddling his lap and kissing his forehead.

"Hadn't decided, got sidetracked talking engines with your Dad, He likes the Cobra. Then I started looking at a few emails and I'd had a couple that I really needed to answer, then I got hijacked by hurricane Sarah." He offers in his defence. "Thoughts of you riding Angel bareback weren't helping much either, I got extremely sidetracked by those….."

"Any more excuses?" I laugh, getting up to raid the freezer. "How about pie, peas and mash or pie and chips?" I wave a big chunky pie at him that came from our engagement hamper. "I'll put it on now and then I'm all yours for at least half an hour, anything you need?" I wiggle my bum at him suggestively as I'm bending over to put the pie in the oven.

"Yeah, little imp. Come with me and you can try a bit more of that bareback riding." He grabs my hand and leads me to our cabin. He strips off his jeans and shirt in record speed and throws himself down dramatically in the middle of the bed. "Come and ride this, my little cowgirl." He growls, pointing himself at the ceiling so that there is no room for misunderstanding. "Bareback and as hard and fast as you want."

"Emm you are such a romantic. How could I possibly resist an offer like that?" I laugh as I enthusiastically shed my own clothes and climb aboard.

After a fun and frantic half hour we head back to the cottage to make chips and cook veggies and we all sit down to eat together. After we've eaten and washed up Dad goes back to the workshop, Joey goes off to meet Ella, Fe and Tiff settle in front of the TV and Emm and I sneak back off to bed.

"Remind me to ring Meave in the morning." Emm says sleepily sometime later as we lie in each other's arms, thoroughly sated. "The princess needs a pony."

"Will do. I bet even she can't believe how quickly you caved on that request. Try Nina too, she might know of one needing a home."

"I'm happy to pay for a well-bred one. It should be more predictable and safer for her."

I lift my head and raise an eyebrow. "How'd that work out when you bought Angel?"

He shrugs. "Fair point, there's always an exception. Angel is that exception. I'll call Nina too. Okay, other than I'm a pushover, which you already knew, what else have we learned lately?"

"Four foot ten girlies won't be able to easily ride your custom-made Arch. How tall are you exactly?"

"Six foot three, I think."

"There, I now know how tall you are. Apart from Jurgen, I have no men in my life under six feet tall, no wonder I am permanently being kissed on top of my head and carried around like a child."

"It's because we all get a cricked neck looking down so far." Emm laughs. "Chaz wouldn't even know you were there if he didn't pick you up. I still can't get over your Charger driving issues." I smack him playfully.

"I also know a little bit more about your life in the band and how well you all work together and that Charlie and Connor are even more talented than I already thought. I know you can charm the pants off every lady in the universe, even grumpy bank managers. I know you trust me with

Angel and I really love you for that. I know you like to have plans; things to look forward to. I got to know a bit about Tiff earlier too. I know Joey is able to ride a horse almost as well as a bike. Wow, I know lots!" I laugh, kissing his nose. "What about you?"

"I know I'm about to marry the most beautiful, kind, thoughtful, funny, clever, crazy and loving, tiny woman and I am an incredibly lucky man. Sleep well, perfect little darlin'." He wraps me in his arms and reaches over to turn off the fairy lights.

CHAPTER 68

"**N**ina's come up trumps again." I tell Emm, waving my phone at him after I've dished up breakfast the next morning. "She's given me the name and number of a family just up the road in Andreas. Their daughter has grown out of her pony and they want to sell it so she can have a horse but the daughter doesn't want it to go off the Island. It's a mare and, according to Nina, she's got a good history and is even the right colour. Do you want me to tell Sal we'll pick little Miss Kryptonite up from school and go and have a look? You can check out her teacher too." I add with a wink.

"I have no desire to check out her teacher." He growls. "Yeah, to picking her up and going to see though."

'I'll ring the owner first.' I do and they happily agree so I call Sal and make arrangements to pick up Sarah and feed her before taking her home. "All sorted, honey. Got to pick her up at three. What's everyone up to today?"

"Workin'." Joey answers. "Gorra get everythin' hired out 'fore we go away."

"Do you need an extra pair of hands?" Felix asks. "Happy to come and help out."

"Cheers, bro. Think we're alright but I'll call ya if we get stuck."

"Stef wanted us to go down the studio for a while, Fe, if you're free."

"All yours, Old Boy." He grins at Tiff. "Tiff wants a day with the horses and she says I can't distract her."

She laughs and nods in agreement. "I'll get everything sorted and ride them all too, except Angel. I'll do the donkeys too if you'll ride him for me Dil."

"No worries, sweetheart. Go easy on that wrist, rest if it starts hurting. Sarah's pony will have to go in with the donkeys so I'll come and move all the food out of that end stall and stash it in the tack room." I reply.

"I'd appreciate your expertise and little hands with a couple of jobs in the workshop, Dilly Girl. Might as well get as much done as I can before 'Dam."

"I'm not going anywhere apart from down the beach, with Angel and the doggies, 'til we fetch Sarah so yell whenever you need me, Daddy dearest."

Everyone finishes eating and drinking and takes off. Joey grabs a big bag of food. "Laters fam. Loves ya!"

"Love you too, ride safe!"

Tiff goes off to start work and Emmett and Felix roam aimlessly around the cottage looking lost. "Where's the car keys, darlin'?"

"In the ignition, babe. You're not in LA anymore." I sass.

"Smartarse!" He replies picking me up for a cuddle and kissing me like he'll be gone for a week. "Can't wait for Fe to hear your song. Stef's talking about releasing a teaser of it to see what the response is like."

"I appreciate the fact that I know absolutely nothing about music and recording but doesn't your record company have any say in who you stick on your tracks? Won't they replace my stuff with their own artist?"

Felix snorts a laugh at me as if I've just said something really stupid. "We *are* the record company. We write, produce, monitor and oversee distribution on all of our own stuff. When you think I'm playing on my phone, I am actually doing my job. Do you two actually ever talk to each other? No, don't answer that; I know what you spend all of your time doing." He holds up his hands in a stop gesture. "Come on, Old Boy, let's go and do some work. We need to show your woman we can earn our keep."

"So Candy Crush is one of your distribution sites is it? What about Babe Station? They must do a lot of work with you from the amount of times I see you on their site. Have fun boys! Drive safe. Love you both." I laugh as Emmett pushes a giggling Felix out of the door.

"Love you too." They yell back.

I pour myself another coffee and hand one to Dad. "Life is so good, Dad." I announce with a sigh.

"It is that, Dilly Girl. You looking forward to Friday?"

"Would it be bad to say I'm kind of looking forward to Friday being done and over with so that we can all get on with normal life? I ask with a grimace.

"Nope, I hear you but you're only going to do it once so you need it to be memorable. You know memories are all you're taking with you into your next life."

"I am excited and I know I'll love it all when it happens but I feel like I'm on a roller coaster and I need to get off for five minutes. It's just been surreal and crazy here ever since Jurgen turned up with his campers. I can't believe you and I were sleeping under canvas ourselves, outside a shell of a cottage, a few months ago. It's like I've reached my final destination and I honestly cannot think of anywhere else I'd rather be but I don't have enough time to relax and enjoy it."

"It has been a frantic few weeks, that's for sure, everything will settle down after Friday and you'll have time to recharge while we're off on the stag do before. Are you still thinking of fostering?"

473

"I've managed to talk Emm into waiting a little while. I need to get my head around being a Mama to Joe and Felix before I add more to the mix but it'll happen soon enough."

"You're a superb Mama to them already but I get that you want a more set routine before taking on anything or anyone else. Come on let's go and get elbow deep in grease, it'll soothe your soul."

We work harmoniously on different bikes Dad has in various states of strip down and get four finished off and ready for collection. Dad rubs his hands together and reaches for his phone to call the owners to collect. "That's my entertainment funds sorted for next week." He laughs.

"Dad tell me if you need any money, we apparently have lots. Emm gave me one of his cards until the new ones for us all come through and you said I have to use it so that I don't hurt his feelings."

"I'm teasing Dil, I'm not short, getting rental money from the other house every month and I've done a fair few jobs in here that have made good money. The guys that are renting our old place have asked if they can buy it when the lease is up. What do you think?"

"Do whatever makes you happy, Dad. I think I've finally found home. Emm's got properties all over the bloody place so we can up sticks and head for the sunshine if winter here gets a bit dreary. We've already made loose plans to all go skiing around Christmastime."

"Sounds perfect, Dilly. I'll let them buy it. They're only young, It's a shame for them to waste all their money on rent."

"There's a fine example of not enough time." I wail, pointing to the green laners we still haven't got out on. "That beautiful Panigale too."

"They're not going anywhere. They'll be there for when you get chance." I kiss his cheek and offer him some lunch. "Whatever you're making, I'll happily eat."

I make some sandwiches and fetch Tiff in for a break.

"I've mucked out and tidied up, cleaned all the tack and found a place for everything, sorted the donkeys and the space for Sarah's pony. Will you need the horsebox to collect her? The boys are all groomed and I'm going to ride Midnight out straight after lunch. Do you want to come with Angel?"

"Thank you for doing the donkeys, I really appreciate that. Did Giles behave himself? The pony is only a few minutes up the road so Sarah can probably ride her back to be honest." I cringe as she shows me a Giles shaped bruise appearing on her shoulder. "Ouch! He's a little bugger, sorry honey. Yes to the ride on Angel, I can do the chucks and all the housework afterwards."

"I'll do the chucks in a minute." Dad offers. "Can you put some washing on? I'm going to need some clean jeans for going away. I'd do it myself but I don't wanna shrink any of the boys' fancy designer gear."

"Don't worry. Washing's on my 'to do' list."

Angel wants to be anything but angelic again and I give up on a saddle as Tiff is already tacked up, mounted and waiting. We have a slightly more sedate ride down the beach than our usual tear arse runs. He torments Midnight and keeps goading him to go faster until we finally concede and give them a mad sprint back to the paddock. "I'm taking Luna now, then Seraph unless you want to take one." Tiff tells me. I agree and have a much more controlled outing on impeccably behaved Seraph with dogs, Dutch and Frank riding shotgun.

Chores time! I select several Era albums to listen to and jamb in my earbuds, sort the washing and get a load on, dust and polish every surface in the cottage, mezzanines and our cabin, vacuum, rearrange all of the beautiful bouquets, do some baking, work through the overflowing ironing basket, change the beds and scrub the bathrooms. I'm just about to collapse with a coffee when I hear the Charger approaching. I set a load of cakes and biscuits on the table and dash off to shower and change ready to get Sarah.

"Good day at the office, darling?" I tease as we're in the car and heading for the school.

"Yeah, we actually got a lot done between us. I had words with Felix because he was disrespectful to you this morning so he's worked his butt off all day to ease his guilt."

"Emm, he wasn't disrespectful. I was ignorant and I imagine he felt a little insulted and then I teased him to make it even worse. You're all really successful and I know nothing about your business. It's me that was being rude, not him."

"We'll agree to disagree there, darlin'. The teasing had him giggling all the way to Jurgen's. Either way we got plenty of work out of him so it's all good." He grins, patting my knee then letting his hand wander up my thigh. "I missed you. I noticed how spotless the cottage and our cabin was and the lovely smell of the fresh beds and huge pile of clean clothes so I won't ask if you've had a fun day."

"Strangely, I enjoy the housework once I get going. I kept myself entertained listening to this band called Era, they're pretty darn good, you know. I did a bit of spannering with Dad, got out with the dogs, Seraph and my favourite four-legged psycho too so, apart from missing you, I had a great day."

"Kinda glad you missed me too, not sure how I'm going to cope for two days without you."

"You'll be having far too much fun with loose women, happy brownies and sex shows to even notice I'm not there. Trust me, The Parkers alone will be more than enough entertainment." I giggle. "You'll be coming home with aching sides from too much laughing."

"Yeah, I imagine the three of them together without you or Sal to keep 'em in line will be an eye opener."

We park in the pub car park next to Sarah's school and go and join the other waiting parents. I notice quite a few moms eyeing up my man but I let it go, I can't blame them for looking. Sarah comes rocketing out of the door and flies into my arms.

"Auntie Dilly, Uncle Emmett, what you doing here? My dinner was really good today, Mommy put one of your muffins in and some Nanny Pat pie but I'm starving now. Are you taking me out for some scran? Can we go to Maccies? I really need a banana milkshake. Does Uncle Emm like milkshake?" I raise my eyes in question and Emm confirms that he does indeed like milkshake. "I made you a card in free time today." She thrusts her empty lunchbox and a big heart shaped card covered in glitter at Emmett. "It's a thank you card for my pony. I know I haven't got my pony yet but you promised and I know you won't break your promise so I made a thank you and an I love you card all in one. Do you want to meet my teacher? She's there telling Jack's mom he's been horrible to Phoebe again. We learned a new song in music today do you want to hear it?" She breaks into a loud rendition of Five little speckled frogs...Sat on a speckled log... Eating some most delicious grubs, yum, yum. I join in with her and Emmett watches us both with an indulgent smile.

The teacher is looking frazzled but has now finished with Jack's mom and waves to get our attention. Sarah begs to get up on Emm's shoulders so that she can be super tall. He lifts her up and we go over to say hi.

"I've been really good today haven't I Miss. Jackson? This is my Auntie Dilly and my Uncle Emm, they're getting married and buying me a pony."

"You have been really good and very helpful all week, Sarah and mentioned about the wedding and the pony a couple of times." She laughs. "It's really good to meet you both, she keeps us all entertained with her tales all about you and the rest of her family."

"Oh dear, that's worrying." I laugh. "Hi, Miss. Jackson, I'm Delilah, her godmother, this is Emmett, my fiancé." He shakes her hand and she looks at him properly for the first time, then looks again.

"Oh my god! You really are *that* Emmett."

"Apparently so." He drawls.

Sarah rolls her eyes, "Miss. Jackson, I already told you that. Are you coming to the wedding or not?"

"Sarah." Emm prompts. "That's a bit of a rude way to speak to your teacher, princess."

"Sorry Miss. Jackson, I thought I told you that Uncle Emmett plays the guitar in a band. My Auntie Dilly rides motorbikes, really fast."

"Is Auntie Dilly who you're named after?"

"Yep." She says proudly. "Auntie Dilly is my second mommy. If my mommy dies Auntie Dilly has to look after me forever. Now, about the wedding, will you be coming because I will need to put a tick or a cross by your name in my wedding book." She looks down into Emm's face to check he's happier with her tone. He pats her leg to show he approves.

Miss Jackson isn't too sure how to respond so I help her out. "You are very welcome to come, Sarah wanted to invite you. It's going to be a very relaxed affair on the beach with music, food, drink and superheroes and occasional dogs, cats, horses, donkeys and rabbits. Whatever stories She's told you, we're probably worse, so don't expect anything formal or re-motely normal. Bring a friend too if you don't want to come alone. We're down at the old white cottage near the beach in Jurby, just follow the noise and you'll find us."

"Oh wow, thank you so much, I would love to come. I can't wait to see Sarah's bridesmaid outfit." She smiles. "It sounds like quite an unusual choice."

"We are an 'unusual' family." I laugh. "Come on then, Snot Monster, we've got a date with a pony."

Her eyes nearly pop out of her head. "What? Now? Today?"

"We're going to look at a pony, see if you like her or would you rather go to Mac D's?" Emm clarifies.

"Pony, pony, pleeeaaase!" She yells, nearly strangling him and kissing him over and over on his head.

We say bye to her teacher and strap her safely in the car and after simultaneously and impulsively bursting into a loud rendition of 'Sorry, Miss Jackson' by OutKast we head for a little smallholding just outside of Andreas.

We are shown the prettiest, immaculate little palomino Connemara pony by a very reluctant young lady who clearly idolises her but has grown far too big to ride.

"This is Dakota. I've had her for four years and she's perfect." She drops her head in her hands and bursts into tears. "I don't want her to go but I can't ride her anymore and she likes to be ridden. It's not fair for her to be bored and lonely in the field all the time."

With a little encouragement from her dad and a lot of reassurance from us, she pulls herself together enough to saddle up Dakota for Sarah to try out. They hit it off right away. Dakota is a spirited little lady and shows plenty of sass but doesn't do anything dangerous. Sarah handles her well and falls in love instantly. The young ownerseems slightly placated by our close proximity, the fact that Dakota will have lots of four legged friends and the open offer to visit any time she wants. Emm chats with the dad about papers and they agree a price and he transfers the money via his phone. We load up a folder full of information, all the extra tack and lots of goodies they throw in like food, brushes, grown out of boots, jodhpurs and helmets into the car and Sarah rides a blissfully happy Dakota the couple of miles to our place while I walk beside her and Emmett heads home in the car planning to make banana milkshakes and cook some burgers ready for our arrival.

We get home to a welcoming committee on the drive. Sarah is in her element, being adored by everyone and the pony laps it all up too. The fact that Joey is taking off his helmet and handing over a couple of very full rucksacks to a sheepish Emm gives away the truth that he'd obviously been dispatched to MacDonald's to buy burgers and milkshake.

Little Dakota is carefully introduced to the donkeys and its love at first sight for Giles, he's so enamored by her that he forgets to bite anyone. Wonky and Isobel hardly look up from their dinner. The big boys make a lot of noise seemingly very excited about a young lady in the vicinity but they seem to calm after a mad run around and a push and shove of each other.

"Looks like they're ready to meet some of Meave's girls." I comment.

Dad yells us for food and we leave Dakota to settle for now. I laugh when I see the table spread with at least two of pretty much every item on the whole Mc D's menu. "How did you get all that in your rucksack, Joe?"

"Took two." He grins. "'Ad one on me back an' one on me front. Better 'ang 'em out else everythin' we pack to go away'll smell like burgers or nana shake." I grab them off the side and peg them out on the line, fetching in the washing from earlier. We all dive in and make short work of clearing the table. I'm just throwing away a mountain of cups and boxes in the bin as Sal and Billy pull up.

"Dave." Bill greets me, kissing the top of my head. "What ya done with me kid? It's too fuckin' quiet in our house."

"She's inside being spoilt rotten and adored by her big bros and their girlies. We were going to bring her home in a while. We were just filling her full of junk food." Sarah hears her dad's voice and comes running out to show them Dakota. She's still wide awake and full of excitement.

Sal watches her and laughs. "Thanks, tart! She's not gonna sleep for a week. Do you want her to stay here for the night?"

"We've got a spare bed." I shrug. "I can get her to school if you and Bill want a night of noisy passion."

She side eyes me. "Are you and Emmett plotting to steal my child?"

"Bugger, you've sussed us already." I giggle and tell her about the conversation with her teacher about the fact that she's mine if Sal dies. "So watch your back, bitch."

She pushes me playfully. "Seriously, Dil, thanks so much for the pony." Then adds with a wink, "And even more for having it here so I don't have to look after it."

We end up breaking out the beers, lighting the fire pit and the torches and having a chilled night, playing on the beach. Joey and Ella take Sarah for a paddle and do a bit of beachcombing then they have a wild game of football with Felix, Tiff, Dad, Billy and the dogs. Frank cuddles up to Sal while Emm cuddles me and Dutch sits on his shoulder, lazily watching everyone. The game morphs into a strange version of volleyball with the girls on the shoulders of the boys; Sarah on Dad, Tiff on Fe and Ella on Billy.

"Eh Ma, gerrup 'ere. We need an extra girl." Joe pulls me up from the blanket then bends forward to lift me onto his shoulders, holding onto both of my hands to steady me. "You, me, Gramps an' Sarah versus Bill, Ell, Fe an' Tiff. First to score five wins, losers 'ave to go for a swim." We thrash out the rules and draw a line on the beach for the net then have an hilarious half hour banging, smashing and crashing the ball around until somehow we manage to get that all important fifth point.

"Ha ha, get in the sea, losers!" Sarah yells from her lofty perch. Billy and Felix strip off and enthusiastically launch themselves straight into the water while the girls gingerly paddle up to their knees. Joey can't help himself and runs in after the boys dropping me off his shoulders and into the cold water when he's deep enough for me to swim then runs back to grab Ella and dunks her too. The dogs think it's a great game and dive in. Tiff's only let off because of the cast on her wrist but she gets more than her fair share of wet dog when they all shake themselves dry next to her.

Dad deposits Sarah on Emm's lap. "Well played partner." He high fives her. "I need beer and they need towels." He laughs heading for the cottage. He's back in a few minutes with fluffy towels, blankets, beer, a couple of bottles of tequila and a cheeky smile.

I look over at Sal. "You staying, honey? I'm sure Joe and Ella will give up their bed for you and Sarah can have the little one. Are the dogs going to be okay?"

"Yes, dogs are fine, Nath was home tonight. I'll text him now. We can have the settee."

Joe and Felix both reply that they'll happily sleep on the settee.

Dad suggests that he has the little bed and Sal, and Billy have his and Sarah will have plenty of room on the settee with the dogs to keep her safe and warm. With that finally settled Sal gets Sarah showered and into one of my t-shirts and my bathrobe. We load up the fire with plenty of driftwood, set half a dozen alarms so that at least one of us gets her highness to school on time and break open the hard stuff. Sarah cuddles up in Joey's arms and goes to sleep whilst Felix leads the way in lots of drinking games he keeps finding on his phone.

We all get into a game of Mr. & Mrs. where partners have to answer questions about each other and if you get it wrong you have to drink a shot. Ella gets legless and Joey doesn't have to drink once. Then it's Bill and Sal's turn and they know everything about each other but keep drinking even when they get the answer right. I'm not a lover of spirits, the taste makes me cringe but I'm up for the game. Emm and I sit back to back and Felix reads the questions.

"What is her favourite colour?"

"Purple or rainbow." Emm replies. Everyone agrees so neither of us have to drink.

"What is Dad's favourite movie?"

"Shit, I have no idea. How about Christine?"

"Good thinking, little darlin' but it's actually Gone in 60 Seconds." I hold my nose and drink.

"What is Dil's favourite place in the world?"

"Here."

"Correct again, baby."

"Does Dad prefer cats or dogs?"

I hold my hands over Dutch's ears so he's not offended. "Dogs."

"Yeah, but I love Dutch and Frank too."

"What is Dil's number-one fear?"

"Wow, that's deep. I don't know. She's fearless. How about Davison's running out of licorice ice cream?"

"Yeah, that is a big one." I laugh. "Drink your tequila, baby."

"Who is his celebrity crush?"

"Oh, I'm bad at this. I have no idea. Angelina Jolie?"

"You got it, darlin'. More specifically, Sway in Gone in 60 seconds."

"What is her proudest moment?"

"Winning a TT?"

"Nope, being asked to adopt Joe." I reply honestly.

"What was his worst mistake?"

"Telling me I'm allowed to drive your sexy cars?" I laugh.

"Nope, marrying Cherry." Felix deadpans. "Drink up Dil."

We carry on until I can't stand to drink any more then start on Felix and Tiff who know a surprising amount about each other and don't come off too badly but then partake in a fair few shots anyway so they don't feel left out.

Sal then begins a game of truth or dare which gets quite out of hand.

"Okay, you bunch of drunkards, bedtime." I yell when she sneakily asks when and where everyone lost their virginity."

Joey carries a fast-asleep Sarah inside and tucks her up on the settee and everyone hugs and kisses 'goodnights' and retires to bed. Emm undresses me and puts me under our duvet as I'm a little inebriated.

"I'm looking forward to getting to know everything about you." I tell him. "When we play that again at our tenth anniversary party, I'll know every single answer."

He climbs in beside me and pulls me into his arms.

"What's your biggest fear then, my darling? Don't think I didn't notice how you avoided that question."

"Losing the people I love." I reply. Emm holds me tightly and whispers something soothing into my hair.

"Can we have drunken sex now?" I mumble sleepily.

CHAPTER 69

I am rudely awoken by what sounds like a thousand tortured demons but turns out to be Emmett's alarm. I throw myself into the shower to clear my head. Emm lets out a loud groan and pulls the pillows back over his. When I get into the cottage Joey is already making breakfast, he hands me a coffee and gives me a quick look over to check I'm fully functioning.

"Great night. 'Ows ya 'ead?"

"I'm all good baby, but Emm may be a little fragile this morning." I laugh, giving him a hug. Ella is patiently braiding a very excited Sarah's hair. "Good morning, my beautiful girlies." I kiss them both on the forehead. There's no sight or sound from Dad or Sal and Billy.

"Can I ride Dakota before I go to school? We've fed her and the donkeys and the big horses their breakfast. Joey said I don't need to clean them out yet. We fed the dogs too and Dutch and Frank and the chickens." She adds.

"Thank you very much, you have all been busy. I don't think we'll have time for a ride until after school, baby but I promise we'll make it a good, long one. What do you want in your lunchbox?"

"Pie and muffins and beer!"

"Hmm, who gave you beer? I don't think we have any left after last night. You'll have to have apple juice or fizzy water, I'm afraid."

"Felix let me have some of his." She rats instantly. "Apple juice is good though."

Joey dives to his brother's defence. "It was only one swig, Ma. Bill okay'd it." He drops a huge plateful of hot, buttered toast on the table and two big glasses of milk for himself and Sarah. "Jam, choccie spread, peanut butter or marmite?" He asks with his head in the larder. "Or fresh eggs we just got from the chucks?"

"Choccie spread!" We all reply. We fill up on toast and I pack Sarah's school bag.

"I can drop 'er off if it's okay to take 'er on the back of me bike." Joey says. "Meetin' Rick at the yard so I gorra pass school."

"Yay! Please can I, Auntie Dilly? Joey can meet Miss. Jackson."

Ella raises and eyebrow. "Should I be worried about him meeting Miss. Jackson?" She asks. "I've got to go the other way, meeting a client in Castletown."

"Nope, unless he's got a thing for ladies who dress like Nanny Pat." I giggle. "I don't think you ever need to worry about him straying, baby. He's as loyal, honest and faithful as they come." She smiles adoringly at him and nods in agreement.

I go outside and dig around in Bill's truck to find one of Sarah's bike jackets and a helmet and get her ready. She gives Ella a big hug and Ella heads off for work. I warn Joe to take it slow and steady and wave bye with strict instructions to text me when he's dropped her off.

"See you later, Auntie Dilly. Love you!"

"Later, babies, love you both too, ride safe." I watch them until they're out of sight then make more coffee and toast and head back to bed.

Emmett groans some more and then perks up a little when he smells the coffee I waft under his nose. "Oh crap! Did Sarah get to school?"

"On her way, as we speak. Joe's taken her. She wants to show him off to her teacher. She just asked for beer in her lunchbox." I tell him with a giggle.

"Is that right? If only she knew how my head felt this morning she might rethink that request." He grimaces.

"Think the tequila may be more to blame than the beer."

"You were in a worse state than me, darlin'. How come you're all cured and lively now? You have no idea what unspeakable things I did to you whilst you were semiconscious." He adds jokingly. "At your request I might add."

I hold up my coffee and toast. "Third coffee and sixth piece of toast with chocolate spread." I shrug. "Lots of sugar. And I'm sure my body enjoyed whatever you did to me last night even if my drink addled brain didn't fully participate."

"You were definitely making all the right noises in the right places." He tells me.

My phone pings to confirm Sarah has got to school safely.

'al gud teechas luv me xxx' I laugh and show Emm. "I love my boys so much my heart hurts." I sigh happily.

"Am I one of your boys?" He asks.

"Yep, definitely, one of my boys and my man so you're extra special." I joke. "Do you want this toast or shall I eat it all?" He gingerly sits up slightly and takes the plate from me. "Dad, Bill and Sal are still comatose; Ricky is going to blame me for disabling his workforce. I'm not sure Fe and Tiff will surface before lunchtime either. How's the head? I can think of a couple of ways we can sweat the alcohol out of your system if you're up to it."

"I like the sound of that but I don't think my head is up for sudden movements just yet so you'll have to do all the work. Climb aboard, little darlin'." He encourages, throwing back the duvet to demonstrate that at least part of him is ready and willing.

"Wake up you lazy tarts, I want a go on your horses." Sal shouts a good while later, throwing the door wide open and dropping a happy Frank on the bed. "Has anyone seen my child this morning? Did I dream it or was your father animatedly discussing the merits of the reverse cowgirl position with your husband and sons at some stage of that Truth or Dare game yesterday evening?"

"Ella got her dressed and presentable and Joey took her to school on time after feeding her so social services won't be round today." I laugh as she jumps on the bed giggling. "Unless they come about the fact she was on the back of his bike and had beer in her lunchbox and yes, that conversation did happen. I remember it all too clearly." I groan. "Where's Bill?"

"Gone to work, Rick woke us up with a round of fucks because he needed something towing somewhere. Where did you find beer for her lunchbox? I thought we ran out last night." She asks pretending to be serious then bursts into fits of giggles when she sees the look on Emm's face. "Can I play on your horses, Emm?" She whines. "I am a responsible adult really. I don't want to ride the mad one though, Dil can ride him."

"Go for it, honey. I need a shower and some Advil before I get involved in anything physical." Emmett smiles, kissing her cheek and climbing out of bed naked to head for the bathroom.

"Oh! I might just stay here a while and admire the view." She sasses. "Are you too hungover for a threesome?" I smack her around the head with a pillow. "Ow, bitch, that hurt. You can't keep all of that for yourself, it's just greedy. You're only little, you don't need that much man. You should share." She jokes. I can hear Emmett chuckling to himself in the shower.

I pull on my shorts and a vest and drag Sal to the paddock. We pass a slightly subdued Dad outside the workshop. "Morning girls. Great night. Did Sarah get to school okay? Where are you off to?"

"She got there fine, Joey and Ella sorted her. We're going to take the horses out before Sal propositions Emm again."

Dad laughs easily. "Ride safe. Love you both."

"Seraph, Luna, Midnight or Angel?" I ask, pointing to each one in turn. Angel comes flying over, snorts all over me and grabs a mouthful of dreadlocks whilst showing Sal the whites of his eyes.

"Not him! He's not right in the head." She exclaims. "Is he a Friesian? He's bloody huge."

"No idea what he is but he's definitely a very special boy. Aren't you my Angel?" I smile, kissing him on the nose.

"You just like him because he's purple." Sal laughs and she's correct; because his coat is so black and shiny he does look a shade of deep, deep purple when the sun catches him right.

"Yes, he is a Friesian, one of the best examples I've ever seen and yes he is 'special' in so many ways." Tiff adds caustically as she reaches the gate. "I will apologise now absolutely and completely for anything I did or said last night." She laughs, holding her hands up. "It was a fun evening. Did Sarah get to school okay?"

"You didn't embarrass yourself in any way, honey. This one has said and done worse in the last half hour. No apologies owed to anyone and Sarah got to school fine." I nod towards a grinning and unrepentant Sal.

"That's good on all counts then." She sighs. "Were you going for a ride? What has Sal done?"

"She's just invited Emm for a threesome." I shrug and poor Tiff isn't sure what to say in reply. "Yeah, we were planning on riding if shithead here will let me near him with a bridle. Are you coming too? Can you grab some tack for Sal?" Tiff tacks up Midnight and Luna and hands me Angel's bridle.

A gorgeous, freshly showered and super sexy Emmett comes sauntering down to join us.

"I'll bring Seraph, grab his stuff, Tiff." He drawls, sharing fuss and polo mints equally between his adoring four-legged fans, canine and equine. I let everyone saddle up and move away a little before coaxing a very bouncy Angel into allowing me to mount. He throws himself around dramatically and zig zags all the way up the path towards the beach, then does a sideways crab walk down to the shoreline. He then proceeds to do a bizarre dressage routine; lifting his knees up high and hopping from foot to foot in an exaggerated march and then goosestepping slowly in circles with his legs alternately stretched out in front as far as he can reach. Tiff, Emm and Sal watch on in wonder.

"See, I told you he was special." I laugh. "Come on, shithead, stop showing off and let's see how fast you can go." He understands exactly what I've said and snorts before dropping his haunches and launching himself down the beach like a maniac.

We ride together at a more sedate pace once everyone has let off some steam and Angel relentlessly torments Seraph by pushing into him and pulling at his bridle.

"I don't think we'll be subjecting Meave's mares to you any time soon, you bloody degenerate." Emm laughs, gently shoving him away. "I think Seraph or Luna are the safest options. What do you think, Tiff?"

"Yes, let's not put her off after one attempt." She laughs. "I think Seraph and Luna will be a gentle and attentive boys, the ladies will love them.

Midnight might be a little aggressive and the 'special one' won't have a clue what to do. If he works out he needs to cover the mare he'll probably stick it in the wrong hole."

"Don't talk about Angel like that." I giggle. "You'll hurt his feelings, he's a very sensitive boy." Just to prove he's anything but he lets out a loud fart and bites Luna on the bum then runs into the sea and splashes everyone.

"He's about as sensitive as a house brick." Tiff sighs.

We head back and Tiff insists that she can groom them all so Emm, Sal and I go in search of food. Felix is lying on the settee with Frank on his chest and Dutch on his head.

"Hi fam, how can you all be so perky after the amount of alcohol we consumed last night? Did Sarah get off okay? Can I fetch her later. I need to meet Miss. Jackson. Why do I keep feeling like I need to sing her name?" We all burst into another rendition of 'Sorry Miss. Jackson'. "Jeez, that's it. Can I fetch her Sal? Pretty sure I'm no longer over the legal drink driving limit. I regained my eyesight about an hour ago." He sits up slowly and tries to focus on us in order to test his theory.

"Course you can if you want to. Her poor teacher will have a breakdown if any more sexy men turn up in her classroom." Sal replies. "I get the feeling she doesn't get much between-the-sheets action."

"She did get a little excited when she realised Emm was really Emm yesterday, you turning up might push her over into complete madness." I laugh. "You might want a shower first; you smell like a feral cat with an alcohol problem." He wraps himself around me, squashing my face into his chest and rubs his stinky body all over me.

"You and your brother are animals! Emmett, have a word with your son." I groan, shoving him back into the chair.

"Felix, don't make your mother smell like a feral cat." Emm says with mock seriousness. "I have to share a bed with her."

"God, it's worse than being in our house." Sal mutters under her breath. "Get the coffee on Dil." Fe wanders off for a wash and we raid the fridge.

"Is everything ready for Friday? Do we need to do anything? I'm pretty sure we must owe you some money." Emmett asks.

"Dil sent me money the other day and you just bought Sarah a bloody pony so I think you're in credit big time."

"That's nothing to do with the wedding. Tell us if we owe for anything. What about the guys you've booked to do the ceremony?"

"All sorted. You just need to squeeze into your sexy outfit and not worry about anything apart from Dil having a panic attack and running for the hills." He looks at me with a raised eyebrow.

"Not gonna happen, baby. I'm not gonna miss seeing you in tights." I reassure him.

His phone rings and it's Stef telling him to have a look at something on a music site. Apparently he's just released a couple of teasers for Era's new album and feedback is pretty favourable. They chat for a few minutes and Emm mooches around looking for his ipad. He logs on and passes it over to me and Sal to read;

'Era fans have just been treated to a sneak preview of their eagerly awaited new album; Watching Waves. The tasty tidbits hint of a more mellow vibe than their last release with hauntingly beautiful woodwind instruments played by the multi-talented Fischer brothers, Charlie and Connor and a mesmerising female voice featuring on one the tracks. The other track is much more classic Era with a heavy guitar and bass presence but somehow sounding a little more relaxed than previous albums. Recent press speculation claims fiercely private guitarist Emmett Wright has filed for divorce from his long time estranged wife, Cherry Martinez. He's been seen, most uncharacteristically, having fun and frolicking around with his son and Era's excellent bass player, Felix, easy going front man Stefan Fischer and a previously unknown lady friend. She's now been identified as feisty and fearless little road racer, Miss. Delilah Blue. Is she responsible for the more laid back sound ? And is it her voice on this track? Who knows? But if it is you Delilah, I strongly suggest you get these talented boys to help you produce your own album. That heavenly voice has been hidden away in a helmet for far too long!'

'None of the band were available for comment but early feedback from fans is looking decent so far.'

We skim through the comments and they are very encouraging with just a few daft ones here and there. Emm is all happy smiles and doesn't seem affected by the remarks on his private life.

"We better get on with the rest of the album. Stef got a bit over excited with this one. We need to get three more tracks down at least."

A much fresher and better smelling Felix rejoins us and we show him. He slaps Emm on the back and kisses my head.

"We're pretty darn good at making music, family. Shall I fetch Sarah in the car or on the bike?"

"If you're going on the bike check with Joey to see if he left her helmet and jacket with her." He grabs his phone and rings Joe who tells him he didn't leave her stuff, it's back in Billy's truck.

"Car it is then." Fe grins. "Laters fam, love you."

I prepare a snack for Sarah then go and brush and tack up a very compliant little Dakota and am just finishing as Felix pulls back in with a very boingy Sarah who dives into his arms as soon as they get out of the car.

"Auntie Dilly, Felix came to fetch me and Miss. Jackson was very surprised and she was surprised too when Joey dropped me off this morning on his bike she went to fetch the other teacher and the lady from the office and they all giggled a lot and liked how he talked." She rolls her eyes. "She said Joey was very handsome and I'll ask her what she thinks of Felix in the morning. He kept making her go red and forget how to talk properly. My lunch was really good. I'm starving. Can I ride Dakota now?" She finally stops for breath and leans right over, flinging her arms around the pony. Fe puts her down gently and stands watching and listening with a daft grin on his face.

"There's a snack on the table then we're ready to ride." She dashes indoors, says a quick hello to everyone, shovels in her food and we all go off for a walk down the beach with her trotting, cantering and galloping around us.

Emmett holds my hand as we walk. "Darlin', I love you more every day. Even drunken you was adorable. How do you feel about making an album? Stef and I can write you some songs."

"You need to concentrate your own songs." I scold. "I have no burning desire to make an album any time soon. Emm, I'm happy being little miss no one on my tiny patch of The Rock."

"You'll be little Mrs. Blue-Wright on Friday." He muses. "I can't wait to have it all signed, sealed and official. Are you going to agree to obey me in your vows?"

"Definitely, I like it when you're all bossy and in charge." I sass. "How about you?"

"I'll certainly love and honour you but I'm still thinking about the 'obey' part. I don't believe you always have your own best interests at heart so if I agree to obey you I might have to do something you ask me to when I don't think it's best for you."

"Oh wow that's deep, you really have been thinking about it, haven't you? Why not promise to love, honour and carnally educate me? Or love, honour and spoil me rotten? You're already doing both."

Felix squashes in between us, putting an arm around us both. "He should agree to love, honour and worship you because he already does."

"Worship? Yeah, I can go for worship, good call, thanks Son."

"Glad to be of service, Old Boy. Have you asked Stef to be your best man?"

"We haven't actually discussed this wedding much, have we?" I comment, looking at Emm.

"I think the 'Batgirl' element may have sidetracked me somewhat. Do I need a best man, Sal?"

"Err yeah, I suppose so, and two witnesses. Rings too, have you got rings?"

I shrug. "Do you even want to wear a wedding ring, honey? Will it get in the way when you're playing?"

"Yeah, I do want one. I want everyone to know I'm yours darlin'. I didn't have one before but I sure as heck want one this time. It shouldn't cause any issues unless you chose one that's so wide I can't bend my finger."

"We better go and find some tomorrow then. You can choose your own so that you know it's right. What else should we have sorted by now, Sal?" I ask.

"Think we're okay. Banns have kind of been read; Chaz helped out with that, food's sorted, Jurgen's chef is making the cake, registrar and druid are sorted, altar and flowers sorted and ribbons for handfasting, think everyone has invited everyone else so guests are sorted, band and DJ sorted, outfits sorted but I suppose you ought to try them on. You've got bridesmaids and Dylan is giving you away, you just need rings, witnesses and a best man." She counts off everything on her fingers. "Oh and I've ordered your stripper poles too."

"Fe and Joe can be witnesses. Stef can be best man and we'll get rings tomorrow. I will obey you and you can worship me or whatever you feel moved to do on the day. All organised." I declare.

"You are the most ungirly girl I have ever met." Felix laughs. "I thought women spent years stressing over their wedding."

"Fe, she'd be down the register office barefoot and in just her knickers if I'd left it to her." Sal comments dryly. "And she'd have forgotten to book the registrar."

I laugh because she knows me so well. "Yep, she's right. If anyone had told me six months ago that I'd ever be getting married I would have slung everything I own in a rucksack and took off on The Duchess. Marriage and commitment is...was a really scary prospect. Shit, who am I kidding? It still is a really, really scary prospect." I admit.

Felix hugs me tighter to his side and kisses my head. "You're gonna be just great at it, Dil. You and Dad are perfect for each other and apart from the Fischers, we're already the happiest and most contented family I've ever known so you've got nothing to worry about. Whatever comes our way we'll handle it, together." He looks to Dad and gets a nod of approval.

"When did my Son get so grown up?" Emm whispers proudly.

"Since we moved here." He replies simply. "It's been a real eye opener."

"Don't worry Auntie Dilly." Sarah pipes up. "You are very brilliant at everything so you'll be alright and I'm going to be there to help you get the wedding stuff right."

"Thank you, my darlings. It means a lot to me that you're all here." I reply, trying not to cry.

"Not getting ready to run again are you, Dilly Girl?" Dad asks seriously.

"God no, it's totally terrifying but in a good way. I'm staying on this ride 'til the very end. I promise."

"Like Felix says, we're all here. If it gets too much talk to us." He adds, still not entirely convinced despite our earlier conversation.

Ella and Joey are home when we get back and Sarah gallops proudly up to them. They put together a couple of makeshift jumps and pretty little Dakota shows us all what a well-rounded pony she is.

CHAPTER 70

"**H**ave you got everything? Who needs what ironing?" I wave the iron at the boys as they run around grabbing washed clothes and shoving them in rucksacks and overnight bags and trying to find matching socks and footwear that the dogs haven't chewed. Dad's sitting at the table, chilling with a coffee; years of drifting on a bike means he knows how to travel light. Ella and Tiff are sitting on the chesterfield looking very forlorn.

"Eh laa, 'av I gorra passport now?" Joey suddenly realises he's missing a vital element of his packing. Ella looks quite hopeful for a second.

"Yep, got it yesterday. Emm's got all of the passports."

"Have I? Oh crap, where have I put them?" Emm asks, looking round frantically.

"In that fancy leather folder thingy. There by the TV." I point. "Last chance for ironing." I yell. "Sal and Kim will be here in ten minutes." Several items are rescued from the ironing basket and thrown at me. I iron and fold them all and they disappear into various bags. "Have you got toothbrushes? I bought you a posh toiletry travel set the other day, Emm. I think it's in the back of the Charger." Dad gets up to go and find it for me and throws it to Emm.

He smiles and kisses me. "Thanks, darlin'. It's perfect. Where's my wedding ring? Can I wear it and pretend we're already married?"

"Doesn't that kind of make all of Sal and Sarah's hard work a bit of a waste?" I laugh. "The good time girlies might not be so forthcoming if you're wearing a shiny, new wedding ring."

"Only one girl I'm interested in." He groans, pulling me in for a more passionate kiss.

We hear the cars approaching and suddenly the cottage is full of bodies. Much hugging and kissing and good-natured tormenting takes place and eventually they're all ready to leave. Joey and Felix hug and kiss me and tell me they love me and I warn them to look out for pickpockets and not eat, drink or smoke anything Dad, Rick, Billy or Chaz haven't approved. I also whisper that they need to use condoms if they partake in any activities that may require one. They listen and promise to do as their told with mock solemn salutes and a chorus of "Yes, Mama Bear!" Once they've had their pep talk they take their girls outside for some last-minute loving.

Dad kisses my head. "Don't worry, Dilly Girl, I'll keep an eye on them all. You enjoy the peace and quiet."

"Rick picks me up and squashes me, whispering, "You better still be here when we get back, Shortarse." In my ear.

Emm looks torn as I hand him the passport folder.

"I really don't want to go without you, Delilah. I can't believe how hard it's going to be to leave you. I'm going to miss you so much, darlin'. Why don't you come with us?"

I wrap my arms around him and rest my head on his chest. "I think that goes against the rules of a stag do." I laugh. "The boys will keep your mind off me and you'll be back before you know. You'll have an amazing time and you have my absolute permission to do whatever you want without feeling guilty or having any regrets. Please enjoy yourself to the max because it's the only stag do you're ever going to have." I add. "Once we're married it'll be forever."

"Good, I want forever and the wedding can't come soon enough. I love you so much my beautiful girl. I'll call you...... lots."

I walk him to the car and Stef gets out to disentangle us. "Come on, bro, put her down now or we'll be late for takeoff." He urges gently. "She'll still be here when you get back. You will still be here won't you, Delilah?" He asks with a smirk.

"Don't even joke about that." Emm groans. "I'm going to Facetime her constantly just so that I can check the background."

They all jump in the cars and Emmett winds down the window, hanging out like a dog. "I love you, Delilah Blue!" He shouts at the top of his voice as they go off down the drive.

The girls look bereft at the loss of their men. I take their hands in mine and lead them inside. "Come on girlies, let's go and find a bottle of something alcoholic and some chocolate and drown our sorrows. Shall we take bets on which one calls or texts first?"

They both laugh and say "Emmett" in unison.

They're on their second bottle of wine and I'm on my third coffee when Sal and Kim return. I hand them both a glass and they get stuck in.

"Okay ladies, what's the plan?" Sal asks. "Are you staying sober, Dil? Someone's gotta get Sarah and fetch Murph and Spudz. I'm staying here. Your Dad, Bill and Rick said I can't let you out of my sight."

"Why?" I laugh. "Where do they think I'm going to go?"

"They're not taking any chances. We all know how well you cope under pressure. You'll be having it away on The Duchess the minute you realise you're going to be getting married in a couple of days."

"Emmett and Stef said I have to stay too." Kim admits with a shrug.

"Me too. Joey made me promise." Ella giggles.

"Lix told me to ring him immediately if you go out alone on 'The Duchess', The Duchess is your bike isn't it?"

"Yeah. Whatever happened to 'girl power' and 'sisterhood'?"

"Honey, you and Emmett are perfect for each other and now he's had a taste of real happiness he will hunt you down if you run so we're just saving us all from lots of worry and heartache." Kim smiles, patting my hand.

"Hm, thanks for having so much faith in me." I remark. "Sal and Sarah can have Dad's bed and Kim can have the little one then."

"No chance! If you're sleeping in your love shack one of us will be sleeping with you." Sal waves her wineglass at me.

"I'm sure everyone will hear The Duchess start up if I try to sneak off, which I am not going to do by the way."

"It'll be too late by then. If you've got her started we won't be catching you." Ella laughs.

Half an hour later, they're all squiffy and I'm buzzing from a caffeine overdose. We have the music on full blast and are learning how to wind, grind and twerk via the power of You Tube. We're in the middle of a very serious discussion about whether booty clapping and twerking are two separate things when Emmett calls.

"Hi baby, are booty clapping and twerking the same or different?"

"What? Bloody hell, darlin' don't make me think of you doing either I'm stuck on a plane right now." He groans. "You didn't tell me you could twerk."

"We're learning right now; how to wind, grind and twerk." I tell him suggestively. "Shall I send you a demo in my daisy dukes when we've perfected it?"

"Mmm yes please." He urges. "Has Kim told you she's going to stay and keep you company?"

"Yep and Ella and Sal and Sarah." I reply. "Honey, do you really think I'm going to run from the best thing that's ever happened to me?"

"Not taking any chances, humour me little imp, I want you to be safe. Gotta go, send that video soon. Love you."

"Love you too. Have fun."

We mess around for a little while longer and perfect the arts of twerking and slow grinding and then record a 'guess whose butt' twerking video for the boys and send it to them all simultaneously. Once we've finished laughing at all the responses we pull ourselves together and get the horses groomed and ridden, the donkeys and Dakota cleaned, fed and watered and I go to fetch more beer and wine, the dogs and Sarah. Kim insists on going with me.

Sarah's teacher looks a little disappointed that the sexy men have been replaced by two huge wolfhounds but Sarah is happy to see the hairy boys and her Auntie Kim.

"Auntie Kim! Uncle Emmett bought me my own pony. Have you come to see her? Has Uncle Stef gone on the shagfest with Daddy and Uncle Ricky and Nathan and everyone else?"

Kim looks a little alarmed and checks Miss. Jackson who has thankfully chosen not to ask. "They've gone to Uncle Emmett's bachelor party, honey. You, me, Ella and your mummy are going to stay with Auntie Dil."

"Yeah I know, it's so she doesn't do a runner before the wedding."

Kim does a strange giggle snort and shrugs at me.

"Let's get back then and you can introduce Auntie Kim to Dakota."

"Yay! See you tomorrow, Miss. Jackson."

The girls have made us dinner when we get back. While we're eating we all get sent a reciprocal 'guess whose butt' game. Unfortunately, the gents don't bother with the twerking or any underwear. Scarily, Sarah quickly and easily identifies her Dad, Rick, Nath, Jurgen, Dad and Joey. I get to about butt number twenty-five....

"How many guys have gone on this shin dig?" I ask.

"I think a few of their mates have flown over from the States. Stef invited everyone. He wanted to make it a memorable event." Kim tells me.

"Paddy and all the Macs were going, Dan and the rest of the band and even DJ Luke and Andrew and John according to our Nathan. In fact Ian might be the only man left on the whole Island." Sal laughs. "Damn, Dil, your man is almost as hot from the back as he is from the front." She adds, studying Emmett's rear view on her phone. The girls all hum in agreement.

"It's even better in the flesh." I reply, then laugh when they all hum in agreement to that too.

"Well I'm pretty sure I don't know all of these bottoms. Oh wait that's Gard and Keanu." Kim points to two very lovely specimens. We all look at the picture and then at Kim. "What? I see a lot of bottoms in my line of work." She shrugs.

I text Emm. 'Has someone just sent us a photo of Keanu Reeves' bottom?'

'Possibly… how the heck did you know it belonged to K?'

'I didn't. Kim told me'

'Hmm.. i'll let Stef know. What u up to?'

'Eating dinner, studying bottoms'

'Sounds like fun xx missing you, love you xx'

'Love you too sexy bum xxx'

We saddle up Dakota and have a long walk on the beach, clearing our heads of the images we've been subjected to and talking about anything and everything whilst throwing endless sticks for the hounds. Kim tells us loads more about her work without naming any clients. Ella updates us on all the places she's sold and leased to Jurgen's associates. Tiff chats about how long she's known Felix but doesn't mention Emm's Karma Sutra tale. Sal tells the others how her and Billy got together and tells me how well Max is doing and how completely hacked off she is that she will be knee deep in her final exams next week so won't make the wedding.

When we've finally worn out Sarah and the dogs we head back and put Dakota, the donkeys, the chickens and the horses to bed. We all get showered and into our pyjamas and settle down in front of the TV to binge watch Sons of Anarchy so that Sal, Ella and Tiff can swoon over Jax and Kim and I can drool over Opie until season five when he gets his head caved in.

As the evening progresses we all get more and more crazy texts and photos from the boys who are clearly embracing everything Amsterdam has to offer. It's amazing how much is going on considering it's only Monday night. We decide it's time for bed when we start to get videos of Dad, Jurgen, Rick and Bill, Chaz, Emm and several others we can't identify, on hired bicycles stark bollock naked, singing 'Raindrops Keep Falling On My Head' and reenacting several scenes from Butch Cassidy and the Sundance Kid.

I manage to convince the girls that I'll still be there in the morning and am eventually allowed to sleep alone in mine and Emm's bed. I snuggle down, planning to go straight to sleep but my mind has other ideas.

Oh no, Delilah, don't even think about it! You've made a dozen promises to everyone that matters in your life that you will not run. What is there to run from or more importantly to run to? Almost everything you've ever wanted is here. Is that true or have I just got a whole lot of stuff and responsibility I never asked for or expected?

The gorgeous, rich and talented man that claims to love me is currently partying with Keanu Reeves. WTF? I've conveniently ignored the fact that he's famous and the reality that he's probably going to be away for long periods of time in the very near future. Do I really love him or is it just lust? How can I fall in love so quickly? Easily, I knew I loved Joey the second time I saw him. That's a totally different love, Delilah. Or do I love the fact that he was such an unexpected surprise and persevered so patiently to break down my defenses? Where's Dutch when I need him? All I have to help is Odin who's missing Emm and busy sniffing his pillows and trying to get under the duvet in order to roll in his scent, and Murphy who's already having happy dreams making little purring noises and running in his sleep.

Come on you stupid woman list three things that you like about Emmett, no, not like, *love*. I love his body, his smile, his patience, his total acceptance of Joey, his love for Felix, his genuine generosity, his enjoyment of sharing, his willingness to listen, the way he makes me feel, the way he tries to understand my weird ideas, the way he loves his music and the way he plays guitar, the way he accepts my family and knows when I'm feeling vulnerable, the way he doesn't give up when I'm being difficult …. Ha, got you now Delilah! You can't argue that all of those are down to lust. You've proved you love pretty much everything about him. Time to go to sleep and look forward to your wedding.

I'm just dropping off when my phone rings. I look at the time and it's just after four in the morning. It's Joey, sounding completely sober. "You awake, Ma?"

"I am now."

"Good. I've just got Emmett back to the 'otel room. 'E's completely arseholed but won't go to bed 'til 'e talks to you." He explains with a chuckle. I hear him patiently trying to coax someone into lying down. "Tell 'im to go to sleep, please." He puts me on speaker phone to a very slurry and sleepy sounding Emmett.

"Hello baby, are you being difficult?"

"Delilah! Jeez I love your voice. Need my girl, Joe's gonna bring the plane now, get to the airport my sexy darlin' I've got something here you'll really like."

I hear a loud groan from Joey who tells him he doesn't want to see his junk.

"'Ow can ya get a 'ard on when ya can't even walk?"

I decide that's a rhetorical question and don't answer. "Have you had a good day, Emm?"

"Er….I think so…can't remember lots… I need you now though. I want to cover you in …."

I cut him off just in case it's not kisses he has in mind. "Have you got a big comfy bed there baby? Why don't you lie down and have a nap?"

"Yeah, I might. I'll lie here and wait for you. Left you a present in your knickers' drawer did you find it? Send me a video."

"No, honey, I haven't needed underwear today." I tell him.

"Ma, don't start 'im off again." Joey laughs.

"Sorry, sweetheart. Thank you for looking out for him. Is everyone else back safely?"

"Yep, reckon so. There's dozens of Americans 'ere. We've pretty much filled the 'otel. I got to share a room with Fe and soft lad 'ere. Fe was easy, just fell on a bed an' 'e's snorin' 'is 'ead off. Emm wouldn't settle til 'e 'eard you. 'E's driftin' off now."

"No, I'm not. I'm waiting for my sexy woman to arrive so that I can…"

"Emmett, the airport is closed for the night darling, shut your eyes and try to get some sleep now. I'll ring you in the morning."

"Don't go, Delilah, pleeease! I love you so much. I can't sleep without you next to me. Sing to me." He wails like his world is ending. I sing him a Bob Marley medley.

Joey finally whispers, "'E's asleep, well most of 'im is. I think Rick gave 'im Viagra cakes earlier." He adds.

"Night Joe. Love you. Don't forget to have some fun yourself."

"I'm 'avin' plenty o' fun watchin' this lot behave like twats." He laughs. "Night Ma, love ya."

I hug the phone to my heart and smile in the darkness. Delilah, you're going nowhere because everything you love, want and need is right here on this Rock. I cuddle up to Odin who is now sound asleep with his head on Emm's pillow.

I'm wide awake at six and indulge is some much-missed and very much needed yoga and meditation with no interruptions. It's absolute bliss and my body and my mind feel so much more balanced for it. Sarah's being fed by Kim when I get into the cottage. I grab a coffee and sit down at the table with them both.

"Did you sleep well?" Kim asks.

"Not really, I was over thinking for half the night and coaxing a very drunken Emmett to bed at four this morning." I laugh. "How about you?"

"I slept like a log until Stef called about the same time to say hello." She giggles. "They sounded like they were having a great time. I dropped back off and woke about half an hour ago."

"Auntie Kim made me eggy toast. Can I take Dakota to school?"

"Sorry, baby. I don't think Miss. Jackson will be very happy about that and she might get lonely whilst you're in lessons or scared by all of the other children. Go and see her now for twenty minutes then it'll be time to get off. Take her and the donkeys some carrots and give her a brush. Watch out for Giles. What do you want in your lunchbox?"

"Pasta and muffins and banana milkshake, please."

"Okay, baby." I hand her some carrots and Kim goes with her. I pack her lunch and her schoolbag and run to get dressed. I find Emm's present in my drawer; a little bullet vibrator with a note attached 'in case you miss me x'. Pervy, but thoughtful, nonetheless.

Sal has surfaced when I go to round up Sarah. "Go over to ours and pick up our outfits. We better try them all on just in case."

"You okay? You look tired. Didn't you sleep."

"Yeah, slept fine until Billy wanted phone sex at four o'clock this morning." She laughs.

I drop Sarah at school and head to Sal's. There's a huge mountain of costumes in the spare room all labelled with everyone's names. I pick up mine, Sal's, Ella's, Kim's and Tiff's and put them in the back of the Charger. Back at home the cottage is full of the girls eating breakfast and giggling at an ipad.

"The boys have made their presence known." Kim laughs. "Let's hope they're all too incapacitated to show Emmett."

'Amsterdam appears to be the chosen venue for the much anticipated bachelor party of rich, renowned, reclusive Era guitarist, Emmett Wright. The City has been taken over by the man himself and all of the other members of the band along with countless famous and infamous male friends and family members. All were in very playful moods and various stages of undress, partying from the early afternoon of yesterday until the wee small hours of this morning. Despite being slightly worse for wear Emmett offered us a very rare few words. When asked why they were celebrating he stated, "I'm getting married to Batgirl on the beach and I really, really love her." We think he may have indulged in a brownie or two!'

The photos are pretty tame considering what they had sent to us. There's a couple of lovely ones of Emm and Stef and the boys holding each other up and giggling. There's also some very famous dudes that I definitely recognise from several bands and films. All of them seem to be very well acquainted. I have to look twice at a lovely snap of Felix who appears to be waltzing up the street with someone who bears a strong resemblance to Alice Cooper.

"Oh Vincent got over, that's nice." Kim comments with a smile. "I wonder if they'll all get over for the wedding. There is a decent golf course nearby, isn't there? Can you book it for Saturday afternoon just in case?"

"What? Who plays golf? Emmett has honestly never mentioned golf."

Kim laughs. "I'm pretty sure that Emmett will be far too occupied the day after his wedding to play golf. Vincent, however, is obsessed and Mark and Justin are pretty keen too. Stef and Charlie like a game when they have time."

Sal gives me a questioning look and I return it with a palms up shrug. Kim sighs affectionately at both of us. "Vincent is Alice Cooper and Mark

Wahlberg and Justin Timberlake are both very clearly in Amsterdam with the boys at this moment."

"Oh, okay then." I accept with a shake of my head. "I'll check with Emmett later. This is all getting far too odd for me now. Who wants to go for a ride?"

"Wheels or legs?" Ella asks. "I wouldn't mind a run on the bike. I've not got to be in work until after lunch."

"I've definitely got an itch to get The Duchess out."

"Can I ride pillion?" Kim inquires. "I loved it last time."

Tiff looks at Sal and Ella. "You can hop in the back of me, honey." Sal offers. "I'm a lot more pillion friendly than the runaway bride here. Can I play on that Panigale?"

"Nope, no pillion seat." I point out. "Have to be Dad's Kwak or Fe's BM." We find kit to fit Tiff and Kim and Sal dig theirs out of the cars. "Tiff's a biking virgin so go easy."

We run over the mountain and down south on empty roads and Kim is so calm and still I forget she's there and just do my thing wherever the fancy takes me. We pull in at Port Erin for a break and tell Kim and Tiff a bit of Island history and check we haven't scared them too much.

Our phones all begin to go off in unison, the guys must have surfaced and couldn't get hold of us. Kim calls Stef and tells him where we are and that we're all fine. I text replies to Emm, Joe and Rick who are all demanding to know where I am. Tiff calls Felix, Ella calls Joey and Sal calls Billy. Emm calls me.

"How come everyone else gets a call and I only get a text?" He whines.

"Morning, sunshine! I thought you head might prefer a text." I reply.

"Hmm, I am feeling a little fragile." He laughs. "We're going to the tattoo museum and some galleries today, going to pace ourselves. What you up to little darlin'?"

"Giving The Duchess a run but don't worry I'm with my bodyguards. I've got Kim on the back and we've popped Tiff's cherry. She's on the back of Sal. Ella's here for a run then she's off to work."

"Rick rang his mates at the port earlier to check you hadn't got on the ferry when we couldn't get anyone on the phone."

"You lot don't have much faith in me do you? Why would I leave? Got everything I've ever wanted and a whole lot more besides. Thank you for my present by the way."

"Have you tried it? Where's my video confirmation?"

"Nope, you were giving Joe enough trouble at the crack of dawn this morning I didn't want to get you any more excited."

"Was I? Oh crap! What did I do?"

"Nothing major, just waved your erect penis at him and told him what you wanted to do to me." He groans and shouts sorry to Joey who laughs and shouts 'hello' to me. "Oh, Kim mentioned that some of your friends might want to play a round of golf if they're coming over for the wedding. Do they want something booked for Saturday and have they got somewhere to stay?"

"There's loads going to stay at Jurgen's place. Mark! Vince! Delilah says do you want a round of golf booked for Saturday?" I hear lots of yells of 'hi Delilah' and 'yes, please' and 'me, too'. "Book for ten please, darlin'. If there's more I'll let you know. I think Stef just invited everyone we know. There's quite a few of us here."

"I gathered that from the number of bottoms we were subjected to yesterday."

"You girls started that!" He argues playfully. "Gotta go, darlin'. Love you. Call me later."

"Will do. Have fun gorgeous. Love you."

We head down to The Sound to see the seals and have a cuppa. Tiff is in awe of the place and can't believe how much it reminds her of Ireland. Ella takes off to work and says she'll be home for tea and we carry on around to Port St. Mary and right into Castletown to mooch around the quaint little shops. I buy a rucksack full of old-fashioned sweets from the fabulous Memory Lane sweetshop to put out on Friday if they last that long.

Kim buys art supplies, pictures and ornaments and then remembers we're on the bike so we arrange to fetch them later. Once she's bought most of the shop we head home to sort dogs and horses before taking the car to fetch Sarah and Kim's purchases.

We get showered and into pjs after tea and Sal decides we need to try on our wedding outfits. Mine is so tight I'm convinced she's mixed it up with Sarah's. Sal throws some talcum powder at me.

"It's like a wet suit. It's meant to be tight." When I do get it on it is pretty amazing and very authentic. Sarah looks like a dream, so cute. Kim's sparkly blue and red Wonder Woman leotard and skirt leave very little to the imagination and I am sure Stef will approve. Ella is super sexy as Catwoman and even has claws to stick on. Sal has decided to be Elastigirl from the Incredibles and looks awesome in her red body suit and thigh length black boots. Tiff is given a choice of Harley Quinn, The Black Widow or The Bride from Kill Bill. She tries them all on and we unanimously vote for Harley Quinn, she looks brilliant and it includes a wig so we don't need to dye her hair. Kim will just have to draw on her tattoos on Friday morning. We send the boys another 'guess the bum' game then get everything put away safely ready for the big day. We get a lot of very appreciative texts, many from totally unknown numbers.

I get to bed at a reasonable hour and am about to have five minutes 'me' time with my present when a very merry Emmett and a club full of people choose to videocall me. "Hello, my beautiful darlin' what you doing?"

"I was going to get some sleep so that I'd be fresh for my 4 a.m. wakeup call."

"Who rang you that early?" He looks incensed on my behalf.

"Err, you did. Well Joe did because you wouldn't go to bed."

"Oh, jeez Delilah, I'm really sorry." He laughs. "I've been telling the guys how sassy and sexy and fabulous you are and they couldn't wait until we get home to meet you."

I wave to twenty odd guys I've never met but I have definitely seen before. "Hi, guys. Having fun?"

A wide-eyed Felix must hear my voice and looms at the screen. "That's my Mom, love you Mom." He's about to wander off. I totally forget Emm's mates are listening.

"Get back here, Felix!" I yell. "Who's given you shit again?"

"Chaz did. I was flaggin'. You're worse than a sniffer dog, love you!" He laughs and wanders off again.

"Don't blame me if your nose drops off you bloody shithead."

"Kim will fix it." He smartmouths back.

"Will she fix the kick in the ass you're going to get when you get home?" I reply. There is plenty of laughter and discussion about my 'sass' and parenting skills.

A Chaz sized man with an abundance of hair, beard and colourful tattoos appears, squinting into the screen with a deep rumbling chuckle. "Emm, man, she's a real sassy doll, I want one of those. Hey lil darlin' I hear you've been offered my job."

"Hey big man, I'm sorry about that, we're you going to be Emmett's wife?"

He roars again. "Not quite darlin', I'm Tiny, I'm the band's security manager."

"Tiny huh? That's original. Your job is safe Tiny, don't worry." I smile.

"You've made it a whole lot easier by getting shot of the crazy lady, thanks for that."

"Thank Chaz and Hans if you can find them. They sorted that out."

"Been talking with them both, cool guys." He replies.

Emm shoves him out of the way. "Stop chatting up my woman, Tiny. Dil, why don't you fly over? I miss you."

"Honey, I think you have plenty of people there to keep you company and you'll be home tomorrow. I was just going to try out my present."

His eyes are instantly full of lust. "Okay baby send me a review. Love you, sleep well."

"Enjoy yourself, stay safe, I'll see you tomorrow. Night darling. Love you."

I record a daft video of me giving Frank a back massage with my bullet and send it off to Emm then snuggle down and sleep like a baby. Delilah Blue, you may be the happiest lady on the planet right now!

CHAPTER 71

C hores all done, Sarah delivered to school and showered and dressed in my white skirt and my 'I am the real Mrs. Wright' t shirt with a rare splash of make-up, I am bouncing around waiting for the girls so that I can get my boys back. I've missed them all so much more than I'm willing to admit.

We all take a separate car as we have no idea how many are coming back and Ella takes Joey's bike for him. We turn up at the airport and Meave and her daughter in laws are there already waiting to claim their boys. We hug and all wait together eagerly by the gate.

Kim points out an extremely impressive plane. "That's ours." Then she points to another two. "That's Vincent's and I'm pretty sure that's Jurgen's." Everyone piles out of several different planes and I smile when I see that Chaz, Rick and Billy are flanking Emmett, Felix, Stef and Joe and looking around for any potential threats as soon as they hit the tarmac. Charlie, Connor and Nathan are behind them with a mountain of a man that I assume is Tiny. Dad is sauntering across with Jurgen and Hans and several others.

I take a run and a flying leap at Emm as soon as he comes through the gate and cling to him like a spider monkey. "I missed you baby." I cry covering him in kisses. He holds onto me tightly and gives me a serious demonstration of how much he's missed me too.

"Man, she's a fast little firecracker, ain't she?" Someone with an American accent drawls.

"Hey little sis." Chaz says patting my bum. "We kept him safe but go easy on him, he's a bit worse for wear. He should be fixed by Friday." I peel myself off Emm and turn to Chaz who takes me on his hip like a small child, pushes my dreads out of my face to look at me and hugs me.

"Hello, Chazman, where are my boys? Did you give Felix shit again?"

"Yep, what you gonna do about it, little one?" He laughs. "The boys are catching up with their girls." He turns to show me that they are safe and well then passes me on to Ricky like I'm part of the luggage. He kisses my head. "Hey Shortarse, how ya doin?"

I hug and kiss him. "All good, honey. I've really missed my boys. Have you shagged everything senseless?" Ricky nods an affirmation.

The mountain man holds out his arms. "Hand her over, Rick. I gotta get me some of this. Come here hot lil mama."

Rick hands me over with a laugh. "Shortarse, meet Tiny." I am completely enveloped in a huge pair of tattooed arms and smothered by a wall of hair and muscle. "Don't underestimate her Tiny, underneath that mass of dreads is a lethal little fucking demon."

"Nice to meet you, Tiny." I say through a mouthful of hair.

"Can I have my woman back now?" Emmett growls playfully. Tiny reluctantly puts me down but I am grabbed from behind in a big hug from Joey.

"Hey, Mama Bear, missed ya." I relax back into his chest and stroke his arms.

"Hello my beautiful, sensible Son. Thank you so much for looking after everyone. Have you had a good time? Where is your stupid big brother?" An unrepentant Felix sweeps me up and crushes me.

"Hey Mom." He grins putting on a really bad accent. "Did ya miss me?" I laugh and can't believe how happy I am to see them all after only two days.

Sal disentangles herself from Billy and he leans over to kiss me. "Still 'ere then, Dave?"

Dad, Jurgen and Hans come strolling through the gate with Alice Cooper and several other guys I don't get chance to see because I'm scooped up by Emmett.

"Oh no, I've shared you enough already. Where's the car? I'm locking you in our place until Friday." He does let me up to hug Dad. I wave hello to the others as I'm carried outside in a fireman's lift.

"Come to mine when you're done cavorting, Liebling, chef is making food." Jurgen yells.

"Who's coming home with us? Joey your lid is in the Cobra." I yell. He puts Ella down and goes to get his kit.

"See y'all at 'ome." He kisses the tank of his bike and Ella climbs on the back. Dad throws his rucksack in the car.

"I'm going straight to Jurgen's. See you in a while." A bus appears and everyone with Jurgen climbs aboard.

Kim, Stef and the boys hug us and say they'll see us later and go off in their hire car. Sal rounds up the Parkers and they go off to unpack then pick up Sarah. Felix and Tiff take the Cobra and me Emm and Tiny are in the Charger.

"Sit in the front, Tiny. I'll jump in the back. Are you fit to drive Emm?" I say.

"Give Tiny the keys, darlin' and get in the back now." Emm growls, pushing me in and getting in after me. "I need my hands on my woman."

"How can you spend two days in Amsterdam and come home horny?" I giggle. "Tiny doesn't know where he's going."

"See to your man, lil lady. I'm pretty resourceful." He rumbles, shaking his head at the fact that the driver's seat practically jammed up the windscreen and I have cushions to lift me up and stick up my back. "Seems like you're pretty resourceful too, honey." He drops the seat back, throws the cushions on the passenger seat and starts the engine.

Emm pulls me into his lap, buries his head in my neck and breathes me in. "God, Darlin', I have missed you so much. I'm never going away for that long without you again."

"Bloody hell, Emm you've only been away two days. How you going to cope when you go on tour?"

"You'll be coming, darlin'. Wedding vows say you have to obey me." He giggles losing his hands up the back of my t shirt. "Arms up."

"Er, no, I don't think so you bloody sex pest. We'll be home in two minutes."

"Don't mind me. Got my eyes on the road." Tiny laughs. "You gotta keep your man happy."

I groan, "Oh lord, I really needed another great big, hairy misogynist in my life."

"You're welcome, lil firecracker." He chuckles deeply. "I like you too. You got a lotta sass."

Emm is shaking with laughter. "I knew you two would get on. Turn up here bro, we're home." He points to the drive.

The Cobra is abandoned at the door to the workshop and Joey's jacket and helmet are on the floor by his bike. "Looks like the boys missed their ladies." I comment as I pick up Joe's stuff and close the driver's door on the Cobra. I open the cottage and the dogs all come bowling out and dive all over Emm.

"Fuck me is that a rabbit?" Tiny exclaims as Frank tries to climb up his leg.

"Yep, that's Frank, Flemish Giant and horse rustler. The big ginger idiot is Jeff, she's harmless and the watcher is Dutch. Do you already know Odin, Thor and Loki?"

"Yeah, but they didn't look this friendly last time I saw them." He marvels.

I put the coffee on and show him the little bedroom. "You might be a lot more comfortable at Jurgen's." I comment. "My bed and you don't look that compatible."

"I wanna be here with you guys, honey. This will do me fine. Slept in far worse places."

"Good." Emm says, "Bathroom is that way, help yourself to food and coffee or there's beer in the fridge." He picks me up and literally runs to our cabin. "Arms up!" He orders pulling at my t shirt and trying to undo his jeans and kick off his boots at the same time. He pushes up my skirt, pins down my wrists and starts kissing me from head to toe. "Darlin' I have missed your body like you would not believe."

We make up for our days apart with plenty of howling and growling and are lying in a post coital stupor when Stef texts to see what time we're going to Jurgen's. I drag myself to the shower and Emm joins me immediately resulting in more howling.

"Bike or car?" I ask waving a dress in one hand and jeans in the other.

He grins and points to the dress. "Car. Go commando, easier access."

"Perv." I sigh, pulling on my dress and boots.

Fe and Tiff are just coming up from feeding the horses. "Coming to Jurgen's?"

"Yeah, I'll go and kick Joe and Ella out of bed." Felix smirks.

"Just send the dogs up." I suggest.

Tiny has made himself at home with the TV on, feet up and a beer in his hand. Tiff kisses his head when she comes in. "Hey, Tiny, long time no see."

"Hey horse lady, how you doing?" They chat for a while and I pour coffee and drop down on the settee. Tiny reaches over a massive hand and pulls me under his arm. "Hey lil mama, you got a real wolf problem round here." He smirks. "Had to put the box on to drown the noise." He points to the TV.

"Yep, the Wright wolves of Blues Cottage." I giggle. "They're getting quite a reputation aren't they Tiff?" She blushes but doesn't comment.

"Tiny, put my woman down and get ya boots on we're going to Jurgen's." Emmett growls.

Joey wanders in fresh from the shower and looking totally chilled, followed by a smiley, blissed out Ella. I introduce her to Tiny.

"Another pocket sized one. They don't breed 'em big over here, do they? Come 'ere lil darlin' you'll fit nicely under this arm." Ella takes one look at him and moves to hide behind Joe. Joey laughs and Tiny shrugs. "More for you then." He wraps both arms around me and squashes me. "You're fearless."

"That's because she knows she could kick your ass if she wants to." Felix tells him. He looks me up and down and laughs. "I'm not kidding, I've seen her take Ricky down."

"You a fighter, lil firecracker?" He asks with a raised eyebrow. "I was sparring with Rick at the hotel. He's no lightweight."

"Bigger they are the harder they fall." I shrug. "Can we go now, I'm starvin'."

Joey and Felix take their bikes and we go in the car. Jurgen's place is lit up like Christmas and there is a huge spread of food out by the lake. Chef is as cheerful as ever and hugs me and tells me all the wonderful things he has planned for Friday. Emm and the boys disappear up to the studio and I catch up with Dad and have a lovely chat with Alice Cooper who is sweet and funny and a perfect gentleman. He's looking forward to his game of golf.

Tiny is getting on like a house on fire with Ricky, Billy and Chaz. "Come 'ere, Shortarse, Tiny thinks we're lying about you being a psycho, demon bitch."

"I am not a psycho, demon bitch. Apart from when you push my bloody buttons. I am grounded, balanced and perfectly sane most of the time." I laugh. "Stop telling fibs to my new big, hairy, misogynistic friend."

Chaz picks me up. "It was little sis here that took out Emmett's stalker."

"I had some help from Thor and you lot for back up."

"What martial arts you into, lil mama?"

"Jiu Jitsu, Kendo, Kenjutsu, Aikido mainly but I have done some Taijutsu, Iaido and a few more."

"I ain't getting involved with swords and big sticks but Jiu Jitsu, that I can get involved in."

"I wouldn't if I were you, Dave. She trained in Brazil with Rickson Gracie."

Tiny blows out a breath. "Impressive credentials, lil mama. You gonna back that up with some sparring."

"Nope."

"Why? You scared?"

"Nope. We can go for it tomorrow."

"What's the difference between now and tomorrow?"

"Are you familiar with Gracie Jiu Jitsu?"

"Yeah, lots of choking and strangle holds. I'll be happy to have your sexy little legs wrapped around my neck any time, firecracker."

"Let's do it tomorrow then...when I'm wearing underwear." They dissolve into hysterics.

"Man, I love this woman." Tiny announces. "What else ya good at? Besides bewitching the Boss."

"She rides her motorbike like the devil is chasing her." Jurgen offers.

"She rides our crazy horse barefoot and bareback." Tiff chimes in.

507

"She cooks the best muffins in the world." Ella says.

"She swims like a mermaid." Fe laughs.

"She sings like an angel." Stefan adds as the boys come back.

"And she's mine, so fuck off, Tiny." Emm adds, taking me out of Chaz's arms. "I can't leave you alone for two minutes, can I?" He adds, kissing my head.

"They started it." I laugh. "Tiny wants to fight me."

"Well that's not going to end well for him is it?"

"Nope. Want to go for a swim?"

"Darlin' I am fit to drop, chasing you for a hundred lengths is going to just about finish me off. Can we just eat, drink and talk bollocks for the next few hours and then go home to bed?"

"Whatever you want, baby. You'll need all your energy to get in your wedding outfit if it's as tight as mine is." I giggle. "Put me down and I'll go and find beer."

Acoustic guitars appear and get passed around with some very subdued, mellow singing and playing, I think the boys may all be feeling the effects of their trip. Emm gets handed a guitar and him and Stef jam for a little while.

I go in search of Kim to check if she needs any help with her unexpected visitors. "You want any beds making?"

"We're fine honey, really. Everything is done. Go enjoy the party."

"It's all feeling a bit surreal. I keep seeing people I know from TV and they're saying, 'Hi Delilah'. I have no idea what to say so I keep running away." I tell her with a groan.

"Emm and the boys didn't faze you. What's different?" She laughs.

"I have no idea." I shake my head. "Maybe it's because they were at our place?"

Tiny looms into the doorway. "Hey Doc, need a hand with anything?"

"I'm good thanks, Tiny." Kim smiles, patting his arm affectionately. "You'll get along fine with Tiny, Dil. Stay close to him, he'll look after you."

I roll my eyes. "Tiny wants to kick my ass." He grins in agreement.

"Oh lord, of course he does! He can't bear the idea that someone can beat him at anything." She swats him playfully. "You may have finally met your match, honey. I bet you never thought it would be a five foot woman."

"She is a lil firecracker but she ain't proved nothin' yet. We're gonna settle it tomorrow."

"Don't you get hurting her! Emmett will not be happy if his bride is damaged." She wags her finger at him and giggles.

Fe sticks his head in the door. "Hey Mom." He smirks. "Dad's having a meltdown because he can't see you. Come and sing with us."

"Definitely not! I am not up for making a complete twat of myself in front of all of your friends." I cry in horror.

"Don't make me have to carry you, Dil." Felix laughs, patting his shoulder.

"Oh god, don't you start with the caveman crap." I groan.

"Let me help you out there, Felix." Tiny offers, sweeping me off the ground and over his shoulder before I can blink.

"Just deliver her to Dad, please." Fe laughs. "He gets in a right state if she's not in his line of sight."

I am unceremoniously dumped in Emmett's lap from a great height. "Hello darlin' are you playing nicely with Tiny?" He kisses me like we've been apart for a month. "Sing with us, baby."

"Oh, Emm no, I don't want to show you up in front of your mates. You play, I'll stay here and listen."

"Thought you were fearless, firecracker? You ain't nothin' but a little girl." Tiny roars with laughter.

"I'll sing if you do." I offer.

"I don't sing." He glowers at me.

"Thought you were fearless, big man?" I counter.

"Tiny appears to have a death wish." Ricky deadpans.

"Do not get into a pissing contest with Delilah, you will lose." Chaz adds some words of advice. "Us three learned that a long time ago. Rick only goes back for more because he's a masochist."

"That's my girl." Dad lifts his bottle to me in salute. "Sing, Dilly girl and Tiny can let us know if he thinks he can beat you."

Felix begins playing Californication and I'm already singing before I realise. Stef and Emm join in and so does everyone else and we mess around morphing into different songs for an hour or so and then Stef says, "Can you remember the words to our new one?" He passes me the ipad just in case. The boys start to play and everyone goes quiet. I look at Emm and concentrate on not making a fool of myself. I get through it and we get a round of applause and plenty of compliments.

"Tiny's turn." Rick shrugs.

Jurgen chimes in. "Sing what you sang in the studio the other day, Liebling. If Tiny can hit the same notes, he wins." Stef nods in amused agreement. "Your Mama's song."

I laugh. "That's really unfair. He can't do that." Tiny growls. I don't think can't is in his vocabulary.

"Let's hear it lil girl. I'll tell you if I can't do it."

"Game on, Tiny!" I laugh, taking a swig of my beer.

Emm is chuckling his head off as he begins to play. 'Lovin' you is easy 'cause you're beautiful..' I deliberately turn to Tiny when I sing the super high notes. I finish and give him a little curtsy. "Your turn."

Everyone starts laughing and teasing him. He shakes his head and smiles.

"I'll give you that one, firecracker but I get to choose the next challenge." I go to shake his hand in agreement and he pulls me into a big bearhug.

"Tiny, get your hands off my woman." Emmett groans. "We really need to find you one of your own."

"I'll get Sarah on it." Sal says. "How about Miss. Jackson?" We all burst into song and then Charlie claims that he has first dibs on Miss. Jackson so Tiny will have to wait.

"I'm just gonna share yours Boss, she's a whole lotta woman for one guy." He jokes.

"Already got enough meat headed perverts, thank you." I remind him, tipping my chin toward The Parkers who raise their bottles and nod happily in agreement. I climb into Emm's lap and kiss him so that there's no doubt where I want to be.

"Is it bedtime, baby? There's a couple of things I'd like to practice for Friday night." I whisper in his ear.

He shakes his head in wonder. "You're gonna be the death of me, little imp. Where are the kids?"

"Skateboarding last time I saw them. They've both got their bikes. Dad are you coming back with us?"

"I'll stay on here, Dilly Girl. Let the big man have my bed." I kiss him and everyone else goodnight, say thanks to Jurgen for having us and after telling the boys and their girlies we're off, we head for the car.

Emmett climbs in the back again and lifts me onto his lap, facing him. He slides up my dress and drives me crazy all the way home.

"Help yourself to the big bed and anything else you need. You want coffee or hot chocolate, Emm?" I say as we get back and I've gained control of my senses.

"No. Bed." Emm barks. "Now."

"Night Tiny."

"Night firecracker, night Boss."

CHAPTER 72

I leave Emmett to sleep off the excesses of his stag do and head for my rock. I stretch and get into quite an intense yoga session trying to re-align my body. The dogs all come thundering down the beach with Tiny who looks like he's going for a run. "Mornin' firecracker. Fancy a run?"

"I was going to swim. Give me two minutes to put some clothes on and I'll run with you."

"Nah, I'll take mine off and swim with you. Bet I can beat you to that buoy and back." He challenges pointing out to sea, pulling off his trainers and t shirt. "Ready, steady...oh my fucking Jesus its cold!" I'm already in and setting my pace. He's a good swimmer for a big guy but clearly not used to the choppy and frigid Irish Sea so I have a huge advantage. He keeps with me to the buoy and then takes off for the shore. I shake my head and maintain my steady pace until I'm nearly back and then sprint past him onto the beach. The dogs are waiting patiently with towels draped over them. I throw one to Tiny.

"Two nil, big man. Want a run now or some breakfast?"

He's wrapped in the towel in a shivering, panting heap.

"You got me again lil mama. I need some of your great coffee."

"Thanks for the towels." I kiss Joey as I go to pour coffees. "Want a full English or a sandwich?"

"The works. Ain't 'ad a decent breakfast in days." He grins. "You want the same Tiny?" He asks digging in the fridge.

"Yeah, whatever it is." Tiny replies. As soon as I start cooking everyone appears as usual.

Felix has a massive scrape down his arm. "What the heck have you done? Shit, is that gravel rash? Is your bike alright? Did you have Tiff on the back?"

"Calm down, Ma, 'e fell off 'is skateboard cos 'e's a divv." Joe informs me.

"It's good to know you're concerned about Tiff and my bike though." Fe laughs, kissing my head. "Drunk in charge of a skateboard never ends well."

"I hope you left your bike at Jurgen's."

"Joe bought me back, Ella rode mine. Stop stressing."

"God, I love you two." I smile. "Eat your breakfasts and bugger off."

I hand a still sleepy Emmett a huge plate of breakfast.

"Thank you darlin'. I haven't given my body so much prolonged abuse for a very long time. I need to stop now."

 I raise an eyebrow. "Is all night sex included in that ban?"

He gives me a big cheeky grin. "No darlin' I'm giving up everything else so that I can keep delivering on the all night sex."

"Eww, too much information." Felix protests.

I empty another pan full of bacon and sausage onto Tiny's plate. Emm shakes his head. "Is she corrupting you too? What happened to your 'my body is a temple' mantra?"

"Soft lad 'ere worked up an appetite perving at Ma while she was doin' 'er 'ippy shite, then the daft twat agreed to swim with 'er." I can hear a hint of 'Parker' warning in his voice.

"I was admiring her flexibility and you could have warned me about the swimmin'." Tiny waves his fork at him with a smirk.

"She got us swimming the minute we got here, I was hooked from then on." Emm smiles and puts his arm around my waist, pulling me into his lap. "She's an amazing woman. *My* amazing woman and if I catch you perving at her I'll let Joey and the Parkers at you." Joe high fives him in agreement.

"What kinda man would I be if I didn't take the time to admire a tiny naked lady, with a perfect body, who can tie herself in knots."

"The kinda man that still has a job?" I sass from the safety of Emmett's lap. They all howl with laughter, including Tiny, thank goodness.

"Jeez Boss, this one is heaven sent. I want one, is there any more where she came from?"

"Only one." Emmett replies. "You'll have quite a wait though she's only four years old. You'll have to answer to The Parkers too, she's Billy's daughter."

"Not gonna be able to wait that long Boss. I'll just keep puttin' your lil firecracker through her paces."

"How many challenges are willing to lose before you give me peace?" I enquire. "I'm pretty sure there's a couple of things Sarah could already beat you at."

"Quit now Tiny, save yourself the embarrassment." Fe advises. "Once she takes you on the back of her bike you realise very quickly that she is 'next level'."

"Not happening! Not ever! Don't say another word Felix Wright unless you want a frying pan upside your head." I shriek and bury my burning face in Emm's chest. Thankfully Emm shuts that down.

"Not happening, Son. Don't even go there." He warns. Fe shrugs and smirks.

"Sounds like Felix knows a weakness, lil mama. I've heard you can ride anything, I'm a Texan so I was born on a horse but I can ride a bike too, shame I don't have my iron steed here."

"We got more than enough to go 'round, bikes an' 'orses." Joey replies, helping to change the focus of the conversation. "Ya losin' though whatever ya got in mind."

Tiff comes in from the paddock. "Are you coming out with the psycho, Dil? He is not conforming at all today. He's took a chunk out of my boot and tried to shove me off my feet half a dozen times while I've brushed and saddled up Luna." She shows us her holey riding boot.

I look at Tiny. "Can you ride bareback, big man?" He snorts in disgust that I would even need to ask. "Tiny will come with you, Tiff."

"I gorra see this." Joey announces, jumping up to wash his plate.

"Give me two minutes to get dressed, you know I'll end up having to ride him." I dig my shorts and a t shirt out of the ironing basket.

"Is that one yours?" Tiny teases when he sees Dakota throwing herself joyfully around the donkey paddock."

"No, that one is hers." Felix laughs pointing to Angel who is on a crazy rampage around his paddock, fighting with Midnight, kicking the fences, snorting and rolling his eyes like a maniac. Luna and Seraph are tethered outside the paddock.

"I fetched them out in case he damaged either of them; Midnight can hold his own." Tiff explains.

"He's all yours, Tiny. Let's see how long it takes you to get a bridle on him. Saddle up Midnight too, I'll take him out." Emm says.

To his credit Tiny climbs straight in and heads to the tack room to get the saddles and bridles and a few crafty carrots for bribery. He turns to come out but an eagle eyed and inquisitive Angel is already in the doorway eyeing him up suspiciously. He really is a natural, he whispers, croons and coaxes and soon talks Midnight into his tack while Angel watches on quietly, lulling Tiny into a completely false sense of security and as soon as he reaches up to put the bridle on, drops his head and butts him very firmly in the chest knocking him on his ass. He then does a flying victory lap around the field. Taking Tiny off his feet a second time and then stamping a challenge at him with his ears turned back and the whites of his eyes showing.

"Enough, come out Tiny before you get hurt." I plead. Tiny climbs over the fence laughing his head off. "He's all yours, firecracker."

I jump in and grab the bridle. "Come here shithead and stop showing off." Angel saunters up to me and snorts into my neck. I put his bridle on and climb up the fence to get onto his back. He drops and bucks and rockets around the paddock like something demented as I hang on and giggle. "Do you want to go a proper run or are we going to just piss about in this field all morning?" I whisper to him. He stands to attention, then does his weird dressage marching thing towards the gate. Tiff opens it to let us out. Angel weighs up everyone then give Joey a big soppy kiss and mugs Emm for polo mints. Tiff mounts Luna.

"Do you want to bring Seraph? He's a pussy cat." She offers to a wide eyed, open mouthed Tiny.

Once he's on the beach Angel takes a flying leap into the sea then screams off like his bum's on fire, along the shoreline at full speed until he runs out of steam. Emm and Midnight keep up with us and Tiny and Tiff aren't hanging around either. We slow and turn back.

"Is that three nil now, big man?" I sass as Angel tries to bite Tiny's knee as we come alongside him and Seraph.

"Yeah, lil mama. I think it is." He rumbles his deep chuckle. "That crazy dude needs gelding." Angel does a whole body shiver as if he understood.

Emm slaps Tiny on the back. "Are you admitting defeat yet?"

"No way Boss, we've only just got started. Nobody's given me game like this in a long while. This is gonna run an' run."

"Oh, deep joy." I groan. "It's like having my very own Cato." I add, thinking of the Pink Panther films.

I groom Angel when we get back and the boys disappear off to Jurgen's for an hour or so. Sal arrives with a car full of stuff and we spend the rest of the day getting ready for tomorrow. Joey and I put together a beautiful, ornate, white metal gazebo and Sal and Tiff cover it in ribbons, flowers and fairy lights. We take the dogs to collect driftwood for the pit and fill the fridge with a mountain of food.

When the boys ring to say they're on the way back we divert them to buy lots of alcohol and collect Sarah. Poor Miss. Jackson truly is going to blow a gasket when Emm, Felix, Tiny and whoever else they have in tow, turn up.

The pole dancing poles arrive and the guys spend some time scratching their heads about how they are going to secure them on the beach. They eventually declare them safe and leave. Dan phones to find out what time we need them and says he'll call Luke too.

Sarah arrives, riding on Tiny's shoulders; dishing out orders to him she helps her mom and Tiff reach the higher bits with the lights and flowers.

"Did Miss. Jackson wee her pants when she saw you all?" I ask as Emmett comes to hug me.

"Pretty much but Sarah was even funnier, Tiny spent ten minutes telling us he scares kids and he should wait in the car but then couldn't resist a look at her teacher. The princess looked him up and down, rolled her eyes and said, 'Has Auntie Dilly found another stray man?' I think between the two of you he's way out of his depth."

I point to the makeshift altar, surrounded by hay bale seating, courtesy of Mr. Jeavons. "Are you getting scared yet? This is all getting very real. By this time tomorrow there'll be no escape."

"Can't come soon enough, Delilah. You already own my heart, body, mind and soul. I want it to be official."

Sarah rides over on Tiny. "Can I take Dakota for a ride, please, Auntie Dilly?"

"Of course you can sweetheart. Are you taking Tiny too?"

"Yep, don't worry, I promise I'll look after him for you." She replies seriously, patting his head.

"Good girl, thank you for that." I smile and watch them head for the field, then return a few minutes later with a saddled up Dakota who tries her best to eat the gazebo flowers before being led off up the beach.

"We've got a shop full of booze in the cars, where do you want it?" Felix asks.

"I don't think there's any room left in the fridge. Put it round by the back door, please." I reply.

"Will do, give us a hand Joe." They take off amiably around the front.

"Have you seen the poles?" I point them out to Emm. "Want a demo?"

"God, yes." He grins. I wrap myself around one and slowly try to recreate the moves I learned at Jurgen's shagfest. Emm plonks himself down on a blanket and watches the show.

"Oi, slapper!" Sal yells. "That's not getting stuff sorted for tomorrow."

"I'm safety testing." I laugh.

"Well, by the look on his face, you're sure as hell not safe from him." She replies, pointing her screwdriver at Emmett.

Ella arrives from work. "Hi everyone, oh fab is that stripper poles? I always wanted to try that. I was too chicken at Jurgen's. Can I have a go?" She watches me for a minute then replicates my moves. "Wow, that's one hell of a core body workout." She laughs, grabbing her sides. "Where's Joey, he needs to have a go at this."

"A go at what? Strippin'? Nah, don't think so."

"Not stripping, pole dancing, it's an art and really good exercise." The boys spend the next half hour falling off the poles and giggling their heads off.

"Right, show me 'ow to do it prop'ly, Ma." Joey requests when he starts getting frustrated. I show him my full routine and he follows it closely and perfectly. "Fuck that ain't as easy as it looks."

Sarah and Tiny return and once they've put Dakota back and settled her and the donkeys she also starts to play on the pole.

"Another challenge for you right here, Tiny." Felix says. "How's your pole dancing skills? Dil rides a mean pole." I slap him round the head.

Tiny shakes his head. "I'm not even gonna go there. Not even gonna say I'd really like to see a demo."

Sal, Ella and I make food for everyone while Tiff and the boys see to the chucks and horses. Dad, Billy and Ricky arrive to see if anything needs manhandling ready for tomorrow. They decide they need to move the gazebo to face in a different direction and ten foot closer to the sea just for the heck of it.

We pile up plates with supper and sit outside with beers, talking bollocks and watching the sun go down. The inevitable pole dancing challenge ensues with Joey and I being crowned victors and Tiny being shown how to do it properly by a very patient Sarah. The impromptu striptease that accompanies Bill and Rick's dance off is something that can never be un-seen, thankfully Sarah is already fast asleep in the arms of her new best friend.

We retire to bed far later than I originally intended. "Are we abstaining on our pre wedding night?" I ask with a giggle.

"You've spent all afternoon and most of the night draped around a strip-per pole, darlin', what do you think?" Emm growls and jumps on me.

CHAPTER 73

D awn is just breaking and I'm sitting on my rock. Okay Delilah, this is it, today is the day that you finally stop running and officially give yourself to Emmett, everything that you are, for better or worse; better I'm sure, in every way. You certainly appear to be richer and not poorer in every sense of the word; love, family, friends, experiences, peace of mind, property and wealth. I pray for much health and very little sickness but I know I will be by Emm's side whatever comes our way. I'm sure Madame Karma has all kinds of interesting shite in store for us in the future. Bring it on, bitch, we're ready for you.

Dutch jumps up next to me and rubs his face against my cheek. "Hey, babe, is it all going to be worth the wait? Is this really what I want?" I ask him quietly. He smacks me between the eyes with his paw and bites my nose then glares at me. "That's a 'yes' then is it? I laugh and he har-rumphs and snuggles back up to my cheek.

"Ya ready to be Mrs. Wright?" Joey asks, dropping down onto the rock and putting an arm around my shoulder. I lean into his chest and he wraps me and Dutch in a warm, comforting embrace. "Told ya second chances are better, didn't I?" He says with his chin on top of my head.

"You did, Joey." I agree. "Thank you for giving me the gentle pushes I've needed. I wouldn't have ever had the confidence to try if it wasn't for your belief in me. You have no idea how much I appreciate you coming into my life, Son."

"Don't get soppy, Ma. Sal'll 'ave to plaster ya in warpaint to 'ide the blotches." He says, wiping his own eyes with the back of his hand.

"I'll be fine, I'm wearing a mask." I remind him through my tears. "What-ever happens next and wherever life takes us this will be home for you and me forever and I will always, always be here for you. I'm the proud-est, most blessed Mama that's ever lived." I sniffle.

"Ya gettin' married not dyin'. Stop talkin' shite an come an' make break-fast." He orders, hugging me tightly and wiping his own tears again. He gets up and holds his hands out to pull me up.

Dad waltzes me around the cottage singing, 'Brown Eyed Girl.' "I can't believe my beautiful daughter is finally getting married. Your Mama will be so happy for you. You're going to be the best wife any man could wish for. What do you want for breakfast?"

"Coffee." I laugh. "Lots of it." Joey hands me a drink in my Mrs. Always Right mug. "Thanks sweetheart. Do you want a full breakfast or a sand-wich?"

"I'll just 'ave toast. Me suit's tight enough already."

"Yeah, mine too." I admit. "I need talcum powder to get it on."

"Better lend Emmett my swiss army knife for later." Dad chuckles. "Where is he? Has he done a runner?"

"He was fast asleep when I left him. He doesn't seem to have any wedding day nerves at all."

"Do you?"

"Nope, talked them all out with my beautiful Son and Dutch." I smile. Joey kisses my head and takes a mug of coffee up to his room for Ella.

Tiny comes out of the little bedroom holding his sides. "Damn man, that pole dancing really does work your core muscles." He chuckles. "Mornin' Dylan, mornin' firecracker, you ready to get hitched?"

"Yep. Ready and waiting." I can feel myself starting to get fidgety.

"Where's ya man? Did you wear him out again?"

"Yep, he's still asleep."

"Wanna let loose on that bike of yours before ya get into all the girly stuff?"

"Great idea, Tiny can take the Panigale." Dad suggests. "I bet Joey'll want to come too."

"Where we goin'?" He asks coming back in.

"A quick blast on the bikes if you're up for it."

"Always." He throws me my leathers and climbs into his own. "Better tell Emm, 'e'll 'ave a breakdown if 'e 'ears The Duchess take off." I creep in and leave him a note on my pillow; 'Gone for a run with Dad, Joe and Tiny. See you at the altar my darling man, love you xx Your Bride xxx'

"Lead the way, lil firecracker." Tiny says. "I gotta get used to this strange European machinery." Needing no further encouragement and once I've paid my dues to the fairy folk I empty my head and ride. I get onto the circuit and do a full lap with Joey following my lines and Dad hanging back a bit for Tiny. We stop at Ramsey square and Tiny gives us his thoughts on Manx roads and Italian bikes.

"Motherfucker! Your roads are thinner than sidewalks with more bends than I've ever seen and this bike is so light and twitchy it's fucking unreal. How can you ride so fast?"

Joey laughs. "She's ridin' slow so's I can keep up an' see 'er lines and poor Gramps ain't got out a third gear. Swap bikes with Dylan and they can 'ave a run an' I'll ride with ya." Tiny willingly obliges. I kiss my thoughtful boy, grin at my lovely Daddy and put my helmet back on.

"Ride safe." I say as I give the Duchess a wrist full and take off towards the hairpin. I actually slow down to shout 'I love you' to Marley and to Jimbob and then accelerate into a mind-blowing run over the mountain with Dad on my back wheel. We stop down at Hillberry and wait for Joe and Tiny.

"This is a nice bit of kit, Dilly Girl." Dad grins. "Feels like the Duchess's posh cousin; more refined and better behaved."

"That's exactly what I thought. When I rode her. She is responsive and still feels exciting but less like she might want to hurt you at any minute." I laugh, patting The Duchess fondly on her tank.

Tiny is apparently impressed with our turn of speed and uses a lot of swear words to express his thoughts. I check my phone, there's a text from Emm 'Ride safe my beautiful bride xx' and one from Sal 'Hairdresser half nine don't be late bitch xx'.

"Got to be at the hairdressers in ten minutes gents so I better get a move on. Ride safe. Love you." They follow me and wave when I turn off.

Alex and Lisa are gowned up, ready and waiting. Sarah and Sal arrive seconds later and Sal has a fit because I'm on The Duchess. "What's the point of getting your hair done then putting a bloody helmet on?" She yells.

"Chill ya beans, honey. I was out for a ride. I'll call Dad when he's had time to get home. He can bring the car and fetch The Duchess."

"Sorry babe, I think I'm more nervous than you." She apologises, giving me a hug. She produces our Batgirl masks out of her bag so that we don't end up with lumpy looking heads. Alex washes and touches up my hair whilst Lisa does a brilliant job of plaiting Sarah's into hundreds of tiny plaits and then spraying on wash out colours that exactly match mine. I call Dad and he and Tiny appear less than half an hour later.

Dad takes The Duchess home for me and Tiny insists he's staying to drive us back. "Boss's orders lil mama, no argument."

"Great, I'm off to sort everything else." Sal says. "See you later." Tiny happily entertains Sarah while they finish her hair and Lisa sorts my wayward eyebrows. Then he growls when I try to get out my purse and pays the bill for us.

"I was going to use Emm's card anyway." I tell him.

"Don't matter, it's my job to take care of you. Come on pretty ladies let's get you to your wedding." He picks up Sarah and puts her on his shoulders.

"Hang on a minute, since when was it your job to take care of me? I thought you were security for Era?"

"I organise security for the band and Emmett and Stefan's families. That includes you and the Doc and this little princess here and Connor's man and Felix's horse lady and your Joey although I have a feelin' he can look after himself." He grins. "I'm sure you can too but we gotta do what the Boss says, right?"

"Apparently we do." I laugh." Lord help me when it's officially in the vows this afternoon he'll be threatening to sue me if I disobey him."

"Only 'cause he loves ya and wants to keep you safe, lil firecracker. I'd have twenty more security guys here if he'd allow me to but he's so chilled over here he says The Parkers and the dogs are enough." He says, buckling Sarah into the car seat. "You'll have to get used to having me around 'cause I ain't goin' away."

Sarah kisses his cheek. "That's good. We like having you around. Don't we Auntie Dilly?"

"Yeah, Sweetie, we do." I agree. He gets in the driver's seat, pats my knee and grins.

Sal is dishing out orders and running around on the beach. Dan's band and Luke are busy setting up and shout and wave. Sarah runs off to show everyone her hair and I go in search of coffee.

"Where's my groom?" I ask Dad.

"Stef took him and Felix to Jurgen's to get ready. This is Morvan who's going to perform your handfasting." Oh wow! Sal wasn't joking when she said she'd booked a sexy druid. I shake hands with a huge, sculped, long haired, full-bearded man with the most powerful green eyes. He's naked from the waist up but wearing a long hooded cloak that matches his eyes. When he speaks it's with a lilting southern Irish accent.

"Hi there, Delilah, it's good to finally meet you, all of your friends and family have told me so much about you." He holds my hand and locks eyes with me. "I can feel that you have a truly beautiful soul."

"Er, thank you." I'm not sure how else to reply.

"Have you chosen which ceremony you would like me to perform?"

"Nope, she's decided she wants to be Batgirl and left everyone else to sort the important stuff." Sal laughs as she comes in. "We have chosen a hand-fasting with full family participation."

"Beautiful, have you written your vows?"

I look at Sal in alarm. "She'll be fine, she's full of shite, she'll say the right stuff at the right time." Sal shrugs.

"In the moment, beautiful. I am already getting so much good energy from this place." Alrighty then I need to be somewhere else now. Tiny saves me from the scarily intense druid.

"Hey lil mama, come and have a word with Angel he's giving horse lady hell." He looks Morvan up and down suspiciously then looks to me for an explanation. "Why is He-Man in our living room, firecracker?"

"This is Morvan, he's going to be performing our handfasting ceremony." I tell him, trying not to giggle.

"Does the Boss know?" He asks, raising an eyebrow.

"He's knows he's getting married; he doesn't know how." I laugh. "Come on big man, what's up with Angel?" I push him out of the cottage.

"Make yourself at home, Morvan." I add as I chase Tiny out.

Angel clearly senses something is going on that he is missing out on and is throwing himself dangerously around the paddock like a toddler having a tantrum. Poor Tiff is in tears. "I can't do a bloody thing with him. Can't even get near him. Should I phone the vet to sedate him?"

"Don't worry, sweetheart. Go and get yourself a cuppa and get ready. I'll sort him. Kim should be here in a bit to do your tattoos."

"Get here, shithead!" I yell at Angel. His ears shoot up and he gives us a wary look as if he thinks he's about to get told off and sent to bed. He approaches me and butts me playfully in the chest. "Are you playing Tiff up, you daft bugger?" He hops from foot to foot and dances around.

"Have I got time to zip him down the beach?" I ask Tiny.

"Do whatever makes ya happy, firecracker. They can't start anythin' without the bride." He grabs the bridle and passes it to me. Angel sucks my dreads as I put it on and seems to understand he's got to behave. We trot up to the beach and weave carefully through everything that is being set up and, when we're clear, shoot up the shoreline at full pelt.

"You better be coming back, bitch!" I hear Sal yell.

Amazingly, my mind doesn't throw up any panic or doubt or stupid suggestions about keeping on running. I pull up Angel when I sense him beginning to slow. "Home, gorgeous I've got a date at the altar with your wonderful Dad."

We get back to find the beach packed. Morvan is staring at me with his hand on his heart. Joey takes Angel's reins and Tiny lifts me down. "You better go an' get ready, lil mama. Joe'll put the crazy dude away." I kiss Joey, tell Angel to behave, and run into our cabin to transform into Batgirl.

"Fucking hell, Dil! Talk about last minute." Sal screeches at me from the bedroom while I'm in the shower. "Do you want knickers or not?"

"Nope. Just talc." I holler back. I dry off and wriggle into my fabulous costume. Sarah comes charging in looking so cute in her own Batgirl outfit and long sparkly purple DMs.

"Uncle Emmett bought us new boots." She announces, handing me a box containing a matching pair. Sarah laces them up for me as Sal puts make up on me and faffs around with my hair and mask. Then bursts into tears and has to take off her Elastigirl mask.

"Oh my god Dil, you look amazing! This is just so you. I can't believe you've finally found your man. It's been a long time coming, honey. Go show 'em the sexiest bride ever." I hug her and thank her for all of her hard work organising the engagement and the wedding and tell her what a brilliant friend she is while she sorts her mask out.

Kim, Ella and Tiff, looking a dream in their outfits, knock the door to fetch us. We admire each other and giggle at the perfect absurdity of it all. Dad, in a full on Superman costume, strides over with his red cape flowing behind him.

"You look stunning Dilly Girl. Are you ready?" We start walking around to the gazebo and Sarah and I are both bouncing with excitement. The girls are right behind us. I catch sight of my sexy man, instantly forget everything Sal told me and just run and jump into his open arms, wrapping my legs around his waist.

"Hello, Batman, you look seriously good in tights, wanna go consumate our marriage?" I purr, kissing him deeply. An older lady in a tweed suit, who is obviously the registrar looks somewhat alarmed by my behaviour but everyone else just howls with laughter.

"Climb down, Delilah, honey. We've gotta get through the services yet." Stef smiles. Emm puts me down but doesn't let me out of his arms, placing me in front of him and kissing the top of my head.

"Stay right there, darlin'." He whispers in my ear. "These tights leave nothing to the imagination." He presses his body against me to help me understand his predicament. Stef and Dad hear him and the giggling starts again. We finally all pull ourselves together and the registrar steps up and begins the ceremony.

"Welcome dearest family and friends of Emmett and Delilah. We have come together today to witness their exchange of vows..." I look around and see that I am surrounded by superheroes; Stef is dressed as Robin, Fe, Charlie, Joey and Connor are standing in a line beside us with their arms folded, visors down and legs apart; Power ranger style, Rick is Deadpool, of course, Billy is Mr. Incredible and Chaz is Thor, complete with hammer. Nathan is keeping with the family theme as Dash. Tiny has tamed his beard and hair into a Wolverine look to match his costume, Jurgen is Antman, Hans is Spiderman and countless others are sitting on the hay bales.

"Delilah?" The registrar brings me back to proceedings.

"What? Oh yes definitely." I say. More laughter and she smiles at me patiently. "Can you repeat after me ..."

"I, Delilah Tallulah Tinkerbell Rainbow Blue, take you Emmett Joseph Woodrow Wright, Joseph? Really? to be my lawfully wedded husband, to have and to hold from this day forward, for better, for worse, for richer, for poorer, in sickness and in health, to love, honour and cherish completely and obey, to some extent, till death us do part. And thereto I pledge myself to you."

"Imp!" Emmett laughs, hugging me. "I, Emmett Joseph Woodrow Wright, take you, Delilah Tallulah Tinkerbell Rainbow Blue to be my lawfully wedded wife, to have and to hold from this day forward, for better, for worse, for richer, for poorer, in sickness and in health, to love, honour and worship, till death us do part. And thereto I pledge myself to you." The registrar doesn't look overly concerned this time when we stop for yet another deep, passionate kiss.

"Not yet, guys. Rings next." Stef shakes his head in mock exasperation. "Oh crap, where did I put them?" Kim steps up, fishes them out of her bra and hands them to him. "Thanks, honey."

We say some more words and exchange our rings.

"Emmett, I give you this ring as a sign of our marriage. With my whole body I honour you, all that I am I give to you, and all that I have I share with you, baby." We get lots of pervy cat calls at my 'whole body' offer. Emm gives me my beautiful little white gold Celtic band that fits perfectly on top of my engagement ring and the registrar pronounces us man and wife. She doesn't have to remind us to kiss.

"Ladies and Gentlemen please put your hands together for Mr. and Mrs. Blue-Wright." Everyone claps and cheers and Sarah enthusiastically throws rose petals all over us. We sign the paperwork whilst everyone gets themselves a drink and some food.

"Darlin' do you think you can get out of that outfit and then back in time for the handfasting? I'm not sure how much longer I can control myself." Emmett groans as I play around the pole dancing pole, taunting him.

"Shortarse! Can you stop that? We're all wearing tights." Ricky shouts.

Morvan appears with a flourish of his cape. "I'm fine to wait if you need to be somewhere else right now." He tells Emmett with an exaggerated wink. Needing no further encouragement, he picks me up and strides up the beach to much cheering and obscenities.

"Don't ruin her outfit you bloody animal." Sal yells.

Emm throws me on the bed and straddles me. "Hello Mrs. Wright, wanna quickie? Keep your mask on it's really sexy." I'm out of the rest of my outfit a lot faster than I got into it and a quickie is definitely what I get.

"Wow, I needed that." We both say at the same time and dissolve into laughter again. We sort ourselves out and Emm zips me back into my suit.

"Delilah, you are the sexiest woman I have ever seen in my whole life. I can't believe you are all mine. My wife."

"Likewise, my gorgeous husband."

Morvan greets us back at the altar with a chuckle. "Are you going be able to get through this now?"

Emm sighs. "Sorry man, but how can I resist this?" He twirls me around like a ballet dancer.

"I feel you, brother. She is a very, very special lady."

"Come on slapper, let's get on with this so we can eat, drink and party." Sal says as she hands over a blue ribbon to Morvan. He claps his hands together to get everyone's attention.

"Dear friends, a handfasting is an ancient Irish wedding tradition that has come to be interpreted literally, as the symbolic act of 'tying the knot'." As he speaks he takes our wedding rings and places them together in Emmett's outstretched right hand and then tells me to put my right hand in Emm's with my left hand on top and Emm's left hand below then binds them loosely with the blue ribbon, knotting it underneath. "I will now invite your loved ones to add strength to your union."

Dad steps forward and adds another blue ribbon, tying it in a knot. "This is to ensure you'll always be as happy as your Mama and me." He kisses us both. Felix steps up and ties a white ribbon.

"White's as close as we could get to Wright." He shrugs. "This is so that you always stay together and keep being the parents I've always wanted." He kisses us.

Joey has another blue ribbon "Stop cryin' Ma." He says, hugging me and wiping his eyes and mine, it's not good crying when your hands are tied up. "This is for being the Mam and Dad I always wanted and givin' me a real 'ome an' family and to keep us all together forever."

Stef and Kim are next with a white ribbon. "You are perfect for him, Delilah. Stay as happy always as you are today, brother." Sarah is next and ties a blue and white striped ribbon, thanks us again for her pony and tells us she loves us both. The process goes on until our hands are completely bound in a huge mass of multi coloured ribbons and everyone is crying happy tears.

Morvan intervenes. "Would you like to exchange vows now?"

"Ladies first." Emmett says, still trying to pull himself together.

"Thanks for that honey." I laugh, looking into his eyes. "Emmett, my darling, patient, talented, caring, loving and incredibly sexy husband. My soul mate. I promise to love you forever and be faithful, honest and true to you. I promise to obey you when it makes sense, talk to you when I'm freaking out, frustrate and challenge you lots, continue to love your Son like my own, quickly dispatch any of your stalkers who have murderous intentions, continue to feed you unhealthy breakfasts and parent our Sons and any subsequent additions to the family in a weird and unorthodox manner. I promise to repair your cars when I break them. I promise I will always look after all of your four legged friends when you bugger off on tour, sing to you any time of the night or day whether you are sober or inebriated, satisfy all of your constant and extremely demanding sexual needs and pole dance for you often. I promise that I will willingly join you in always embarrassing our children as I grow old disgracefully with you." I kiss him as he cries and laughs at the same time.

"Darlin' Delilah, how can I follow that? My perfect wife, I promise I will love you until the end of time. I will be faithful and never lie to you, I will support you in every way and provide for you and my family, whether you all like it or not. I will always protect you, even though you don't need it. I will be forever grateful that you came into my life. I will continue to be amazed and frustrated by you. I will always ask your advice and listen to it. I will treat you to licorice and banoffee ice creams often. I will be good humoured when you beat me….at everything. I promise to also satisfy your constant and extremely demanding sexual needs and never ever discourage you from behaving disgracefully even when we're a hundred and ten. God I love you so much." He adds with a deep kiss. We get a round of applause and several offers of other things we could have included.

Morvan chuckles softly as he carefully removes the mass of ribbons and pulls it tightly to form one huge knot. We replace each other's rings and he hands us the knotted ribbon.

"This cord of ribbons symbolizes so much. It is your life, your love and the eternal connection that the two of you have found with each other. The ties of this handfasting are formed not by these ribbons or even by the knots connecting them. They are formed by your vows, your pledge, your souls and your two hearts, now forever bound together as one." He turns to all of our guests. "Emmett and Delilah are clearly made for loving each other and this bond will stay strong because they have chosen to make their home in a magical place and have so much love and support from you all. Please congratulate them on this beautiful union." We are crushed in a sea of hugs.

"Okay, someone give him a guitar before they disappear again." Stef shouts to Dan and after some serious heavy petting we get some music started and the food and drink flowing freely.

Emm and I get to the microphone and thank everyone for being here and celebrating with us and then Emmett says. "After much consideration and lots of discussion Dil and I are pretty sure this is our song and begins to sing 'I was made for lovin' you baby…You were made for lovin' me…'" I sing with him and then hand the microphone back to Stef, happily stand back and watch my gorgeous husband do his thing.

Billy drops his arm around my shoulder, hands me a beer and kisses me on the head. "Fuck me Dave, looks like yow finally got a life! We gotta sort our kid now."

There's a playlist of all the music included in Get a Life! Delilah Blue available

AND

Look out for Get a Wife! Ricky Parker....coming soon....